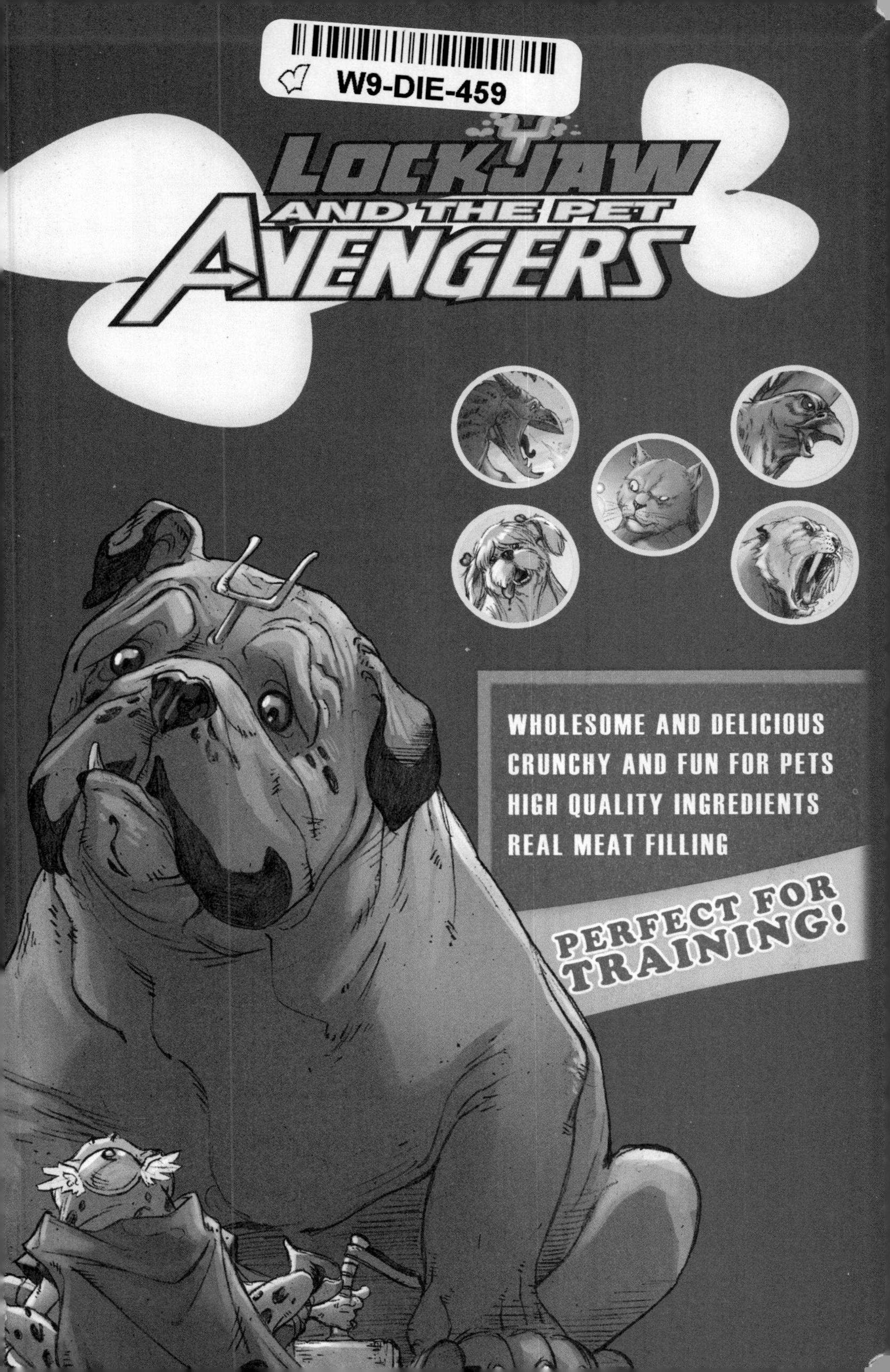
LOCKJAW
AND THE PET
AVENGERS
WHOLESOME AND DELICIOUS
CRUNCHY AND FUN FOR PETS
HIGH QUALITY INGREDIENTS
REAL MEAT FILLING
PERFECT FOR TRAINING!

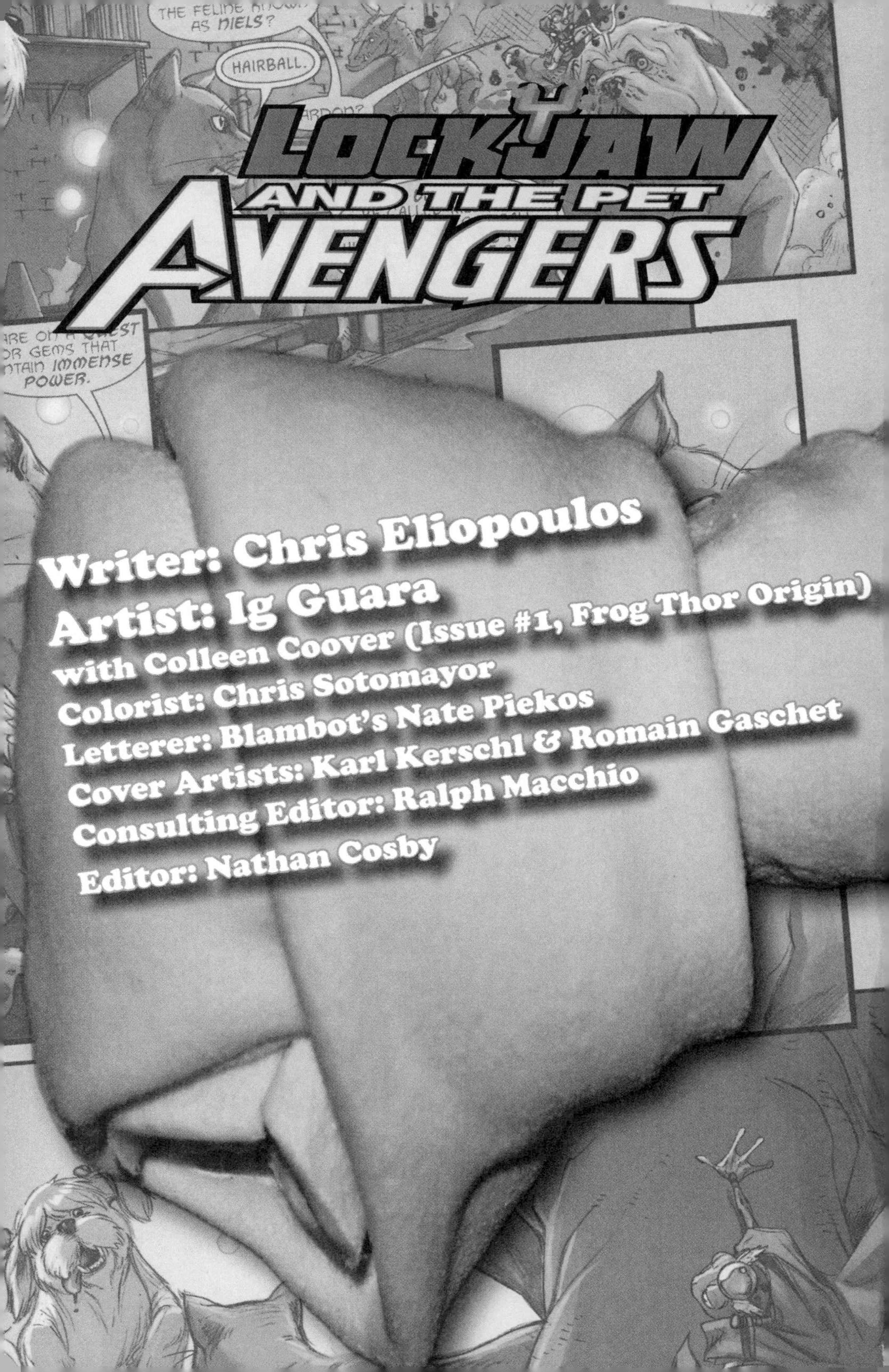
HAIRBALL.

# LOCKJAW AND THE PET AVENGERS

**Writer: Chris Eliopoulos**

**Artist: Ig Guara**

**with Colleen Coover (Issue #1, Frog Thor Origin)**

**Colorist: Chris Sotomayor**

**Letterer: Blambot's Nate Piekos**

**Cover Artists: Karl Kerschl & Romain Gaschet**

**Consulting Editor: Ralph Macchio**

**Editor: Nathan Cosby**

**Tails of the Pet Avengers #1**
Writers: Chris Eliopoulos, Scott Gray,
Colleen Coover, Joe Caramagna
& Buddy Scalera
Artists: Ig Guara and Chris Sotomayor,
GuriHiru, Colleen Coover
& Chris Eliopoulos
Letterers: Chris Eliopoulos, Dave Sharpe
& Colleen Coover
Cover Artists: Humberto Ramos
& Chris Sotomayor
Assistant Editor: Michael Horwitz
Editor: Nathan Cosby

**Marvel Pets Handbook**
Head Writer/Coordinator: Michael Hoskin
Writers: Madison Carter, Sean McQuaid, Stuart Vandal,
Gabriel Shechter, David Wiltfong, Ronald Byrd,
Eric J. Moreels, Jacob Rougemont, Markus Raymond,
Jeff Christiansen, Mark O'English, Mike O'Sullivan,
Chris Biggs & Rob London
Cover Artists: Karl Kerschl & Romain Gaschet

Collection Editor: Cory Levine
Assistant Editor: Alex Starbuck
Associate Editor: John Denning
Editors, Special Projects: Jennifer Grünwald
& Mark D. Beazley
Senior Editor, Special Projects: Jeff Youngquist
Senior Vice President of Sales: David Gabriel
Editor in Chief: Joe Quesada
Publisher: Dan Buckley
Executive Producer: Alan Fine

SO
CAN I
COME?

# 1

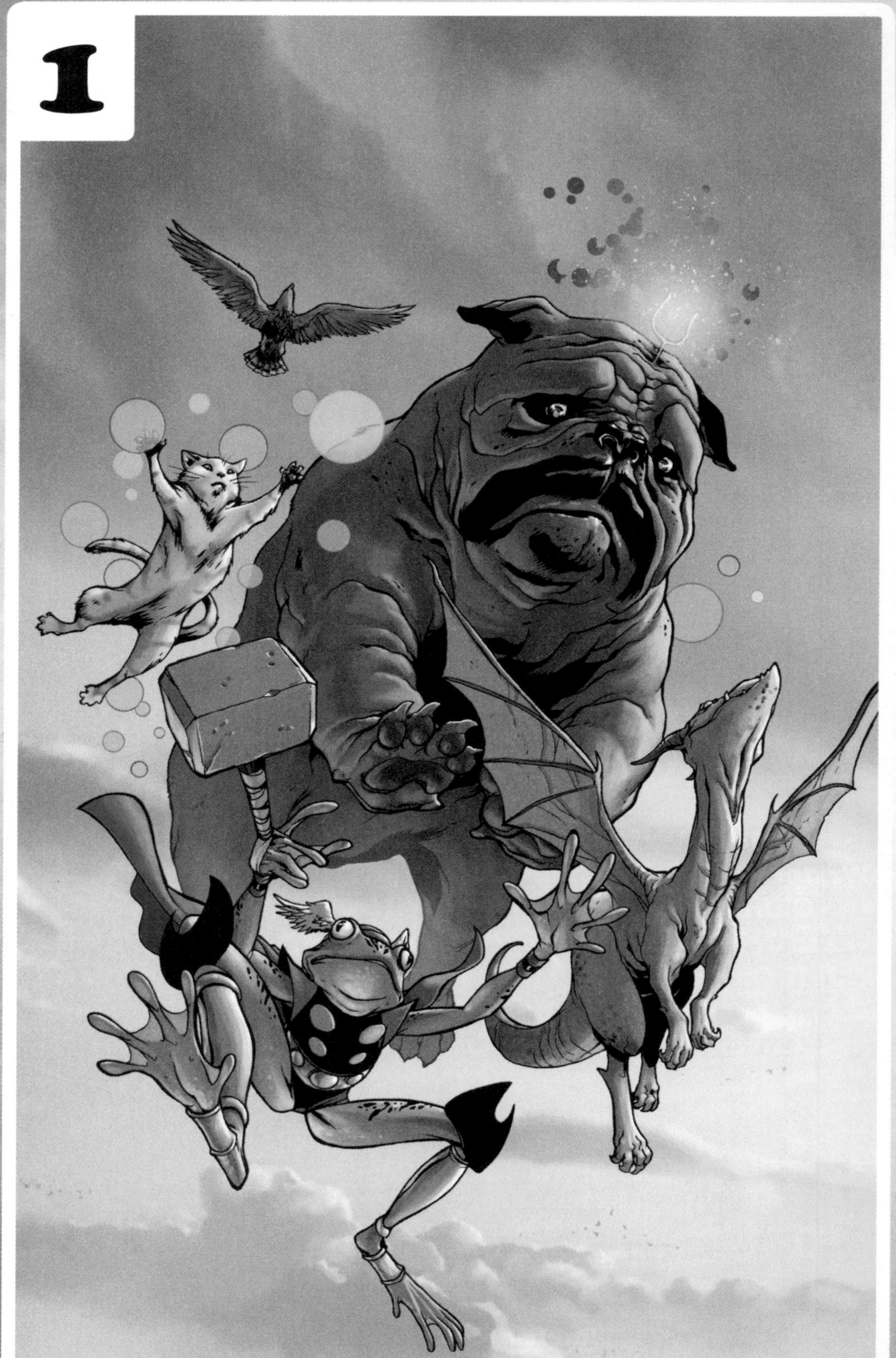

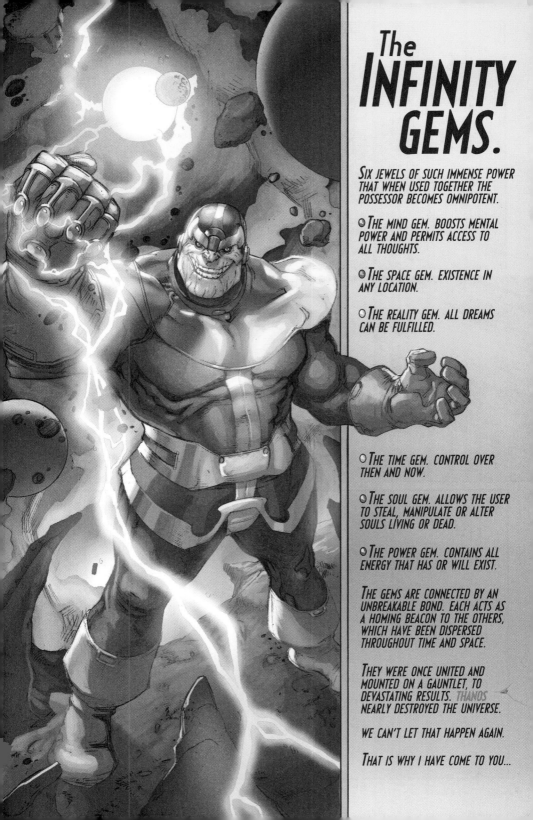

# The INFINITY GEMS.

Six jewels of such immense power that when used together the possessor becomes omnipotent.

- The mind gem. Boosts mental power and permits access to all thoughts.

- The space gem. Existence in any location.

- The reality gem. All dreams can be fulfilled.

- The time gem. Control over then and now.

- The soul gem. Allows the user to steal, manipulate or alter souls living or dead.

- The power gem. Contains all energy that has or will exist.

The gems are connected by an unbreakable bond. Each acts as a homing beacon to the others, which have been dispersed throughout time and space.

They were once united and mounted on a gauntlet, to devastating results. Thanos nearly destroyed the universe.

We can't let that happen again.

That is why I have come to you...

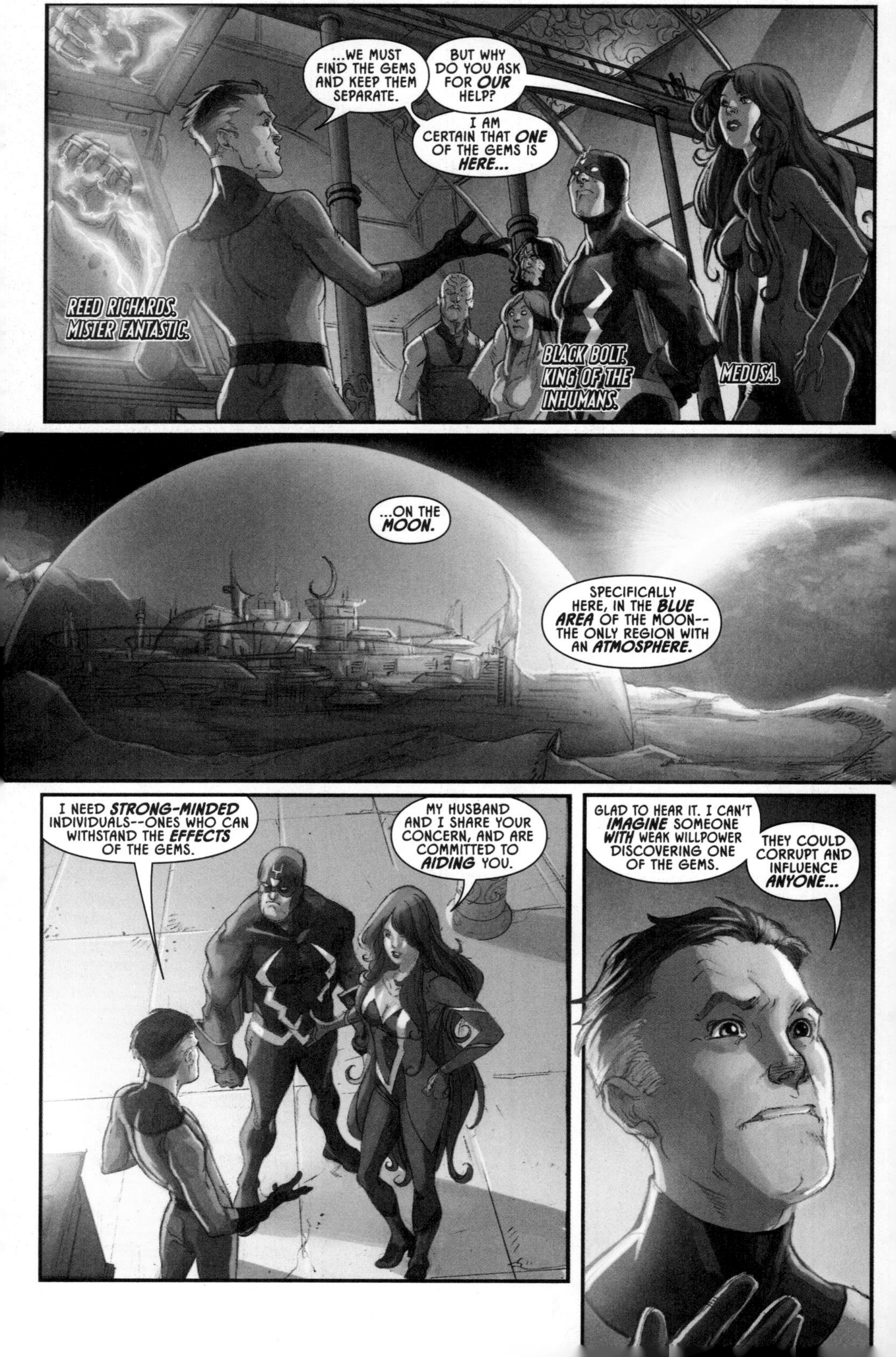
...WE MUST FIND THE GEMS AND KEEP THEM SEPARATE.
BUT WHY DO YOU ASK FOR OUR HELP?
I AM CERTAIN THAT ONE OF THE GEMS IS HERE...
REED RICHARDS. MISTER FANTASTIC.
BLACK BOLT. KING OF THE INHUMANS.
MEDUSA.
...ON THE MOON.
SPECIFICALLY HERE, IN THE BLUE AREA OF THE MOON-- THE ONLY REGION WITH AN ATMOSPHERE.
I NEED STRONG-MINDED INDIVIDUALS--ONES WHO CAN WITHSTAND THE EFFECTS OF THE GEMS.
MY HUSBAND AND I SHARE YOUR CONCERN, AND ARE COMMITTED TO AIDING YOU.
GLAD TO HEAR IT. I CAN'T IMAGINE SOMEONE WITH WEAK WILLPOWER DISCOVERING ONE OF THE GEMS.
THEY COULD CORRUPT AND INFLUENCE ANYONE...

"...EVEN THE *SIMPLEST* OF CREATURES."

WHOOF!

SNFF SNFF

SNFF SNFF SNFF

SKTCH SKTCH SKTCH

MRF.

GLP

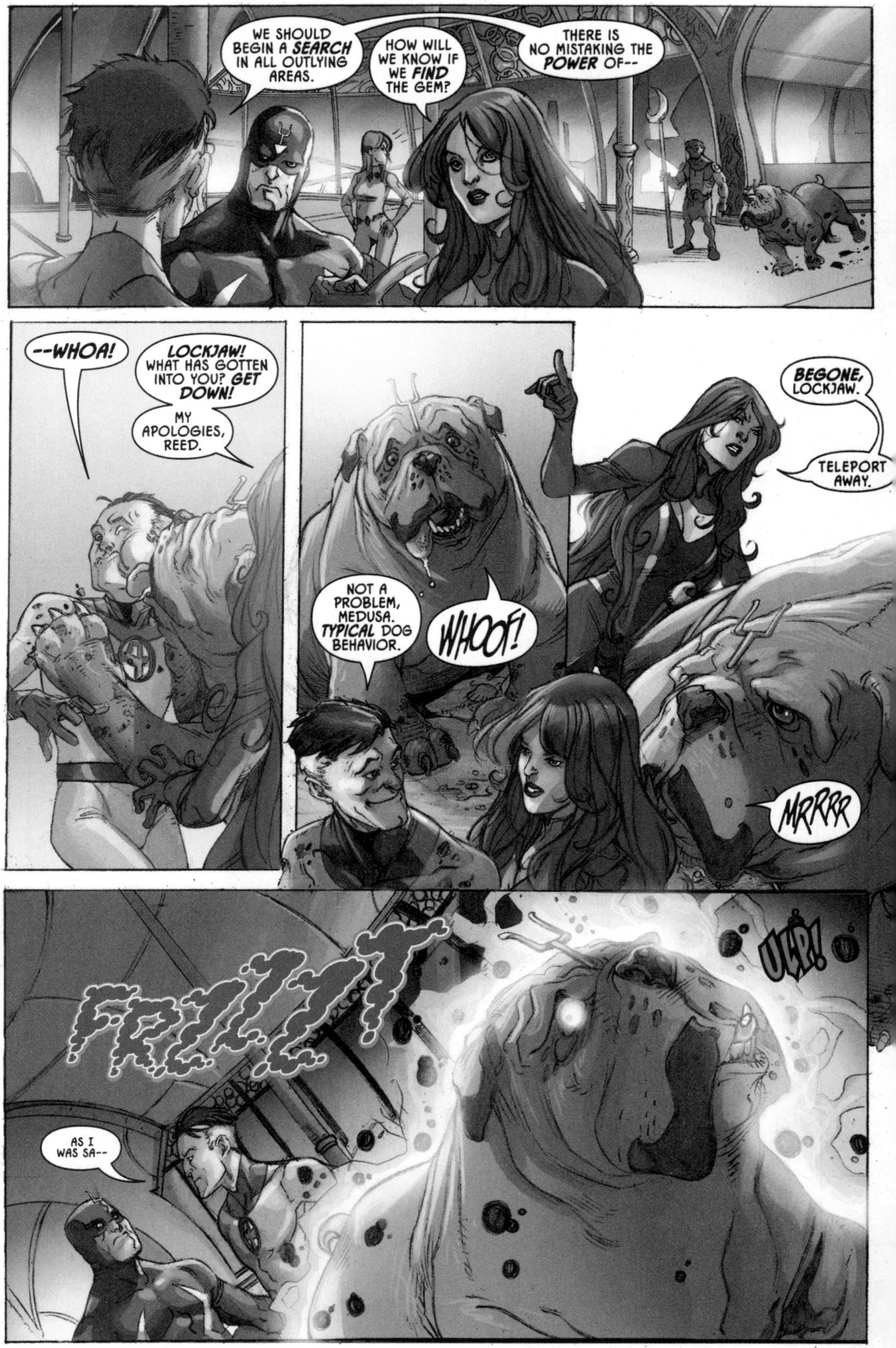

WE SHOULD BEGIN A **SEARCH** IN ALL OUTLYING AREAS.
HOW WILL WE KNOW IF WE **FIND** THE GEM?
THERE IS NO MISTAKING THE **POWER** OF--
--WHOA!
**LOCKJAW!** WHAT HAS GOTTEN INTO YOU? **GET DOWN!**
MY APOLOGIES, REED.
NOT A PROBLEM, MEDUSA. **TYPICAL** DOG BEHAVIOR.
WHOOF!
**BEGONE,** LOCKJAW.
TELEPORT AWAY.
MRRRR
FRZZZT
ULP!
AS I WAS SA--

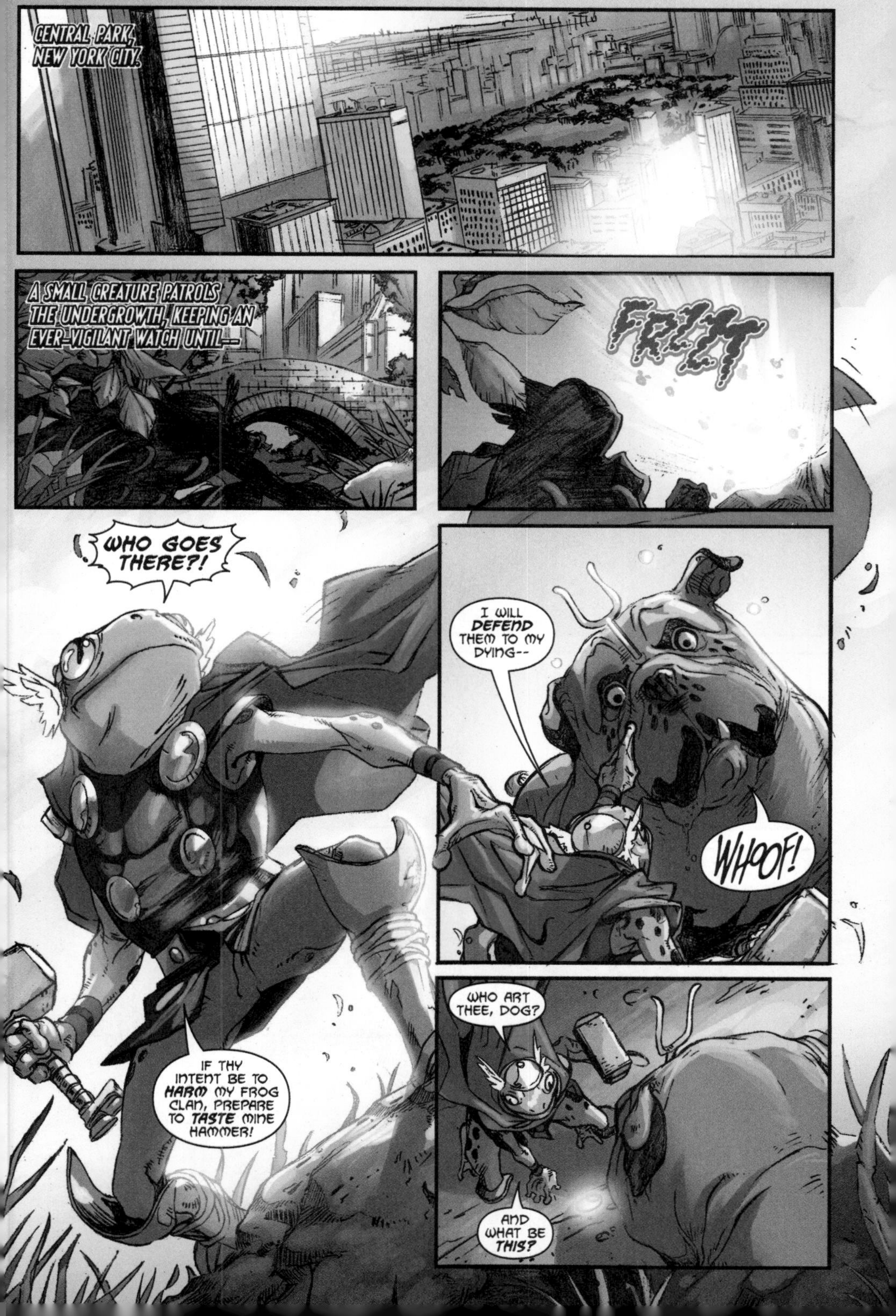
CENTRAL PARK, NEW YORK CITY.
A SMALL CREATURE PATROLS THE UNDERGROWTH, KEEPING AN EVER-VIGILANT WATCH UNTIL--
FRZZT
WHO GOES THERE?!
IF THY INTENT BE TO HARM MY FROG CLAN, PREPARE TO TASTE MINE HAMMER!
I WILL DEFEND THEM TO MY DYING--
WHOOF!
WHO ART THEE, DOG?
AND WHAT BE THIS?

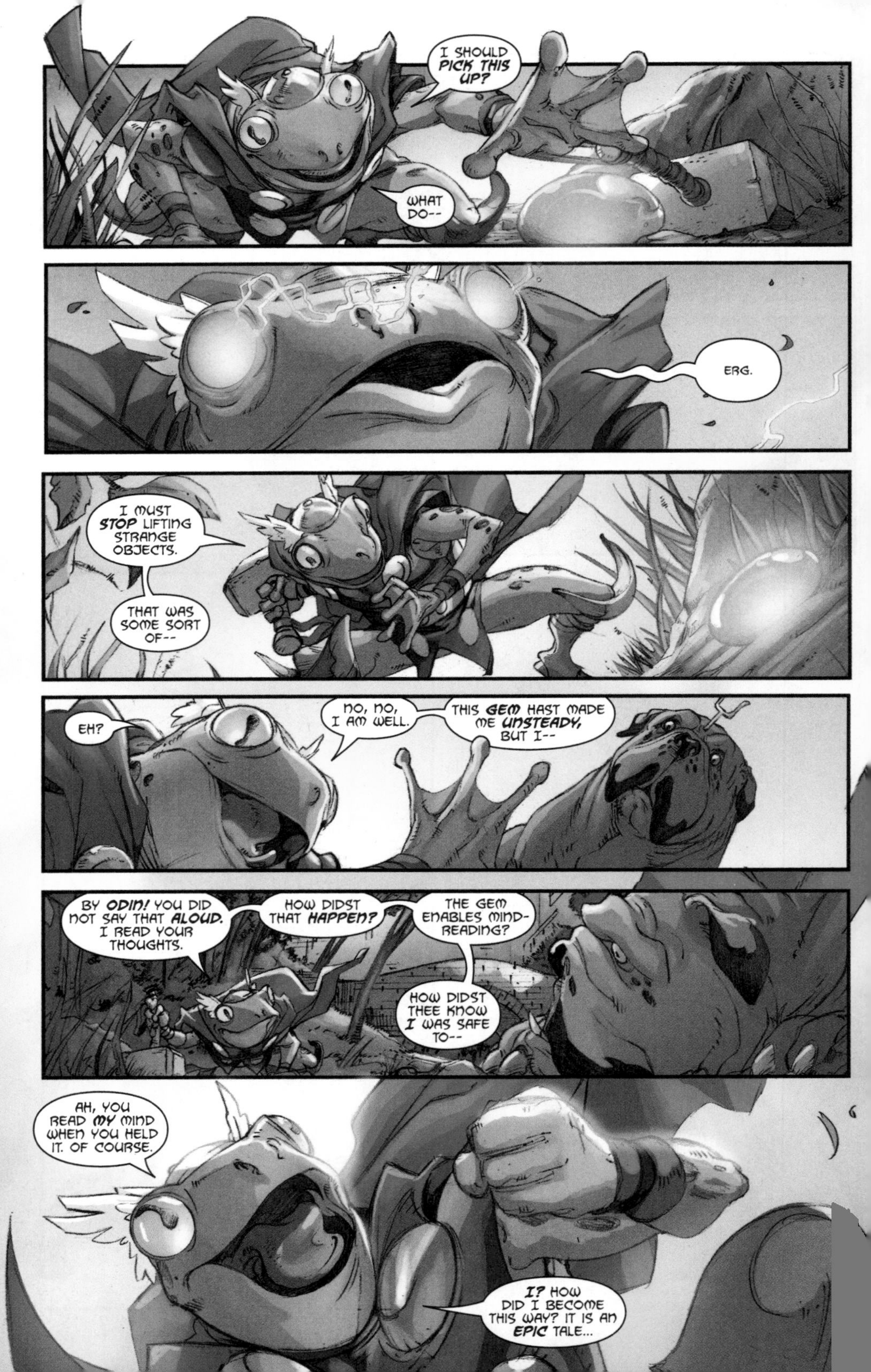
I SHOULD PICK THIS UP?
WHAT DO--
ERG.
I MUST STOP LIFTING STRANGE OBJECTS.
THAT WAS SOME SORT OF--
EH?
NO, NO, I AM WELL.
THIS GEM HAST MADE ME UNSTEADY, BUT I--
BY ODIN! YOU DID NOT SAY THAT ALOUD. I READ YOUR THOUGHTS.
HOW DIDST THAT HAPPEN?
THE GEM ENABLES MIND-READING?
HOW DIDST THEE KNOW I WAS SAFE TO--
AH, YOU READ MY MIND WHEN YOU HELD IT. OF COURSE.
I? HOW DID I BECOME THIS WAY? IT IS AN EPIC TALE...

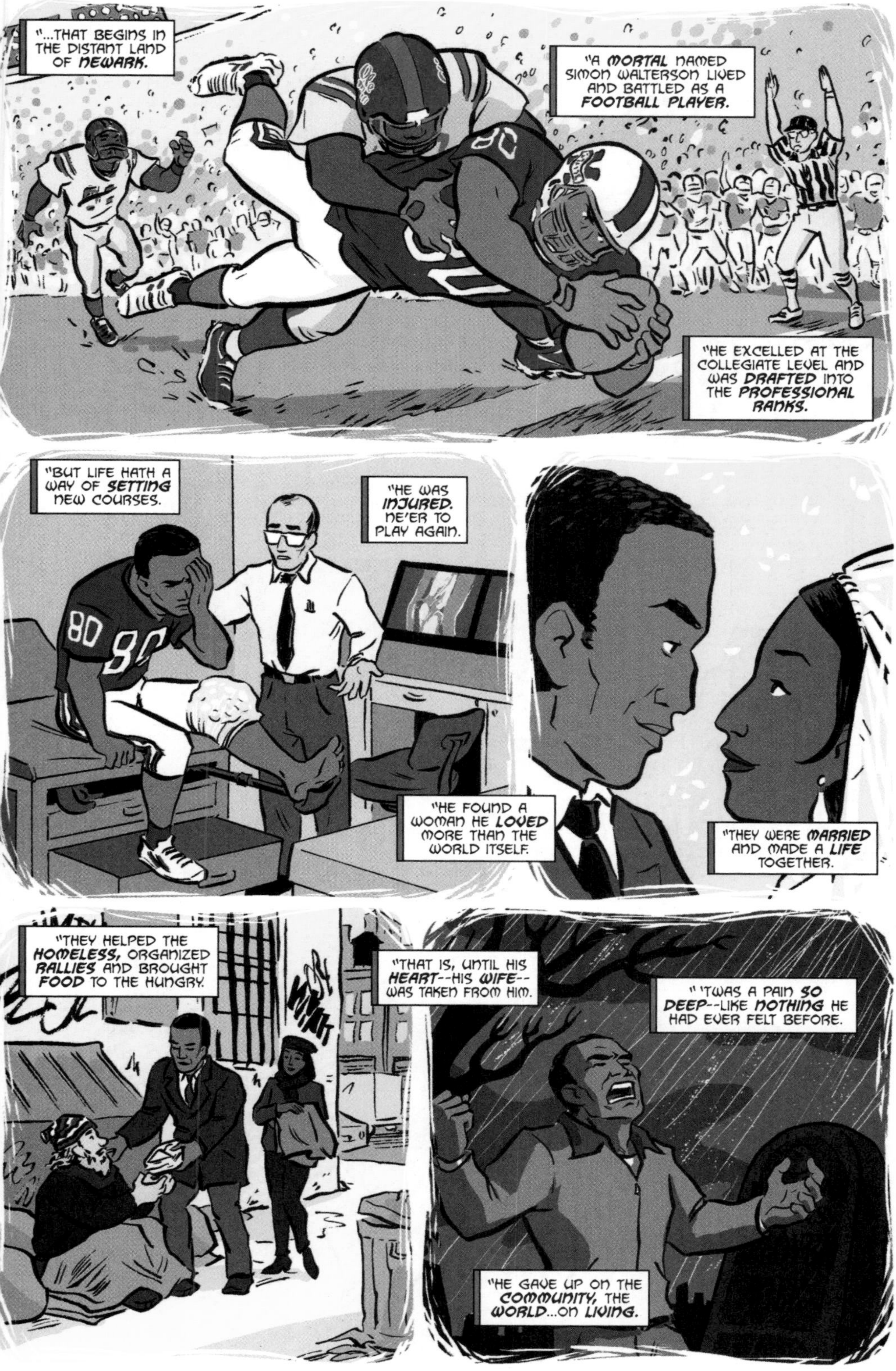
"...THAT BEGINS IN THE DISTANT LAND OF NEWARK.
"A MORTAL NAMED SIMON WALTERSON LIVED AND BATTLED AS A FOOTBALL PLAYER.
"HE EXCELLED AT THE COLLEGIATE LEVEL AND WAS DRAFTED INTO THE PROFESSIONAL RANKS.
"BUT LIFE HATH A WAY OF SETTING NEW COURSES.
"HE WAS INJURED. NE'ER TO PLAY AGAIN.
80
"HE FOUND A WOMAN HE LOVED MORE THAN THE WORLD ITSELF.
"THEY WERE MARRIED AND MADE A LIFE TOGETHER.
"THEY HELPED THE HOMELESS, ORGANIZED RALLIES AND BROUGHT FOOD TO THE HUNGRY.
"THAT IS, UNTIL HIS HEART--HIS WIFE--WAS TAKEN FROM HIM.
"'TWAS A PAIN SO DEEP--LIKE NOTHING HE HAD EVER FELT BEFORE.
"HE GAVE UP ON THE COMMUNITY, THE WORLD...ON LIVING.

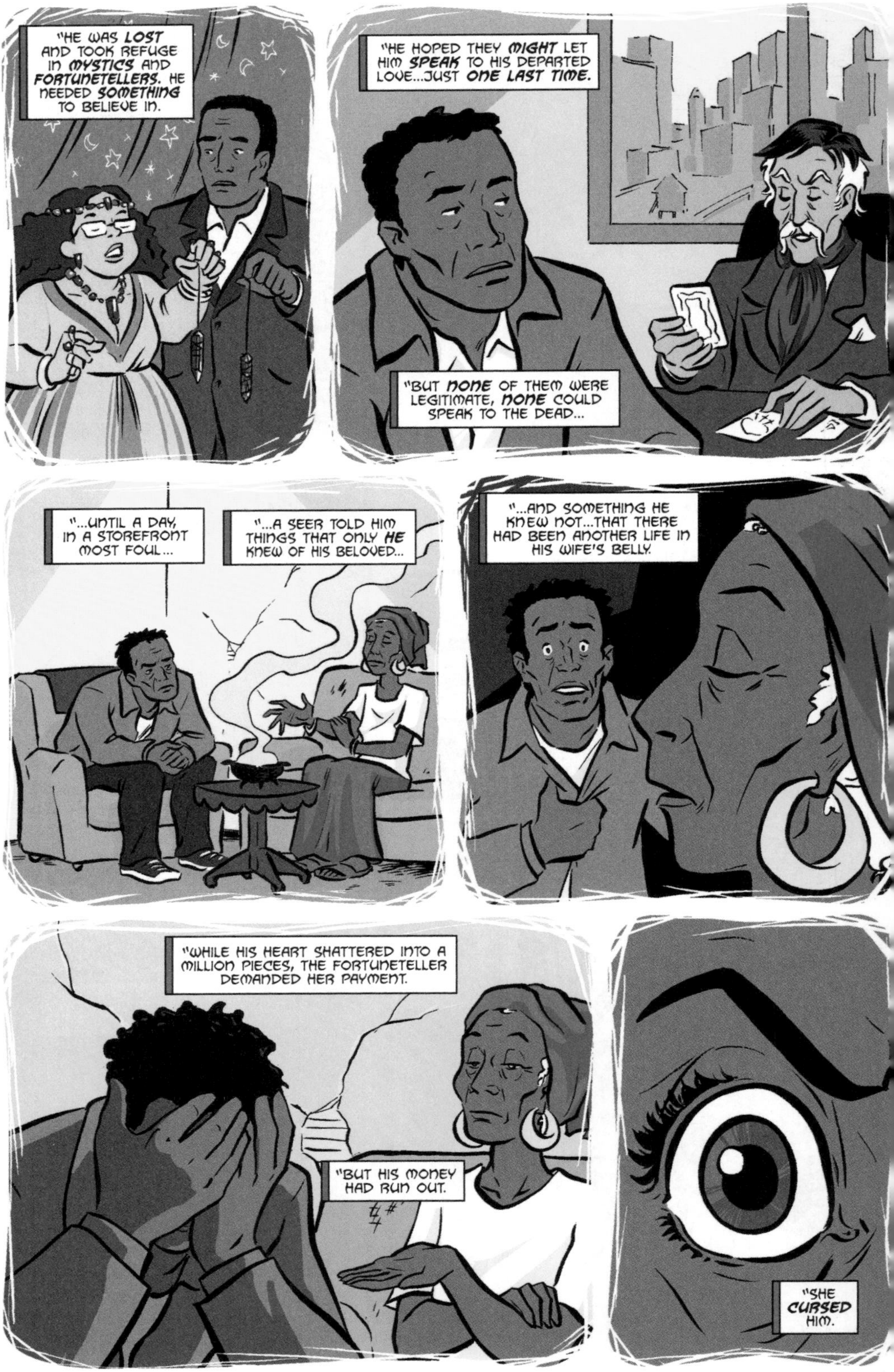
"HE WAS LOST AND TOOK REFUGE IN MYSTICS AND FORTUNETELLERS. HE NEEDED SOMETHING TO BELIEVE IN.
"HE HOPED THEY MIGHT LET HIM SPEAK TO HIS DEPARTED LOVE...JUST ONE LAST TIME.
"BUT NONE OF THEM WERE LEGITIMATE, NONE COULD SPEAK TO THE DEAD...
"...UNTIL A DAY, IN A STOREFRONT MOST FOUL...
"...A SEER TOLD HIM THINGS THAT ONLY HE KNEW OF HIS BELOVED...
"...AND SOMETHING HE KNEW NOT...THAT THERE HAD BEEN ANOTHER LIFE IN HIS WIFE'S BELLY.
"WHILE HIS HEART SHATTERED INTO A MILLION PIECES, THE FORTUNETELLER DEMANDED HER PAYMENT.
"BUT HIS MONEY HAD RUN OUT.
"SHE CURSED HIM.

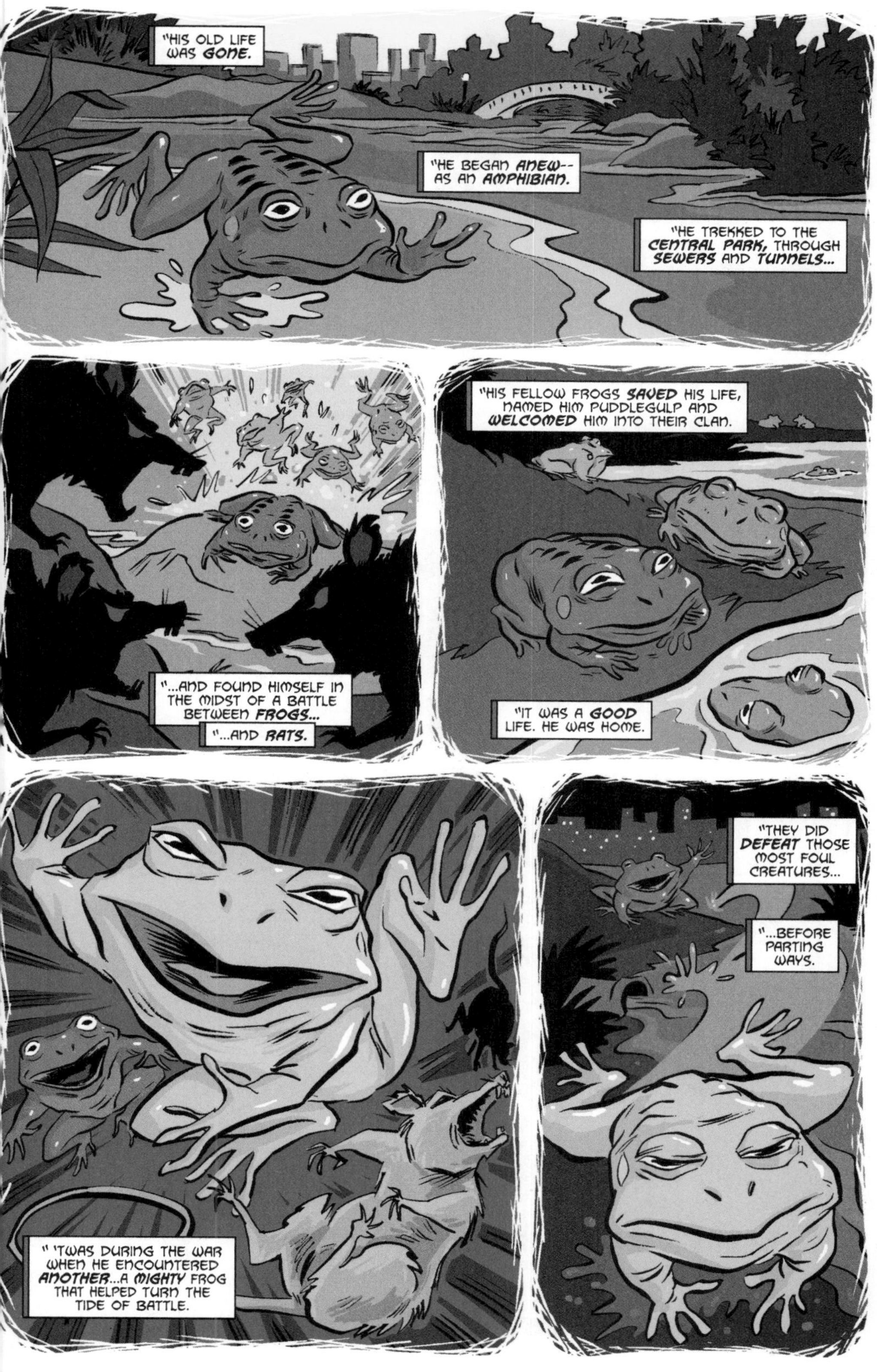
"HIS OLD LIFE WAS GONE.
"HE BEGAN ANEW-- AS AN AMPHIBIAN.
"HE TREKKED TO THE CENTRAL PARK, THROUGH SEWERS AND TUNNELS...
"...AND FOUND HIMSELF IN THE MIDST OF A BATTLE BETWEEN FROGS...
"...AND RATS.
"HIS FELLOW FROGS SAVED HIS LIFE, NAMED HIM PUDDLEGULP AND WELCOMED HIM INTO THEIR CLAN.
"IT WAS A GOOD LIFE. HE WAS HOME.
" 'TWAS DURING THE WAR WHEN HE ENCOUNTERED ANOTHER...A MIGHTY FROG THAT HELPED TURN THE TIDE OF BATTLE.
"THEY DID DEFEAT THOSE MOST FOUL CREATURES...
"...BEFORE PARTING WAYS.

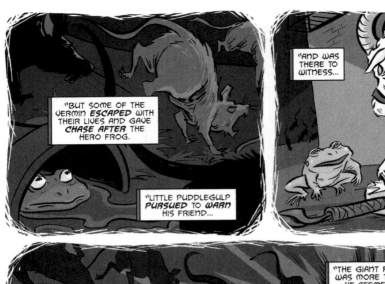

"BUT SOME OF THE VERMIN *ESCAPED* WITH THEIR LIVES AND GAVE *CHASE AFTER* THE HERO FROG.

"LITTLE PUDDLEGULP *PURSUED* TO *WARN* HIS FRIEND...

"AND WAS THERE TO WITNESS...

"THE GIANT FROG WAS MORE THAN HE SEEMED!

KRAKADOOOUM!!

"HE WAS ACTUALLY *THOR, THE GOD OF THUNDER,* TRAPPED AS A FROG, JUST LIKE HE!

"THOR'S LOYAL GOATS, *TOOTHGNASHER* AND *TOOTHGRINDER,* WHISKED HIM BACK TO HIS HOMELAND, LEAVING BEHIND THE RATS...

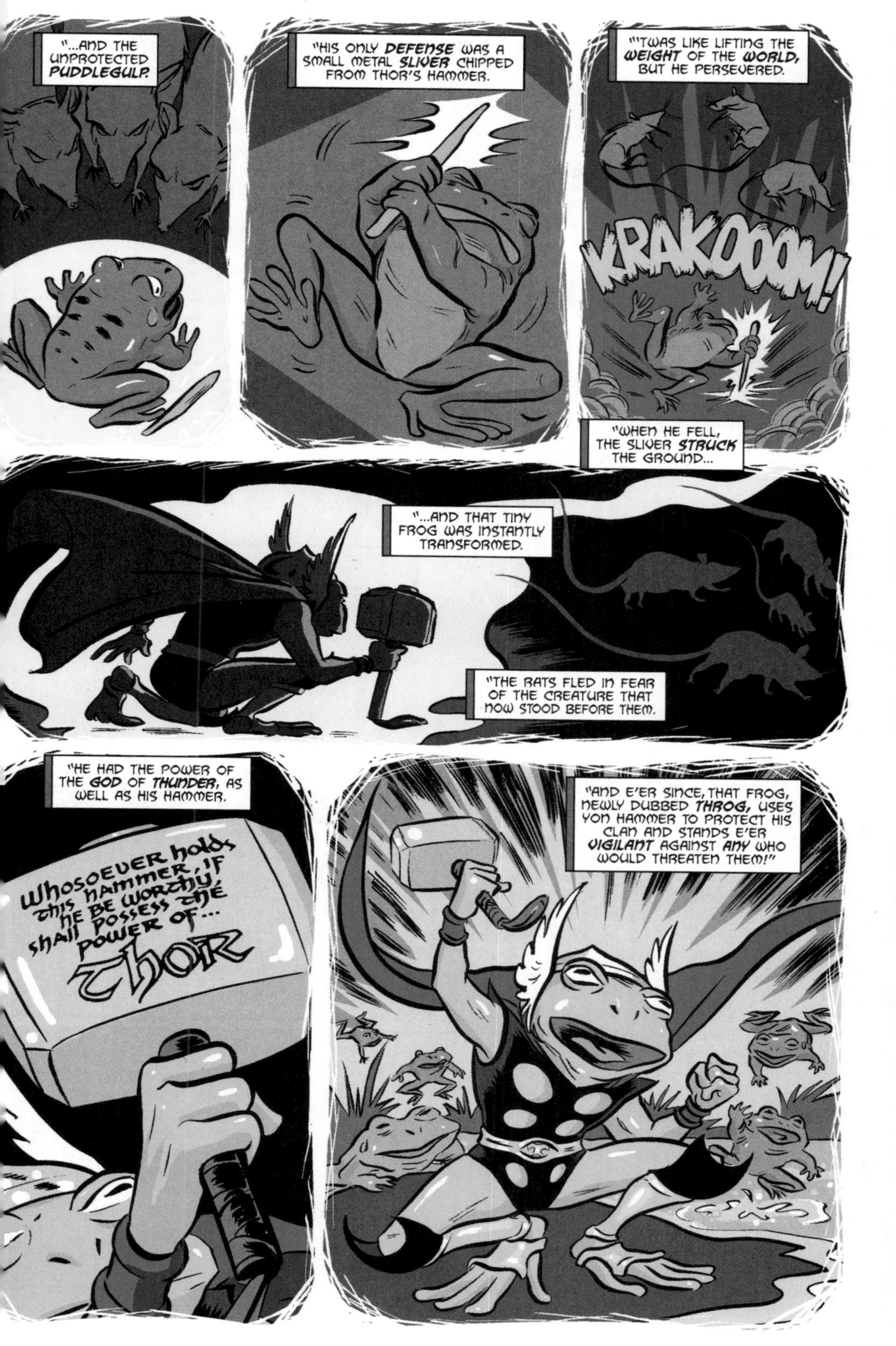
"...AND THE UNPROTECTED PUDDLEGULP.
"HIS ONLY DEFENSE WAS A SMALL METAL SLIVER CHIPPED FROM THOR'S HAMMER.
"'TWAS LIKE LIFTING THE WEIGHT OF THE WORLD, BUT HE PERSEVERED.
KRAKOOOM!
"WHEN HE FELL, THE SLIVER STRUCK THE GROUND...
"...AND THAT TINY FROG WAS INSTANTLY TRANSFORMED.
"THE RATS FLED IN FEAR OF THE CREATURE THAT NOW STOOD BEFORE THEM.
"HE HAD THE POWER OF THE GOD OF THUNDER, AS WELL AS HIS HAMMER.
Whosoever holds this hammer, if he be worthy, shall possess the power of... THOR
"AND E'ER SINCE, THAT FROG, NEWLY DUBBED THROG, USES YON HAMMER TO PROTECT HIS CLAN AND STANDS E'ER VIGILANT AGAINST ANY WHO WOULD THREATEN THEM!"

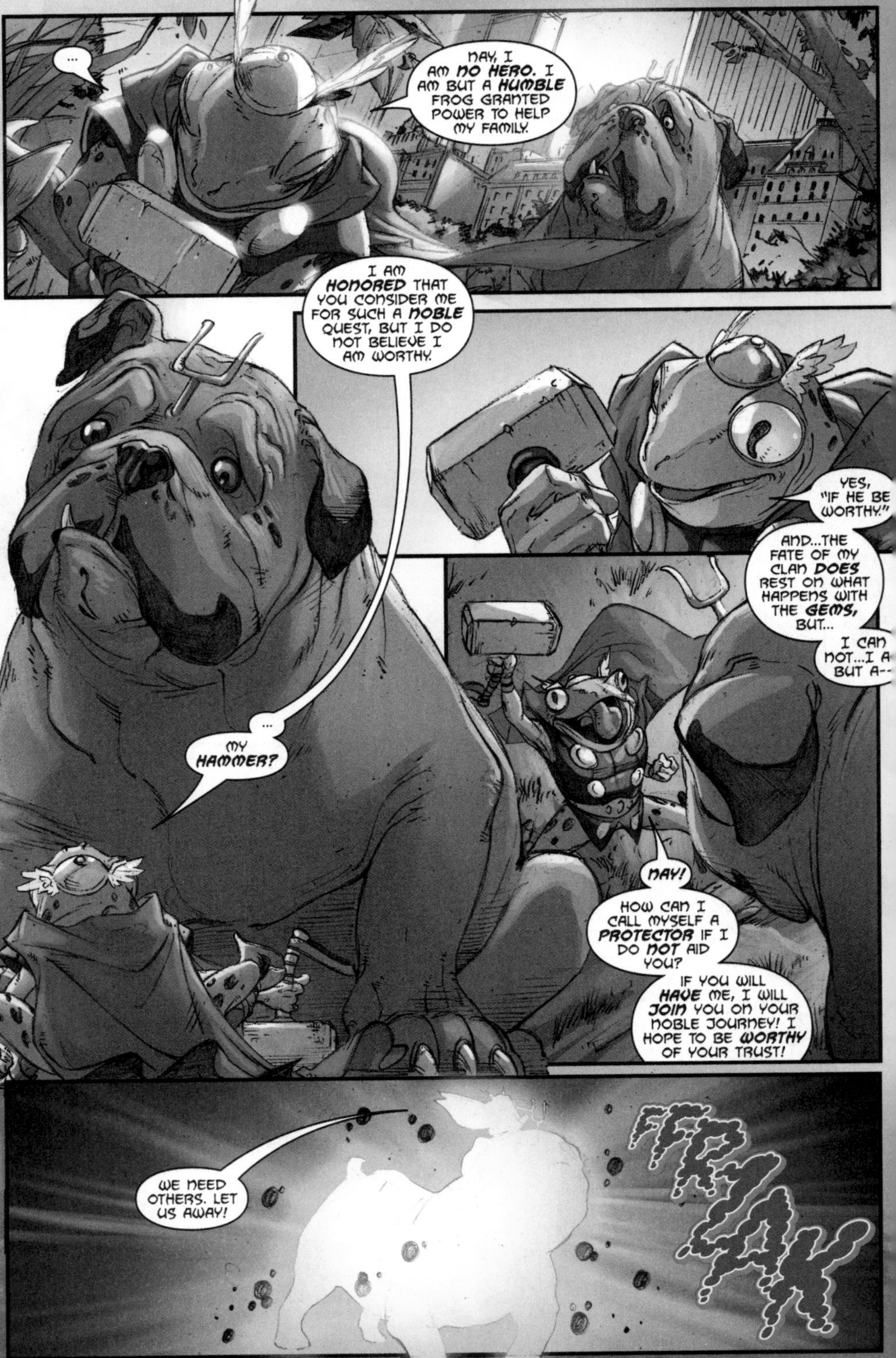
...
NAY, I AM NO HERO. I AM BUT A HUMBLE FROG GRANTED POWER TO HELP MY FAMILY.
I AM HONORED THAT YOU CONSIDER ME FOR SUCH A NOBLE QUEST, BUT I DO NOT BELIEVE I AM WORTHY.
YES, "IF HE BE WORTHY."
AND...THE FATE OF MY CLAN DOES REST ON WHAT HAPPENS WITH THE GEMS, BUT...
I CAN NOT...I A BUT A--
...
MY HAMMER?
NAY!
HOW CAN I CALL MYSELF A PROTECTOR IF I DO NOT AID YOU?
IF YOU WILL HAVE ME, I WILL JOIN YOU ON YOUR NOBLE JOURNEY! I HOPE TO BE WORTHY OF YOUR TRUST!
WE NEED OTHERS. LET US AWAY!
FFR4ZAK!

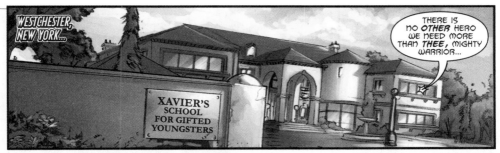

WESTCHESTER, NEW YORK...

XAVIER'S SCHOOL FOR GIFTED YOUNGSTERS

THERE IS NO *OTHER* HERO WE NEED MORE THAN *THEE*, MIGHTY WARRIOR...

...MIGHTY *LOCKHEED.*

I...I HAVE FOUGHT FOR *MANY...* BATTLED ALONGSIDE *FRIENDS* AND *COMRADES,* BUT IN THE END ALL IT HAS CAUSED IS *DEATH* AND *LONELINESS.*

I HAVE LOST *EVERYONE* ON MY PLANET... AND THE *ONE* PERSON ON EARTH I CALLED FRIEND IS *GONE...*AND I COULDN'T SAVE HER.

*WHY* GO THROUGH THIS AGAIN? WHY *BOTHER?* IT ONLY CAUSES *DESPAIR.*

LOCKJAW HAS TOLD ME OF THE MANY *BATTLES* YOU HAVE FOUGHT AND OF YOUR *GRACIOUS SPIRIT* AND I CANNOT, I *WILL* NOT, BELIEVE THAT THOU WOULDST *TURN AWAY* IN A TIME OF NEED.

I DO NOT BELIEVE THOSE YOU *LOVED* MOST WOULD WANT TO SEE YOU *THIS* WAY-- GIVING UP ON ALL. THEY KNEW YOU TO BE *STRONG* AND *DEVOTED.*

WE DO NOT ASK *MUCH,* BUT IT IS SOMETHING ONLY ONE SUCH AS *YOU* CAN PERFORM.

...

VERY WELL. I WILL *HELP.* NOT FOR *YOU,* NOT FOR THE *UNIVERSE...*

...BUT FOR THE *MEMORY* OF THOSE I *CRY* FOR EVERY DAY.

FRYAAAKK

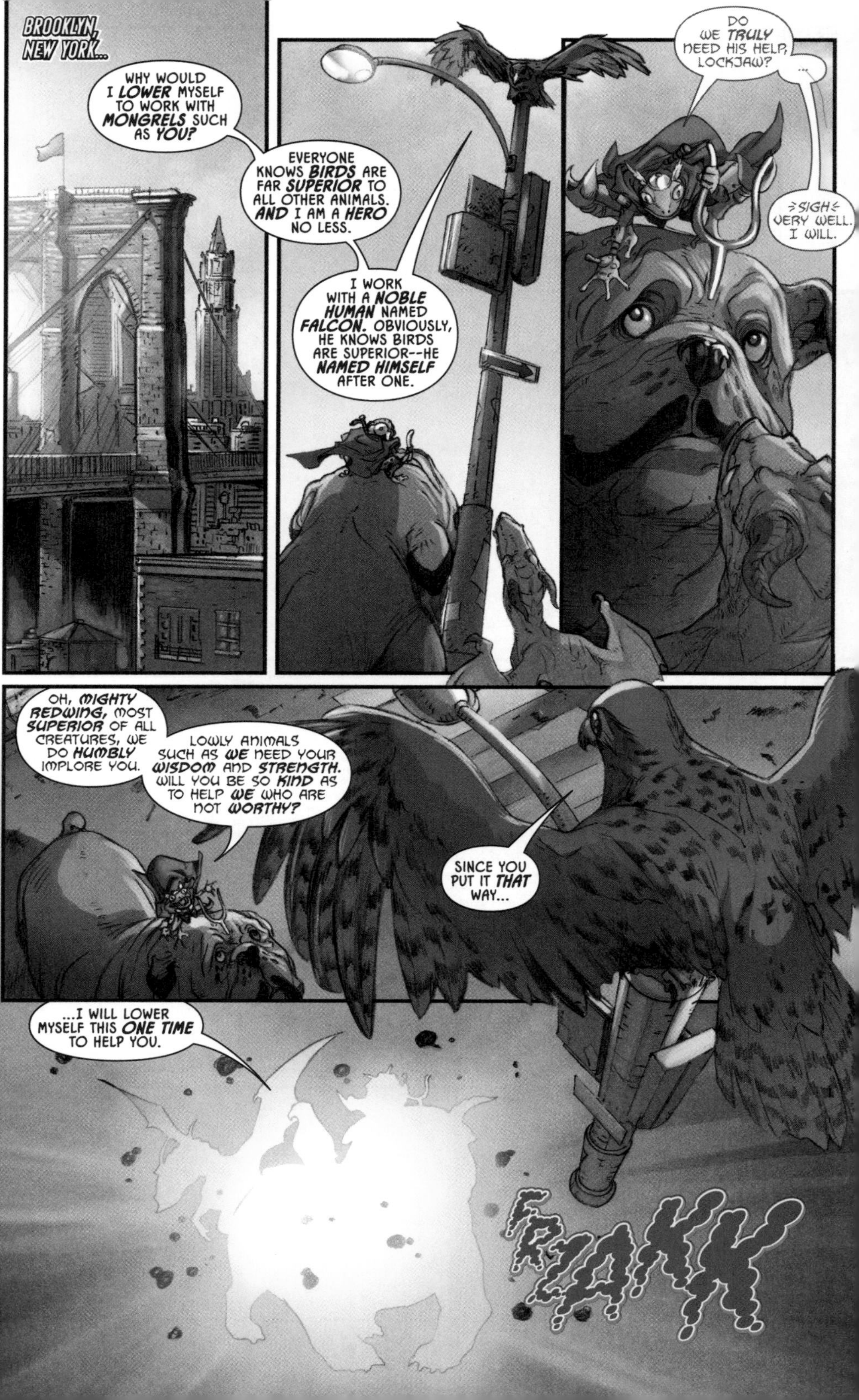
BROOKLYN, NEW YORK...
WHY WOULD I LOWER MYSELF TO WORK WITH MONGRELS SUCH AS YOU?
EVERYONE KNOWS BIRDS ARE FAR SUPERIOR TO ALL OTHER ANIMALS. AND I AM A HERO NO LESS.
I WORK WITH A NOBLE HUMAN NAMED FALCON. OBVIOUSLY, HE KNOWS BIRDS ARE SUPERIOR--HE NAMED HIMSELF AFTER ONE.
DO WE TRULY NEED HIS HELP, LOCKJAW?
...
SIGH VERY WELL. I WILL.
OH, MIGHTY REDWING, MOST SUPERIOR OF ALL CREATURES, WE DO HUMBLY IMPLORE YOU.
LOWLY ANIMALS SUCH AS WE NEED YOUR WISDOM AND STRENGTH. WILL YOU BE SO KIND AS TO HELP WE WHO ARE NOT WORTHY?
SINCE YOU PUT IT THAT WAY...
...I WILL LOWER MYSELF THIS ONE TIME TO HELP YOU.
FRZAKK

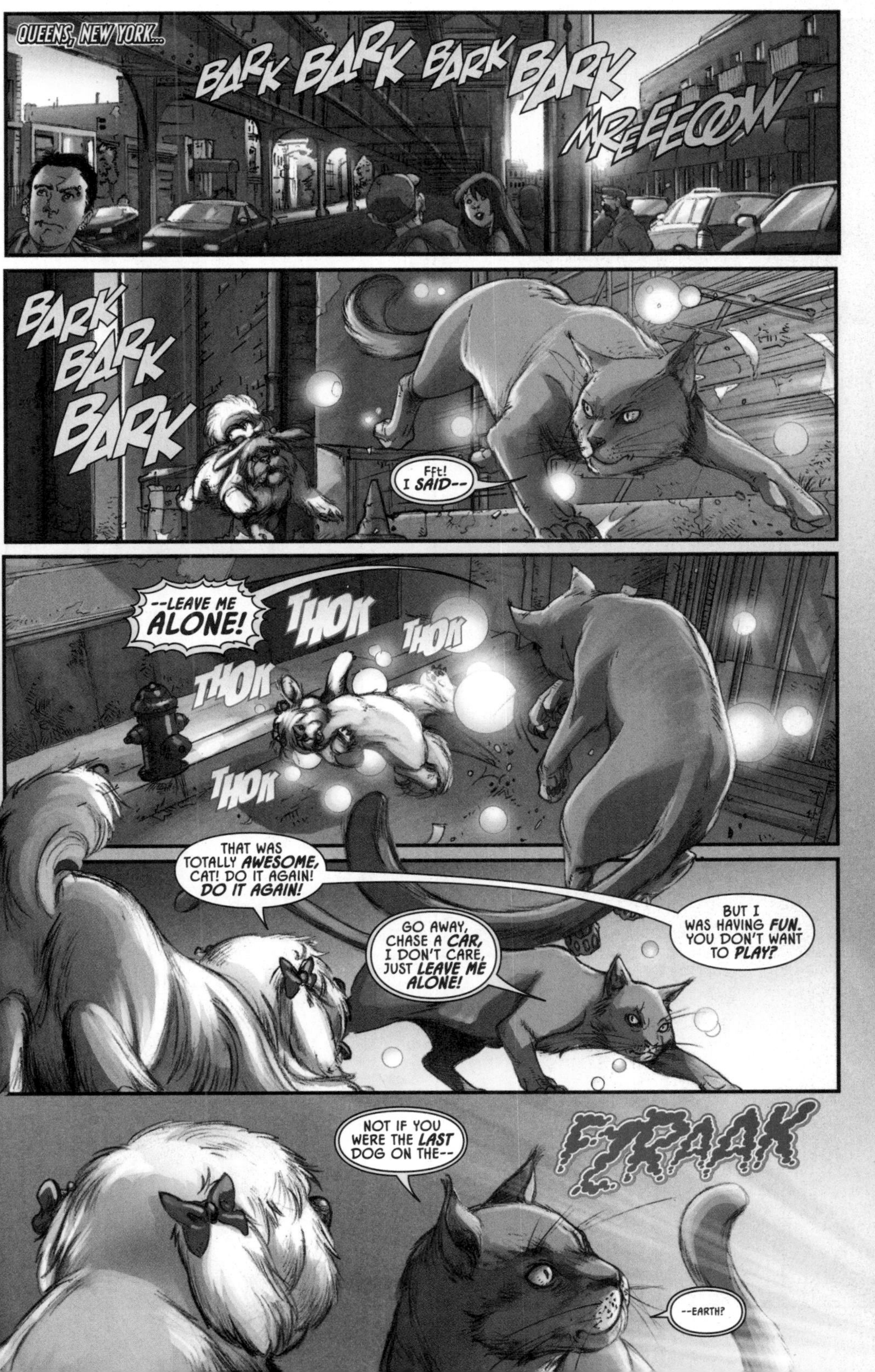
QUEENS, NEW YORK...
BARK BARK BARK BARK
MREEEOOW
BARK BARK BARK
Fft! I SAID--
--LEAVE ME ALONE!
THOK
THOK
THOK
THOK
THAT WAS TOTALLY AWESOME, CAT! DO IT AGAIN! DO IT AGAIN!
GO AWAY, CHASE A CAR, I DON'T CARE, JUST LEAVE ME ALONE!
BUT I WAS HAVING FUN. YOU DON'T WANT TO PLAY?
NOT IF YOU WERE THE LAST DOG ON THE--
FZRAAK
--EARTH?

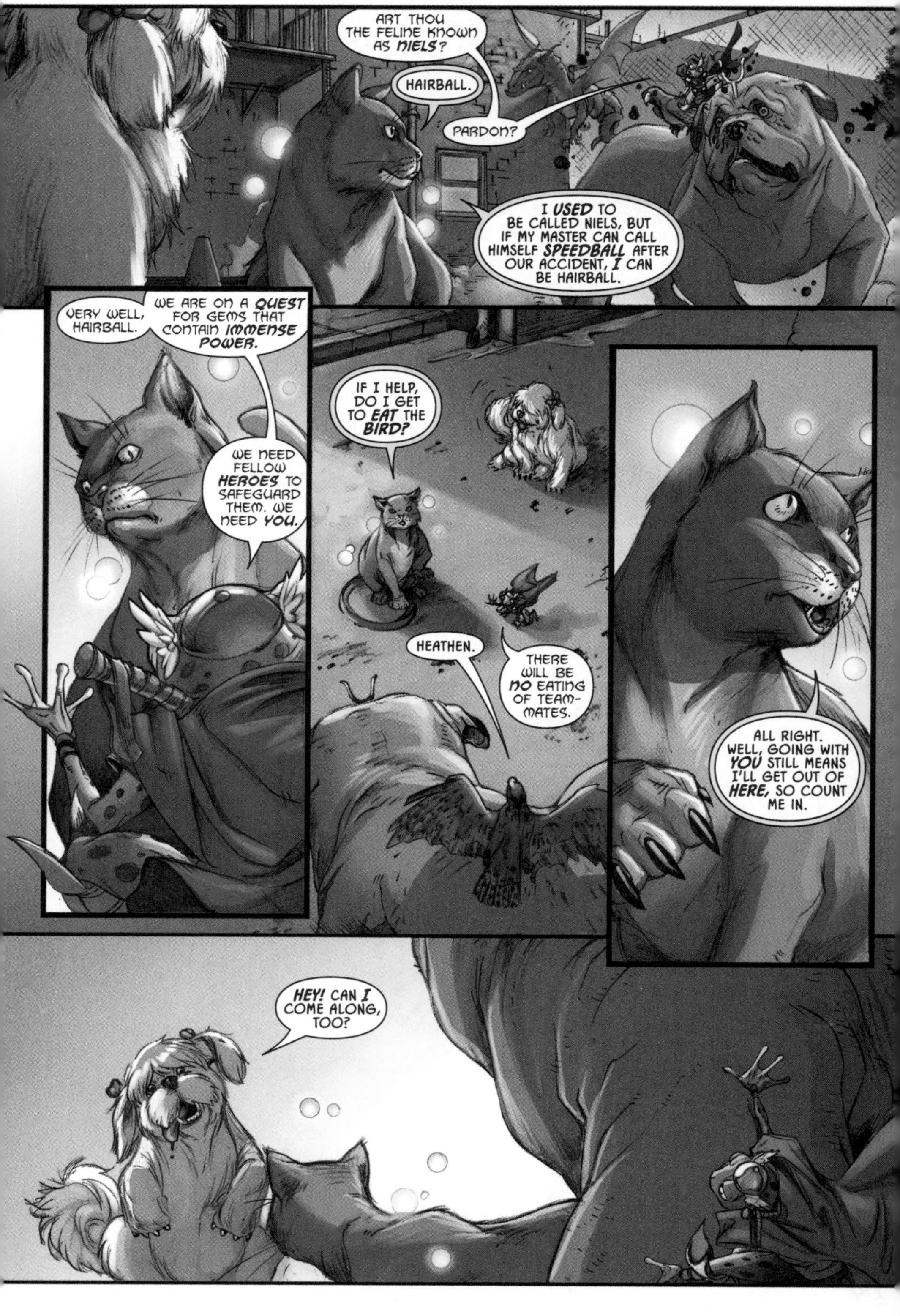
ART THOU THE FELINE KNOWN AS *NIELS*?
HAIRBALL.
PARDON?
I *USED* TO BE CALLED NIELS, BUT IF MY MASTER CAN CALL HIMSELF *SPEEDBALL* AFTER OUR ACCIDENT, *I* CAN BE HAIRBALL.
VERY WELL, HAIRBALL.
WE ARE ON A *QUEST* FOR GEMS THAT CONTAIN *IMMENSE POWER.*
WE NEED FELLOW *HEROES* TO SAFEGUARD THEM. WE NEED *YOU.*
IF I HELP, DO I GET TO *EAT* THE *BIRD?*
HEATHEN.
THERE WILL BE *NO* EATING OF TEAM-MATES.
ALL RIGHT. WELL, GOING WITH *YOU* STILL MEANS I'LL GET OUT OF *HERE,* SO COUNT ME IN.
*HEY!* CAN *I* COME ALONG, TOO?

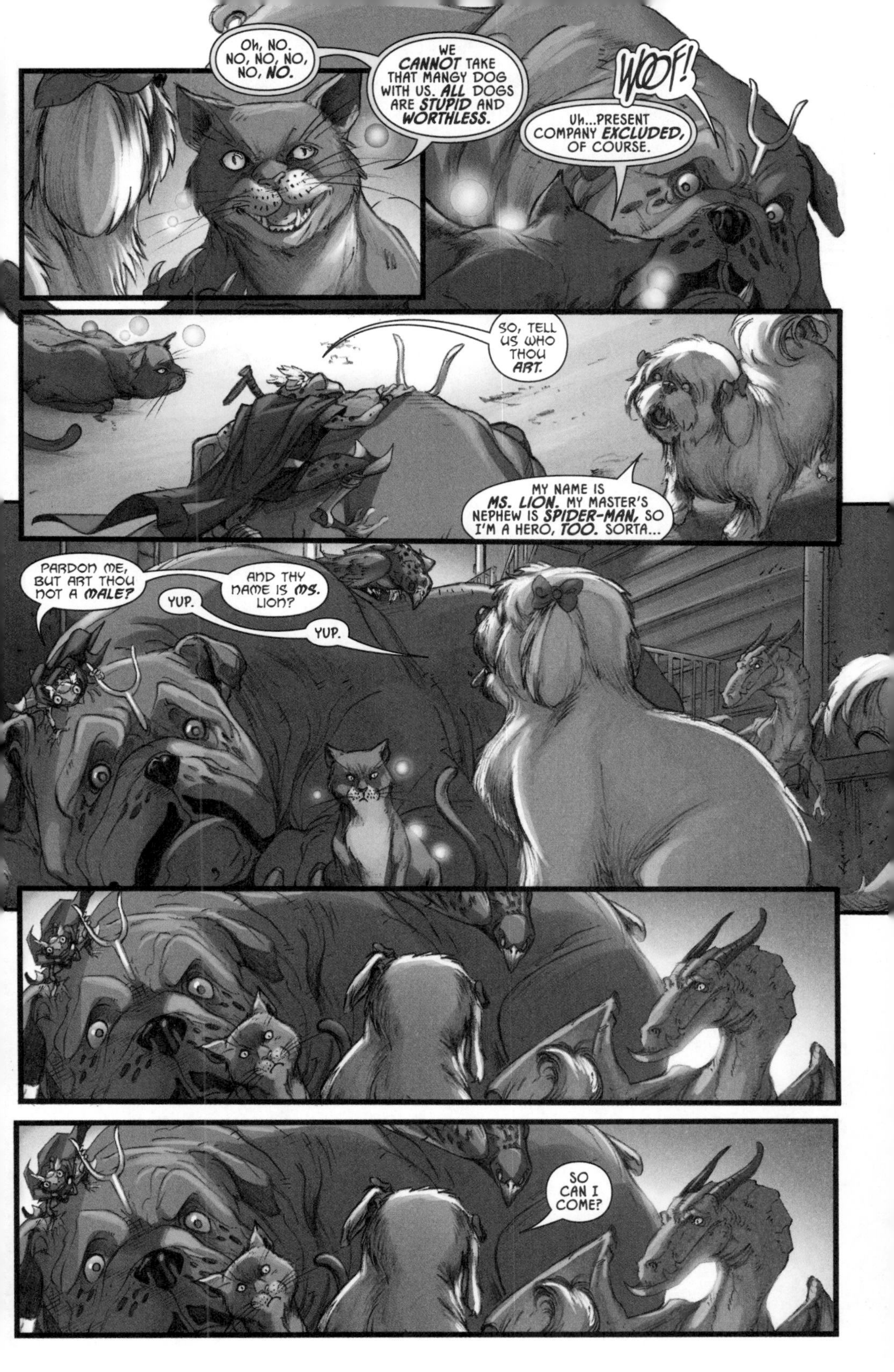
Oh, NO. NO, NO, NO, NO, NO.
WE CANNOT TAKE THAT MANGY DOG WITH US. ALL DOGS ARE STUPID AND WORTHLESS.
WOOF!
Uh...PRESENT COMPANY EXCLUDED, OF COURSE.
SO, TELL US WHO THOU ART.
MY NAME IS MS. LION. MY MASTER'S NEPHEW IS SPIDER-MAN, SO I'M A HERO, TOO. SORTA...
PARDON ME, BUT ART THOU NOT A MALE?
YUP.
AND THY NAME IS MS. LION?
YUP.
SO CAN I COME?

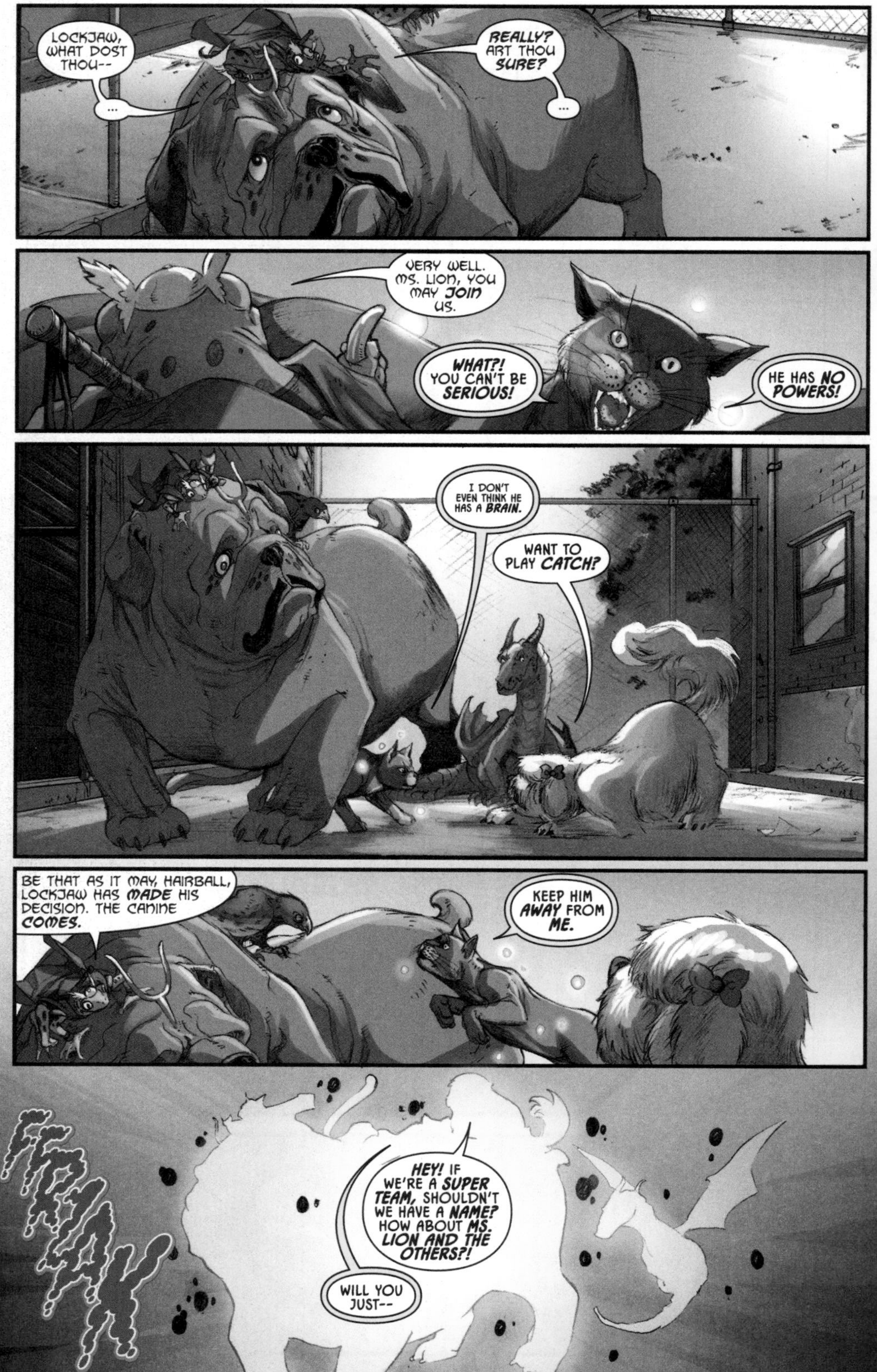

LOCKJAW, WHAT DOST THOU--
...
REALLY? ART THOU SURE?
...
VERY WELL. MS. LION, YOU MAY JOIN US.
WHAT?! YOU CAN'T BE SERIOUS!
HE HAS NO POWERS!
I DON'T EVEN THINK HE HAS A BRAIN.
WANT TO PLAY CATCH?
BE THAT AS IT MAY, HAIRBALL, LOCKJAW HAS MADE HIS DECISION. THE CANINE COMES.
KEEP HIM AWAY FROM ME.
FRRZAK
HEY! IF WE'RE A SUPER TEAM, SHOULDN'T WE HAVE A NAME? HOW ABOUT MS. LION AND THE OTHERS?!
WILL YOU JUST--

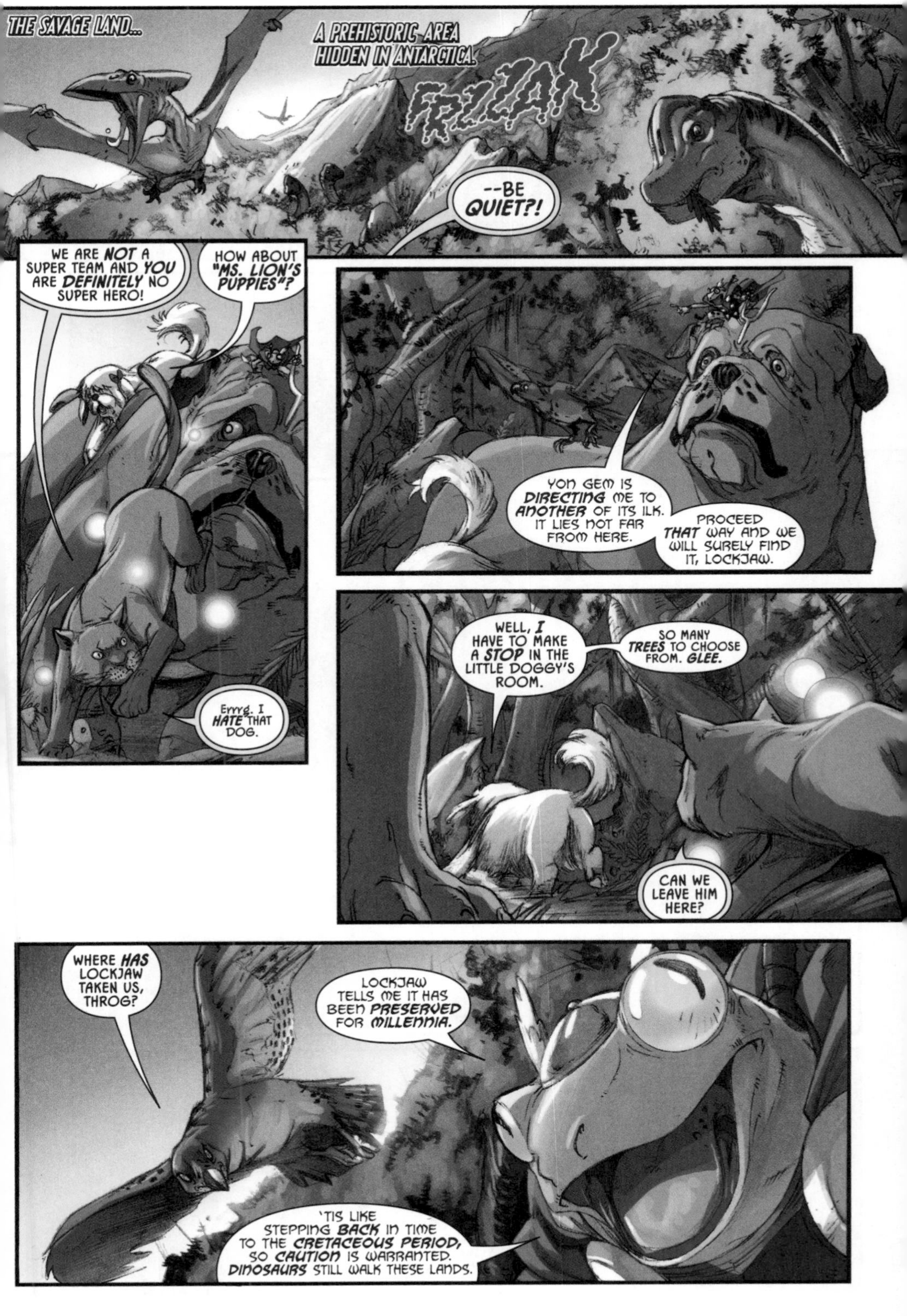
THE SAVAGE LAND...
A PREHISTORIC AREA HIDDEN IN ANTARCTICA.
FRZZAK
--BE QUIET?!
WE ARE NOT A SUPER TEAM AND YOU ARE DEFINITELY NO SUPER HERO!
HOW ABOUT "MS. LION'S PUPPIES"?
Erryg. I HATE THAT DOG.
YON GEM IS DIRECTING ME TO ANOTHER OF ITS ILK. IT LIES NOT FAR FROM HERE.
PROCEED THAT WAY AND WE WILL SURELY FIND IT, LOCKJAW.
WELL, I HAVE TO MAKE A STOP IN THE LITTLE DOGGY'S ROOM.
SO MANY TREES TO CHOOSE FROM. GLEE.
CAN WE LEAVE HIM HERE?
WHERE HAS LOCKJAW TAKEN US, THROG?
LOCKJAW TELLS ME IT HAS BEEN PRESERVED FOR MILLENNIA.
'TIS LIKE STEPPING BACK IN TIME TO THE CRETACEOUS PERIOD, SO CAUTION IS WARRANTED. DINOSAURS STILL WALK THESE LANDS.

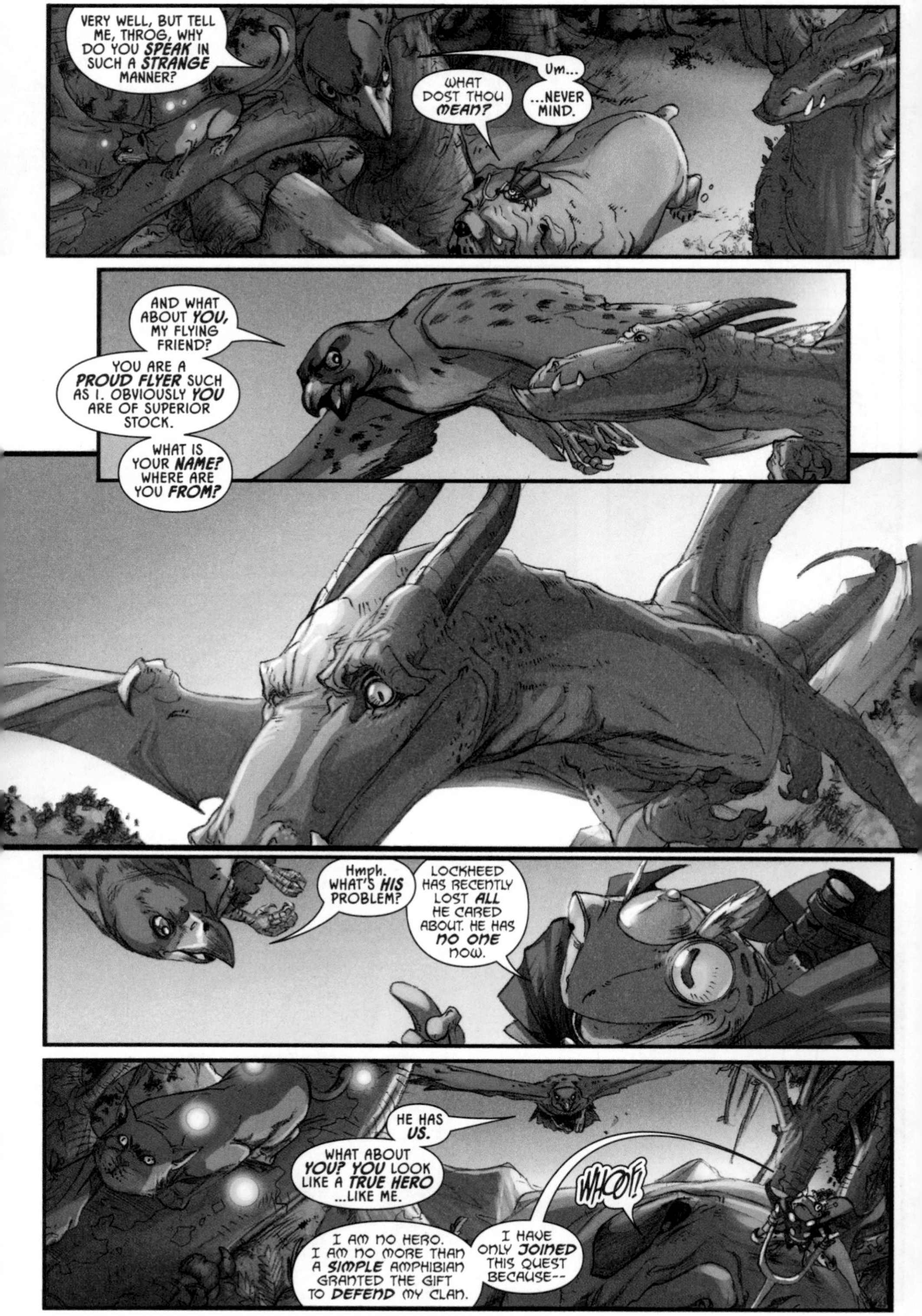
VERY WELL, BUT TELL ME, THROG, WHY DO YOU SPEAK IN SUCH A STRANGE MANNER?
WHAT DOST THOU MEAN?
Um...
...NEVER MIND.
AND WHAT ABOUT YOU, MY FLYING FRIEND?
YOU ARE A PROUD FLYER SUCH AS I. OBVIOUSLY YOU ARE OF SUPERIOR STOCK.
WHAT IS YOUR NAME? WHERE ARE YOU FROM?
Hmph. WHAT'S HIS PROBLEM?
LOCKHEED HAS RECENTLY LOST ALL HE CARED ABOUT. HE HAS NO ONE NOW.
HE HAS US.
WHAT ABOUT YOU? YOU LOOK LIKE A TRUE HERO ...LIKE ME.
WHOOF!
I AM NO HERO. I AM NO MORE THAN A SIMPLE AMPHIBIAN GRANTED THE GIFT TO DEFEND MY CLAN.
I HAVE ONLY JOINED THIS QUEST BECAUSE--

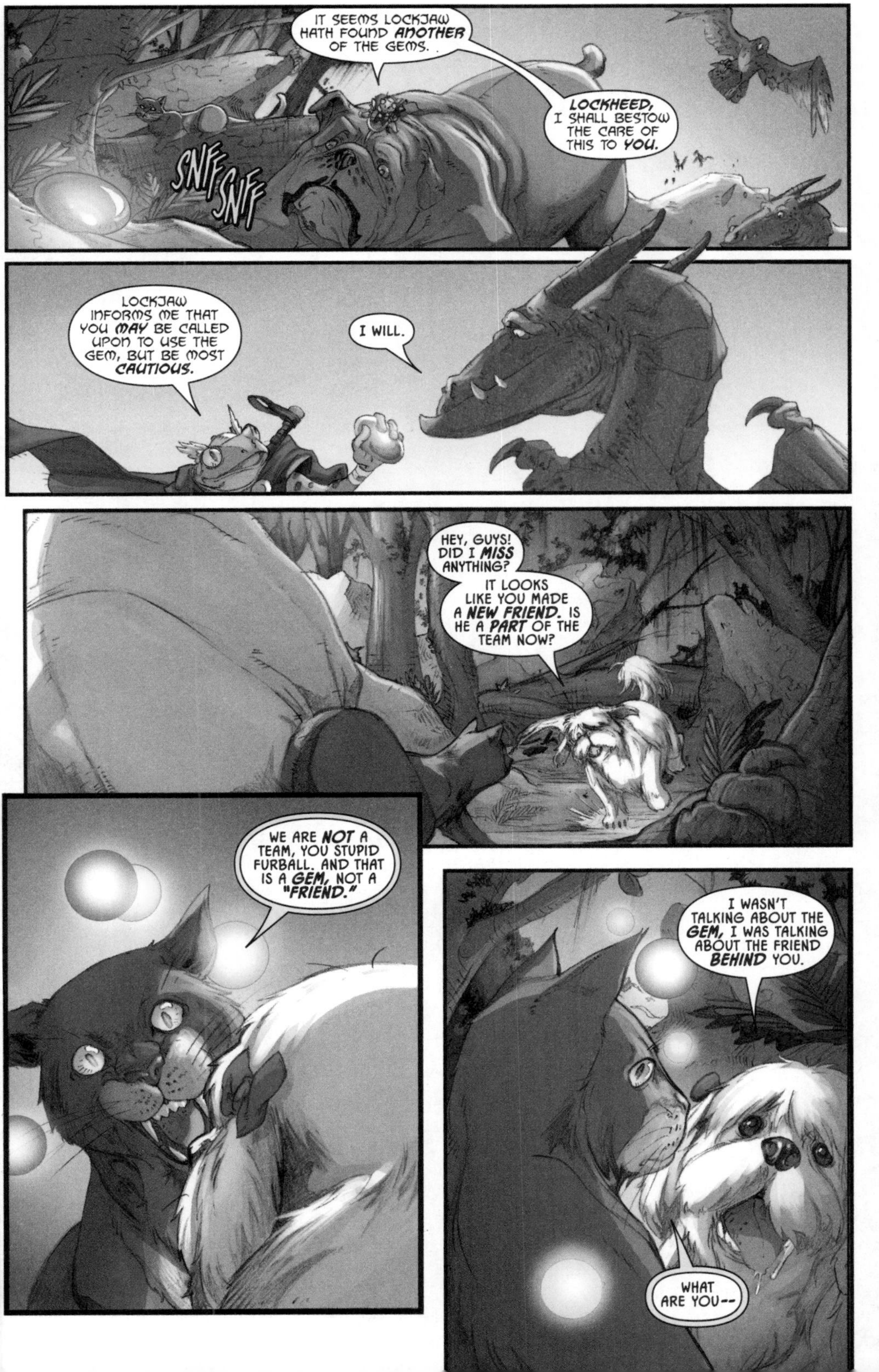
IT SEEMS LOCKJAW HATH FOUND ANOTHER OF THE GEMS.
SNIFF SNIFF
LOCKHEED, I SHALL BESTOW THE CARE OF THIS TO YOU.
LOCKJAW INFORMS ME THAT YOU MAY BE CALLED UPON TO USE THE GEM, BUT BE MOST CAUTIOUS.
I WILL.
HEY, GUYS! DID I MISS ANYTHING?
IT LOOKS LIKE YOU MADE A NEW FRIEND. IS HE A PART OF THE TEAM NOW?
WE ARE NOT A TEAM, YOU STUPID FURBALL. AND THAT IS A GEM, NOT A "FRIEND."
I WASN'T TALKING ABOUT THE GEM, I WAS TALKING ABOUT THE FRIEND BEHIND YOU.
WHAT ARE YOU--

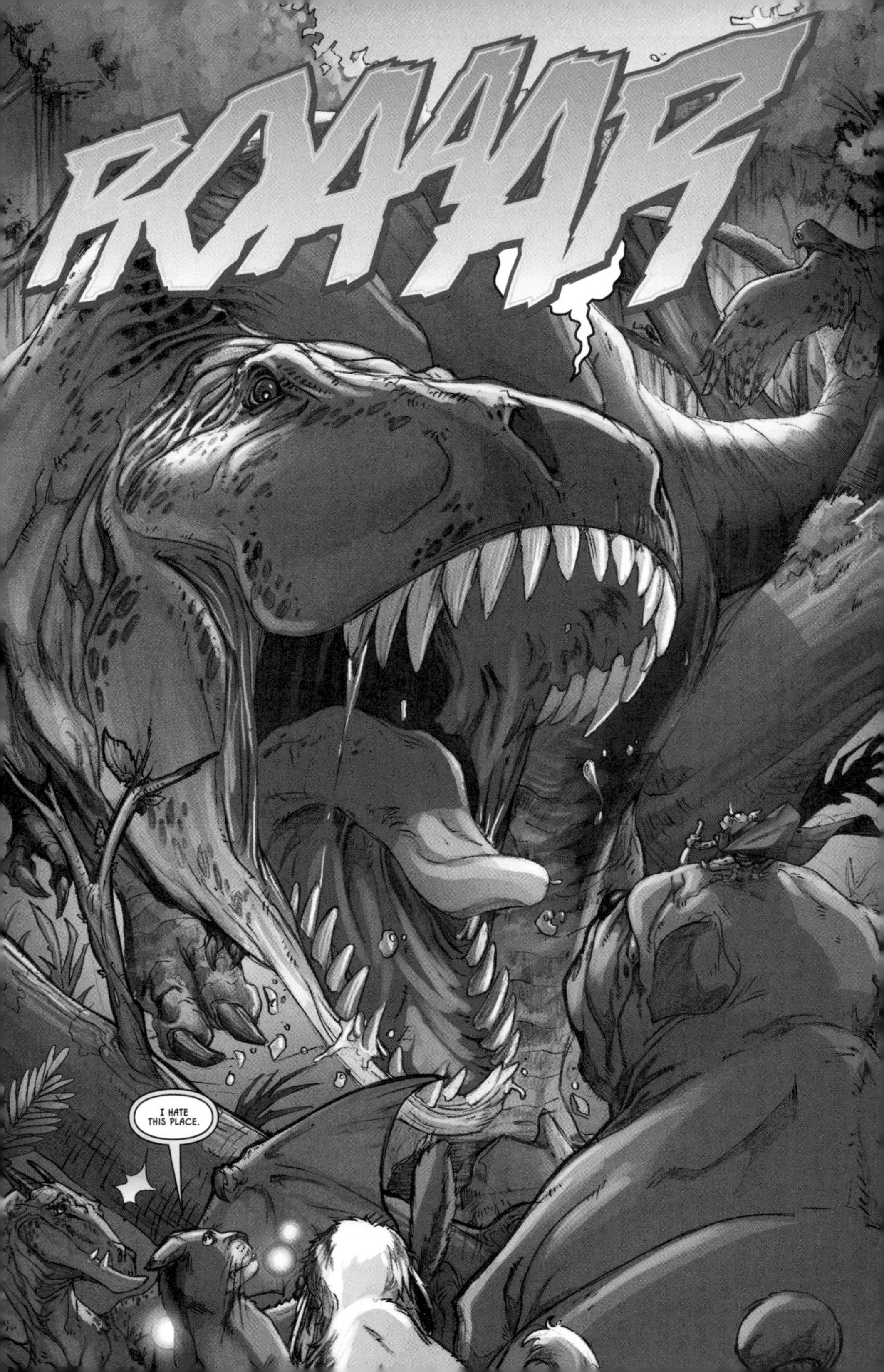
ROAAAR
I HATE THIS PLACE.

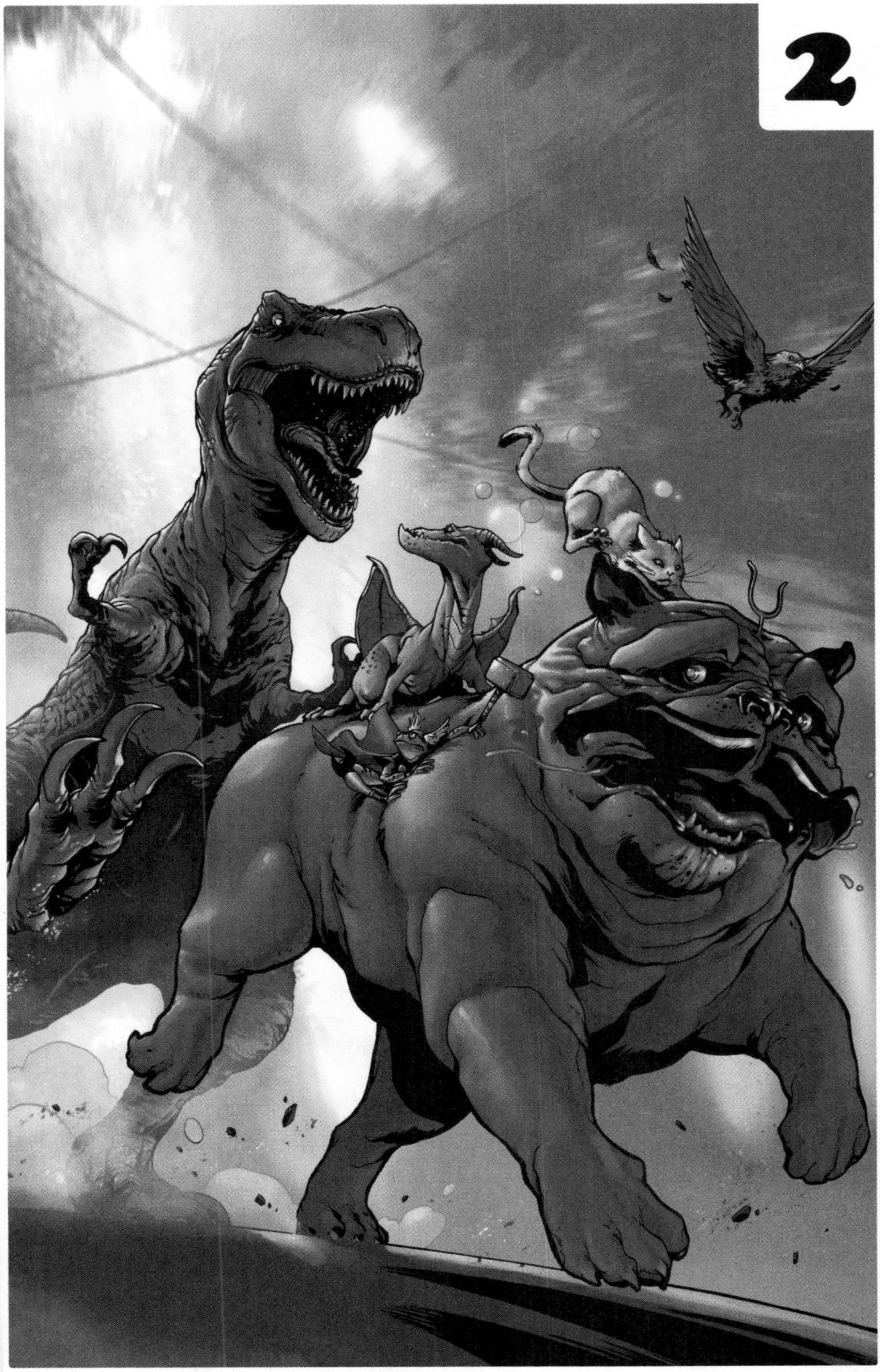
2

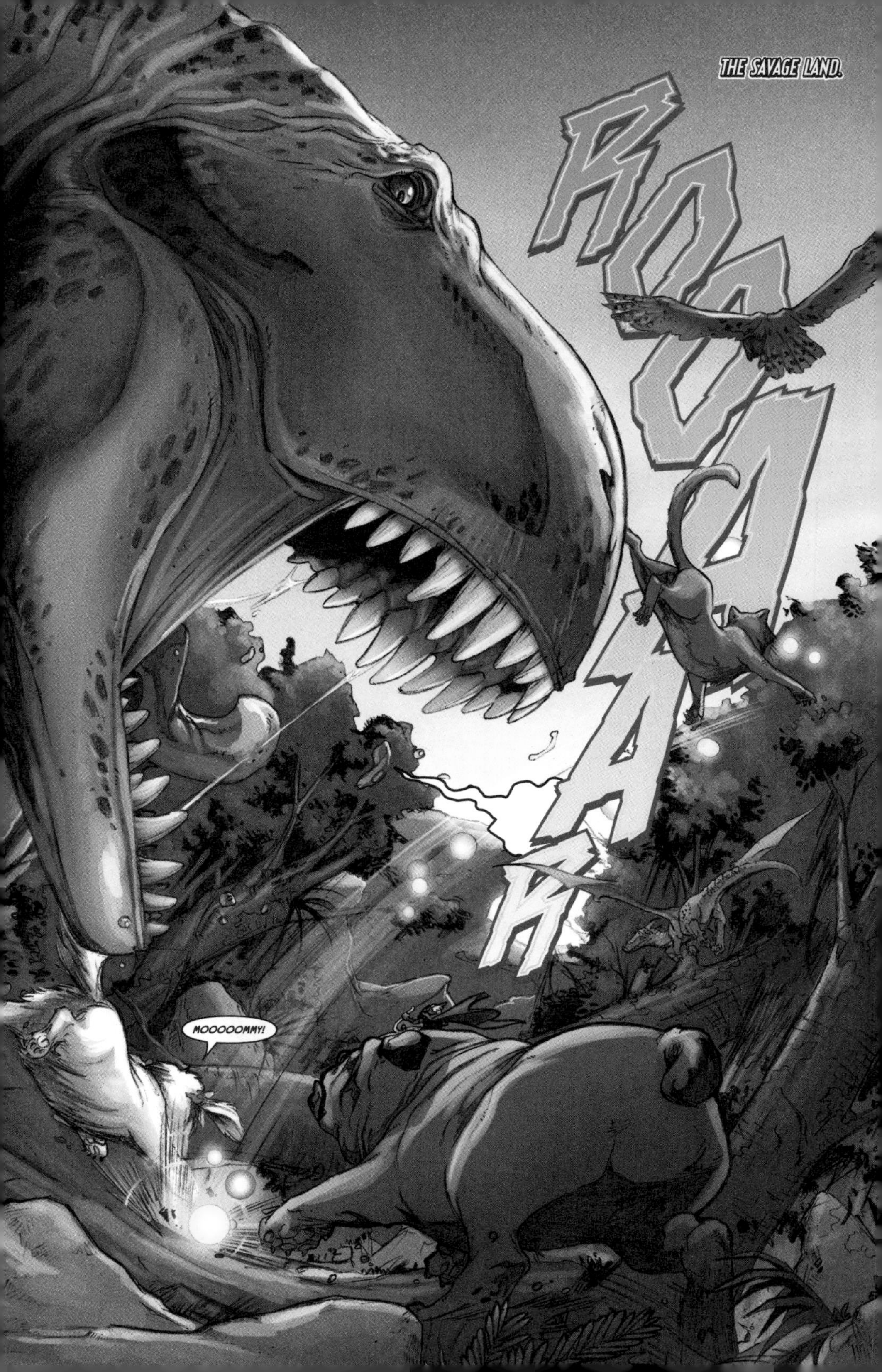
THE SAVAGE LAND.
ROOOAAAAK!
MOOOOOMMY!

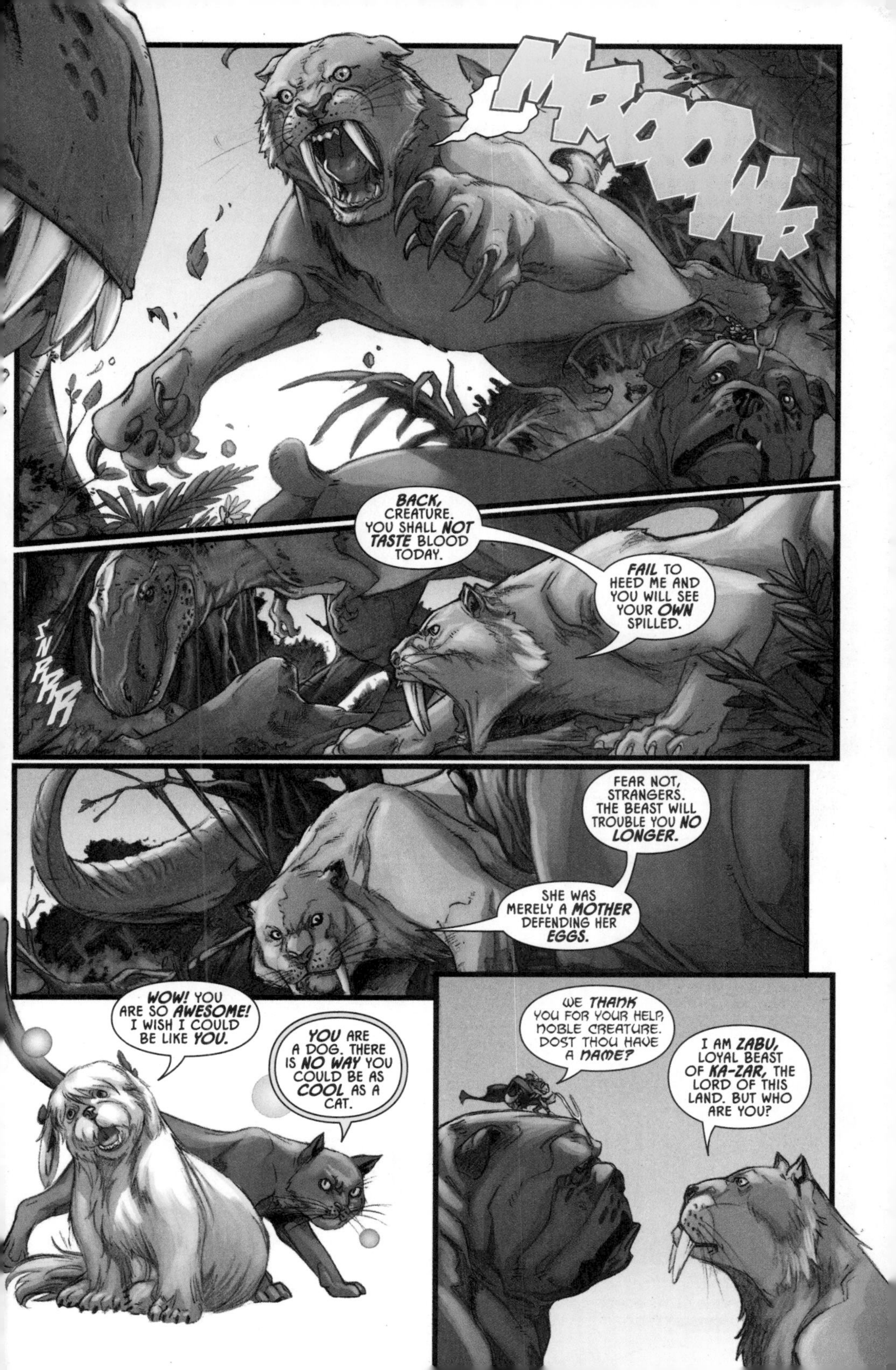
MROOWR
BACK, CREATURE. YOU SHALL NOT TASTE BLOOD TODAY.
FAIL TO HEED ME AND YOU WILL SEE YOUR OWN SPILLED.
SNRRRR
FEAR NOT, STRANGERS. THE BEAST WILL TROUBLE YOU NO LONGER.
SHE WAS MERELY A MOTHER DEFENDING HER EGGS.
WOW! YOU ARE SO AWESOME! I WISH I COULD BE LIKE YOU.
YOU ARE A DOG. THERE IS NO WAY YOU COULD BE AS COOL AS A CAT.
WE THANK YOU FOR YOUR HELP, NOBLE CREATURE. DOST THOU HAVE A NAME?
I AM ZABU, LOYAL BEAST OF KA-ZAR, THE LORD OF THIS LAND. BUT WHO ARE YOU?

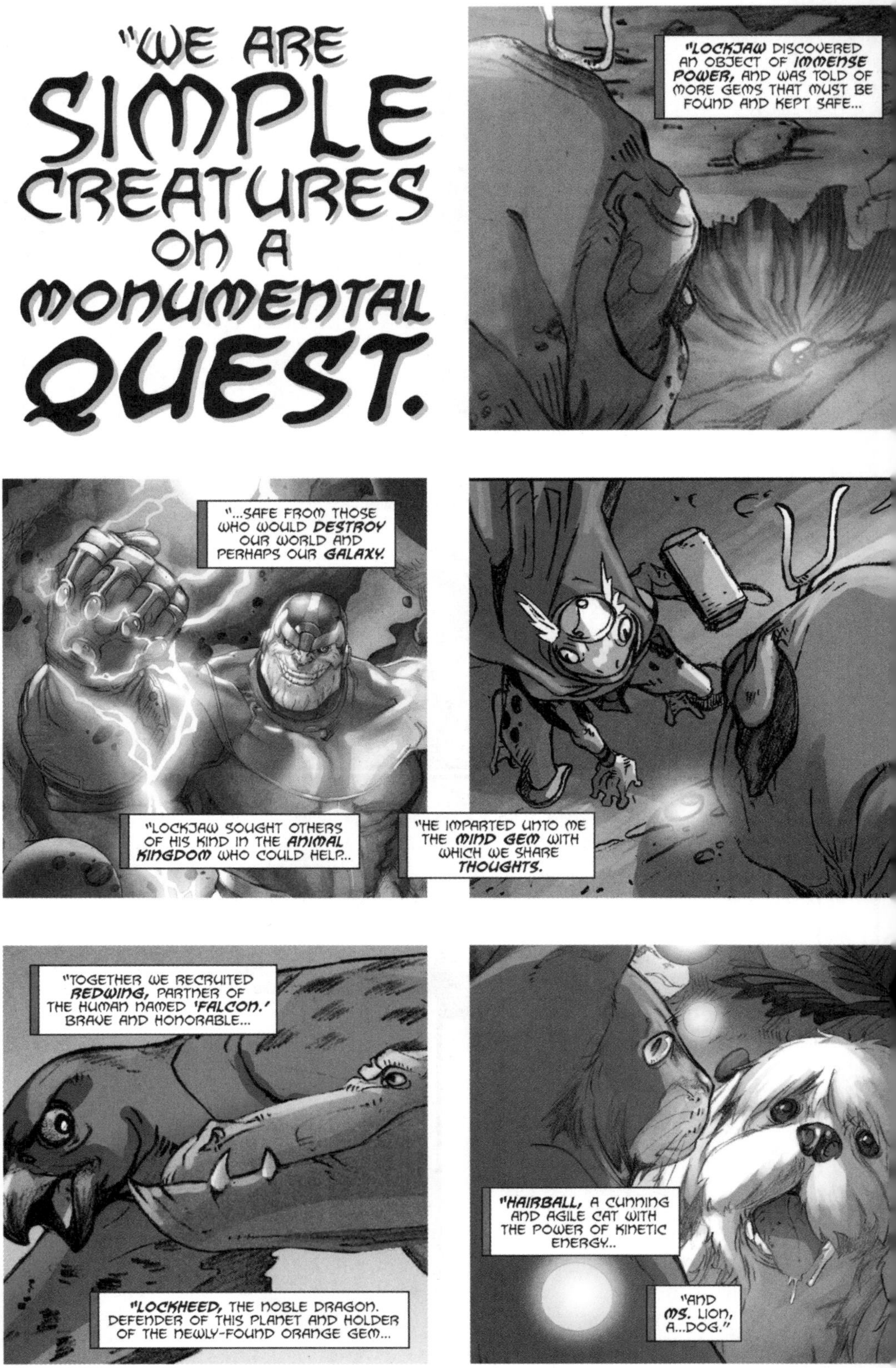
"WE ARE SIMPLE CREATURES ON A MONUMENTAL QUEST.
"LOCKJAW DISCOVERED AN OBJECT OF IMMENSE POWER, AND WAS TOLD OF MORE GEMS THAT MUST BE FOUND AND KEPT SAFE...
"...SAFE FROM THOSE WHO WOULD DESTROY OUR WORLD AND PERHAPS OUR GALAXY.
"LOCKJAW SOUGHT OTHERS OF HIS KIND IN THE ANIMAL KINGDOM WHO COULD HELP...
"HE IMPARTED UNTO ME THE MIND GEM WITH WHICH WE SHARE THOUGHTS.
"TOGETHER WE RECRUITED REDWING, PARTNER OF THE HUMAN NAMED 'FALCON.' BRAVE AND HONORABLE...
"LOCKHEED, THE NOBLE DRAGON. DEFENDER OF THIS PLANET AND HOLDER OF THE NEWLY-FOUND ORANGE GEM...
"HAIRBALL, A CUNNING AND AGILE CAT WITH THE POWER OF KINETIC ENERGY...
"AND MS. LION, A...DOG."

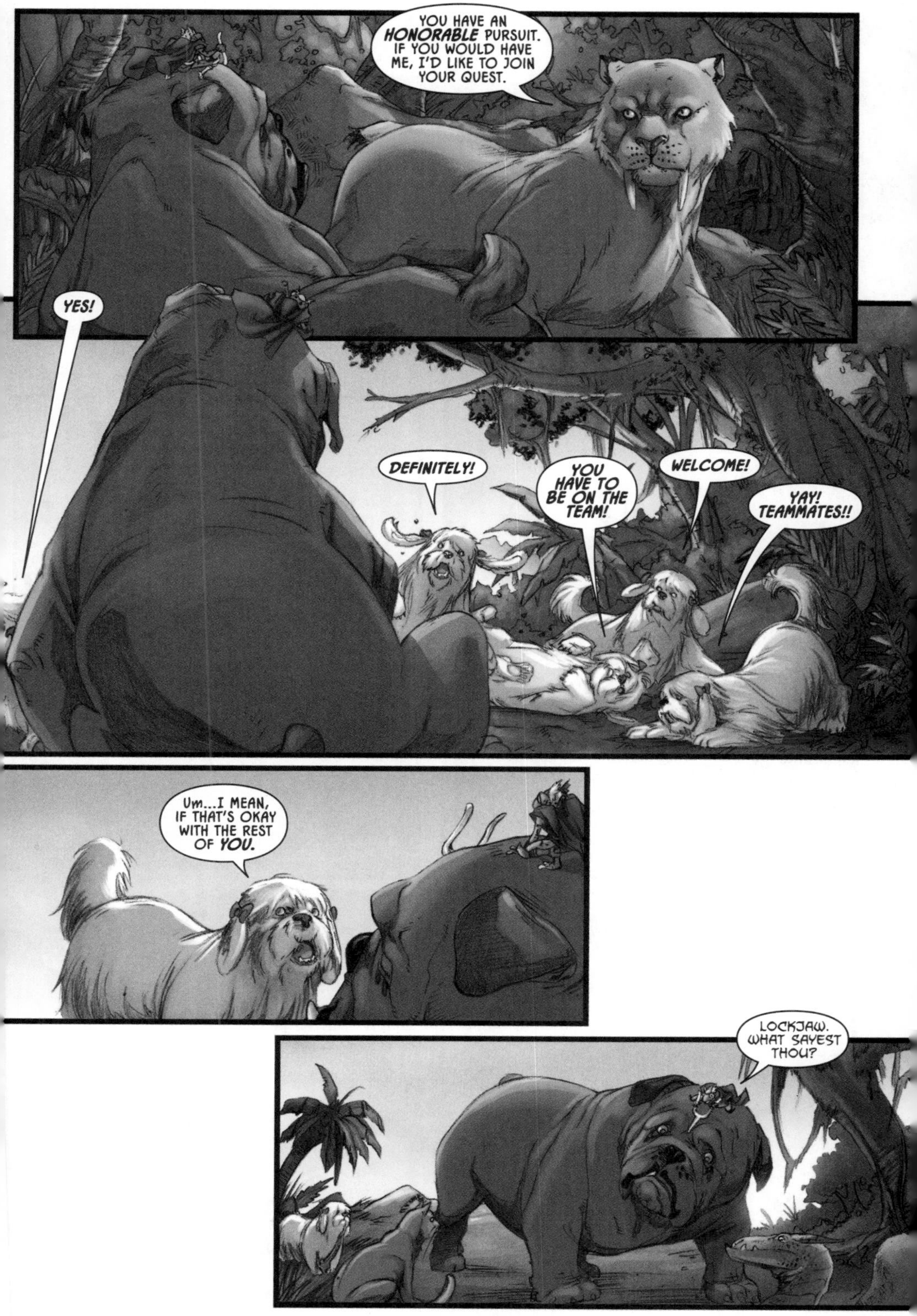
YOU HAVE AN HONORABLE PURSUIT. IF YOU WOULD HAVE ME, I'D LIKE TO JOIN YOUR QUEST.
YES!
DEFINITELY!
YOU HAVE TO BE ON THE TEAM!
WELCOME!
YAY! TEAMMATES!!
Um...I MEAN, IF THAT'S OKAY WITH THE REST OF YOU.
LOCKJAW. WHAT SAYEST THOU?

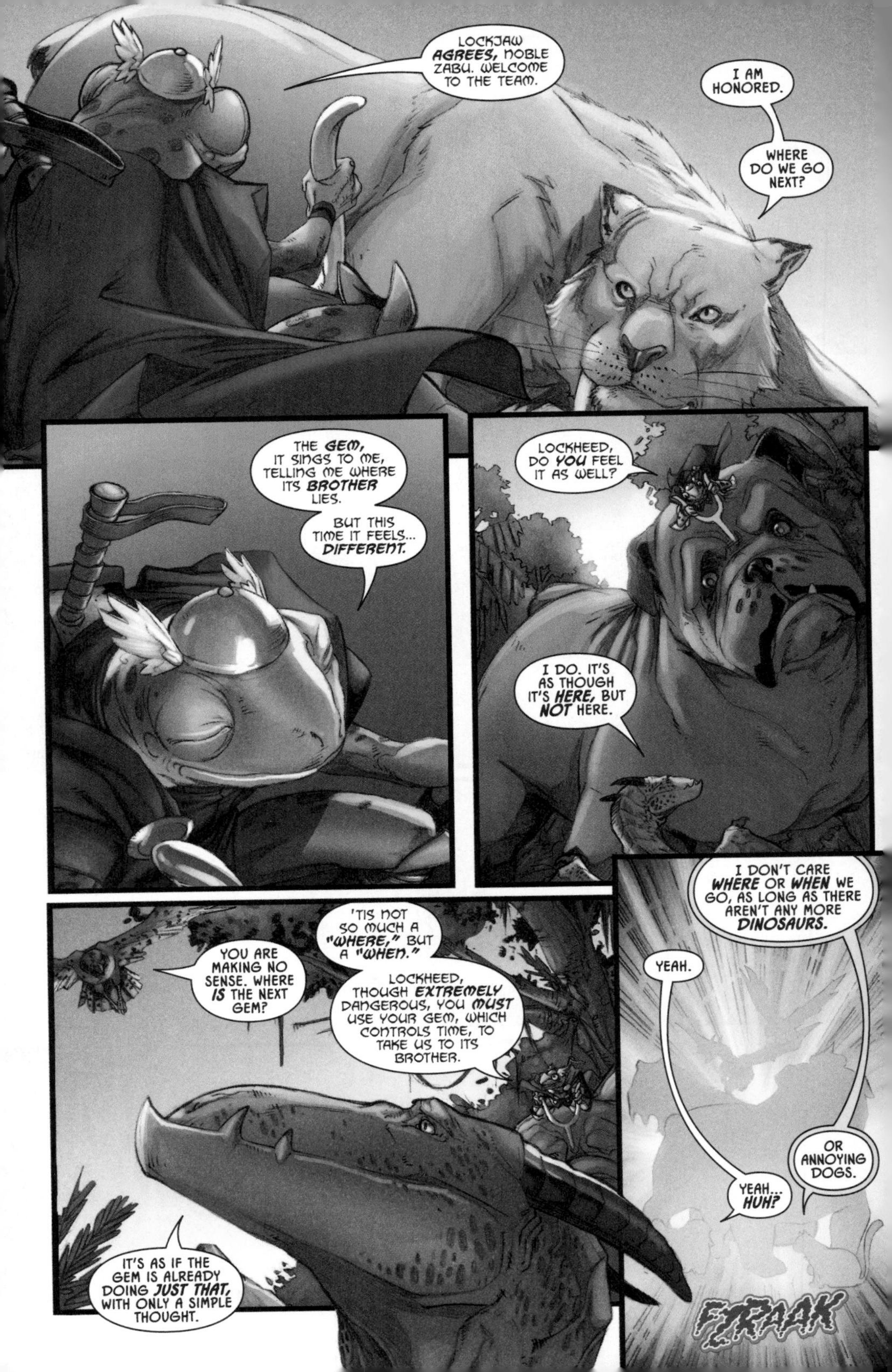
LOCKJAW AGREES, NOBLE ZABU. WELCOME TO THE TEAM.
I AM HONORED.
WHERE DO WE GO NEXT?
THE GEM, IT SINGS TO ME, TELLING ME WHERE ITS BROTHER LIES.
BUT THIS TIME IT FEELS... DIFFERENT.
LOCKHEED, DO YOU FEEL IT AS WELL?
I DO. IT'S AS THOUGH IT'S HERE, BUT NOT HERE.
YOU ARE MAKING NO SENSE. WHERE IS THE NEXT GEM?
'TIS NOT SO MUCH A "WHERE," BUT A "WHEN."
LOCKHEED, THOUGH EXTREMELY DANGEROUS, YOU MUST USE YOUR GEM, WHICH CONTROLS TIME, TO TAKE US TO ITS BROTHER.
IT'S AS IF THE GEM IS ALREADY DOING JUST THAT, WITH ONLY A SIMPLE THOUGHT.
I DON'T CARE WHERE OR WHEN WE GO, AS LONG AS THERE AREN'T ANY MORE DINOSAURS.
YEAH.
OR ANNOYING DOGS.
YEAH... HUH?
FZRAAK

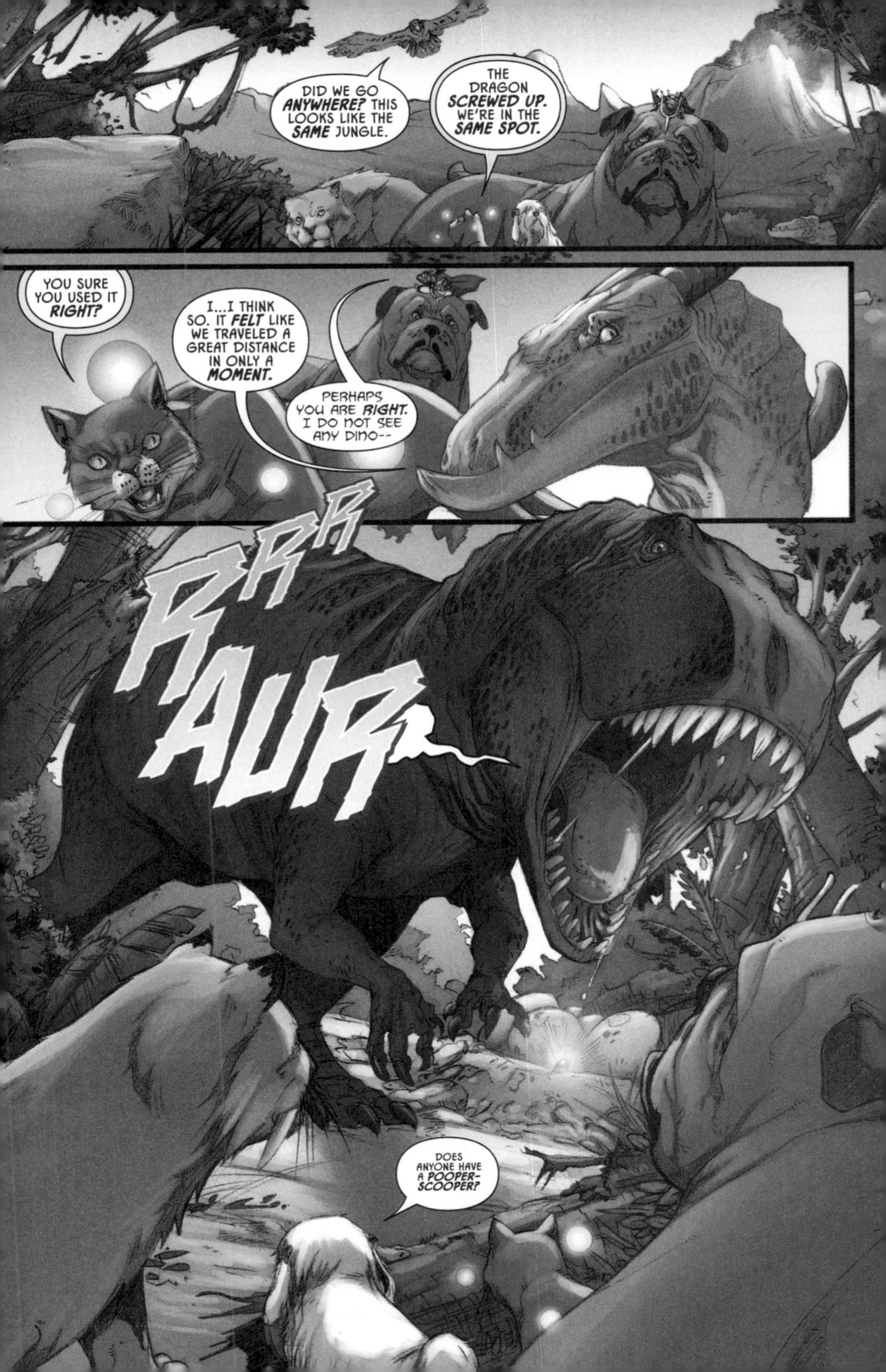
DID WE GO ANYWHERE? THIS LOOKS LIKE THE SAME JUNGLE.
THE DRAGON SCREWED UP. WE'RE IN THE SAME SPOT.
YOU SURE YOU USED IT RIGHT?
I...I THINK SO. IT FELT LIKE WE TRAVELED A GREAT DISTANCE IN ONLY A MOMENT.
PERHAPS YOU ARE RIGHT. I DO NOT SEE ANY DINO--
RRRRAUR
DOES ANYONE HAVE A POOPER-SCOOPER?

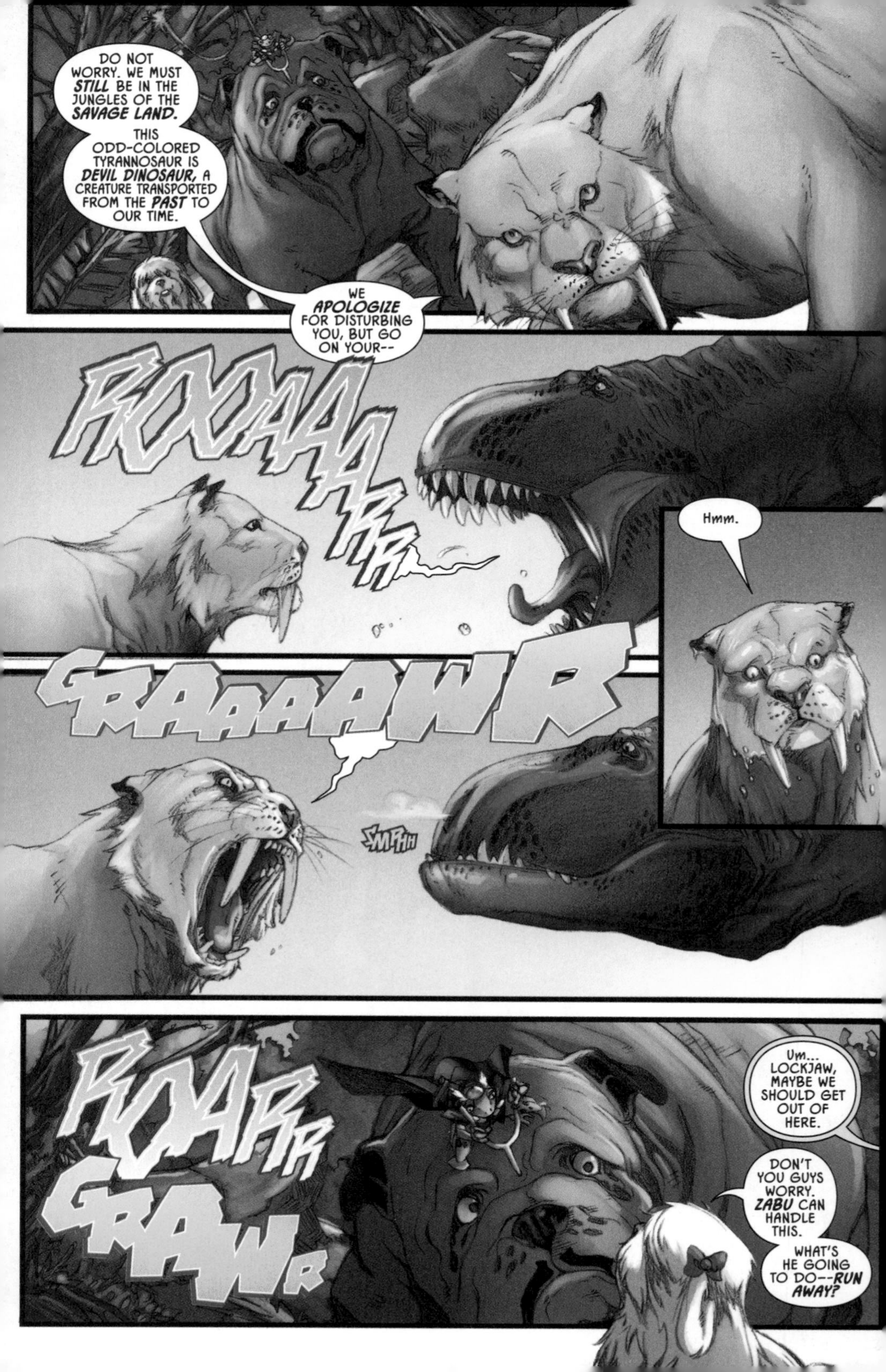
DO NOT WORRY. WE MUST STILL BE IN THE JUNGLES OF THE SAVAGE LAND.
THIS ODD-COLORED TYRANNOSAUR IS DEVIL DINOSAUR, A CREATURE TRANSPORTED FROM THE PAST TO OUR TIME.
WE APOLOGIZE FOR DISTURBING YOU, BUT GO ON YOUR--
ROOAAARR
Hmm.
GRAAAAAWR
SMPHH
ROOARRR
GRAWR
Um... LOCKJAW, MAYBE WE SHOULD GET OUT OF HERE.
DON'T YOU GUYS WORRY. ZABU CAN HANDLE THIS.
WHAT'S HE GOING TO DO--RUN AWAY?

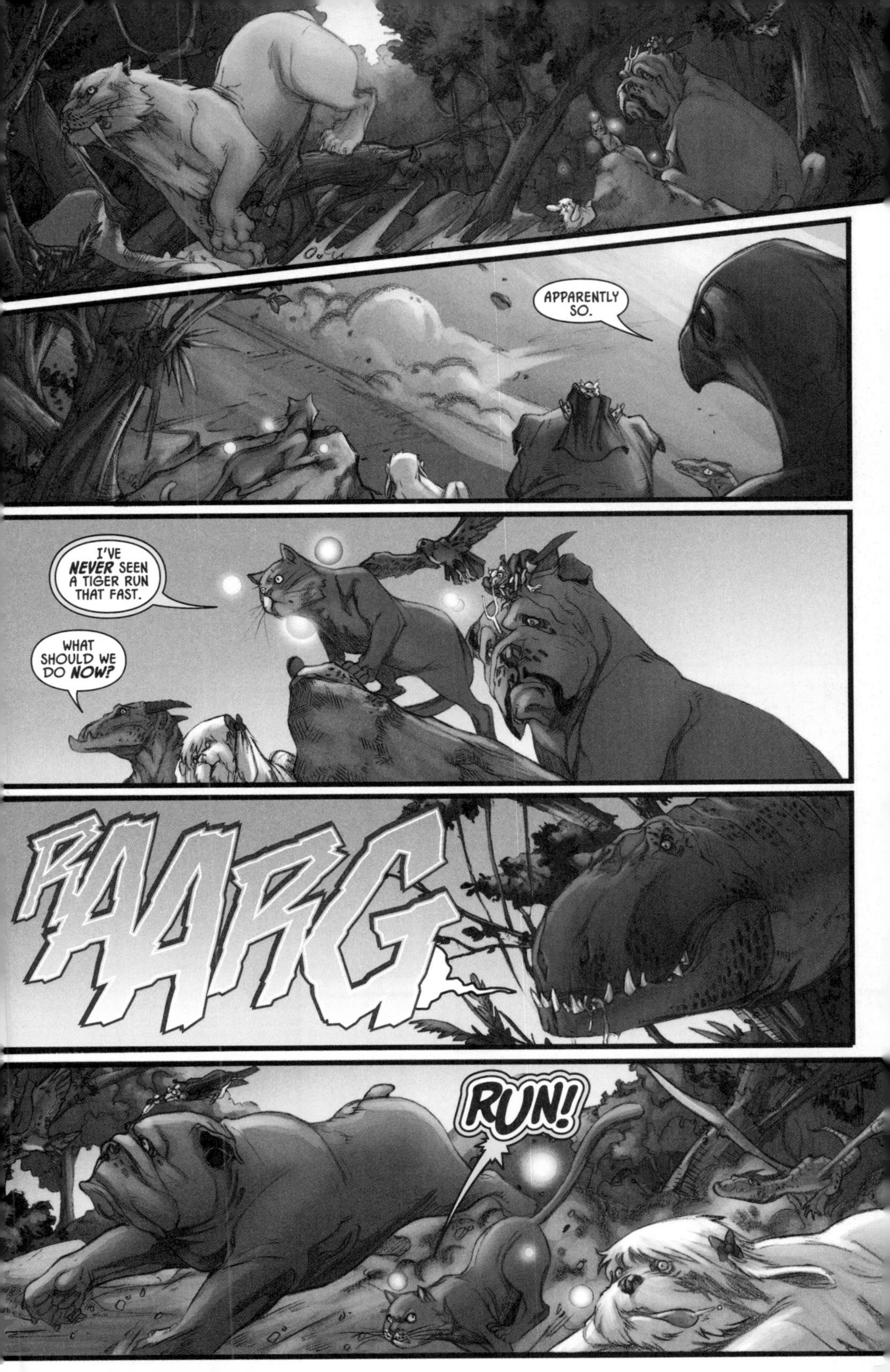
APPARENTLY SO.
I'VE NEVER SEEN A TIGER RUN THAT FAST.
WHAT SHOULD WE DO NOW?
RAARG
RUN!

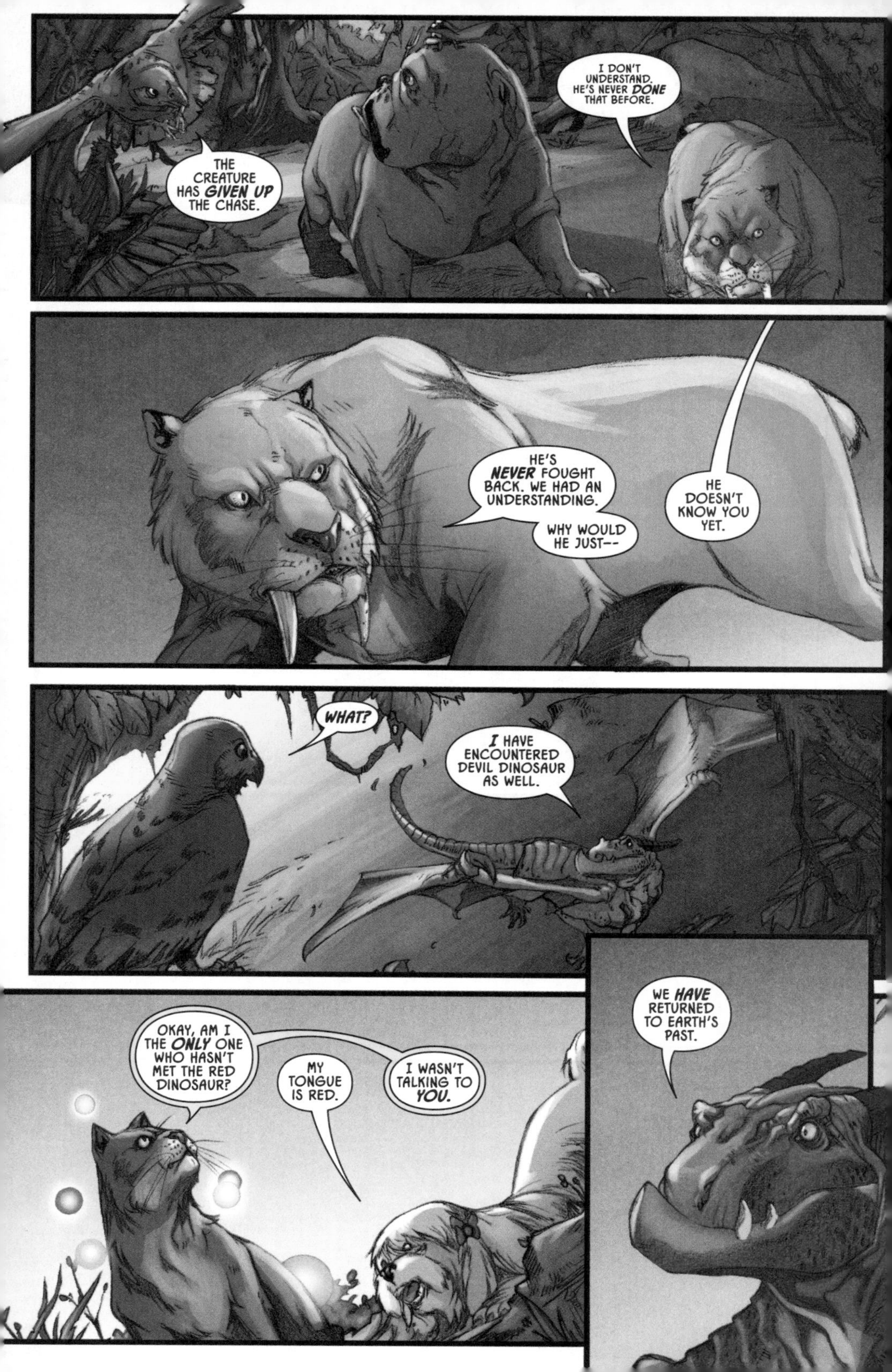
THE CREATURE HAS *GIVEN UP* THE CHASE.
I DON'T UNDERSTAND. HE'S NEVER *DONE* THAT BEFORE.
HE'S *NEVER* FOUGHT BACK. WE HAD AN UNDERSTANDING.
WHY WOULD HE JUST--
HE DOESN'T KNOW YOU YET.
*WHAT?*
*I* HAVE ENCOUNTERED DEVIL DINOSAUR AS WELL.
OKAY, AM I THE *ONLY* ONE WHO HASN'T MET THE RED DINOSAUR?
MY TONGUE IS RED.
I WASN'T TALKING TO *YOU.*
WE *HAVE* RETURNED TO EARTH'S PAST.

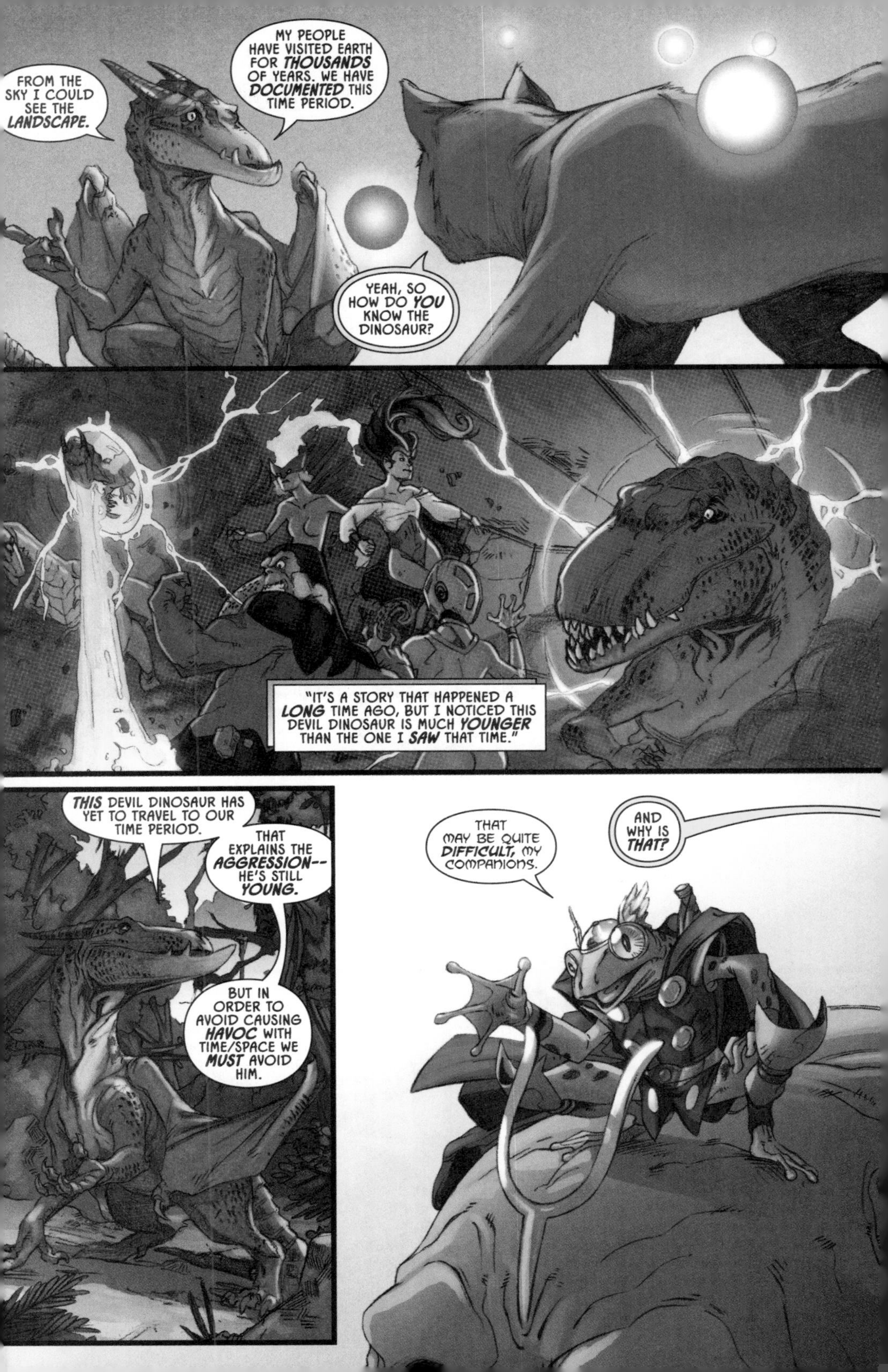

FROM THE SKY I COULD SEE THE LANDSCAPE.
MY PEOPLE HAVE VISITED EARTH FOR THOUSANDS OF YEARS. WE HAVE DOCUMENTED THIS TIME PERIOD.
YEAH, SO HOW DO YOU KNOW THE DINOSAUR?
"IT'S A STORY THAT HAPPENED A LONG TIME AGO, BUT I NOTICED THIS DEVIL DINOSAUR IS MUCH YOUNGER THAN THE ONE I SAW THAT TIME."
THIS DEVIL DINOSAUR HAS YET TO TRAVEL TO OUR TIME PERIOD.
THAT EXPLAINS THE AGGRESSION-- HE'S STILL YOUNG.
BUT IN ORDER TO AVOID CAUSING HAVOC WITH TIME/SPACE WE MUST AVOID HIM.
THAT MAY BE QUITE DIFFICULT, MY COMPANIONS.
AND WHY IS THAT?

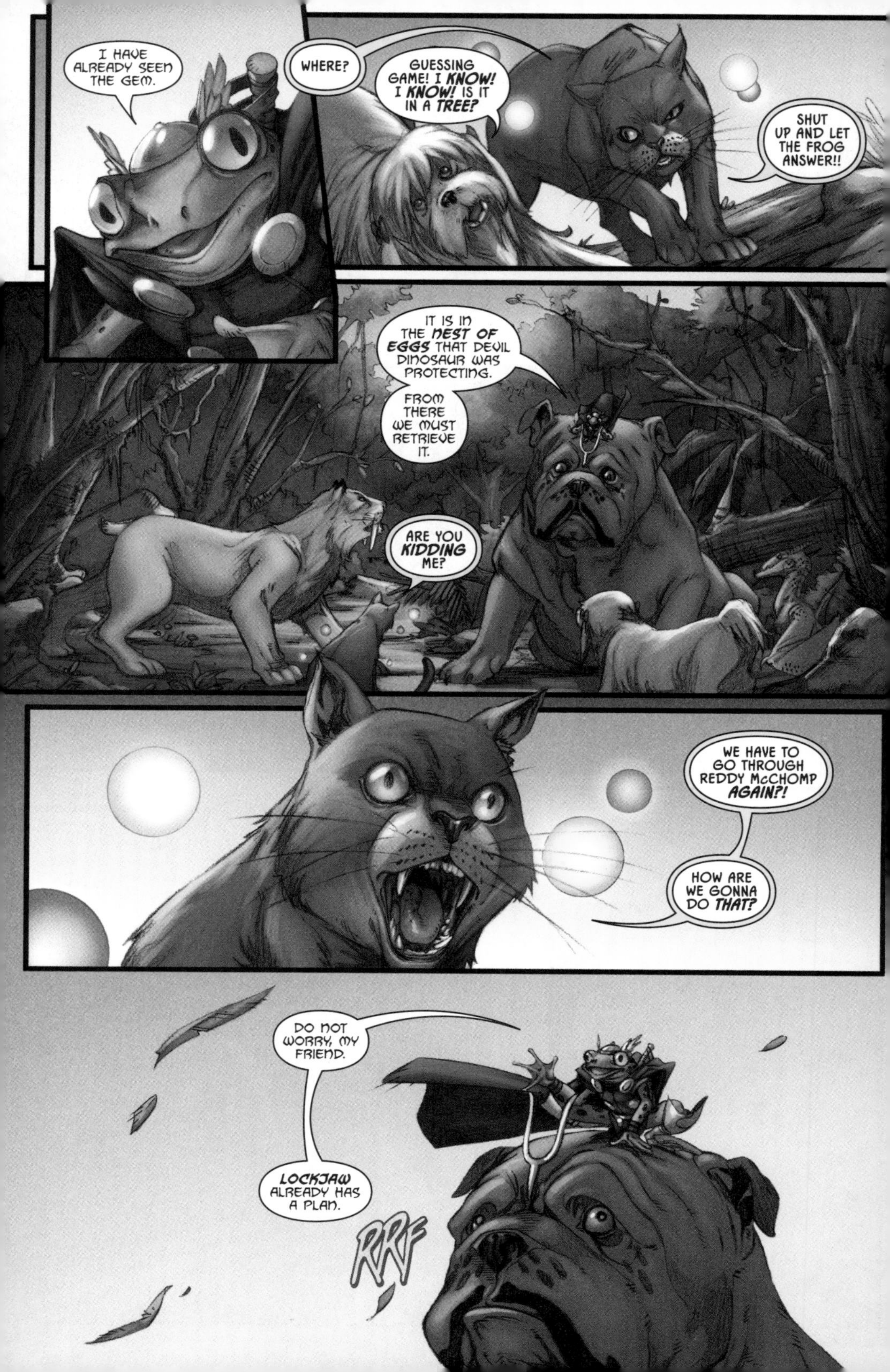
I HAVE ALREADY SEEN THE GEM.
WHERE?
GUESSING GAME! I KNOW! I KNOW! IS IT IN A TREE?
SHUT UP AND LET THE FROG ANSWER!!
IT IS IN THE NEST OF EGGS THAT DEVIL DINOSAUR WAS PROTECTING.
FROM THERE WE MUST RETRIEVE IT.
ARE YOU KIDDING ME?
WE HAVE TO GO THROUGH REDDY McCHOMP AGAIN?!
HOW ARE WE GONNA DO THAT?
DO NOT WORRY, MY FRIEND.
LOCKJAW ALREADY HAS A PLAN.
RRF

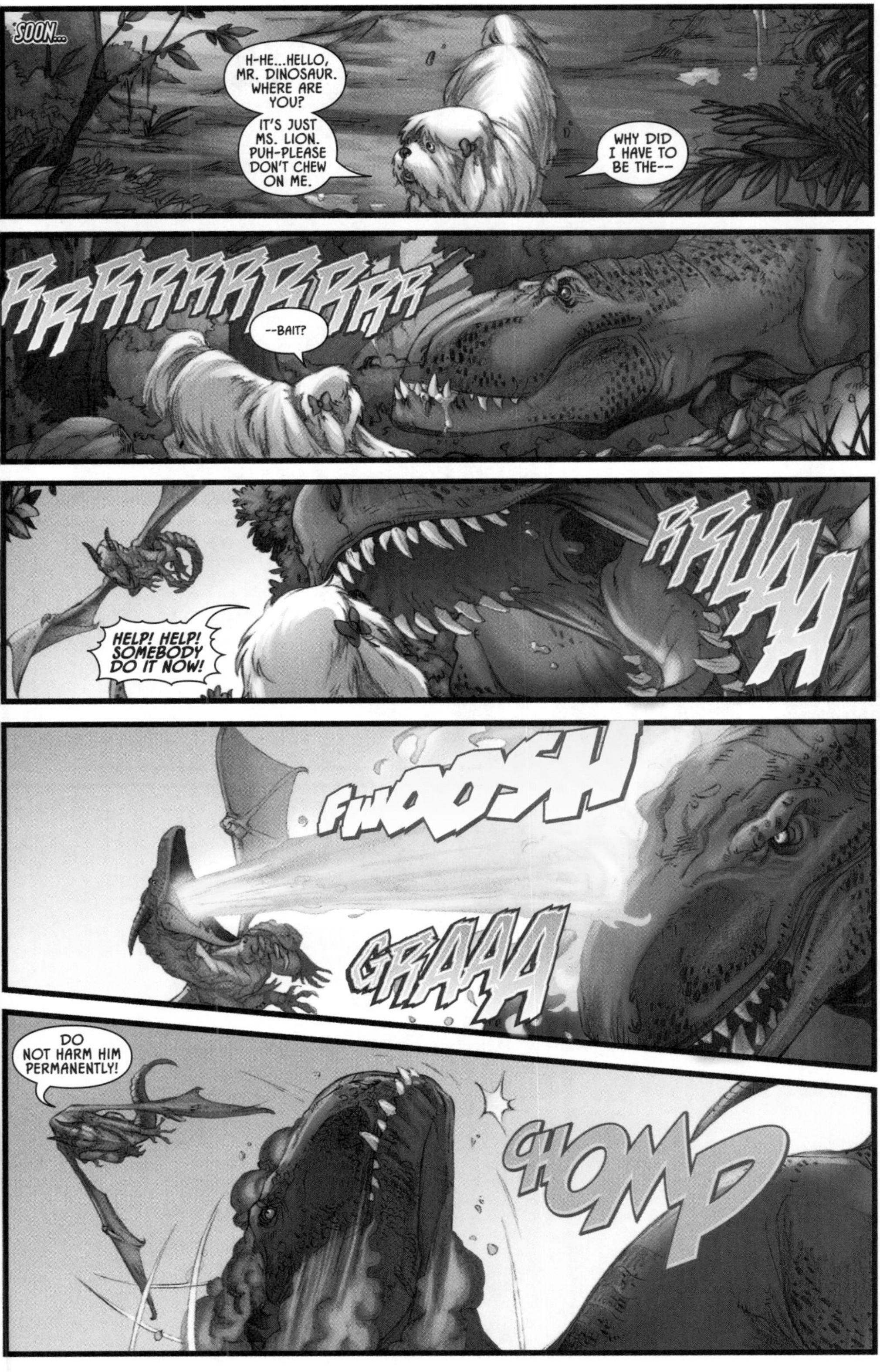
SOON...
H-HE...HELLO, MR. DINOSAUR. WHERE ARE YOU?
IT'S JUST MS. LION. PUH-PLEASE DON'T CHEW ON ME.
WHY DID I HAVE TO BE THE--
RRRRRRRRRRR
--BAIT?
RRUAA
HELP! HELP! SOMEBODY DO IT NOW!
FWOOSH
GRAAA
DO NOT HARM HIM PERMANENTLY!
CHOMP

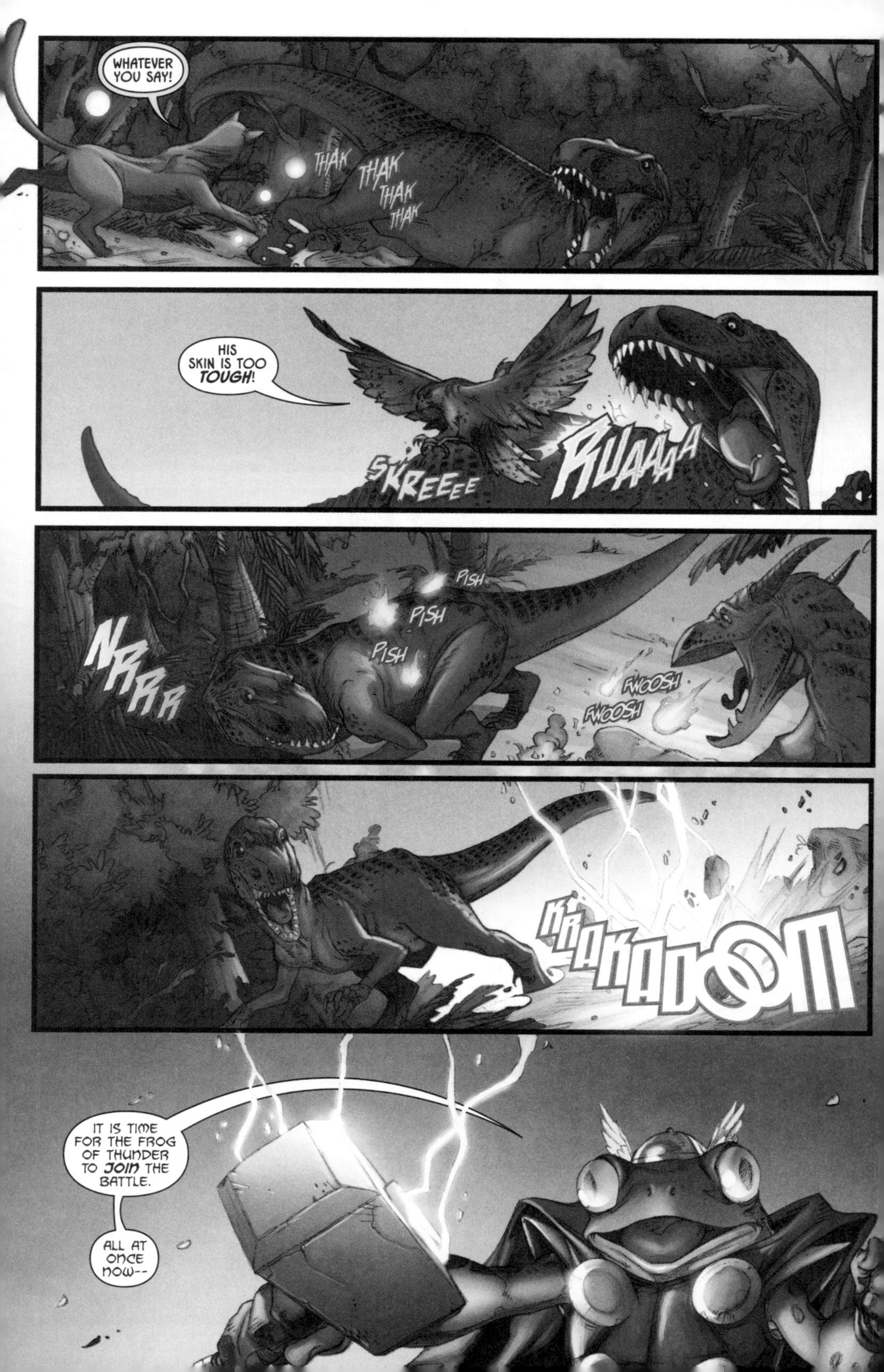

WHATEVER YOU SAY!
THAK
THAK THAK THAK
HIS SKIN IS TOO TOUGH!
SKREEEE
RUAAAA
NRRR
PISH
PISH
PISH
FWOOSH
FWOOSH
KRAKADOOM
IT IS TIME FOR THE FROG OF THUNDER TO JOIN THE BATTLE.
ALL AT ONCE NOW--

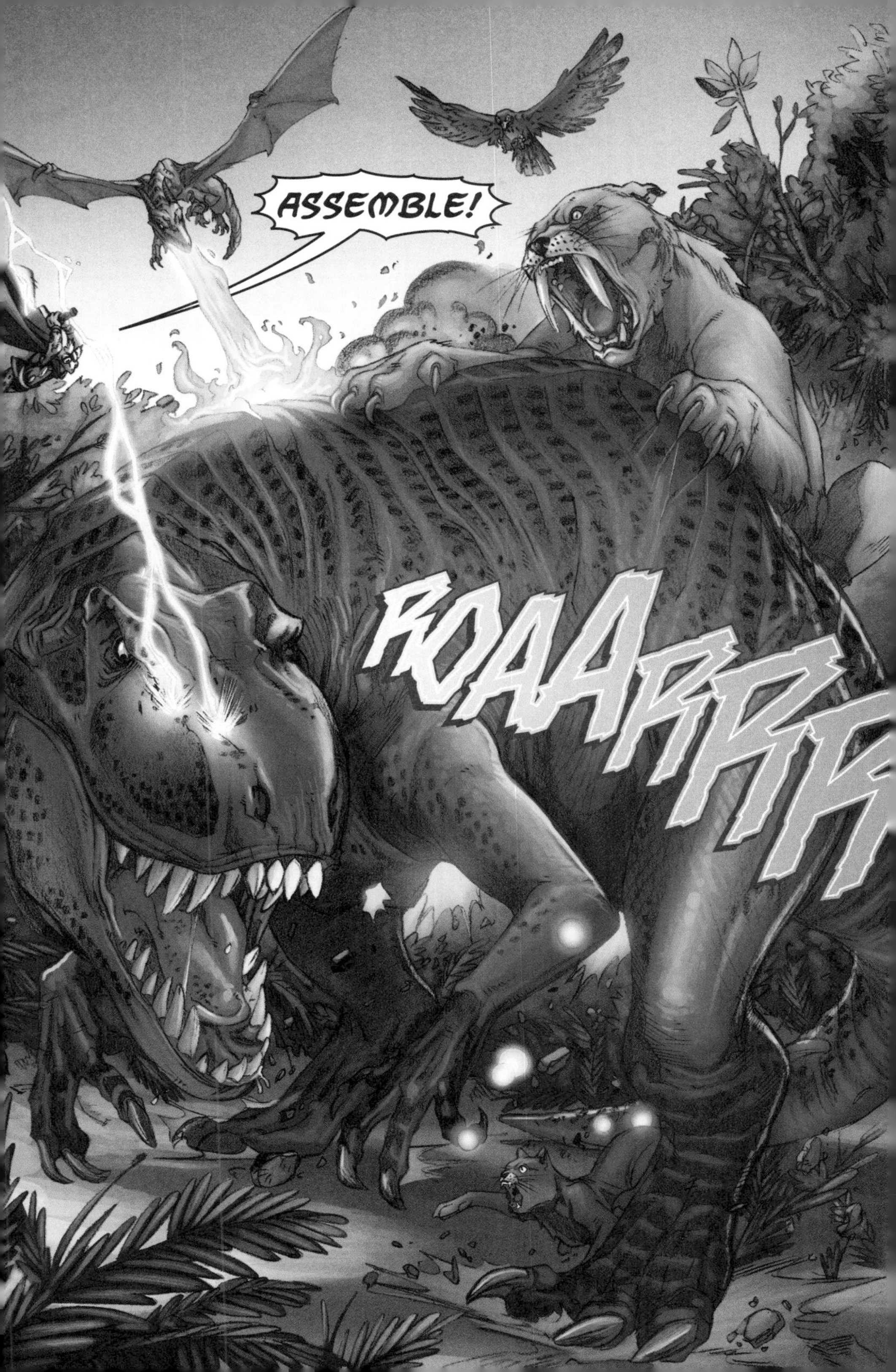
ASSEMBLE!
ROAARRRR

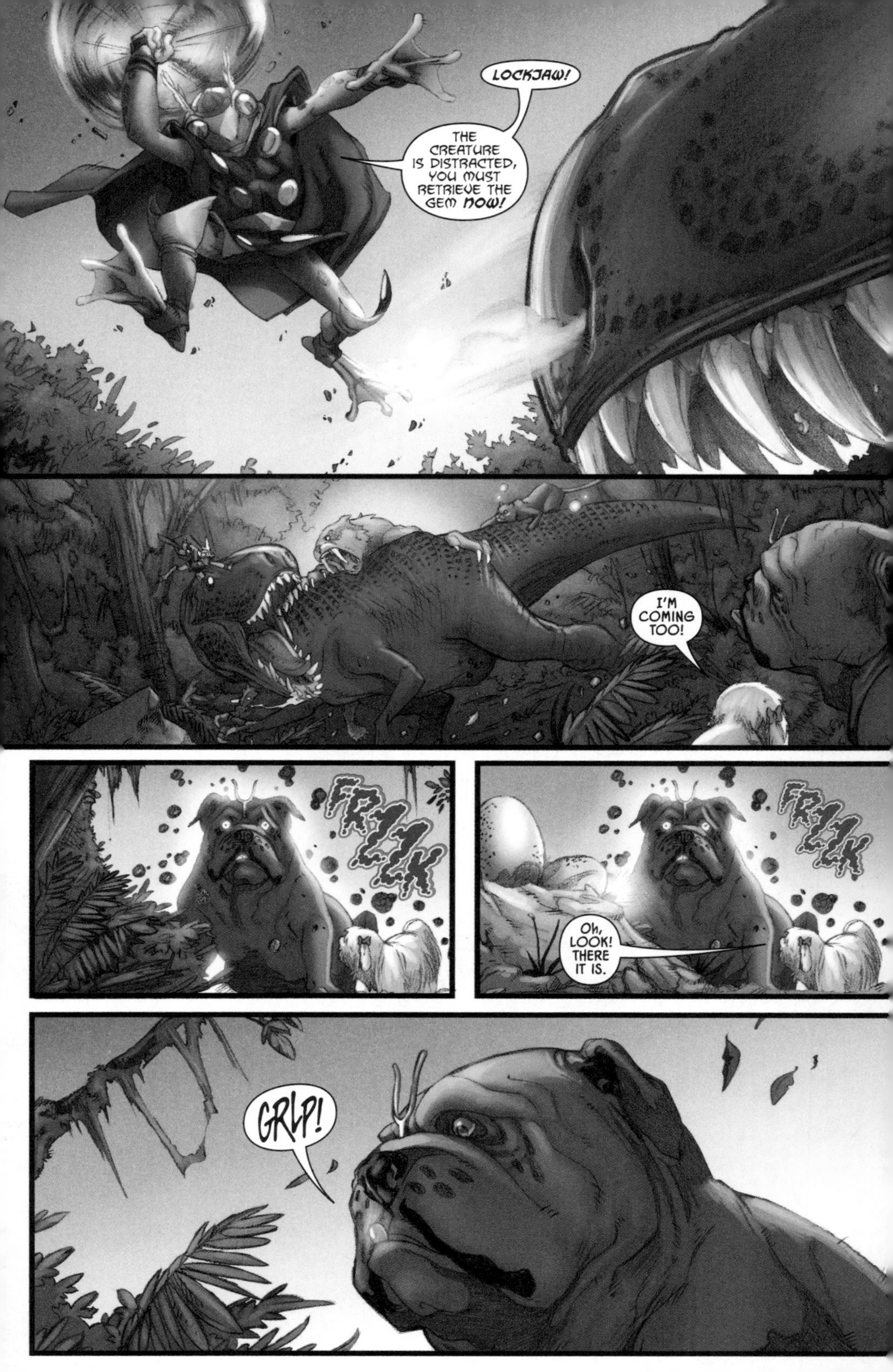
LOCKJAW!
THE CREATURE IS DISTRACTED, YOU MUST RETRIEVE THE GEM NOW!
I'M COMING TOO!
FRZZK
FRZZK
Oh, LOOK! THERE IT IS.
GRLP!

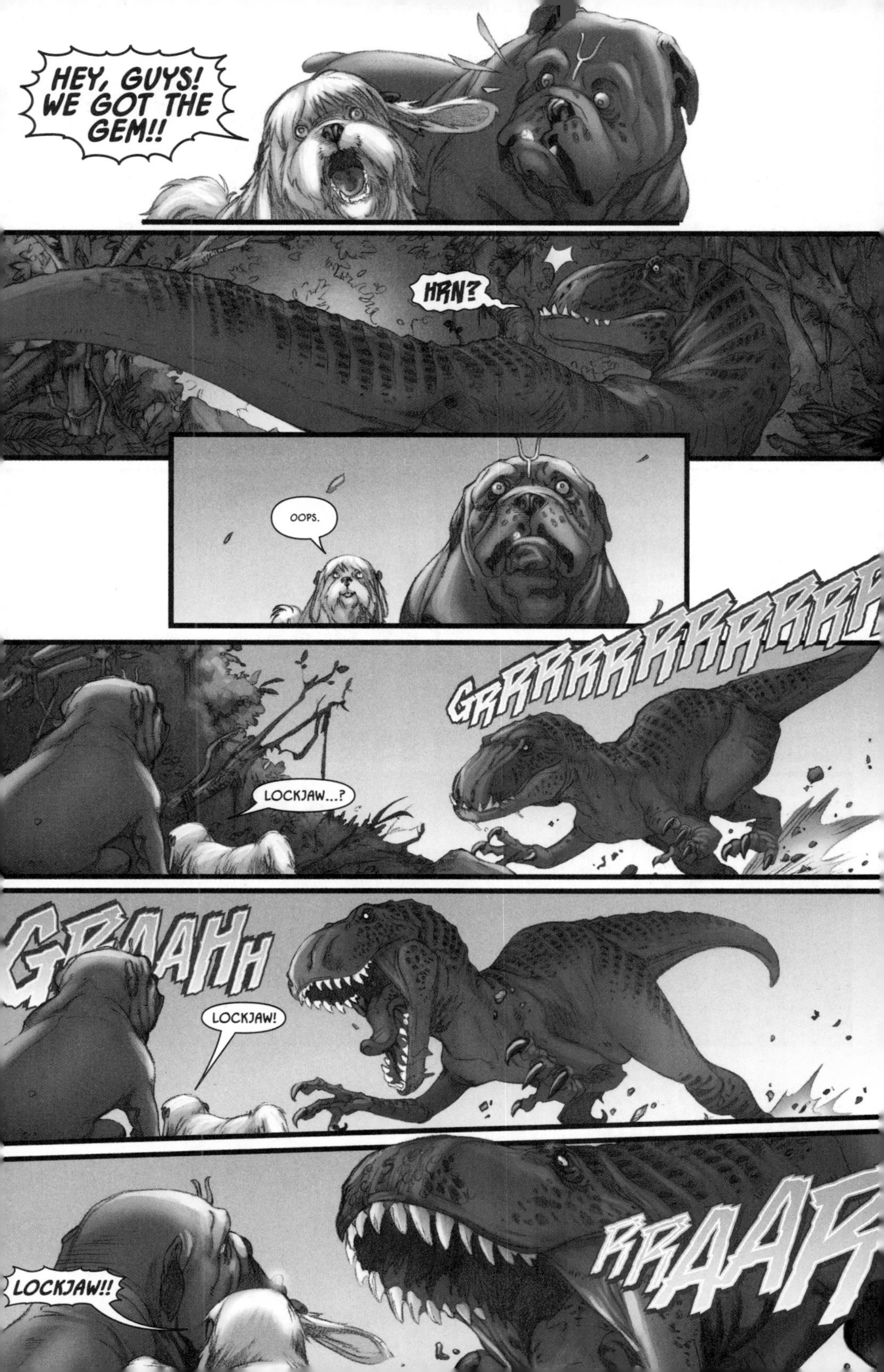
HEY, GUYS! WE GOT THE GEM!!
HRN?
OOPS.
GRRRRRRRRRRRR
LOCKJAW...?
GRAAHH
LOCKJAW!
RRAAR
LOCKJAW!!

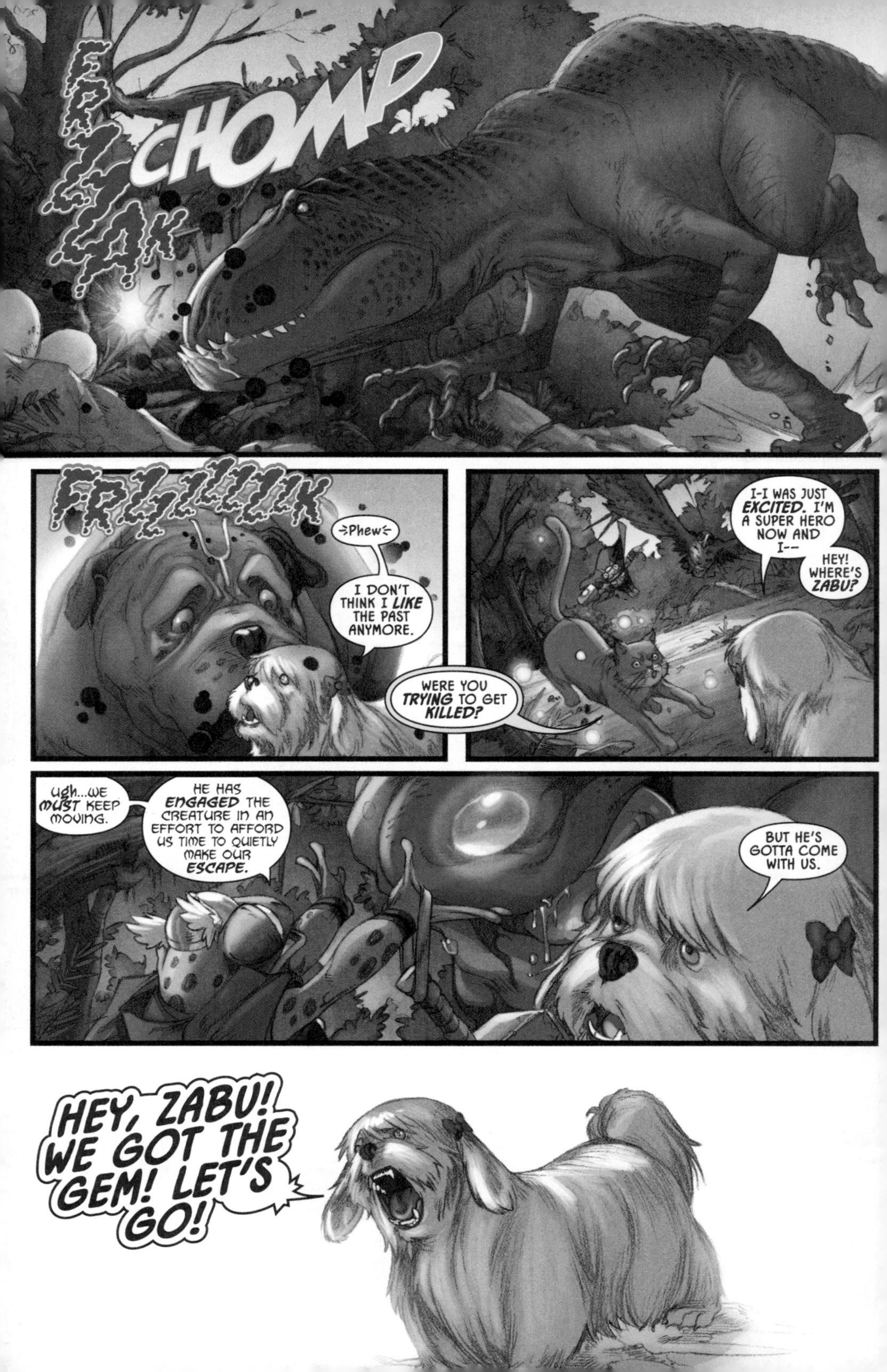
FRZZAK
CHOMP
FRZZZZZZK
Phew
I DON'T THINK I LIKE THE PAST ANYMORE.
WERE YOU TRYING TO GET KILLED?
I-I WAS JUST EXCITED. I'M A SUPER HERO NOW AND I--
HEY! WHERE'S ZABU?
ugh...WE MUST KEEP MOVING.
HE HAS ENGAGED THE CREATURE IN AN EFFORT TO AFFORD US TIME TO QUIETLY MAKE OUR ESCAPE.
BUT HE'S GOTTA COME WITH US.
HEY, ZABU! WE GOT THE GEM! LET'S GO!

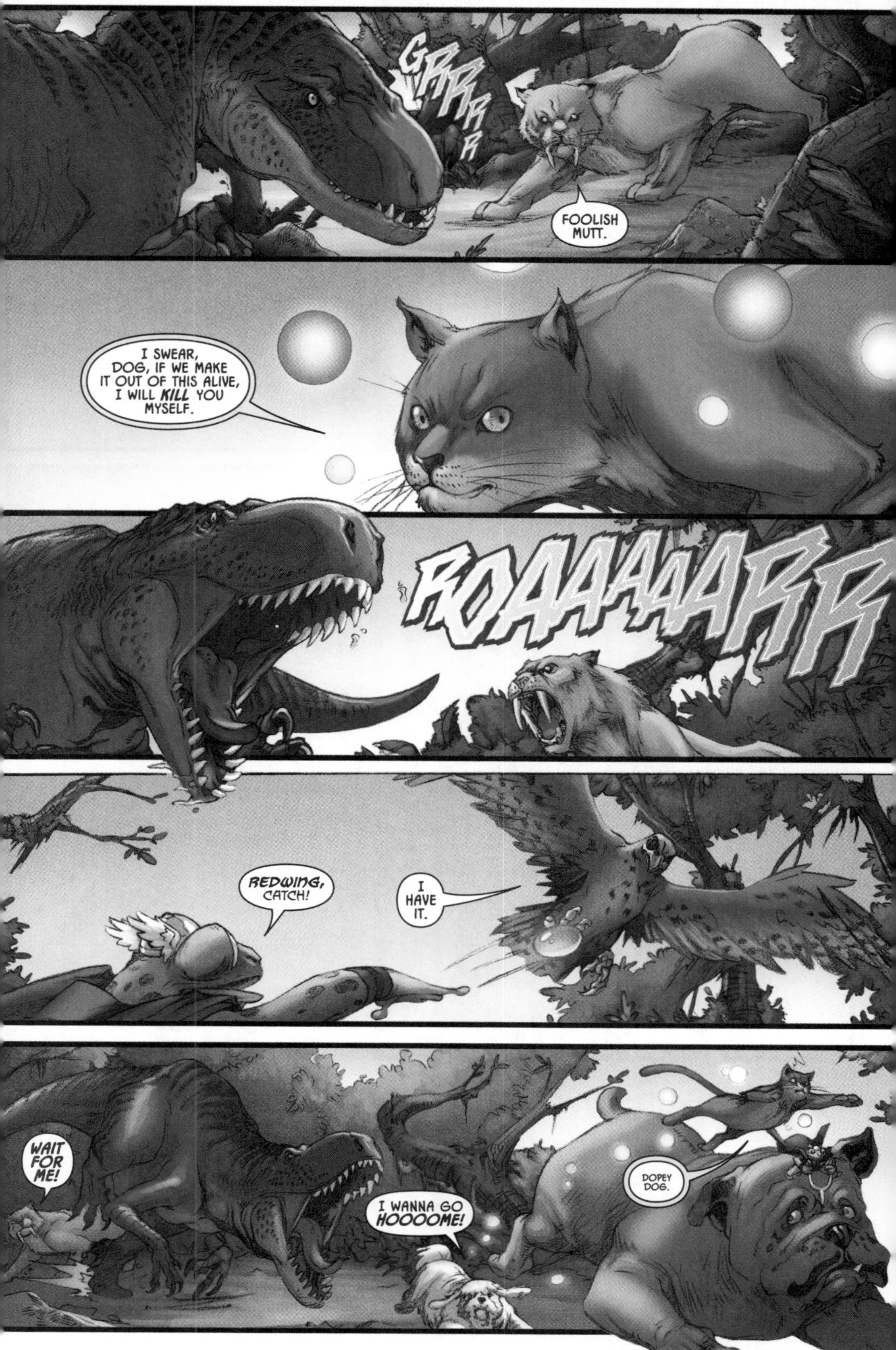
GRRRR
FOOLISH MUTT.
I SWEAR, DOG, IF WE MAKE IT OUT OF THIS ALIVE, I WILL KILL YOU MYSELF.
ROAAAARR
REDWING, CATCH!
I HAVE IT.
WAIT FOR ME!
I WANNA GO HOOOOME!
DOPEY DOG.

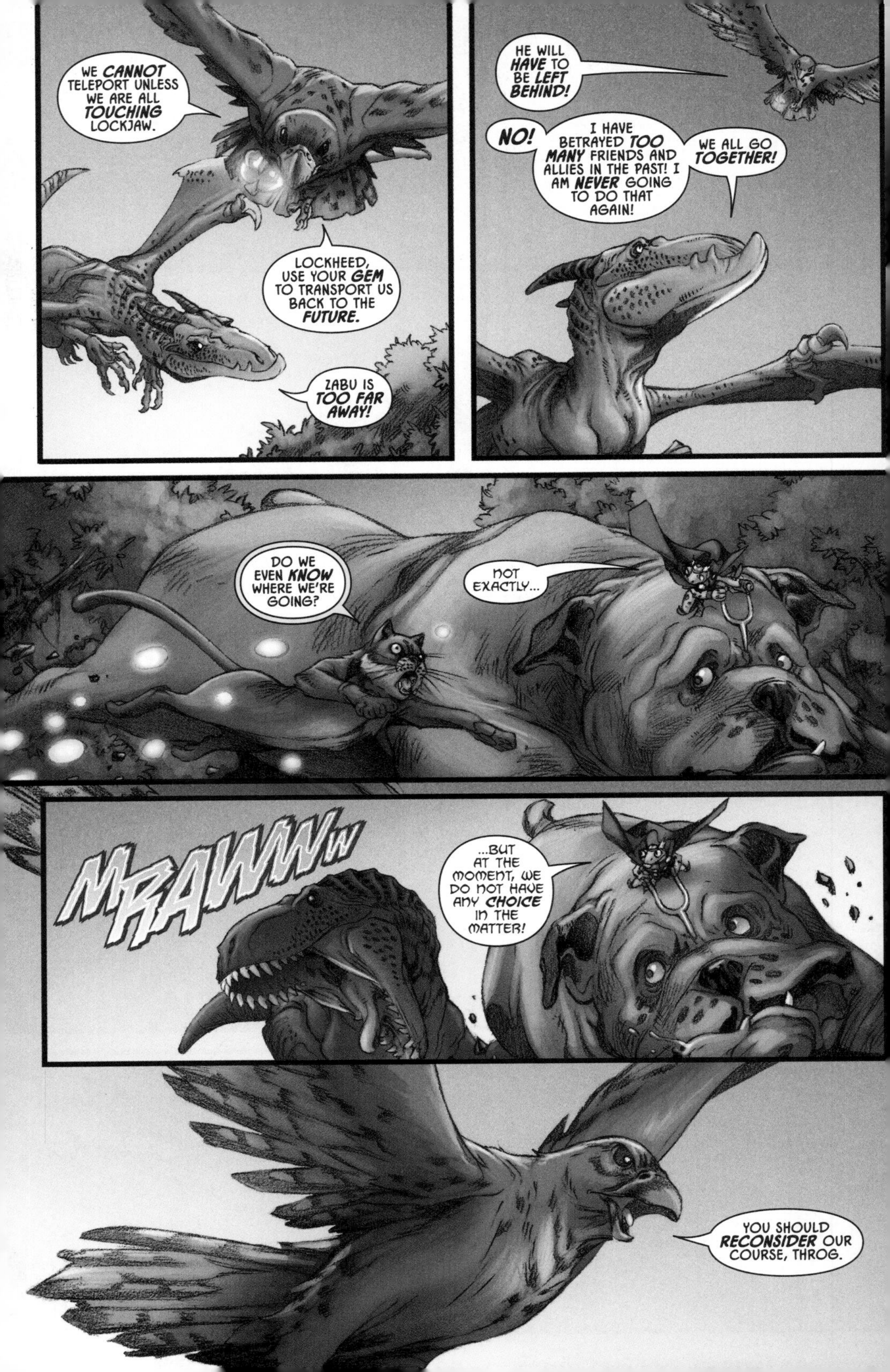
WE CANNOT TELEPORT UNLESS WE ARE ALL TOUCHING LOCKJAW.
LOCKHEED, USE YOUR GEM TO TRANSPORT US BACK TO THE FUTURE.
ZABU IS TOO FAR AWAY!
HE WILL HAVE TO BE LEFT BEHIND!
NO!
I HAVE BETRAYED TOO MANY FRIENDS AND ALLIES IN THE PAST! I AM NEVER GOING TO DO THAT AGAIN!
WE ALL GO TOGETHER!
DO WE EVEN KNOW WHERE WE'RE GOING?
NOT EXACTLY...
MRAWWW
...BUT AT THE MOMENT, WE DO NOT HAVE ANY CHOICE IN THE MATTER!
YOU SHOULD RECONSIDER OUR COURSE, THROG.

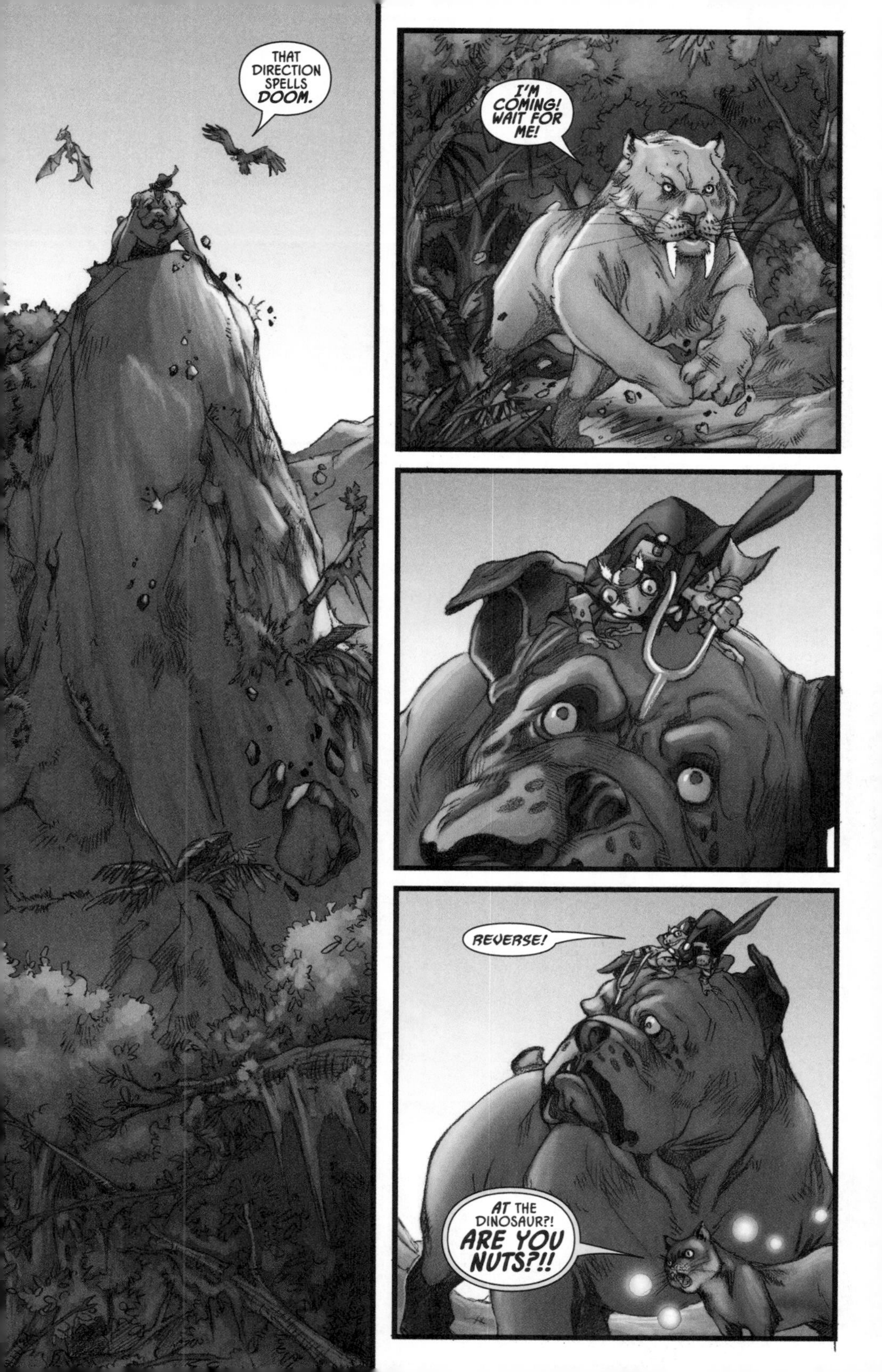
THAT DIRECTION SPELLS DOOM.
I'M COMING! WAIT FOR ME!
REVERSE!
AT THE DINOSAUR?! ARE YOU NUTS?!!

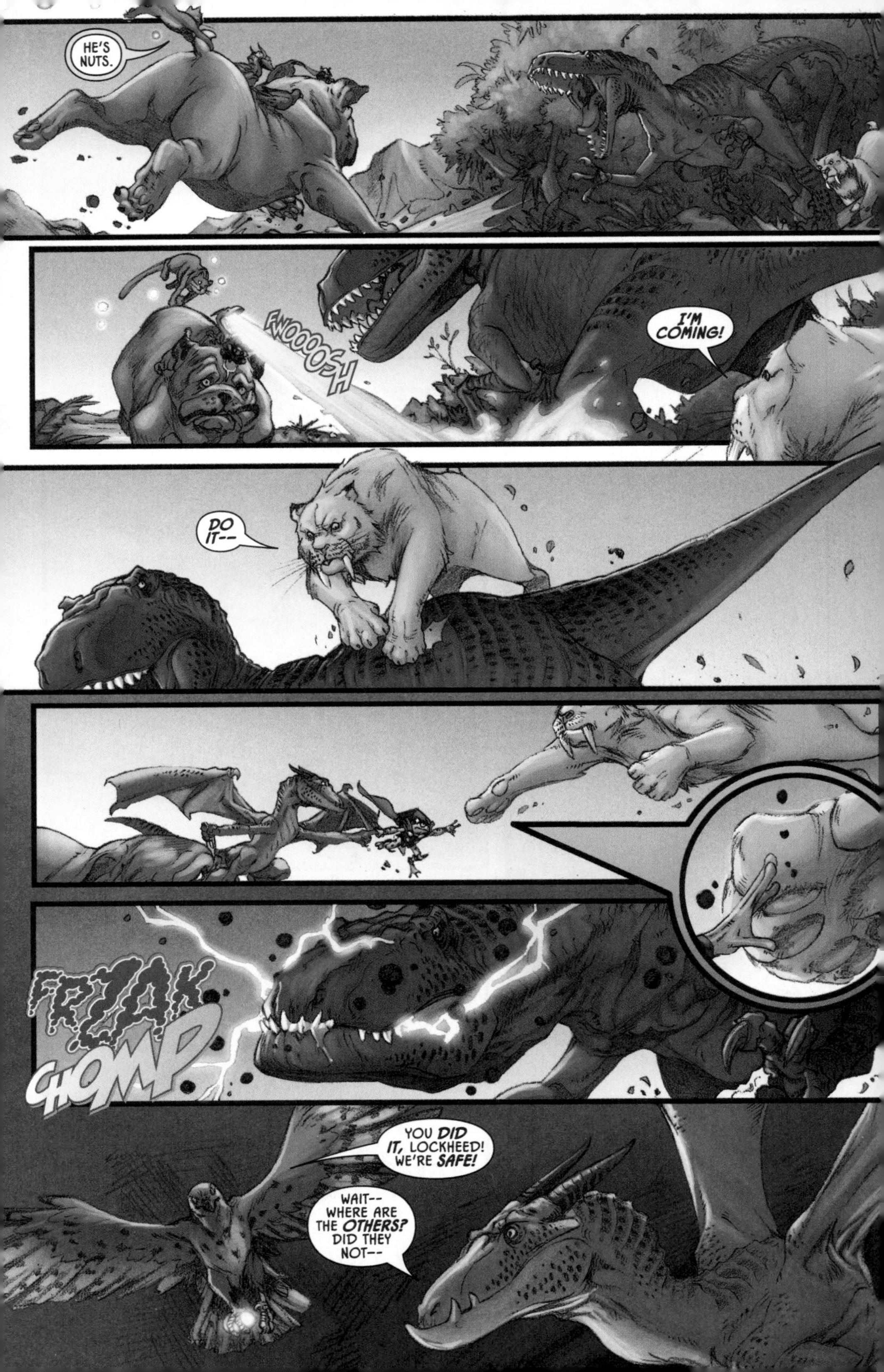
HE'S NUTS.
FWOOOOSH
I'M COMING!
DO IT--
FRZAK
CHOMP
YOU DID IT, LOCKHEED! WE'RE SAFE!
WAIT-- WHERE ARE THE OTHERS? DID THEY NOT--

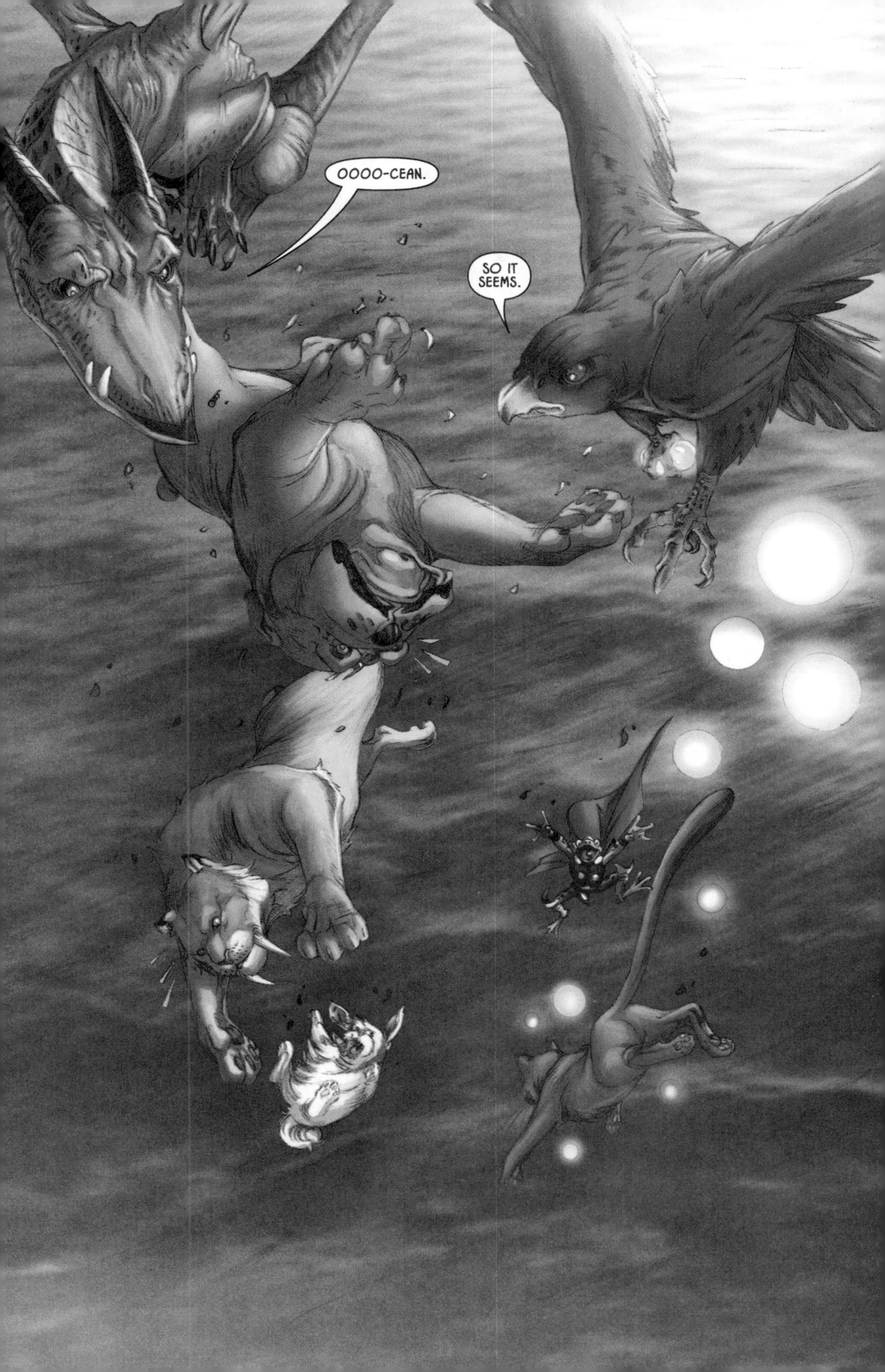
OOOO-CEAN.
SO IT SEEMS.

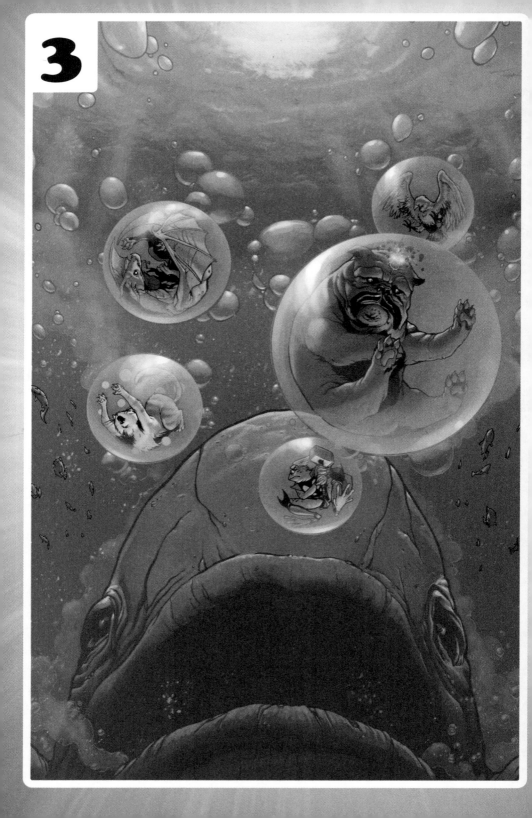

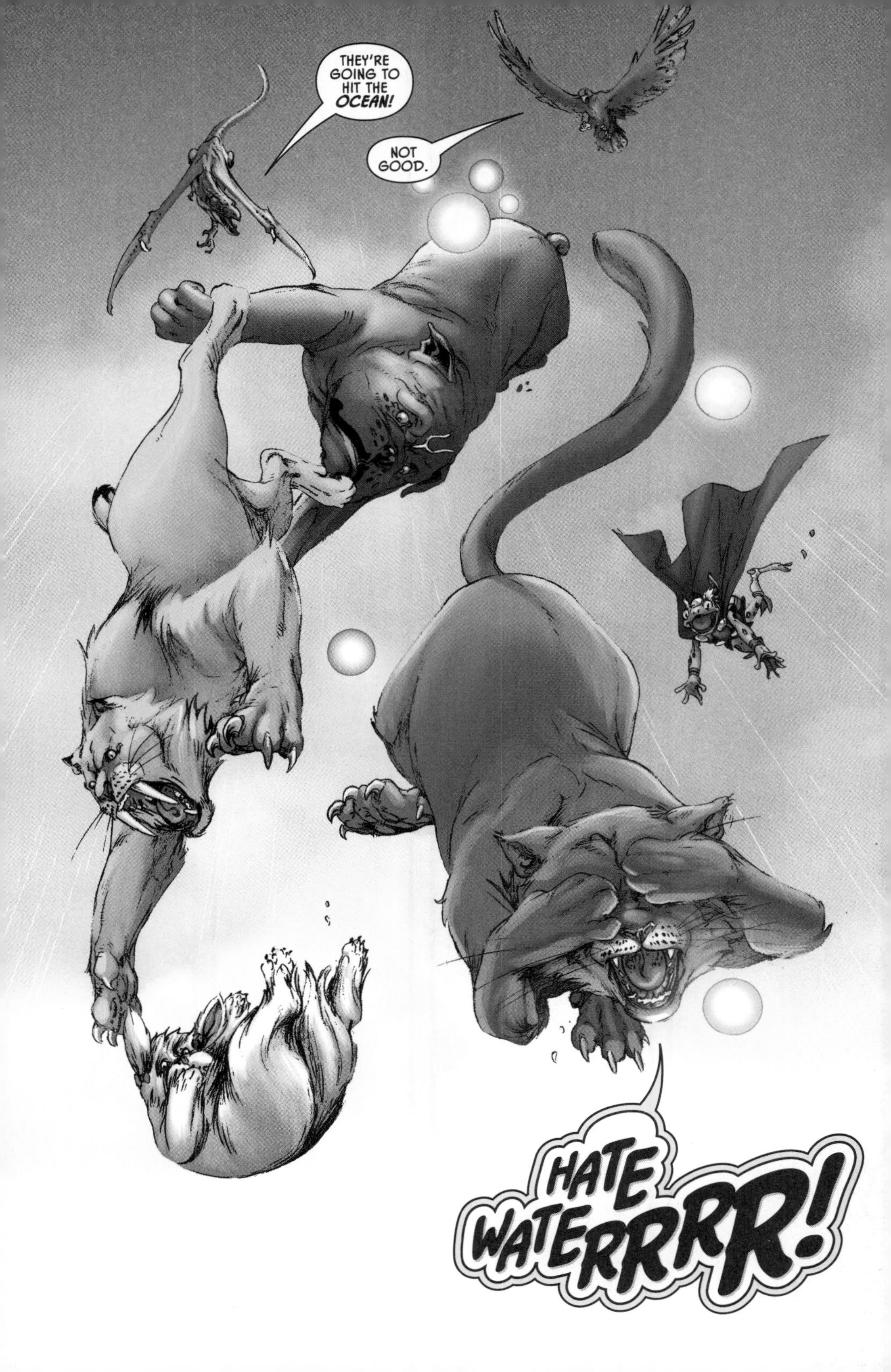
THEY'RE GOING TO HIT THE OCEAN!
NOT GOOD.
HATE WATERRRR!

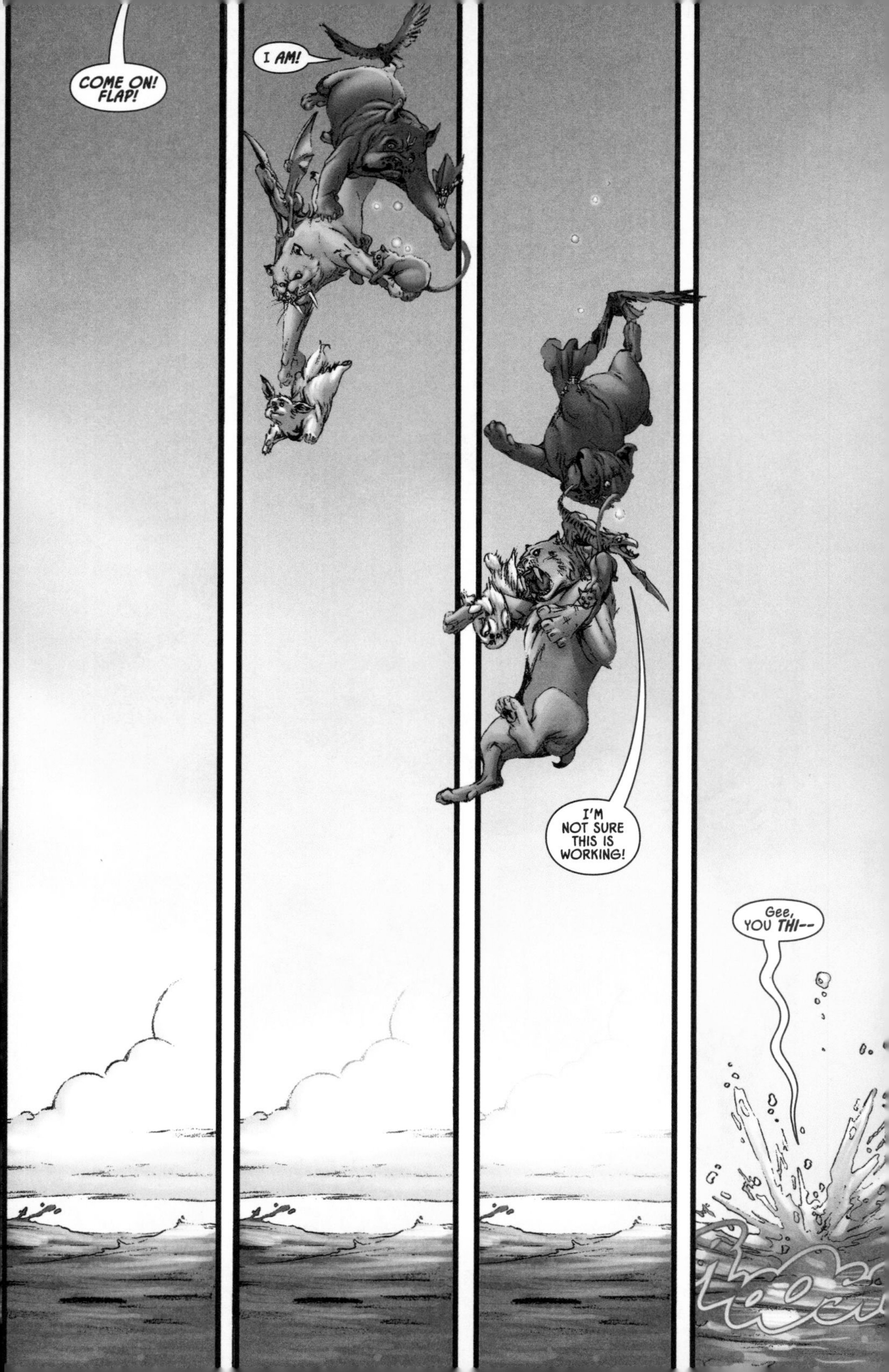
COME ON! FLAP!
I AM!
I'M NOT SURE THIS IS WORKING!
Gee, YOU THI--

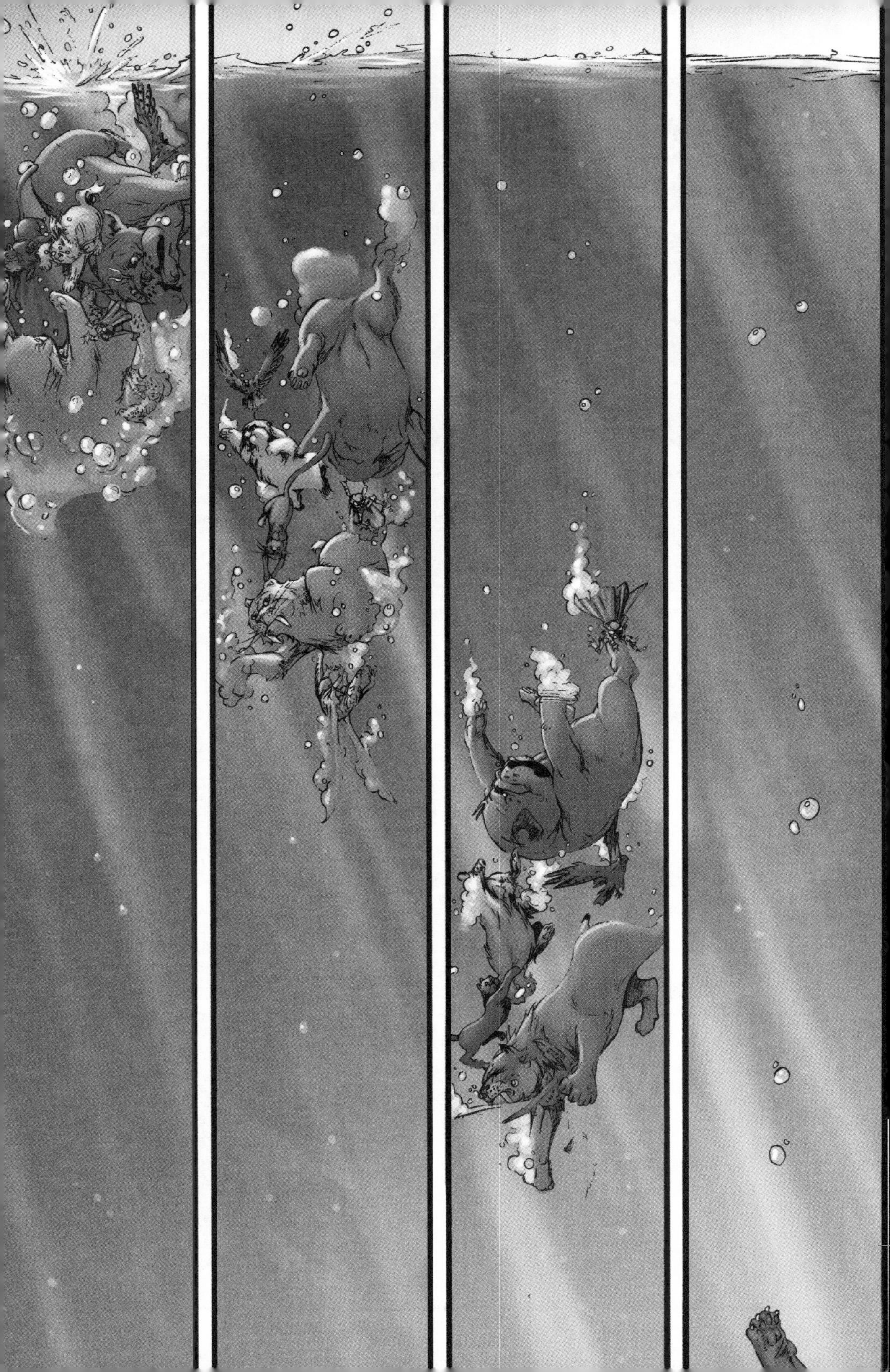

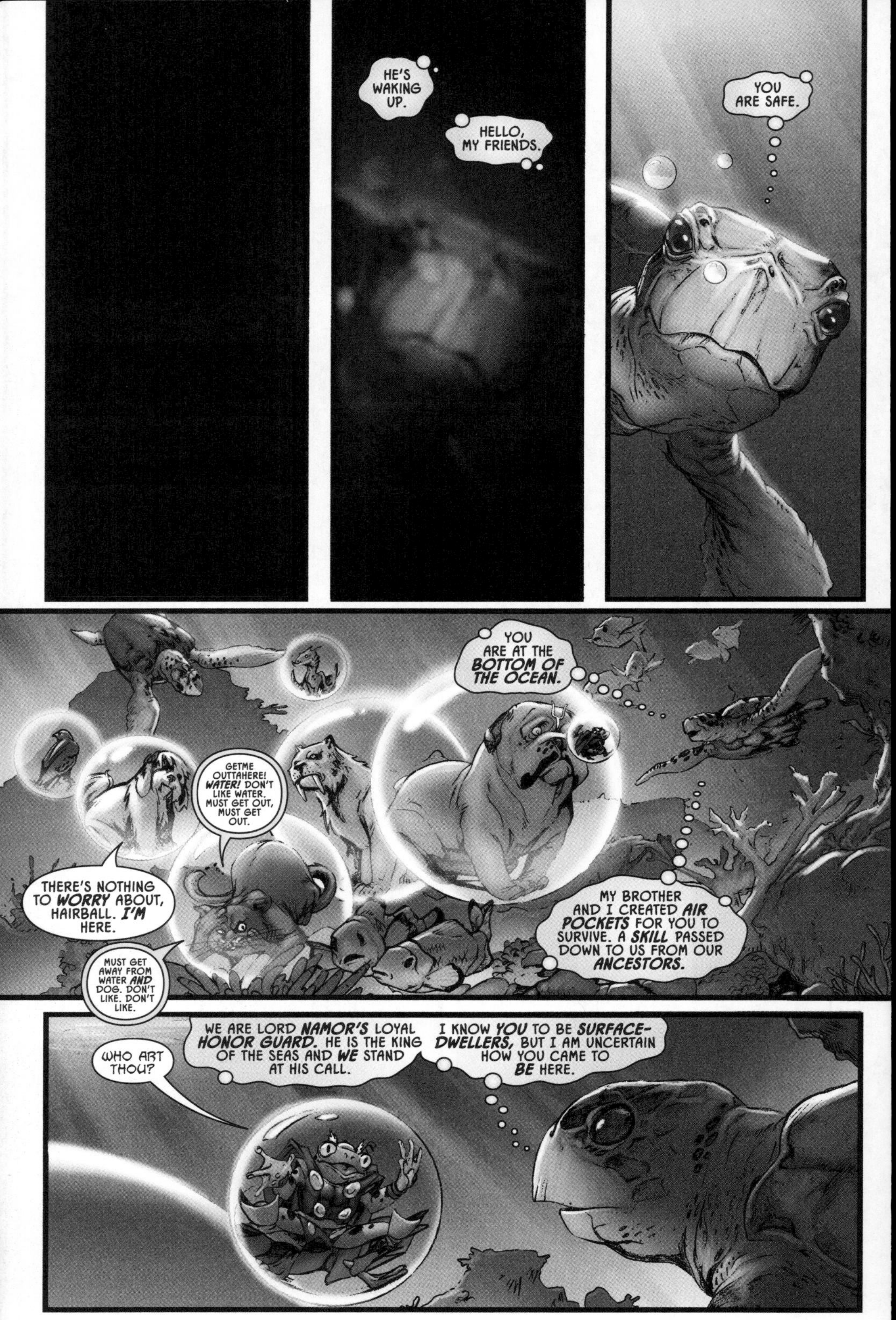
HE'S WAKING UP.
HELLO, MY FRIENDS.
YOU ARE SAFE.
YOU ARE AT THE BOTTOM OF THE OCEAN.
GETME OUTTAHERE! WATER! DON'T LIKE WATER. MUST GET OUT, MUST GET OUT.
THERE'S NOTHING TO WORRY ABOUT, HAIRBALL. I'M HERE.
MY BROTHER AND I CREATED AIR POCKETS FOR YOU TO SURVIVE. A SKILL PASSED DOWN TO US FROM OUR ANCESTORS.
MUST GET AWAY FROM WATER AND DOG. DON'T LIKE. DON'T LIKE.
WHO ART THOU?
WE ARE LORD NAMOR'S LOYAL HONOR GUARD. HE IS THE KING OF THE SEAS AND WE STAND AT HIS CALL.
I KNOW YOU TO BE SURFACE-DWELLERS, BUT I AM UNCERTAIN HOW YOU CAME TO BE HERE.

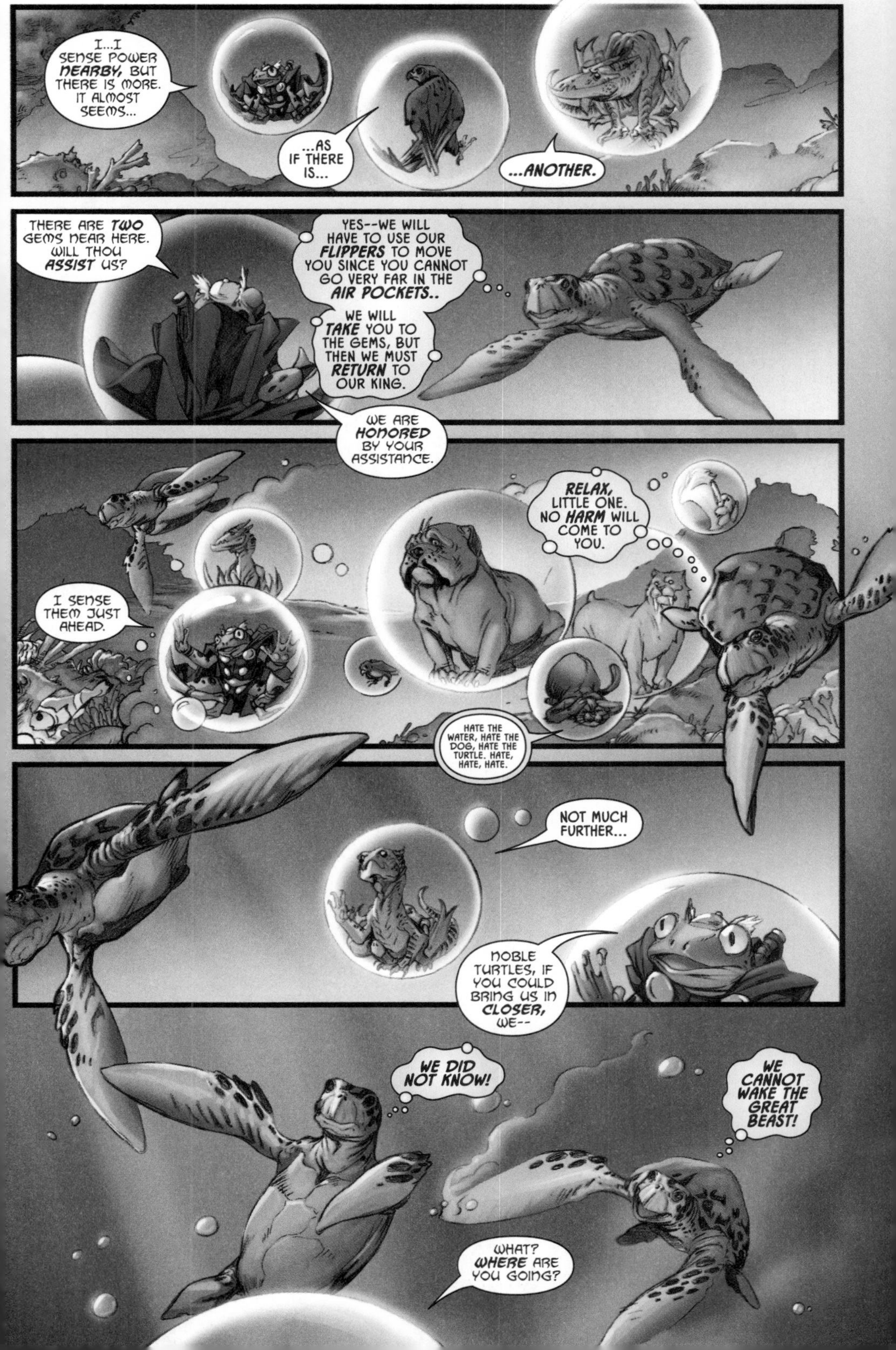
I...I SENSE POWER NEARBY, BUT THERE IS MORE. IT ALMOST SEEMS...
...AS IF THERE IS...
...ANOTHER.
THERE ARE TWO GEMS NEAR HERE. WILL THOU ASSIST US?
YES--WE WILL HAVE TO USE OUR FLIPPERS TO MOVE YOU SINCE YOU CANNOT GO VERY FAR IN THE AIR POCKETS..
WE WILL TAKE YOU TO THE GEMS, BUT THEN WE MUST RETURN TO OUR KING.
WE ARE HONORED BY YOUR ASSISTANCE.
RELAX, LITTLE ONE. NO HARM WILL COME TO YOU.
I SENSE THEM JUST AHEAD.
HATE THE WATER, HATE THE DOG, HATE THE TURTLE. HATE, HATE, HATE.
NOT MUCH FURTHER...
NOBLE TURTLES, IF YOU COULD BRING US IN CLOSER, WE--
WE DID NOT KNOW!
WE CANNOT WAKE THE GREAT BEAST!
WHAT? WHERE ARE YOU GOING?

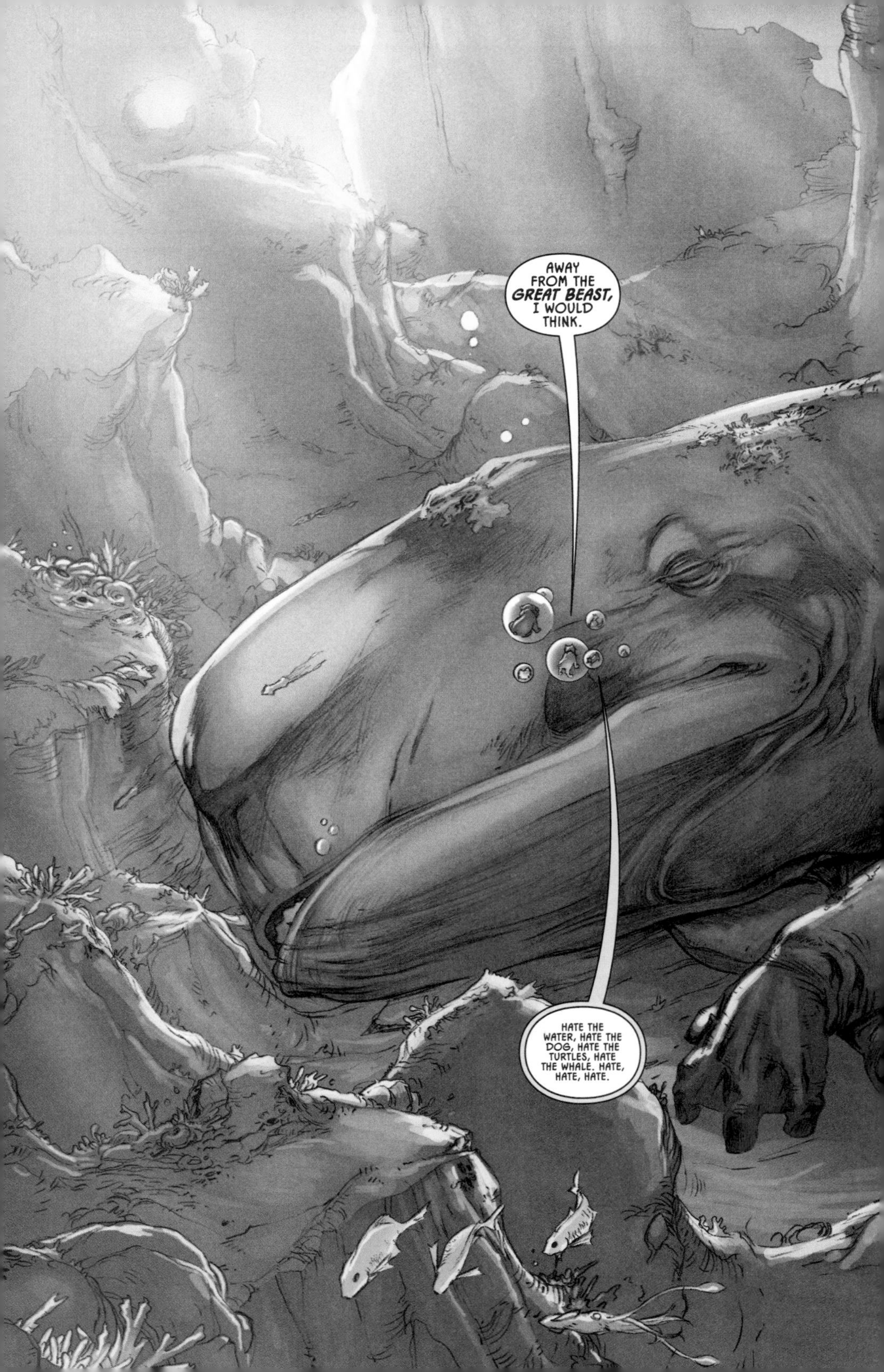
AWAY FROM THE GREAT BEAST, I WOULD THINK.
HATE THE WATER, HATE THE DOG, HATE THE TURTLES, HATE THE WHALE. HATE, HATE, HATE.

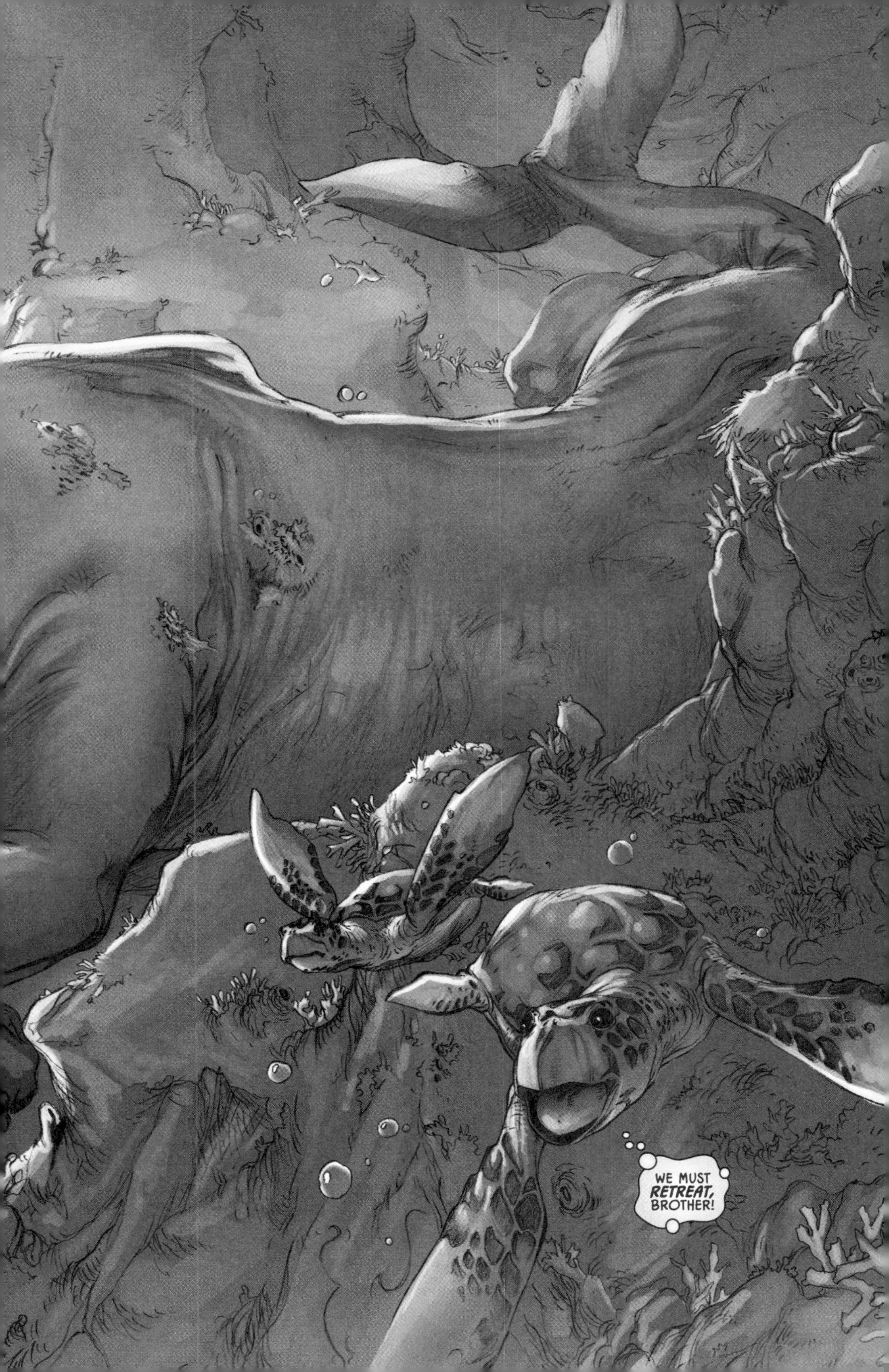
WE MUST RETREAT, BROTHER!

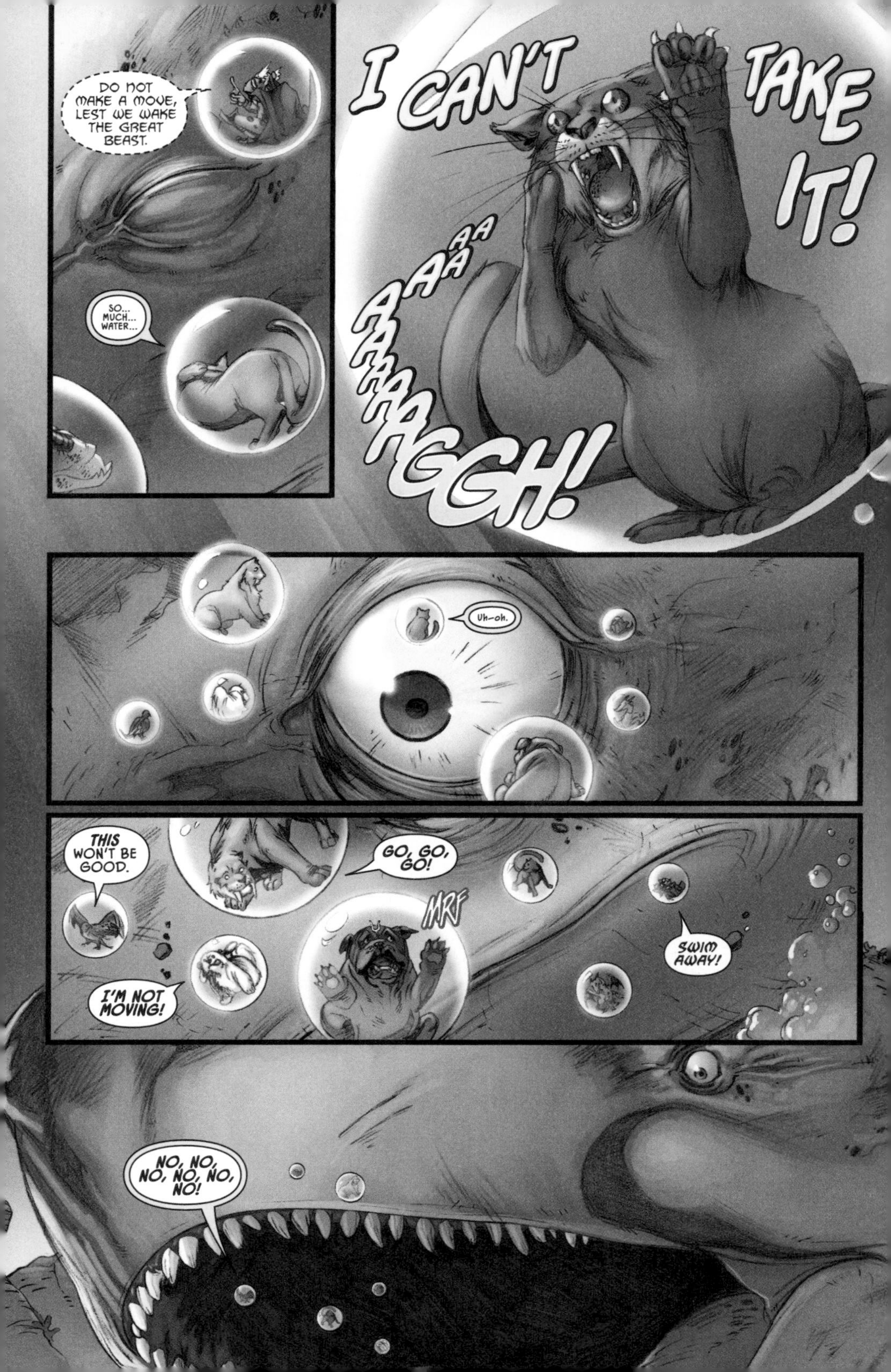
DO NOT MAKE A MOVE, LEST WE WAKE THE GREAT BEAST.
SO... MUCH... WATER...
I CAN'T TAKE IT!
AAAAAAAAAGGH!
Uh-oh.
THIS WON'T BE GOOD.
GO, GO, GO!
MRF
SWIM AWAY!
I'M NOT MOVING!
NO, NO, NO, NO, NO, NO!

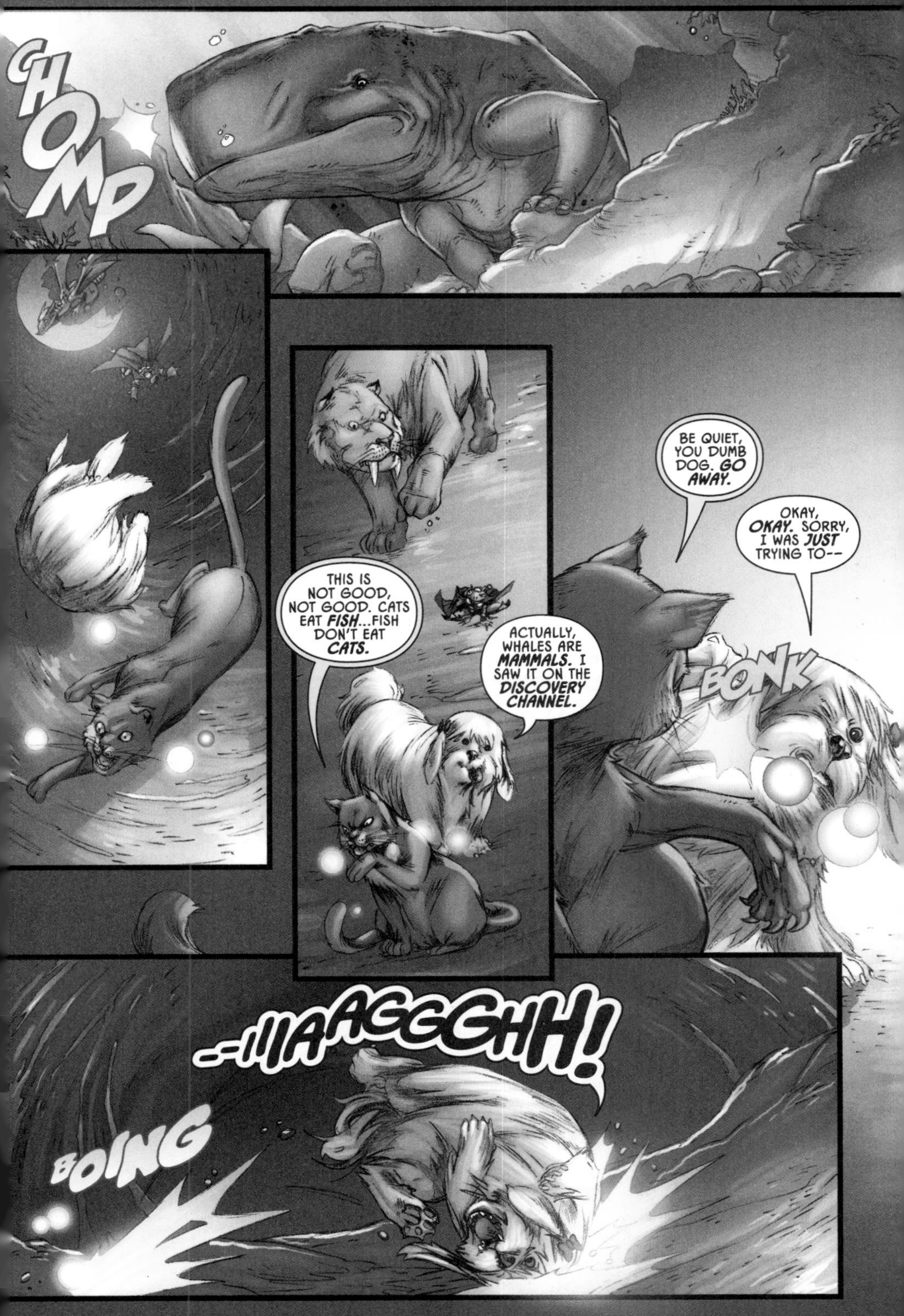
CHOMP
THIS IS NOT GOOD, NOT GOOD. CATS EAT FISH...FISH DON'T EAT CATS.
ACTUALLY, WHALES ARE MAMMALS. I SAW IT ON THE DISCOVERY CHANNEL.
BE QUIET, YOU DUMB DOG. GO AWAY.
OKAY, OKAY. SORRY, I WAS JUST TRYING TO--
BONK
--IIIAAGGGHH!
BOING

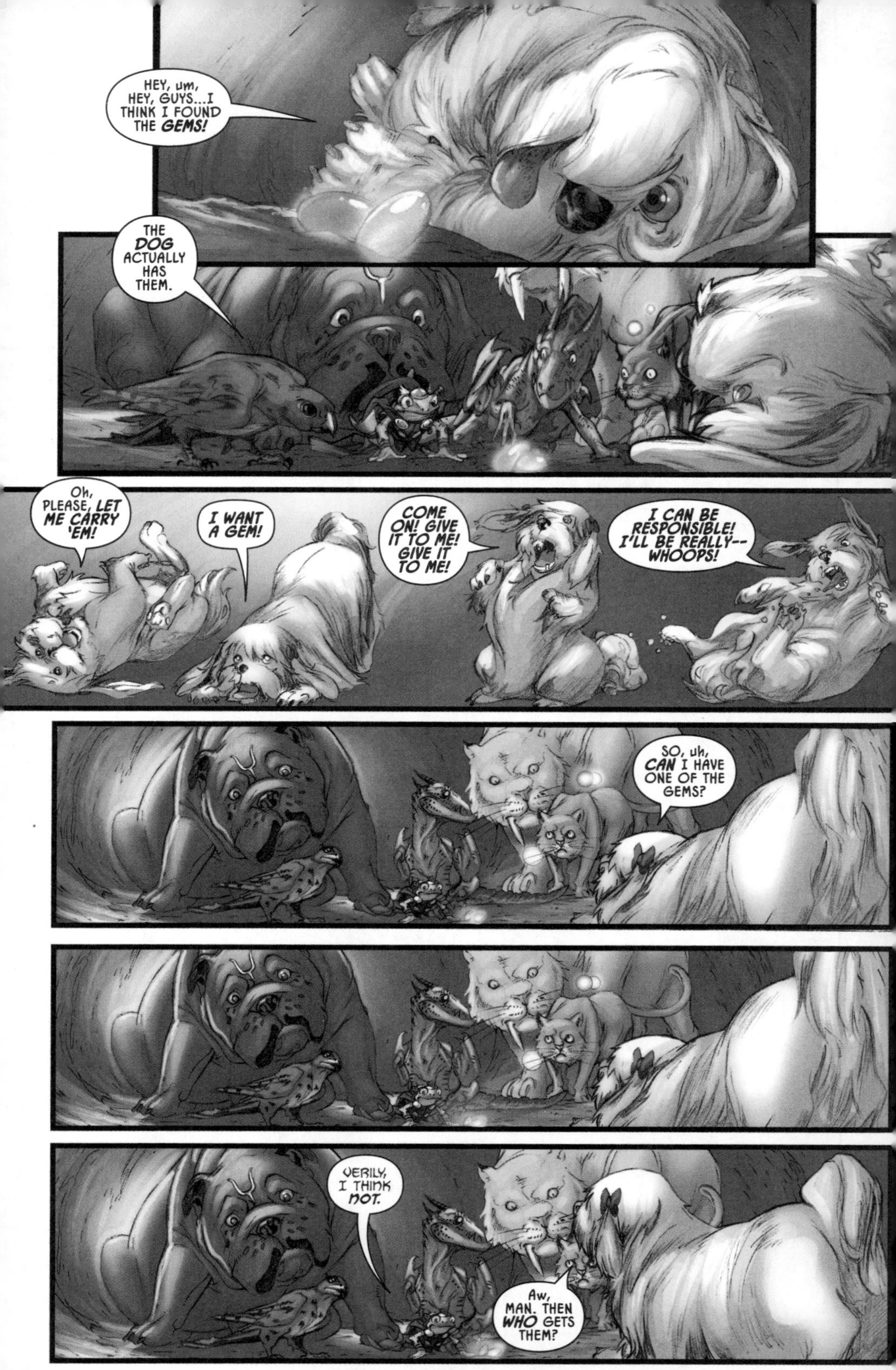

HEY, um, HEY, GUYS...I THINK I FOUND THE GEMS!
THE DOG ACTUALLY HAS THEM.
Oh, PLEASE, LET ME CARRY 'EM!
I WANT A GEM!
COME ON! GIVE IT TO ME! GIVE IT TO ME!
I CAN BE RESPONSIBLE! I'LL BE REALLY--WHOOPS!
SO, uh, CAN I HAVE ONE OF THE GEMS?
VERILY, I THINK NOT.
Aw, MAN. THEN WHO GETS THEM?

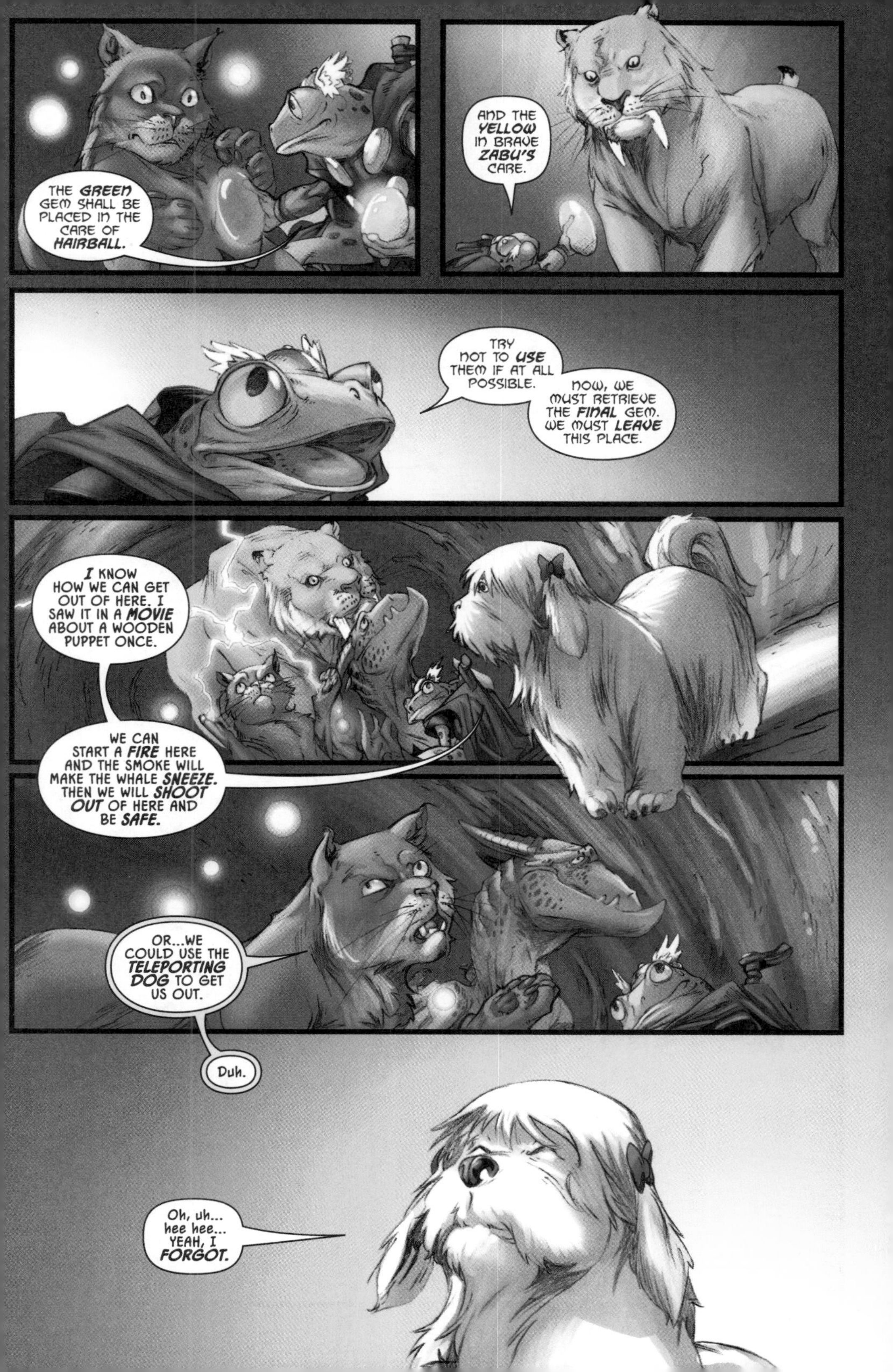
THE GREEN GEM SHALL BE PLACED IN THE CARE OF HAIRBALL.
AND THE YELLOW IN BRAVE ZABU'S CARE.
TRY NOT TO USE THEM IF AT ALL POSSIBLE.
NOW, WE MUST RETRIEVE THE FINAL GEM. WE MUST LEAVE THIS PLACE.
I KNOW HOW WE CAN GET OUT OF HERE. I SAW IT IN A MOVIE ABOUT A WOODEN PUPPET ONCE.
WE CAN START A FIRE HERE AND THE SMOKE WILL MAKE THE WHALE SNEEZE. THEN WE WILL SHOOT OUT OF HERE AND BE SAFE.
OR...WE COULD USE THE TELEPORTING DOG TO GET US OUT.
Duh.
Oh, uh... hee hee... YEAH, I FORGOT.

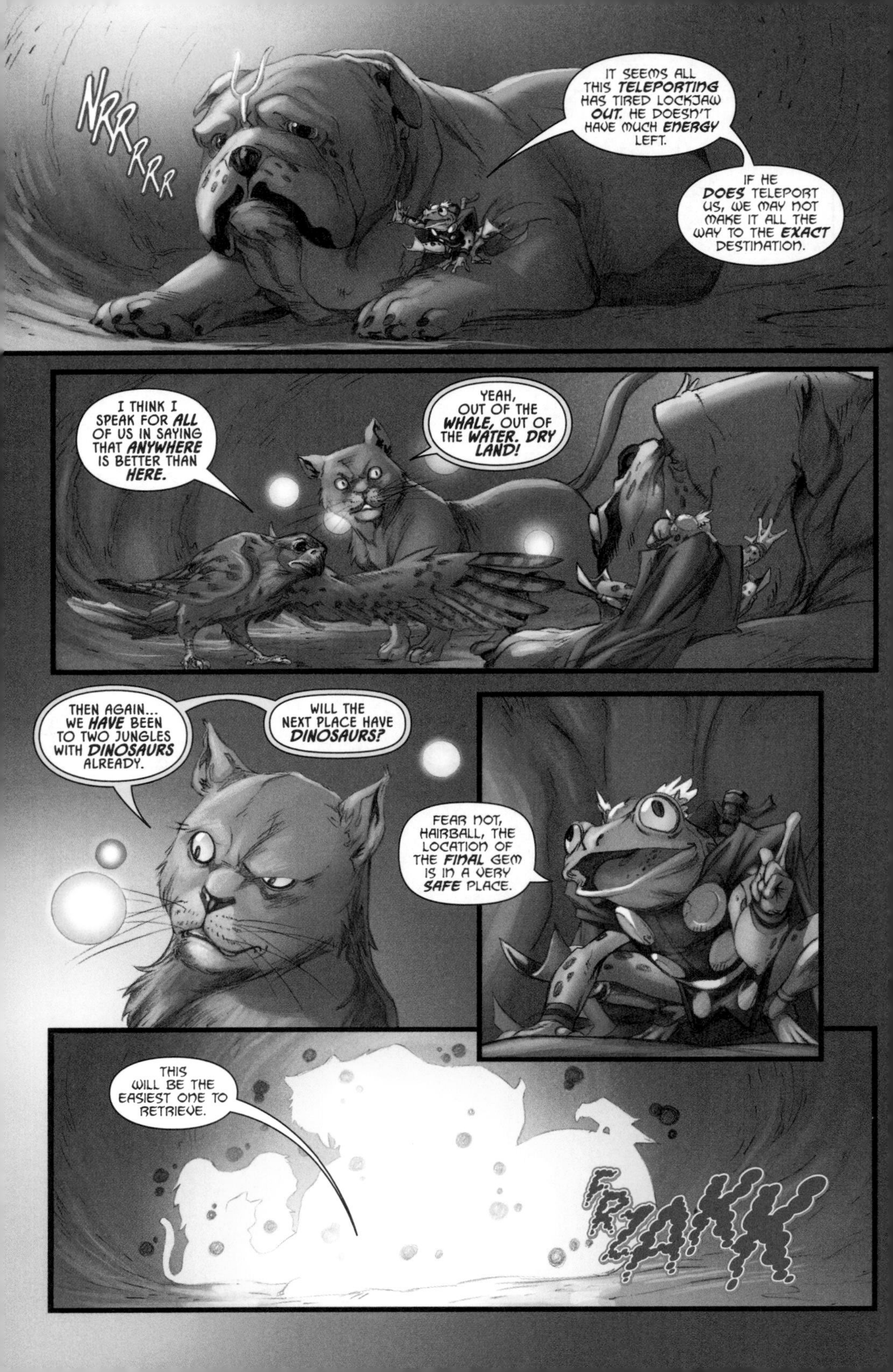
NRRRRRR
IT SEEMS ALL THIS TELEPORTING HAS TIRED LOCKJAW OUT. HE DOESN'T HAVE MUCH ENERGY LEFT.
IF HE DOES TELEPORT US, WE MAY NOT MAKE IT ALL THE WAY TO THE EXACT DESTINATION.
I THINK I SPEAK FOR ALL OF US IN SAYING THAT ANYWHERE IS BETTER THAN HERE.
YEAH, OUT OF THE WHALE, OUT OF THE WATER. DRY LAND!
WILL THE NEXT PLACE HAVE DINOSAURS?
THEN AGAIN... WE HAVE BEEN TO TWO JUNGLES WITH DINOSAURS ALREADY.
FEAR NOT, HAIRBALL, THE LOCATION OF THE FINAL GEM IS IN A VERY SAFE PLACE.
THIS WILL BE THE EASIEST ONE TO RETRIEVE.
FRZAKK

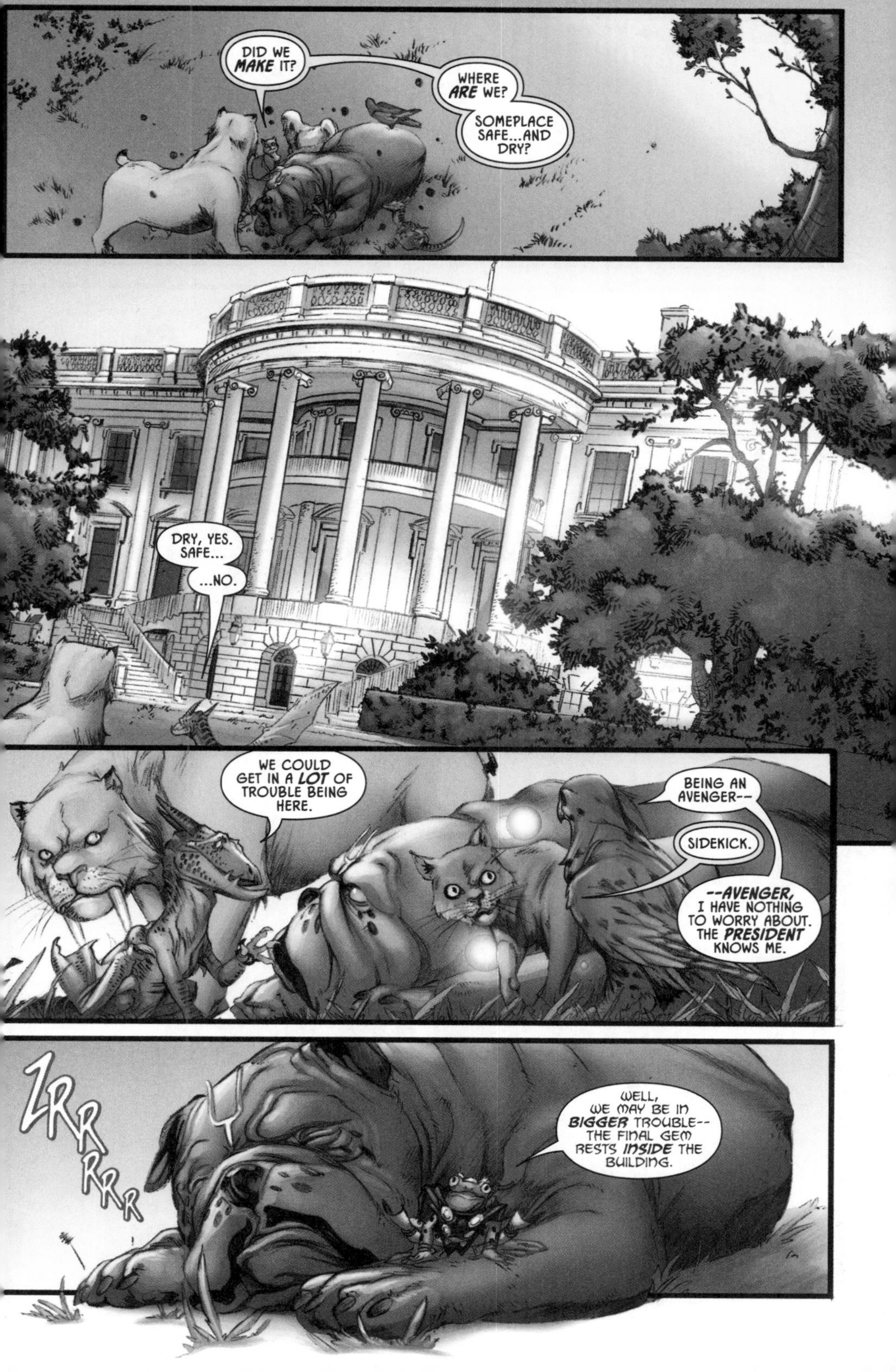
DID WE MAKE IT?
WHERE ARE WE?
SOMEPLACE SAFE...AND DRY?
DRY, YES. SAFE...
...NO.
WE COULD GET IN A LOT OF TROUBLE BEING HERE.
BEING AN AVENGER--
SIDEKICK.
--AVENGER, I HAVE NOTHING TO WORRY ABOUT. THE PRESIDENT KNOWS ME.
ZRRRRRR
WELL, WE MAY BE IN BIGGER TROUBLE-- THE FINAL GEM RESTS INSIDE THE BUILDING.

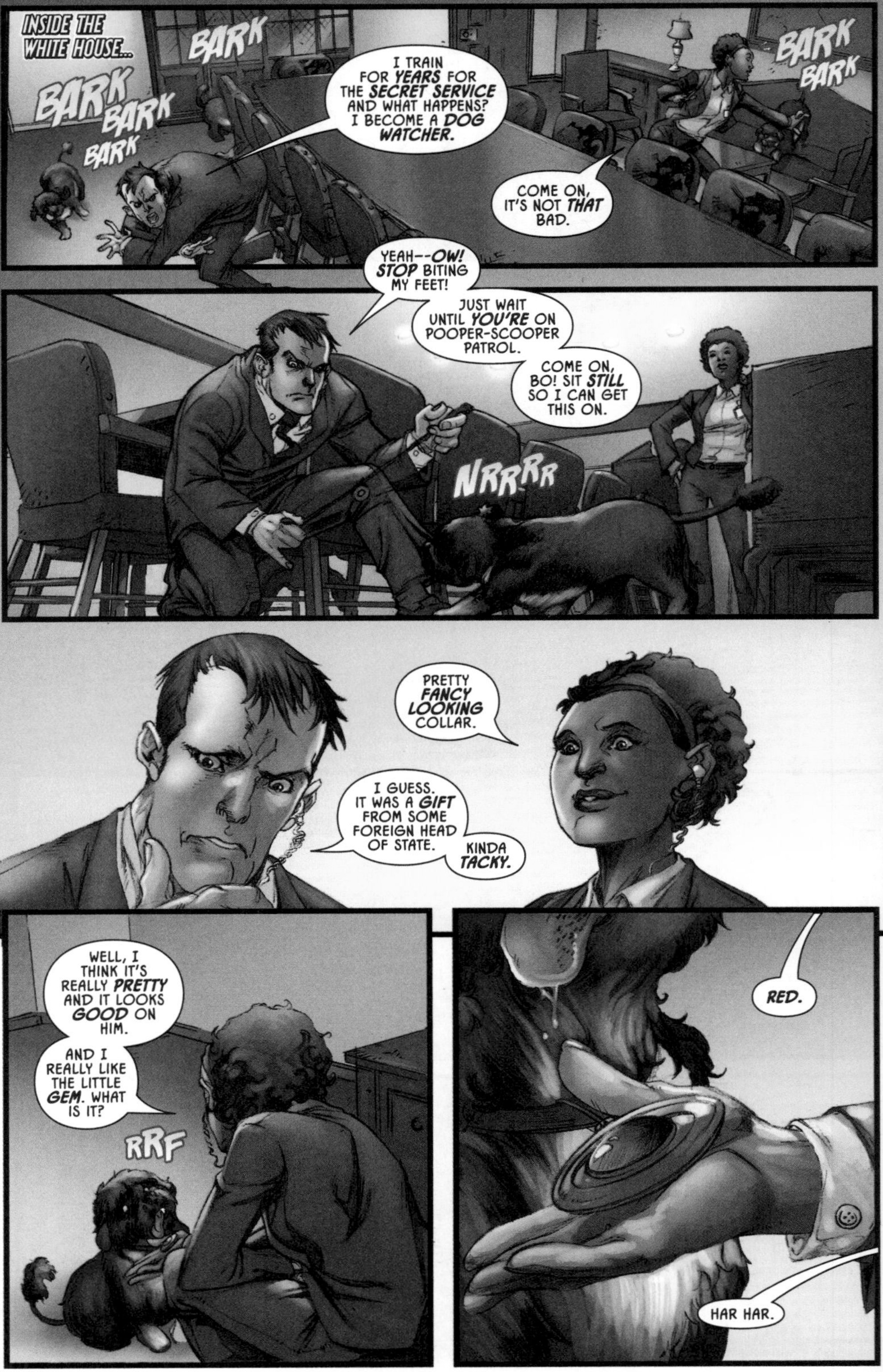
INSIDE THE WHITE HOUSE...
BARK
BARK BARK BARK
I TRAIN FOR YEARS FOR THE SECRET SERVICE AND WHAT HAPPENS? I BECOME A DOG WATCHER.
BARK BARK
COME ON, IT'S NOT THAT BAD.
YEAH--OW! STOP BITING MY FEET!
JUST WAIT UNTIL YOU'RE ON POOPER-SCOOPER PATROL.
COME ON, BO! SIT STILL SO I CAN GET THIS ON.
NRRRR
PRETTY FANCY LOOKING COLLAR.
I GUESS. IT WAS A GIFT FROM SOME FOREIGN HEAD OF STATE.
KINDA TACKY.
WELL, I THINK IT'S REALLY PRETTY AND IT LOOKS GOOD ON HIM.
AND I REALLY LIKE THE LITTLE GEM. WHAT IS IT?
RRF
RED.
HAR HAR.

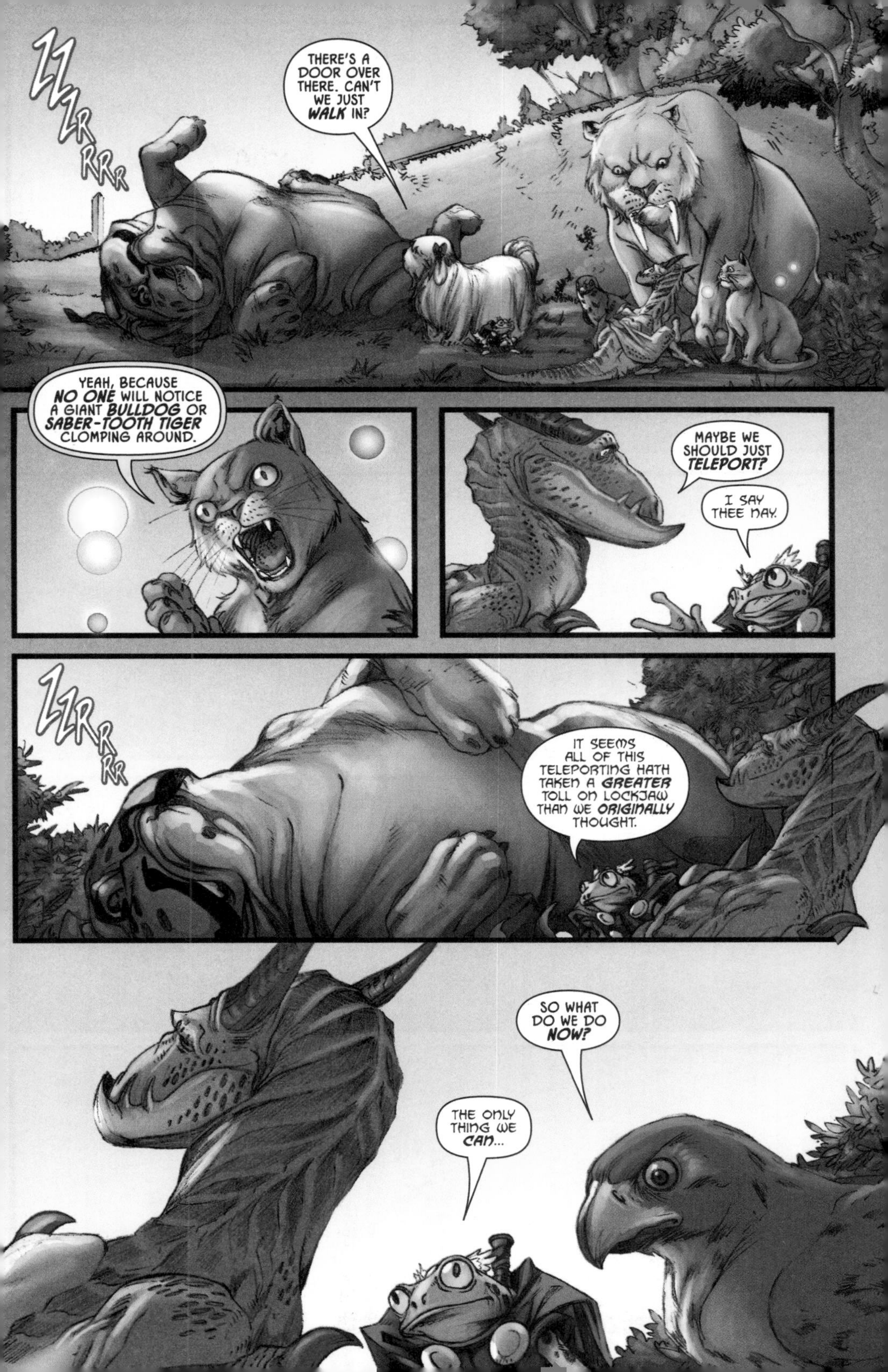
ZZZRRRR
THERE'S A DOOR OVER THERE. CAN'T WE JUST WALK IN?
YEAH, BECAUSE NO ONE WILL NOTICE A GIANT BULLDOG OR SABER-TOOTH TIGER CLOMPING AROUND.
MAYBE WE SHOULD JUST TELEPORT?
I SAY THEE NAY.
ZZRRRR
IT SEEMS ALL OF THIS TELEPORTING HATH TAKEN A GREATER TOLL ON LOCKJAW THAN WE ORIGINALLY THOUGHT.
SO WHAT DO WE DO NOW?
THE ONLY THING WE CAN...

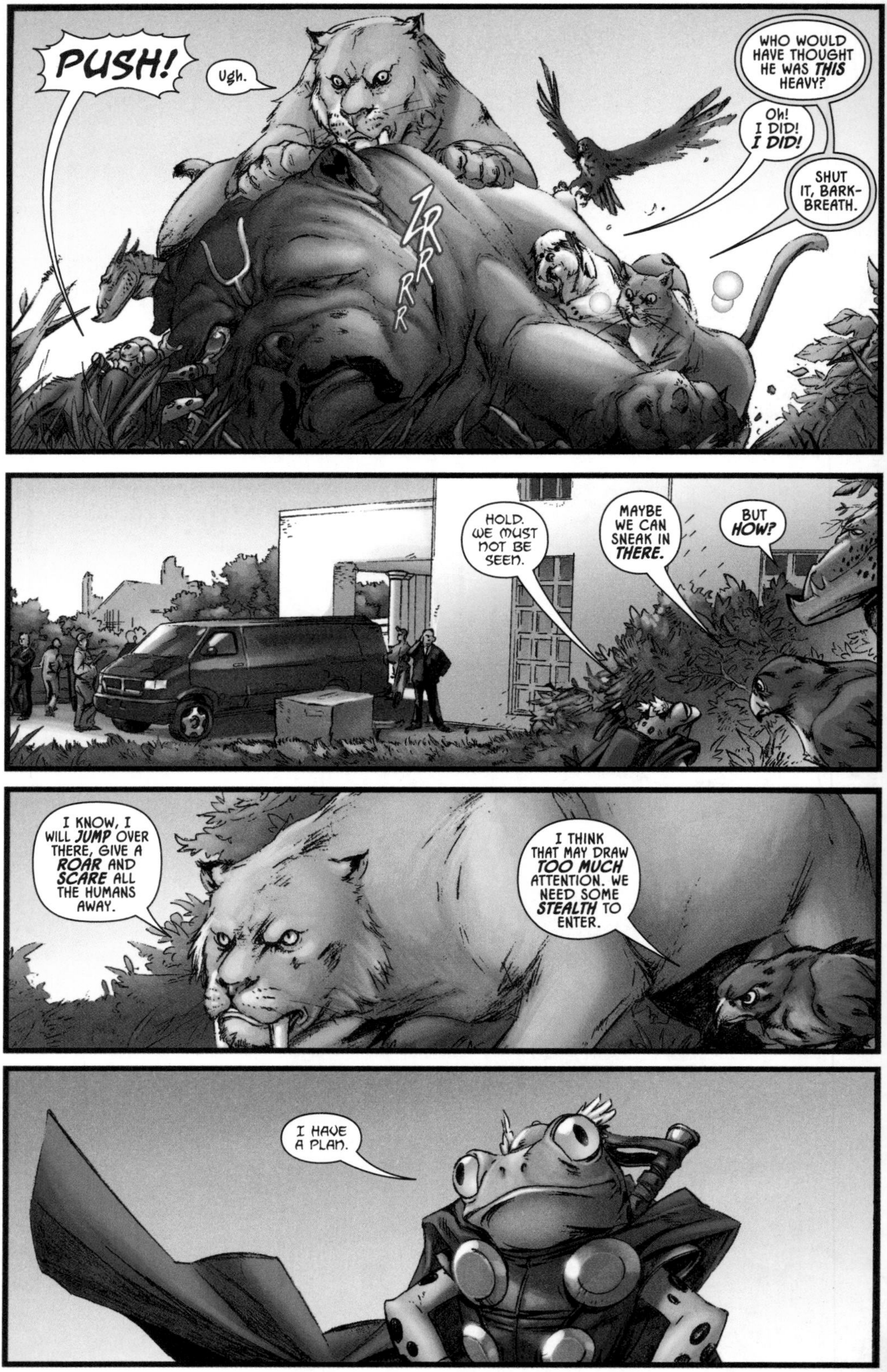
PUSH!
Ugh.
WHO WOULD HAVE THOUGHT HE WAS THIS HEAVY?
Oh! I DID! I DID!
SHUT IT, BARK-BREATH.
ZRRRR
HOLD. WE MUST NOT BE SEEN.
MAYBE WE CAN SNEAK IN THERE.
BUT HOW?
I KNOW, I WILL JUMP OVER THERE, GIVE A ROAR AND SCARE ALL THE HUMANS AWAY.
I THINK THAT MAY DRAW TOO MUCH ATTENTION. WE NEED SOME STEALTH TO ENTER.
I HAVE A PLAN.

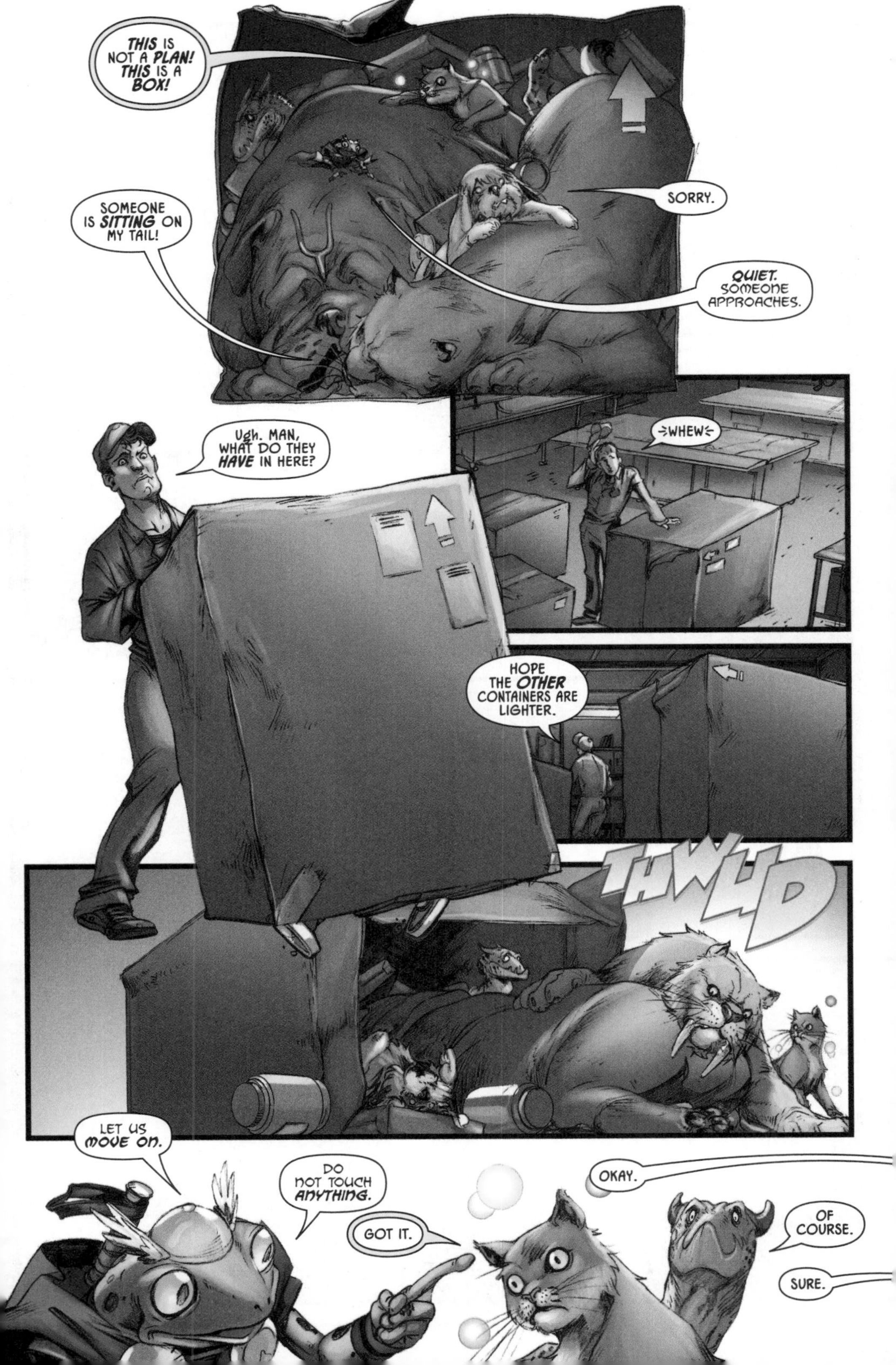
THIS IS NOT A PLAN! THIS IS A BOX!
SOMEONE IS SITTING ON MY TAIL!
SORRY.
QUIET. SOMEONE APPROACHES.
Ugh. MAN, WHAT DO THEY HAVE IN HERE?
WHEW
HOPE THE OTHER CONTAINERS ARE LIGHTER.
THWUD
LET US MOVE ON.
DO NOT TOUCH ANYTHING.
GOT IT.
OKAY.
OF COURSE.
SURE.

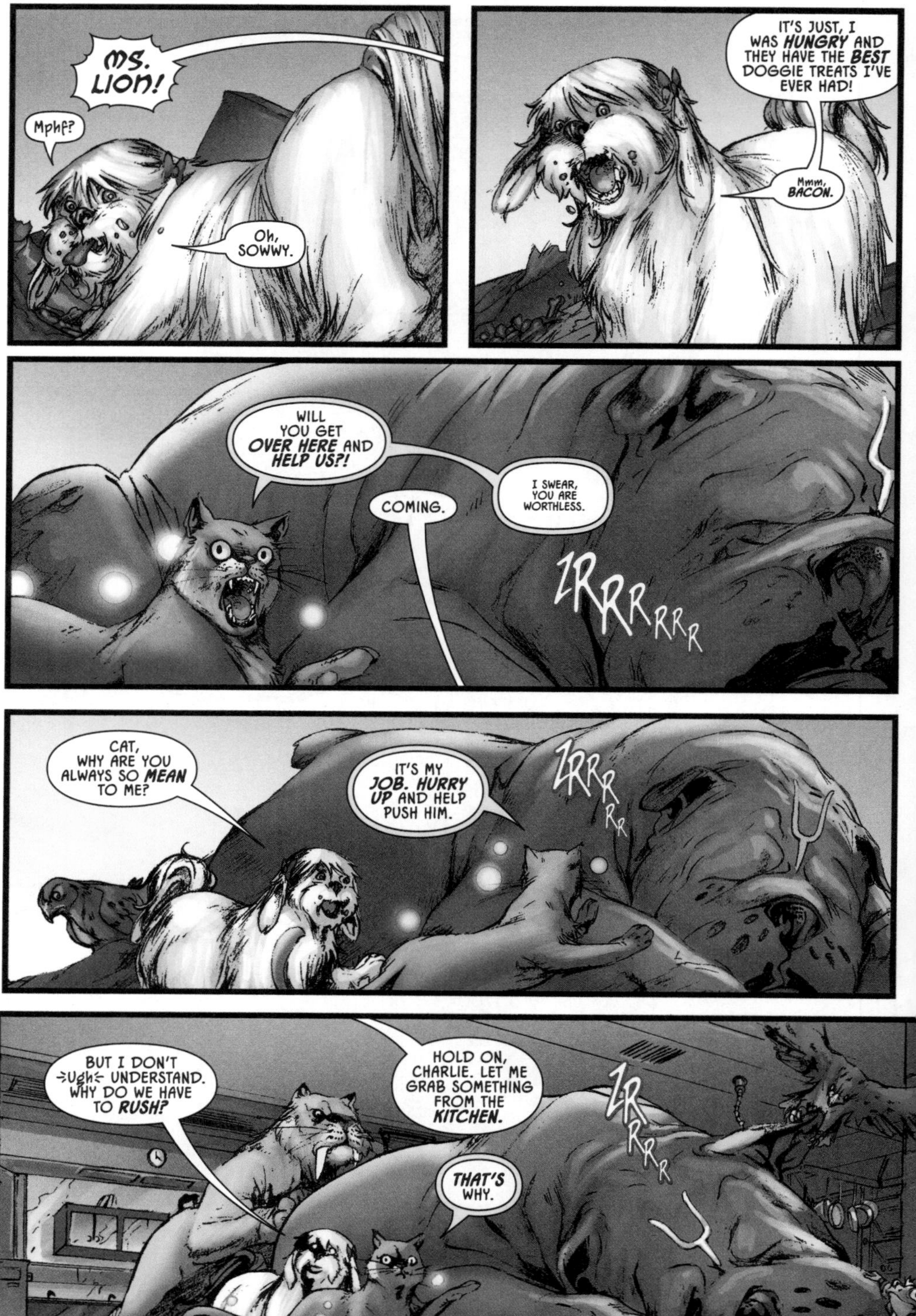
MS. LION!
Mphf?
Oh, SOWWY.
IT'S JUST, I WAS HUNGRY AND THEY HAVE THE BEST DOGGIE TREATS I'VE EVER HAD!
Mmm, BACON.
WILL YOU GET OVER HERE AND HELP US?!
I SWEAR, YOU ARE WORTHLESS.
COMING.
ZRRRRRR
CAT, WHY ARE YOU ALWAYS SO MEAN TO ME?
IT'S MY JOB. HURRY UP AND HELP PUSH HIM.
ZRRRRR
BUT I DON'T ~Ugh~ UNDERSTAND. WHY DO WE HAVE TO RUSH?
HOLD ON, CHARLIE. LET ME GRAB SOMETHING FROM THE KITCHEN.
THAT'S WHY.
ZRRRR

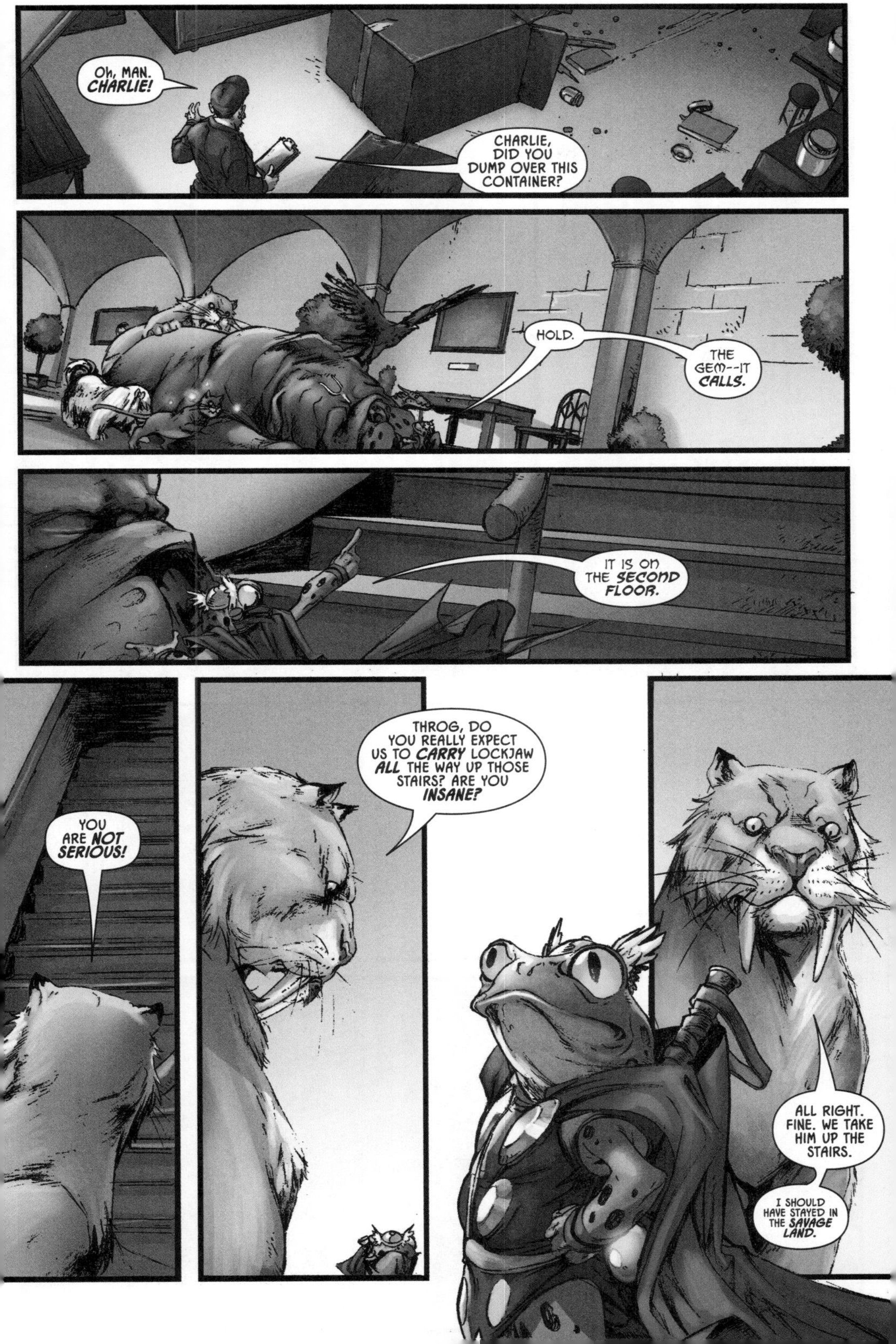
Oh, MAN. CHARLIE!
CHARLIE, DID YOU DUMP OVER THIS CONTAINER?
HOLD.
THE GEM--IT CALLS.
IT IS ON THE SECOND FLOOR.
YOU ARE NOT SERIOUS!
THROG, DO YOU REALLY EXPECT US TO CARRY LOCKJAW ALL THE WAY UP THOSE STAIRS? ARE YOU INSANE?
ALL RIGHT. FINE. WE TAKE HIM UP THE STAIRS.
I SHOULD HAVE STAYED IN THE SAVAGE LAND.

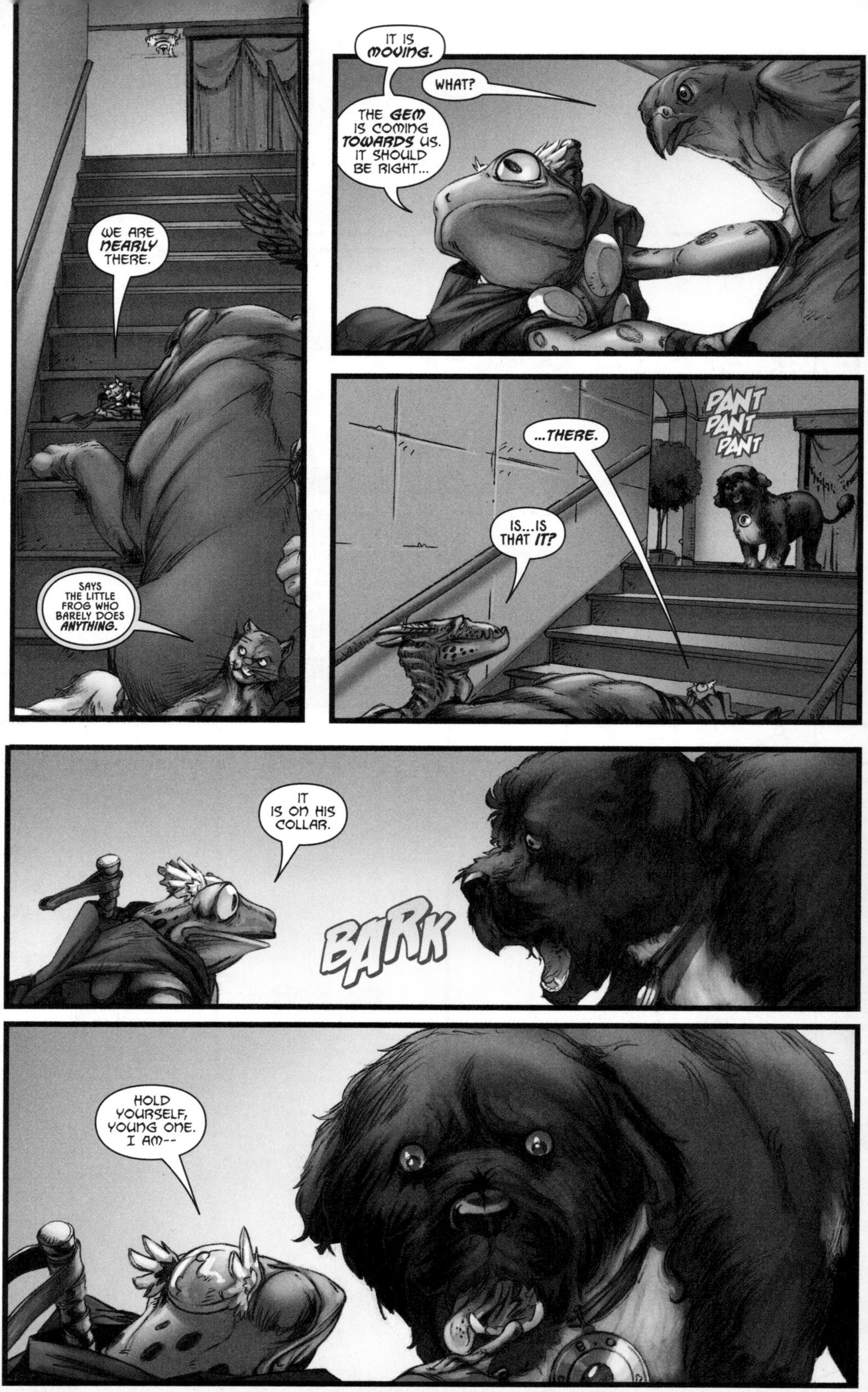

WE ARE NEARLY THERE.
SAYS THE LITTLE FROG WHO BARELY DOES ANYTHING.
IT IS MOVING.
WHAT?
THE GEM IS COMING TOWARDS US. IT SHOULD BE RIGHT...
...THERE.
PANT PANT PANT
IS...IS THAT IT?
IT IS ON HIS COLLAR.
BARK
HOLD YOURSELF, YOUNG ONE. I AM--

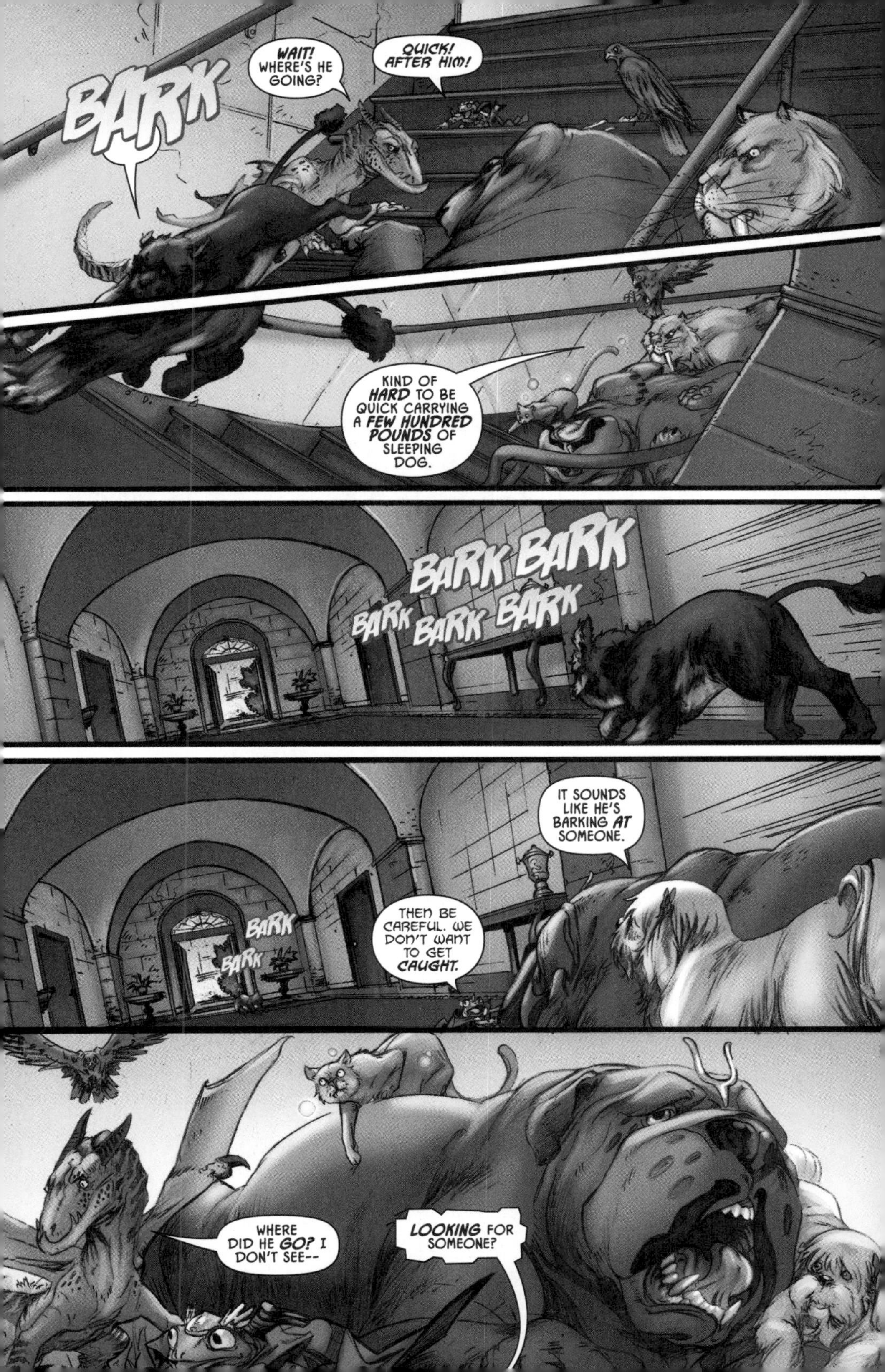
BARK
WAIT! WHERE'S HE GOING?
QUICK! AFTER HIM!
KIND OF HARD TO BE QUICK CARRYING A FEW HUNDRED POUNDS OF SLEEPING DOG.
BARK BARK
BARK BARK BARK
IT SOUNDS LIKE HE'S BARKING AT SOMEONE.
THEN BE CAREFUL. WE DON'T WANT TO GET CAUGHT.
BARK
BARK
WHERE DID HE GO? I DON'T SEE--
LOOKING FOR SOMEONE?

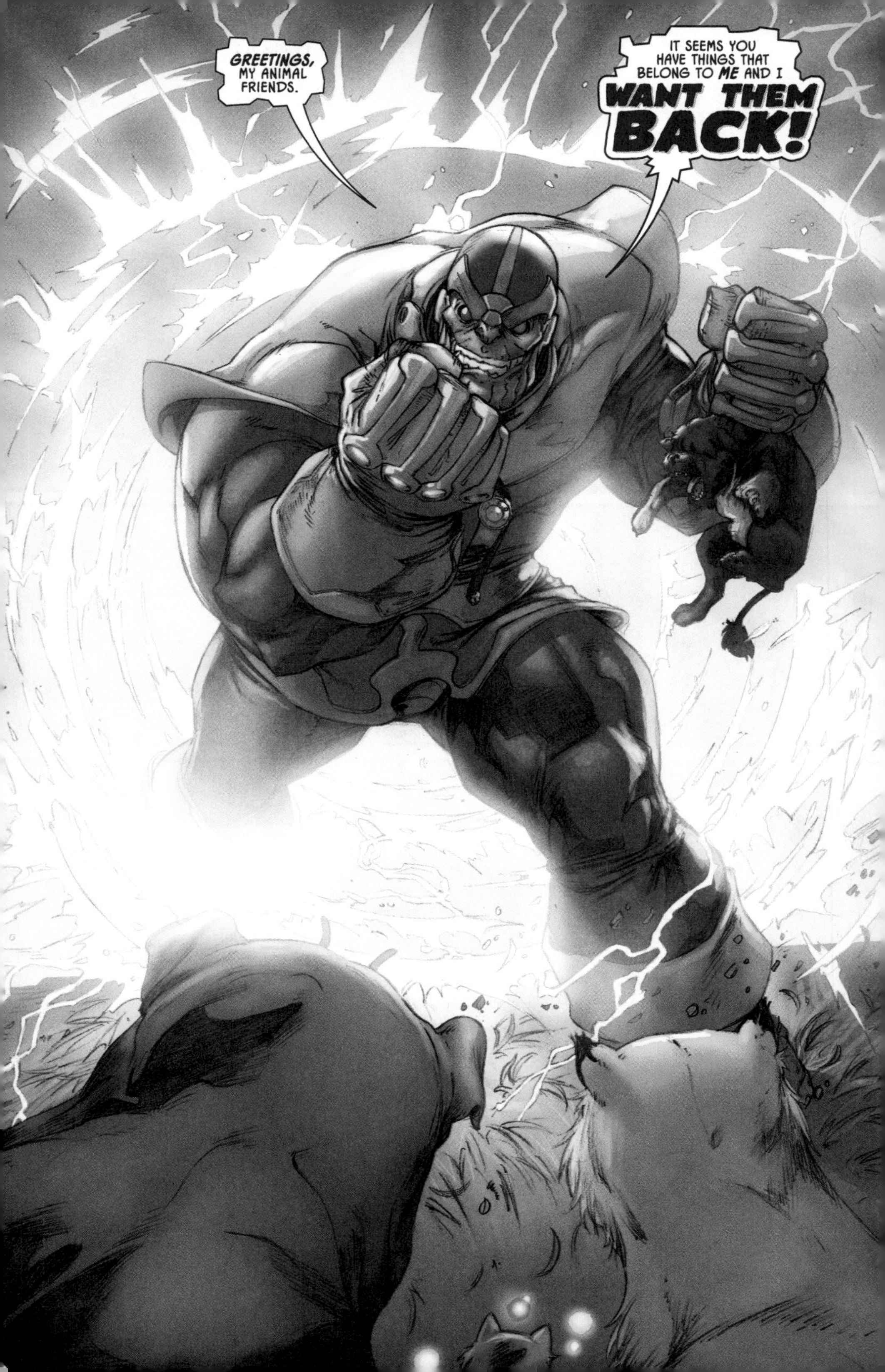
GREETINGS, MY ANIMAL FRIENDS.
IT SEEMS YOU HAVE THINGS THAT BELONG TO ME AND I WANT THEM BACK!

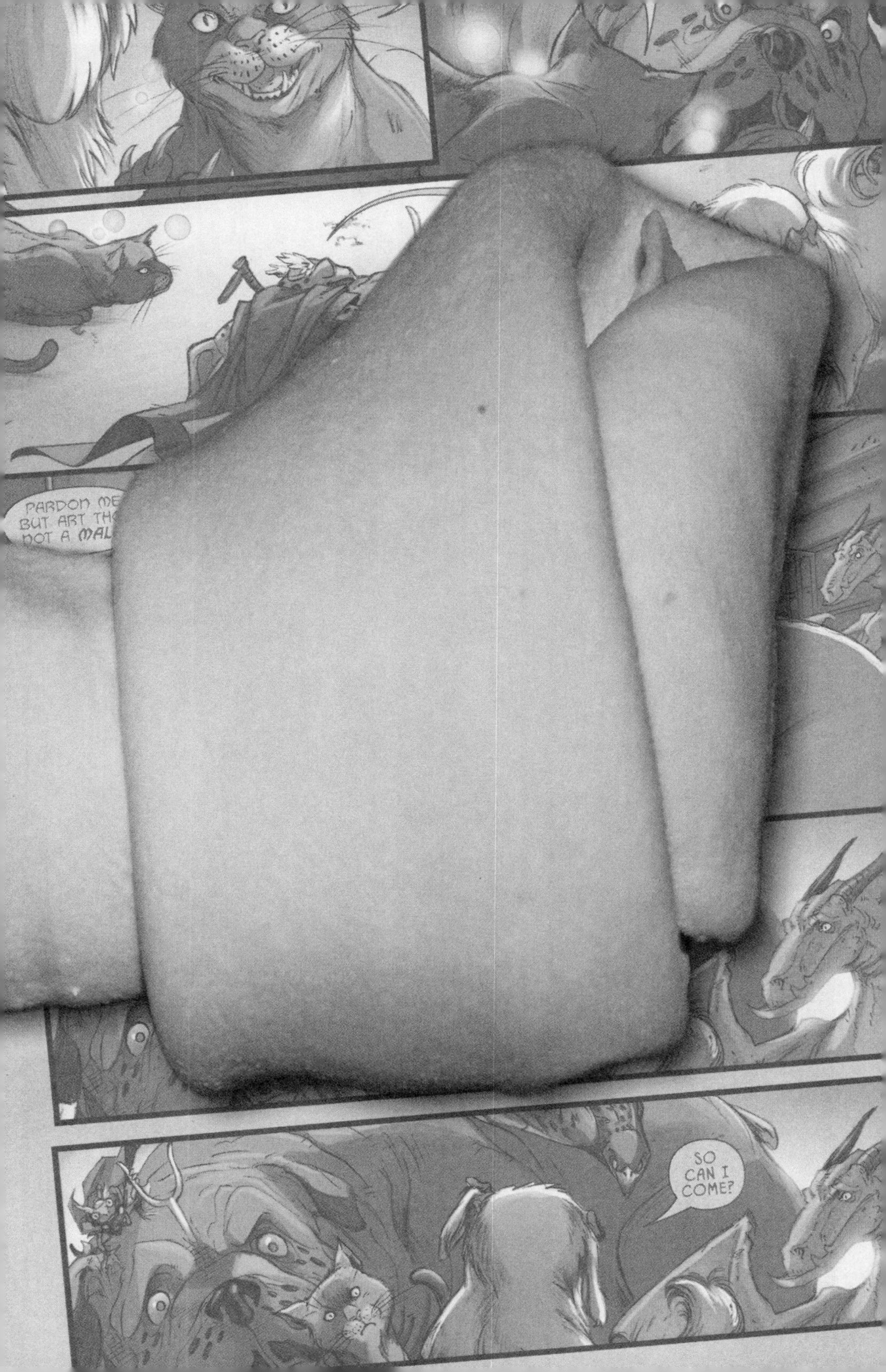
PARDON ME
BUT ART THO
NOT A MAL
SO CAN I COME?

4

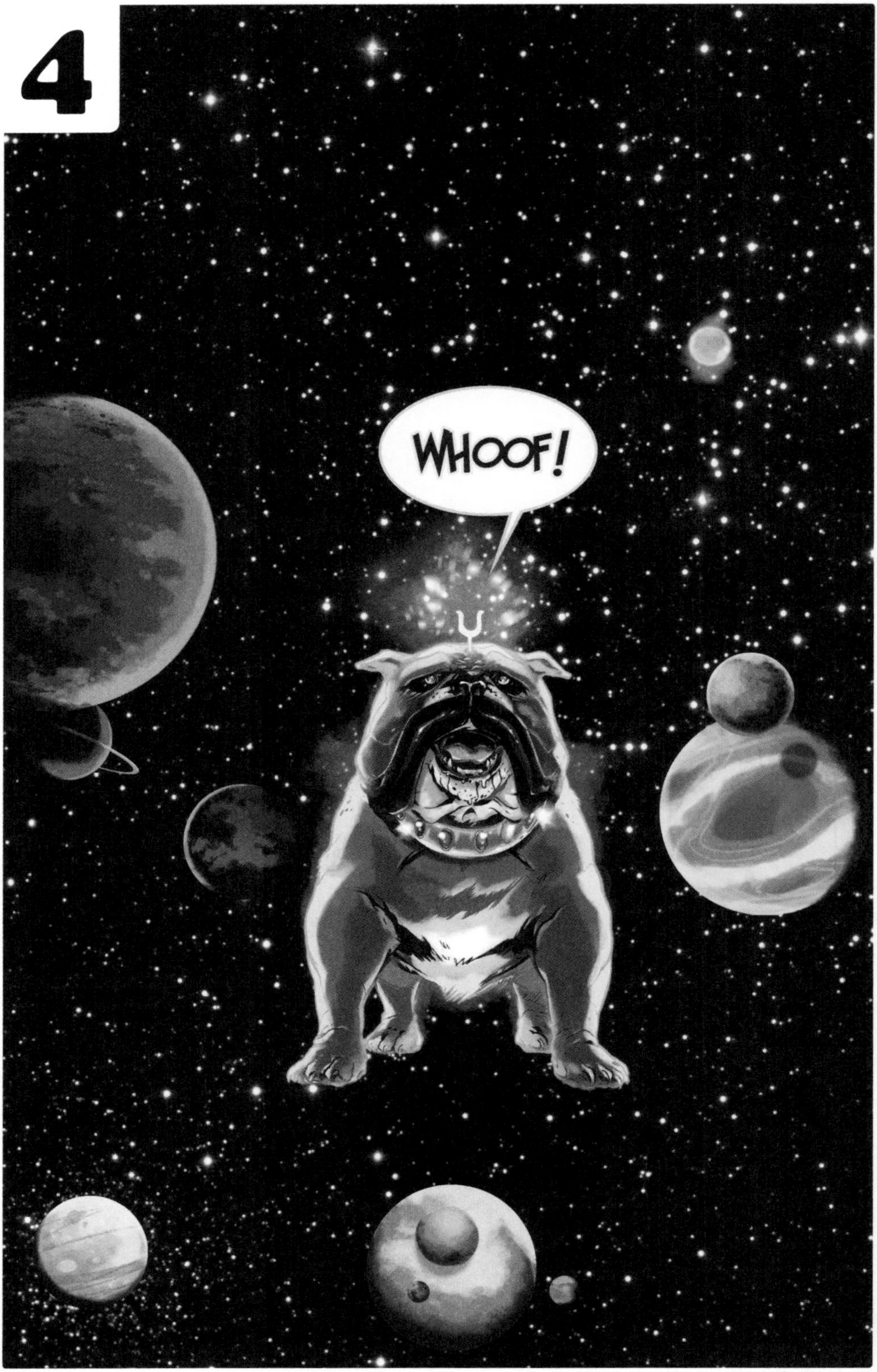
WHOOF!

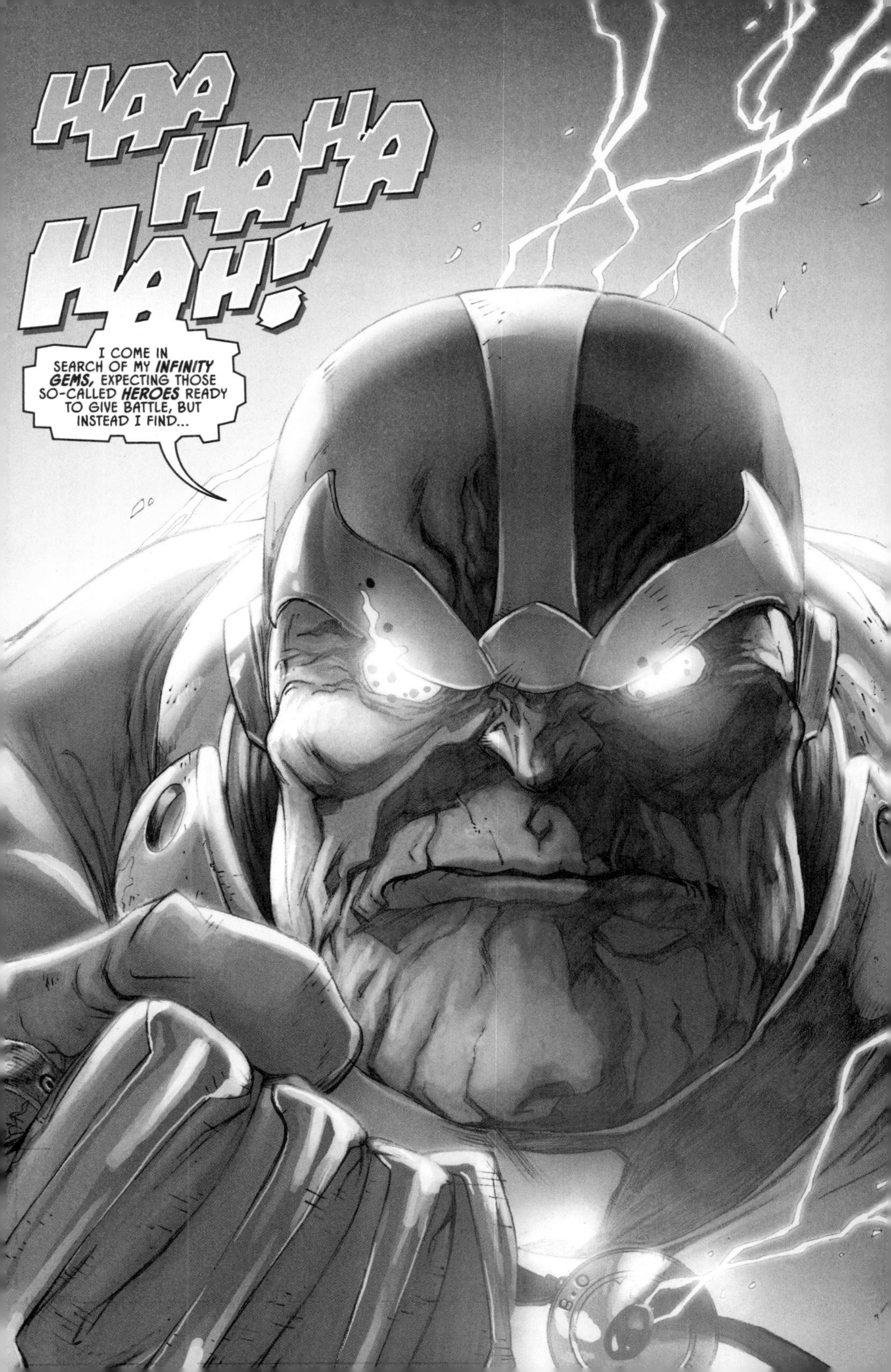
HAA HAHA HAH!
I COME IN SEARCH OF MY INFINITY GEMS, EXPECTING THOSE SO-CALLED HEROES READY TO GIVE BATTLE, BUT INSTEAD I FIND...

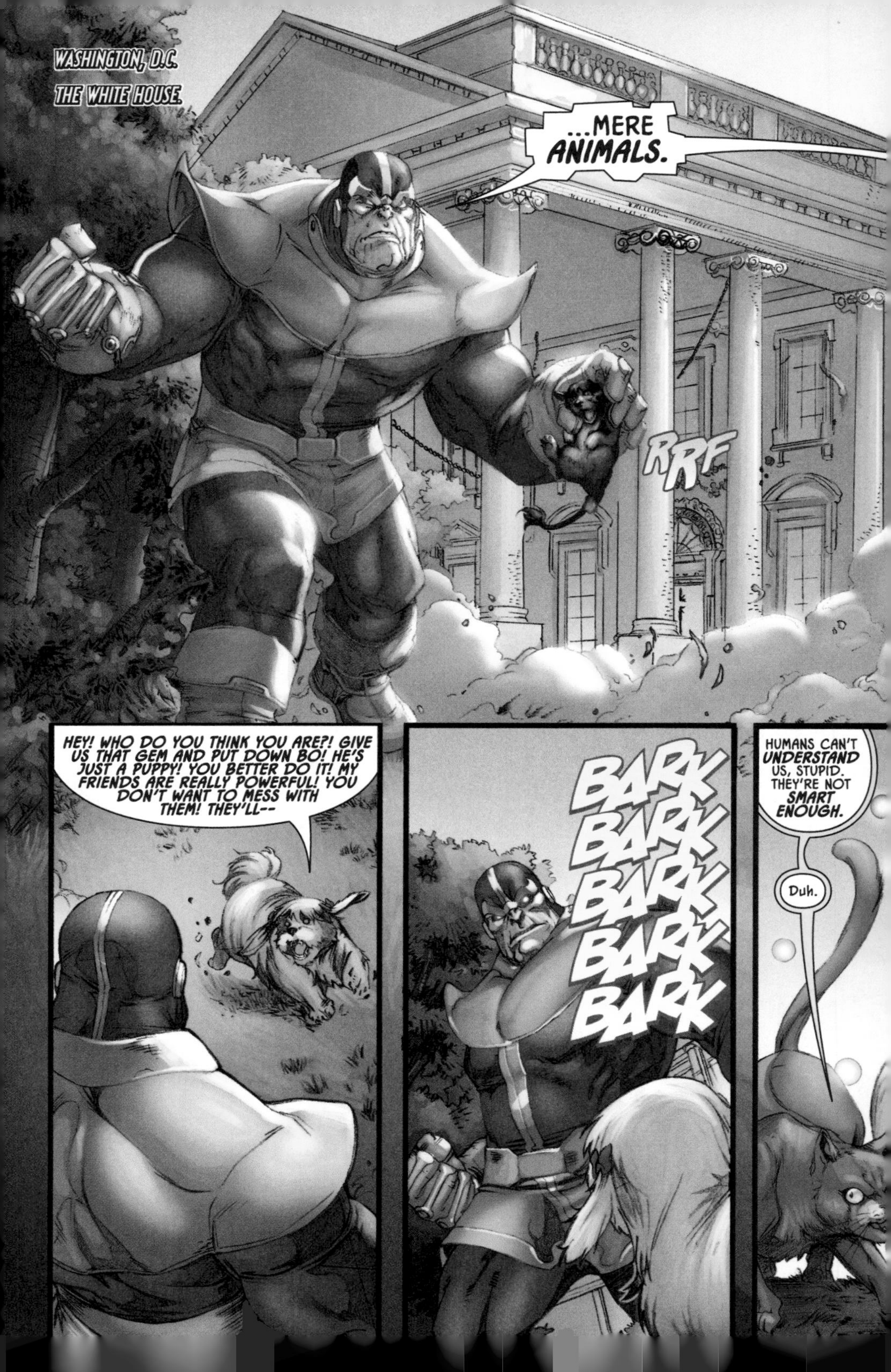
WASHINGTON, D.C.
THE WHITE HOUSE.
...MERE ANIMALS.
RRF
HEY! WHO DO YOU THINK YOU ARE?! GIVE US THAT GEM AND PUT DOWN BO! HE'S JUST A PUPPY! YOU BETTER DO IT! MY FRIENDS ARE REALLY POWERFUL! YOU DON'T WANT TO MESS WITH THEM! THEY'LL--
BARK BARK BARK BARK BARK
HUMANS CAN'T UNDERSTAND US, STUPID. THEY'RE NOT SMART ENOUGH.
Duh.

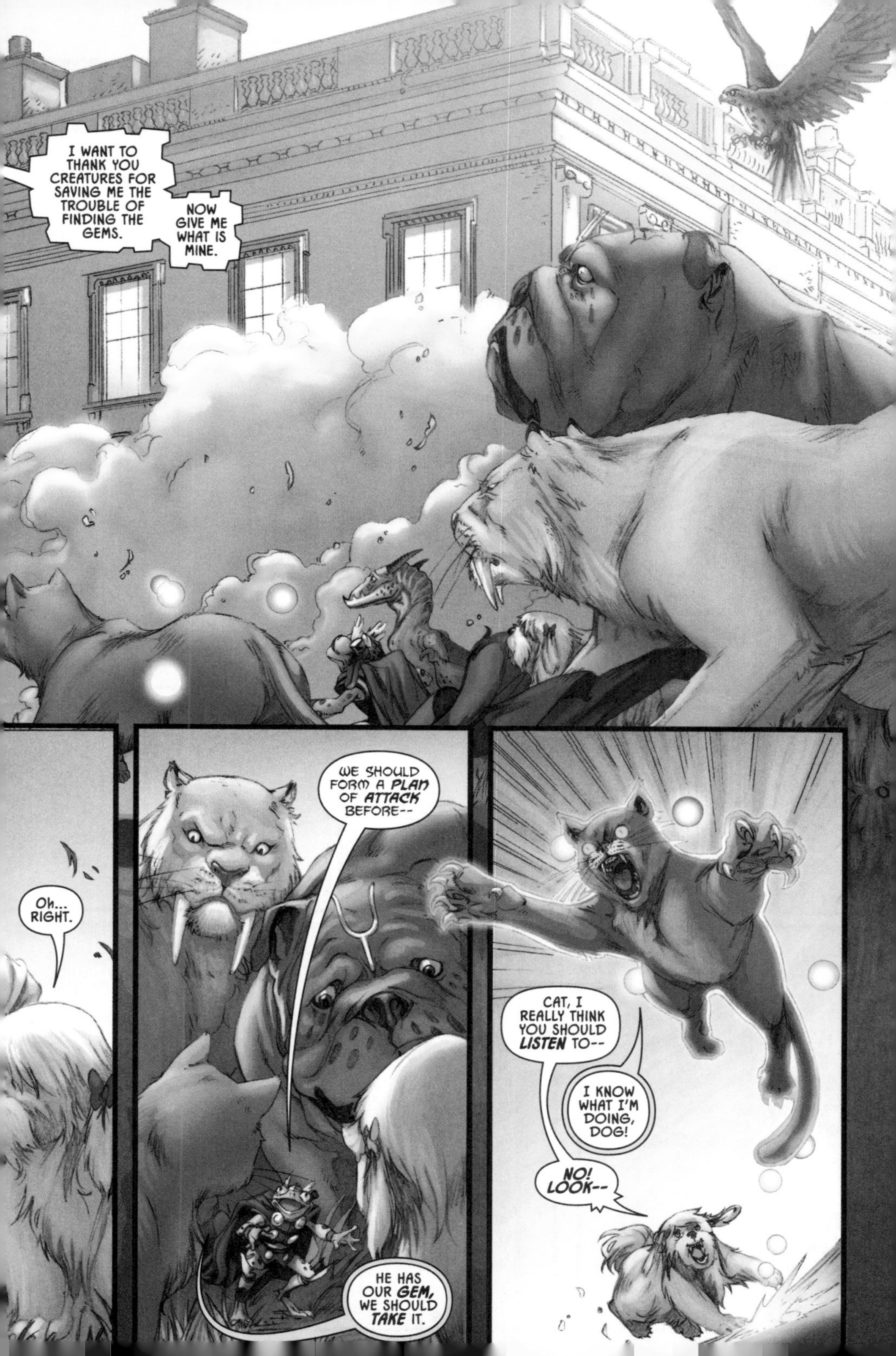
I WANT TO THANK YOU CREATURES FOR SAVING ME THE TROUBLE OF FINDING THE GEMS.
NOW GIVE ME WHAT IS MINE.
Oh... RIGHT.
WE SHOULD FORM A PLAN OF ATTACK BEFORE--
HE HAS OUR GEM, WE SHOULD TAKE IT.
CAT, I REALLY THINK YOU SHOULD LISTEN TO--
I KNOW WHAT I'M DOING, DOG!
NO! LOOK--

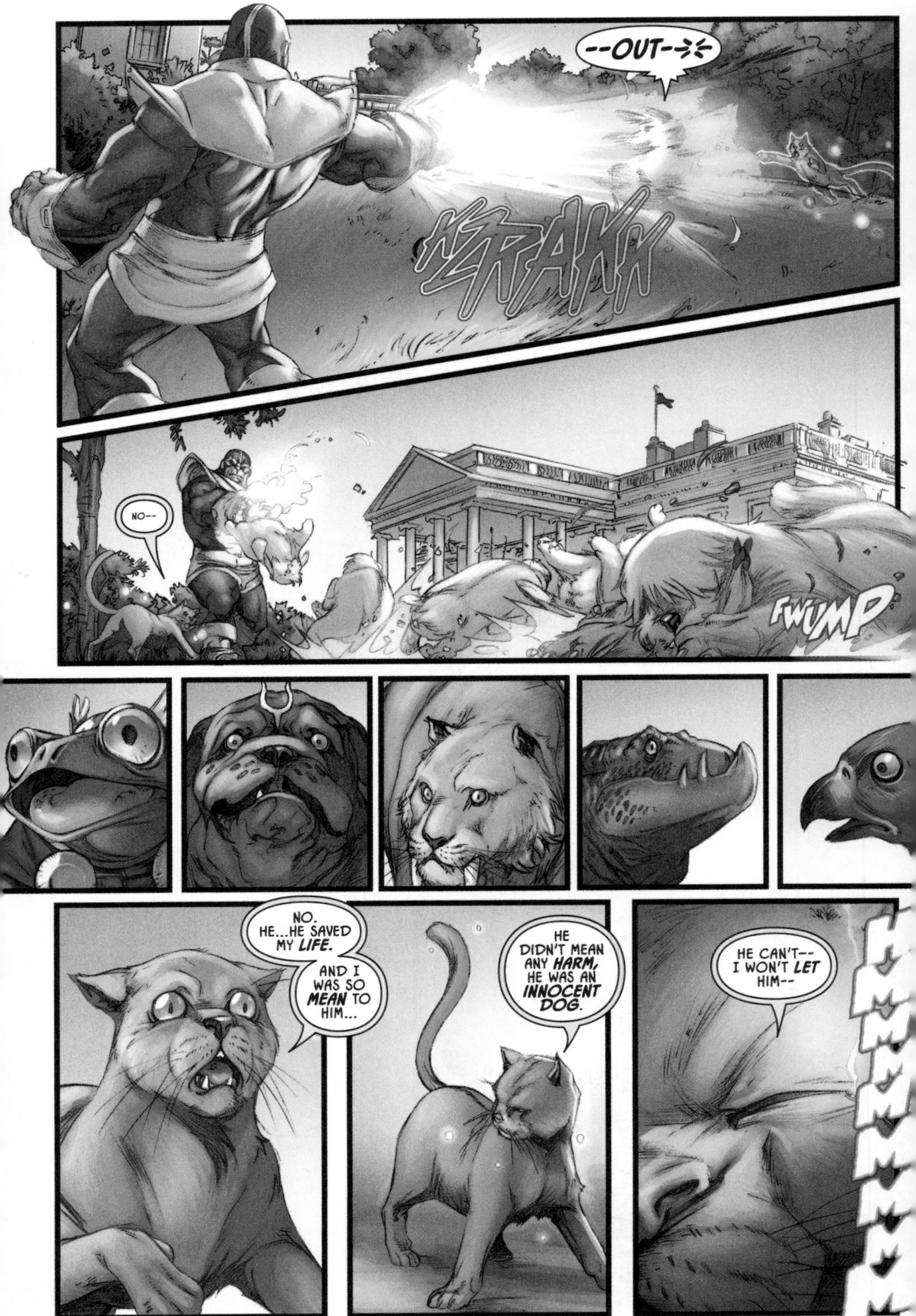
--OUT--
KRAKK
NO--
FWUMP
NO.
HE...HE SAVED MY LIFE.
AND I WAS SO MEAN TO HIM...
HE DIDN'T MEAN ANY HARM, HE WAS AN INNOCENT DOG.
HE CAN'T--
I WON'T LET HIM--

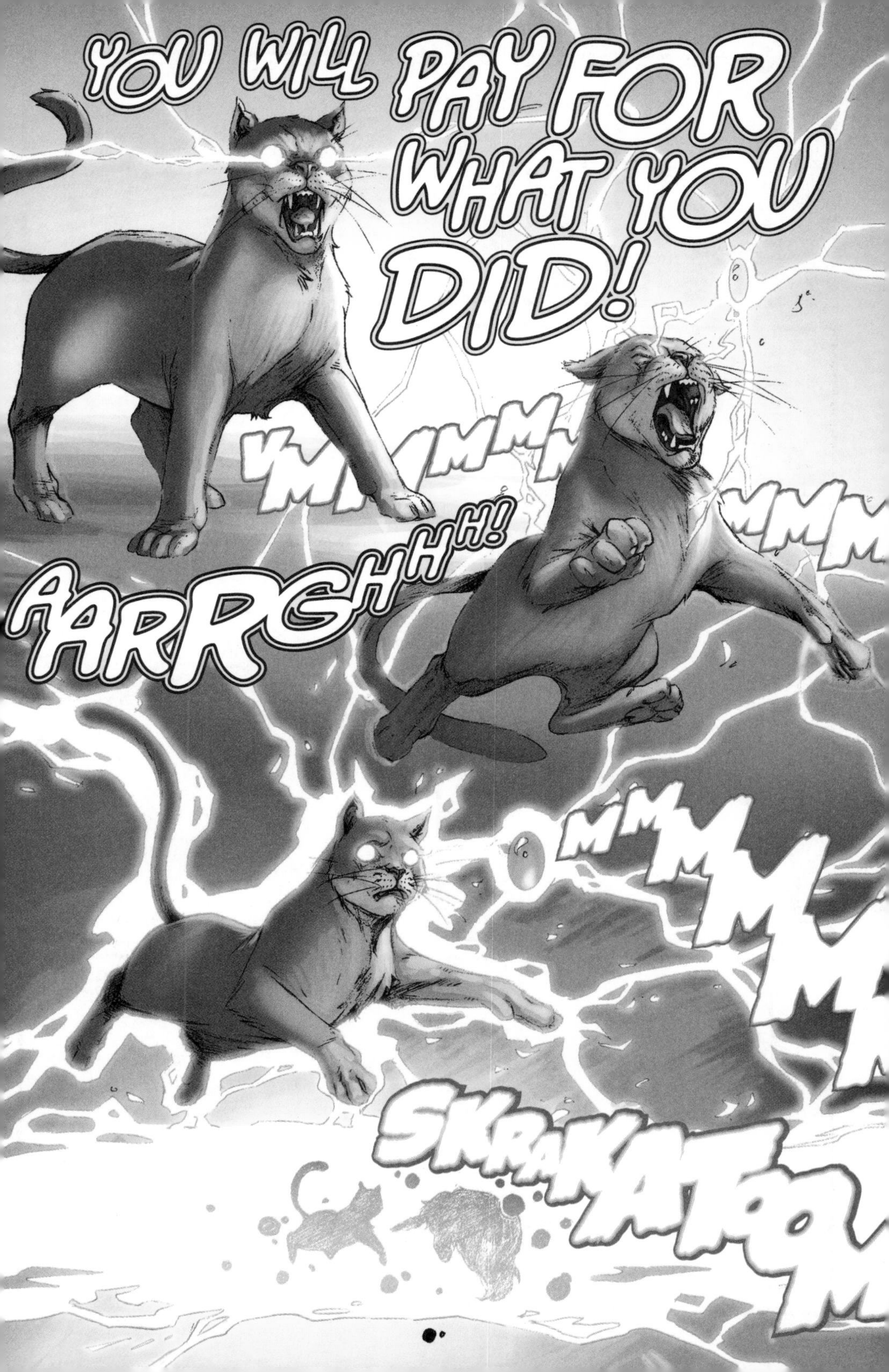
YOU WILL PAY FOR WHAT YOU DID!
VMMMMMMMMMMM
AARRGHHH!
OMMMMMMM
SKRAKATOOM

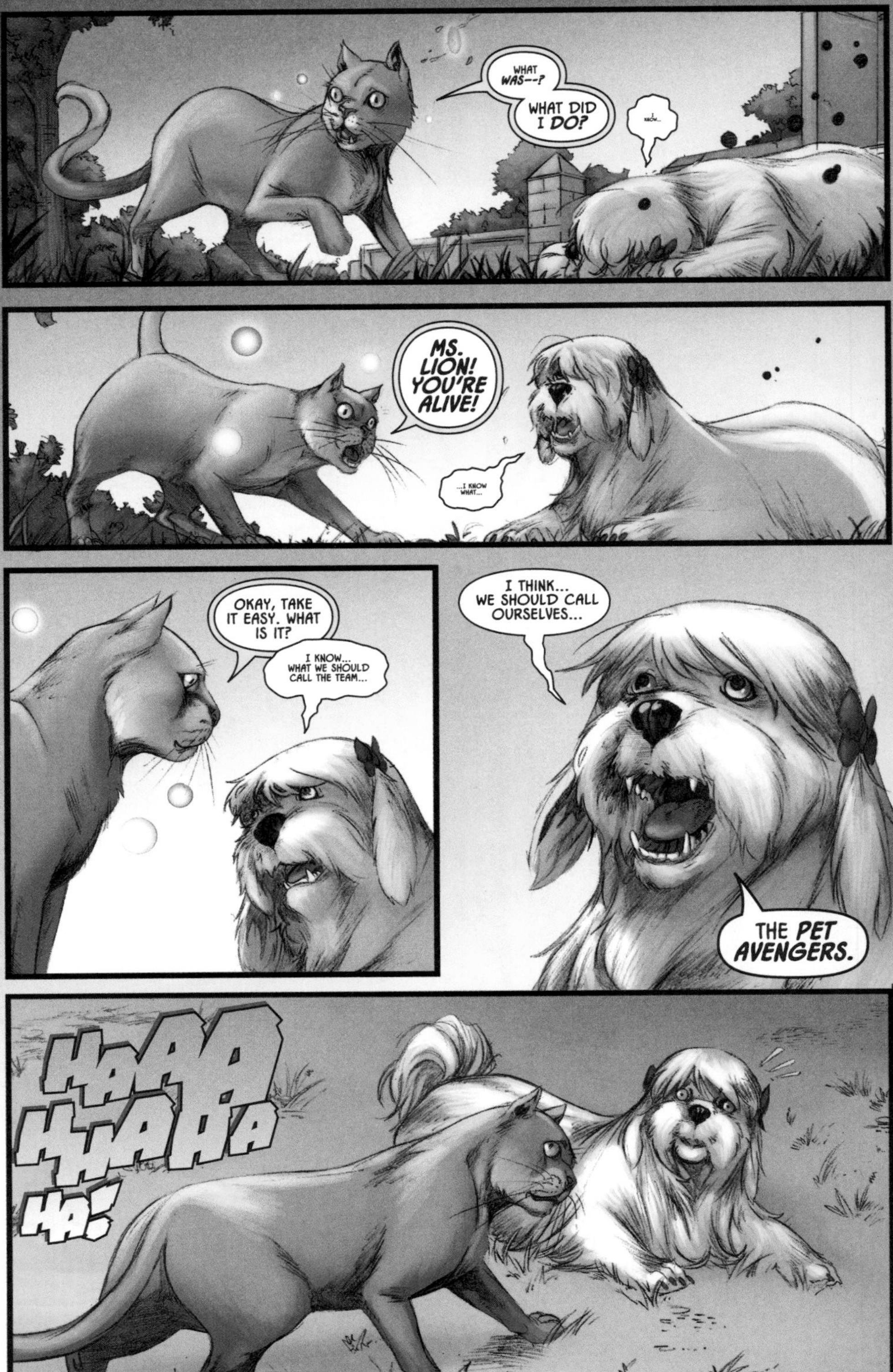

WHAT WAS--?
WHAT DID I DO?
I KNOW...
MS. LION! YOU'RE ALIVE!
...I KNOW WHAT...
OKAY, TAKE IT EASY. WHAT IS IT?
I KNOW... WHAT WE SHOULD CALL THE TEAM...
I THINK... WE SHOULD CALL OURSELVES...
THE PET AVENGERS.
HAHA HWAHA HA!

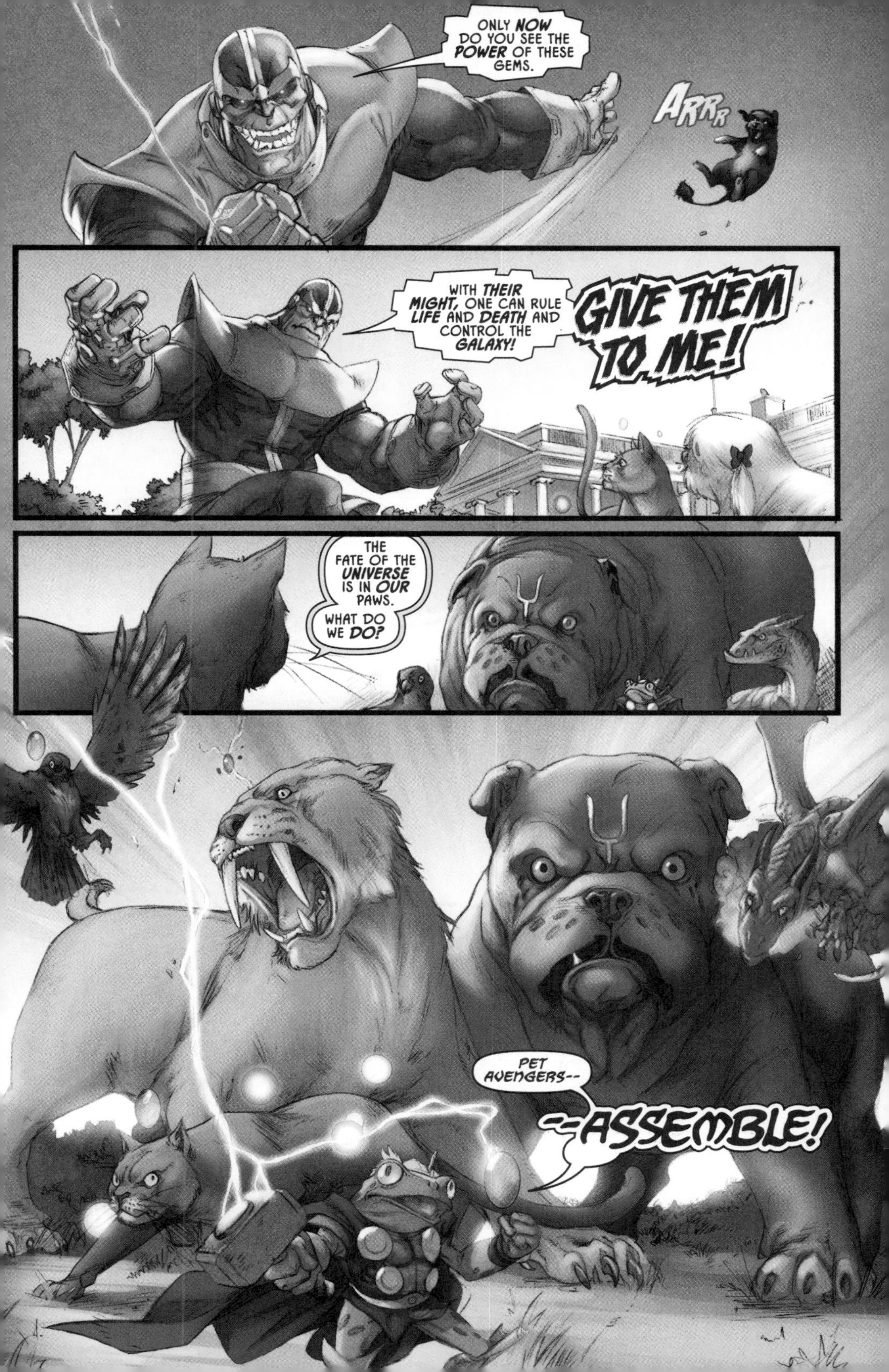
ONLY NOW DO YOU SEE THE POWER OF THESE GEMS.
ARRR
WITH THEIR MIGHT, ONE CAN RULE LIFE AND DEATH AND CONTROL THE GALAXY!
GIVE THEM TO ME!
THE FATE OF THE UNIVERSE IS IN OUR PAWS.
WHAT DO WE DO?
PET AVENGERS--
--ASSEMBLE!

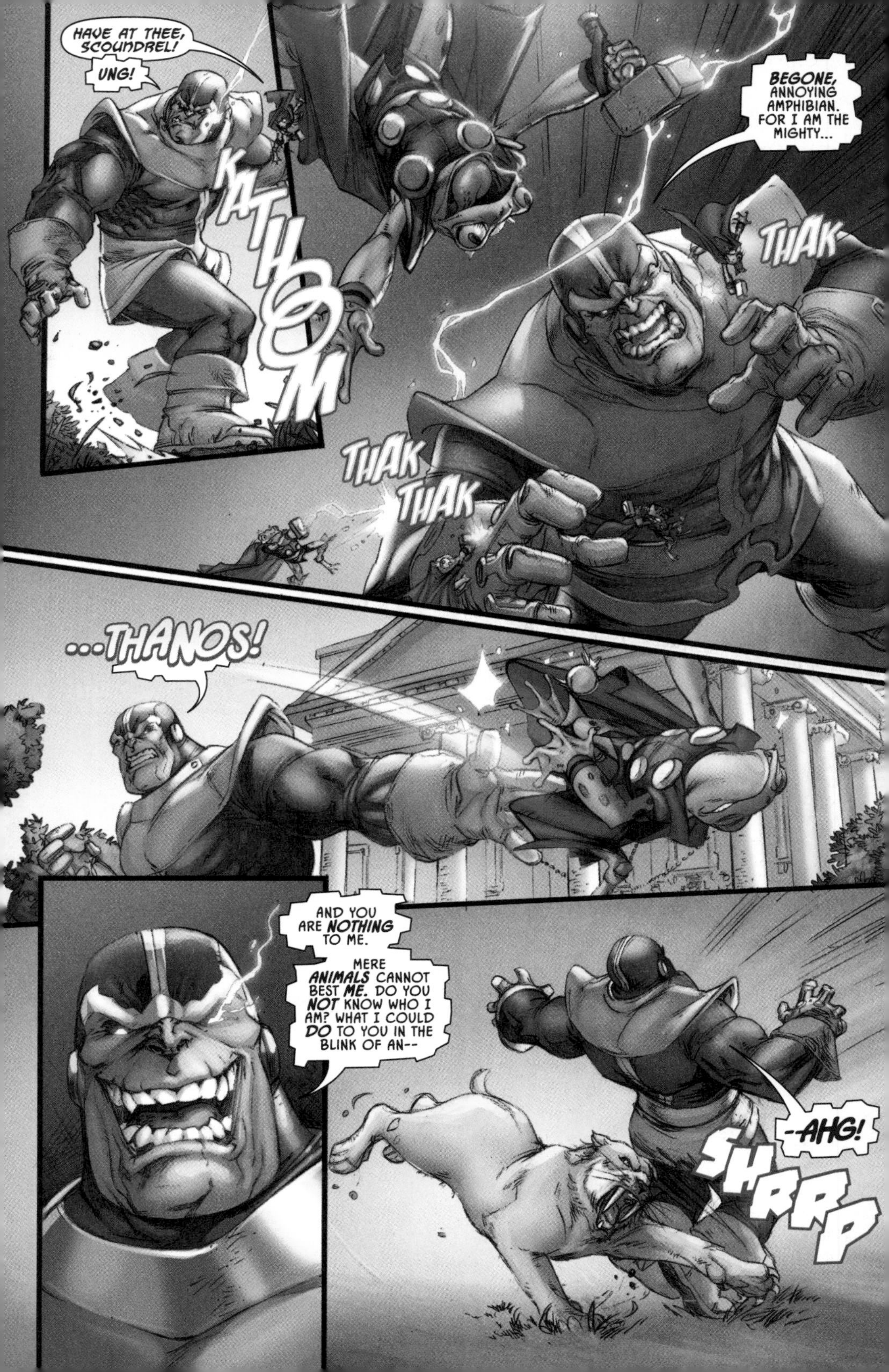
HAVE AT THEE, SCOUNDREL!
UNG!
KATHOOM
BEGONE, ANNOYING AMPHIBIAN. FOR I AM THE MIGHTY...
THAK
THAK
THAK
...THANOS!
AND YOU ARE NOTHING TO ME.
MERE ANIMALS CANNOT BEST ME. DO YOU NOT KNOW WHO I AM? WHAT I COULD DO TO YOU IN THE BLINK OF AN--
--AHG!
SHRRP

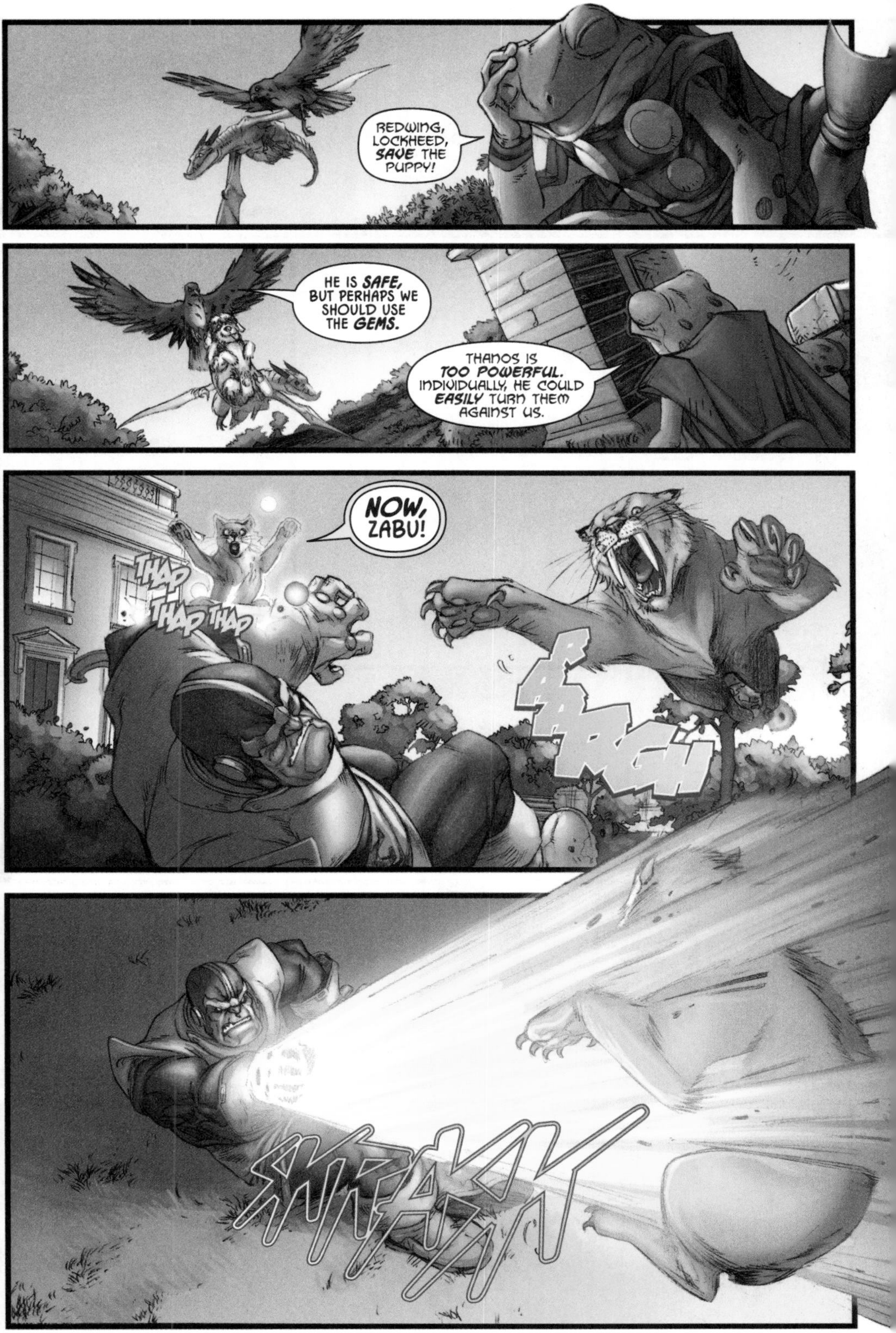
REDWING, LOCKHEED, SAVE THE PUPPY!
HE IS SAFE, BUT PERHAPS WE SHOULD USE THE GEMS.
THANOS IS TOO POWERFUL. INDIVIDUALLY, HE COULD EASILY TURN THEM AGAINST US.
NOW, ZABU!
THAP THAP THAP THAP
RARGH

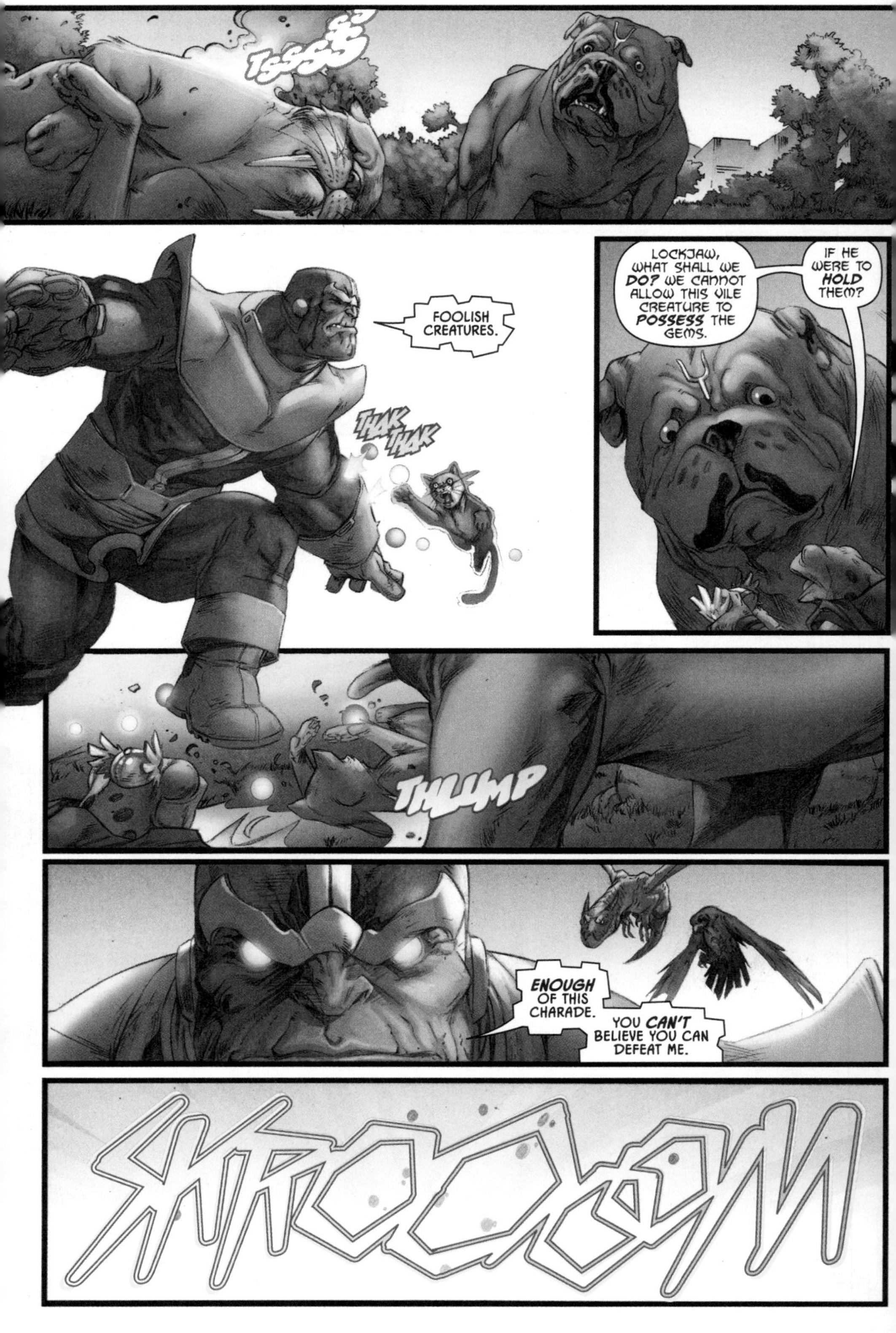
TSSSSS
FOOLISH CREATURES.
LOCKJAW, WHAT SHALL WE DO? WE CANNOT ALLOW THIS VILE CREATURE TO POSSESS THE GEMS.
IF HE WERE TO HOLD THEM?
THAK THAK
THUMP
ENOUGH OF THIS CHARADE.
YOU CAN'T BELIEVE YOU CAN DEFEAT ME.
SHROOOOM

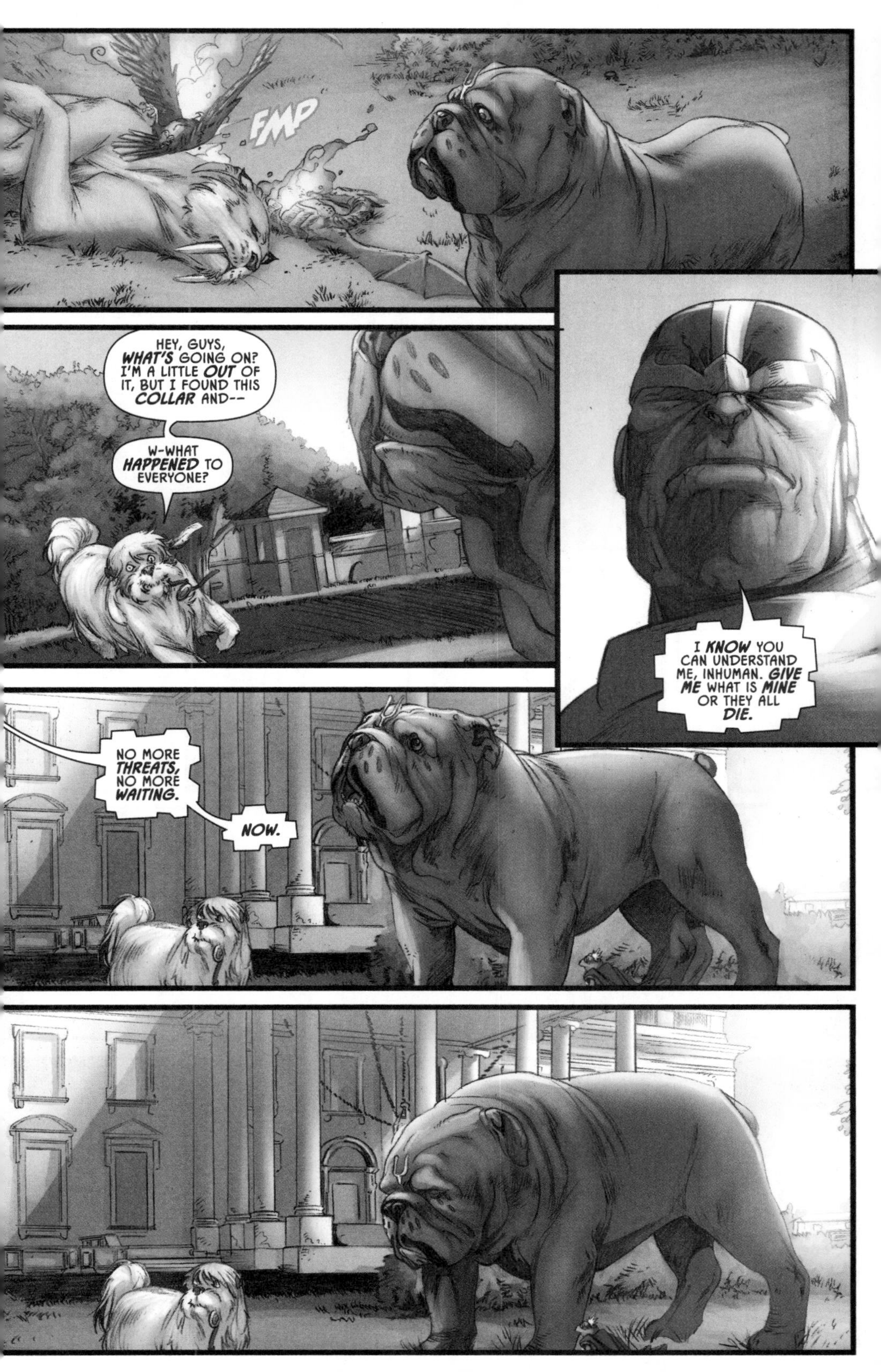
FMP
HEY, GUYS, WHAT'S GOING ON? I'M A LITTLE OUT OF IT, BUT I FOUND THIS COLLAR AND--
W-WHAT HAPPENED TO EVERYONE?
I KNOW YOU CAN UNDERSTAND ME, INHUMAN. GIVE ME WHAT IS MINE OR THEY ALL DIE.
NO MORE THREATS, NO MORE WAITING.
NOW.

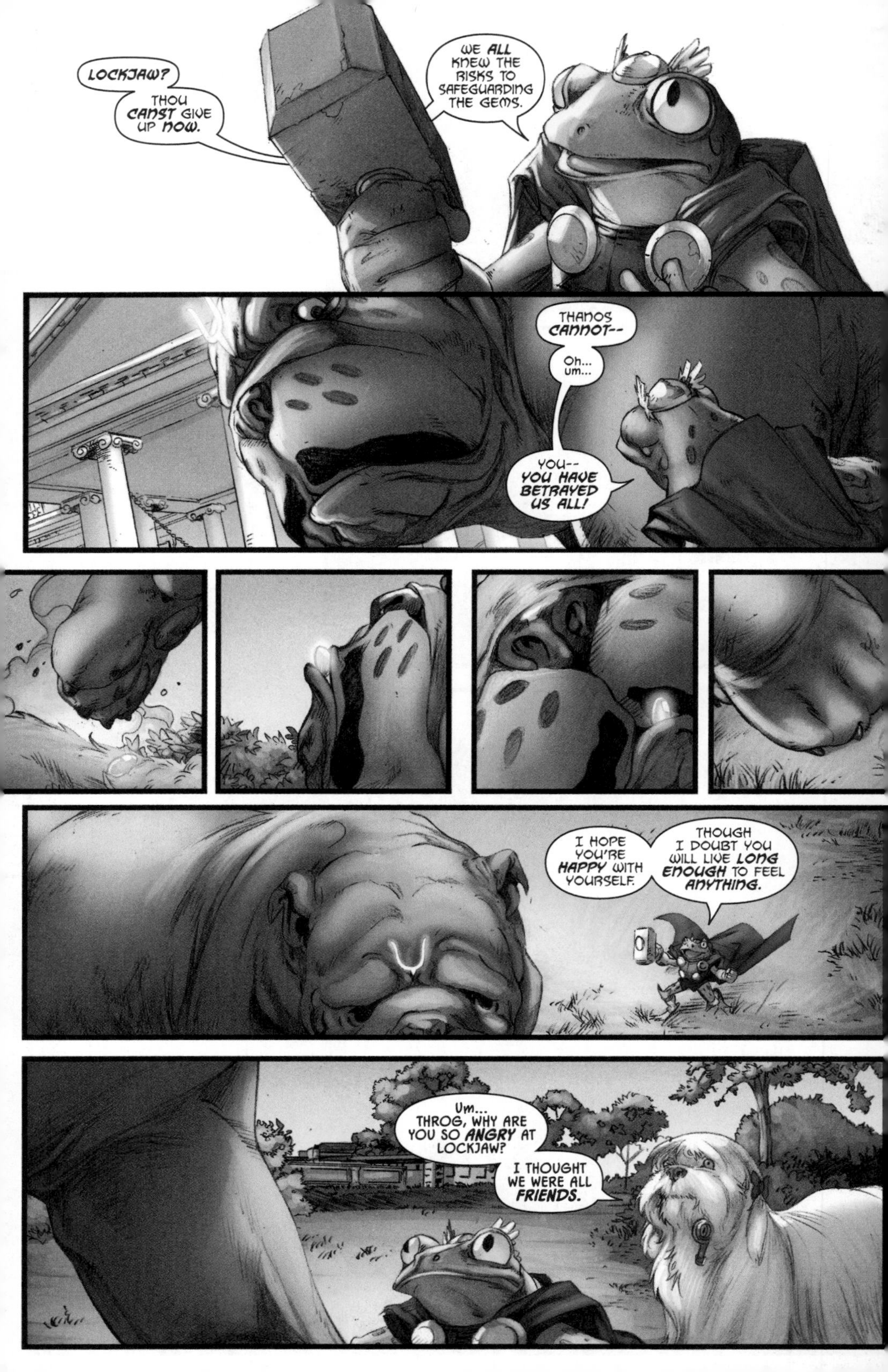

LOCKJAW?
THOU CANST GIVE UP NOW.
WE ALL KNEW THE RISKS TO SAFEGUARDING THE GEMS.
THANOS CANNOT--
Oh... um...
YOU-- YOU HAVE BETRAYED US ALL!
I HOPE YOU'RE HAPPY WITH YOURSELF.
THOUGH I DOUBT YOU WILL LIVE LONG ENOUGH TO FEEL ANYTHING.
Um... THROG, WHY ARE YOU SO ANGRY AT LOCKJAW?
I THOUGHT WE WERE ALL FRIENDS.

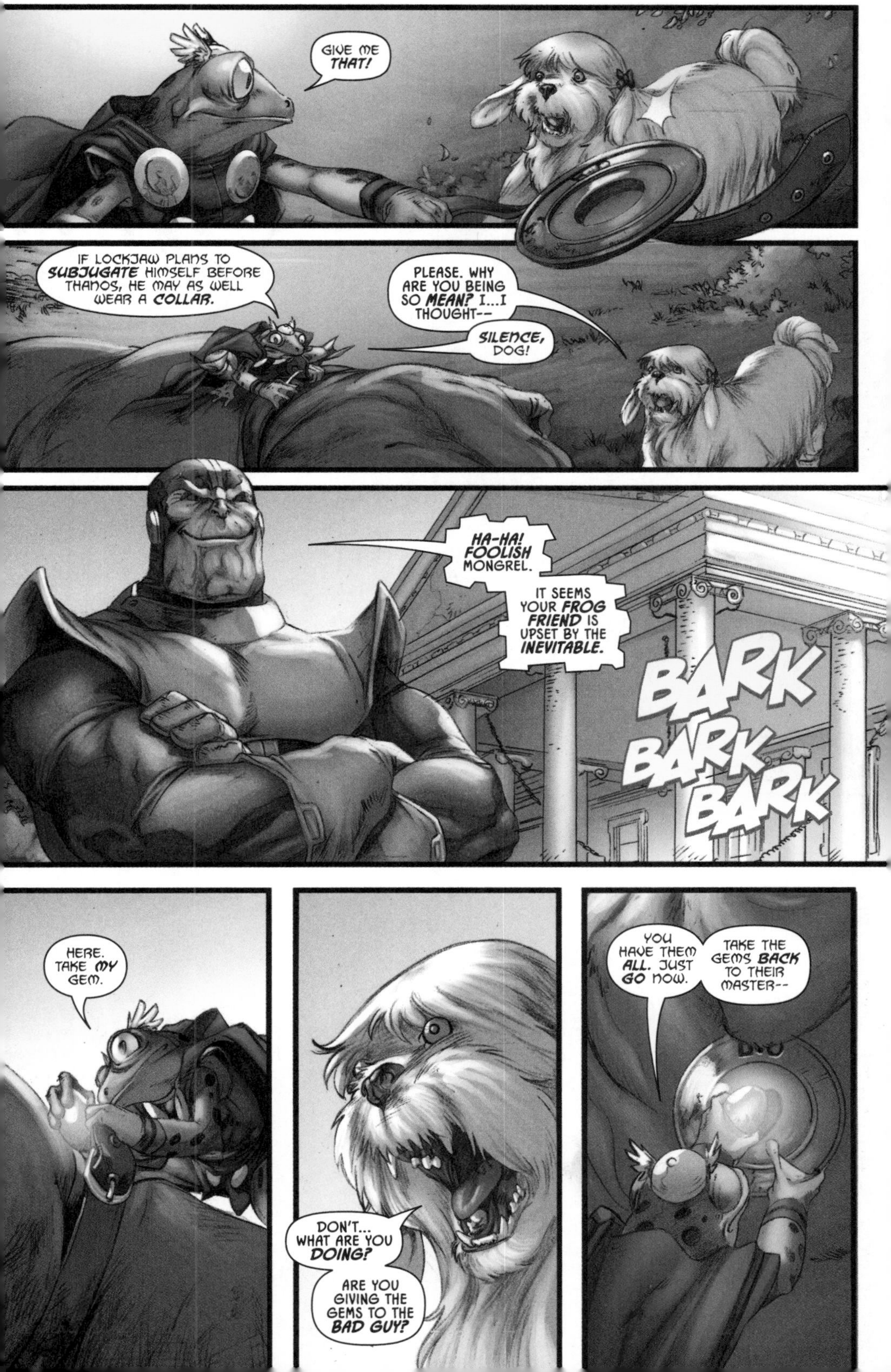
GIVE ME THAT!
IF LOCKJAW PLANS TO SUBJUGATE HIMSELF BEFORE THANOS, HE MAY AS WELL WEAR A COLLAR.
PLEASE. WHY ARE YOU BEING SO MEAN? I...I THOUGHT--
SILENCE, DOG!
HA-HA! FOOLISH MONGREL.
IT SEEMS YOUR FROG FRIEND IS UPSET BY THE INEVITABLE.
BARK BARK BARK
HERE. TAKE MY GEM.
DON'T... WHAT ARE YOU DOING?
ARE YOU GIVING THE GEMS TO THE BAD GUY?
YOU HAVE THEM ALL. JUST GO NOW.
TAKE THE GEMS BACK TO THEIR MASTER--

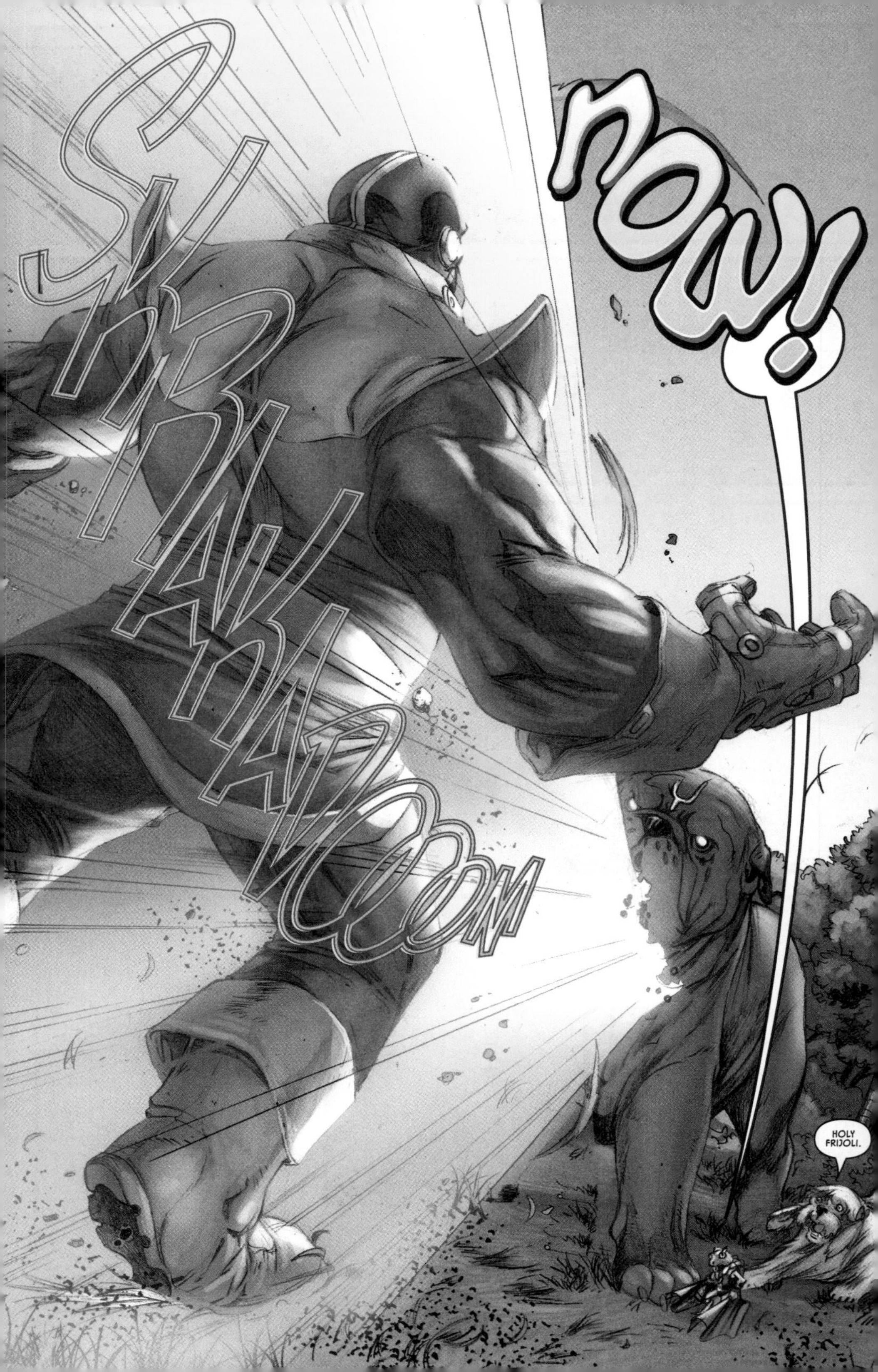
NOW!
HOLY FRIJOLI.

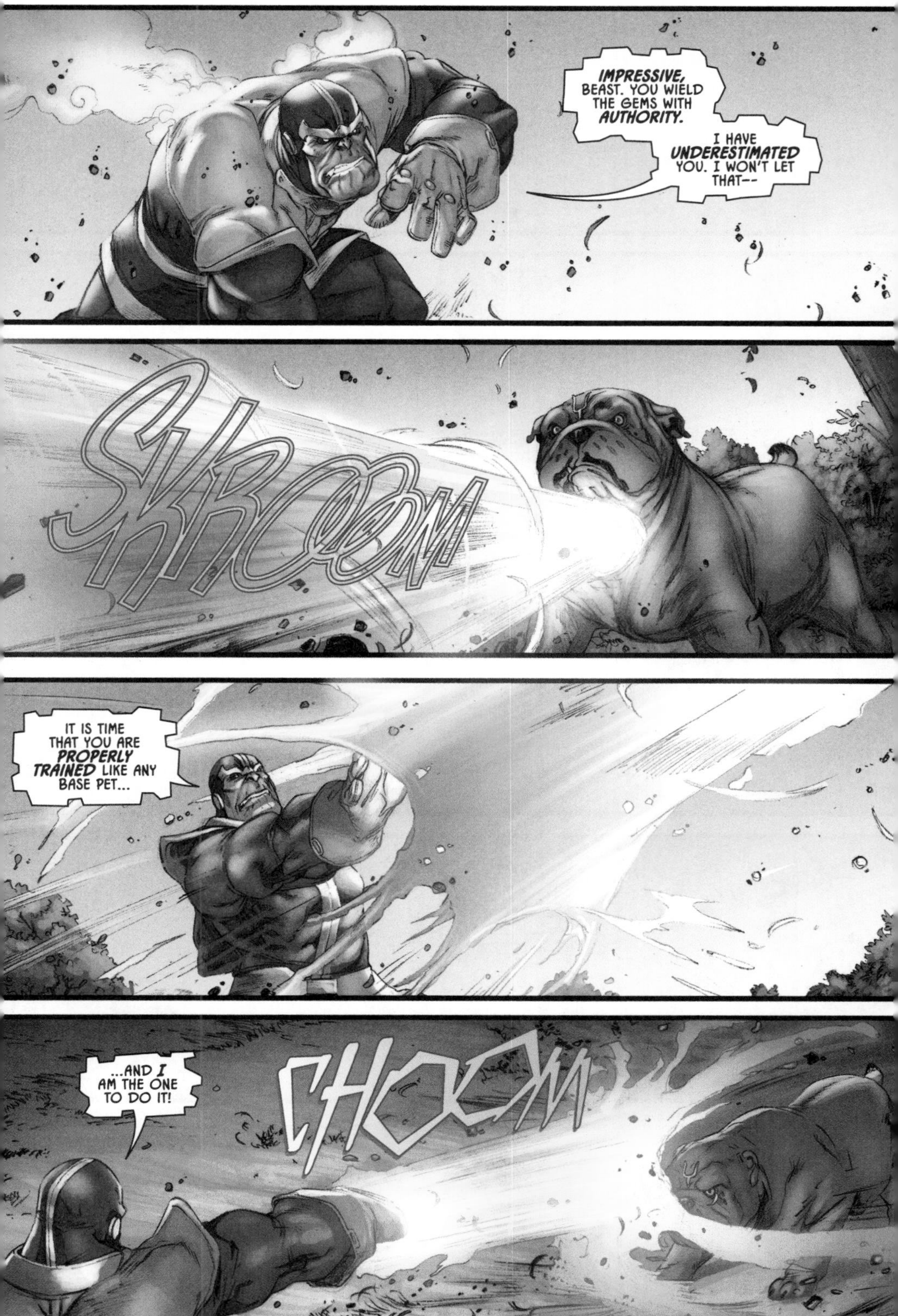
IMPRESSIVE, BEAST. YOU WIELD THE GEMS WITH AUTHORITY.
I HAVE UNDERESTIMATED YOU. I WON'T LET THAT--
SKROOM
IT IS TIME THAT YOU ARE PROPERLY TRAINED LIKE ANY BASE PET...
...AND I AM THE ONE TO DO IT!
CHOOM

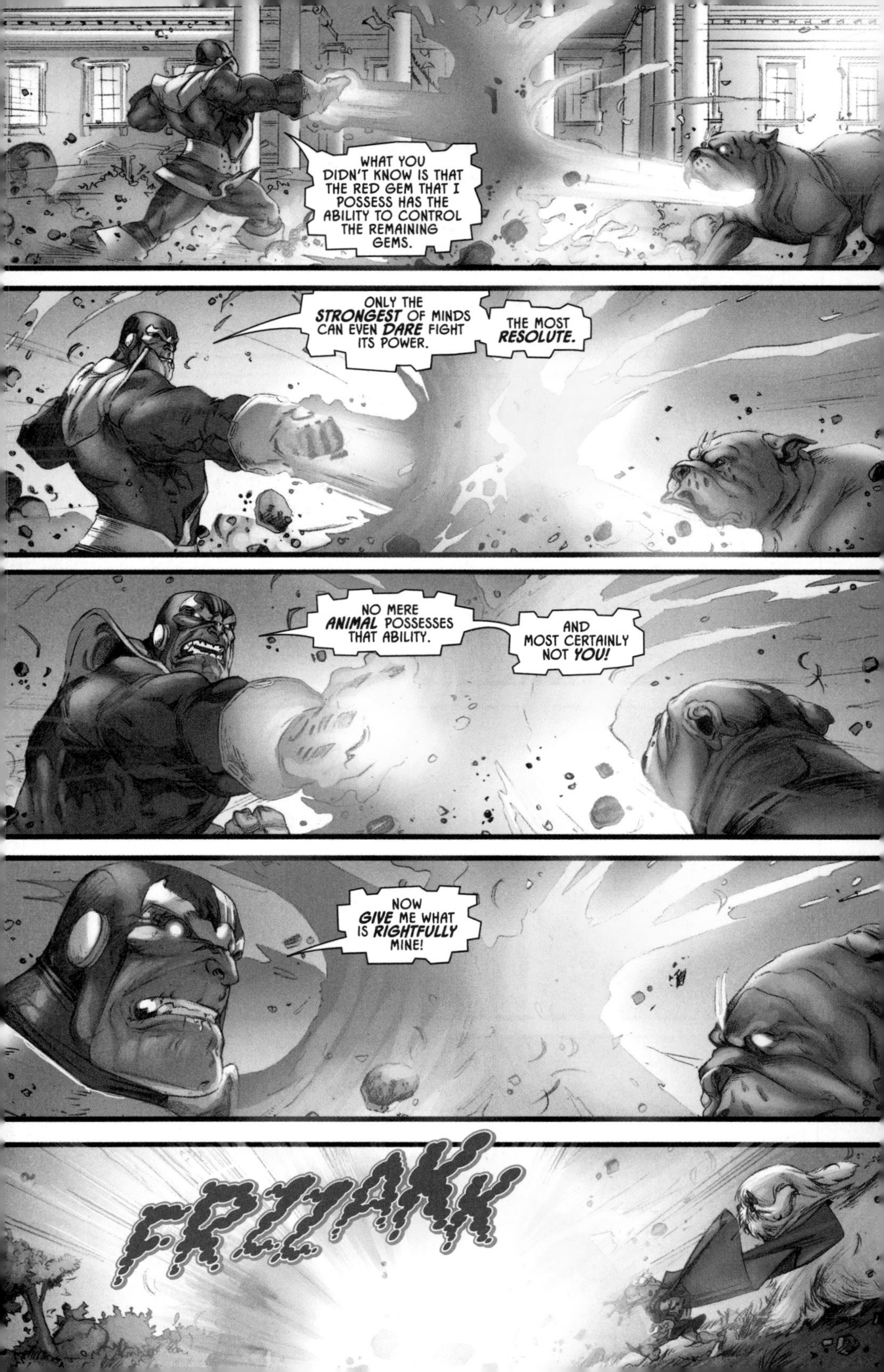
WHAT YOU DIDN'T KNOW IS THAT THE RED GEM THAT I POSSESS HAS THE ABILITY TO CONTROL THE REMAINING GEMS.
ONLY THE STRONGEST OF MINDS CAN EVEN DARE FIGHT ITS POWER.
THE MOST RESOLUTE.
NO MERE ANIMAL POSSESSES THAT ABILITY.
AND MOST CERTAINLY NOT YOU!
NOW GIVE ME WHAT IS RIGHTFULLY MINE!
FRZZAKK

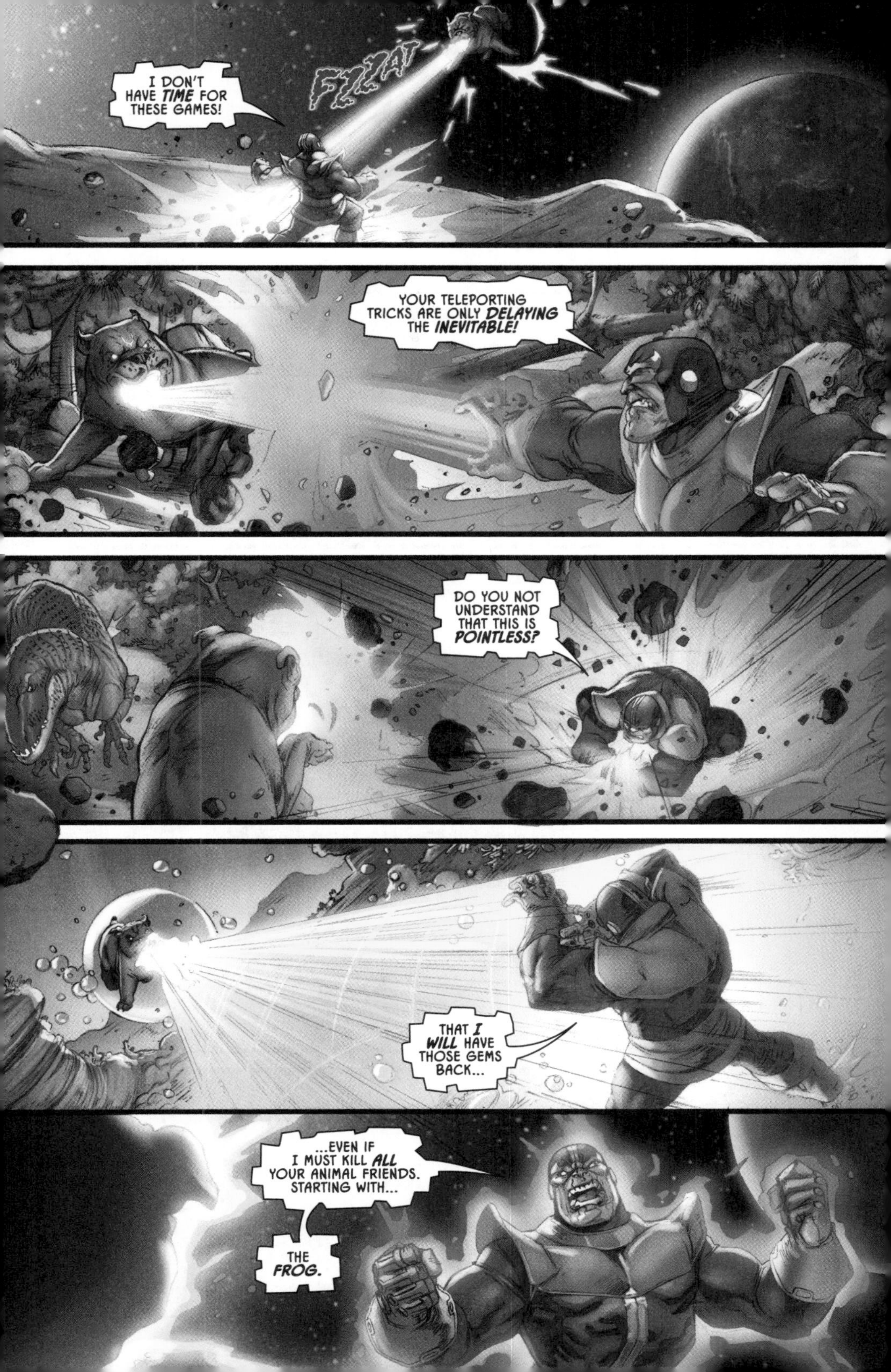
I DON'T HAVE TIME FOR THESE GAMES!
FZZAT
YOUR TELEPORTING TRICKS ARE ONLY DELAYING THE INEVITABLE!
DO YOU NOT UNDERSTAND THAT THIS IS POINTLESS?
THAT I WILL HAVE THOSE GEMS BACK...
...EVEN IF I MUST KILL ALL YOUR ANIMAL FRIENDS. STARTING WITH...
THE FROG.

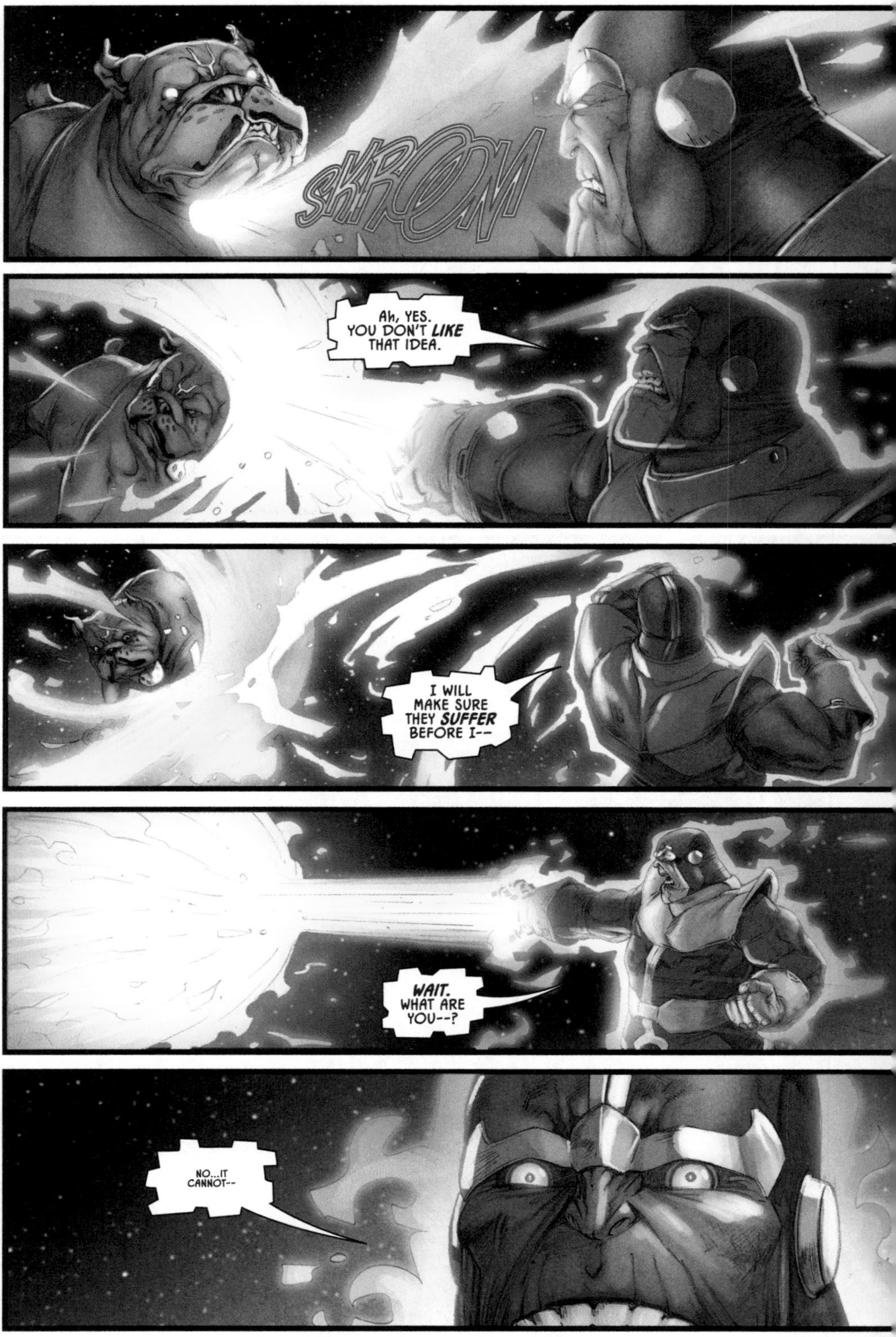
SKROOM
Ah, YES. YOU DON'T LIKE THAT IDEA.
I WILL MAKE SURE THEY SUFFER BEFORE I--
WAIT. WHAT ARE YOU--?
NO...IT CANNOT--

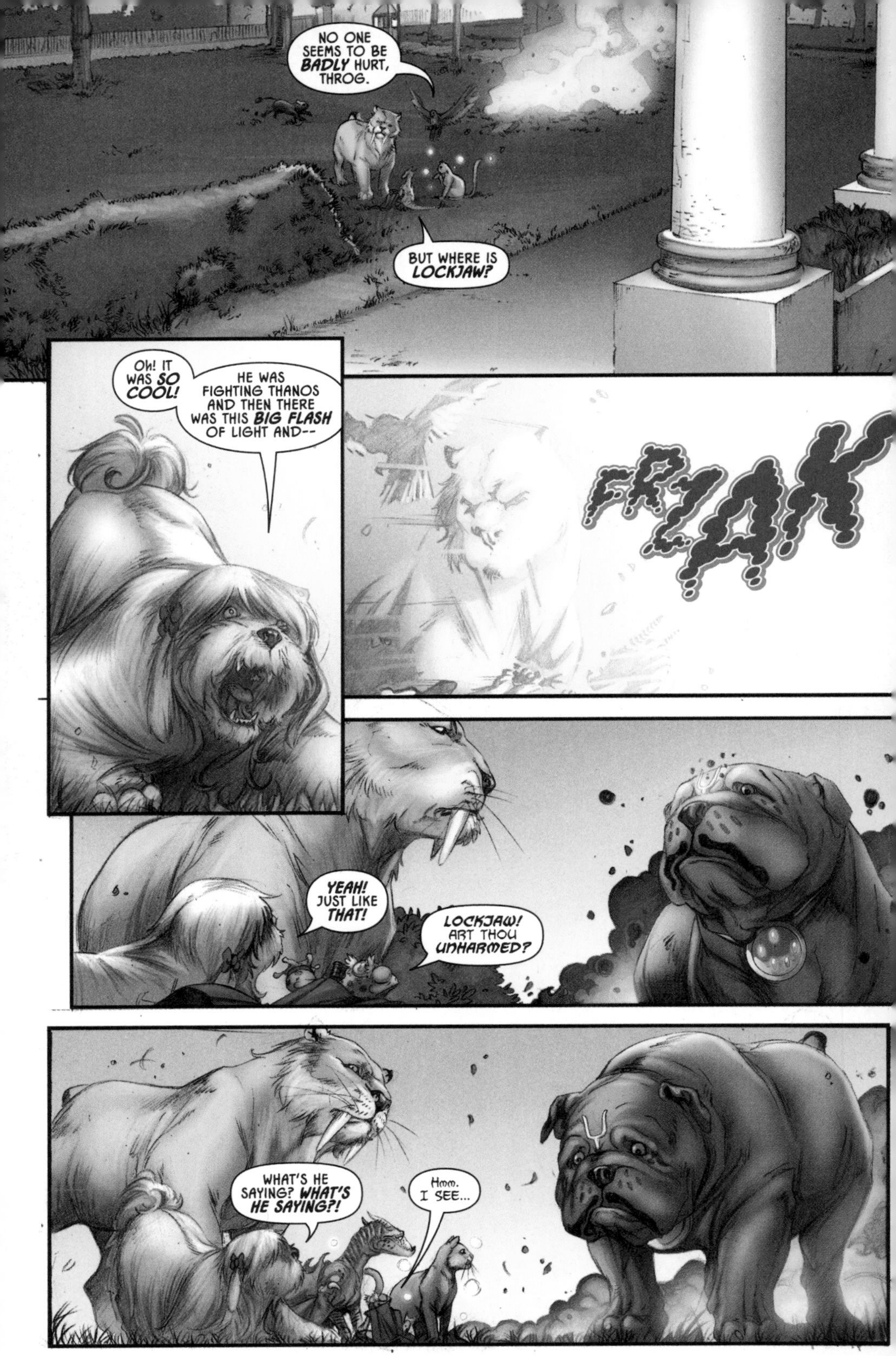
NO ONE SEEMS TO BE BADLY HURT, THROG.
BUT WHERE IS LOCKJAW?
Oh! IT WAS SO COOL!
HE WAS FIGHTING THANOS AND THEN THERE WAS THIS BIG FLASH OF LIGHT AND--
FRZAK!
YEAH! JUST LIKE THAT!
LOCKJAW! ART THOU UNHARMED?
WHAT'S HE SAYING? WHAT'S HE SAYING?!
Hmm. I SEE...

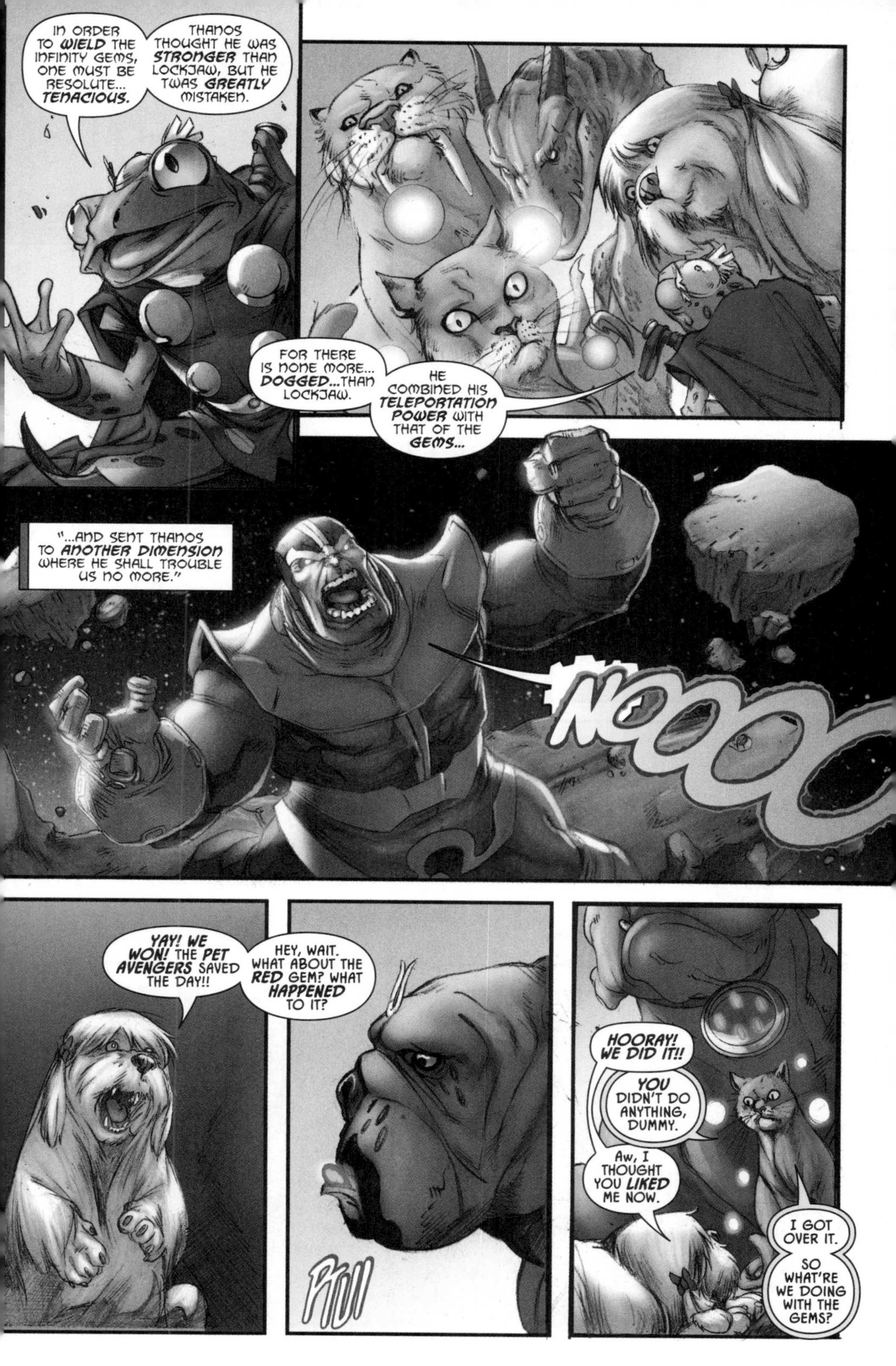

IN ORDER TO WIELD THE INFINITY GEMS, ONE MUST BE RESOLUTE... TENACIOUS.
THANOS THOUGHT HE WAS STRONGER THAN LOCKJAW, BUT HE TWAS GREATLY MISTAKEN.
FOR THERE IS NONE MORE... DOGGED...THAN LOCKJAW.
HE COMBINED HIS TELEPORTATION POWER WITH THAT OF THE GEMS...
"...AND SENT THANOS TO ANOTHER DIMENSION WHERE HE SHALL TROUBLE US NO MORE."
YAY! WE WON! THE PET AVENGERS SAVED THE DAY!!
HEY, WAIT. WHAT ABOUT THE RED GEM? WHAT HAPPENED TO IT?
HOORAY! WE DID IT!!
YOU DIDN'T DO ANYTHING, DUMMY.
AW, I THOUGHT YOU LIKED ME NOW.
I GOT OVER IT.
SO WHAT'RE WE DOING WITH THE GEMS?

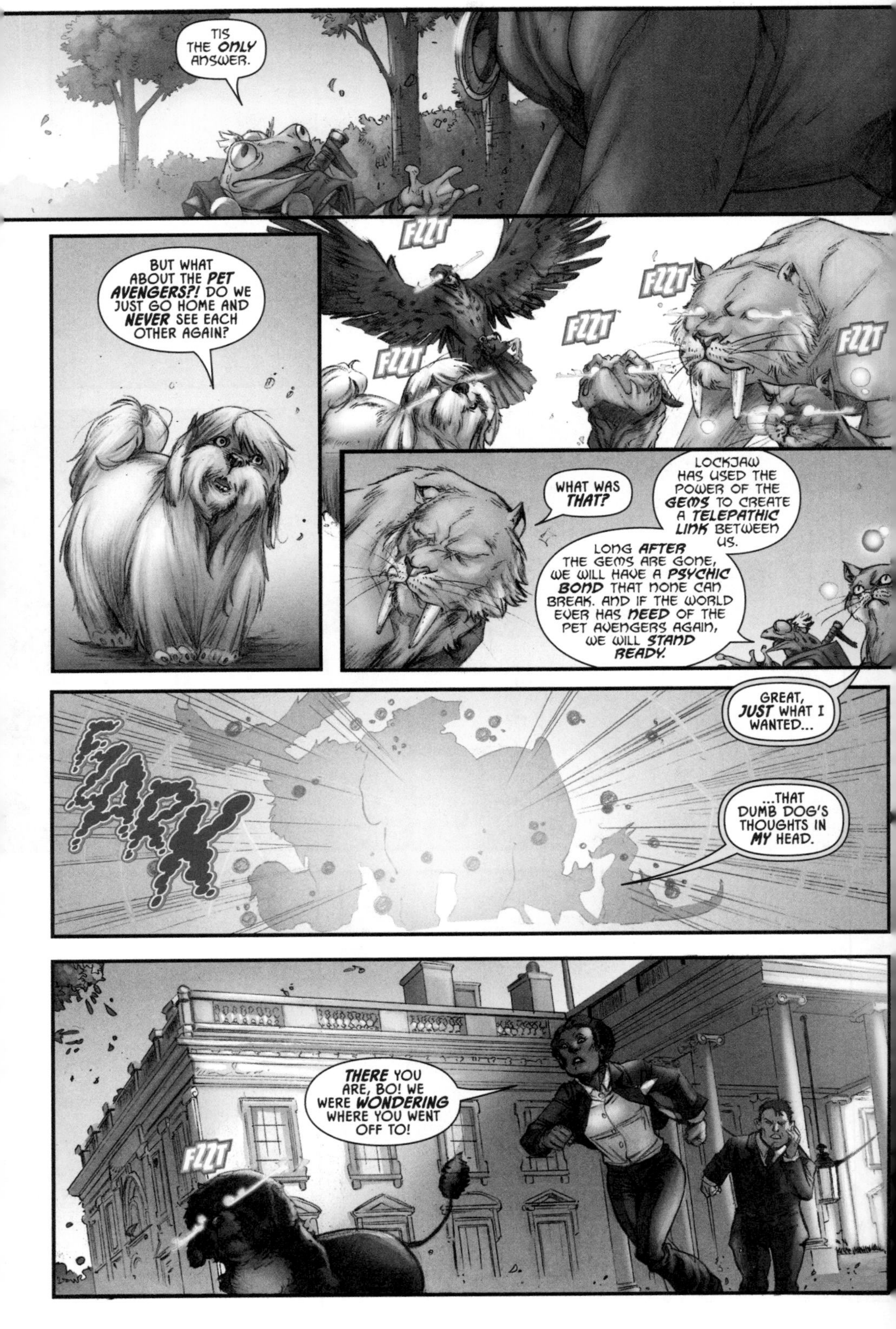
TIS THE ONLY ANSWER.
FZZT
BUT WHAT ABOUT THE PET AVENGERS?! DO WE JUST GO HOME AND NEVER SEE EACH OTHER AGAIN?
FZZT
FZZT
FZZT
FZZT
WHAT WAS THAT?
LOCKJAW HAS USED THE POWER OF THE GEMS TO CREATE A TELEPATHIC LINK BETWEEN US.
LONG AFTER THE GEMS ARE GONE, WE WILL HAVE A PSYCHIC BOND THAT NONE CAN BREAK. AND IF THE WORLD EVER HAS NEED OF THE PET AVENGERS AGAIN, WE WILL STAND READY.
GREAT, JUST WHAT I WANTED...
...THAT DUMB DOG'S THOUGHTS IN MY HEAD.
THERE YOU ARE, BO! WE WERE WONDERING WHERE YOU WENT OFF TO!
FZZT

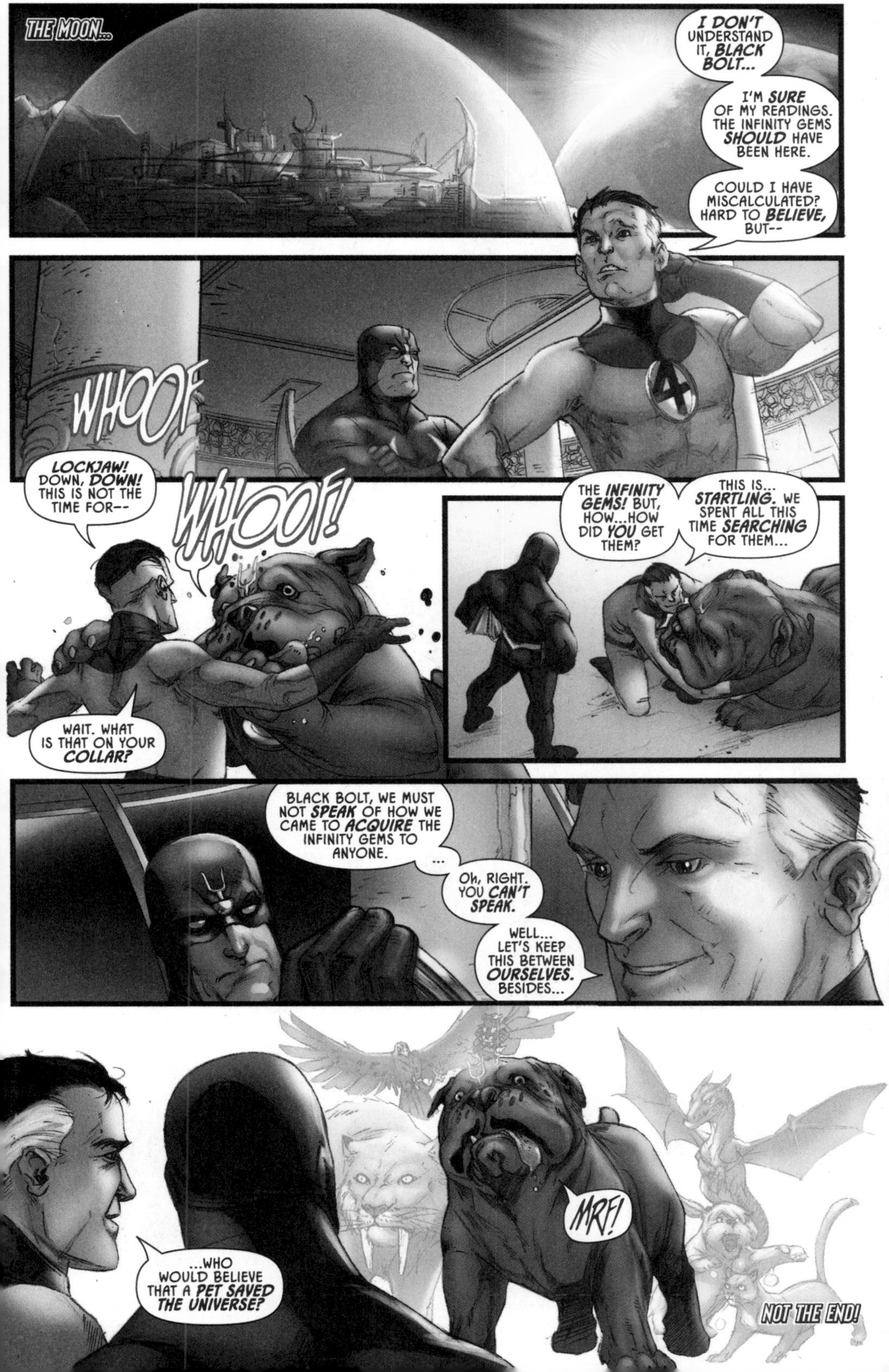
THE MOON...
I DON'T UNDERSTAND IT, BLACK BOLT...
I'M SURE OF MY READINGS. THE INFINITY GEMS SHOULD HAVE BEEN HERE.
COULD I HAVE MISCALCULATED? HARD TO BELIEVE, BUT--
WHOOF
LOCKJAW! DOWN, DOWN! THIS IS NOT THE TIME FOR--
WHOOF!
WAIT. WHAT IS THAT ON YOUR COLLAR?
THE INFINITY GEMS! BUT, HOW...HOW DID YOU GET THEM?
THIS IS... STARTLING. WE SPENT ALL THIS TIME SEARCHING FOR THEM...
BLACK BOLT, WE MUST NOT SPEAK OF HOW WE CAME TO ACQUIRE THE INFINITY GEMS TO ANYONE.
...
Oh, RIGHT. YOU CAN'T SPEAK.
WELL... LET'S KEEP THIS BETWEEN OURSELVES. BESIDES...
MRF!
...WHO WOULD BELIEVE THAT A PET SAVED THE UNIVERSE?
NOT THE END!

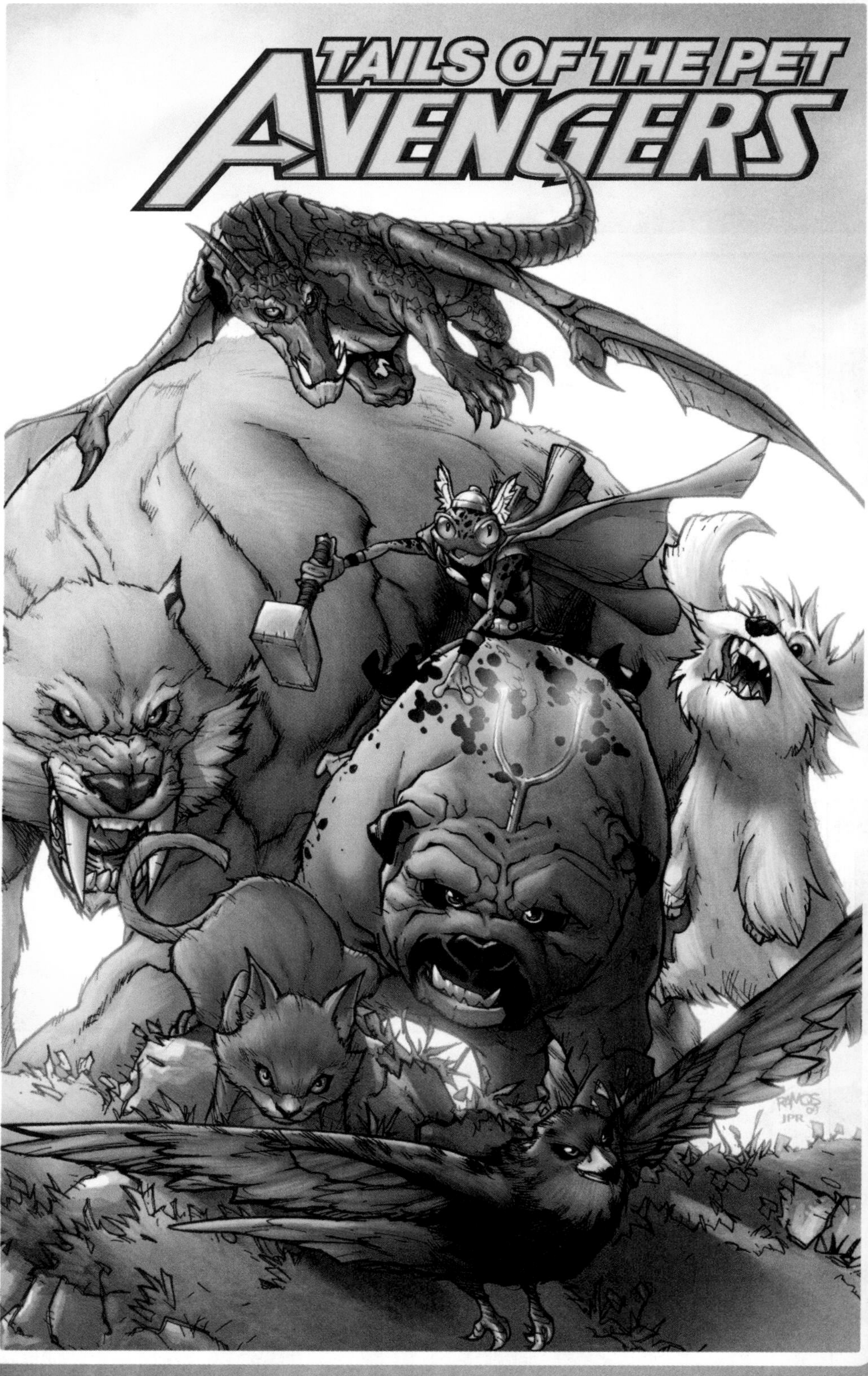
TAILS OF THE PET
AVENGERS

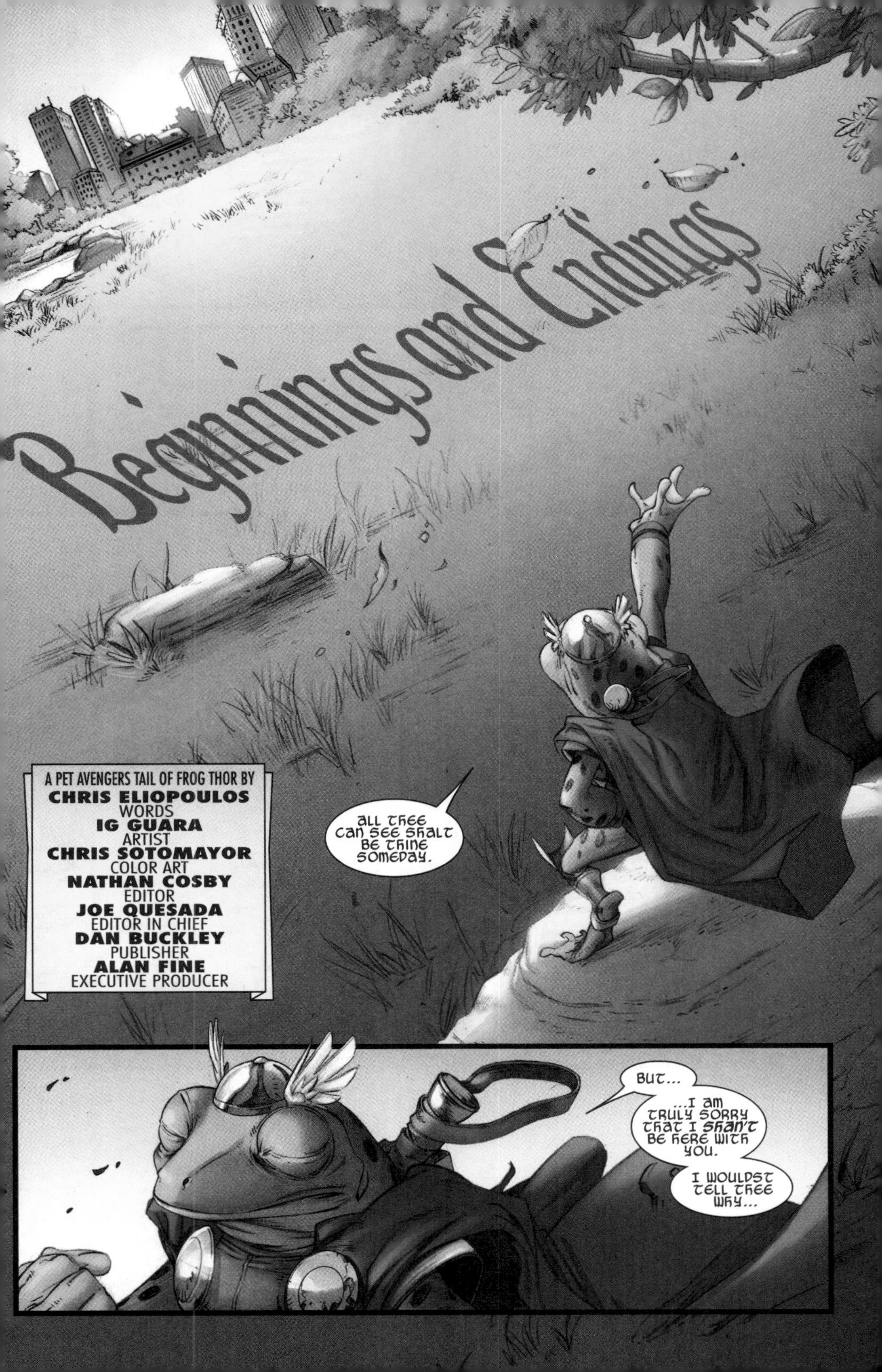

Beginnings and Endings
A PET AVENGERS TAIL OF FROG THOR BY
CHRIS ELIOPOULOS
WORDS
IG GUARA
ARTIST
CHRIS SOTOMAYOR
COLOR ART
NATHAN COSBY
EDITOR
JOE QUESADA
EDITOR IN CHIEF
DAN BUCKLEY
PUBLISHER
ALAN FINE
EXECUTIVE PRODUCER
ALL THEE CAN SEE SHALT BE THINE SOMEDAY.
BUT...
...I AM TRULY SORRY THAT I SHAN'T BE HERE WITH YOU.
I WOULDST TELL THEE WHY...

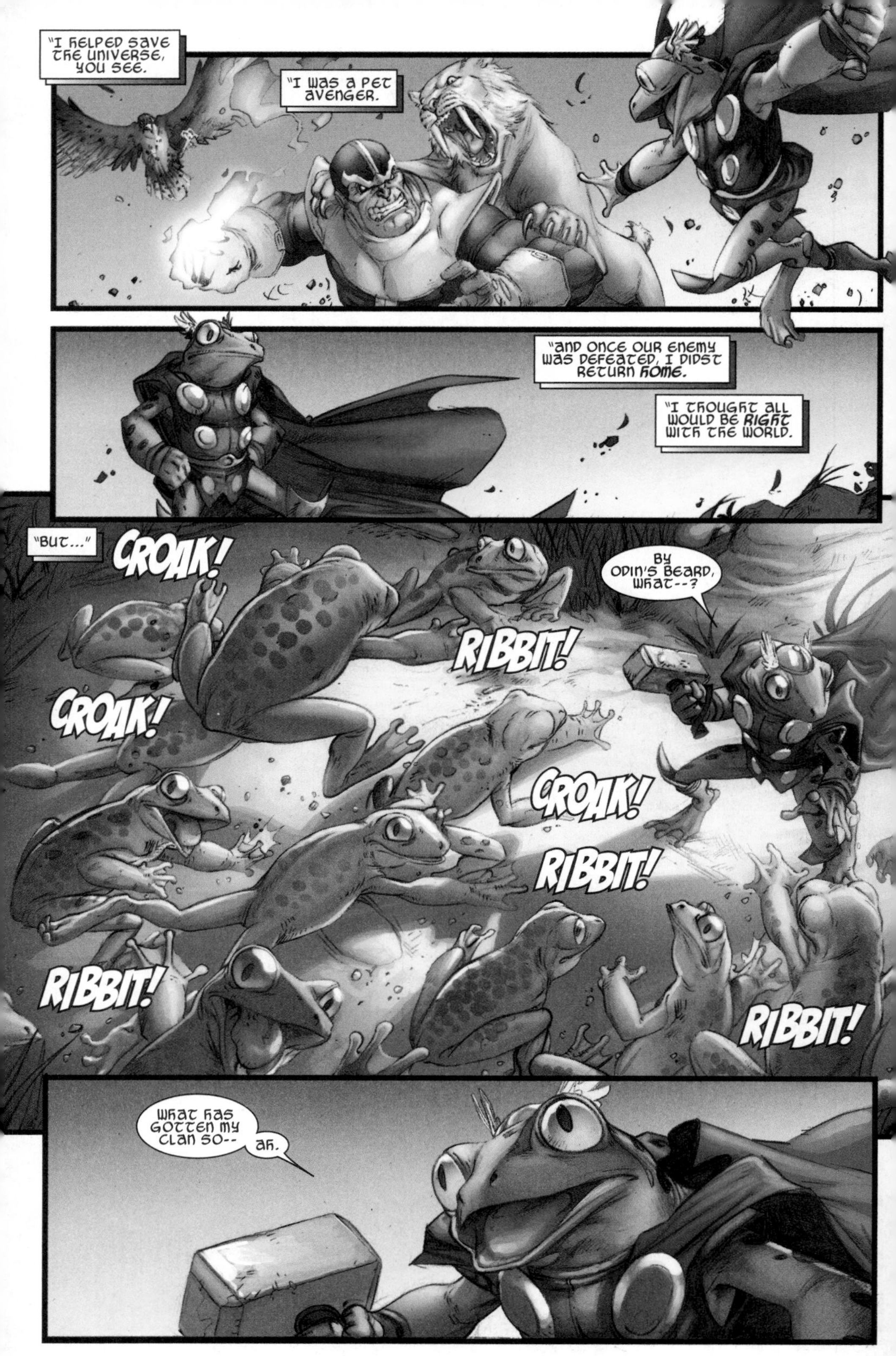
"I HELPED SAVE THE UNIVERSE, YOU SEE.
"I WAS A PET AVENGER.
"AND ONCE OUR ENEMY WAS DEFEATED, I DIDST RETURN HOME.
"I THOUGHT ALL WOULD BE RIGHT WITH THE WORLD.
"BUT..."
CROAK!
BY ODIN'S BEARD, WHAT--?
RIBBIT!
CROAK!
CROAK!
RIBBIT!
RIBBIT!
RIBBIT!
WHAT HAS GOTTEN MY CLAN SO--
AH.

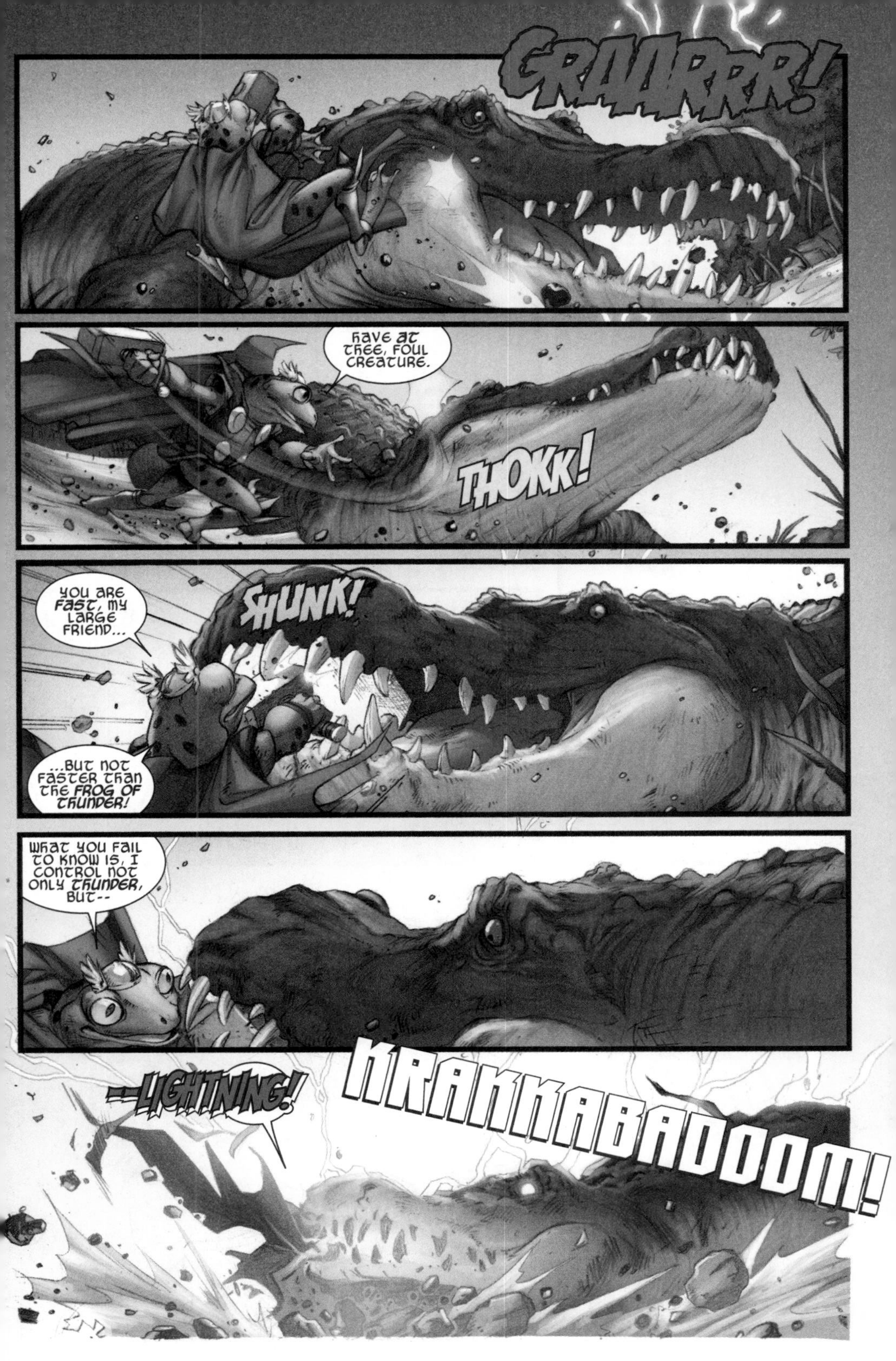
GRAARRR!
HAVE AT THEE, FOUL CREATURE.
THOKK!
SHUNK!
YOU ARE FAST, MY LARGE FRIEND...
...BUT NOT FASTER THAN THE FROG OF THUNDER!
WHAT YOU FAIL TO KNOW IS, I CONTROL NOT ONLY THUNDER, BUT--
--LIGHTNING!
KRAKKABADOOM!

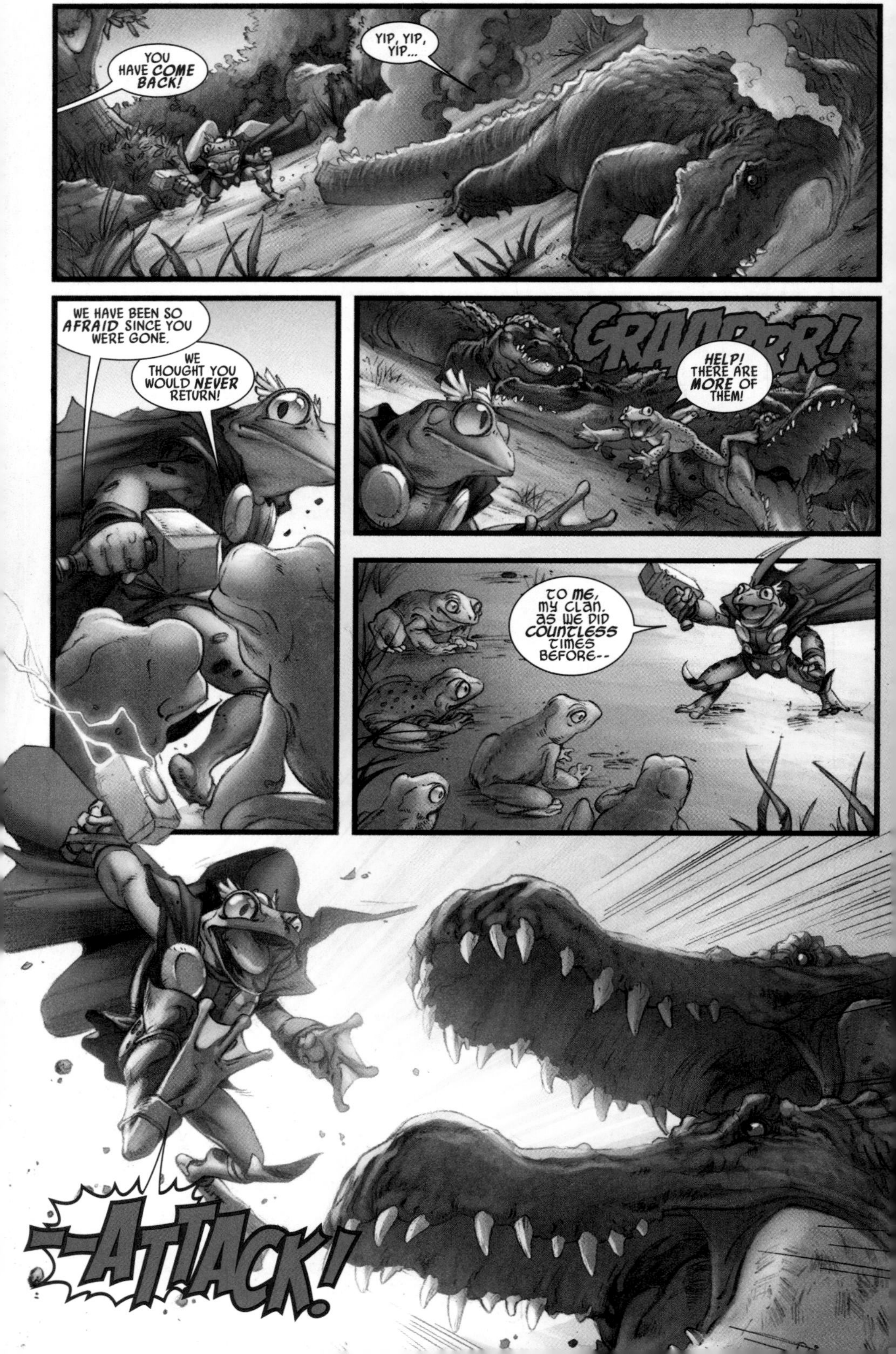
YOU HAVE COME BACK!
YIP, YIP, YIP...
WE HAVE BEEN SO AFRAID SINCE YOU WERE GONE.
WE THOUGHT YOU WOULD NEVER RETURN!
GRAAARR!
HELP! THERE ARE MORE OF THEM!
TO ME, MY CLAN, AS WE DID COUNTLESS TIMES BEFORE--
--ATTACK!

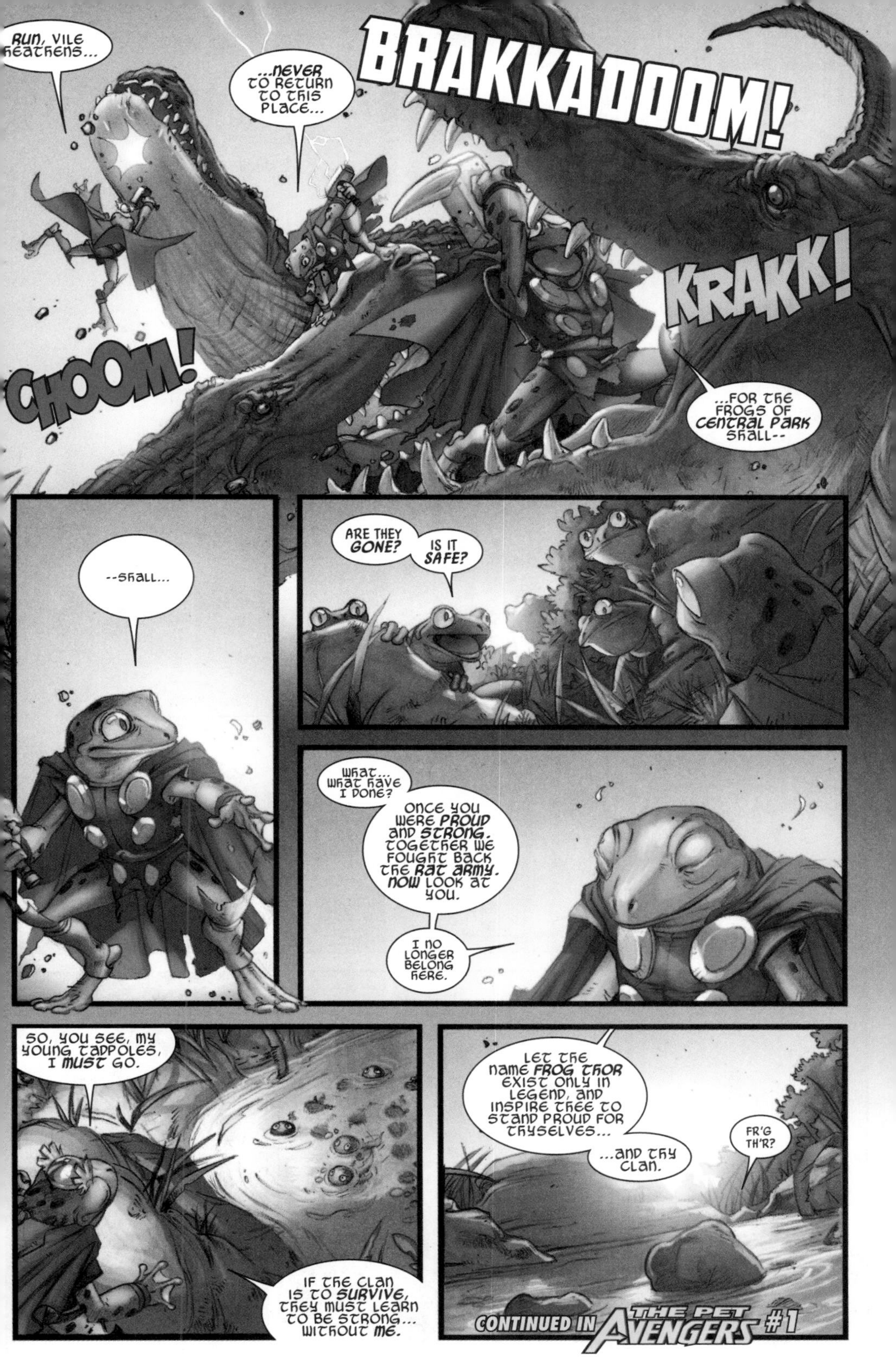
BRAKKADOOM!
RUN, VILE HEATHENS...
...NEVER TO RETURN TO THIS PLACE...
CHOOM!
KRAKK!
...FOR THE FROGS OF CENTRAL PARK SHALL--
--SHALL...
ARE THEY GONE?
IS IT SAFE?
WHAT... WHAT HAVE I DONE?
ONCE YOU WERE PROUD AND STRONG. TOGETHER WE FOUGHT BACK THE RAT ARMY. NOW LOOK AT YOU.
I NO LONGER BELONG HERE.
SO, YOU SEE, MY YOUNG TADPOLES, I MUST GO.
IF THE CLAN IS TO SURVIVE, THEY MUST LEARN TO BE STRONG... WITHOUT ME.
LET THE NAME FROG THOR EXIST ONLY IN LEGEND, AND INSPIRE THEE TO STAND PROUD FOR THYSELVES...
...AND THY CLAN.
FR'G TH'R?
CONTINUED IN THE PET AVENGERS #1

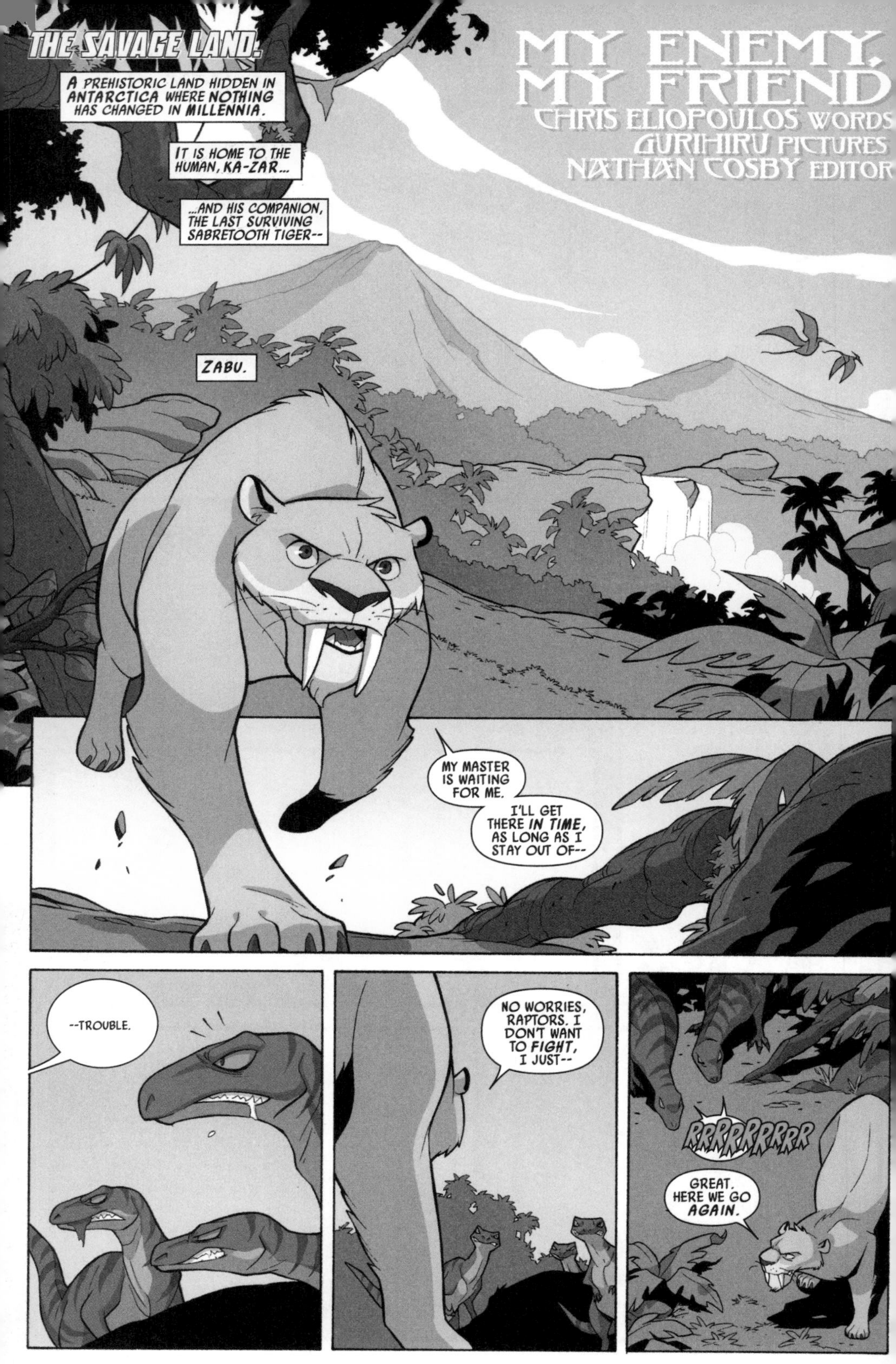
THE SAVAGE LAND.
A PREHISTORIC LAND HIDDEN IN ANTARCTICA WHERE NOTHING HAS CHANGED IN MILLENNIA.
IT IS HOME TO THE HUMAN, KA-ZAR...
...AND HIS COMPANION, THE LAST SURVIVING SABRETOOTH TIGER--
ZABU.
MY ENEMY, MY FRIEND
CHRIS ELIOPOULOS WORDS
GURIHIRU PICTURES
NATHAN COSBY EDITOR
MY MASTER IS WAITING FOR ME.
I'LL GET THERE IN TIME, AS LONG AS I STAY OUT OF--
--TROUBLE.
NO WORRIES, RAPTORS. I DON'T WANT TO FIGHT, I JUST--
RRRRRRRRR
GREAT. HERE WE GO AGAIN.

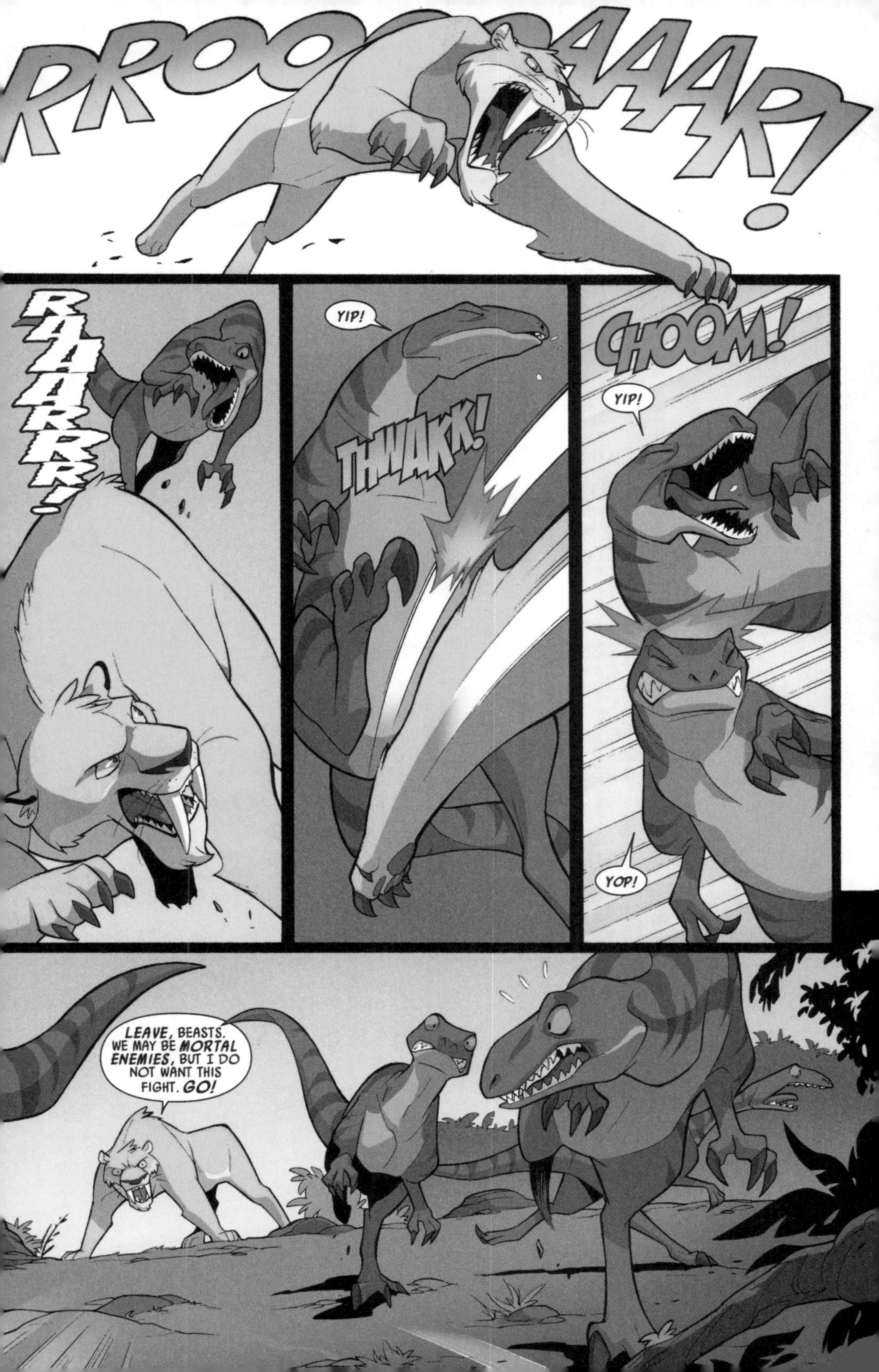
RROOOOAAAAR!
RAAARRR!
YIP!
THWAKK!
CHOOM!
YIP!
YOP!
LEAVE, BEASTS. WE MAY BE MORTAL ENEMIES, BUT I DO NOT WANT THIS FIGHT. GO!

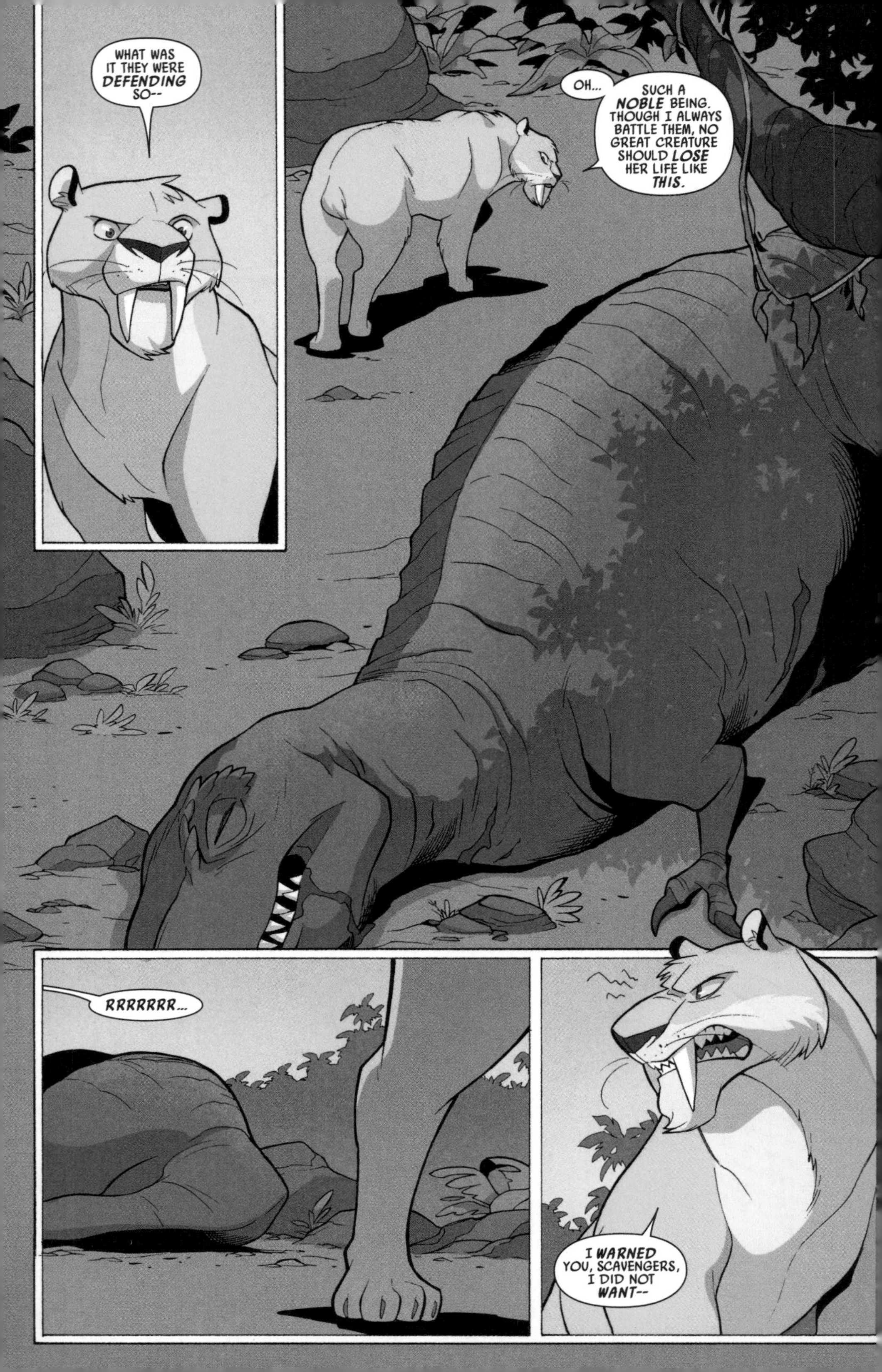
WHAT WAS IT THEY WERE DEFENDING SO--
OH...
SUCH A NOBLE BEING. THOUGH I ALWAYS BATTLE THEM, NO GREAT CREATURE SHOULD LOSE HER LIFE LIKE THIS.
RRRRRRR...
I WARNED YOU, SCAVENGERS, I DID NOT WANT--

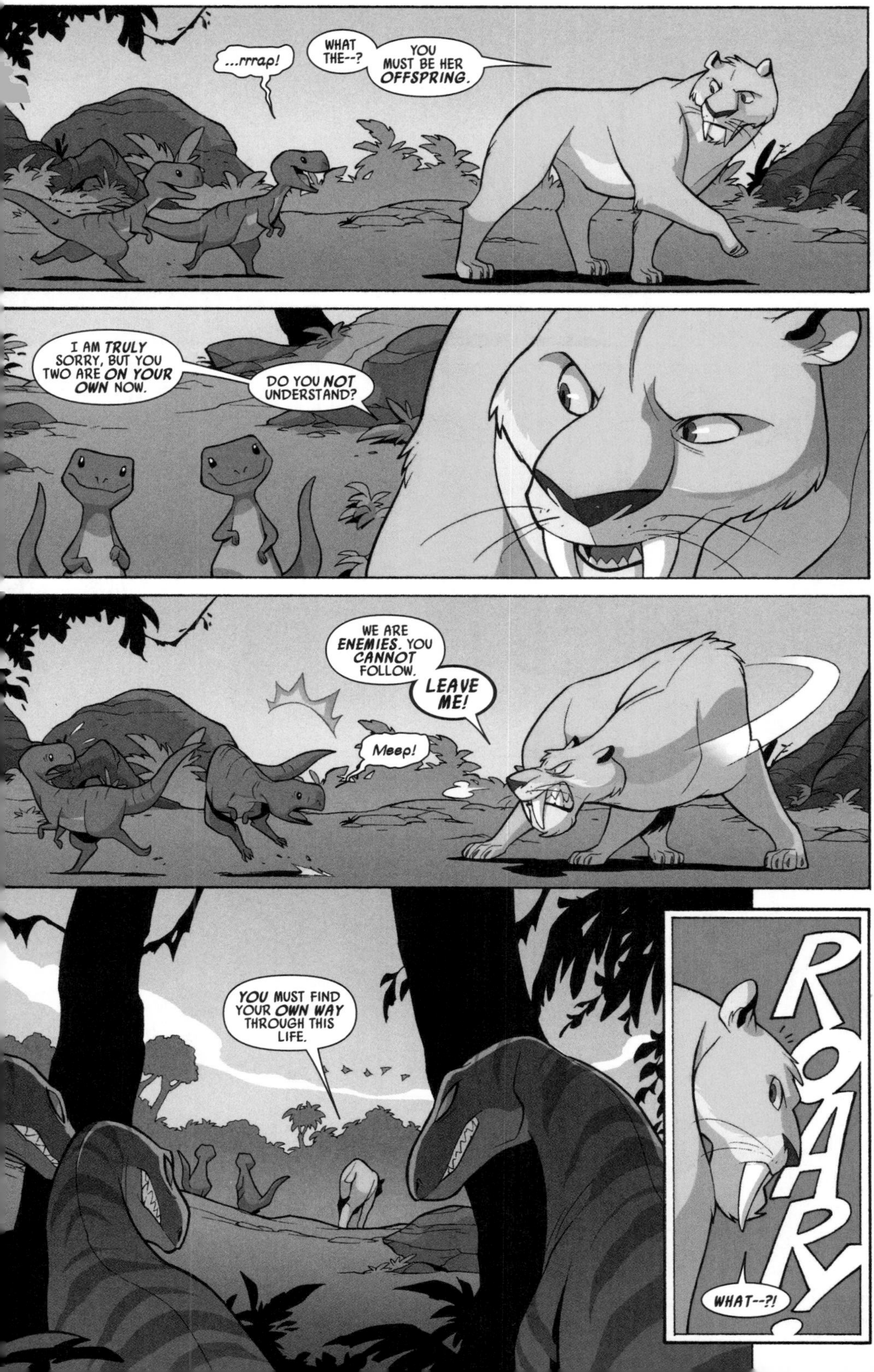

...rrrap!
WHAT THE--?
YOU MUST BE HER OFFSPRING.
I AM TRULY SORRY, BUT YOU TWO ARE ON YOUR OWN NOW.
DO YOU NOT UNDERSTAND?
WE ARE ENEMIES. YOU CANNOT FOLLOW.
LEAVE ME!
Meep!
YOU MUST FIND YOUR OWN WAY THROUGH THIS LIFE.
ROAARY
WHAT--?!

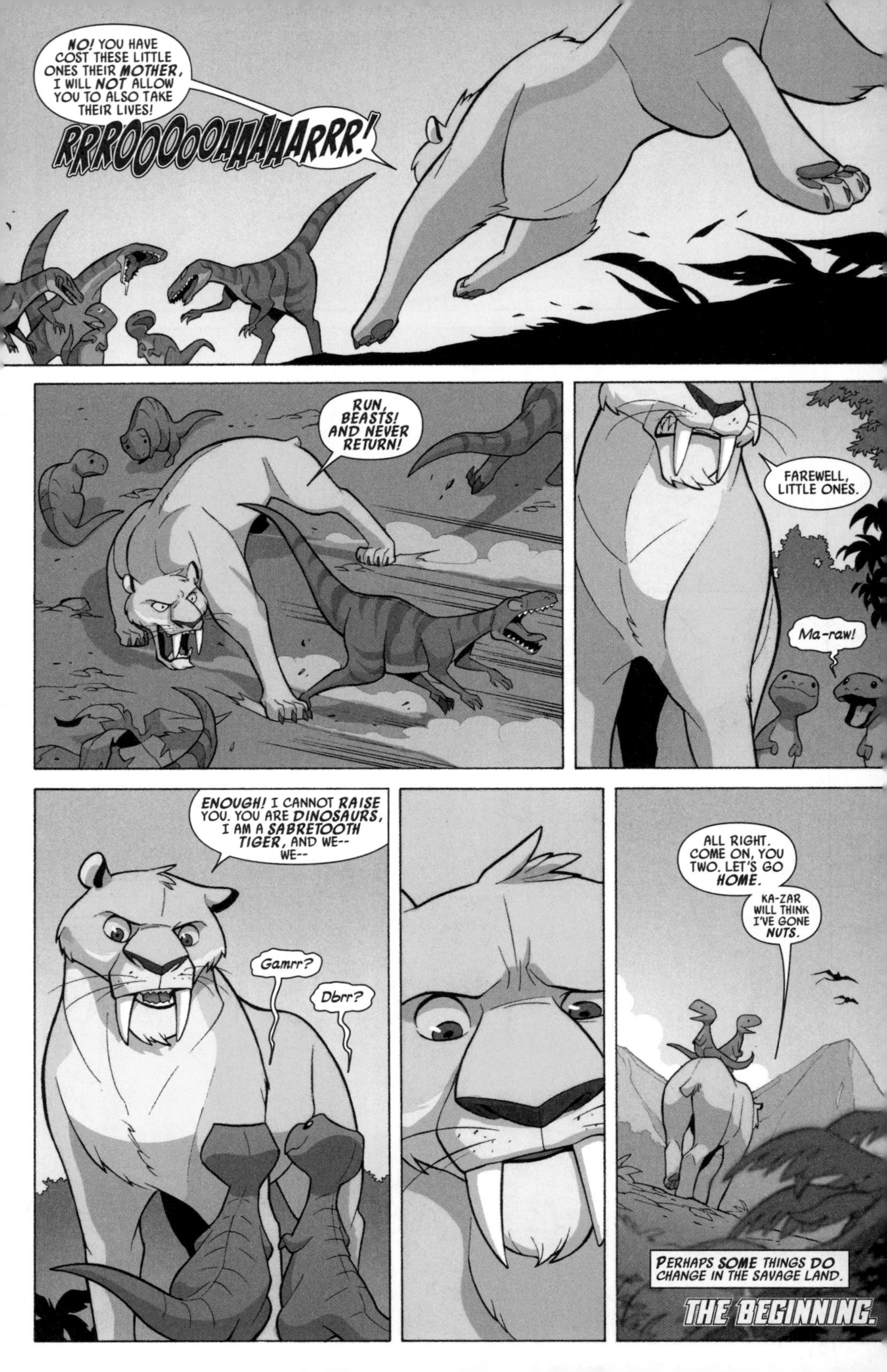
NO! YOU HAVE COST THESE LITTLE ONES THEIR MOTHER, I WILL NOT ALLOW YOU TO ALSO TAKE THEIR LIVES!
RRROOOOOOAAAAARRR!
RUN, BEASTS! AND NEVER RETURN!
FAREWELL, LITTLE ONES.
Ma-raw!
ENOUGH! I CANNOT RAISE YOU. YOU ARE DINOSAURS, I AM A SABRETOOTH TIGER, AND WE-- WE--
Gamrr?
Dbrr?
ALL RIGHT. COME ON, YOU TWO. LET'S GO HOME.
KA-ZAR WILL THINK I'VE GONE NUTS.
PERHAPS SOME THINGS DO CHANGE IN THE SAVAGE LAND.
THE BEGINNING.

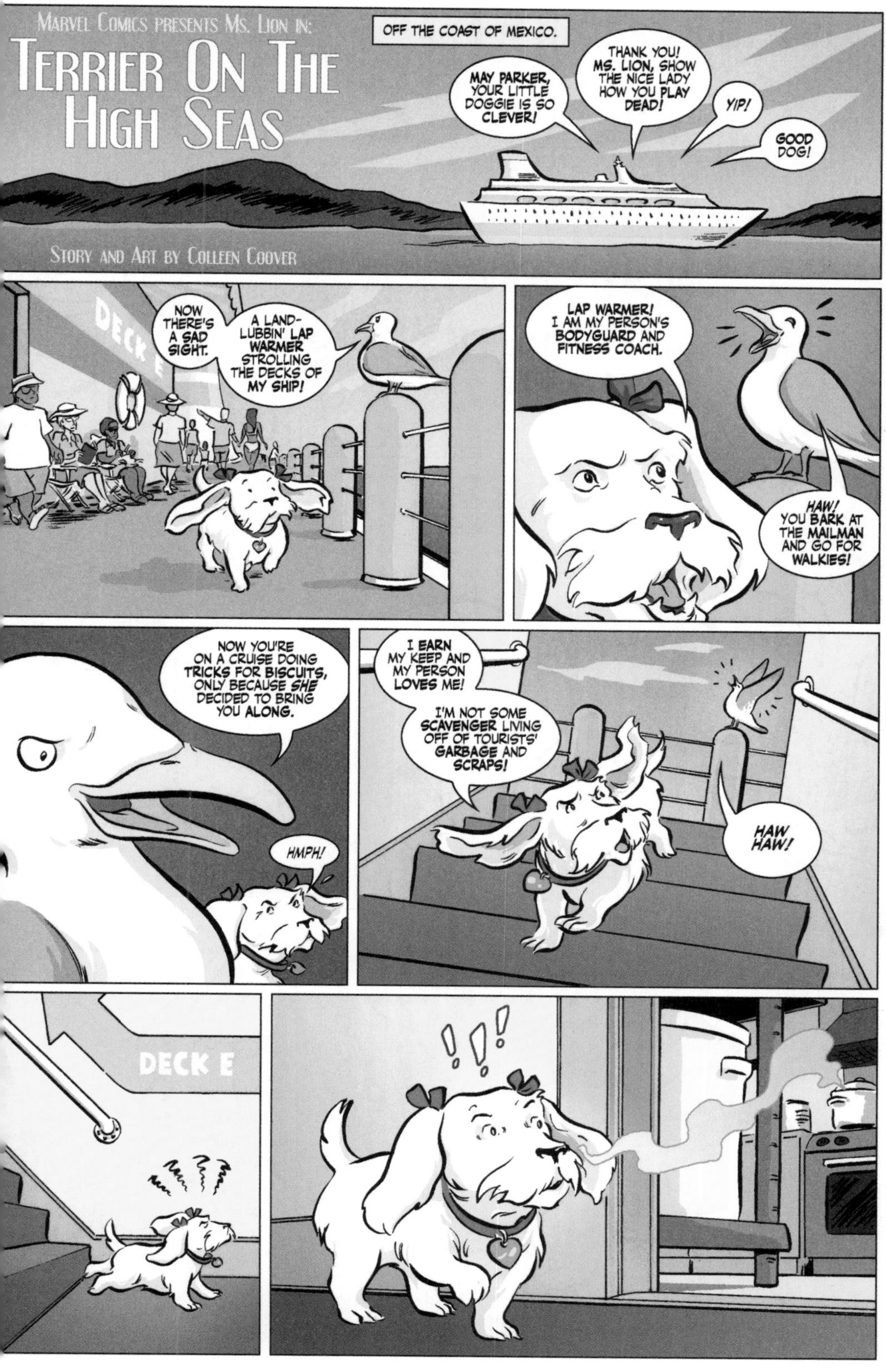

Marvel Comics presents Ms. Lion in:
Terrier On The High Seas
Story and Art by Colleen Coover
OFF THE COAST OF MEXICO.
MAY PARKER, YOUR LITTLE DOGGIE IS SO CLEVER!
THANK YOU! MS. LION, SHOW THE NICE LADY HOW YOU PLAY DEAD!
YIP!
GOOD DOG!
DECK E
NOW THERE'S A SAD SIGHT.
A LAND-LUBBIN' LAP WARMER STROLLING THE DECKS OF MY SHIP!
LAP WARMER! I AM MY PERSON'S BODYGUARD AND FITNESS COACH.
HAW! YOU BARK AT THE MAILMAN AND GO FOR WALKIES!
NOW YOU'RE ON A CRUISE DOING TRICKS FOR BISCUITS, ONLY BECAUSE SHE DECIDED TO BRING YOU ALONG.
HMPH!
I EARN MY KEEP AND MY PERSON LOVES ME!
I'M NOT SOME SCAVENGER LIVING OFF OF TOURISTS' GARBAGE AND SCRAPS!
HAW HAW!
DECK E
!!!

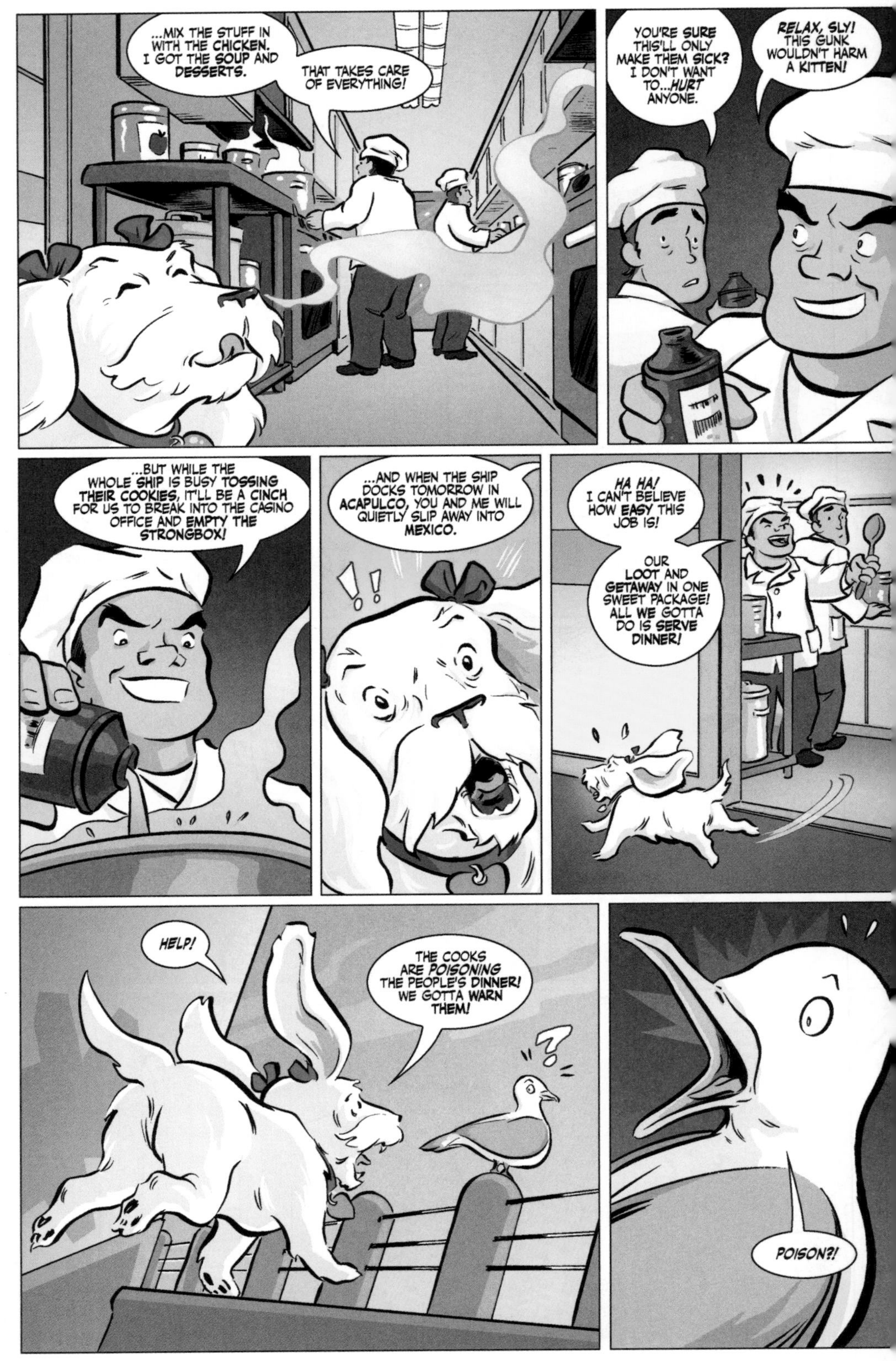
...MIX THE STUFF IN WITH THE CHICKEN. I GOT THE SOUP AND DESSERTS.
THAT TAKES CARE OF EVERYTHING!
YOU'RE SURE THIS'LL ONLY MAKE THEM SICK? I DON'T WANT TO...HURT ANYONE.
RELAX, SLY! THIS GUNK WOULDN'T HARM A KITTEN!
...BUT WHILE THE WHOLE SHIP IS BUSY TOSSING THEIR COOKIES, IT'LL BE A CINCH FOR US TO BREAK INTO THE CASINO OFFICE AND EMPTY THE STRONGBOX!
...AND WHEN THE SHIP DOCKS TOMORROW IN ACAPULCO, YOU AND ME WILL QUIETLY SLIP AWAY INTO MEXICO.
!!
HA HA! I CAN'T BELIEVE HOW EASY THIS JOB IS!
OUR LOOT AND GETAWAY IN ONE SWEET PACKAGE! ALL WE GOTTA DO IS SERVE DINNER!
HELP!
THE COOKS ARE POISONING THE PEOPLE'S DINNER! WE GOTTA WARN THEM!
?
POISON?!

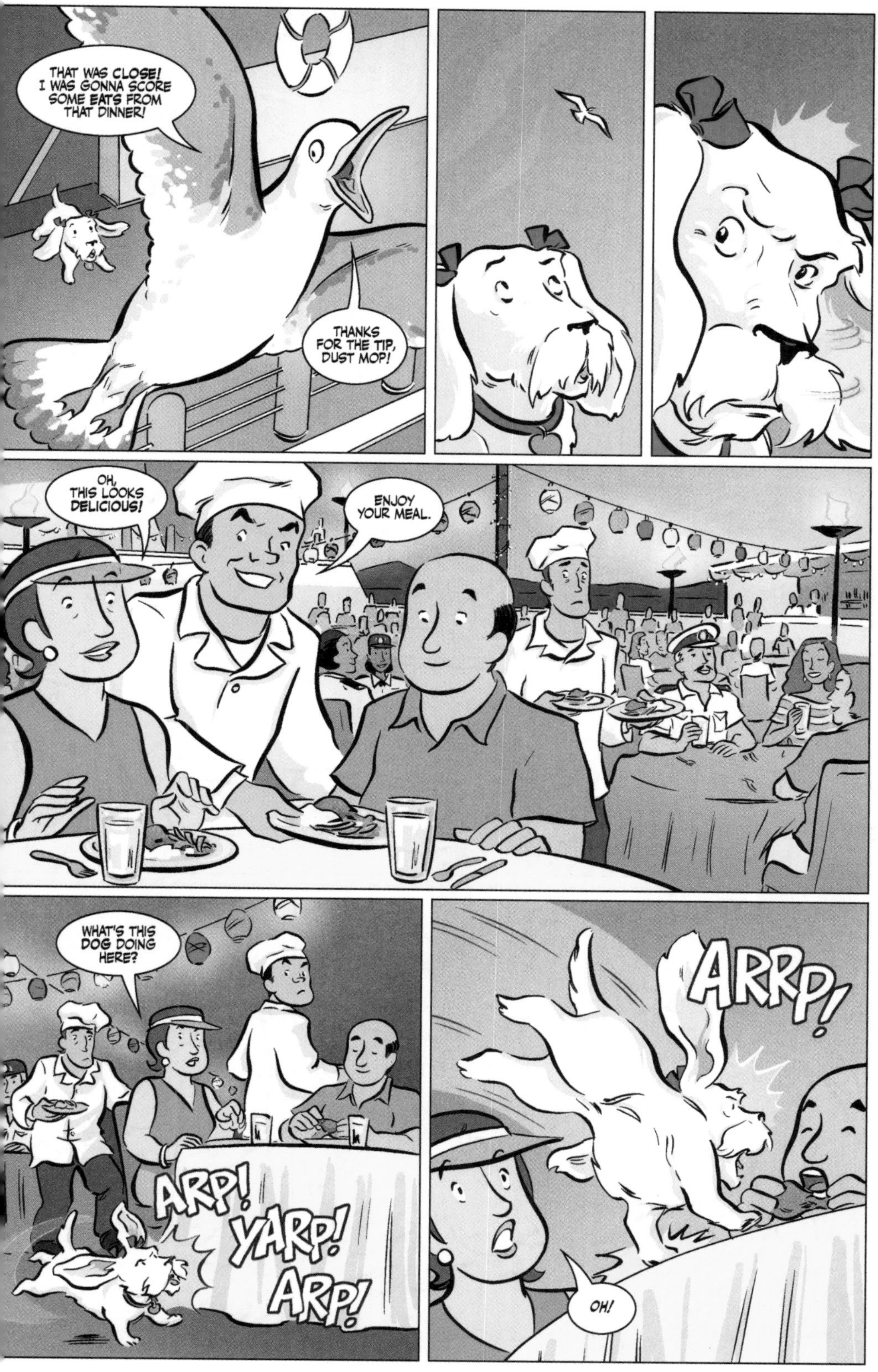
THAT WAS CLOSE! I WAS GONNA SCORE SOME EATS FROM THAT DINNER!
THANKS FOR THE TIP, DUST MOP!
OH, THIS LOOKS DELICIOUS!
ENJOY YOUR MEAL.
WHAT'S THIS DOG DOING HERE?
ARP!
YARP!
ARP!
ARRP!
OH!

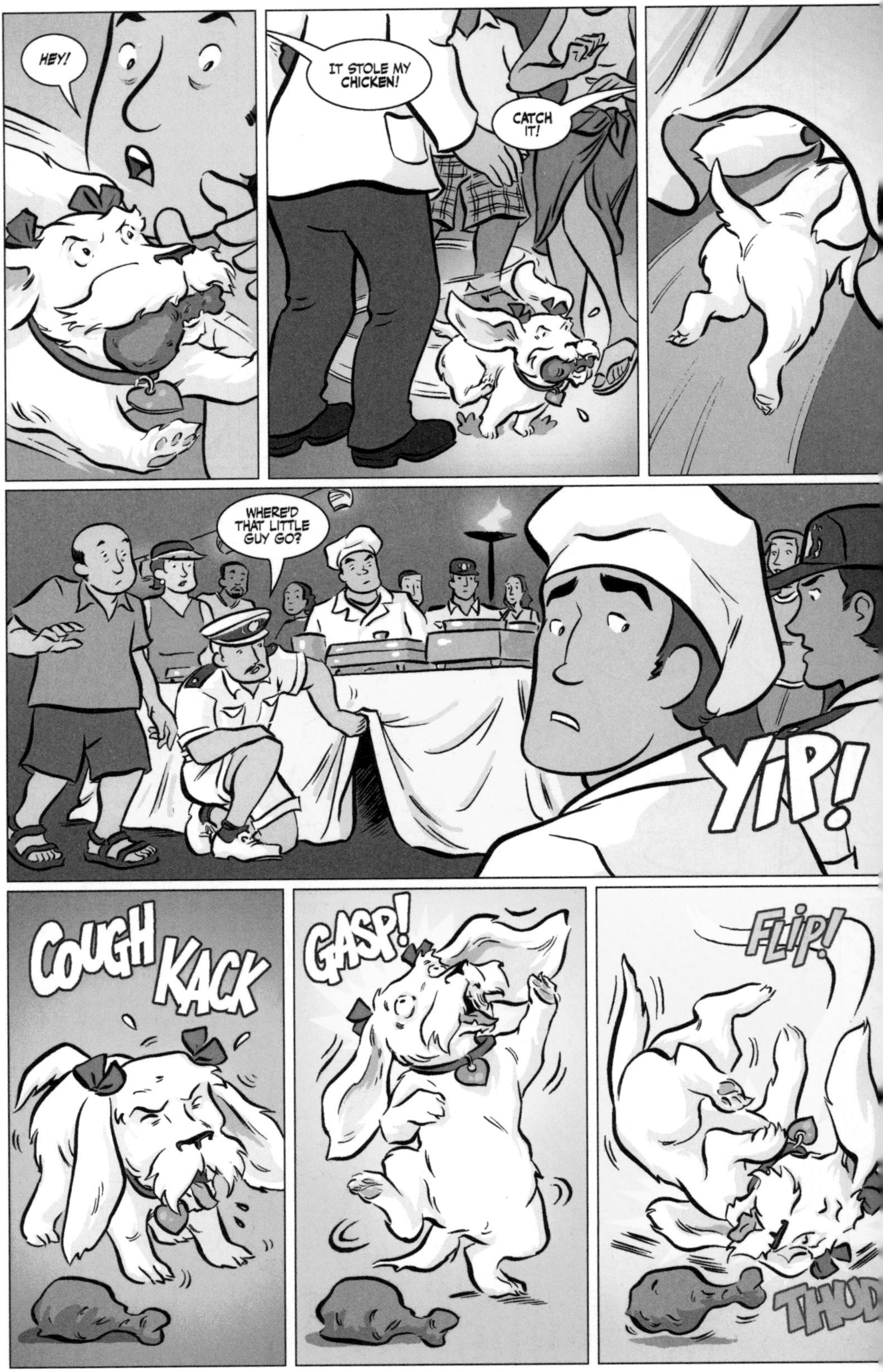
HEY!
IT STOLE MY CHICKEN!
CATCH IT!
WHERE'D THAT LITTLE GUY GO?
YIP!
COUGH
KACK
GASP!
FLIP!
THUD

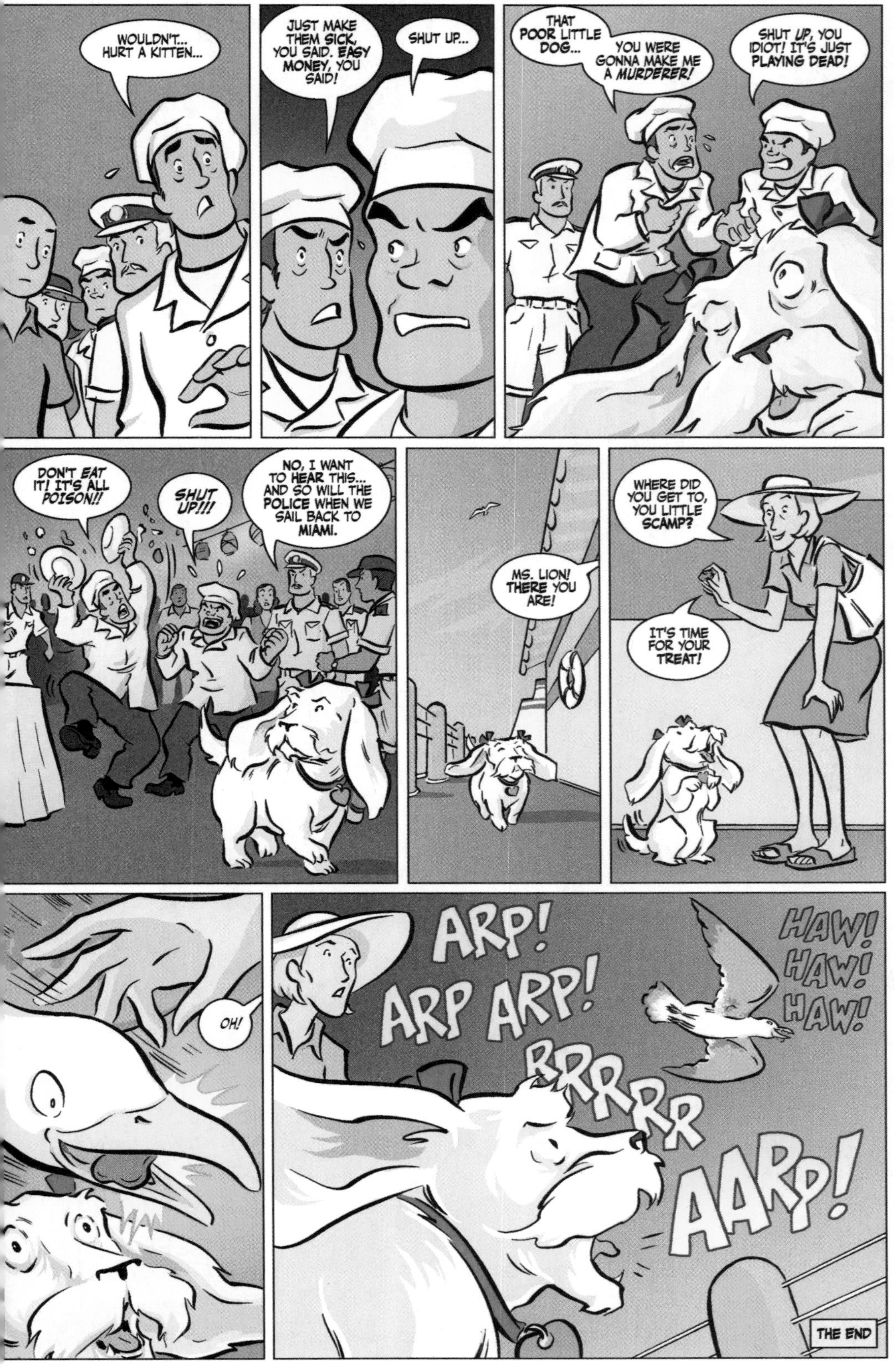

WOULDN'T... HURT A KITTEN...
JUST MAKE THEM SICK, YOU SAID. EASY MONEY, YOU SAID!
SHUT UP...
THAT POOR LITTLE DOG...
YOU WERE GONNA MAKE ME A MURDERER!
SHUT UP, YOU IDIOT! IT'S JUST PLAYING DEAD!
DON'T EAT IT! IT'S ALL POISON!!
SHUT UP!!!
NO, I WANT TO HEAR THIS... AND SO WILL THE POLICE WHEN WE SAIL BACK TO MIAMI.
MS. LION! THERE YOU ARE!
WHERE DID YOU GET TO, YOU LITTLE SCAMP?
IT'S TIME FOR YOUR TREAT!
OH!
ARP! ARP ARP! RRRRRR AARP!
HAW! HAW! HAW!
THE END

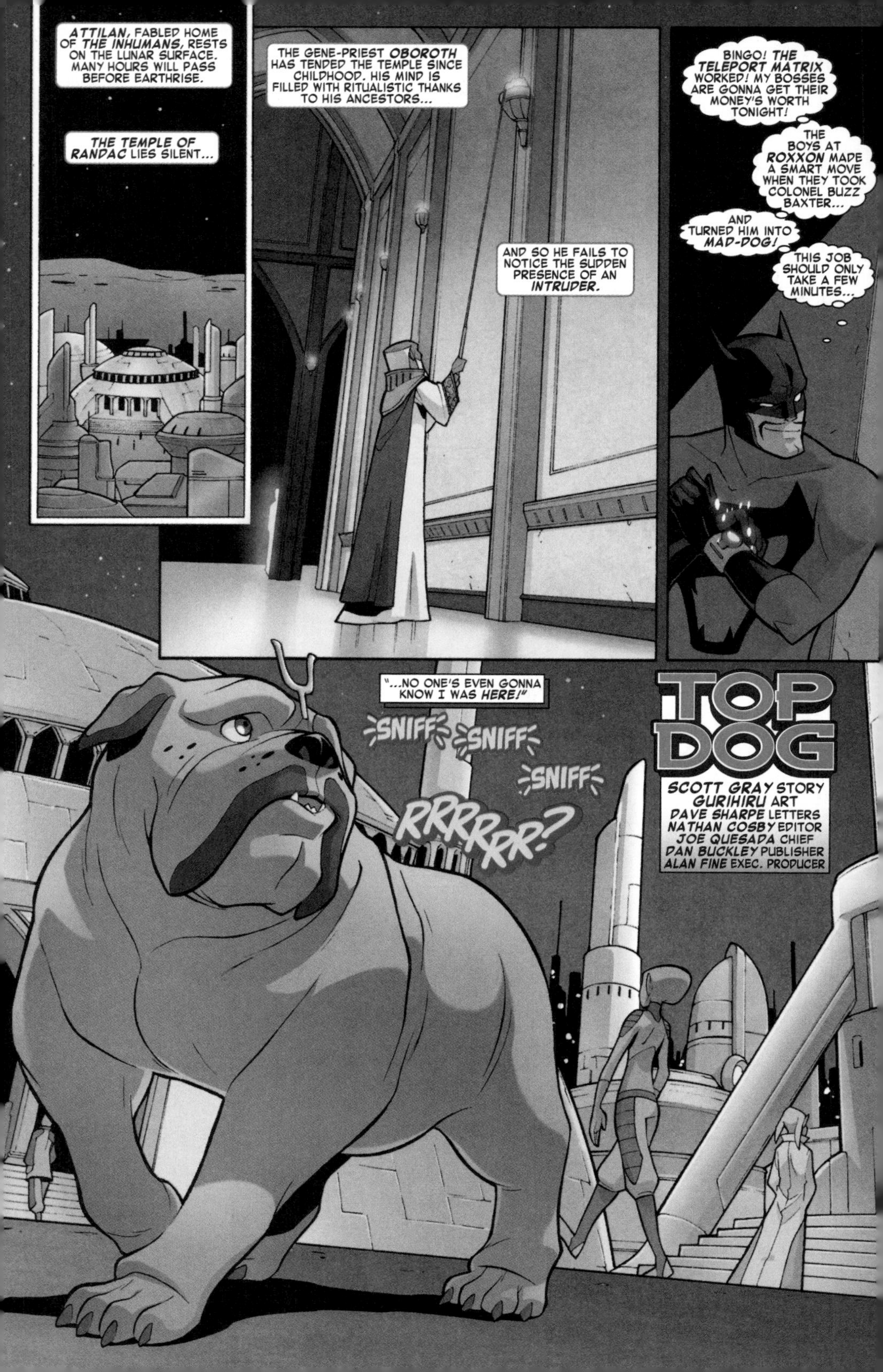
ATTILAN, FABLED HOME OF THE INHUMANS, RESTS ON THE LUNAR SURFACE. MANY HOURS WILL PASS BEFORE EARTHRISE.
THE TEMPLE OF RANDAC LIES SILENT...
THE GENE-PRIEST OBOROTH HAS TENDED THE TEMPLE SINCE CHILDHOOD. HIS MIND IS FILLED WITH RITUALISTIC THANKS TO HIS ANCESTORS...
AND SO HE FAILS TO NOTICE THE SUDDEN PRESENCE OF AN INTRUDER.
BINGO! THE TELEPORT MATRIX WORKED! MY BOSSES ARE GONNA GET THEIR MONEY'S WORTH TONIGHT!
THE BOYS AT ROXXON MADE A SMART MOVE WHEN THEY TOOK COLONEL BUZZ BAXTER...
AND TURNED HIM INTO MAD-DOG!
THIS JOB SHOULD ONLY TAKE A FEW MINUTES...
"...NO ONE'S EVEN GONNA KNOW I WAS HERE!"
SNIFF SNIFF
SNIFF
RRRRRR?
TOP DOG
SCOTT GRAY STORY
GURIHIRU ART
DAVE SHARPE LETTERS
NATHAN COSBY EDITOR
JOE QUESADA CHIEF
DAN BUCKLEY PUBLISHER
ALAN FINE EXEC. PRODUCER

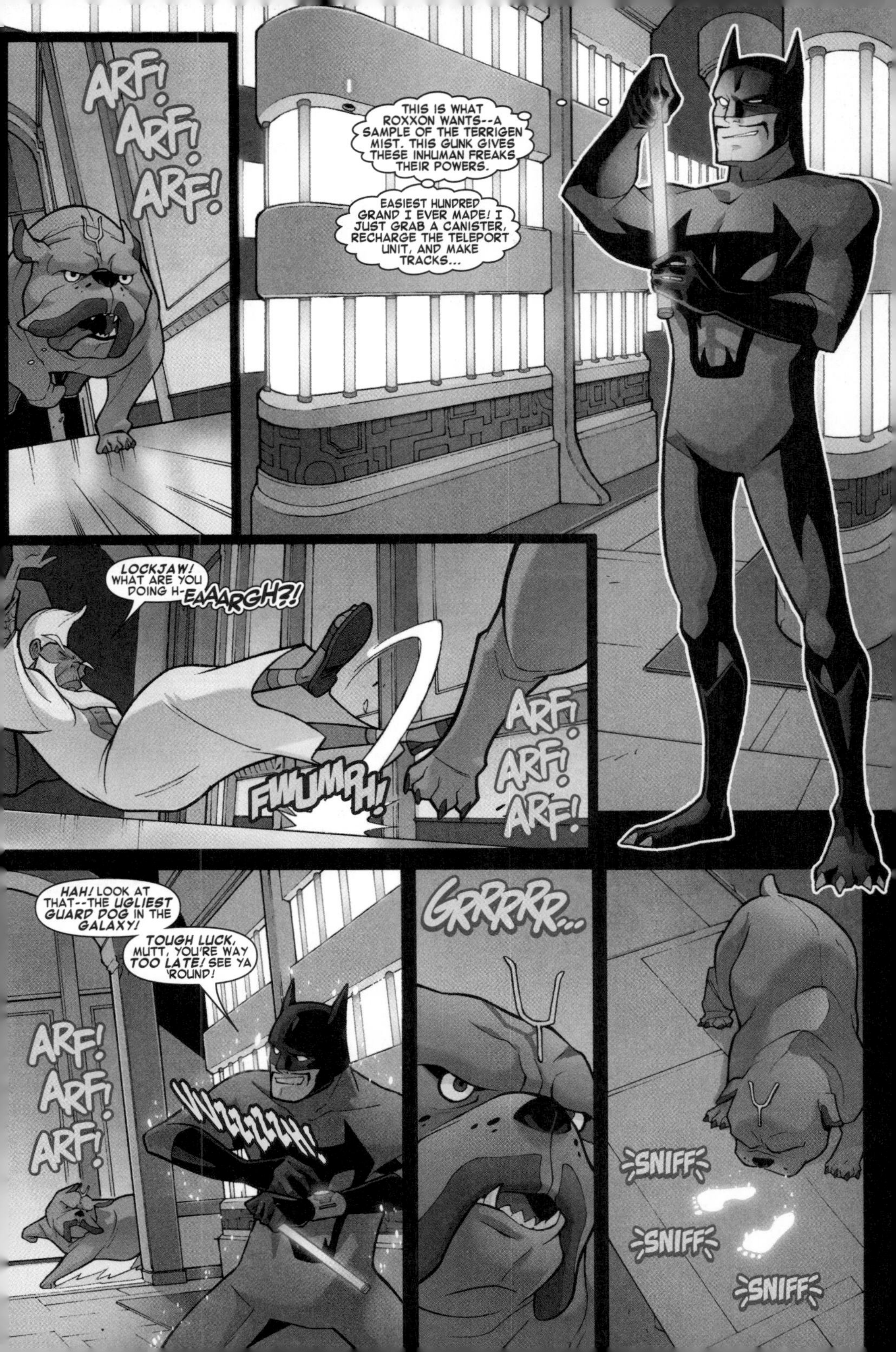
ARF! ARF! ARF!
THIS IS WHAT ROXXON WANTS--A SAMPLE OF THE TERRIGEN MIST. THIS GUNK GIVES THESE INHUMAN FREAKS THEIR POWERS.
EASIEST HUNDRED GRAND I EVER MADE! I JUST GRAB A CANISTER, RECHARGE THE TELEPORT UNIT, AND MAKE TRACKS...
LOCKJAW! WHAT ARE YOU DOING H-EAAARGH?!
FWUMPH!
ARF! ARF! ARF!
HAH! LOOK AT THAT--THE UGLIEST GUARD DOG IN THE GALAXY!
TOUGH LUCK, MUTT, YOU'RE WAY TOO LATE! SEE YA 'ROUND!
ARF! ARF! ARF!
VVZZZZZZH!
GRRRRR...
SNIFF
SNIFF
SNIFF

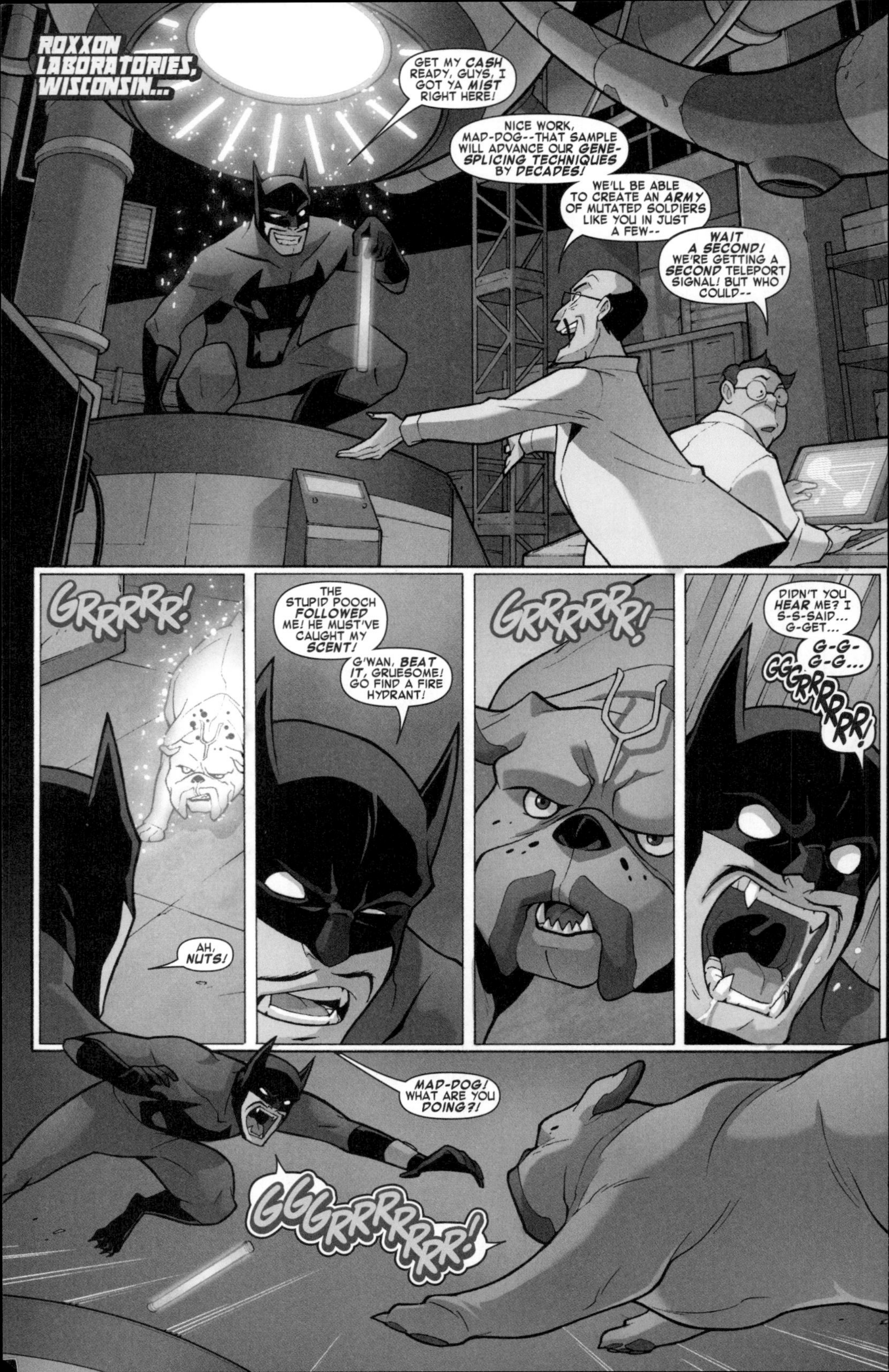
ROXXON LABORATORIES, WISCONSIN...
GET MY CASH READY, GUYS, I GOT YA MIST RIGHT HERE!
NICE WORK, MAD-DOG--THAT SAMPLE WILL ADVANCE OUR GENE-SPLICING TECHNIQUES BY DECADES!
WE'LL BE ABLE TO CREATE AN ARMY OF MUTATED SOLDIERS LIKE YOU IN JUST A FEW--
WAIT A SECOND! WE'RE GETTING A SECOND TELEPORT SIGNAL! BUT WHO COULD--
GRRRRR!
AH, NUTS!
THE STUPID POOCH FOLLOWED ME! HE MUST'VE CAUGHT MY SCENT!
G'WAN, BEAT IT, GRUESOME! GO FIND A FIRE HYDRANT!
GRRRRRR!
DIDN'T YOU HEAR ME? I S-S-SAID... G-GET...
G-G-G-G...
GGGRRRRRR!
MAD-DOG! WHAT ARE YOU DOING?!
GGGRRRRRRR!

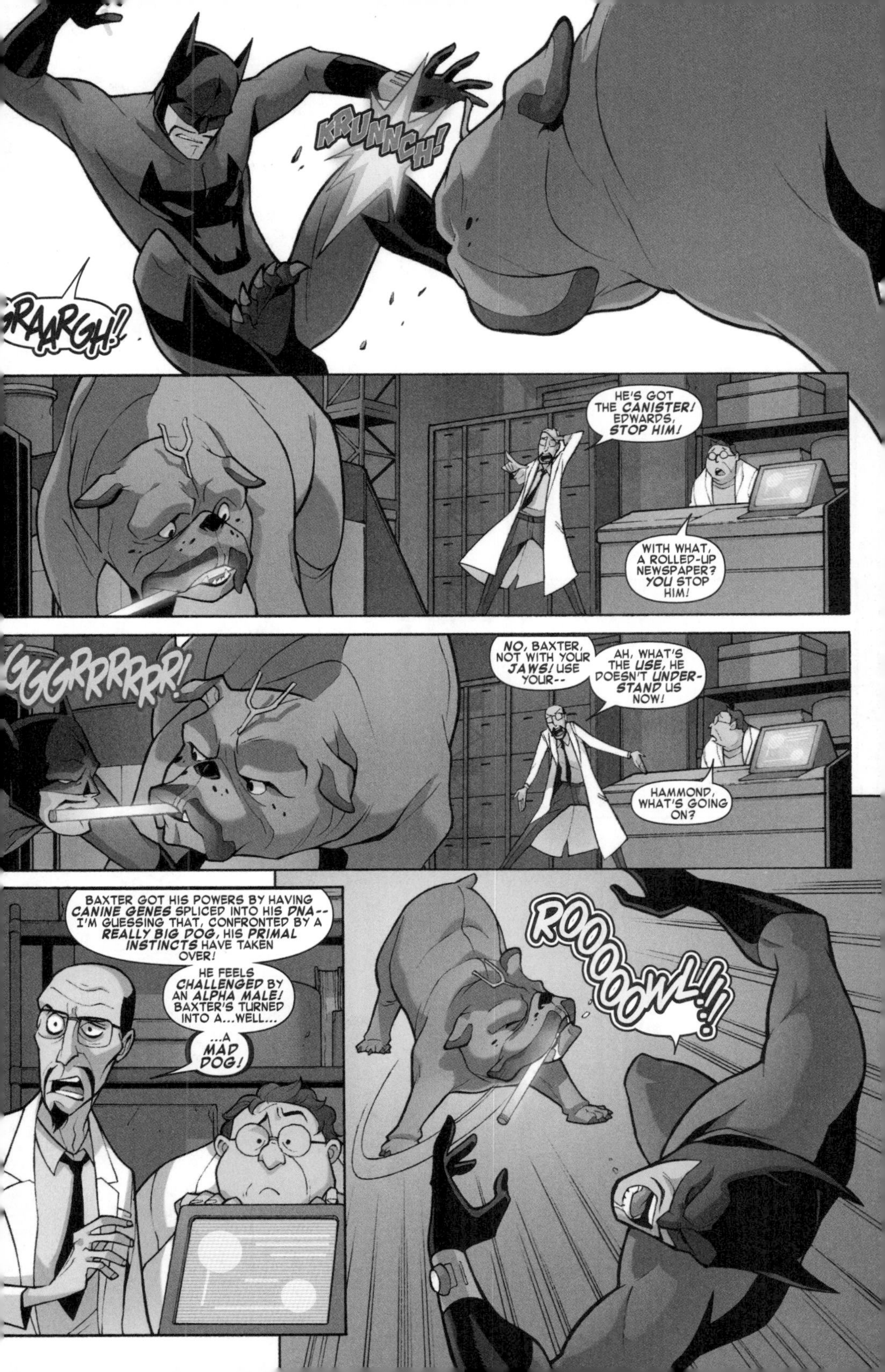
KRUNNCH!
GRAARGH!!
HE'S GOT THE CANISTER! EDWARDS, STOP HIM!
WITH WHAT, A ROLLED-UP NEWSPAPER? YOU STOP HIM!
GGGRRRRRR!
NO, BAXTER, NOT WITH YOUR JAWS! USE YOUR--
AH, WHAT'S THE USE, HE DOESN'T UNDERSTAND US NOW!
HAMMOND, WHAT'S GOING ON?
BAXTER GOT HIS POWERS BY HAVING CANINE GENES SPLICED INTO HIS DNA-- I'M GUESSING THAT, CONFRONTED BY A REALLY BIG DOG, HIS PRIMAL INSTINCTS HAVE TAKEN OVER!
HE FEELS CHALLENGED BY AN ALPHA MALE! BAXTER'S TURNED INTO A...WELL...
...A MAD DOG!
ROOOOOWL!!

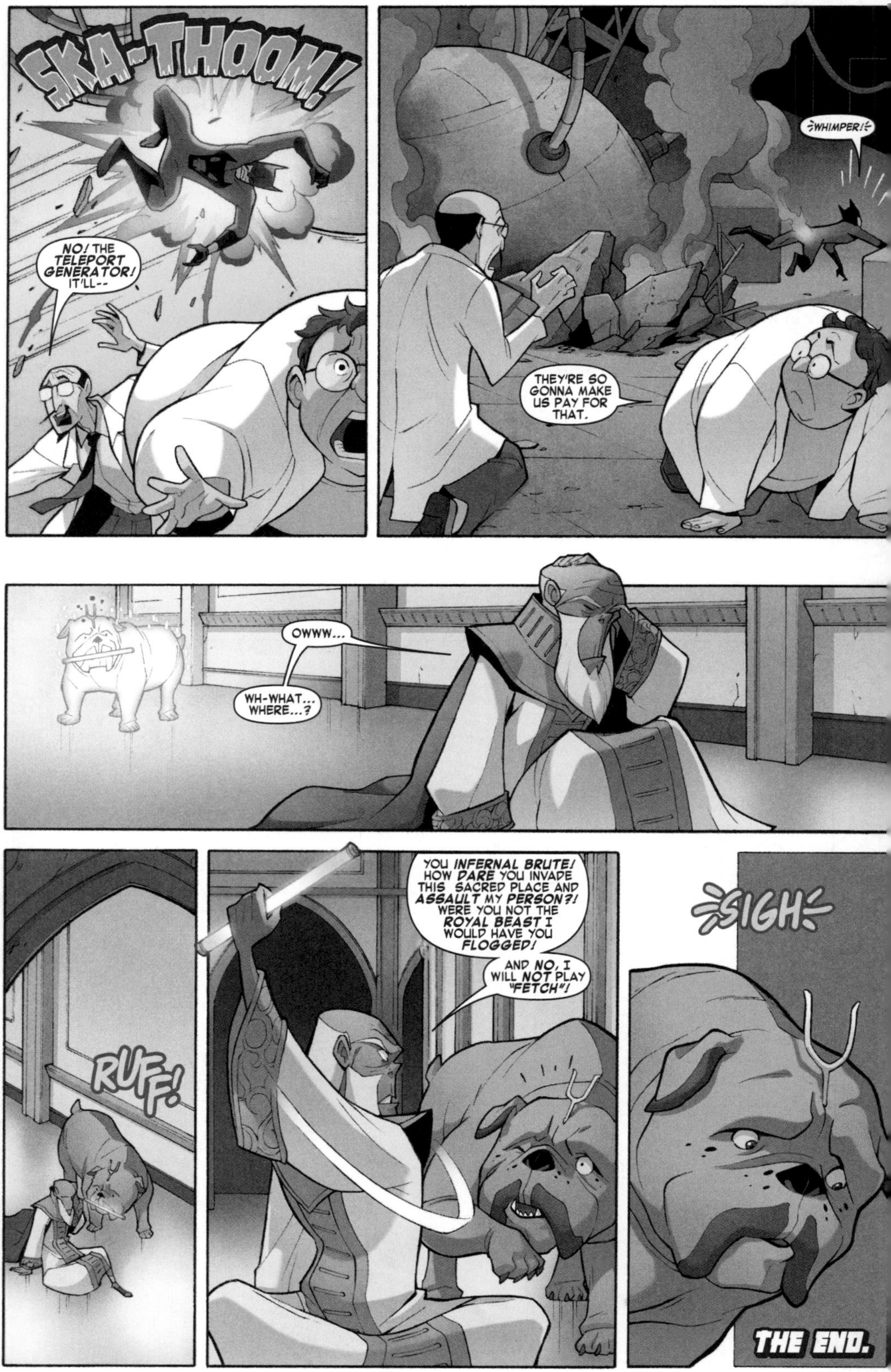
SKA-THOOM!
NO! THE TELEPORT GENERATOR! IT'LL--
THEY'RE SO GONNA MAKE US PAY FOR THAT.
WHIMPER!
OWWW...
WH-WHAT... WHERE...?
RUFF!
YOU INFERNAL BRUTE! HOW DARE YOU INVADE THIS SACRED PLACE AND ASSAULT MY PERSON?! WERE YOU NOT THE ROYAL BEAST I WOULD HAVE YOU FLOGGED!
AND NO, I WILL NOT PLAY "FETCH"!
SIGH
THE END.

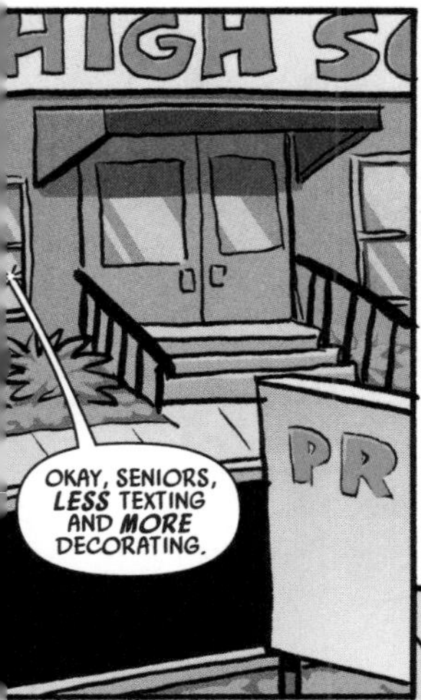
HIGH S
PR
OKAY, SENIORS, *LESS* TEXTING AND *MORE* DECORATING.

# Prom Queen

A TAIL OF THE **PET AVENGERS** STARRING **LOCKHEED**

**BUDDY SCALERA** WITH **CHRIS ELIOPOULOS**
WRITERS

**CHRIS ELIOPOULOS**
ARTIST

**SOTOCOLOR'S C. GARCIA**
ARTIST

**NATHAN COSBY**
EDITOR

**JOE QUESADA**
EDITOR IN CHIEF

**DAN BUCKLEY**
PUBLISHER

**ALAN FINE**
EXECUTIVE PRODUCER

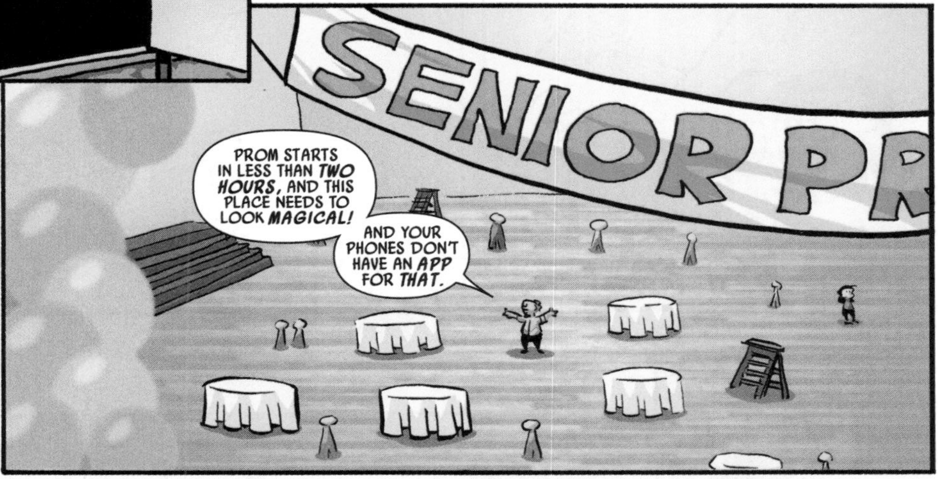
SENIOR PR
PROM STARTS IN LESS THAN *TWO HOURS*, AND THIS PLACE NEEDS TO LOOK *MAGICAL*!
AND YOUR PHONES DON'T HAVE AN *APP* FOR *THAT*.

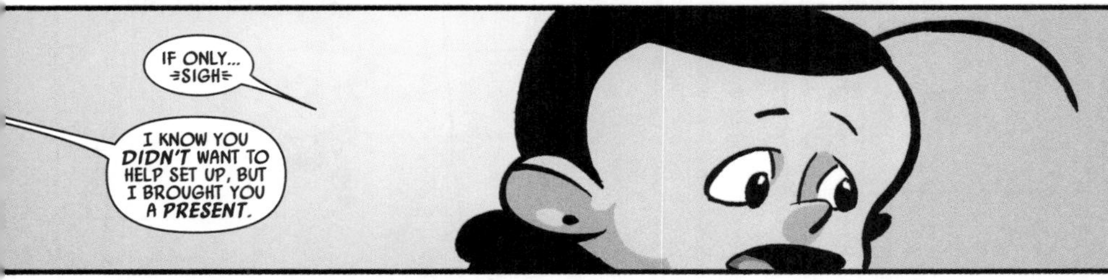
IF ONLY... =SIGH=
I KNOW YOU *DIDN'T* WANT TO HELP SET UP, BUT I BROUGHT YOU A *PRESENT*.

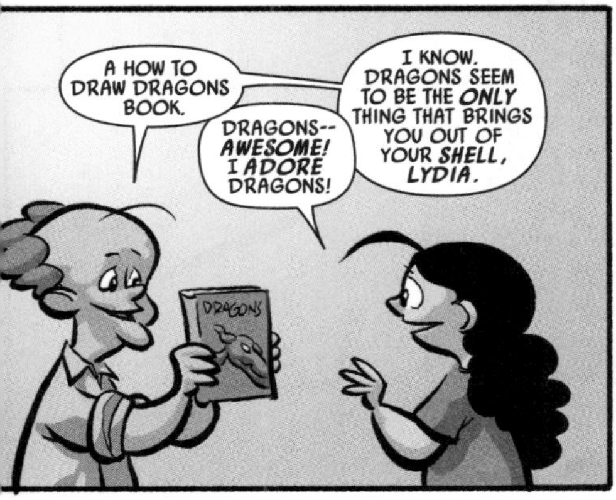
A HOW TO DRAW DRAGONS BOOK.
DRAGONS-- *AWESOME!* I *ADORE* DRAGONS!
I KNOW. DRAGONS SEEM TO BE THE *ONLY* THING THAT BRINGS YOU OUT OF YOUR *SHELL*, *LYDIA*.
DRAGONS

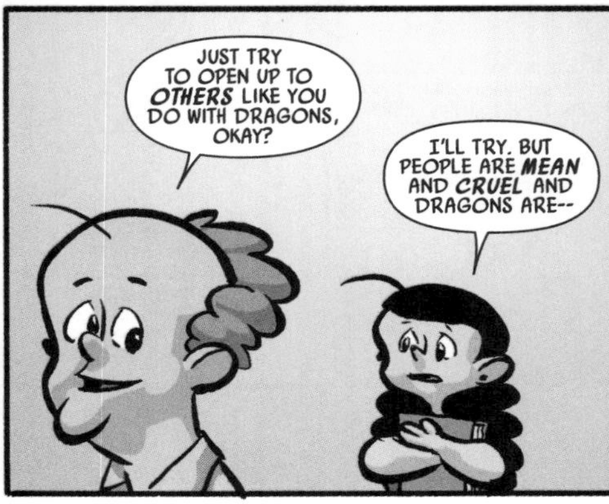
JUST TRY TO OPEN UP TO *OTHERS* LIKE YOU DO WITH DRAGONS, OKAY?
I'LL TRY. BUT PEOPLE ARE *MEAN* AND *CRUEL* AND DRAGONS ARE--

OOOOH. LOOK! LYDIA HAS A *NEW BOOK* ON DRAGONS!

HEY! GIVE THAT BACK!

WHAT A SURPRISE, *DRAGON GIRL.*

DRAGON GIRL! DRAGON GIRL!

PLEASE, JUST--

OKAY. *WHAT'S GOING ON HERE?*

DON'T YOU GIRLS HAVE TO *FINISH DECORATING?*

YES, MR. DUCOT.

HERE, *TAKE* YOUR DUMB DRAGON BOOK.

TIME TO *GROW UP--* THERE *ARE* NO SUCH THING AS DRAGONS.

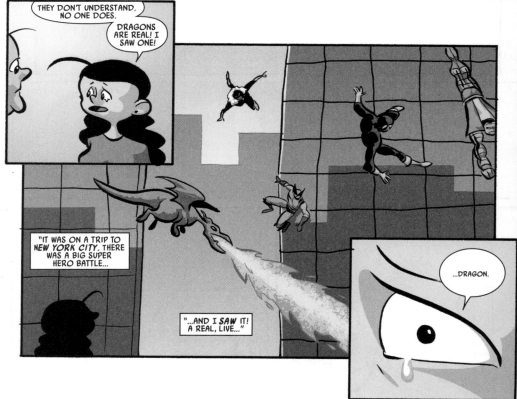

THEY DON'T UNDERSTAND. NO ONE DOES.

DRAGONS ARE REAL! I SAW ONE!

"IT WAS ON A TRIP TO *NEW YORK CITY.* THERE WAS A BIG SUPER HERO BATTLE...

"...AND I *SAW* IT! A REAL, LIVE..."

...DRAGON.

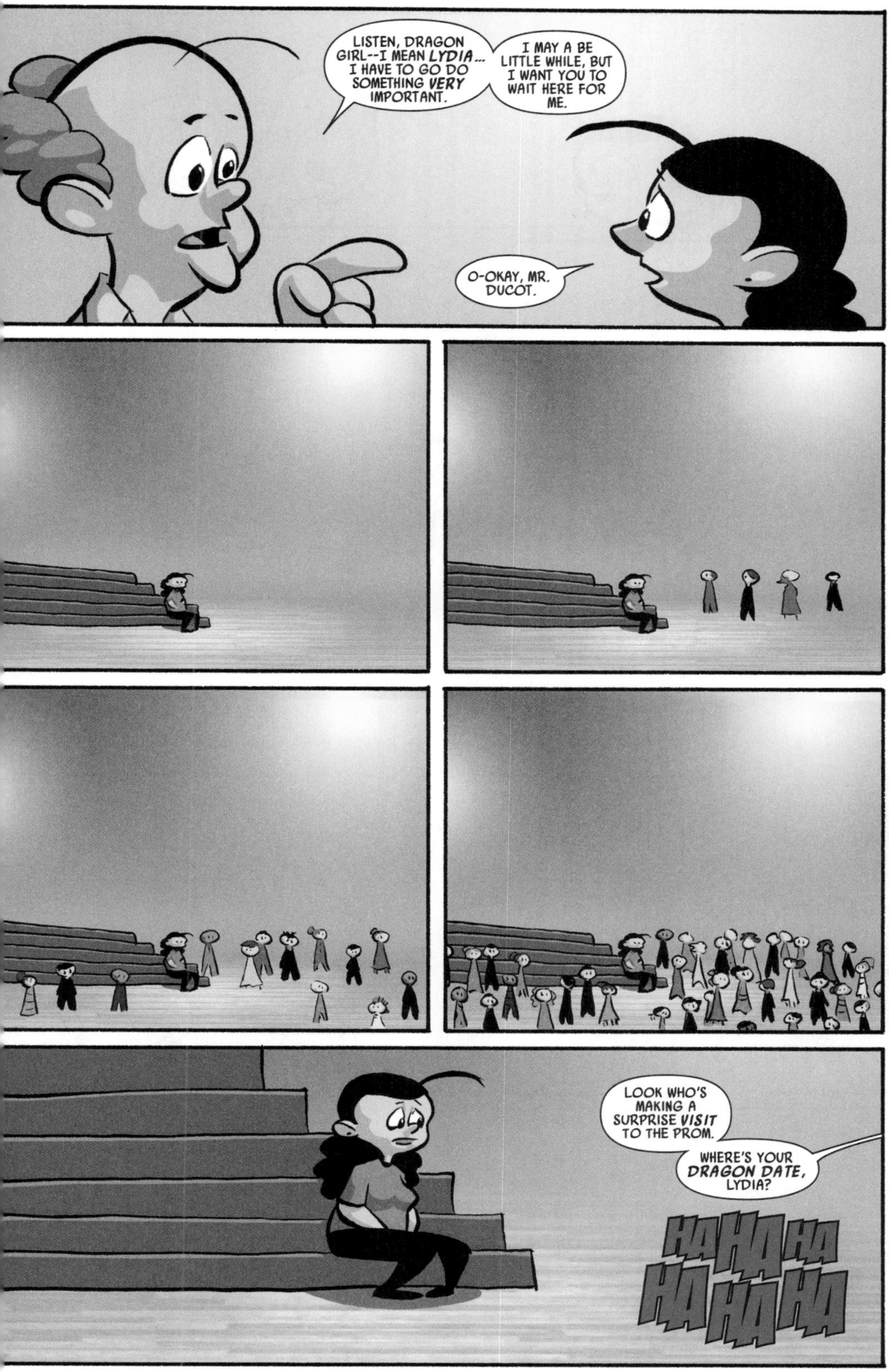
LISTEN, DRAGON GIRL--I MEAN LYDIA... I HAVE TO GO DO SOMETHING VERY IMPORTANT.
I MAY A BE LITTLE WHILE, BUT I WANT YOU TO WAIT HERE FOR ME.
O-OKAY, MR. DUCOT.
LOOK WHO'S MAKING A SURPRISE VISIT TO THE PROM.
WHERE'S YOUR DRAGON DATE, LYDIA?
HA HA HA HA HA HA

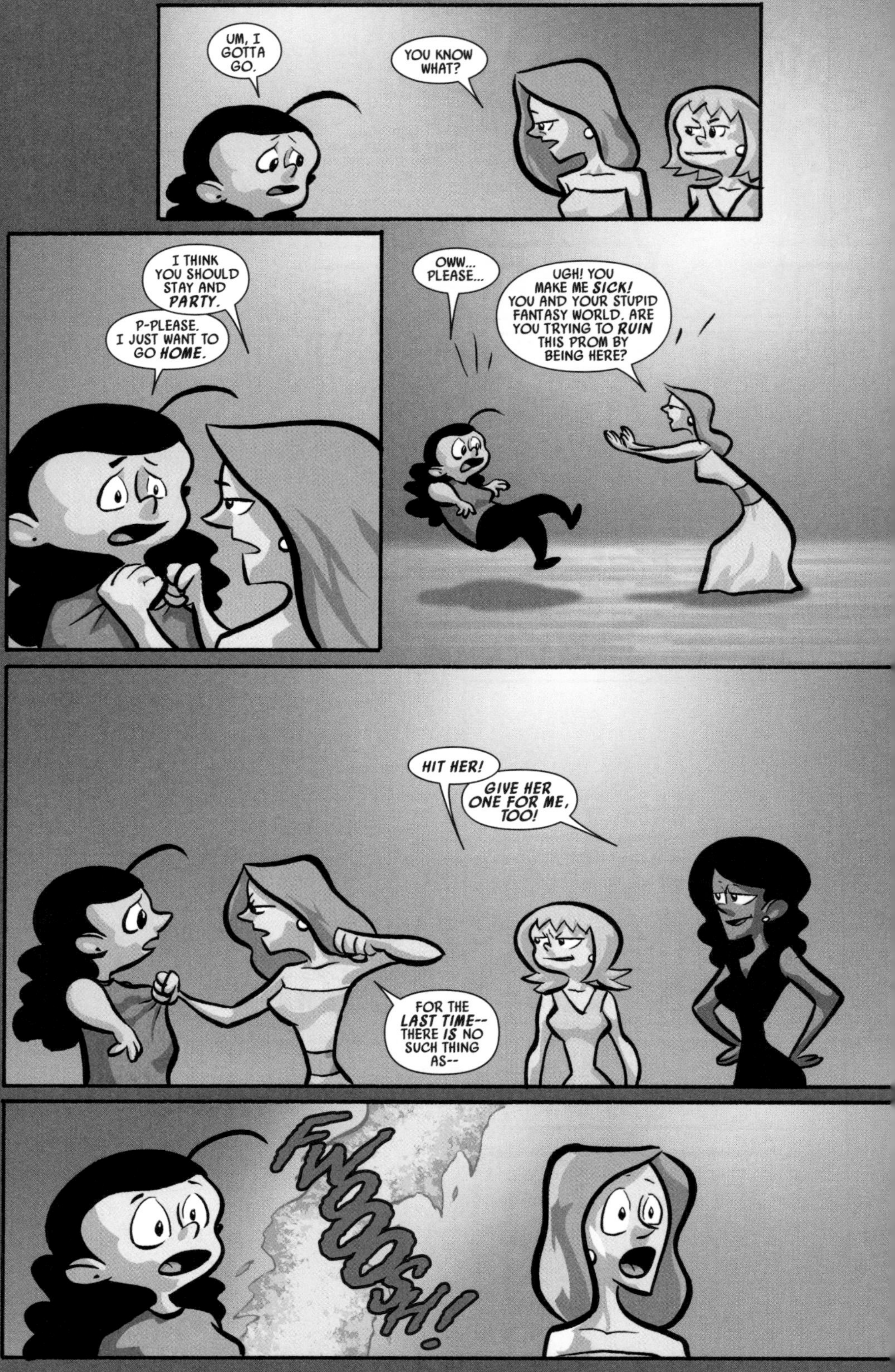
UM, I GOTTA GO.
YOU KNOW WHAT?
I THINK YOU SHOULD STAY AND PARTY.
P-PLEASE. I JUST WANT TO GO HOME.
OWW... PLEASE...
UGH! YOU MAKE ME SICK! YOU AND YOUR STUPID FANTASY WORLD. ARE YOU TRYING TO RUIN THIS PROM BY BEING HERE?
HIT HER!
GIVE HER ONE FOR ME, TOO!
FOR THE LAST TIME-- THERE IS NO SUCH THING AS--
FWOOOSH!

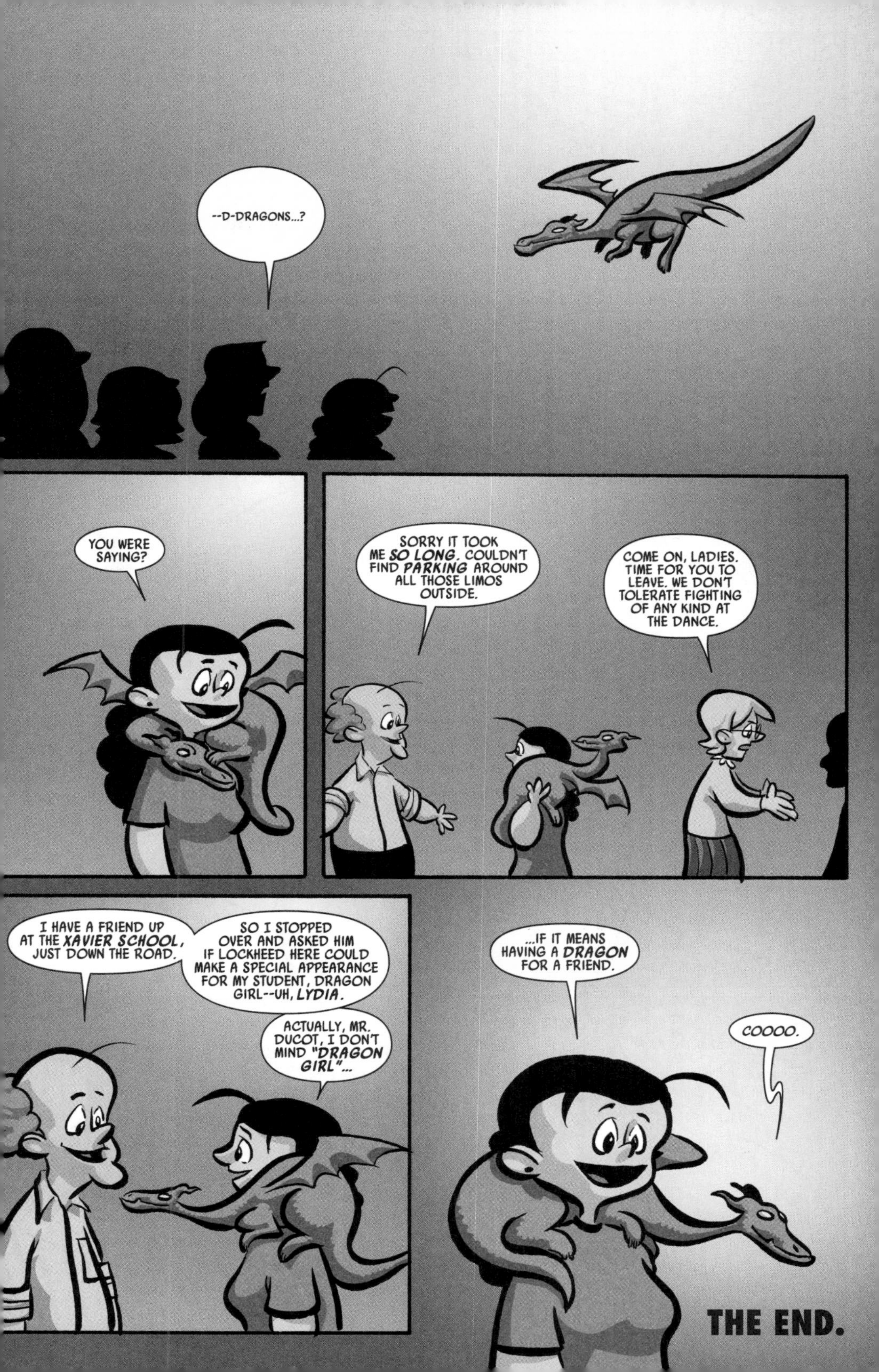
--D-DRAGONS...?
YOU WERE SAYING?
SORRY IT TOOK ME SO LONG. COULDN'T FIND PARKING AROUND ALL THOSE LIMOS OUTSIDE.
COME ON, LADIES. TIME FOR YOU TO LEAVE. WE DON'T TOLERATE FIGHTING OF ANY KIND AT THE DANCE.
I HAVE A FRIEND UP AT THE XAVIER SCHOOL, JUST DOWN THE ROAD.
SO I STOPPED OVER AND ASKED HIM IF LOCKHEED HERE COULD MAKE A SPECIAL APPEARANCE FOR MY STUDENT, DRAGON GIRL--UH, LYDIA.
ACTUALLY, MR. DUCOT, I DON'T MIND "DRAGON GIRL"...
...IF IT MEANS HAVING A DRAGON FOR A FRIEND.
COOOO.
THE END.

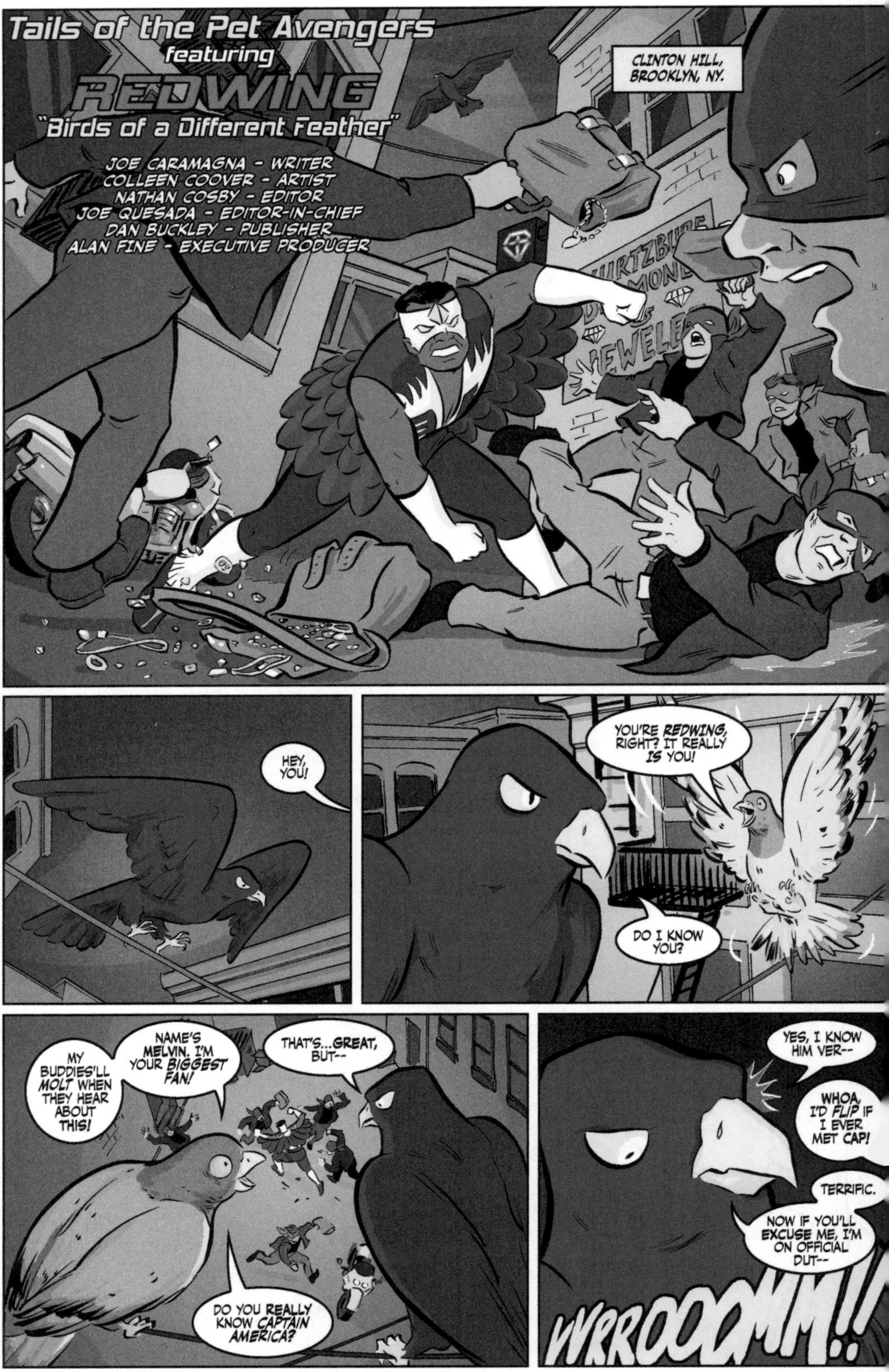

Tails of the Pet Avengers
featuring
REDWING
"Birds of a Different Feather"
JOE CARAMAGNA - WRITER
COLLEEN COOVER - ARTIST
NATHAN COSBY - EDITOR
JOE QUESADA - EDITOR-IN-CHIEF
DAN BUCKLEY - PUBLISHER
ALAN FINE - EXECUTIVE PRODUCER
CLINTON HILL, BROOKLYN, NY.
HEY, YOU!
YOU'RE REDWING, RIGHT? IT REALLY IS YOU!
DO I KNOW YOU?
NAME'S MELVIN. I'M YOUR BIGGEST FAN!
MY BUDDIES'LL MOLT WHEN THEY HEAR ABOUT THIS!
THAT'S...GREAT, BUT--
DO YOU REALLY KNOW CAPTAIN AMERICA?
YES, I KNOW HIM VER--
WHOA, I'D FLIP IF I EVER MET CAP!
TERRIFIC.
NOW IF YOU'LL EXCUSE ME, I'M ON OFFICIAL DUT--
VVRROOOMM!!

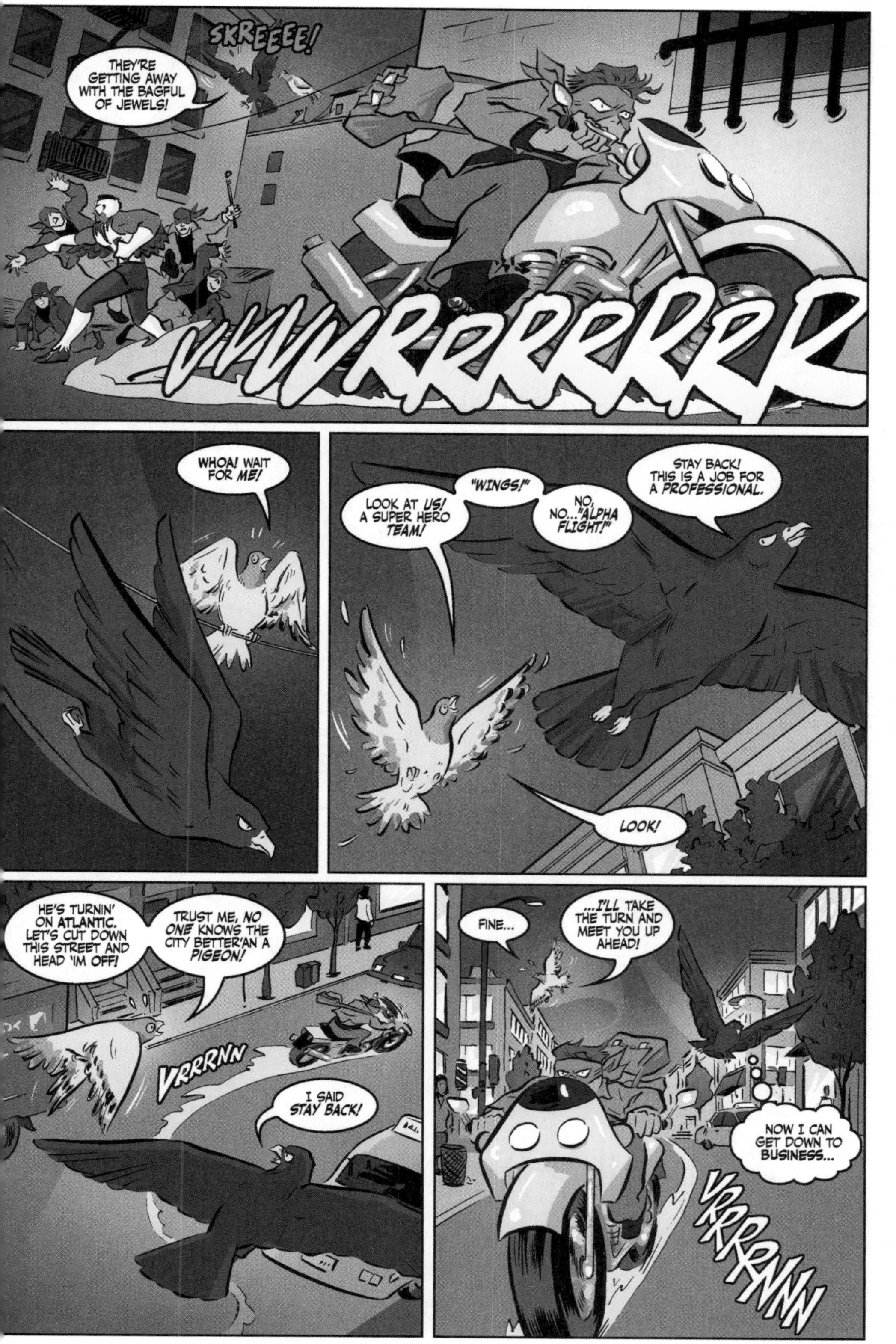
SKREEEEE!
THEY'RE GETTING AWAY WITH THE BAGFUL OF JEWELS!
VVVVVRRRRRRRRRR
WHOA! WAIT FOR ME!
LOOK AT US! A SUPER HERO TEAM!
"WINGS!"
NO, NO..."ALPHA FLIGHT!"
STAY BACK! THIS IS A JOB FOR A PROFESSIONAL.
LOOK!
HE'S TURNIN' ON ATLANTIC. LET'S CUT DOWN THIS STREET AND HEAD 'IM OFF!
TRUST ME, NO ONE KNOWS THE CITY BETTER'AN A PIGEON!
VRRRNN
I SAID STAY BACK!
FINE...
...I'LL TAKE THE TURN AND MEET YOU UP AHEAD!
NOW I CAN GET DOWN TO BUSINESS...
VRRRNNN

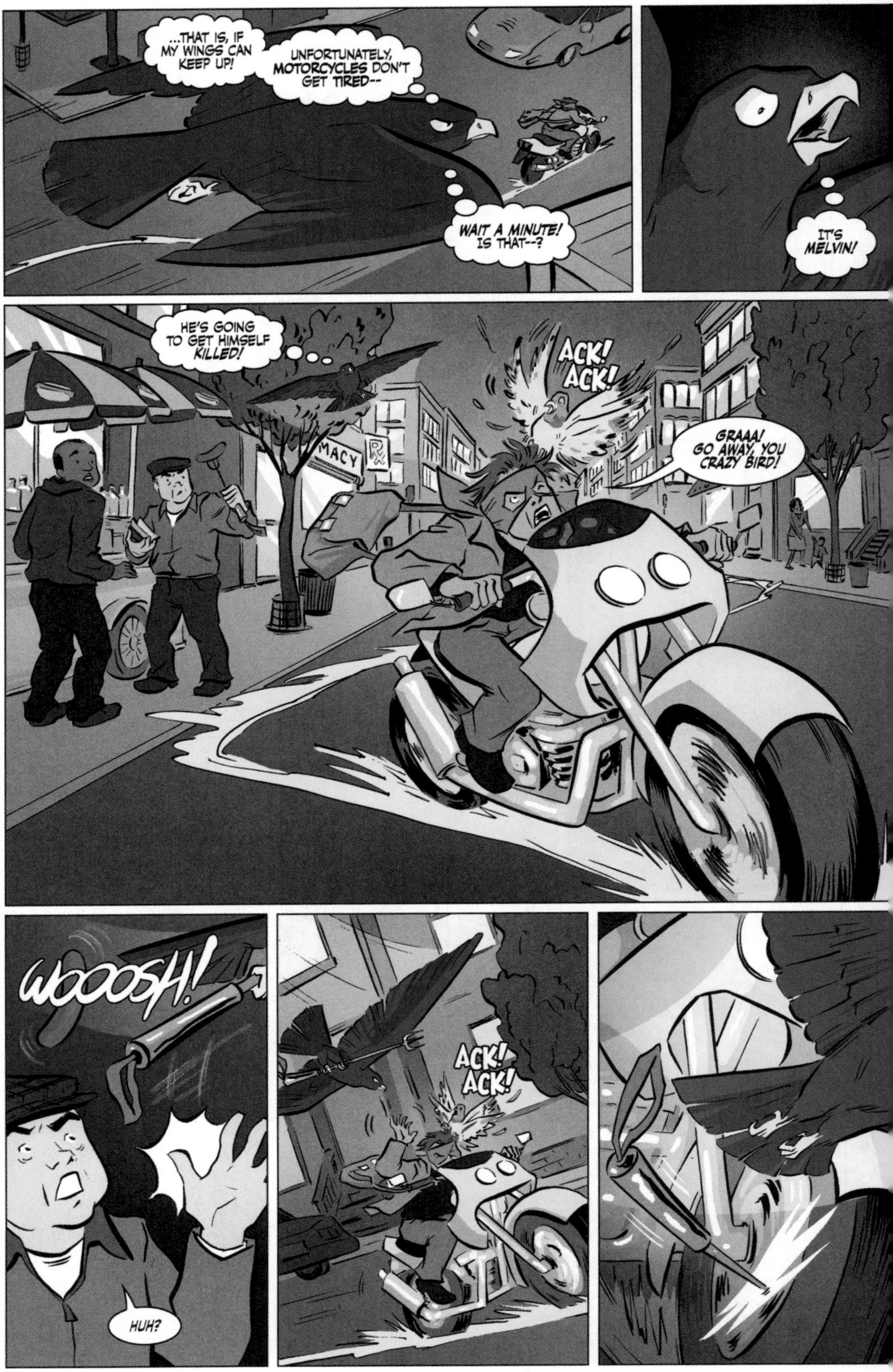

...THAT IS, IF MY WINGS CAN KEEP UP!
UNFORTUNATELY, MOTORCYCLES DON'T GET TIRED--
WAIT A MINUTE! IS THAT--?
IT'S MELVIN!
HE'S GOING TO GET HIMSELF KILLED!
ACK! ACK!
MACY
Rx
GRAAA! GO AWAY, YOU CRAZY BIRD!
WOOOSH!
HUH?
ACK! ACK!

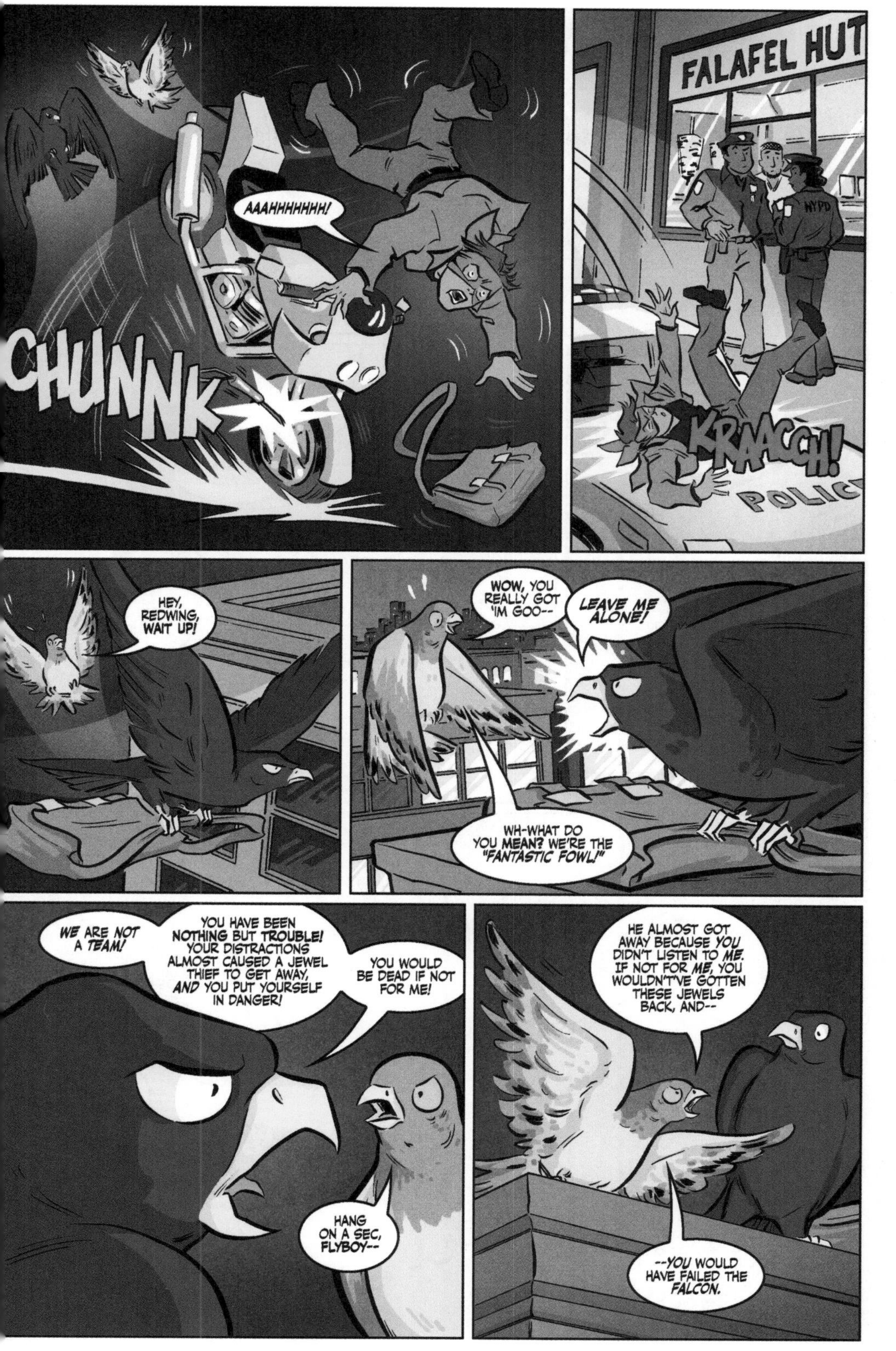
AAAHHHHHHHH!
CHUNNK
FALAFEL HUT
NYPD
KRAACCH!
POLIC
HEY, REDWING, WAIT UP!
WOW, YOU REALLY GOT 'IM GOO--
LEAVE ME ALONE!
WH-WHAT DO YOU MEAN? WE'RE THE "FANTASTIC FOWL!"
WE ARE NOT A TEAM!
YOU HAVE BEEN NOTHING BUT TROUBLE! YOUR DISTRACTIONS ALMOST CAUSED A JEWEL THIEF TO GET AWAY, AND YOU PUT YOURSELF IN DANGER!
YOU WOULD BE DEAD IF NOT FOR ME!
HANG ON A SEC, FLYBOY--
HE ALMOST GOT AWAY BECAUSE YOU DIDN'T LISTEN TO ME. IF NOT FOR ME, YOU WOULDN'T'VE GOTTEN THESE JEWELS BACK, AND--
--YOU WOULD HAVE FAILED THE FALCON.

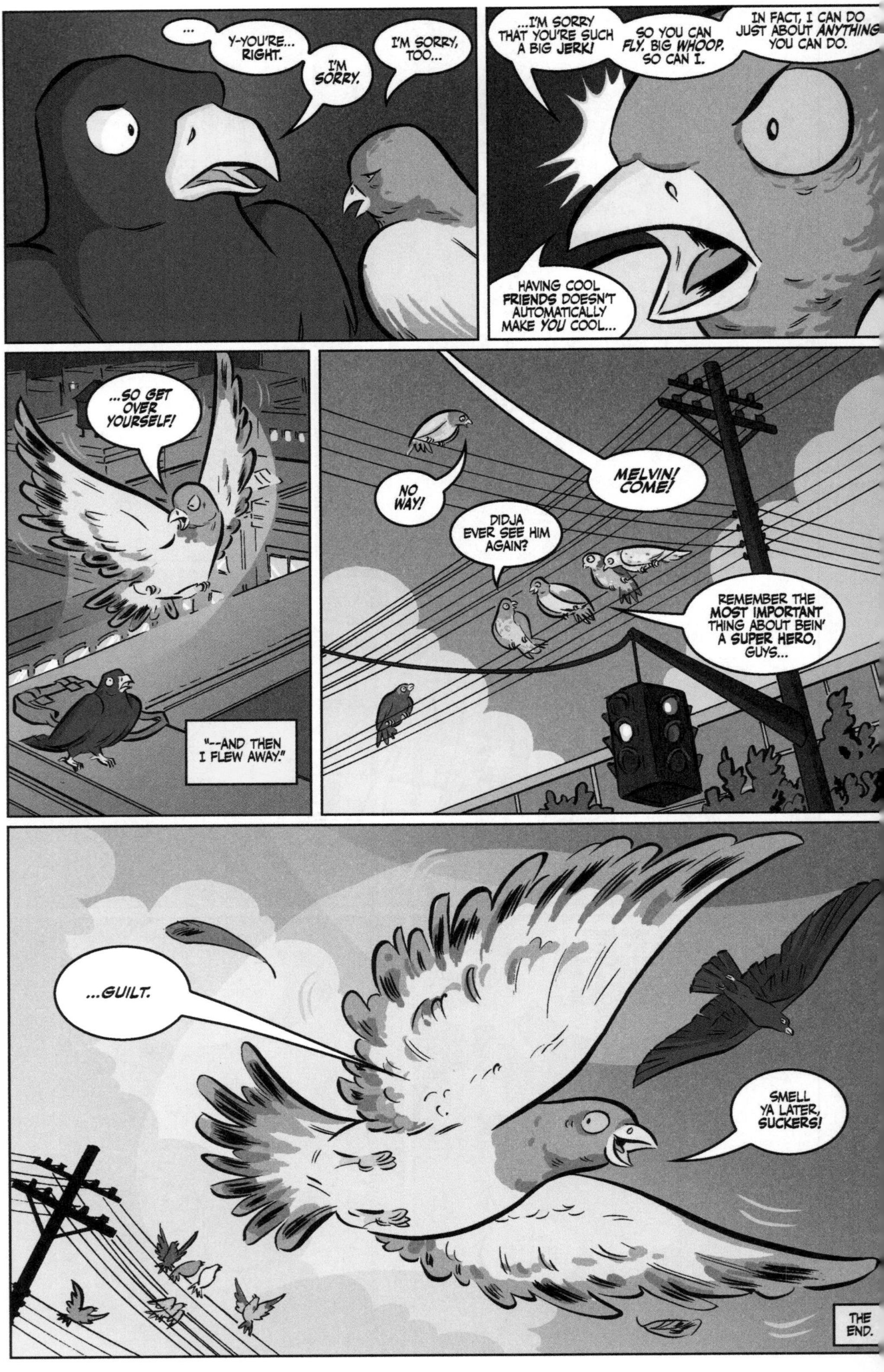
...
Y-YOU'RE... RIGHT.
I'M SORRY.
I'M SORRY, TOO...
...I'M SORRY THAT YOU'RE SUCH A BIG JERK!
SO YOU CAN FLY. BIG WHOOP. SO CAN I.
IN FACT, I CAN DO JUST ABOUT ANYTHING YOU CAN DO.
HAVING COOL FRIENDS DOESN'T AUTOMATICALLY MAKE YOU COOL...
...SO GET OVER YOURSELF!
"--AND THEN I FLEW AWAY."
MELVIN! COME!
NO WAY!
DIDJA EVER SEE HIM AGAIN?
REMEMBER THE MOST IMPORTANT THING ABOUT BEIN' A SUPER HERO, GUYS...
...GUILT.
SMELL YA LATER, SUCKERS!
THE END.

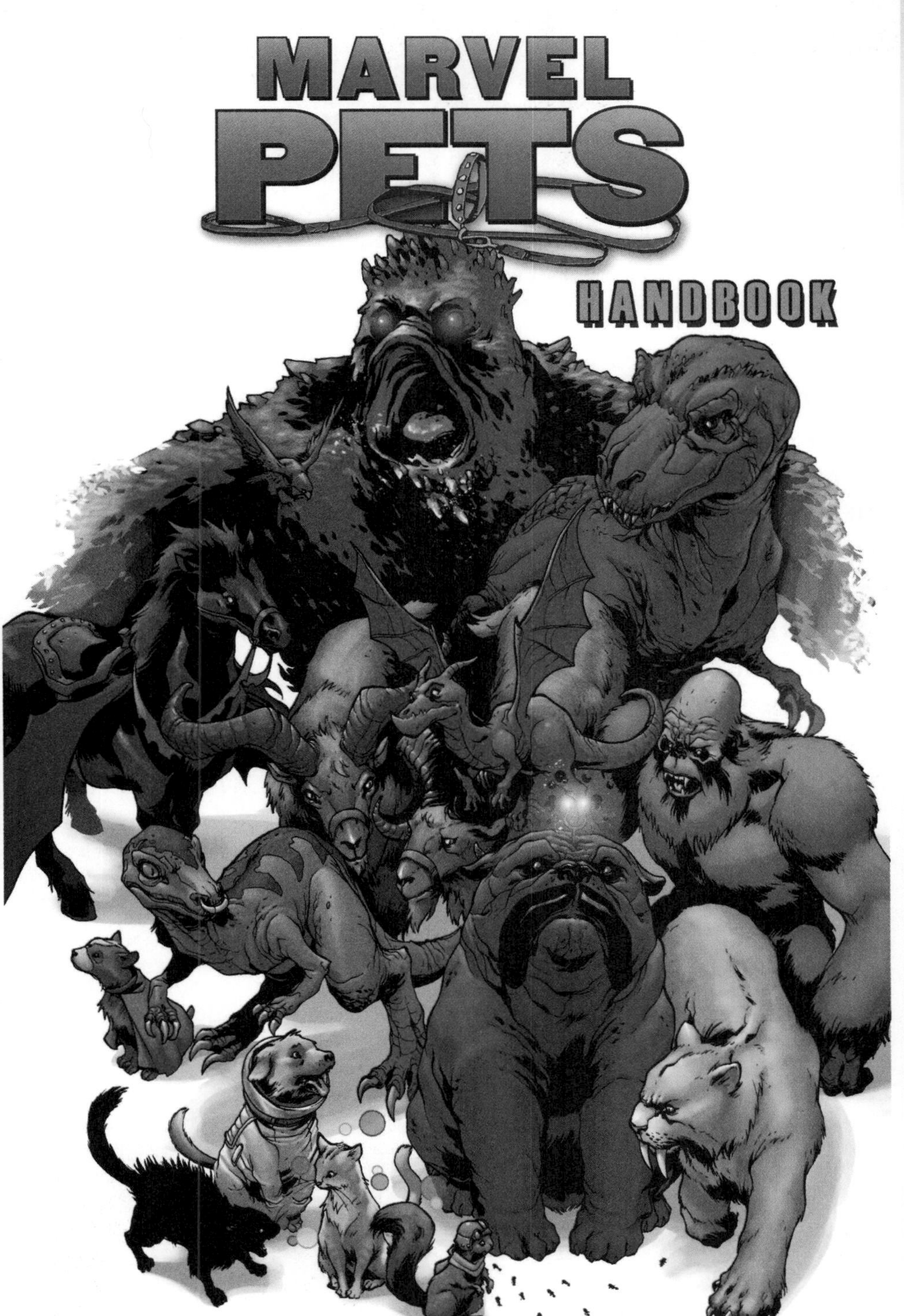
MARVEL
PETS
HANDBOOK

# MARVEL PETS HANDBOOK

**HEAD WRITER/COORDINATOR** . . . . . . . . . . . . . . . . . . . . . . . . . . . . . . . . . . . . . . MICHAEL HOSKIN

**WRITERS** . . . . . . . . MADISON CARTER, SEAN MCQUAID, STUART VANDAL, GABRIEL SHECHTER, DAVID WILTFONG, RONALD BYRD, ERIC J. MOREELS, JACOB ROUGEMONT, MARKUS RAYMOND, JEFF CHRISTIANSEN, MARK O'ENGLISH, MIKE O'SULLIVAN, CHRIS BIGGS & ROB LONDON

**ART REFURBISHMENT** . . . . . . MIKE FICHERA, JASON LEWIS, GALLY ARTICOLA & COURTNEY VIA

**COVER ARTIST** . . . . . . . . . . . . . . . . . . . . . . . . . . . . . . . . . . . . . . . . . . . . . . . . KARL KERSCHL

**COVER DESIGN** . . . . . . . . . . . . . . . . . . . . . . . . . . . . . . . . . . . . . . . . . . . . . . . SPRING HOTELING

**ART RECONSTRUCTION** . . . . . . . . . . . . . . . . . . . . . . . . . . . . . . . POND SCUM & NELSON RIBEIRO

**SELECT COLORING** . . . . . . . . . . . . . . . . . . . . . . . . . . . . . . . . . . . . . . . . . . . . . . . TOM SMITH

**PRODUCTION** . . . . . . . . . . . . . . . . . . . . . . . . . . . . . NELSON RIBEIRO & JERRON QUALITY COLOR

**EDITOR** . . . . . . . . . . . . . . . . . . . . . . . . . . . . . . . . . . . . . . . . . . . . . . . . . JEFF YOUNGQUIST

**EDITORS, SPECIAL PROJECTS** . . . . . . . . . . . . . . . . . . . . MARK D. BEAZLEY & JENNIFER GRÜNWALD

**ASSISTANT EDITORS** . . . . . . . . . . . . . . . . . . . . . . . . . . . . . . . JOHN DENNING & CORY LEVINE

**EDITORIAL ASSISTANT** . . . . . . . . . . . . . . . . . . . . . . . . . . . . . . . . . . . . . . ALEX STARBUCK

**COPY EDITOR** . . . . . . . . . . . . . . . . . . . . . . . . . . . . . . . . . . . . . . . . . . . . BRIAN OVERTON

**SENIOR VICE PRESIDENT OF SALES** . . . . . . . . . . . . . . . . . . . . . . . . . . . . . . . DAVID GABRIEL

**EDITOR IN CHIEF** . . . . . . . . . . . . . . . . . . . . . . . . . . . . . . . . . . . . . . . . . . . . . JOE QUESADA

**PUBLISHER** . . . . . . . . . . . . . . . . . . . . . . . . . . . . . . . . . . . . . . . . . . . . . . . . DAN BUCKLEY

**EXECUTIVE PRODUCER** . . . . . . . . . . . . . . . . . . . . . . . . . . . . . . . . . . . . . . . . . . ALAN FINE

Special thanks to the guys at the Appendix (www.marvunapp.com), www.g-mart.com, Tom Brevoort, Chris Allo, Art Adams, Joe Casey, Paul Cornell, Craig Dylke, Mike Fichera, Christos N. Gage, Jess Nevin, Priest & Jim Starlin.

Dedicated to the Official Pets of the Marvel Pets Authors — Michael: Dusky and Silver; Jeff: Willow, Rainman, Consuela, Elvis, Lamont, Shaniqua and Yolanda; Mike O': Lockheed and Pancake; Chris: Heba, Diamond, Tiger Lily, Phineas, Venus and Cija; David: Rizzo, Buffy and Shelby; Rob: Kippy & Patches; Gabriel: Jesse and Mocha; Jacob: Cricket; Markus: Schnurli; Sean: Lil, Book and Buffy; Eric: Pepe, Pikachu and Astro; Mark O': Molly and Heidi

The Official Handbook of the Marvel Universe Frequently Asked Questions page — including data corrections and explanations, complete bibliographies, and Power Grid legends: http://www.marvel.com/universe/OHOTMU

## "Why?"

### A Brief History of Marvel Pets

It began as a back-and-forth between the writing and editorial staff of the Official Handbook of the Marvel Universe. Wouldn't it be cute to do an entire handbook on Marvel Pets? And somewhere in that back-and-forth, so many names were brought up that realization began to sink in: this could actually be viable.

About two years later, here we are at a time when Marvel Pets are clearly on the rise! Between Chris Eliopoulous' Lockjaw and the Pet Avengers and the Marvel Pets trade paperback (a handsome collection of tales featuring all of your favorite Marvel Pets), this was clearly the time for a Marvel Pets Handbook!

Although there are many Marvel characters who keep pets, the notion of a super-pet – one who shares the powers/appearance of its master – is particular to the publications of a certain Distinguished Competitor. But just as Marvel Apes demonstrated that they are no longer the leader in all things simian, the dawning of the age of Marvel Pets sees Marvel Comics taking the lead in comics on super-pets!

In the early days of Marvel Comics when Jack Kirby would etch his drawings on cavern walls with a smilodon fang, only a few Marvel heroes kept pets. The pet horse is, of course, a must for western heroes and from the 40s to the 70s there were several (see the Appendix: Cowboy Horses for the highlights). Jungle heroes like the original Ka-Zar had their own furry friends, notably the lion Zar. Strangely, pets were also popular with detectives such as Terry Vance with his pet monkey Dr. Watson and the Ferret with his pet ferret (duh) Nosey. At a particular point of the late 40s and early 50s a number of four-footed friends received their own stories, including Blaze the Wonder Collie, Diablo the grizzly, Man-oo the gorilla and Nimo the mountain lion! Sadly, this fad was over faster than the 3-D craze.

Fast forward to the 1960s, the era where Stan Lee's new tie-dye coloring process revolutionized the industry. Appropriately, the very comic to usher in the Marvel Age of Comics – Fantastic Four #1 – spotlighted one of the most iconic pets of them all: the Mole Man's monster, who we later learned was named Giganto! Before long we had met the Red Ghost's Super-Apes as well! Not to leave the heroes shorn of pets, Stan and Jack gave us an all-new Ka-Zar with his fanged friend Zabu, who would eventually grow popular enough to command his own solo features! And

when the Fantastic Four met the Inhumans and their pet dog Lockjaw it was slobberin' time!

MS. LION

As time went on we saw a veritable fleet of flying horses serving Black Knight and Valkyrie much as the Cowboy horses of old did their masters. Perhaps the most momentous new Marvel Pet find was Kitty Pryde's friend Lockheed the dragon! Known as the "Wolverine of Marvel Pets," Lockheed has repeatedly demonstrated an ability to increase sales of any comic or specialty merchandise by his mere presence. Speedball's friend Niels the cat was another notable latter-day Marvel Pet. Recent years have gifted us with such notables as Amadeus Cho's coyote pup Kerberos and Sentry's ever-lovable Watchdog!

All these pets are fine, but many of the most popular Marvel heroes have never had a pet to call their own. No pet skunk for Wolverine, no Mexican hairless for Professor X, not even a goldfish for Captain America. In the world of animation, this led to two instances of newly-fashioned Marvel Pets. Fans of the 1980s series Spider-Man and his Amazing Friends will recall that Aunt May kept a pet dog, Ms. Lion. Ms. Lion would even join in the exploits of Spider-Man, Iceman and Firestar. Memorably, in the episode "Seven Little Super Heroes" she saved the Amazing Friends, Shanna, Dr. Strange, the Sub-Mariner and Captain America from the Chameleon! Ms. Lion has made two forays into the non-animated environment, appearing in a comic book adaptation of the TV show and in the aforementioned Pet Avengers.

But at the same time in the 1980s, plans had been made for Daredevil to make the leap to Saturday morning television! Sadly, the proposed series never materialized, but it would have given Daredevil a canine sidekick: Lightning the Super Dog! Being that Daredevil is a blind man in his alter ego of Matthew Murdock, it actually made good sense for Murdock to adopt a Seeing Eye dog. Although Lightning never made it off the drawing board, his spirit eventually lived on in the comics via the 1990s pooch Deuce, the Devil Dog!

So, for the purposes of this book, what is a "Marvel Pet?" We allowed the concept some flexibility to allow any character who is treated like a pet, but allowed some creatures which are wild animals. Although Cerberus has demonstrated at least as much intelligence as his foe Hercules, Cerberus is clearly a pet to his master Pluto and so a Marvel Pet is he. On the other hand, the New Men created by the High Evolutionary are one-time animals but are clearly now sentient and self-willed; they are not Marvel Pets. Devil Dinosaur and Cosmo are both clearly above the average pet, but emerged from humble pet-like roots. For some of the lesser Marvel Pets we didn't have space to grant full coverage, please see the Appendix: Miscellaneous Pets.

DAREDEVIL and LIGHTNING THE SUPER DOG!

# ARAGORN

**REAL NAME:** Aragorn
**ALIASES:** None
**IDENTITY:** No dual identity
**OCCUPATION:** Steed of the Valkyrie
**CITIZENSHIP:** Property of Samantha Parrington
**PLACE OF BIRTH:** Castle Garrett, Washington DC, USA
**KNOWN RELATIVES:** None
**GROUP AFFILIATION:** None
**EDUCATION:** No formal education
**FIRST APPEARANCE:** Avengers #48 (1968)

**HISTORY:** Aragorn was a horse kept at Castle Garrett, home of the criminal scientist the Black Knight (Nathan Garrett) who developed the means to grant a horse wings capable of flight. When Garrett died, his own horse was lost (becoming the Hellhorse steed of Dreadknight) and his secrets were passed on to his nephew, Dane Whitman. Whitman decided to redeem his uncle's work and became a heroic Black Knight, using Garrett's work to grant Aragorn wings. Whitman soon tested himself and Aragorn in battle when he attempted to aid the Avengers against the mutant Magneto (Max Eisenhardt). Aragorn also joined his master as he infiltrated Ultron-5's Masters of Evil to aid the Avengers. Later they engaged in an aerial battle with le Sabre (Paul Richarde) and his own mount, a flying gargoyle. Aragorn also aided his master and Dr. Stephen Strange against the extradimensional sorcerer Tiboro and flew the Black Knight and Hawkeye (Clint Barton) to a battle with the fire demon Surtur. Aragorn also led his master to battles with Arkon, Imperion of extradimensional Polemachus; Amora the Enchantress; and Olympian war god Ares.

After the Black Knight's body was transformed into stone while his spirit was cast back to the 12th century, Aragorn fell into the possession of the Valkyrie (Brunnhilde) who rode him into battle as a member of the Defenders. Jack Norriss, who believed Valkyrie to be his wife Barbara, learned to care for Aragorn in an attempt to demonstrate support to her. Aragorn once carried Valkyrie and Namorita into battle against the robot Omegatron, creation of the extradimensional world Yann's scientist supreme, Yandroth. While the Defenders were based at Dr. Strange's Sanctum Sanctorum, Aragorn was kept in a hidden courtyard. After the wealthy Nighthawk (Kyle Richmond) joined the team, he procured stables at a secluded Long Island locale soon dubbed the Richmond Riding Academy where Aragorn could be properly cared for. Over the time Valkyrie spent with the Defenders, Aragorn aided her in battles with threats such as the Meteor Man (aka the Looter), the Headmen, the Red Rajah, Lunatik (Arisen Turk), the Anything Man (Jeff Colt, empowered by Omegatron), the Mandrill and Nebulon. Aragorn was once duplicated by the Defenders' foe Casiolena, who created a false Valkyrie to ride her ersatz Aragorn. Although Aragorn was not always friendly to Valkyrie's teammates, he once permitted Clea to ride him. When the Defenders relocated to the Aerie base of their new member Angel (Warren Worthington), Aragorn went with them. Eventually, Valkyrie seemingly perished in battle with her one-time teammate Moondragon, possessed by the Dragon of the Moon.

However, Valkyrie eventually returned to life and Aragorn sought her out, reclaiming its role as her steed. Valkyrie was now based primarily in Asgard where Aragorn was welcome amongst the Valkyries' other winged horses. After the mortal Samantha Parrington was transformed into a near-replica of Brunnhilde as the new Valkyrie, Brunnhilde gifted her with Aragorn as she joined a reformed team of Defenders. Aragorn aided Parrington and the other Defenders in battles against the likes of Attuma, the Wayfinder and the Headmen. When the Defenders' own Dr. Strange, Silver Surfer, Sub-Mariner and Hulk (Bruce Banner) became corrupted by their foe Yandroth, Aragorn aided Parrington and the other Defenders against them. Recently, Parrington joined the Lady Liberators, a team formed by She-Hulk to combat the mysterious red Hulk. Aragorn continues to serve as Parrington's steed in her ongoing adventures.

*NOTE: The Vatican's Black Knight also possessed a flying horse named Aragorn, which was ultimately slain by the insane Kraven the Hunter (Alyosha Kravinoff).*

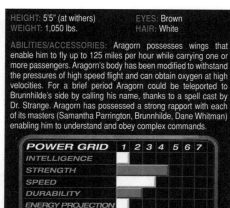

**HEIGHT:** 5'5" (at withers)      **EYES:** Brown
**WEIGHT:** 1,050 lbs.      **HAIR:** White

**ABILITIES/ACCESSORIES:** Aragorn possesses wings that enable him to fly up to 125 miles per hour while carrying one or more passengers. Aragorn's body has been modified to withstand the pressures of high speed flight and can obtain oxygen at high velocities. For a brief period Aragorn could be teleported to Brunnhilde's side by calling his name, thanks to a spell cast by Dr. Strange. Aragorn has possessed a strong rapport with each of its masters (Samantha Parrington, Brunnhilde, Dane Whitman) enabling him to understand and obey complex commands.

| POWER GRID | 1 | 2 | 3 | 4 | 5 | 6 | 7 |
|---|---|---|---|---|---|---|---|
| INTELLIGENCE | | | | | | | |
| STRENGTH | | | | | | | |
| SPEED | | | | | | | |
| DURABILITY | | | | | | | |
| ENERGY PROJECTION | | | | | | | |
| FIGHTING SKILLS | | | | | | | |

# BRIGHTWIND

**HISTORY:** One of the sacred winged horses of the Asgardian Valkyrior (who transported the valorous dead to Valhalla), Brightwind was rescued from a group of hunters and named by the New Mutants' Mirage (Danielle Moonstar) during a trip to Asgard. Quickly developing a bond with Danielle, Brightwind chose her as its rider, bestowing the Valkyrie honor and abilities upon her. After riding Brightwind into battle against Loki, the Valkyrior made Danielle one of their own and allowed her to bring Brightwind to Earth when she returned. Brightwind often carried Danielle into battle as well as coming to her aid on a few occasions, such as when he saved Danielle from a group of thugs by attacking them and led then-Xavier's School headmaster Magneto (Max Eisenhardt) back to their location. The psychic bond shared by horse and rider made Danielle and Brightwind as close as family, with Moonstar often confiding her problems to Brightwind, whose mood and even appearance reflected Moonstar's own emotions.

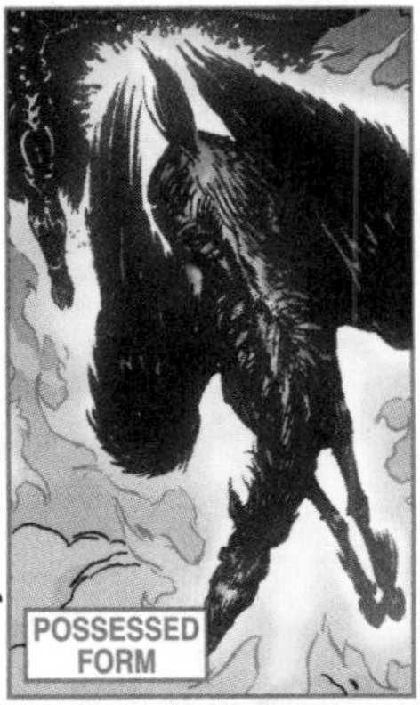

POSSESSED FORM

After Danielle received a brief power increase via the High Evolutionary's machines, Danielle took Brightwind into the air and tested her newfound power, creating a solid form of a female horse from Brightwind's mind, causing a distracted Brightwind to drop her. Brightwind returned soon after, however, once again aiding Moonstar by scaring off a police officer. Shortly thereafter, when the New Mutants merged their group with the X-Factor trainees known as the X-Terminators, Brightwind accompanied Mirage to X-Factor's sentient Ship. Both Brightwind and Mirage were soon attacked by the Asgardian death goddess Hela, who cast a spell that allowed a spirit to possess Dani's form, altering Brightwind as well due to their psychic bond. Hela then summoned them to Asgard as part of her attempt to take over the realm during the All-Father Odin's slumber, but Hela was defeated and both Brightwind and Mirage were returned to their previous states. While the other New Mutants returned to Earth, Mirage opted to stay with Brightwind in Asgard to make up for the damage she had unwillingly caused.

Upon their return to Earth, Moonstar posed as a villain within Reignfire's Mutant Liberation Front (MLF), her sudden personality change physically transforming Brightwind. Moonstar renamed him Darkwind, and he accompanied her during her early missions with the MLF. Once Reignfire discovered that Moonstar was secretly working against the MLF, he attacked her and as she ran towards Darkwind, Reignfire incinerated the winged horse before Moonstar's horrified eyes. As Darkwind died, Moonstar ended her bond with the horse, allowing Brightwind's spirit to return home to Asgard.

*Art by Bret Blevins*

**REAL NAME:** Brightwind
**ALIASES:** Darkwind
**IDENTITY:** The general public of Earth was unaware of Brightwind's existence
**OCCUPATION:** Sacred mount of the Valkyrior
**CITIZENSHIP:** Property of Danielle Moonstar
**PLACE OF BIRTH:** Asgard
**KNOWN RELATIVES:** None
**GROUP AFFILIATION:** None
**EDUCATION:** No formal education
**FIRST APPEARANCE:** New Mutants Special Edition #1 (1985)

**HEIGHT:** 5'4" (at withers)
**WEIGHT:** 1300 lbs.
**EYES:** Red
**HAIR:** White; Red (transformed by Hela); Black (as Darkwind)

**ABILITIES/ACCESSORIES:** Brightwind had feathered wings capable of flight. The maximum altitude that he could fly at was undetermined. Due to his Asgardian nature, Brightwind also possessed greater physical attributes than that of an ordinary Earth horse. His stamina and durability allowed him to fly for nearly 24 hours without rest, as well as withstand the extreme cold and pressure of flying at high altitudes. His strength was also higher than a typical Earth horse, allowing him to carry numerous passengers at once without tiring.

Brightwind shared a mystical, empathic, and psychic bond with Danielle Moonstar, often sharing her emotional states and losing consciousness whenever she did. If her emotions changed dramatically enough, Brightwind's body would physically alter itself to reflect her emotions. For example, when Mirage was possessed, Brightwind transformed into a decaying, skeletal form surrounded by hellfire, which it could project during times of extreme anger. As Darkwind, he was dark-haired and had demonic, bat-like wings.

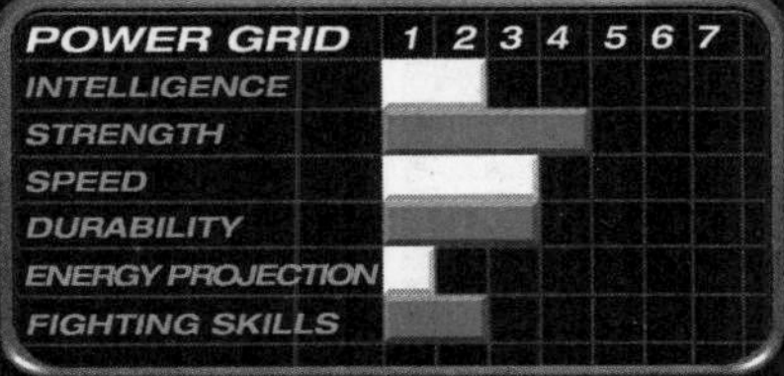
POWER GRID
1 2 3 4 5 6 7
INTELLIGENCE
STRENGTH
SPEED
DURABILITY
ENERGY PROJECTION
FIGHTING SKILLS

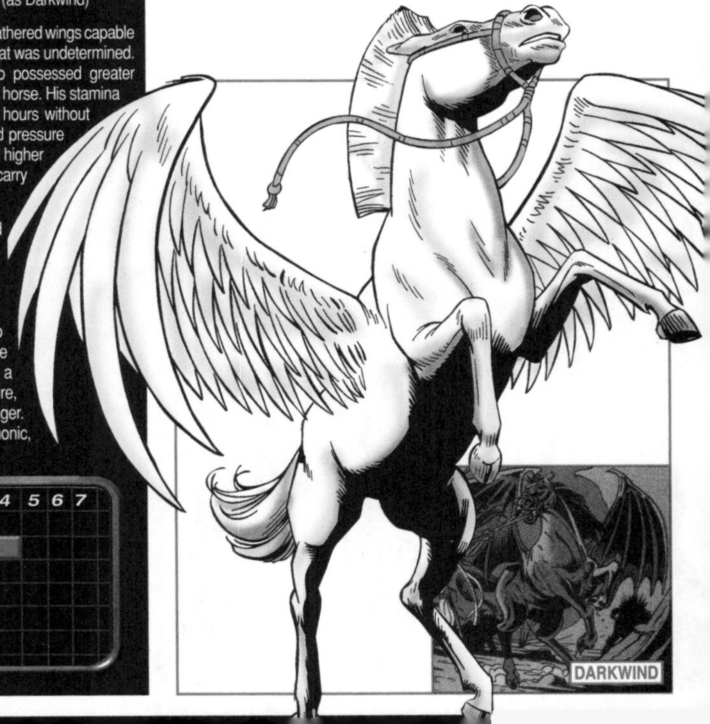

DARKWIND

# CERBERUS

**REAL NAME:** Cerberus
**ALIASES:** Kerberos, Hellhound
**IDENTITY:** No dual identity
**OCCUPATION:** Guardian of Hades
**CITIZENSHIP:** Property of Pluto
**PLACE OF BIRTH:** Arima
**KNOWN RELATIVES:** Typhon (father), Echidna (mother), Lernaean Hydra, Nemean Lion, Ladon, Orthrus (brothers, deceased), Chimera (brother), Sphinx (sister, deceased), Gaea, Tartarus (grandparents), others
**GROUP AFFILIATION:** None
**EDUCATION:** None
**FIRST APPEARANCE:** Thor #130 (1966)

**HISTORY:** Cerberus is the spawn of Typhon the Titan and Echidna, one of many monsters born into the world to punish Zeus' offspring for having vanquished Typhon in the early days of the Olympian gods. After the fall of the Titans, Cerberus was claimed by the death god Pluto and taken to his realm Hades to serve as his watchdog. Cerberus was charged with guarding the portals to Hades to prevent the dead from escaping and the unwelcome living from entering. However, for all of Cerberus' might, he was tricked by the hero Orpheus, whose music mesmerized the hellhound allowing Orpheus to safely pass into Hades. Later, as one of the fabled twelve labors assigned by his cousin Eurystheus, the demigod Hercules (Heracles) overcame Cerberus in battle, then delivered the dog to Eurystheus; terrified by Cerberus, Eurystheus ran and hid. Cerberus was later returned to Hades.

In recent times, Hercules was tricked into accepting rule of Hades by Pluto; the Asgardian god Thor came to Hercules' rescue, defeating Cerberus to enter Hades. Later, when Pluto conspired with Ares to wed Hercules to the Amazon queen Hippolyta, Cerberus was sent to Los Angeles to capture Hercules but was bested by Hercules and the Ghost Rider (Johnny Blaze). When Zeus turned against Hercules' mortal allies the Avengers, he had them sent to Hades to be punished by Pluto. Cerberus helped bring the Avengers to his master, but the Sub-Mariner eluded him and engineered his fellow Avengers' escape; the Avengers eventually overcame Cerberus and escaped Hades. Under unrevealed circumstances, Cerberus was bound to an arrow called the Havoc-Bringer, which came into the possession of the human Albert McGee; when McGee cut himself on the arrow, his blood released Cerberus who took over McGee's body. Hercules ultimately drove Cerberus from McGee and back into the arrow.

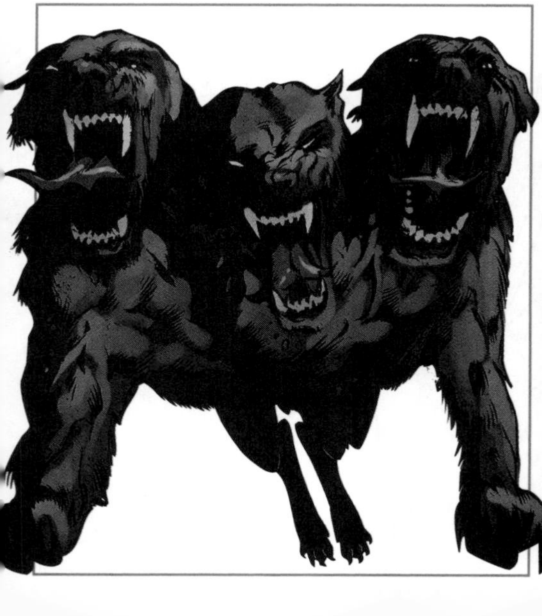

Cerberus was later made a pawn of the Asgardian death goddess Hela, who captured him from Pluto to teach her fellow death god a lesson. Cerberus briefly guarded Hela's realm Niffleheim and fought with Clea, Dr. Stephen Strange and the Scarlet Witch when they sought an audience with Hela. Returned to Hades, Cerberus was chosen by the wicked light elf the Flame (Hrinmeer) as his steed when he agreed to assist Pluto and Loki in their plot to slay both Thor and Hercules. The Flame and Cerberus battled Thor and paralyzed him with poison from Cerberus' fangs, but when the Flame menaced Loki's wife Sigyn, Loki turned against him and helped revive Thor, who quickly bested the Flame and Cerberus. When Pluto and Hippolyta captured the heroine Caledonia and brought her to Hades, her friends Bounty, Franklin Richards, Marvel Girl (Valeria Richards) and the dog Puppy pursued her; Cerberus barred their way, aided by Hippolyta, Yellow-Crested Titans, Centaurs and Myrmidons, but the battle was called off when Pluto's wife Persephone intervened on the outsiders' behalf. When Hercules descended to Hades to visit the spirits of his dead wife and children, Cerberus attempted to bar his path, but Hercules swiftly beat him. Cerberus remains the guardian of Hades.

***NOTE:*** *Cerberus should not be confused with any of the creatures named in honor of him, including the coyote Kerberos, the wolf/dog pet of O.Z. Chase, the pets of Oliver Stroker, the Cerberus created by Dr. Zeus or the Cerberus robot built by Dr. Demonicus.*

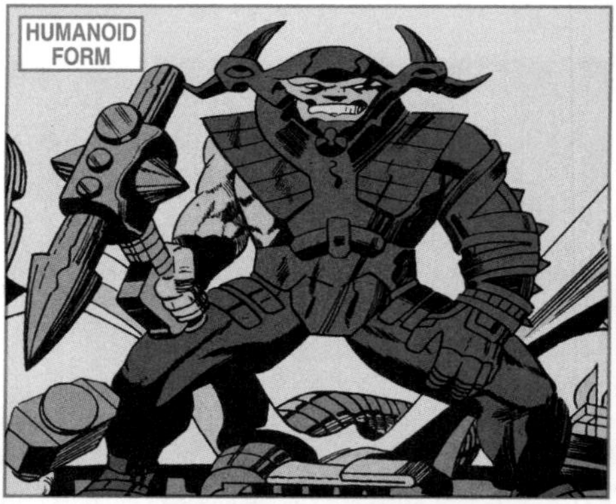
HUMANOID FORM

*Art by Jack Kirby*

**HEIGHT:** Variable
**WEIGHT:** Variable
**EYES:** Yellow (both)
**HAIR:** Brown

**ABILITIES/ACCESSORIES:** Cerberus can change between humanoid and canine forms. As a canine, Cerberus possesses three heads and sets of poisoned fangs and claws. As a humanoid, Cerberus has superhuman strength (lifting up to 80 tons) and durability, wears armor and carries a war hammer crafted from Adamantine. In each of his forms, Cerberus can alter his size and mass to become more than 30' tall.

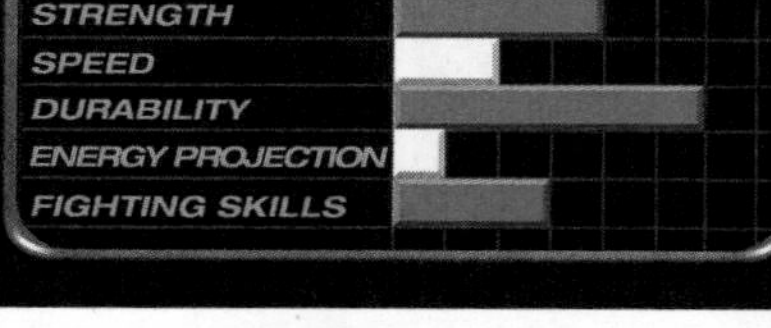
POWER GRID
1 2 3 4 5 6 7
INTELLIGENCE
STRENGTH
SPEED
DURABILITY
ENERGY PROJECTION
FIGHTING SKILLS

# COLLECTOR'S CREATURES

**HISTORY:** The Collector (Taneleer Tivan) is one of the Elders of the Universe, a handful of ancient and powerful extraterrestrials whose longevity stems in part from their obsessive devotion to certain pursuits. Tivan, specifically, is obsessed with collecting things, including a wide variety of living creatures procured from throughout the universe.

Tivan maintains zoos at various locations, and has even converted entire worlds into specimen habitats, or created artificial planets for that purpose — for instance, a Prison World the Collector built to house endangered alien races, until well-intentioned adventurers Aria and Wolverine (Logan/James Howlett) sabotaged that world's security system and unwittingly caused its subsequent consumption by the planet-eater Galactus, a disaster with relatively few survivors. Tivan also stores much of his collection in his vast personal interstellar spacecraft; though it has been wrecked repeatedly, the Collector always replaces it or rebuilds it. He can locate virtually anything using his cosmic viewer, shift targets from other time periods using his time probe, and beam acquisitions into his ship using teleportation technology. At least one of his spacecraft was specially modified for the long-term housing of ancient specimens, and its interior somehow preserved any living inhabitants for many years beyond their natural lifespan, but these beings would decay into dust within seconds if they left the ship. Most of that vessel's inhabitants were lost during the Collector's clash with three rebellious, monstrous new acquisitions: The Hulk (Bruce Banner), the Man-Thing (Ted Sallis) and the Glob (Joe Timms).

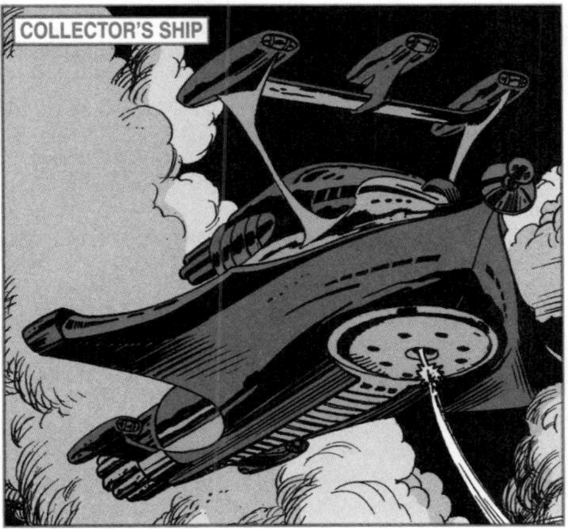
COLLECTOR'S SHIP
Art by John Buscema

The Collector's various headquarters usually include containment devices to restrain his collected captives, notably stasis tubes, which place their occupants in a state of suspended animation; seemingly conventional cages with bars and locks; transparent domed enclosures; various chains and manacles, notably "stasis-shackles," which incapacitate their occupants; assorted transparent display cases, some with interiors modified to simulate the natural environment of each case's inhabitant(s); aquarium tanks; and force fields. Some of the Collector's acquisitions become trained pets or loyal servants, and may then be allowed to wander his facilities freely; others might be mentally enslaved via Tivan's "obedience potion" and granted enough mobility to perform whatever tasks the Collector requires of them.

Tivan stores larger groups or entire populations of living beings within his starship by shrinking them to tiny size and housing them in his Vivarium, where a series of artificial miniature ecosystems duplicate each race's respective natural environments, complete with extensive flora and fauna. His miniature ecosystems are so detailed that some of his specimens don't even realize they are living in an artificial environment. The bacteria-spawned warrior race known as the Brethren were among the Vivarium's inhabitants until the Collector allowed them to break out as part of an elaborate plot against Earth; the Brethren slaughtered the inhabitants of multiple Vivarium ecosystems during their escape, though apparently their victims were all lesser acquisitions deemed expendable by the Collector.

The Collector's various facilities and spaceships have always contained many live creatures, such as giant birds, ape-like simians and small domesticated reptiles or mammals. Notable creatures in Tivan's collections over the years have included the following:

The **Bruruthian Paramecium Rex** is an unusually large and aggressive single-celled organism housed within the Collector's Vivarium. This extremely rare, adhesive-tentacled entity tried to consume the Collector and his longtime foes, the Avengers, when they entered the Vivarium at reduced size to investigate the Brethren's escape. Avengers member Quasar (Wendell Vaughn) drove off the creature with a quantum energy blast.

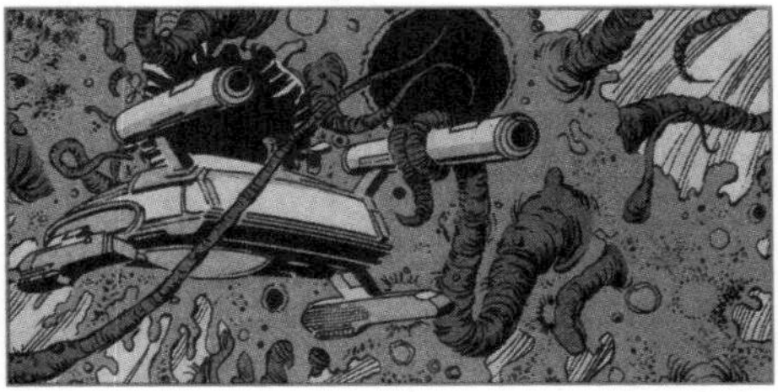
Art by Steve Epting

The rare **Jupiterian Sauro-Beast**, treated like a prize pet by the Collector, was a seemingly reptilian quadruped with clawed feet, a tail, and a snake-like neck and head. Slightly larger than a cat and sensitive to noise, it was actually a large species of insect; it therefore proved susceptible to the insect-controlling powers of the Wasp (Janet Van Dyne), who once compelled the Sauro-Beast to help her and her fellow Avengers escape their cells on the Collector's ship. As that ship was destroyed during the ensuing battle, the Sauro-Beast is presumed dead.

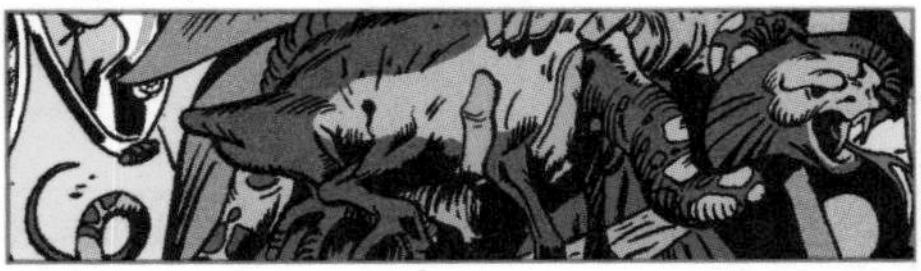
Art by John Buscema

The **Pearl of Great Price** or "Pearl" for short is a huge, oyster-like shellfish containing a proportionately huge pearl. Pearl is able to open and close its shell at will and can trap humanoids or other prey within its confines. Pearl can also sprout four legs for locomotion when rapid motion is required. Pearl battled Spider-Man (Peter Parker) when the Collector tried to capture that hero, but was restrained by Spider-Man's webbing.

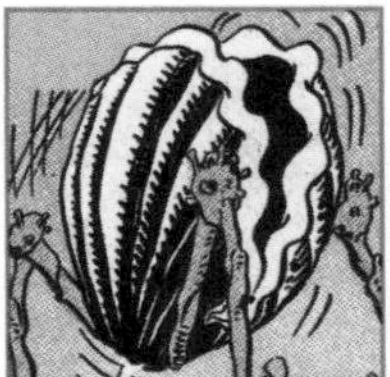
Art by Paul Neary

The Collector has acquired at least one **pterosaur** (winged reptile) of unrevealed origin (possible sources include Earth's prehistoric past, the hidden jungles of the Savage Land in Antarctica, or various alien worlds). Capable of flight via its wings and

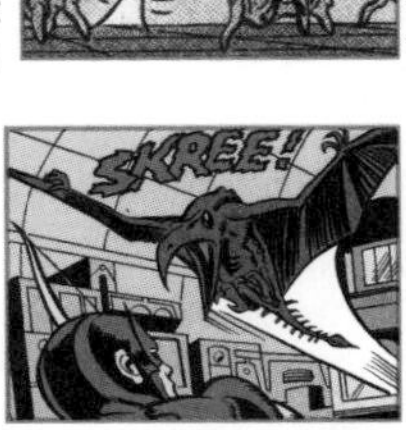
SKREEE!
Art by Dave Wenzel

housed in a transparent case on the Collector's ship, the pterosaur was released to hunt the Collector's foe Hawkeye (Clint Barton), but the archer subdued the creature by entangling its wings with a bola arrow.

Art by Paul Neary

**Snake Eyes** is a Xanthian Boulder Crusher, a cobra-like giant snake with a powerful hypnotic gaze that places its viewers in a suggestible trance. The Collector uses a mystical Kymellian flute to control the snake's actions, but even with the flute's aid he is still susceptible to the serpent's hypnotic gaze. To counteract this, Collector usually uses one of his Triplets, three highly hypnosis-resistant primates, as an intermediary through which he sees the snake while his own vision is blocked by the primate's hands. Without the flute's influence, Snake Eyes is uncontrollable and prone to destructive rampages; it escaped the Collector's ships during a battle with Spider-Man and Canadian super-team Alpha Flight, living in Earth's oceans until subdued by amphibious Alphan Marrina and Power Pack, who deposited it in the Arctic, where the freezing cold sent Snake Eyes into hibernation.

Art by Paul Neary

The **Triplets** are a trio of monkey-like simians, apparently siblings, named See-No-Evil, Hear-No-Evil and Speak-No-Evil. One constantly covers his eyes with his hands, the second covers his ears, and the third covers his mouth; this trio or similar creatures may have inspired visually similar recurring images of monkeys in Earth culture over the centuries. The Triplets are unusually resistant to hypnosis, and the Collector uses See-No-Evil to aid him in handling the giant hypnotic serpent Snake Eyes; more specifically, See-No-Evil will cover the Collector's eyes while the Collector apparently continues to see through the simian's eyes, directing the snake's actions. The Triplets will eventually fall into a trance, but usually slowly enough for the Collector to issue Snake Eyes' commands during the time available.

Art by Bob Brown

The Collector once unleashed a horde of large, bloodthirsty **vampire bats** while battling the Avengers at his Rutland, Vermont hideout. He produced the bats by loudly striking together a large pair of round stones, releasing sound waves that somehow transformed into thousands of fanged, vicious bats. While the bats were temporarily disoriented by an ultrasonic assault from Iron Man (Tony Stark), which muddled their sonar-based navigational abilities, they could only be dispelled by striking the stones together again. Penetrating the Collector's elaborate defensive devices, the Avengers' ally Mantis seized the stones and struck them together, causing the bats to vanish.

The **Venusian Retriever-Anemone**, like its Earthly aquatic counterpart the sea anemone, was a predatory creature that ensnared its prey in its many tentacles. The Venusian Retriever-Anemone was much larger, however, capable of ensnaring multiple full-sized humanoids simultaneously in its tentacles, which exude a powerful adhesive. The Collector's Retriever-Anemone had a "playful" tendency to ensnare visitors in its tentacles, and the Collector would discipline it with a "stun beam" forcing it to drop its prey. The Collector once rescued the captive Avengers from this creature in that fashion, though the Avengers' subsequent escape destroyed the Collector's ship, presumably destroying the Retriever-Anemone aboard it.

Art by John Buscema

The **Venusian Shock-Flies** are small, capsule-shaped insects, red with one white stripe. Capable of flight and able to rapidly eat through substances such as Spider-Man's webbing, they swarm their targets and release a powerful stunning energy charge, then drain energy from their victims. The Collector has kept a container of Shock-Flies on his ship and once used them to subdue Spider-Man.

Art by Paul Neary

The **Vultures of Nepenthe** are birds with electrically charged talons, hatched from tiny spherical capsules called "birth stones." The Collector planned to hatch four vultures at his Rutland base to attack the Avengers, but raucous Halloween partiers prevented this.

In addition to his many animals, the Collector has also captured various humans and other forms of sentient life over the years. His former subterranean base in Canada housed numerous giant monsters, many of them intelligent, until a jealous Mole Man's assault set them all loose. This facility's former inmates included Droom, Fin Fang Foom, Gargantus, Goom, Grogg, Groot, Grottu, Rommbu, Taboo, Tragg, Vandoom's Monster and others. Since then, the Collector's primary obsession in terms of Earth-based collecting has been the Avengers super-hero team, though they always escape. Avengers he has temporarily captured include Black Panther, Black Widow, Captain America (Rogers), Captain Marvel (Mar-Vell), Hawkeye (Barton), Hercules, Hulk, Invisible Woman, Iron Man (Stark), Jocasta, Mantis, Marrina, Moondragon, Quicksilver, Scarlet Witch, She-Hulk, Spider-Man (Parker), Thor, Two-Gun Kid, Vision (Shade), Wasp (Van Dyne), Wolverine (Logan/Howlett), Wonder Man and Yellowjacket (Pym). Other beings captured by the Collector include body-snatching alien adventurer Aria, the Beetle (Abe Jenkins), Captain Horatio Cutlass and his pirate crew (shrunken and trapped within a genuine ship in a bottle for 300 years), a Drakion Destructoid, an orange-skinned giant humanoid savage, Gamora, the Glob (Timms), ex-boxer Happy Hogan and his wife Pepper, the Man-Thing, Quasar (Phyla-Vell), a Robotoid (a giant robot from another solar system), the Starjammers, Storm (Ororo Munroe), Thundra and Vakyrie (Samantha Parrington), as well as various members of alien races such as the Brethren, the Dire Wraiths, the Plodex and the Skrulls (notably the warriors Jazinda and Lyja).

**FIRST APPEARANCE:** (Collector and his collection) Avengers #28 (1966); (Collector's Ship, Sauro-Beast, Retriever-Anemone) Avengers #51 (1968); (Bats, Vultures) Avengers #119 (1974); (Pterosaur) Avengers #174 (1978); (Pearl, Snake Eyes, Triplets, Shock-Flies) Marvel Team-Up Annual #7 (1984); (Vivarium) Avengers #334 (1991); (Bruruthian Paramecium Rex) Avengers #335 (1991).

**HISTORY:** Cosmo is a Golden Retriever/Labrador mix dog. How he came to the space station Knowhere, the apparent "last place in creation" housed inside the decapitated head of a Celestial at the edge of the universe, is unrevealed. Possibly he was once part of the Union of Soviet Socialist Republic (currently the Russian Rebublic's) space exploration program; if so then the same unrevealed process that gave Cosmo psionic powers, heightened intelligence, and the ability to talk also lengthened his lifespan as well. At some point after arriving on Knowhere, Cosmo became its chief of security, using his powers as needed to help keep order among the many visitors coming to Knowhere to study the end of the universe from a safe place.

When the Luminals, the super-powered global protectors of the planet Xarth Three, secretly brought their archenemy, the gigantic mystic-powered Abyss, to Knowhere to cast him out into the edge of the universe to finally be rid of him, they instead unleashed terror on Knowhere. Imprisoned in a coffin-like box, Abyss managed to free just enough of himself to begin taking over the minds of Knowhere's citizens. Tracking Abyss' energy readings to the Xarthian sector (though not yet aware who was causing them), Cosmo confronted the head Luminal, Cynosure, over what was inside the box, but Cynosure arrogantly denied anything wrong. Unable to legally search the sector on suspicion alone, Cosmo left Cynosure with a stern warning that further trouble would get them kicked off Knowhere. When Abyss caused deadly mass hallucinations and turned some of the citizens into zombie-like "meat puppets" as his defenders, Cosmo ordered an emergency lockdown and got everyone he could to safety inside a dimensional envelope housed within a tesseracted

storage crystal on Cosmo's collar. Searching again for the cause of the hauntings, Cosmo instead found the recently arrived Nova (Richard Rider) and the Xandarian Worldmind, whose mission to find a means of freeing the Kree Empire of a Phalanx invasion had landed them there. Cosmo informed Nova of the killings, giving the Worldmind enough

**REAL NAME:** Cosmo
**ALIASES:** None
**IDENTITY:** No dual identity
**OCCUPATION:** Chief of security on Knowhere
**CITIZENSHIP:** Knowhere
**PLACE OF BIRTH:** Unrevealed, possibly Russia
**KNOWN RELATIVES:** None
**GROUP AFFILIATION:** Knowhere's security forces
**EDUCATION:** Unrevealed
**FIRST APPEARANCE:** Nova #8 (2008)

information to inform Cosmo of Abyss' existence. Now with a main suspect, Cosmo and Nova entered the Xarthian sector to find Abyss, only to realize Abyss had turned the Luminals into his zombie puppets. Cosmo fought off the zombies long enough for Nova to repair Abyss' prison, containing him once more and allowing Knowhere to return to normal. In gratitude, Cosmo used Knowhere's main teleportation center, the Continuum Cortex, to plot a course to the planet Kvch, long-lost homeworld of both the Phalanx and their creators, the Technarch. In return, Nova left Cosmo with a parting gift of a chewy bone, which Cosmo gleefully accepted.

Later, when Star-Lord (Peter Quill) formed a new Guardians of the Galaxy team, Cosmo allowed them to make their base on Knowhere, allowing them access to the Core Continuum's teleportation facilities. Cosmo also allowed a group of pacifist Skrulls, followers of the martyr Princess Anelle, to use Knowhere as a destination to escape the militaristic jihad the Skrull government was mounting. To keep from betraying them, Cosmo had the Skrulls wipe his mind after each run through the Cortex, so he could truly say he knew nothing about them. However, when an agent of the Skrull jihad found the railroad and tried to shut it down he succeeded only in damaging the Cortex and leaving the bodies of some dead Skrulls, officially alerting Knowhere's citizens to their presence. When Knowhere's Administrative Council began investigating the disruptions the Guardian's presence on the station brought, Cosmo was given no choice but to temporarily confine them to quarters until things with the alleged Skrull invasion were settled. While Cosmo went to have his memory restored, Guardians member Drax the Destroyer used brain synapse disruptor charges to temporarily "kill" everyone on board Knowhere to flush out the Skrulls (since Skrulls revert to their true form after dying). Cosmo was forced to defend the pacifist Skrulls against the Guardians and a new team of Luminals before he was able to reveal the truth to them. While sympathetic to the Guardians and their goals, Cosmo's first job will always be to defend Knowhere, even against those he considers friends. Cosmo and the Guardians soon found themselves drawn into a war between the Kree Empire and the Shi'ar Imperium, whose superweapons threated to destroy the already weakened fabric of space. Cosmo aided Mantis and Moondragon (Heather Douglas) in coordinating their unsuccessful efforts to convince both sides to stop the so-called " war of kings", but when both sub-teams inadvertently allowed the Shi'ar Imperial Guard and Kree rulers the Inhumans onto Knowhere, Cosmo was forced to fight both invading teams to defend his home.

**HEIGHT:** 23" (at withers) **EYES:** Brown
**WEIGHT:** 70 lbs. **FUR:** Golden-yellow

**ABILITIES/ACCESSORIES:** Cosmo has psionic abilities, including both telepathy and telekinetic powers. While the upper limits of these abilities are unrevealed, he can use his telepathy to read minds, even eavesdropping on conversations between Nova and the Worldmind when it was housed in Nova's head. Cosmo can telekinetically throw several people across a room at once, even stunning them when needed. He can create shields wide enough to block a corridor and strong enough to deflect energy blasts. In addition to having the heightened senses of a normal dog, Cosmo has access to all of Knowhere's technology and information resources when he needs it.

| POWER GRID | 1 | 2 | 3 | 4 | 5 | 6 | 7 |
|---|---|---|---|---|---|---|---|
| INTELLIGENCE | | | | | | | |
| STRENGTH | | | | | | | |
| SPEED | | | | | | | |
| DURABILITY | | | | | | | |
| ENERGY PROJECTION | | | | | | | |
| FIGHTING SKILLS | | | | | | | |

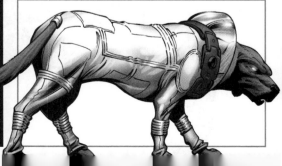

# DEVIL DINOSAUR

REAL NAME: Devil
ALIASES: "Devil-Beast," "Red Devil"
IDENTITY: No dual identity
OCCUPATION: Hunter
CITIZENSHIP: Inapplicable
PLACE OF BIRTH: Valley of Flame, Earth-78411
KNOWN RELATIVES: Unidentified mother (deceased), two unidentified siblings (both deceased), Moon-Boy (adopted brother)
GROUP AFFILIATION: Partner of Moon-Boy; formerly Tibolt Circus, Fallen Angels
EDUCATION: None
FIRST APPEARANCE: Devil Dinosaur #1 (1978)

HISTORY: In Reality-78411 on what other timelines would consider 21st century Earth, primitive hominids ("Dawn-Men") share the planet with a variety of dinosaurs. In the Valley of Flame, two mutants were born to two very different species. One was a Small-Folk child, a peaceful hominid tribe; deeply inquisitive, his fellows dubbed him Moon-Boy. The second, possessing heightened intelligence and durability, belonged to the Devil Beasts, a Tyrannosaur-like species. The Devil Beast child, his mother and two of his siblings were lured into a pit trap by the Killer-Folk tribe; the rest of his family was slain, but the child fought back. Before a minor volcanic eruption scared them away, the Killer-Folk tried to burn the child, the intense heat triggering a mutative pigment change that turned him red. Having witnessed the end of the assault, Moon-Boy helped the child to water to soothe his wounds, and found him fruit to eat, dubbing him Devil because of his unique appearance. When an earth tremor forced the pair to flee, Moon-Boy instinctively jumped on Devil's back as he passed, riding him to safety. Insisting they were now brothers as they had saved one another's lives, Moon-Boy took Devil back to the Small-Folk, but they fled in terror, and Moon-Boy became an outcast. Growing swiftly, Devil became the valley's dominant predator; he even scouted the valley, learning which natural features might prove useful against potential future foes. He slew Killer-Folk on sight, so when Seven-Scars seized control of that tribe, he decided to eliminate the "Devil-Beast," luring him into a pit

full of sharpened stakes, and when that failed, triggering an avalanche that buried him and trapped Moon-Boy. Believing their tormentor dead, the Killer-Folk planned to sacrifice Moon-Boy to the Long-Legs (a giant tarantula). However, Devil survived and used a burning branch to set alight the grass around the Killer-Folk, trapping them between the fire and the Long-Legs, then rescued Moon-Boy and carried him to safety. A short while later Devil battled one of the Giant-Folk, a hominid nearly Devil's own size, who was hunting for his wayward child Ruka. Devil lured him into a bog, but when Moon-Boy asked him to show mercy, Devil pulled the giant free before he drowned in the mud. Reunited with his child, the giant left in peace.

A short while later a spaceship landed, discharging hostile extraterrestrial robots ("Sky Demons"). Having moved close to the landing ship to investigate, Devil and Moon-Boy were attacked, and Moon-Boy was taken captive. As the robots rounded up both dinosaurs and hominids for chemical processing, two Hill-Folk tribe survivors, Stone-Hand and White-Hair, helped Devil destroy one of the robots, earning his friendship. Realizing the robots were too strong for a frontal assault, Devil headed for the Tower of Death, home of the valley's giant ants. En route he destroyed another pursuing robot by luring it over a natural geyser, then kicking a boulder into the geyser, triggering a massive water spout that shorted its energy pack. Judging Devil a threat, further robots were dispatched to destroy him with a "land crusher," but Devil and his allies took refuge inside the ant's tower, fighting off the voracious horde until the crusher brought the tower down. Forgetting the intruders, thousands of enraged ants swarmed the robots' ship, destroying it and all the robots. Only part of the ship's computer, which the locals decided was a Demon Tree, survived; with its old programming redundant, it offered sanctuary to Stone-Hand, White-Hair and a third hominid, the female Eev of the Forest Folk, then imprisoned them inside a force field for their own protection. Having reunited with Moon-Boy, Devil smashed through the force field, overloading the damaged computer, though not before White-Hair died from radiation poisoning inadvertently caused by the computer.

Moon-Boy and Devil found the Small-Folk hiding from Dino-Riders who rode dinosaurs broken to their will. Wanting to make Devil into a steed, the Riders overpowered him, but Moon-Boy rallied the Small-Folk to attack them and free Devil. Soon afterwards, Moon-Boy and Devil investigated a region of deep pits, ignoring the crone-like Hag of the Pits' warnings. Stumbling into one of the pits, Devil triggered an interdimensional portal, and appeared in Earth-616's Nevada. He wandered into Zuma City, where the terrified locals attacked him; back on Earth-78411 the Hag and her son helped Moon-Boy reopen the portal, allowing Devil to return home. News reports of Devil's visit eventually led to a movie being made about him on Earth-616, coincidentally titled "Devil Dinosaur," presumably naming him after his red hide and savage nature. Devil briefly revisited 616 again when he and Moon-Boy were transported there for a few seconds by Dr. Yesterday. A short while later Devil battled an alien Skrull shapeshifter, and the Small Folk offered to reunite Moon-Boy with his mother Kirba and provide him a mate, but asked him to choose between the tribe and Devil; he chose his friend. Soon after, Devil watched over his friend when Moon-Boy came down with a serious fever.

On Earth-616 the kaiju (giant monster) Godzilla was captured by SHIELD (Supreme Headquarters, International Espionage, Law-Enforcement Division) after being shrunk in size using Pym-particles. SHIELD tried using the Fantastic Four's time machine to send the Kaiju into the prehistoric past, but Godzilla's irradiated form interfered, and he was instead transported to Earth-78411. Godzilla appeared the Valley of Flame, where, after an initial misunderstanding, he assisted Moon-Boy and Devil in battling the invading Lizard Riders and their tame dinosaurs, luring them into the Pits, transporting them

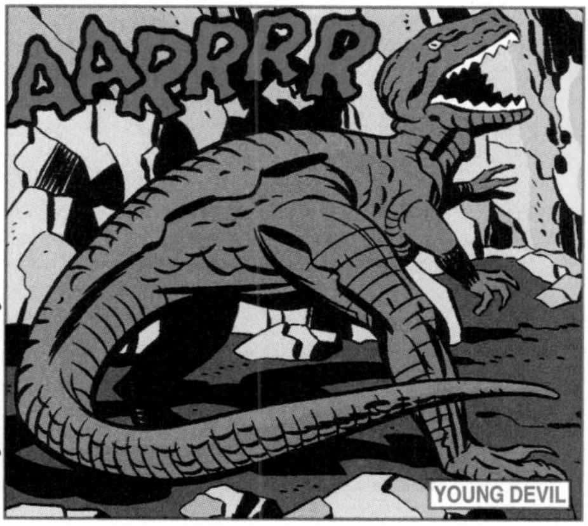
AARRRR
YOUNG DEVIL

Art by Jack Kirby

elsewhere, before the Pit energies transported him home. When two immature Celestials, Gamiel and Devron, observed the valley, Devron viewed Devil as a wonderful exception to the natural order, but Gamiel felt he was a disruptive aberration, and transported Earth-616's Hulk (Bruce Banner) to the valley to destroy him. The Killer-Folk convinced the Hulk to attack Devil, but after defeating the dinosaur, he was convinced by Moon-Boy's pleas to spare his opponent. Discovering what his fellow Celestial had done, Devron remotely evolved Devil to level the playing field, but the two Celestials soon realized the mutagenic and gamma radiations being released by the two behemoths battling would draw disapproving attention from senior Celestials, and transported the pair into a cell on board their ship. Unhappy with being caged, the pair immediately broke free and rampaged, until elder Celestials arrived, devolving Devil back to his normal state and returning both monsters to their respective homes.

On Earth-616, the extraterrestrial Ariel had been secretly charged by the people of her homeworld, Coconut Grove, to procure mutants for examination, and joined the Fallen Angels, a gang consisting of several mutants, a human cyborg (Gomi), and two cyborg lobsters (Bill and Don, the latter a mutant too). Learning of Devil via his movie and locating his reality, Ariel took the Fallen Angels there to recruit him. Taking a liking to the young humans, Devil and Moon-Boy returned to Earth-616 with them, but with a giant dinosaur and tiny lobsters on the same team, tragedy was inevitable, and Devil accidentally stepped on Don, crushing him; a guilt-stricken Devil grieved for his teammate. Later visiting Coconut Grove, the Angels were taken prisoner, but escaped and returned to Earth. Devil remained with the Angels for a while, until the Conservator took Devil to his private wildlife reverse, Castillo; when the Conservator captured Wolverine (Logan/James Howlett), Ka-Zar (Kevin Plunder), Shanna, and Namor, Ka-Zar's ally Zabu asked Devil to free them, and afterwards Moon-Boy had Ariel return them home. Devil returned to Earth-616 when the extradimensional Technet accidentally transported him to the lighthouse base of the British Excalibur team, but was soon returned home. When Wolverine and the Beast (Hank McCoy) arrived on Earth-78411 pursuing a "time arrow" created by Kang the Conqueror, Devil and Moon-Boy provided assistance in destroying the device. Later the sorceress Jennifer Kale, trying to send Howard the Duck back to his native reality, accidentally sent him to Earth-78411 instead. Mistaking him for lunch, Devil and Moon-Boy pursued him back through Kale's portal to Earth-616, where they battled Johnny Blaze and police task force Code: Blue before the Ghost Rider (Danny Ketch) subdued them.

Taken into custody, the pair was studied by scientist Dr. Thomas Maries; ethical treatment and comfortable quarters turned them into contented visitors, but eventually the Ringmaster (Maynard Tiboldt) gained a court order granting their freedom and hypnotized them into joining his Circus. Their performances provided a diversion for Circus members to burgle with impunity, until Spider-Man (Peter Parker) exposed the ruse and freed the pair. On his suggestion, Dr. Maries transported Devil and Moon-Boy to the Savage Land; the scientist later wrote an article detailing the history of the two. Having retained their mutant abilities following the mass mutant depowering on M-Day, Devil and Moon-Boy joined Ka-Zar, Shanna, Zabu, Stegron and the Savage Land Mutates in defending their new home from the Roxxon company's deprivations. Through unrevealed means, perhaps spontaneous gender change and parthogenesis, Devil laid a clutch of eggs, jealously defending them even from Moon-Boy. Meanwhile SHIELD (now Strategic Hazard Intervention Espionage Logistics Directorate) scientists concluded Moon-Boy's DNA might provide cures for numerous illnesses, and sent the Heroes for Hire and mercenary Paladin to procure him. Devil tried to defend his old friend, but forced to choose between his eggs and Moon-Boy, with great heartache he reluctantly chose the former. The loss of his friend plunged Devil into a life threatening depression, leading Stegron to try and rescue Moon-Boy from SHIELD; though he failed, the hero Reptil learned the cause of Stegron's mission, and smuggled Moon-Boy back to his friend.

***NOTE:*** *Roxxon's subsidiary the Nth Command once sought to siphon fossil fuels from Earth-78411, but were stopped by Quasar (Wendell Vaughn) and the Thing (Ben Grimm), who did not encounter Devil or Moon-Boy. Accounts from one of those visitors may well have influenced the Devil Dinosaur movie's plot. The Thing was present however when a mutated kaiju destroyed the Devil robot being used to film the Devil Dinosaur movie. The terrorist SILENT organization was allegedly run by a clone of Devil before he was slain by the Nextwave Squad.*

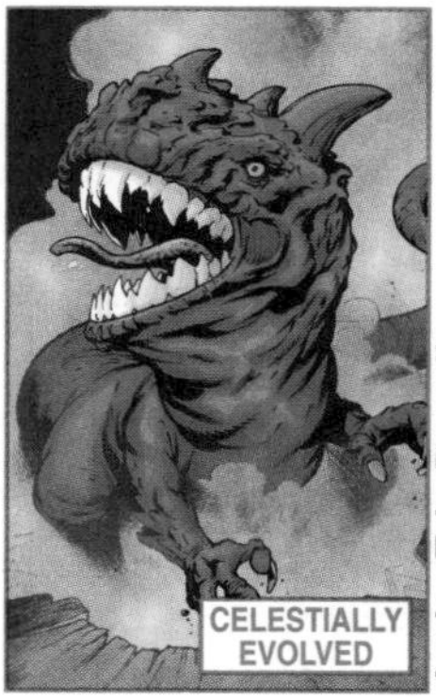
CELESTIALLY EVOLVED

Art by Eric Powell

**HEIGHT:** 20' **EYES:** Red
**WEIGHT:** 3 tons **HAIR:** None

**ABILITIES/ACCESSORIES:** Devil is a mutant member of a species resembling Tyrannosaurus rex. Standing a little over 20 feet tall, his tail adds an additional 20 feet to his overall length. His hide is exceptionally thick and his bones unusually dense, rendering him bulletproof and resistant to impact and heat. His jaws are full of razor-sharp teeth and can lift around 25 tons, while his legs are strong enough for him to leap over 20 feet from a standing start; his arms, though weaker, are still far stronger than a human's. He can track and identify people by their scent. Though he prefers meat, he is omnivorous. Devil's greatest power, however, is his brain. He is capable of careful, at-least human level, reasoning, and is a master tactician, planning ahead and using knowledge of his home terrain to lure opponents into traps. He fights using not only his deadly jaws, but also his tail and legs, protecting his entire perimeter in battle. He proved immune to the mind-disruption powers of the Technet's Scatterbrain.

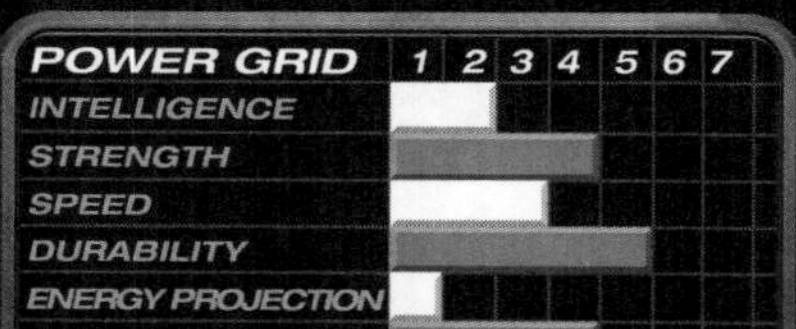
POWER GRID
1 2 3 4 5 6 7
INTELLIGENCE
STRENGTH
SPEED
DURABILITY
ENERGY PROJECTION
FIGHTING SKILLS

**REAL NAME:** Garm
**ALIASES:** The Doom of Tyr, Fiercest of Hounds, Gorm, the Hel-Hound, Hound of Hela
**IDENTITY:** No dual identity
**OCCUPATION:** Guardian of the entrance to Hel, servant of Hela
**CITIZENSHIP:** Hel, Asgard
**PLACE OF BIRTH:** Unrevealed
**KNOWN RELATIVES:** None
**GROUP AFFILIATION:** None
**EDUCATION:** Unrevealed
**FIRST APPEARANCE:** Thor Annual #5 (1976)

**HISTORY:** Garm is an enormous wolf who guards the entrance to Hel, the Asgardian land of the dead, in the service of the death goddess Hela. Sometimes chained to the entrance itself, he permits anyone to enter but is covered in the blood of the many who have tried to escape. It is prophesied that at Ragnarok he will break his chains and devour Tyr, the god of war, but be killed himself as well.

The Asgardian warrior Greyval Grimson visited Hel during a quest to retrieve the lost Raven Banner, a mystical item that ensured victory in battle. He met Garm at Hel's entrance, and was permitted to pass. Later, after Loki arranged for Balder the Brave to be struck by an enchanted arrow, Garm witnessed Balder's descent into Hel. But though Balder's soul had entered the land of the dead, his body was kept alive by Odin's magic. Against impossible odds, Balder fought his way past Garm and legions of Hela's forces and returned to the land of the living.

When Hela stole many mortal souls from Earth, Thor led an expedition to retrieve them and return them to their rightful bodies. Thor, along with Balder, the Einherjar (mortal heroes who had earned a place in Valhalla), and Skurge the Executioner, met Garm at Hel's entrance. Garm permitted them to cross into the land of the dead but warned he would not be so kind should he see them again. After Thor defeated Hela and retrieved

the souls, Garm sought to prevent the heroes' escape. Thor knocked Garm unconscious with a blow from his hammer, Mjolnir, and led his victorious forces back to Asgard. Soon after, Thor employed the Destroyer armor and returned to force Hela to lift a curse she had placed on him. Garm defended his mistress but was easily struck down by the powerful Destroyer, and Hela acquiesced to Thor's demands.

Hela later used a spell to control the Asgardian Valkyrior as part of her plan to conquer Asgard. This brought her into conflict with the New Mutants (Boom Boom/Tabith Smith, Cannonball/Sam Guthrie, Mirage/Dani Moonstar, Rictor, Sunspot, the Technarch Warlock, and Wolfsbane/Rahne Sinclair), who found the spell had affected one of their own. As Garm watched the Valkyries lead several captured New Mutants into Hel, his appearance unnerved Wolfsbane, who perceived him as a dark reflection of her own nature. In a subsequent plot, Hela tried to control the Destroyer armor only to have it possessed by the spirit of the departed Asgardian goddess Lorelei. Using the armor, Lorelei imprisoned Hela within a crystal and encased Garm in solid rock when he tried to defend her. When Sif and Balder arrived in Hel searching for the recently-exiled Thor, Garm informed them of what had transpired and directed them to a sword that could free Hela. Sif and Balder prevailed when the Destroyer fell into a pit of great beasts, freeing Hela and Garm from their imprisonment. Hela later instilled the Destroyer with the consciousness of both Garm and the artificial Donald Blake construct and sent the armor to Earth to gain vengeance on Thor. With Garm's mind dominant, the Destroyer fought both Thor and Thunderstrike, getting the better of them until the Donald Blake construct's will asserted itself, causing the Destroyer armor to stall momentarily. Thor and Thunderstrike took advantage and struck the Destroyer down, sending Garm's consciousness back to Hel. Later, when Kurse temporarily took control of Hel, he defeated Garm before taking a legion of undead monsters to the surface to search for his enemy, Malekith. Garm played a small role in Kurse's downfall, aiding the lady Sif in alerting Hela, who recalled her minions back to the underworld. At the conclusion of this crisis, Hela coerced Thor into becoming her servant, leading Balder and the Hulk (Bruce Banner) to Hel to rescue him. Garm fought against Balder while the Hulk and Thor battled across Hel. Hela was eventually convinced to release Thor from her service, and he and the Hulk knocked Garm unconscious to aid Balder before departing. Garm later perished alongside all of Asgard during Ragnarok. His status since the return of the Asgardians remains unclear.

**HEIGHT:** 40' (at the shoulder)
**WEIGHT:** 8000 lbs.
**EYES:** Solid yellow (no visible iris or pupil)
**HAIR:** Brown

**ABILITIES/ACCESSORIES:** Garm is of immense stature and possesses great strength. He has powerful jaws full of sharp teeth and an extremely acute olfactory sense, allowing him to perceive the presence of beings invisible to the eye. Though his form is that of a wolf, he possesses human level intelligence. He is completely loyal to Hela and will gladly rip to pieces anyone who tries to escape the land of the dead. He has sometimes been chained to the entrance of Hel, thereby limiting his mobility, but has at other times stood unchained beside Hela herself.

| POWER GRID | 1 | 2 | 3 | 4 | 5 | 6 | 7 |
|---|---|---|---|---|---|---|---|
| INTELLIGENCE | | | | | | | |
| STRENGTH | | | | | | | |
| SPEED | | | | | | | |
| DURABILITY | | | | | | | |
| ENERGY PROJECTION | | | | | | | |
| FIGHTING SKILLS | | | | | | | |

**HISTORY:** Giganto, though often referred to as a singular creature, is actually a race of whale-like leviathans lurking deep in the ocean. Theories about the race's origins range from them being Deviant mutates, products of Atlantean sorcery or evolutionary offshoots of the order Cetacea.

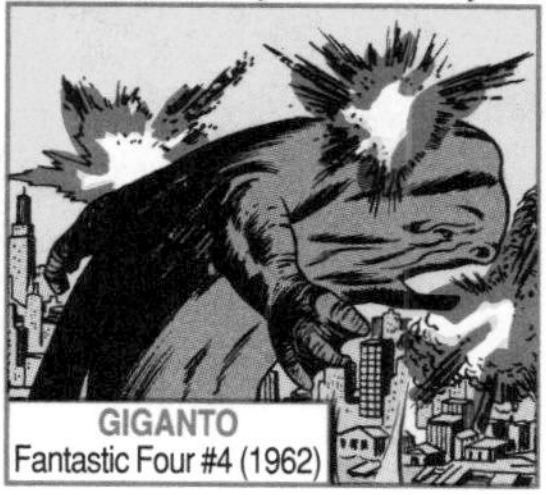
GIGANTO
Fantastic Four #4 (1962)
Art by Jack Kirby

The first known encounter with a Giganto occurred in the 19th century, when an albino Giganto attacked the Pequod, a ship helmed by immortal monster hunter Ulysses Bloodstone. This confrontation inspired author Herman Melville to write the novel "Moby Dick."

In the modern era, Namor the Sub-Mariner, only recently having regained his memories after decades of amnesia, ventured to the ocean floor to find a weapon capable of gaining revenge against the surface world, who he erroneously believed caused the destruction of Atlantis. Finding a Giganto sleeping on the sea bed and the Horn of Proteus buried near it, Namor blew the Horn, awakening the creature. Giganto rampaged across Manhattan at Namor's command, but when the monster fell asleep, the Fantastic Four's

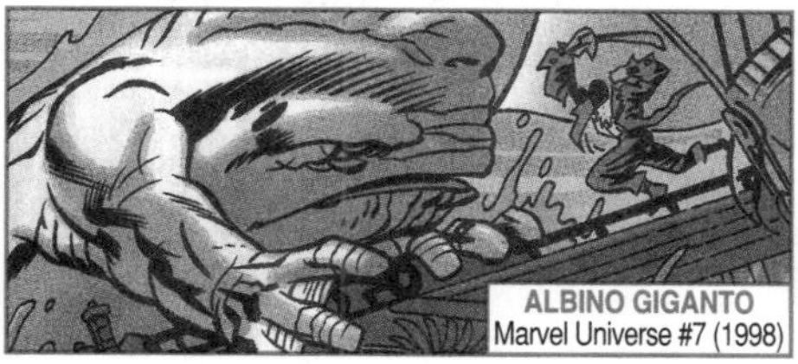
ALBINO GIGANTO
Marvel Universe #7 (1998)
Armstrong

Thing (Ben Grimm) entered Giganto's body through its mouth carrying a nuclear warhead. The bomb exploded, killing this Giganto. Not long after, Dr. Doom (Victor von Doom) gained control of the Horn and called forth an even larger Giganto and other sea monsters. Iron Man (Tony Stark) took possession of the Horn and lured the creatures back out to sea. After Doom gained the power of Galactus, this Giganto was among the Atlantean armies that Namor led against the power-mad monarch, but they were all quickly defeated.

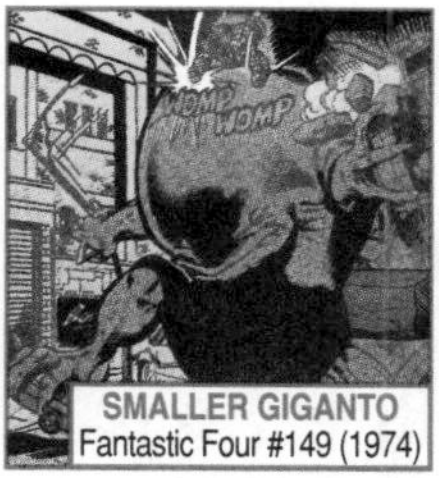
WOMP
WOMP
SMALLER GIGANTO
Fantastic Four #149 (1974)
Art by Bill Sienkiewicz

In a later attempt to force the FF's Mr. Fantastic (Reed Richards) and Invisible Girl (Sue Richards) to reconcile with each other, Namor feigned an attack on New York with the help of the Inhuman Triton. Another Giganto, this one much smaller (approximately 35' tall), was among Namor's mock invasion, and while the creature was defeated by the Thing, Namor's plan ultimately worked. This Giganto was soon called forth by Captain Barracuda, who sent it into Manhattan, where it again encountered the Fantastic Four before Namor intervened, sending Giganto and the other sea monsters back into the ocean.

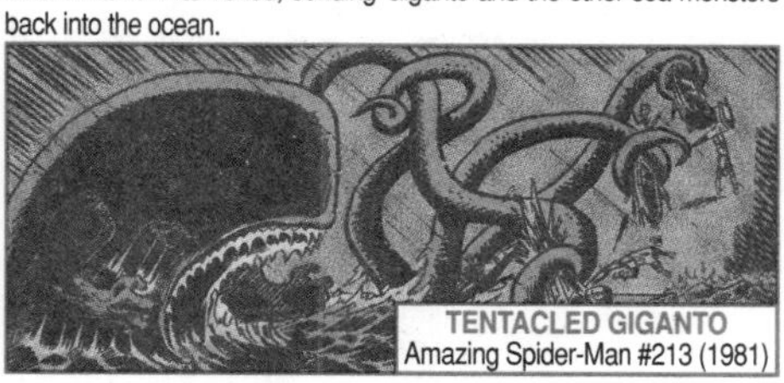
TENTACLED GIGANTO
Amazing Spider-Man #213 (1981)
Art by John Romita Jr.

**FIRST APPEARANCE:** Fantastic Four #4 (1962)

**TRAITS:** Gigantos most often resemble oversized bipedal sperm whales with immeasurable strength. They range in size from 35' to approximately 200'. They possess echolocation (the emission of sound waves) and the ability to emit hard blasts of water via their blowholes, both strong enough to injure smaller beings. Some Gigantos possess unique abilities, and most can be controlled by the Proteus Horn.

---

A markedly different Giganto was utilized by the Lemurian Llyra in helping the Wizard (formerly William Bentley) escape the authorities. This Giganto had red skin and its lower half ended in four tentacles. Much later, Namor built a robot duplicate of Giganto, using it in a ploy to help his friends the Human Torch (Jim Hammond) and Anne Raymond locate the island Raymond's husband Toro (Thomas Raymond) had seemingly perished on. This robot was destroyed by the Torch, though another real Giganto emerged from the ocean depths soon after. Called forth by Llyra in an attempt to discredit Namor, Giganto and other ocean monsters assaulted the city before being turned back by Namor.

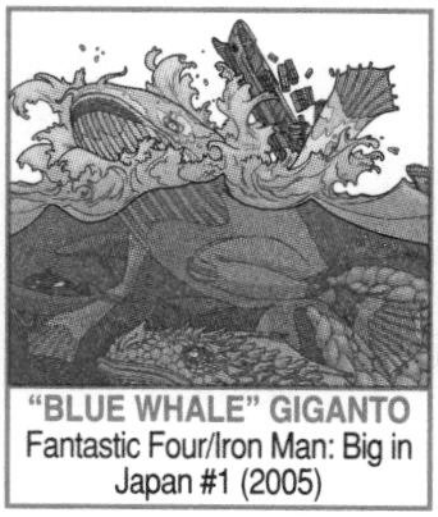
"BLUE WHALE" GIGANTO
Fantastic Four/Iron Man: Big in Japan #1 (2005)
Art by Seth Fisher

Another of the Giganto race, this one more closely resembling a blue whale than a sperm whale, was among the giant monsters that attacked Tokyo after being driven mad by the impending arrival of the Apocalypse

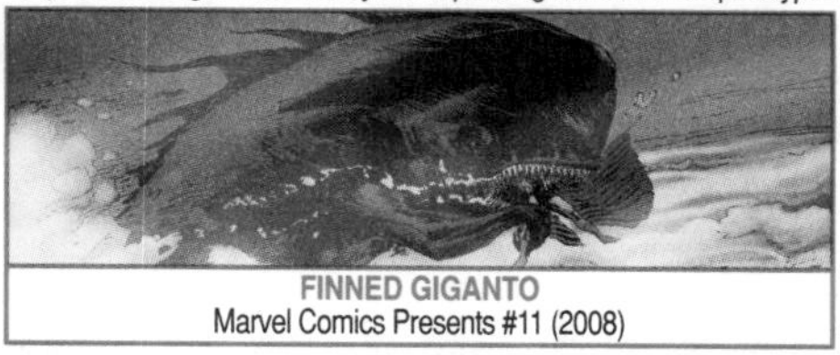
FINNED GIGANTO
Marvel Comics Presents #11 (2008)
Art by Lee Weeks

Beast. The monster Grogg regained its senses and led this Giganto and the other creatures back to the sea. Squirrel Girl later defeated a Giganto (presumably the same one Llyra had recently called forth) before it returned to the ocean, where Namor commanded it and other creatures to safeguard a small tropical island upon which the Black Panther (T'Challa) and Storm (Ororo Munroe) were celebrating their honeymoon. The super-villain Tiger Shark stole the Horn, but he, Giganto and other creatures called forth were defeated by a team of Avengers led by Iron Man. The Avenger Stingray encountered a finned Giganto while helping a shipwreck salvage crew. It seemingly choked to death trying to swallow the hero, and Stingray escaped its body soon after.

**NOTE:** *Alternate reality counterparts of the Giganto race have been seen on Earth-311, where one confronted the Four of the Fantasticks during the 17th century; on Earth-700089, where one was revived from its ocean slumber by Gamma Ray (a mutated Professor Gamma); and on Earth-928, where a green Giganto variation was summoned by the Sub-Mariner (Roman) before being sent back to the sea by Spider-Man (Miguel O'Hara). This particular Giganto possessed low-level hydrokinesis, which allowed it to draw and maintain a depth of water within its surroundings to support its mass.*

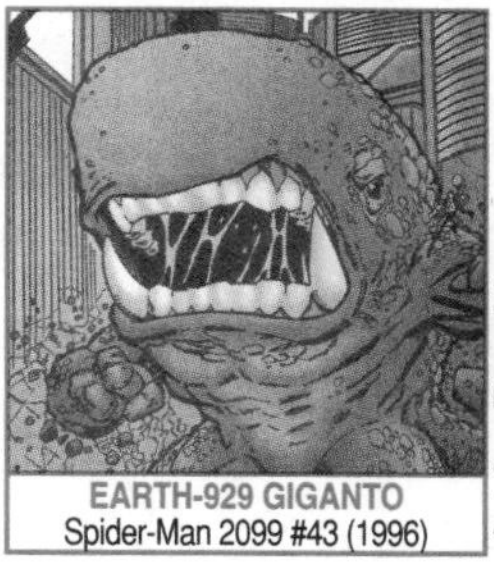
EARTH-929 GIGANTO
Spider-Man 2099 #43 (1996)
Art by Ron Lim

# HELLSTORM'S DEMON-STEEDS

**CURRENT MEMBERS:** Hegal, Malah, Zulum, possibly others
**FORMER MEMBERS:** Amon, Hecate, Set
**BASE OF OPERATIONS:** Fire Lake, Greentown, Massachusetts; formerly Satan (Marduk Kurios)'s realm of Hell
**FIRST APPEARANCE:** (Amon, Hecate, Set) Marvel Spotlight #12 (1973); (Hegal, Malah, Zulum) Punisher #2 (1998)

HEGAL, MALAH & ZULUM

Art by Bernie Wrightson

Art by Peter Gross

AMON & SET

**TRAITS:** The Demon-Steeds are demons bound into equine form. They serve the wielder of the Satanic Trident, carrying their master aboard the Satanic Chariot. Unlike earthly horses, which consume primarily grains and grasses, largely fermenting and digesting them in their cecum ("hindgut"), the Demon-Steeds are carnivorous beasts, magically transforming the flesh they consume into energy to power their demonic forms; only their master's supervision prevents them from devouring any bodies or limbs that come within reach of their mouths. They are unlimited by other mortal needs, such as warmth and respiration, and are resistant to non-mystical injury. They are equally able to travel on land, underwater, and in the air or in space. They can also traverse dimensional barriers, though usually only via pre-existing portals. They are superhumanly strong, swift, and durable, with undefined upper limits. Rather than hooves, they have clawed, two-toed feet, and their tails are thick, muscular and long. The steeds have varied their colors, though whether this is an inherent ability or whether they were changed by Daimon is uncertain.

The steeds can coat themselves with hellfire, able to burn objects like conventional fire and/or cause spiritual pain or disrupt other magical forces. They are boarded in a subterranean cavern fathoms below Fire Lake, Massachusetts, near Daimon Hellstrom's mansion, which contains a portal to Hell. The steeds magically enter and exit the cavern via flying into or out of the lake itself; upon their entrance into the lake, Hellstrom

is transported to his mansion's doorsteps. The chariot is presumably composed of the highly durable nether metal ("Netheranium," a bane to other demons) and can carry as many people as can fit in it, at least four passengers. Hellstrom allegedly can transform the chariot (and possibly the steeds) into other methods of transport, though he claims to prefer the chariot due to a fondness for the movie "Ben Hur."

**HEIGHT:** 5' (at the withers)
**WEIGHT:** 1300 lbs.
**EYES:** Red iris, yellow sclera (variable)
**HAIR:** (Amon, Hegal) gray; (Hecate, Malah) black; (Set) magenta; (Zulum) sorrel — all variable

**HISTORY:** Long ago, Marduk Kurios, one of many demons using the alias Satan, bound demons into equine form forced to obey the wielder of Kurios' Satanic Trident. In recent years, however, the Son of Satan (Daimon Hellstrom, aka Hellstorm), usurped his father's trident and thus summoned the Steeds Amon, Hecate and Set, using them to escape from Hell and boarding them beneath his Fire Lake mansion. Hellstrom subsequently used the steeds for transportation as needed across Earth and to and from Hell, sometimes carrying Hellstrom's Defenders allies or others with him. When Daimon sought to help a trio of Damned Souls gain entrance to Heaven, he summoned the Demon-Steeds and transported them along the only path he could: Through Hell itself. As they crossed the planes of Purgatorius towards Mt. Qaf, which ascended to the pearly gates, they were assaulted by massive demon hordes sent by Daimon's father, who wished to reclaim the souls for Hell. Daimon escaped with his passengers by accessing his full demonic power, but the steeds fell before the savage onslaught. Daimon subsequently outfitted a new trio of steeds, Hegal, Malah and Zulum, to drive his chariot.

AMON, HECATE & SET

# LOBO

**HISTORY:** The Lobo name has been given to several wolves who were each the companion to the Red Wolf, a succession of heroes chosen by the wolf god Owayodata. The first Red Wolf known to have a pet wolf was Johnny Wakely in the 1870s. When Wakely first found the tomb of the deceased Red Wolf Wildrun, he discovered a wolf in the premises, wounded by an arrow. Wakely treated the wolf's wound and called him Lobo. When Owayodata called Wakely to become the new Red Wolf, Lobo followed Wakely into battle, aiding him against the renegade Cheyenne led by Burning Tree. From then on, Lobo aided his master in many adventures, notably aiding him against Ursa the Man-Bear, who kept a pack of bears. Wakely was still accompanied by Lobo as late as 1885 when he aided a team of heroic outlaws against Clay Riley's Nightriders. Another Red Wolf (possibly Wakely himself) died and was immediately replaced by a successor who took the fallen Red Wolf's Lobo as his own companion. In the 1970s, Thomas Thunderhead was summoned as the new Red Wolf. Owayodata presented him with a new Lobo who possessed supernatural abilities. Together, the duo fought criminals such as Clayton Bickford and King Cycle.

In recent years, Will Talltrees assumed the guise of Red Wolf. As he set out to begin his service to Owayodata, Talltrees came across a female wolf who attacked him. Talltrees was forced to kill the wolf, then found she had been protecting a cub. Talltrees adopted the cub and it became the new Lobo. As Lobo matured, he aided his friend against the forces of Cornelius Van Lunt. When the Hulk (Bruce Banner) fell under the control of the Corruptor, the Hulk's friend Rick Jones sent out a distress call to the Avengers. However, the call was diverted and instead gathered Red Wolf, Lobo, the Phantom Rider (Hamilton Slade), Firebird (Bonita Juarez), Texas Twister and Shooting Star, all heroes based in the western United States. The team held up against the Hulk, and it was ultimately Lobo who defeated the Corruptor. Afterward, the western heroes banded together as the Rangers. Sometime later after Firebird had begun an affiliation with the Avengers, Shooting Star was possessed by the demon Riglevio. The demon's presence on the Rangers had an adverse effect upon their personalities and Lobo even developed demonic powers, including the power to grow in size. When Riglevio was exposed and defeated by the Avengers, Lobo and the other Rangers returned to normal.

Talltrees was hunted down by the Bengal, a vengeful young man who blamed him for the slaughter of his family. During his fight with Red Wolf he killed Lobo. Talltrees barely pulled through himself and afterward skinned Lobo's corpse, donning his hide as his new uniform so that they would remain together. When a group of drunken hunters massacred a mother wolf and her cubs, Red Wolf punished the hunters; finding a sole surviving cub, Talltrees adopted him as the new Lobo. The youthful Lobo would follow Talltrees on his adventures in spite of Red Wolf's precautions, once encountering the infant "Bucky" (later Julia Winters) when Talltrees fought Bucky's foster father Nomad (Jack Monroe). Eventually growing to maturity, Lobo aided Red Wolf in battle against the Maggia and other foes.

After the adoption of the Superhuman Registration Act, the Rangers were reassembled as the official super hero team of Texas. Red Wolf and Lobo rejoined their comrades, but the Skrulls had been preparing for a mass invasion of the USA and replaced a member of each state's team. The Skrulls kidnapped Lobo, replacing him with an imposter who was later exposed by the 3-D Man (Delroy Garrett); used his abilities to detect its presence; Shooting Star killed the Skrull. The real Lobo was subsequently retrieved from the Skrulls and reunited with Red Wolf.

**REAL NAME:** Lobo
**ALIASES:** "Wolf Brother," "Furry Brother," "Brother Owayo"
**IDENTITY:** No dual identity
**OCCUPATION:** Pet, adventurer
**CITIZENSHIP:** Property of William Talltrees
**PLACE OF BIRTH:** Wolf Point, Montana
**KNOWN RELATIVES:** Unidentified mother (deceased), four siblings (deceased)
**GROUP AFFILIATION:** Rangers
**EDUCATION:** Trained by William Talltrees
**FIRST APPEARANCE:** (Wakely's) Marvel Spotlight #1 (1971); (Thunderhead's) Red Wolf #7 (1973); (Talltrees' first) Avengers #80 (1970); (Talltrees' second) Marvel Comics Presents #72 (1991)

**HEIGHT:** 2'11" (at the shoulder) **EYES:** Black
**WEIGHT:** 65 lbs. **HAIR:** Brown

**ABILITIES/ACCESSORIES:** Like most wolves, Lobo possesses a keen sense of smell, making him an excellent tracker. He has claws on each paw and sharp teeth, which he uses in combat. Each Lobo has had a special bond to his particular Red Wolf, following his instructions and faithfully assisting him in combat. The Lobo owned by Thomas Thunderhead could teleport and become immaterial.

| POWER GRID | 1 | 2 | 3 | 4 | 5 | 6 | 7 |
|---|---|---|---|---|---|---|---|
| INTELLIGENCE | ■ | | | | | | |
| STRENGTH | ■ | ■ | ■ | ■ | | | |
| SPEED | ■ | ■ | ■ | ■ | ■ | ■ | ■ |
| DURABILITY | ■ | ■ | ■ | ■ | | | |
| ENERGY PROJECTION | ■ | | | | | | |
| FIGHTING SKILLS | ■ | ■ | | | | | |

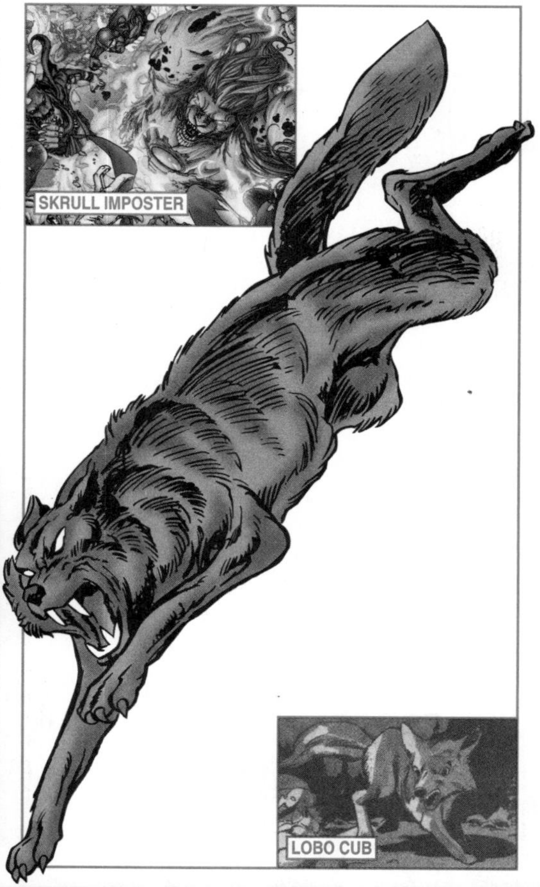
SKRULL IMPOSTER
LOBO CUB

*Art by John Buscema with Harvey Tolibao (Skrull) & Javiar Saltares (cub)*

# LOCKHEED

**REAL NAME:** Unrevealed, possibly inapplicable
**ALIASES:** "Dragon"; "Young Dragling"
**IDENTITY:** No dual identity
**OCCUPATION:** Spy; former adventurer, warrior
**CITIZENSHIP:** Formerly Flock with criminal record
**PLACE OF BIRTH:** Flock homeworld
**KNOWN RELATIVES:** None
**GROUP AFFILIATION:** SWORD; formerly X-Men, Excalibur, Flock
**EDUCATION:** Unrevealed
**FIRST APPEARANCE:** Uncanny X-Men #166 (1983)

**HISTORY:** One of the greatest warriors of the alien race the Flock, Lockheed battled the alien Brood on their homeworld where he encountered the young Earth mutant Kitty Pryde. Secretly returning to Earth with Kitty and her X-Men teammates, Lockheed found a nest of alien Sidri beneath the X-Men's mansion and, along with Kitty and her teammate Colossus, defeated them. Kitty named Lockheed after a character in a fairytale, which itself was named after the X-Men's SR-71 Lockheed Blackbird jet, and the pair quickly became inseparable friends, developing an empathic bond between each other. On the alien Battleworld, Lockheed befriended a female green dragon, later nicknamed "Puff," and after the X-Men unwittingly brought her to Earth she grew to gigantic size and caused chaos in Tokyo until Lockheed defused the situation, after which she inexplicably disappeared in a massive energy discharge.

Lockheed later joined Kitty and others in founding the British super-team Excalibur. During a battle with the despotic Dr. Doom (Victor von Doom), Lockheed was severely wounded while protecting Kitty. After undergoing surgery, his astral form was transported aboard the spaceship that carried the collective transient souls of his entire space-faring race. There, Lockheed was placed on trial for abandoning not only his people, but his intended bride on their wedding day. Lockheed defended his decision to leave, but during his speech the ship's pilots fell asleep. Lockheed regained control of the ship, thus preventing his people's souls from dissipating. The court still found him guilty; however, they commuted the death sentence and instead exiled him from the Flock.

Lockheed recovered, and after Kitty returned to the X-Men, he was injured during a fight after which he was taken in by a pair of sister witches. After discovering they were terrorizing their town with their powers, Lockheed joined a rival witch in opposing them. She helped him locate Kitty, who had since left the X-Men and was attending university, and he rejoined her there. After Kitty returned to the X-Men once more, Lockheed was recruited by the espionage agency SWORD, which deals with extraterrestrial matters, to act as a mole to observe and report on the X-Men's activites in exchange for SWORD's help in resolving pressing homeworld issues. Lockheed rejoined the X-Men in time to aid in opposing the alien Ord. Lockheed was then alerted to Puff's reappearance in Tokyo where, having returned to normal size, she was kidnapped by the Path of Destiny cult. With Kitty's help, Lockheed rescued her. When the X-Men were taken by SWORD to the Breakworld to oppose their intended destruction of Earth, they learned of Lockheed's SWORD agent status. Lockheed aided the X-Men against the Breakworld, but lost Kitty when she apparently sacrificed herself to save Earth.

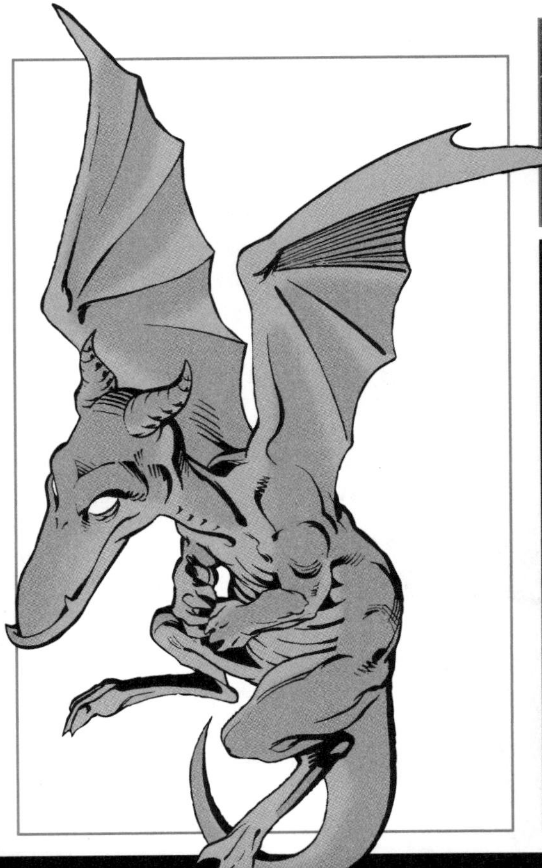

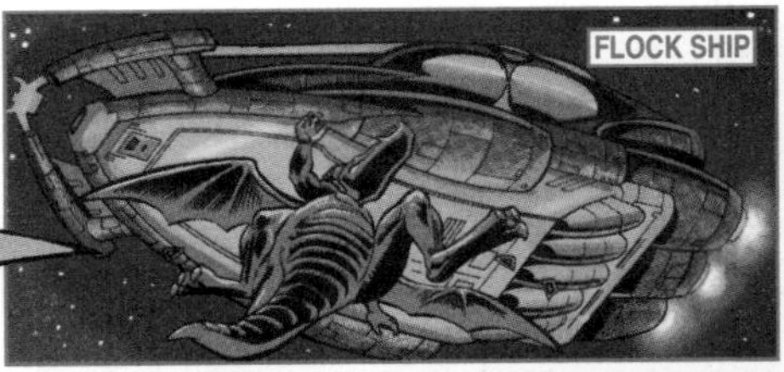
FLOCK SHIP

Art by Dave Hoover

**HEIGHT:** 15" (at shoulder)
**WEIGHT:** 20 lbs.
**EYES:** Yellow, no visible irises
**HAIR:** None

**ABILITIES/ACCESSORIES:** Lockheed is a purple-skinned alien with a dragon-like appearance, including small forepaws and wings. He can fly and breathe fire. Lockheed is immune to the intense heat and flames he can generate, as well as that from external sources within certain limits. Lockheed has been seen to withstand immersion in molten lava with no ill effects. He also possesses five lungs of unknown function.

Lockheed's mind is capable of resisting telepathic probes from even the most powerful telepaths. Like all members of his race, Lockheed can sense the emotions of others via empathy. He has learned several Earth languages including English, though he rarely speaks, and is skilled in the piloting of his race's astral starship. Lockheed once wore an image inducer on a collar around his neck that created the holographic illusion of him being a housecat.

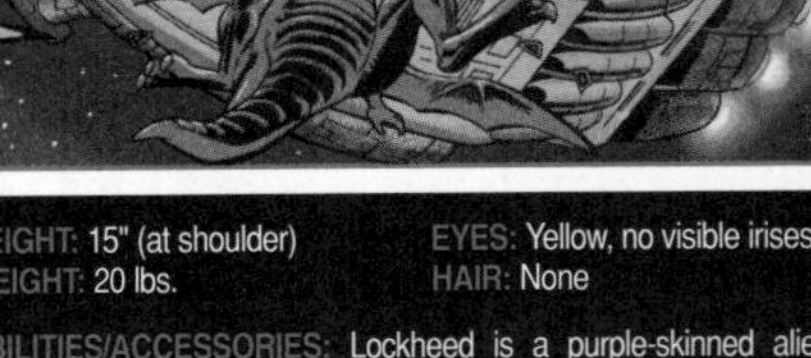
POWER GRID
1 2 3 4 5 6 7
INTELLIGENCE
STRENGTH
SPEED
DURABILITY
ENERGY PROJECTION
FIGHTING SKILLS

Art by Alan Davis

# LOCKJAW

**REAL NAME:** Lockjaw
**ALIASES:** "Slobberchops," "Sparky," "Droopy," "Puppy Boy"
**IDENTITY:** No dual identity
**OCCUPATION:** Companion to the Inhumans' Royal Family
**CITIZENSHIP:** Attilan
**PLACE OF BIRTH:** Island of Attilan, Atlantic Ocean
**KNOWN RELATIVES:** None
**GROUP AFFILIATION:** Inhumans
**EDUCATION:** Unrevealed
**FIRST APPEARANCE:** Fantastic Four #45 (1965)

**HISTORY:** Lockjaw is escort and companion to the Inhumans' Royal Family, and has been at least since Crystal was a young child. Lockjaw has a special fondness for Crystal and is highly protective of her; he has a similar relationship with her daughter Luna, and, to a lesser degree, with the Fantastic Four's Thing (Ben Grimm) and with the Inhumans' king, Black Bolt (the latter may be due to the antennae each have on their brow). Lockjaw serves as the Royal Family's unofficial transportation; he will almost always do as asked by Crystal, Luna, or Bolt, but the other Inhumans may have to be more persuasive to gain Lockjaw's cooperation, though he seems always reliable in emergencies.

When the Inhuman Royal Family traveled out into modern society in search of their amnesiac Medusa, Lockjaw went with them, there meeting the Fantastic Four. After his family was trapped behind a "negative space" barrier, Lockjaw traveled for several weeks with Johnny Storm and Wyatt Wingfoot seeking a way to traverse the barrier, but the Inhumans freed themselves. Lockjaw has thrice been mind-controlled and used against his family or friends, twice by Maximus and once by Esteban Diablo, but each event was short-lived.

Lockjaw has had a great influence on his family — when Crystal was heartbroken at leaving Johnny Storm, Lockjaw brought her to the wounded Quicksilver; they eventually married, though the pairing would eventually sour. On another occasion, the Sphinx (Anath-Na Mut) captured the Royal Family until Lockjaw freed them. Lockjaw has stayed with the family and Crystal as they've moved Attilan between the Atlantic Ocean, the Himalayas, the moon's Blue Area, and even deep space several times (on one of those occasions Lockjaw actually moved the city himself when Black Bolt routed all of Attilan's power through him); he became part of the Avengers' extended family when Crystal joined them. Lockjaw also briefly stayed with the Thing in his short-lived Atlas Towers penthouse.

The most controversial element of Lockjaw's life occurred when he appeared to speak to convince Quicksilver not to expose the infant Luna to mutative Terrigen Mists. Quicksilver later claimed that his "speech" was a joke played by Gorgon and Karnak on Ben Grimm (actually a trick played on Quicksilver for Crystal's benefit; Ben was an innocent bystander), although both Inhumans were in plain sight when Quicksilver alleged they were using hidden transmitters. Nonetheless, Lockjaw has not spoken otherwise, and no other evidence exists that he can.

Though Lockjaw usually remains with his family or friends, he occasionally acts alone — he once aided the New York Police Department in rescuing homeless families from an arsonist. When Lockjaw was forced to choose between Luna and Crystal after Quicksilver misled their daughter, he chose to briefly flee rather than disobey either.

**NOTE:** *The one-time Fantastic Four companion Puppy appears to be somewhat similar to a younger Lockjaw, complete with forehead antennae. On Earth-6513, a similar looking Puppy is said to be the grandson of that world's Lockjaw; however, no connections have been established between Earth-616's Lockjaw and Puppy.*

**HEIGHT:** 5' (at the shoulder) **EYES:** Brown
**WEIGHT:** 1240 lbs. **HAIR:** Brown

**ABILITIES/ACCESSORIES:** Lockjaw can teleport distances as little as ten feet and as much as 24,000 miles (from Earth to the moon); it is unclear if he can teleport further. Lockjaw can also teleport interdimensionally, and has teleported across time on very rare occasions. When teleporting he can bring along up to a dozen individuals or a ton of mass, though all being teleported must be within a radius of 14 feet of him (the closer the better; physical contact makes it easier). He cannot teleport others without teleporting himself. His teleportation is accompanied by a bright sparkling white flash. Certain types of fields, notably the Inhumans' "negative space" barriers, can inhibit Lockjaw's teleporting.

Lockjaw has limited telekinetic abilities. He has used these to move rocks and to create force shields to protect the Royal Family; these exhaust him and he uses them rarely. The antennae on Lockjaw's and Black Bolt's foreheads allow the two to combine their powers; they once created a dimensional gateway, something neither can do alone. Lockjaw has limited and erratic empathic abilities as well; he sometimes senses when those he cares for are in danger or need, no matter their distance. Lockjaw can also track beings he knows, even across interdimensional space.

Lockjaw's intelligence fluctuates from little more than canine at times to comprehending complex language. Lockjaw's strength is significantly greater than that of a normal being of his size and build, and his jaws are able to grab and hold up to 90 tons; he has held the Silver Surfer at a standoff. Lockjaw's teeth and digestive system are similarly strengthened — whereas normal dogs chew on and digest bone, Lockjaw chews on metal.

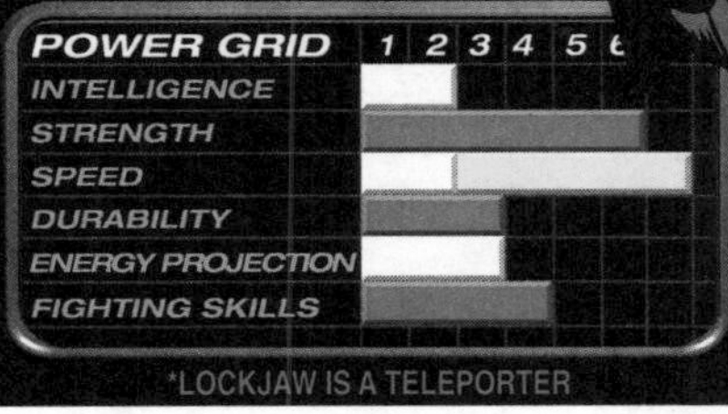
POWER GRID
1 2 3 4 5
INTELLIGENCE
STRENGTH
SPEED
DURABILITY
ENERGY PROJECTION
FIGHTING SKILLS
*LOCKJAW IS A TELEPORTER

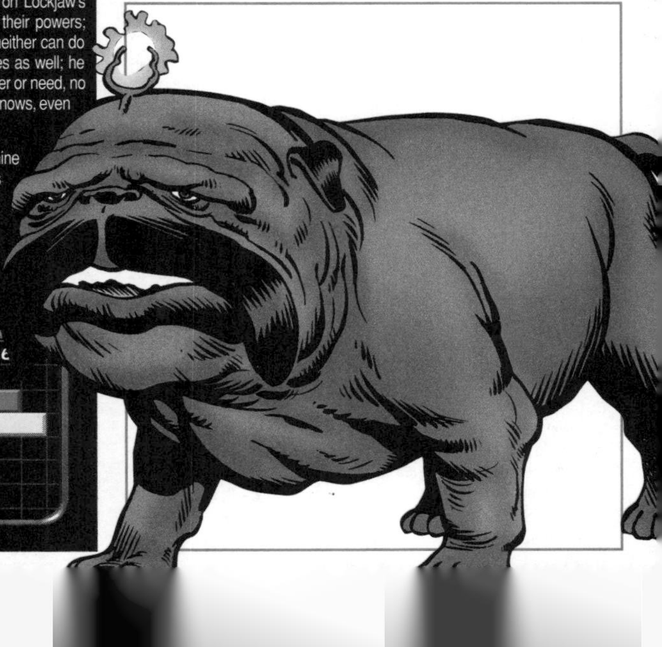

# MOLE MAN'S MONSTERS

FIRST APPEARANCE: Fantastic Four #1 (1961)

HISTORY: The creatures known as Mole Man's monsters are mostly genetic mutates created by the Deviants decades ago and now controlled by the Mole Man (Harvey Rupert Elder). During his surface world exploits under various guises the Deviant warlord Kro helmed the creation of these beasts; many of them are mutated Deviants, though some may be technologically mutated terrestrial animals. In the 1950s, the Eternal Makkari and his fellow Monster Hunters opposed Kro's plans to invade the surface. During this conflict, would-be rival adventurer Elder followed the Monster Hunters for his own reasons and became stranded on what would be dubbed Monster Island (aka Monster Isle) in the Sea of Japan, one of several similar islands linked via Subterranea, a complex system of underground passageways originally leading to the Deviants' home of Lemuria. Exploring the island's caves, Elder fell into the Valley of Diamonds; nearly blinded by its light and maddened by his failures, Elder became the Mole Man, taking command of the Moloids, a subhuman race of beings also engineered by the Deviants, and many of the mutates Kro had abandoned in the area after his plans failed.

The Mole Man spent subsequent decades mastering the Deviants' abandoned technology and plotting to use it against the world that had scorned him, slowly fueling rumors in the outside world of Monster Island's existence. At some point, the government operation CONTROL may have begun depositing giant monsters on the island as well. Having taken over much of Subterranea, the Mole Man eventually tried to conquer the world. He had an enormous Giganto monster destroy various atomic plants around the world, believing humanity would be helpless against him without nuclear power; however, the newly formed Fantastic Four tracked Giganto back to Monster Island, and after defeating monsters Tricephalous, Ugu the Neolithic and Giganto, they escaped before Mole Man seemingly destroyed the island to avoid capture. Monster Island survived, though, and the Fantastic Four soon began using it to imprison various monsters they had encountered and defeated, including the alien dragon Fin Fang Foom; Klagg and Gruto, two peace-loving aliens who had returned to Earth and fought the Fantastic Four in unrevealed encounters; the giant ape creature Gorgilla; and the giant alien child Googam.

Not content with his army of Deviant mutates, the Mole Man began actively recruiting other creatures into his menagerie. Discovering the Elder of the Universe known as the Collector held a large zoo of creatures in his base below Canada, the Mole Man assaulted it; however, he only managed to free the monsters, not capture them, and they subsequently terrorized Manhattan until the Thing (Ben Grimm), the Hulk (Bruce Banner), the Beast (Henry McCoy) and Giant-Man (Hank Pym) stopped them. Since then, the Mole Man has been more resigned to establishing his own kingdom, and many of his creatures have remained on Monster Island, only venturing into the outside world under unique circumstances, usually when Mole Man dispatched Giganto to aid in his various vendettas.

Without the Mole Man's leadership, many of the monsters in Subterranea, along with their Moloid and Lava Men neighbors, were targeted by the High Evolutionary's Purifiers, who sought to purge these offshoot races. Many were saved by the intervention of the mutant team X-Factor. Not long after, the rogue Watcher Aron dispatched his Fantastic Four clones to the island, where they viciously beat the creatures in an attempt to recreate the real FF's first encounter with the Mole Man. When the Skrull De'Lila fled to Earth, a crew of Skrulls chasing her landed on Monster Island and took control of many of its larger monsters, sending them to rampage throughout the world, hoping to draw their target out. Aided by the original Fantastic Four and a temporary "replacement" FF team comprised of Ghost Rider (Dan Ketch), Hulk (Bruce Banner), Spider-Man (Peter Parker) and Wolverine (Logan/James Howlett), the Mole Man drove the Skrulls from the island and freed his monsters from their control. After a violent war between various factions within Subterranea, which the Deviant Brutus sought to re-conquer, the Mole Man sought allies and allowed the Infinity Watch to reside on Monster Island. That group often interacted with the island's creatures. When Morgan Le Fay massively disrupted sea levels while raising Atlantis, many of the Mole Man's monsters fled to Subterranea to escape the deluge. Monster Island survived the disaster, and many of the creatures returned to the surface. Soon after, the emergence of Chtylok the Che-K'n Kau from its slumber far below Monster Island sent many of the creatures into a panic. Again seeking revenge against the world, the Mole Man led his monsters in attacking Manhattan, but the Fantastic Four shrank the creatures to a miniature size. More concerned about the protection of his "family" than revenge, the Mole Man retreated with his monsters, and they soon returned to normal size back on Monster Island. Seeking the Ultimate Nullifier, which had been placed on the island as part of a contest between the Grandmaster and a powerful scientist from a distant cosmos, that reality's league of champions defeated multiple monsters to retrieve the Nullifier. The monsters were later driven into a frenzy by the ancient Apocalypse Beast's imminent arrival, with many of them attacking Tokyo alongside other giant monsters before being calmed and sent home by the dragon Grogg. When the Apocalypse Beast reached Monster Island, many of the Mole Man's faithful Moloids sacrificed themselves to destroy it, saving the island and its creatures. Though he tried to keep his kingdom separate from the outside world, the Mole Man soon led an army of monsters against Manhattan in retaliation for the murder of many of his creatures and Moloids through the machinations of mad robot Ultron. The monsters fought the Avengers before Ultron's arrival drove them back into Subterranea, though many were killed in the process. Mole Man's remaining monsters continue to reside on Monster Island and in Subterranea, trying to live as peacefully as possible. For a time, the Mole Man kept a working relationship with SHIELD; in exchange for aid from him and his monsters' occasional aid, SHIELD would often place creatures unsuitable for their Howling Commandos program on Monster Island. With the dismantling of SHIELD in the wake of a Skrull invasion, it is undetermined if the various giant monsters in SHIELD's care were returned to Monster Island.

**BRUTE THAT WALKS**
Journey Into Mystery #65 (1961)

*Art by Jack Kirby*

Howard Avery, aka the **BRUTE THAT WALKS**, was a scientist whose love for Sally Barton led him to create a growth serum in hopes of giving himself a better physique to impress her. The faulty serum instead turned him into a giant rampaging monster, but eventually it wore off and he regained human form. Years later, Avery somehow reverted to his Brute form, even larger than before, and was confined to Monster Island, where he encountered the Infinity Watch.

The extraterrestrial dragon **FIN FANG FOOM** has resided on Monster Island at least twice, following his various defeats by the likes of the Fantastic Four and Iron Man. While on Monster Island, Foom hired Jennifer Walters (She-

**FIN FANG FOOM**
Strange Tales #89 (1961)

*Art by Walter Simonson*

*Art by Jack Kirby*

Art by Art Adams and Chris Weston

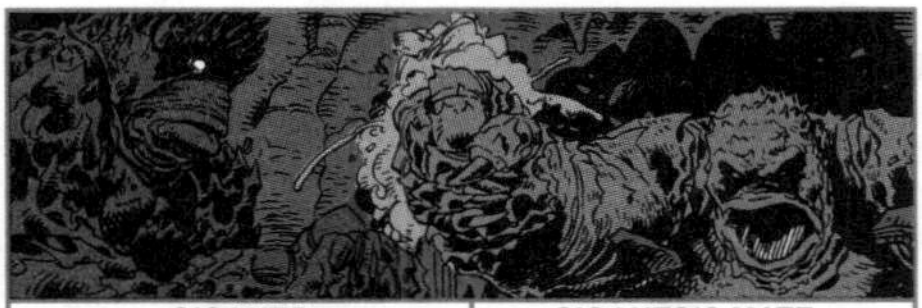

GIGANTO
Fantastic Four #1 (1961)

GIGANTO'S MATE
Fantastic Four #348 (1991)

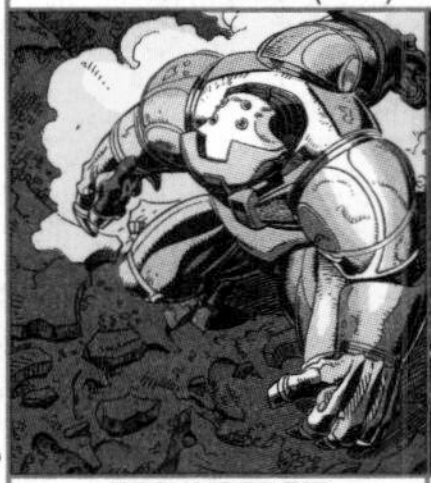

TECHNOTROID
Fantastic Four #349 (1991)

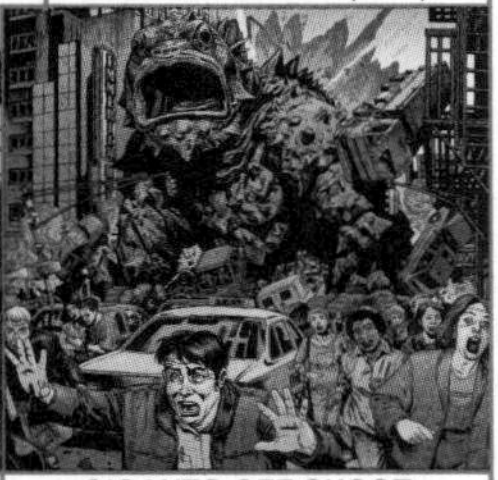

GIGANTO OFF-SHOOT
Fantastic Four: First Family #3 (2006)

Hulk) as a lawyer to aid in his parole and subsequent placement in human society. Though Foom is not known to have worked with the Mole Man during his time on the island, he was among the giant monsters who fought an extradimensional league of heroes who came there seeking the Ultimate Nullifier.

Mole Man's most powerful monster, **GIGANTO**, should not be confused with the undersea whale-like race who share that name. Giganto is a large, powerful, semi-reptilian creature that can burrow through the earth with ease. A Deviant mutate, Giganto has been essential to many of the Mole Man's schemes, often tunneling beneath large buildings or cities. The creature's bulletproof hide is near-impervious to most conventional military weapons. After its initial encounter with the Fantastic Four, Giganto continued to serve the Mole Man over the years, aiding him against not only the Fantastic Four, but Alden Mass and the Avengers. After being captured by Hercules as part of a re-creation of the Olympian's legendary twelve labors, Giganto was sent by the Moloids to capture people dressed like Santa Claus in an effort to find their missing master, who had actually left for an unannounced vacation to Santa Barbara. Giganto has a **FEMALE MATE** who physically resembles him. The two were present during De'Lila's scheme to control the **INORGANIC TECHNOTROID**, though the artificial being was "born" within the hands of Giganto's mate, thus imprinting her as its "mother." It presumably still resides with the two. At least one more of Giganto's race has been documented. This creature, more lizard-like than the other known Gigantos, followed the Fantastic Four back to New York after their first clash with the Mole Man and was driven off by them. The inexperienced FF believed the creature to be the same as the one previously encountered, though its appearance is distinguished by its spikier hide and the tendency to walk on all four legs.

Art by Jack Kirby

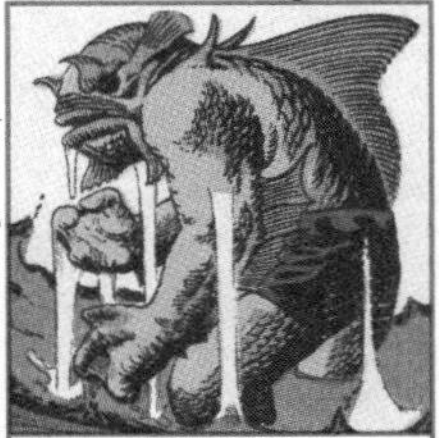

GIGANTUS
Journey Into Mystery #63 (1960)

**GIGANTUS** is a large amphibious creature originally claiming to hail from the undersea kingdom of Mu, but was actually a Deviant mutate who resided in the waters surrounding Monster Island.

A criminal on his home planet ("Planet X"), **GOOM** arrived on Earth in hopes of conquering the world, but was soon captured and returned home by members of his race. Goom found himself back on Earth as part of the Collector's zoo underneath Canada, but was freed by the Mole Man. After rampaging through Manhattan, Goom was sent to the Negative Zone. Escaping from there, he was remanded to Monster Island, but departed for space before returning yet again and being forced into service with SHIELD's Howling Commandos unit.

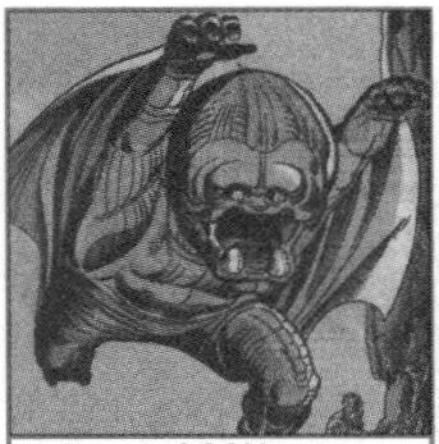

GOOM
Tales of Suspense #15 (1961)

Art by Jack Kirby

During his first Earth visit, Goom left behind his son, **GOOGAM**. Following in his father's footsteps, Googam also sought world conquest, but was defeated by Billy Langley, the son of Mark Langley, the man who initially brought Goom to Earth. Googam recovered but was again defeated, this time by the Fantastic Four in one of their earliest adventures. Googam was exiled to Monster Island, where he resided for years before Fin Fang Foom's legal battle allowed the two of them to be shrunk to human size and brought into human civilization.

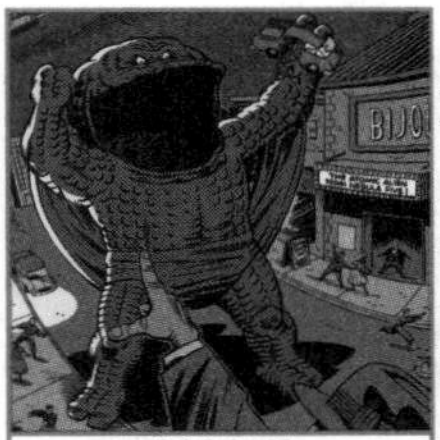
BIJO

GOOGAM
Tales of Suspense #17 (1961)

Art by Roger Langridge

**KRAA** was a normal unidentified human and a member of the Wazubi tribe in Africa who was mutated by Russian atomic testing. Growing in size into a hideous monster, he assumed the role of Kraa, a god in local mythology. After an encounter with an American teacher left Kraa believed dead, he was transported to Monster Island, where his mutation continued to cause him to grow to even greater proportions during his residence there. Later returning to his original mutated size, he was recruited into SHIELD's Howling Commandos unit.

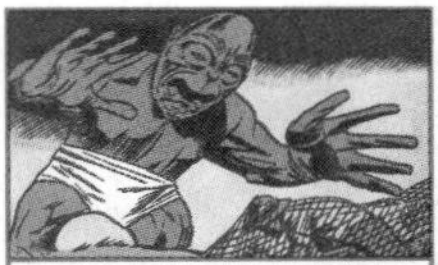

KRAA THE UNHUMAN
Tales of Suspense #18 (1961)

Art by Jack Kirby

A being resembling a **KROGARRIAN** alien was among the legion of creatures who greeted the Infinity Watch's arrival on Monster Island. As this creature was several stories tall, while the creatures from Krogarr are much smaller, it is undetermined if this was an actual Krogarrian or possibly a mutate of the race confined to the island upon its arrival on Earth.

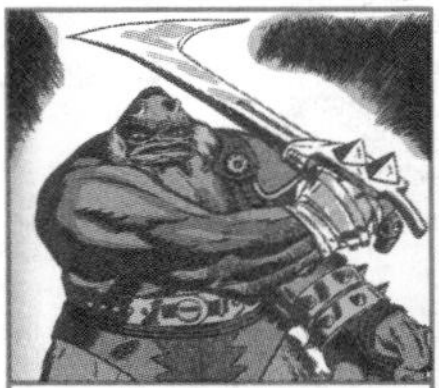

KROGARRIAN
Tales to Astonish #25 (1961)

Art by Jack Kirby

**RHEDOLLANTE** is reptillian in nature, though it has plant-like aspects to its biology. It was sent to raze Mexico City by the Skrulls searching for De'Lila and was later among the creatures defeated by an extradimensional league of heroes.

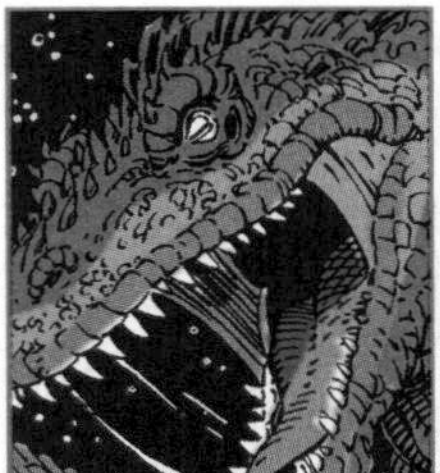

RHEDOLLANTE
Fantastic Four #347 (1991)

Art by Art Adams

A giant semi-humanoid monster with a moth-like appearance, **SKREEAL** was controlled by the Skrulls searching for De'Lila and sent to terrorize Washington, DC before it returned home after fighting the "replacement" Fantastic Four. It has been seen numerous times since, though it very rarely interacts with Monster Island's various visitors and intruders.

Another race of creatures called **SKREEAL** have served as Mole Man's flying steeds. These creatures, of which at least four have been documented, resemble winged slugs. Mole Man rode one to locate the Fantastic Four shortly after the emergence of the Apocalypse Beast. While these may be larvae of the larger moth-like Skreeal, this remains speculation until confirmed.

**SLUGMON** is a burrower that uses its tentacles and snake-like appendages to search for food on the surface. It encountered the Infinity Watch's Pip the Troll during an attempted picnic, and when he tried to drive away what he believed to be a snake, Slugmon attacked and swallowed him before Pip teleported to safety.

Little is known about the giant creature **TANAKADON** other than it has some faint ursine- and canine-like qualities. It was among the creatures subjugated to Skrull control and sent to attack San Francisco.

**TRICEPHALOUS** is a three-headed winged reptilian Deviant mutate. Like Giganto, Tricephalous is one of Mole Man's leading defenders and has battled his master's foes numerous times. It was among the monsters defeated by the extradimensional league of heroes. A similar creature, dubbed **BICEPHALOUS**, was present when Aron the Watcher's clone FF assaulted Monster Island and was severely beaten by the clone of the Thing (Ben Grimm). Other three-headed dragon-like creatures have been seen on Monster Island, but whether these are related to Tricephalous remains unrevealed.

**UGU THE NEOLITHIC**'s stone-like exterior has chameleon-like properties, allowing it to camouflage itself among its surroundings. Not as large as many of the other monsters, Ugu often stays close to the Mole Man as his personal guard.

**VANDOOM's MONSTER** was originally a large wax statue built by Ludwig Vandoom to serve as the centerpiece of his museum in Transylvania (now Romania). A stray lightning bolt brought the statue to life, and its appearance caused the local villagers to attack it. It lived long enough to stave off a race of aliens who arrived in the town in preparation for world conquest, but it collapsed and died shortly thereafter. Humbled, the villagers buried the monster and allowed Vandoom to sculpt another statue in its likeness. At some point, the original Vandoom Monster was somehow revived and captured by the Collector. After it joined numerous other giant monsters in fighting Beast, Giant-Man, Hulk and Thing, it was expelled to the Negative Zone before returning to Earth, where it found a permanent home on Monster Island.

**X THE THING THAT LIVED** (aka **X THE UNKNOWABLE**) was a creature originally brought to life through a mysterious typewriter bought in Europe by Marvel Comics writer Charles Bentley. Though it tried to destroy Bentley, he defeated it by writing its death on the typewriter. At some point, X was brought back into the real world, much larger than before, and was contained on Monster Island, where it confronted the Infinity Watch. It would later be re-created yet again by a young boy named Tomi, who created his own manga comic based on Bentley's original. Alpha Flight defeated this incarnation of X.

An **UNIDENTIFIED MONSTER** wandered away from Monster Island and rampaged through Manhattan before being defeated by the combined efforts of the Fantastic Four and the X-Men.

Other giant monsters that have resided on Monster Island and in the care of the Mole Man include the dinosaur mutate Godzilla and the extradimensional alien monsters Antlar and Miclas, though their status as current residents, and how they ended up on Monster Island to begin with, remain unrevealed. In addition, several dinosaurs and scores of other unidentified monsters have been documented on Monster Island.

*Art by Art Adams*

SKREEAL
Fantastic Four #347 (1991)

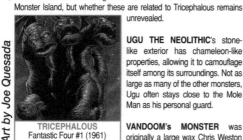

*Art by Seth Fisher*

SKREEAL (STEEDS)
Fantastic Four/Iron Man: Big in Japan #3 (2006)

*Art by Rita Fagani*

SLUGMON
Marvel Comics Presents #112 (1992)

*Art by Art Adams*

TANAKADON
Fantastic Four #347 (1991)

*Art by Joe Quesada*

TRICEPHALOUS
Fantastic Four #1 (1961)

*Art by Jack Kirby*

UGU THE NEOLITHIC
Fantastic Four #1 (1961)

*Art by Jack Kirby*

VANDOOM'S MONSTER
Tales to Astonish #17 (1961)

*Art by Jack Kirby*

X THE THING THAT LIVED
Tales to Astonish #20 (1961)

*Art by John Cassaday*

UNIDENTIFIED MONSTER
Astonishing X-Men #7 (2005)

**HISTORY:** The beings who would become the Outcasts were originally the normal flora and fauna in the desert of New Mexico. When Bruce Banner's gamma bomb exploded at Los Diablos missile base ("Desert Base"), most of the creatures in the surrounding area were killed by the radiation. Those who survived were changed by the experience; both plants and animals grew larger, some stood up on two legs, some became wise, and some even learned how to speak. They were shunned by their own species, and attacked by any human they approached. They eventually found one of Bruce Banner's abandoned Desert Labs and settled there. They chose the transformed rattlesnake, Rattilore, as their leader, and some learned to speak English from the lab's computers. Many of the Outcasts had seen Banner's transformation into the Hulk from afar and awaited the return of "the Green One." During this time, they may have encountered the children Jason Berg and Cara LeBlanc, who later developed radiation-spawned abilities themselves.

Rick Jones, having been transformed into a version of the Hulk that emerged at night, sought out Desert Lab to imprison himself in its containment chamber. When he entered the lab, the reclusive and fearful Outcasts surprised and overpowered him, told him of their origins, and tried to lock him up. However, the moon began to rise, and Rick turned into the Hulk. After a brief struggle, the Rick Hulk and the Outcasts realized they could be friends. Rick lived with the Outcasts for several days, teaching them to use the lab's machines by day, assisting them with his gamma-spawned strength by night, and enjoying the companionship of others unwelcome in normal society. Their peace was interrupted when Bruce Banner, one of the only people who knew that Rick was the Hulk, arrived at Desert Lab to look for his old friend. SHIELD, who sought to capture the new Hulk, had been keeping tabs on Banner, and followed him. Banner arrived at dusk, just as Rick was transforming into the Hulk, in which form he introduced Banner to his new friends, moments before SHIELD arrived. Instantly enraged by their presence, the Rick Hulk hurled a boulder to try to drive them off, leading the soldiers to

**CURRENT MEMBERS:** Ech (cactus), Falco (falcon), Gil (gila monster), Iggo (rock creature), Kir (bat), Kkk-Kkk (ant), Rattilore (rattlesnake), Sting (scorpion), Vult (vulture), many others
**FORMER MEMBERS:** Eeek (small mammal, deceased)
**BASE OF OPERATIONS:** Desert Laboratory, New Mexico
**FIRST APPEARANCE:** Incredible Hulk #329 (1987)

Art by Al Milgrom

return fire, and a battle ensued. The Outcasts put forth a valiant effort to defend themselves, but the superior fire-power of SHIELD soon forced them to give ground and many of their number were injured or killed. The Rick Hulk sprung to his friends' defense, smashing SHIELD's tanks and other weapons and driving off their agents. However, Rattilore and the other Outcasts realized that this was only a temporary measure, and that the humans would return in greater force within a short time. Though the Rick Hulk wanted to stay to protect his newfound friends, Rattilore told him that before his arrival they had been left alone; as long as the Rick Hulk stayed there, men would return to hunt him. Rattilore asked the Hulk to leave, or else the Outcasts would have to flee their home. The Rick Jones Hulk understood and sadly agreed to leave. The friends parted ways, the Outcasts descending into the deepest tunnels to dwell in darkness.

*NOTE: Several other creatures were transformed by the gamma bomb as well, including a plant in the New Mexico Desert which infected Ephraim Soles when he consumed it, and eventually seeded the area with gamma spores. The spores went on to infect many life forms and expand at an alarming rate before being halted by the Defenders. Similarly, a race of lizards was evolved by government atomic testing into intelligent humanoid forms as the Saurians. The Saurians lived in isolation, and much of their population was eventually slaughtered by Dire Wraiths; the survivors relocated to the Savage Land. However, these creatures were not members of the Outcasts, but a separate group of beings altogether.*

THE OUTCASTS WITH RICK JONES HULK

Art by Al Milgrom

# RED GHOST'S SUPER-APES

**CURRENT MEMBERS:** Igor, Miklho, Peotor
**FORMER MEMBERS:** Alpha, Beta, Dmitri
**BASE OF OPERATIONS:** Mobile
**FIRST APPEARANCE:** Fantastic Four #13 (1963)

---

**HISTORY:** The Red Ghost's Super-Apes are a trio of primates who accompanied Russian cosmonaut Ivan Kragoff into space on a mission to duplicate the accident that granted the Fantastic Four their powers. Bombarded by cosmic radiation, Kragoff and the three simians each developed a different superhuman ability. While Kragoff gained the ability to become intangible as the Red Ghost, his allies' powers are as follows:

Miklho, the gorilla, possesses superhuman strength. Although he was initially able to lift only one ton, over the years Miklho's strength has increased and he can now lift up to 85 tons.

Peotor, the orangutan, can project magnetic force, enabling him to attract or repel objects containing iron or steel. The force of Peotor's magnetism is roughly equal to that of Miklho's superhuman strength.

Igor, the baboon, can transform his shape to mimic any object or animal he can imagine. It is unclear whether or not he can alter his mass while changing his shape.

Landing their vessel on the moon, the Red Ghost and the Super-Apes quickly tested out their powers and soon engaged the Fantastic Four in battle for the first time, only to meet defeat. They later kidnapped the Fantastic Four and transported them back to the moon for a rematch, only to fail again. Although Red Ghost and his Super-Apes became career criminals, Red Ghost would often omit the simians from his plots, considering their behavior too "unpredictable." After Red Ghost and his Super-Apes were among the many villains to invade Mr. Fantastic and the Invisible Girl's wedding, Red Ghost went a lengthy period without employing his original primates at all.

The Red Ghost trained two new apes, Alpha and Beta, empowering them with Tony Stark's stolen Cosmic Intensifier Ray: Alpha gained superhuman strength, and Beta could control minds. The trio clashed with Iron Man (Stark) but when the Ghost tried to empower an ape army, Beta, possessing a superior intellect, stopped him and had Alpha destroy the intensifier; Alpha and Beta returned to the wild, and Red Ghost eventually reunited with Miklho, Peotor and Igor. Red Ghost and Super-Apes continued to battle various foes, including Captain Marvel (Mar-Vell), Spider-Man (Peter Parker) and Power Pack. Red Ghost once attempted to force the thief Black Fox to aid the Super-Apes in a series of robberies, but the Fox wound up giving up the Red Ghost to Spider-Man.

At one point, the Super-Apes began to harness each other's powers and also gained the ability to speak along with human-level intelligence. At the same time, the Red Ghost suffered a lapse in his own intellect, creating a reversal of their usual structure. This was apparently due to prolonged proximity to each other since the original cosmic radiation exposure. The Super-Apes sought to develop nerve gas, intending to assault Times Square. However, the extra-powered and intelligent Super-Apes fared no better against the Fantastic Four. Although the foursome regained their normal power levels, the Super-Apes retained their human-level intellect. The Super-Apes were briefly joined by fourth primate, Dmitri.

The Red Ghost and Super-Apes later formed an alliance with Dr. Erich Paine in the African nation Niganda, attempting to seize control of the state, only to be thwarted by the Black Panther (T'Challa) and the X-Men. The Red Ghost developed a new series of Super-Apes while there and left at least one of these apes behind; it eventually joined forces with Erik Killmonger when he took control of Niganda. The original Super-Apes finally had themselves legally freed from Red Ghost's custody and were retroactively pardoned for their crimes. Developing a means to enhance the intellects of other animals, the Super-Apes tested their methods at the private zoo of John Burrows in Salina, Kansas. The Super-Apes and their enhanced allies battled the New Warriors but finally reached an understanding, and the Super-Apes were left in control of the zoo.

ALPHA & BETA

Art by George Tuska

**HISTORY:** Purchased and named in Rio de Janeiro by Samuel "Snap" Wilson, Redwing was brought to the Isle of Exiles when Wilson attempted to hijack and crash a mob plane full of money. Soon after he crashed, Wilson's mind and body were altered by the Red Skull (Johann Shmidt) in a plot to create an agent that would befriend and eventually betray Captain America (Steve Rogers). Using a Cosmic Cube, the Red Skull reverted Sam to his pre-criminal mindset and secretly gave him a telepathic link with Redwing, as well as planting a desire for heroics. After aiding Sam and Captain America (who was, at the time, in the Red Skull's body) against the Exiles and the Red Skull, Redwing accompanied Sam (now the crimefighter known as the Falcon) back to Harlem, New York, where the Falcon set himself up as a solo crimefighter. Shortly thereafter, the Falcon began a partnership with Captain America, with Redwing aiding them against several villains including Diamond Head (Rocky the Lynx), Advanced Idea Mechanics' (AIM)'s Bulldozer android, the gangster Stone Face, and Dr. Erik Gorbo. Redwing was even briefly turned to stone during a battle with the Grey Gargoyle. During a battle against the Grey Gargoyle (Jordan Dixon), Redwing failed to retrieve the antidote to the Viper's poison, prompting the Falcon to train Redwing heavily in retrieval thereafter, first revealing the psychic bond between the two when the Falcon managed to telepathically summon Redwing against the SHIELD "Wild Bill robot."

Shortly thereafter, Redwing was captured by archer Mortimer Freebish, who attempted to hold the bird hostage in an effort to defeat Falcon and thereby, become rich and famous. Once Redwing was freed however, the duo made short work of Freebish. The Falcon soon joined the Avengers, bringing Redwing along into battles against the Absorbing Man and the Grey Gargoyle, where Redwing was once again briefly turned to stone. Following his transportation into space alongside the Falcon during the Grandmaster and Death's "Contest of Champions," Redwing joined the Falcon in numerous cases involving the Serpent Society, Apocalypse (En Sabah Nur)'s Horseman Famine (Autumn Rolfson), and a breakout at the Vault superhuman prison. During the reconstruction of the then-destroyed Avengers Mansion, Redwing and the construction crew

**REAL NAME:** Redwing
**ALIASES:** "Brother Bird," "Brother Redwing"
**IDENTITY:** No dual identity
**OCCUPATION:** Adventurer
**CITIZENSHIP:** Property of Samuel Wilson
**PLACE OF BIRTH:** Rio de Janeiro, Brazil
**KNOWN RELATIVES:** None
**GROUP AFFILIATION:** None
**EDUCATION:** Trained by Samuel Wilson
**FIRST APPEARANCE:** Captain America #117 (1969)

managed to take down Stilt-Man (Wilbur Day) who, along with other super-villains, was attempting to sabotage the construction. Redwing and the Falcon soon learned that due to their psychic link, the Falcon was able to telepathically "see" through the eyes of Redwing and other birds in his vicinity, an ability that allowed him to eventually defeat Mr. Hyde (Calvin Zabo) with the aid of the Avengers. While Falcon was with the Avengers, Redwing aided them in tracking down the missing half of the cosmic In-Betweener's psyche, defeating a new incarnation of Scorpio, and bringing the Scarecrow (Ebenezer Laughton) to justice. Redwing's connection with the Falcon was also instrumental in exposing US Secretary of Defense Dell Rusk as the Red Skull when Redwing acted as a spy to discover Rusk's true nature.

The Falcon and Redwing next aided Captain America in restoring the Winter Soldier (Bucky Barnes)'s memories, as well as siding with Captain America during the superhuman civil war that erupted upon the enactment of the Superhuman Registration Act. Following Captain America's death at the end of the war, the Falcon registered with the US government, along with Redwing, and the two remain crimefighters in the Harlem area.

**LENGTH:** 10" (22" wingspan)
**WEIGHT:** 3.9 oz.
**EYES:** Yellow
**PLUMAGE:** Red-Brown

**ABILITIES/ACCESSORIES:** Redwing possesses the abilities typical of a highly trained American Kestrel falcon, including thin tapered wings capable of flight and quick change of aerial direction. Redwing also has exceptional vision, able to spot a target from several miles away, and sharp talons capable of rending flesh. Like most birds, Redwing also has a sharp beak, sufficient enough to cut a leather whip in two.

Redwing shares a telepathic link with his trainer/partner, the Falcon. This link also allows Redwing to understand orders given to him in English, whether verbally or telepathically by the Falcon. Due to the link, the Falcon can telepathically "see" through the eyes of Redwing and other birds in his vicinity, allowing him to psychically "see" what Redwing sees.

Redwing has also been extensively trained by the Falcon in aerial combat and maneuvering, including doing loop-de-loops around enemies and hovering in front of a moving car's windshield without being hit to provide distractions. He is also trained to retrieve items on command, such as disarming a gun-toting enemy.

| POWER GRID | 1 | 2 | 3 | 4 | 5 | 6 | 7 |
|---|---|---|---|---|---|---|---|
| INTELLIGENCE | | | | | | | |
| STRENGTH | | | | | | | |
| SPEED | | | | | | | |
| DURABILITY | | | | | | | |
| ENERGY PROJECTION | | | | | | | |
| FIGHTING SKILLS | | | | | | | |

# TOOTHGNASHER & TOOTHGRINDER

**REAL NAMES:** Tanngrisnir and Tanngnjostr
**ALIASES:** None
**IDENTITY:** No Dual Identity
**OCCUPATION:** Leading the chariot of Thor
**CITIZENSHIP:** Property of Thor
**PLACE OF BIRTH:** Asgard
**KNOWN RELATIVES:** None
**GROUP AFFILIATION:** None
**EDUCATION:** Unrevealed
**FIRST APPEARANCE:** Thor Annual #5 (1976)

**HISTORY:** For centuries, the mystical Asgardian goats Toothgnasher and Toothgrinder have pulled Thor Odinson's chariot, appearing to him whenever summoned. According to legend, when Thor's travels have made him weary, he can eat Toothgnasher and Toothgrinder for a meal, and they will return to life as long as their bones remain unbroken. Long ago, in the days of Ancient Greece, they transported Thor, Balder, and a small company of Asgardian warriors to Athens to claim it in the name of Asgard. However, upon arriving, the Asgardians found that Odin had temporarily stripped Thor's hammer, Mjolnir, of its power as part of a peace treaty he had made with Zeus. Toothgnasher and Toothgrinder bore their master back to Asgard empty-handed.

Many years later, when the people of Thor's ally Beta Ray Bill were pursued across the universe by a horde of bloodthirsty fire demons from Surtur's realm, Muspelheim, Toothgnasher and Toothgrinder carried Thor, Beta Ray Bill, and the lady Sif into battle. While Sif held the demons at bay, Toothgnasher and Toothgrinder carried their remaining two passengers to the portal from which the demons emanated. After Thor and Beta Ray Bill destroyed the portal, the faithful steeds took the warriors back to Asgard. Thor later summoned them to carry him to battle against the dragon Fafnir of Nastrond. The two goats transported Thor from Antarctica to New York's South Bronx where Thor and his ally Eilif slew the dragon, but only at the cost of Eilif's life.

Toothgnasher and Toothgrinder pulled Thor's chariot as he led his forces to Hel to reclaim mortal souls stolen by the death goddess Hela. They rode past Garm, the hell-hound that guards the entrance to the underworld, and on for a further nine days and nights, across the river Gjoll and over the bridge Gjallerbru before arriving in Hel. After Thor defeated Hela in personal combat and won back the souls, Toothgnasher and Toothgrinder pulled several wagons carrying the souls as they departed Hel. However, Hela reneged on her deal with Thor and sent her undead warriors to block the Asgardian's exit. As Thor prepared to sacrafice himself to give the Asgardians time to escape, he was knocked unconcious by Skruge the Executioner, who took Thor's place, perishing before Hela's warriors while Balder steered Toothgnasher and Toothgrinder back to the land of the living, with the mortal souls and their unconcious master in tow. Toothgnasher and Toothgrinder carried their master to Earth where he dispatched the souls to their bodies. While on Earth, Thor bid Toothgnasher and Toothgrinder to wait for him in an alley, but was transformed into a frog by Loki before he could return. Toothgnasher and Toothgrinder waited for their master, and proved able to communicate with the transformed Thor, advising him to lift his hammer. Thor complied, and was transformed into a humanoid frog with Thor's powers. Toothgnasher and Toothgrinder took their altered master back to Asgard, the journey taking several days because the rainbow bridge, Bifrost, which connected Earth to Asgard, had been shattered. Thor soon defeated Loki and regained his true form.

After Hogun the Grim had been mortally wounded by the Wrecking Crew, Balder employed Toothgnasher and Toothgrinder to carry him to Earth with a healing elixir. They were attacked by the frost giant Pentigaar, but the villain was defeated by Beta Ray Bill, and the elixir was delivered in time. Soon after, when Surtur returned, Odin rode a chariot pulled by Toothgnasher and Toothgrinder and opposed his ancient enemy. Odin and the steeds met Surtur in an immense clash, which left Odin dead, and Toothgnasher and Toothgrinder reduced to skeletons. Though Toothgnasher and Toothgrinder soon regenerated, Odin remained dead, and Thor ascended to the throne of Asgard.

When Loki and his forces brought Ragnarok to Asgard and decimated its inhabitants, Thor departed the Asgardians to gain his father's wisdom. Toothgnasher and Toothgrinder carried him to the mountain Hildstalft and waited for his return as he underwent a series of rituals. While waiting, they were killed and eaten by Loki, who broke their bones so they could not regenerate. All Asgard was subsequently destroyed in the war against Surtur's armies. Their status since the return of the Asgardians remains unclear.

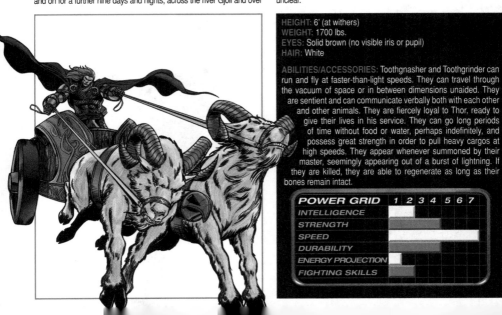

**HEIGHT:** 6' (at withers)
**WEIGHT:** 1700 lbs.
**EYES:** Solid brown (no visible iris or pupil)
**HAIR:** White

**ABILITIES/ACCESSORIES:** Toothgnasher and Toothgrinder can run and fly at faster-than-light speeds. They can travel through the vacuum of space or in between dimensions unaided. They are sentient and can communicate verbally both with each other and other animals. They are fiercely loyal to Thor, ready to give their lives in his service. They can go long periods of time without food or water, perhaps indefinitely, and possess great strength in order to pull heavy cargos at high speeds. They appear whenever summoned by their master, seemingly appearing out of a burst of lightning. If they are killed, they are able to regenerate as long as their bones remain intact.

| POWER GRID | 1 | 2 | 3 | 4 | 5 | 6 | 7 |
|---|---|---|---|---|---|---|---|
| INTELLIGENCE | | | | | | | |
| STRENGTH | | | | | | | |
| SPEED | | | | | | | |
| DURABILITY | | | | | | | |
| ENERGY PROJECTION | | | | | | | |
| FIGHTING SKILLS | | | | | | | |

**HISTORY:** Valinor was originally the property of the 12th century sorcerer Hassan ibn Sabbah, who presumably magically created Valinor's wings. Hassan once employed his servant Karna astride Valinor to abduct the time traveler Black Knight (Dane Whitman in the body of Eobar Garrington), who at the time was in the service of King Richard the Lion-Hearted. Hassan hoped to recruit the Black Knight to his cause, but the Knight refused and ultimately departed from Hassan's fortress with Valinor. From then on, Whitman used Valinor as his own steed. The Black Knight brought Valinor with him when he journeyed to the realm of Avalon. As Avalon was placed under siege by the Fomor, the druid Amergin and his descendant Dr. Druid brought Whitman's allies the Avengers to Avalon's past to help defend the realm. After Avalon was saved, Amergin returned Whitman to his own era alongside Valinor. However, when the Nethergod Necromon sought to invade Otherworld, Merlyn the magician sent Dane and Valinor to find the missing hero Captain Britain (Brian Braddock); succeeding, they entered Otherworld and ultimately triumphed over Necromon. After returning to Earth and taking up residence in Castle Garrett, Valinor became sick as his magical wings and related adaptations became unstable and began to kill him. Whitman's friend Dr. Strange came to Valinor's aid and magically removed the wings to save his life. Valinor remained at the stables of Castle Garrett.

Unfortunately, Whitman soon fell under the curse of his enchanted Ebony Blade and was transformed into stone. In an attempt to restore him to life, magic practitioner Victoria Bentley performed a ceremony that placed the spirit of Whitman's ancestor Sir Percy of Scandia within his body. At the same time, this spell restored Valinor's enchantments and brought him back to perfect health. Valinor bore Sir Percy/Whitman into battle with the Dreadknight, Balor of the Fomor and Morgan Le Fay before Sir Percy's spirit was cast into the Ebony Blade, curing Whitman. Whitman continued to use Valinor on occasion, including a battle with the Crusader (Arthur Blackwood) and rode him on some adventures with the Avengers, including an encounter with the Swordsman (Phillip Javert) and Magdalene of the Gatherers.

Sadly, the curse of the Ebony Blade persisted, and its growing wickedness evidently took a toll upon Valinor, causing him to become restless. When Whitman's squire Sean Dolan took up the Ebony Blade in an attempt to save Victoria Bentley's life, he became consumed by its curse and transformed into the Bloodwraith. Taking Valinor as his steed, the Bloodwraith set out to find new victims for the blade, clashing with the Black Knight as he tried to cure his friend. Dolan was finally separated from the Ebony Blade when it was trapped behind

**REAL NAME:** Valinor
**ALIASES:** None
**IDENTITY:** No dual identity
**OCCUPATION:** Former steed of the Bloodwraith and Black Knight (Dane Whitman)
**CITIZENSHIP:** Property of Sean Dolan
**PLACE OF BIRTH:** Iran
**KNOWN RELATIVES:** None
**GROUP AFFILIATION:** None
**EDUCATION:** No formal education
**FIRST APPEARANCE:** Avengers #226 (1982)

a barrier beneath Attilan, home of the Inhumans. Valinor brought the powerless Dolan to the Avengers, but he became possessed by the Ebony Blade of Earth-374's Proctor, a darker version of his own sword; under this enchantment, Bloodwraith transformed Valinor into a skeletal demonic creature. However, Valinor bore the Avengers' Crystal to the first Ebony Blade and had her return it to Dolan, placing the curse under control again. Dolan was later imprisoned within the nation of Slorenia by the Scarlet Witch; the fate of Valinor is unrevealed.

Art by M.C. Wyman

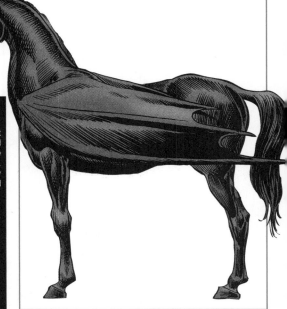

**HEIGHT:** 5'4" (at withers)        **EYES:** Brown
**WEIGHT:** 1200 lbs.        **HAIR:** Black

**ABILITIES/ACCESSORIES:** Valinor possesses wings that enable him to fly while supporting one or more riders. Valinor had a strong rapport with each of his masters (Sean Dolan and Dane Whitman), enabling him to understand and obey their commands. While Bloodwraith was under the control of Proctor's Ebony Blade, Valinor assumed a fiery skeletal appearance and could teleport.

| POWER GRID | 1 | 2 | 3 | 4 | 5 | 6 | 7 |
|---|---|---|---|---|---|---|---|
| INTELLIGENCE | | | | | | | |
| STRENGTH | | | | | | | |
| SPEED | | | | | | | |
| DURABILITY | | | | | | | |
| ENERGY PROJECTION | | | | | | | |
| FIGHTING SKILLS | | | | | | | |

**REAL NAME:** Unrevealed
**ALIASES:** Dominatrix
**IDENTITY:** Secret
**OCCUPATION:** Pet, former crimelord
**CITIZENSHIP:** UK
**PLACE OF BIRTH:** Unrevealed
**KNOWN RELATIVES:** None
**GROUP AFFILIATION:** None
**EDUCATION:** Unrevealed
**FIRST APPEARANCE:** (mentioned) Captain Britain #3 (1976); (voice) The Daredevils #4 (1983); (seen) The Daredevils #9 (1983)

**HISTORY:** Formerly the British underworld's self-proclaimed top dog, the Vixen controlled her organization with ruthless efficiency, feared by her men who knew that failure was rewarded by torture. Extravagant, vain, violently intolerant of any perceived slight, given to flamboyant outfits and preferring for her lackies to address her as "Dominatrix," her organization and name became well known to the police, but not her appearance or true identity. She planned a series of gold bullion robberies, raiding London banks, but an assault on the Chambers St Bank went awry when a silent alarm triggered, drawing Chief Inspector Dai Thomas' armed CID Flying Squad to the scene. Pinned down by the police, the robbers were caught off guard by new super hero Captain Britain (Brian Braddock), who made his public debut overpowering them. A few weeks later another of Vixen's bank raid teams was apprehended by the hero and police detective Kate Fraser. At some point Vixen decided her ultimate goal was to become the UK's self-appointed monarch. Her criminal espionage network infiltrated the British spy agency STRIKE (Special Tactical Reserve for International Key Emergencies), covertly placing people in top positions; however, STRIKE's Psi-Division discovered this, and the Vixen hired the assassin Arcade to eliminate them. The telepaths went on the run, but were rapidly picked off by Arcade's subcontractor, Slaymaster, until he was stopped by Captain Britain, called in by one of the surviving psis, his sister Betsy Braddock. Vixen swiftly consolidated her control over STRIKE before the remaining psis could expose her. Soon after, the insane reality-warping mutant Sir James Jaspers manipulated the UK government to order STRIKE to round up all super heroes into concentration camps. Initially happy to facilitate this, when Jaspers became Prime Minister and Britain rapidly devolved into a police state, Vixen became concerned that Jaspers' excesses would draw international interest. She tried to eliminate Jaspers, but he casually slew her guards, then turned Vixen into a small fox.

Jaspers was soon slain, and STRIKE was discredited and dissolved; Vixen reverted to normal, though she retained nightmarish memories of her experience. A few months later Slaymaster captured Captain Britain and delivered him to Vixen; however Vixen refused to hand over the hero's power-enhancing costume to Slaymaster, insisting her own scientists would examine and duplicate it, and tortured the hero, treatment Slaymaster felt was dishonorable. Captain Britain subsequently escaped after Slaymaster stole his costume from Vixen's lab. Betsy Braddock later became the new Captain Britain, prompting Brian to retire; finding this new hero and her allies RCX (Resources Control Executive, STRIKE's successors) equally meddlesome, Vixen furnished Slaymaster with a power-enhancing suit created using the data they had gathered, and lured Betsy into an ambush. Slaymaster crippled Betsy, but when an enraged Brian arrived and gained the upper hand, Vixen beat a hasty retreat. Shortly after Captain Britain (Brian once more) joined new super group Excalibur, Vixen made a failed attempt to capture young mutant Colin McKay (later Kylun), and was hired to break a prisoner out of Crossmoor Prison, which proved to be a police trap; to escape, she released the imprisoned Juggernaut (Cain Marko) and dozens of other inmates to act as a distraction. Some time later Vixen was again lured into a trap, this time by banker Nigel Frobisher, an agent of extradimensional deposed tyrant Sat-Yr9, who saw Vixen's organization as a conveniently pre-built new powerbase; Sat-Yr9's other agent, the reality warping Jamie Braddock, transformed Vixen into a fox again (presumably sensing the pattern left by Jaspers), and Frobisher into a doppelganger of Vixen's human form. Frobisher kept up his pretense until Sat-Yr9 was in a position to openly take control of the organization, at which point she ambushed Excalibur. When Frobisher challenged Sat-Yr9's authority during this mission, she fatally stabbed him; soon after Excalibur rallied, and Jamie was captured. The fate of Vixen, who had accompanied the assault as Jamie's docile pet, remains unrevealed.

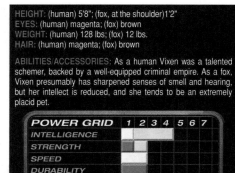

**HEIGHT:** (human) 5'8"; (fox, at the shoulder)1'2"
**EYES:** (human) magenta; (fox) brown
**WEIGHT:** (human) 128 lbs; (fox) 12 lbs.
**HAIR:** (human) magenta; (fox) brown

**ABILITIES/ACCESSORIES:** As a human Vixen was a talented schemer, backed by a well-equipped criminal empire. As a fox, Vixen presumably has sharpened senses of smell and hearing, but her intellect is reduced, and she tends to be an extremely placid pet.

| POWER GRID | 1 | 2 | 3 | 4 | 5 | 6 | 7 |
|---|---|---|---|---|---|---|---|
| INTELLIGENCE | | | | | | | |
| STRENGTH | | | | | | | |
| SPEED | | | | | | | |
| DURABILITY | | | | | | | |
| ENERGY PROJECTION | | | | | | | |
| FIGHTING SKILLS | | | | | | | |

YELLOW BARS INDICATE HUMAN FORM'S LEVELS

**HISTORY:** Zabu is the last member of the Smilodon (saber-toothed tiger) species known to survive in the Savage Land, an artificial preserve for prehistoric wildlife located in Antarctica. As a cub, Zabu was made an orphan by the Man-Apes, neanderthal-like creatures who slaughtered his mother and siblings. Zabu was found by the wolf Zagah who brought him to his mate Thana for food, but instead Thana adopted Zabu as her own cub and he grew up beside her children Jhet and Fheta. Jhet grew to resent Zabu and hated Fheta for admiring him; when Jhet slew Fheta, Zabu was forced to kill him in combat, estranging him from Zagah and Thana. At the age of one, Zabu met a female Smilodon and took her to be his mate. She became pregnant with Zabu's litter, but one day while he was out hunting, the Man-Apes burst into their cave and killed his mate.

Enraged, Zabu pursued the Man-Apes and came upon them just as they had slain the outsider Robert Plunder and were about to kill his son Kevin. Zabu's arrival saved Kevin's life and when the Man-Ape's chief Maa-Gor was about to strike Zabu from behind, Kevin shot Maa-Gor with his father's pistol, returning Zabu's favor. Both deprived of family, Zabu and Kevin adopted each other. Zabu taught Kevin how to survive in the Savage Land and their bond earned Kevin a new name from the locals — "Son of the Tiger" or, "Ka-Zar." Ka-Zar and Zabu made their first home in the Place of Mists and the unusual gases there retarded Zabu's aging so that by the time Ka-Zar was an adult male, Zabu was still in the prime of his life.

Over time more outsiders came to the Savage Land, notably the X-Men who befriended Ka-Zar and Zabu. When Ka-Zar's existence became known to the outside world, he made the first of several excursions to his homeland alongside Zabu. The duo's adventures in the outside world included encounters with Kraven the Hunter (Sergei Kravinoff), AIM, the Man-Thing (Ted Sallis), Gemini (Joshua Link) and Ka-Zar's brother the Plunderer. Zabu also befriended Ka-Zar's allies including Tongah, SHIELD agent Bobbi Morse, Shanna the She-Devil (Shanna O'Hara), Bernard Kloss and Wolverine (Logan/James Howlett). Ka-Zar and Zabu soon met Leanne, queen of Lemura who possessed a pet giant cat named Felina; although Ka-Zar and Zabu were respectively taken with Leanne and Felina, Ka-Zar ultimately married Shanna. Zabu was briefly abducted by the Impossible Man as part of a "scavenger hunt," but was returned to the Savage Land by the X-Men. The Savage Land was eventually destroyed by Jorro, a Deviant wearing the armor of Terminus. Zabu lived with Ka-Zar and Shanna in the outside world until the Savage Land's restoration at the High Evolutionary's hands, at which time Zabu rejoined Ka-Zar, Shanna and their son Matthew in the Savage Land.

Zabu continued to aid Ka-Zar and Shanna both in adventuring about the Savage Land and protecting their homeland from exploitation.

**REAL NAME:** Zabu
**ALIASES:** "Tiger-Brother"
**IDENTITY:** No dual identity
**OCCUPATION:** Pet, adventurer
**CITIZENSHIP:** Property of Kevin Plunder
**PLACE OF BIRTH:** The Savage Land
**KNOWN RELATIVES:** Unidentified mate (deceased), Mara (mother, deceased), unidentified siblings (deceased)
**GROUP AFFILIATION:** None
**EDUCATION:** None
**FIRST APPEARANCE:** X-Men #10 (1965)

When the Plunderer sent the villainous Gregor to the Savage Land to abduct Matthew, Zabu was badly injured after taking an energy blast intended for Ka-Zar. Eventually besting the Plunderer, Ka-Zar and Zabu were later held up in New York by legalities, but were released thanks to Everett K. Ross and the Black Panther (T'Challa). Zabu once mysteriously disappeared, driving Ka-Zar to attempt to recruit Jessica Jones to find him, but Ka-Zar ultimately found Zabu himself.

Zabu was one of the first beings on Earth to learn about the Skrull's "Secret Invasion" when attacked along with Ka-Zar and Shanna by Skrulls posing as SHIELD agents at their Vibranium mining operation in the Savage Land. Zabu was later caught by Hercules (Heracles) as part of the demi-gods televised new Twelve Labors, but he was eventually returned to Ka-Zar. Zabu later joined many of the Savage Land's people in repelling an attempted invasion by Roxxon Oil and the Plunderer. After a Skrull ship crash landed in the Savage Land filled with Skrulls believing themselves to be Earth heroes, Zabu followed Ka-Zar, Spider-Man (Peter Parker) and many others into combat against the threat and was badly beaten by Pitt'o Nili, the Skrull posing as Captain America. Zabu soon joined the Avengers along with his friends and helped kill the remaining Skrull invaders within the Savage Land after they were exposed by Mr. Fantastic (Reed Richards).

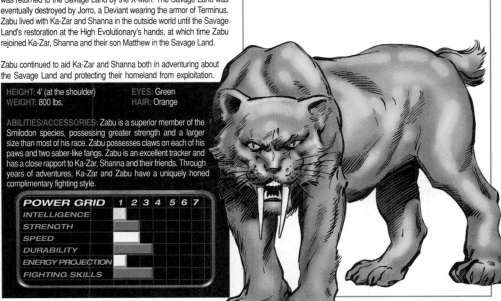

**HEIGHT:** 4' (at the shoulder)
**WEIGHT:** 800 lbs.
**EYES:** Green
**HAIR:** Orange

**ABILITIES/ACCESSORIES:** Zabu is a superior member of the Smilodon species, possessing greater strength and a larger size than most of his race. Zabu possesses claws on each of his paws and two saber-like fangs. Zabu is an excellent tracker and has a close rapport to Ka-Zar, Shanna and their friends. Through years of adventures, Ka-Zar and Zabu have a uniquely honed complimentary fighting style.

| POWER GRID | 1 | 2 | 3 | 4 | 5 | 6 | 7 |
|---|---|---|---|---|---|---|---|
| INTELLIGENCE | | | | | | | |
| STRENGTH | | | | | | | |
| SPEED | | | | | | | |
| DURABILITY | | | | | | | |
| ENERGY PROJECTION | | | | | | | |
| FIGHTING SKILLS | | | | | | | |

# ANT-MAN'S ANTS

**CURRENT MEMBERS:** None
**FORMER MEMBERS:** (Pym's) Korr (deceased), Melanie, Nash (deceased), Nash XII (deceased); (Lang's) Axel, Blixen, Emma, Gambit (deceased), Indy, James, Jezebel, Kenny G, Mara, Martha, Prince (deceased), Purdey, Silver, Silver Streak, Steed, Van Halen, Vixen (deceased), Whitmore; (both) thousands of others
**BASE OF OPERATIONS:** Mobile, depending on Ant-Man's activities
**FIRST APPEARANCE:** Tales to Astonish #27 (1962)

**HISTORY:** When genius biochemist Henry Pym became Ant-Man, he used his cybernetic helmet to regularly recruit hundreds of ants to assist him. As one of his era's earliest super heroes, Pym was much depended upon by police, and he stationed ants at police stations and elsewhere throughout Manhattan to, via relay system, inform him of major developments. Pym's nemesis Egghead (Elihas Starr) tried to turn Pym's ants against him, but the ants, supposedly dedicated to justice, refused. When Voice (Jason Cragg) almost sent Pym to his death, ants even rescued him without instructions. When Pym and his partner Wasp (Janet van Dyne) were attacked by Trago, Korr, a longtime ant ally, rescued them, then perished fighting off a Trago-controlled snake. Korr's death perhaps contributed to Pym's change to Giant-Man, in which identity he relied far less on ants. He subsequently took new identities as Goliath and Yellowjacket.

Several years after Pym first became Ant-Man, Scott Lang absconded with his equipment to rescue Dr. Erica Sondheim; Lang rallied hundreds of ants to assist; the two most notable he dubbed "Emma" and "Steed." Pym approved Lang's new super-hero career, which set Lang against Taskmaster, Odd John, Shellshock, and others. Like Pym, Lang stationed ants as listeners, and a response to one eavesdropping incident led to a microversal adventure with the Thing (Ben Grimm). When Lang relocated to California, he regularly deployed ant Indy as his flying steed. Returning to Manhattan and joining

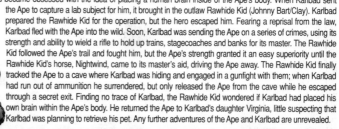

*Art by Bob Layton*

the Fantastic Four, Lang relied more on upgraded equipment than on ants. When Pym's Project: BIG (Biotechnically Induced Growth) was disrupted by Kosmosians, however, Lang, with ants Van Halen and Kenny G as lieutenants, again led ant armies to support Pym. Lang joined the Avengers but perished when the Scarlet Witch went mad.

Lang's "Ant-Brigades" included Blixen and Vixen, the latter slain by Odd John's mutated insects; Purdey, who was grown to giant size to help Lang against Taskmaster; Gambit, who perished under laser fire from renegade AI GARD (Graduated Automatic Radical Defense); Prince, who died ignominiously in a young boy's "food fight"; Axel, who carried a shrunken Goliath (Erik Josten) to police custody; Mara, who acted as Lang's confidante/sounding board; and steeds Silver Streak, Jezebel, Whitmore, James, Martha, and Silver.

# APE

**REAL NAME:** None
**ALIASES:** None
**IDENTITY:** No dual identity
**OCCUPATION:** Trained animal, experimental subject; former carnival performer
**CITIZENSHIP:** Property of Kurt Karlbad

**PLACE OF BIRTH:** Unrevealed
**KNOWN RELATIVES:** None
**GROUP AFFILIATION:** None
**EDUCATION:** Performance training
**FIRST APPEARANCE:** Rawhide Kid #39 (1964)

**HISTORY:** The Ape was part of a traveling carnival when it was discovered by scientist Kurt Karlbad in 1872. Interested in the Ape's particular adaptability to human commands, Karlbad became obsessed with the idea of placing a human brain inside of the Ape's body. When Karlbad sent

*Art by Herb Trimpe*

the Ape to capture a lab subject for him, it brought in the outlaw Rawhide Kid (Johnny Bart/Clay). Karlbad prepared the Rawhide Kid for the operation, but the hero escaped him. Fearing a reprisal from the law, Karlbad fled with the Ape into the wild. Soon, Karlbad was sending the Ape on a series of crimes, using its strength and ability to wield a rifle to hold up trains, stagecoaches and banks for its master. The Rawhide Kid followed the Ape's trail and fought him, but the Ape's strength granted it an easy superiority until the Rawhide Kid's horse, Nightwind, came to its master's aid, driving the Ape away. The Rawhide Kid finally tracked the Ape to a cave where Karlbad was hiding and engaged in a gunfight with them; when Karlbad had run out of ammunition he surrendered, but only released the Ape from the cave while he escaped through a secret exit. Finding no trace of Karlbad, the Rawhide Kid wondered if Karlbad had placed his own brain within the Ape's body. He returned the Ape to Karlbad's daughter Virginia, little suspecting that Karlbad was planning to retrieve his pet. Any further adventures of the Ape and Karlbad are unrevealed.

**HEIGHT:** 5'7"
**WEIGHT:** 340 lbs.

**EYES:** Brown
**HAIR:** Brown

**ABILITIES/ACCESSORIES:** Like most gorillas, the Ape was stronger than an average human, skilled at climbing and was specially trained to follow verbal commands, respond to musical signals and operate human instruments such as a rifle.

**INTELLIGENCE:** 2 **STRENGTH:** 3 **SPEED:** 2 **DURABILITY:** 3
**ENERGY PROJECTION:** 1 **FIGHTING SKILLS:** 3

# THE BEASTS OF BERLIN

**MEMBERS:** None named
**BASE OF OPERATIONS:** Budapest, Hungary; formerly a laboratory in Berlin, Germany

**FIRST APPEARANCE:** Tales to Astonish #60 (1964)

**HISTORY:** Communist scientists in Berlin accidentally created a ray projector that could increase animal intelligence, using it to endow gorillas with human-like intellect. Unable to analyze or duplicate the ray projector, the communists kept it under heavy guard at a laboratory within a secret facility. Dubbed the "Beasts of Berlin," the super-intelligent apes served as guards at this facility. Hearing rumors of a new communist super-weapon, ex-FBI agent Lee Kearns investigated, but the communists captured him. Kearns had left word of his mission with his friend Hank Pym, alias Giant-Man, who followed him to Berlin. Pym quickly found and freed Kearns, who briefed Pym regarding the situation. While Pym and Kearns fought their way to the lab, subduing a gorilla en route, the communist facility's troops prepared to create an entire army of super-intelligent apes. Before they could do so, Pym and Kearns invaded the lab, where Pym evaded six more super-gorillas and turned the ray projector against the troops, temporarily reducing them to animalistic simpletons since the ray had an opposite effect on humans. Realizing the gorillas were gradually losing their intelligence without further exposure to the ray, Pym smashed the ray projector to smithereens. Their mission accomplished, Pym and Kearns fled Berlin. Years later, communist scientists re-created the animal intelligence ray and mentally augmented a new ape army, now capable of speech. These Beasts of Berlin joined other communist super-operatives in forming the People's Security Forces (PSF). While allied with Hungarian communists and a then-mad Quicksilver, the PSF battled the Avengers, but were defeated. The Beyond Corporation later created their own version of the Beasts, sending them and other ersatz copies of various super-beings against the Nextwave Squad.

Art by Al Milgrom

ORIGINAL UNIFORM

Art by Dick Ayers

# BILL & DON

**REAL NAME:** Bill & Don
**ALIASES:** None
**IDENTITY:** The general public is unaware of Bill & Don's existence
**OCCUPATION:** Adventurers; former laboratory test subjects
**CITIZENSHIP:** Property of Alphonsus Lefszycic

**PLACE OF BIRTH:** Unrevealed; possibly the Atlantic Ocean
**KNOWN RELATIVES:** None
**GROUP AFFILIATION:** Fallen Angels
**EDUCATION:** Trained by Alphonsus Lefszycic
**FIRST APPEARANCE:** Fallen Angels #2 (1987)

**HISTORY:** Despite Don's mutant blue hue, Bill & Don were unremarkable marine crustaceans that genius college seniors Ramon Lipschitz and Tadashi Fujita turned into cyborgs as part of their cybernetics research. Between experiments, Lipschitz's cousin Alphonsus Lefszycic (nicknamed Gomi), who the seniors also turned into an unwilling cyborg, cared for Bill & Don, the three developing a close-knit friendship. When the Fallen Angels — a group of superhuman adolescent petty criminals — invited the three cyborgs to join, the trio voted two to one to join. The Fallen Angels had no specific mission or purpose, remaining together mostly for each other's company. The group was headquartered in New York City's Beat St. Club and had misadventures on and off-planet. However, during one of the team's outings, Don was killed when his reptilian teammate Devil Dinosaur accidentally stepped on him. After harboring a grudge and a desire for revenge, Bill finally forgave Devil Dinosaur and honored Don's memory by continuing to help others. Bill's current activities and location are unrevealed, although he and Gomi were noted by Tony Stark as potential Initiative recruits.

**LENGTH:** 1'2" (including tail)
**WEIGHT:** 4.5 lbs.; (as cyborg) 10 lbs.

**EYES:** (Bill) green; (Don) blue
**HAIR** (trichoid sensillae): (Bill) green; (Don) blue

Art by Kerry Gammill

**ABILITIES/ACCESSORIES:** Bill's cybernetic implants greatly enhance his intelligence and durability, while also amplifying his strength to a degree that he can lift logs or knock over a standing human being. The devices also enable him to survive out of water for extended periods of time, and greatly enhance his claw's crushing grip. He can crawl briskly on the ocean floor and swim backwards with great speed; it is unrevealed if his cybernetics have enhanced these abilities. He also has hair-like trichoid sensillae along his body which function as sensors for touch, pressure, motion and changes in ambient chemicals. Via uncertain means, Bill is able to communicate with humans. Don's blue color marked him as a rare mutant lobster, though no evidence of him having mutant powers existed.

**INTELLIGENCE:** 3 **STRENGTH:** 2 **SPEED:** 2 **DURABILITY:** 3
**ENERGY PROJECTION:** 1 **FIGHTING SKILLS:** 2

# BLAZE THE WONDER COLLIE

**REAL NAME:** Blaze, Son of Fury
**ALIASES:** None
**IDENTITY:** No dual identity
**OCCUPATION:** Companion; former search-and-rescue dog
**CITIZENSHIP:** Property of Dr. Glenn Forest; former property of US Army, Lynlan Kennels
**PLACE OF BIRTH:** Springdale, Maine
**KNOWN RELATIVES:** Fury (father, presumed deceased)
**GROUP AFFILIATION:** Formerly American Red Cross, K-9 Corps
**EDUCATION:** K-9 training, Red Cross training
**FIRST APPEARANCE:** Blaze the Wonder Collie #2 (1949)

**HISTORY:** In 1944, after winning "Best in the Show" for Lynlan Kennels, Blaze was stolen and sold to an army camp. Blaze excelled at most K-9 instruction, but innate friendliness made him a poor student for attack dog training. Transferred to Red Cross service, Blaze was sent to Normandy, France. Assigned to Captain Glenn Forest, whom he instinctively recognized as his destined "Master," Blaze located injured men on the battlefield, also saving Forest's life by pushing him away from plane gunfire. He also detected Nazi spies, and, with Forest, retrieved WAC Judy Stanton from enemy hands. By war's end, Blaze had earned Legion of Merit, Croix de Guerre, and other medals, and Forest's superiors allowed him to retain Blaze as a pet. Forest set up medical practice in Springdale, Maine, where wealthy Glenda Stanton, Lynlan Kennels' owner, recognized Blaze and forced authorities to retrieve him. While Forest sought legal recourse, Blaze pined for his master until Glenda's daughter Judy, the WAC he had rescued, took him to visit Glenn. When a saboteur planted a bomb at Glenda's defense plant, Blaze killed the saboteur and led Glenn to rescue Judy from flames. Glenda returned Blaze to Forest, who became guardian to young Tad, whom Blaze rescued from a bull. Glenda, retaining a grudge, supported Dr. Lawrence Cheney as town doctor, but when he misdiagnosed a town outbreak, Cheney was fired and Forest promoted in his stead. Last heard of in the early 1950s, Blaze is presumably long dead, but he earned widespread public acclaim during his lifetime, although his many adventures remain mostly unrecorded.

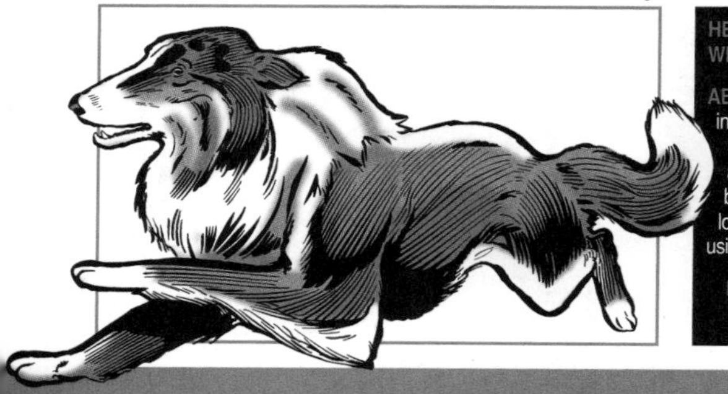

**HEIGHT:** 2'4" (at the shoulder)
**WEIGHT:** 83 lbs.
**EYES:** Brown
**HAIR:** Gold and white

**ABILITIES/ACCESSORIES:** Blaze possessed remarkable courage, intelligence, and devotion, particularly to his master and friends. Understanding spoken language far better than most animals, he adapted quickly to any training and could perform remarkable feats beyond those of almost any other dog. Although possessing a deep love for humanity, he could be a savage opponent when necessary, using teeth and claws in combat.

**INTELLIGENCE:** 3 **STRENGTH:** 3 **SPEED:** 3 **DURABILITY:** 2
**ENERGY PROJECTION:** 1 **FIGHTING SKILLS:** 4

# CR'REEE

**REAL NAME:** Cr'reee
**ALIASES:** Cr+eee
**IDENTITY:** No dual identity
**OCCUPATION:** Space pirate
**CITIZENSHIP:** Lupus
**PLACE OF BIRTH:** Lupus
**KNOWN RELATIVES:** Lt'al (mate), unidentified offspring
**GROUP AFFILIATION:** Starjammers
**EDUCATION:** Unrevealed
**FIRST APPEARANCE:** X-Men #104 (1977); (identified) Uncanny X-Men #158 (1982)

**HISTORY:** After his mate became pregnant, the Lupine Cr'reee feared he was not ready for parenthood and so fled his homeworld Lupus. He soon encountered the Saurid Ch'od and his companions, the human Corsair and the Mephitisoid Hepzibah who had recently fled Shi'ar imprisonment and banded together as the space pirates called the Starjammers. Cr'reee took an instant liking to Ch'od, who seemed to be the only non-Lupine to understand Cr'reee's language. Cr'reee eventually joined the Starjammers and was regularly referred to as Ch'od's pet, given that he would often sit on Ch'od's shoulder. During the Starjammers' quest to find the legendary Phalkon, Cr'reee returned to Lupus to recover a pod that contained part of a map to Phalkon. Arrested for his past social crime and imprisoned, Cr'reee quickly escaped and, after learning that the pod had been taken to a museum, enlisted the aid of his old friend Flex in retrieving it. After Flex was arrested, Cr'reee went to his aid, convincing Cr'reee's mate to forgive him and drop the charges against him. After she recovered the pod for him, Cr'reee reconciled with her and returned to the Starjammers with her and their offspring. Attacked by the Shi'ar, explosive decompression blew Cr'reee into open space, but he was rescued by the Starjammer's sentient artificial intelligence Waldo and returned in time to save Corsair from the Shi'ar Imperial Guardsman Quasar. The Starjammers ultimately located the Phalkon on Earth, which led to a clash with the Shi'ar Imperial Guard during which Cr'reee and his family overwhelmed Guardsman Nightside. Cr'reee's mate and their offspring ultimately returned to Lupus while Cr'reee remained with the Starjammers.

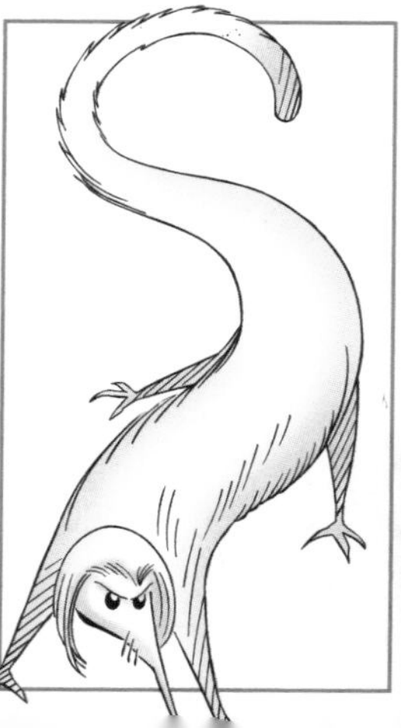

Art by Dave Cockrum

**HEIGHT:** 1'4"
**WEIGHT:** 8 lbs.
**EYES:** Black (no visible pupil)
**HAIR:** White

**ABILITIES/ACCESSORIES:** Cr'reee possesses various animalistic traits, including heightened senses and swiftness as well as natural fangs and claws.

**INTELLIGENCE:** 3 **STRENGTH:** 2 **SPEED:** 3 **DURABILITY:** 2
**ENERGY PROJECTION:** 1 **FIGHTING SKILLS:** 2

# CURRS

**KNOWN MEMBERS:** None named
**BASE OF OPERATIONS:** The Negative Zone and Annihilation Wave-controlled worlds
**FIRST APPEARANCE:** Annihilation: Silver Surfer #1 (2006)

**TRAITS:** Curs are dog-like beings native to the Negative Zone. They possess the Opposing Force, the Negative Zone's version of the Power Cosmic. They have long tentacle-like sensory organs in place of eyes, sharp claws, and large mouths filled with several rows of sharp teeth. Two to three Currs are bonded to each member of Ravenous' Seekers via an umbilical cord at the back of each Curr's neck, which grants the Seeker the power of the Opposing Force. They are attuned to the Power Cosmic, allowing them to track it and its possessors across entire galaxies. If mortally wounded, a Curr reverts to a larval form, then regenerates from the cord into its adult form within minutes; while the Curr is reconstituting itself, the Seeker to which it is bonded loses his connection to the Opposing Force. The Currs also power the Seekers' Star Sleds, which are capable of intergalactic travel.

**HEIGHT:** 2'2" (at haunches)
**WEIGHT:** 170 lbs.
**EYES:** None
**SKIN:** Blue

**HISTORY:** The origin of the Currs, and how they came to serve Ravenous, remains a mystery. Ravenous and his Seekers brought their Currs with them into the positive-matter universe as part of Annihilus' invasion force. Seeking out the Power Cosmic, they encountered two of Galactus' former heralds amidst the ruins of Xandar: the Silver Surfer (Norrin Radd) and the android Air-Walker (Gabriel Lan). The Currs mortally wounded the Air-Walker, but the Surfer escaped. While another group of Currs brought Terrax the Tamer to heel in the Eudorian Reach, Ravenous' Currs were driven away from the Surfer by Red Shift and Firelord, but tracked the Surfer to Galactus himself. Ravenous and his Curs were badly beaten by the Surfer, who had been freshly empowered by the world-devourer, and fled back to Annihilus empty-handed. The Seekers and their Currs later attacked Nova (Richard Rider) and his allies on Daedalus 5, helping to drive them off the planet. The Currs eventually met defeat on the Kree homeworld Hala at the hands of Ronan the Accuser and the Super-Skrull (Kl'rt). The Currs presumably retreated to the worlds granted to Ravenous after Annihilus' defeat and seeming death.

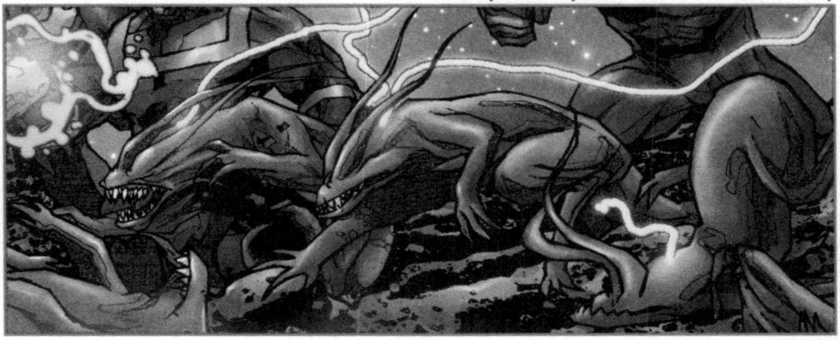
Art by Renato Arlem

# DEUCE

**REAL NAME:** Deuce
**ALIASES:** The Devil-Dog
**IDENTITY:** Inapplicable
**OCCUPATION:** Pet; former guide & police dog
**CITIZENSHIP:** Property of Weasel
**PLACE OF BIRTH:** Unrevealed
**KNOWN RELATIVES:** None
**GROUP AFFILIATION:** None
**EDUCATION:** Trained police & guide dog
**FIRST APPEARANCE:** Daredevil #361 (1997)

**HISTORY:** Deuce was an old, retired police dog that Franklin "Foggy" Nelson bought for Matt Murdock. Deuce was supposed to be Matt's guide dog in public and help Matt fight crime in his heroic Daredevil persona, but Matt didn't like the idea and let Foggy keep the dog. Despite his age, Deuce proved his heroism on several occasions, saving the lives of Foggy and his friends. After a pizza and a few drinks too many, Foggy lost Deuce in a poker game to Deadpool's partner Weasel. Deadpool in return gave the dog and some meat to his prisoner Blind Al. Deuce liked Blind Al a lot since Deadpool hid food everywhere in Al's home, but she couldn't stand the dog, rightfully feeling that Deadpool had given her the dog to torture her. After another of Deadpool's pranks involving Deuce, Blind Al had enough and tied up Deuce with duct tape; as a result he got fleas and had to be fitted with an E-Collar. During this period, Al and Deadpool took Deuce to the Bay City Aquarium, but when Al tried to have Deuce lead her home, the dog ran back without her, where he was found by Weasel. Deuce took Weasel back to the aquarium, arriving moments after Deadpool and Al became lost in time. They eventually returned, but learning Deuce had eaten her slippers, Blind Al's hatred of the dog endured. When Deadpool learned that Weasel was visiting Blind Al, only Deuce escaped his punishments. After escaping Deadpool's Box torture chamber, Blind Al gave Deuce to Weasel, and together the pair started a new chapter in their lives.

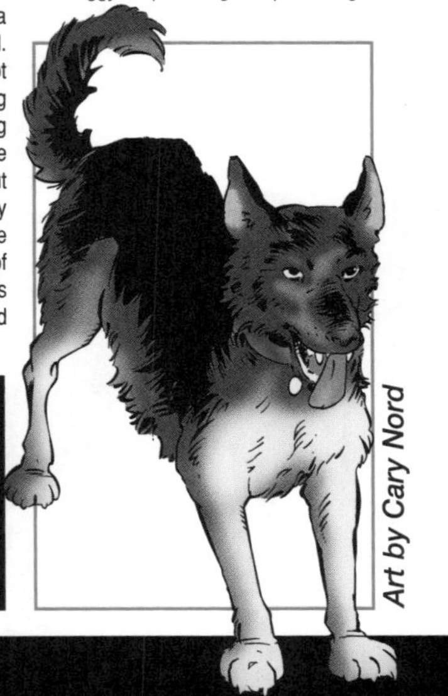
Art by Cary Nord

**HEIGHT:** 2' (at the shoulder)
**WEIGHT:** 77 lbs.
**EYES:** Blue
**HAIR:** Brown, black and white

**ABILITIES/ACCESSORIES:** Deuce runs around 30 mph and was trained to understand a variety of commands. Due to his age Deuce isn't able to act according to his police dog training anymore and only jumps at enemies to distract them instead of biting and holding them down.

**INTELLIGENCE:** 1 **STRENGTH:** 2 **SPEED:** 3 **DURABILITY:** 2
**ENERGY PROJECTION:** 1 **FIGHTING SKILLS:** 1

# DIABLO

**REAL NAME:** Diablo
**ALIASES:** None
**IDENTITY:** No dual identity
**OCCUPATION:** Hunter
**CITIZENSHIP:** None
**PLACE OF BIRTH:** Renegade's Peak, Montana
**KNOWN RELATIVES:** None
**GROUP AFFILIATION:** None
**EDUCATION:** No formal education
**FIRST APPEARANCE:** Blaze the Wonder Collie #2 (1949)

**HISTORY:** Diablo was a powerful grizzly who lived around Renegade's Peak, feasting mainly upon ants and fish. Diablo befriended Len Crabtree, a lone gold prospector in the mountains. When the outlaw Sam Derringer threatened Crabtree's life, thinking his gold prospecting had paid off, Diablo attacked Derringer and wound up killing him. Crabtree collected the reward on Derringer and shared his wealth with Diablo on special food, including honey. A forest fire around Renegade's Peak once drove Diablo high into the mountains where he tried to claim a mountain goat for food, only to fail at catching the creature. Diablo also tried to slay an elk, but wound up siding with the elk against the wolf Fang and his pack, mutual enemies; Diablo presented the dead wolves to Crabtree, who sold them to trapper Jack Crazyhorse for more money. Diablo was also an enemy of the cougar Slasher, the bull Caesar and the grizzly Blackbeard, who threatened to kill both Diablo and Crabtree until Diablo slew him. Despite the bear's friendship with Crabtree, the rancher Wes Ambler once tried to hunt Diablo for sport, but ultimately chose to respect Diablo's place in the wild. Diablo had an occasionally feisty spirit and once feasted upon Crabtree's apple cider; caught in a drunken stupor, the bear tore apart Crabtree's home and covered himself with flour. When Crabtree returned, he mistook Diablo for a polar bear.

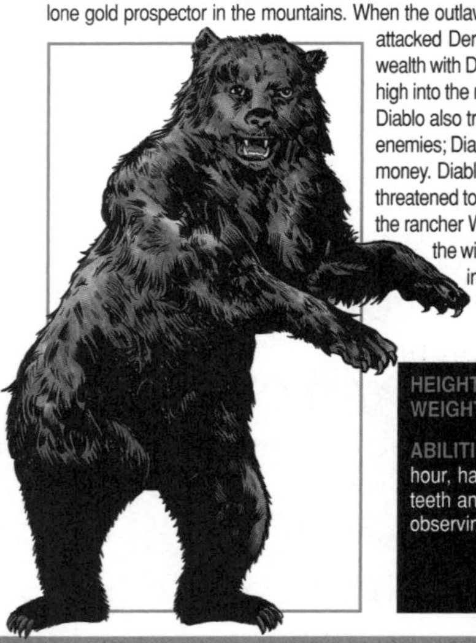

**HEIGHT:** 10'
**WEIGHT:** 420 lbs.
**EYES:** Brown
**HAIR:** Black

**ABILITIES/ACCESSORIES:** Like most grizzly bears, Diablo could run at a peak of 40 miles per hour, had a sense of smell superior to that of humans, possessed claws on each paw, sharp teeth and could stand on his hind legs for brief periods. Diablo could duplicate some tasks by observing the behavior of humans, such as opening bottles.

**INTELLIGENCE:** 1 **STRENGTH:** 3 **SPEED:** 2 **DURABILITY:** 3
**ENERGY PROJECTION:** 1 **FIGHTING SKILLS:** 2

# DREAMSTALKER

**REAL NAME:** Dreamstalker
**ALIASES:** None
**IDENTITY:** Existence not consciously known to general public
**OCCUPATION:** Steed of Nightmare
**CITIZENSHIP:** Property of Nightmare
**PLACE OF BIRTH:** Nightmare World, Dream Dimension
**KNOWN RELATIVES:** None
**GROUP AFFILIATION:** None
**EDUCATION:** No formal education
**FIRST APPEARANCE:** Strange Tales #110 (1963)

**HISTORY:** Dreamstalker is the dark spectral horse serving Nightmare. Used for transportation throughout dimensions, Dreamstalker was present during many of Nightmare's battles with his arch-foe, Dr. Stephen Strange, whose Eye of Agamotto the steed always feared, and with Nightmare met many other beings. After failing to live a mortal life on Earth, Nightmare decided to commit suicide and gave his realm and Dreamstalker to Dr. Strange and the Lilin Sister Nil, but Dr. Strange saved Nightmare from himself. Some time later Nightmare and Dreamstalker got trapped in the Land of the Dead, but Nightmare eventually escaped. In another failed Earth conquest plot, Nightmare rode Dreamstalker into battle against the "Marvel Knights." The steed was later stolen from Nightmare by the Hulk (Bruce Banner), who beat Nightmare on his earthly base, Nightmare Island. Later, Hellstorm seemingly destroyed several dark spectral horses that attacked Dr. Strange in Greenwich Village. Nightmare later led on Dreamstalker a mounted army in conquering the Land of Fiction, until the Fantastic Four stopped them. How many horses have been active as Dreamstalker during Nightmare's existence is unrevealed.

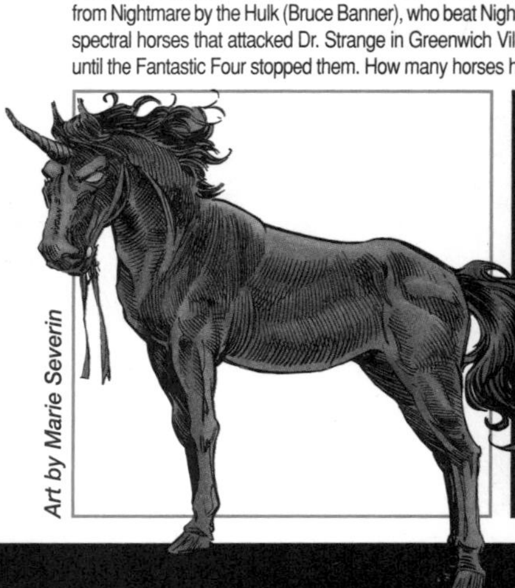

*Art by Marie Severin*

**HEIGHT:** 5'2" (at withers) **EYES:** Variable
**WEIGHT:** Variable **HAIR:** Black (variable)

**ABILITIES/ACCESSORIES:** Dreamstalker is a dark spectral horse from the Dream Dimension. These horned horses are, according to Nightmare, immortal. The male's horn's sting is deadly and they can run on air currents and the ground at approximately 80 mph. Though they possess some immunity to magic they are afraid of bright light and can temporarily be destroyed by powerful magic spells or Hellfire. Nightmare can summon Dreamstalker at any time and place and change his appearance at will. Over the years Dreamstalker has had varied manes (black, grey, burning or spiked), teeth (sometimes with prominent canine teeth, like a carnivore), eyes (red, green, grey, black or hollow) or hair color (mostly black). On some occasions Nightmare added bird-like or bat-like wings to Dreamstalker. There were even instances when Dreamstalker looked like a normal Earth horse.

**INTELLIGENCE:** 1 **STRENGTH:** 2 **SPEED:** 3 **DURABILITY:** 7
**ENERGY PROJECTION:** 2 **FIGHTING SKILLS:** 2

# DROOG

**REAL NAME:** Droog
**ALIASES:** Friend, "Droogi"
**IDENTITY:** No dual identity
**OCCUPATION:** Companion, bodyguard, enforcer
**CITIZENSHIP:** None
**PLACE OF BIRTH:** Bitterfrost, Siberia

**KNOWN RELATIVES:** Kondrati Yurivich Topolov (Gremlin, creator, deceased)
**GROUP AFFILIATION:** None
**EDUCATION:** No formal education
**FIRST APPEARANCE:** Incredible Hulk #188 (1975)

**HISTORY:** Droog is apparently a dog bioengineered into monstrous form and raised from a pup by the young Russian mutant genius Gremlin. As the peerless Gremlin designed weaponry for the Russian government, Droog — named for the Russian word for friend — was his only companion. Droog also enforced the diminutive Gremlin's will among the soldiers, occasionally "reprimanding" a disobedient Russian. After the Gremlin captured and brainwashed Major Glenn Talbot, his superior, General "Thunderbolt" Ross worked to rescue Talbot alongside SHIELD. Bruce Banner stowed away on the rescue mission, eventually joining them as the Hulk in the field. Captured by Ross' forces, the Gremlin summoned Droog, his loyal pet. The Hulk occupied Droog while the other Americans escaped via jet. Droog battered the Hulk, hurling him from heights and smashing him through walls while taunting him with rhymes. As the struggle caused Bitterfrost to collapse around them, SHIELD obliterated the surface facility, leaving only a crater to mark their violent times. The Gremlin, Hulk and Droog would each recover, though unbeknownst to each other. Gremlin later died battling Iron Man (Tony Stark), and Droog found a new master — it was Megacephalo, an ultra-genus who answered game show trivia from his Manhattan apartment, better and faster.

*Art by Herb Trimpe*

**HEIGHT:** 6'6" (at withers); 12'6" (on hind legs)
**WEIGHT:** 5210 lbs.
**EYES:** White
**HAIR:** None

**ABILITIES/ACCESSORIES:** Biped or quadruped, Droog is immensely durable and strong, has gifted human-level intellect, razor-sharp claws and a semi-prehensile tail, and speaks both Russian and English — rhyming all day long.

**INTELLIGENCE:** 4 **STRENGTH:** 7 **SPEED:** 2 **DURABILITY:** 7
**ENERGY PROJECTION:** 1 **FIGHTING SKILLS:** 4

# EBONY

**REAL NAME:** Ebony
**ALIASES:** None
**IDENTITY:** No dual identity
**OCCUPATION:** Familiar of Agatha Harkness
**CITIZENSHIP:** Property of Agatha Harkness

**PLACE OF BIRTH:** Unrevealed
**KNOWN RELATIVES:** None
**GROUP AFFILIATION:** None
**EDUCATION:** Unrevealed
**FIRST APPEARANCE:** Fantastic Four #94 (1970)

DEMONIC FORM

**HISTORY:** Ebony is the familiar to Agatha Harkness, one of the powerful witches of New Salem, Colorado. Although Harkness has been a practicing witch for centuries, the origins of Ebony are unrevealed. When Agatha and Ebony were living in Whisper Hill, New York, Agatha was chosen by Reed and Susan Richards to serve as governess to their son Franklin Richards. The Richards' enemies in the Frightful Four saw an opportunity to kidnap the child. However, they had not realized that Agatha was a true witch; Agatha and Ebony unleashed their powers upon the foursome, terrifying and vanquishing them. Ebony later helped defend Agatha and the Scarlet Witch against Necrodamus, although it was ultimately the Scarlet Witch who bested him. Later, Ebony helped the Avengers escape the grasp of the demon Mephisto, though the Hell-lord nearly turned Ebony inside-out in the process; later still, Ebony and Agatha aided Tigra (Greer Nelson) against the New Men's Tabur who was reverted to his original housecat form, in which he was easily beaten by Ebony.

**HEIGHT:** 9" (variable)
**WEIGHT:** 9 lbs. (variable)
**EYES:** Yellow (variable)
**HAIR:** Black (variable)

**ABILITIES/ACCESSORIES:** Typically in the form of a normal-sized domestic shorthair cat, Ebony can transform into a powerful, demonic cat-like creature, demonstrating phenomenal strength and speed in addition to large, razor-sharp claws and canine teeth. In one of these forms, Ebony resembles a giant panther; in his other form, Ebony is almost humanoid in shape and can breathe fire. In all his forms, Ebony demonstrates greater intelligence than normal housecats and appears to possess mystical senses. He also assists Agatha Harkness in casting her spells, utilizing an unrevealed form of communication (presumably telepathy); Agatha is able to extend her magic into locations where Ebony is present, even other dimensions.

*Art by Jack Kirby*

**INTELLIGENCE:** 2 **STRENGTH:** 4 **SPEED:** 2 **DURABILITY:** 7
**ENERGY PROJECTION:** 4 **FIGHTING SKILLS:** 2

# FREKI & GERI

**REAL NAMES:** Freki & Geri
**ALIASES:** (Freki) Freke, Ravenous; (Geri) Gere, Greedy
**IDENTITY:** No dual identities
**OCCUPATION:** Guardians
**CITIZENSHIP:** Property of the Asgardian throne
**PLACE OF BIRTH:** Asgard
**KNOWN RELATIVES:** Unrevealed
**GROUP AFFILIATION:** None
**EDUCATION:** Unrevealed
**FIRST APPEARANCE:** Thor #275 (1978); (Geri identified) Thor #344 (1984); (Freki identified) Official Handbook of the Marvel Universe #9 (1985)

**HISTORY:** Freki & Geri are Asgardian Dire Wolves that faithfully served Odin, later the monarch of Asgard, and accompanied Odin into battle and remained at his side when addressing Asgard. They were present when Odin used the Odinpower to restore Balder to life in an attempt to forestall Ragnarok, at Loki's trial for his attempt to cause Ragnarok and when Balder was proclaimed ruler of Asgard. Their fate since the destruction and recreation of Asgard is unrevealed.

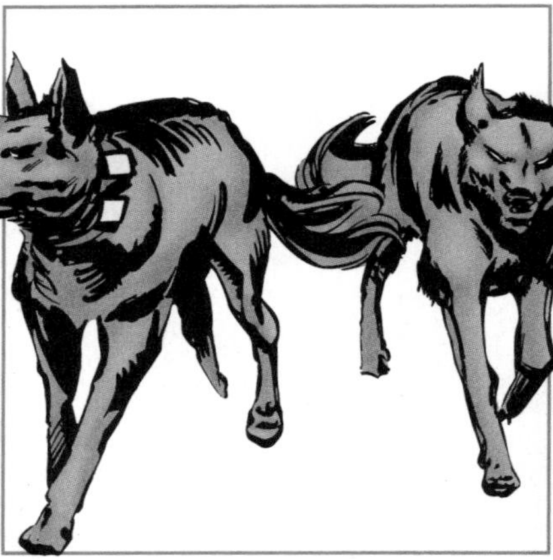

Art by John Buscema

**HEIGHT:** (Both, at the shoulder) 4'2"
**WEIGHT:** (Both) 220 lbs.
**EYES:** (Both) Red
**HAIR:** (Both) Dark gray

**ABILITIES/ACCESSORIES:** Freki & Geri possesses superhuman strength (can carry approximately 2 tons), speed, stamina, agility and reflexes. They can run at peak speed of 55 mph for approximately one hour before tiring. They can see into the infrared portions of the electromagnetic spectrum allowing them to see in complete darkness. They can smell the approach of others within 100 feet of themselves and can track a scent across almost any terrain. Freki & Geri can judge a person's emotional state and can detect any changes through observing the heat patterns and scents that person gives off. Their hearing is sensitive enough to enable them to hear sounds beyond the range of human hearing. They also possess razor-sharp claws on all four feet able to rend flesh and light wood. Their natural fur protects them from extreme cold conditions.

**INTELLIGENCE:** 2 **STRENGTH:** 4 **SPEED:** 2 **DURABILITY:** 3
**ENERGY PROJECTION:** 1 **FIGHTING SKILLS:** 3

# THE FROGS OF CENTRAL PARK

**CURRENT MEMBERS:** Bugeye, Dewlap, Queen Greensong and her son, Puddlegulp, many others
**FORMER MEMBERS:** King Glugwort (deceased), Gullywhump (deceased)
**BASE OF OPERATIONS:** Central Park, Manhattan, New York City
**FIRST APPEARANCE:** Thor #364 (1986)

**HISTORY:** For years, a society of frogs has lived in Central Park, making their home in the reservoir. Presided over by their monarch, King Glugwort, and his daughter, Princess Greensong, the frogs avoided the tunnels beneath the park where the alligators lived, and shared a bitter enmity with the rats of Central Park, ultimately leading to war between the two. One of the frogs, Puddlegulp, was once a man until being transformed by a vindictive witch. After the Asgardian thunder god, Thor, had been turned into a frog by his evil step-brother Loki's magic, he met Puddlegulp and followed him to the safety of the reservoir. On their way, Thor and Puddlegulp saw King Glutwort and his body guards under assault from the rats. They quickly moved to defend the king, but although they were successful in driving off the rats, they were too late to save him. The dying king warned them of the rats' plot to poison the reservoir and begged Thor to aid his subjects. The frogs followed Thor's plan: they attacked the rats and then strategically retreated while Thor descended into the sewers and lured alligators to the surface. They then led the rats into a trap where their ranks were decimated by the alligators. The frogs wanted Thor to remain as their new king, but he declined, and departed after thanking the frogs for their kindness. Puddlegulp said goodbye to Thor, revealing his own origin as a man, and informing Thor that he had surmised his true identity from the beginning. When Thor later returned to Central Park in his true form, Puddlegulp and Bugeye informed him of violence in the tunnels beneath the city. Thor entered the tunnels to investigate and fought the Marauders who had massacred the resident mutant civilization, the Morlocks. The Frogs of Central Park later witnessed a battle between the X-Men and Mojo in Manhattan's Delacorte Theatre, and assisted Dr. Stephen Strange after Dormammu had transformed him into a rat. Though they initially attacked Strange out of fear, they aided him in a ritual to summon the Earth goddess Gaea after he explained the situation. Later still, the frogs approached Thor on the eve of his battle with Onslaught to bid him farewell in case he should perish.

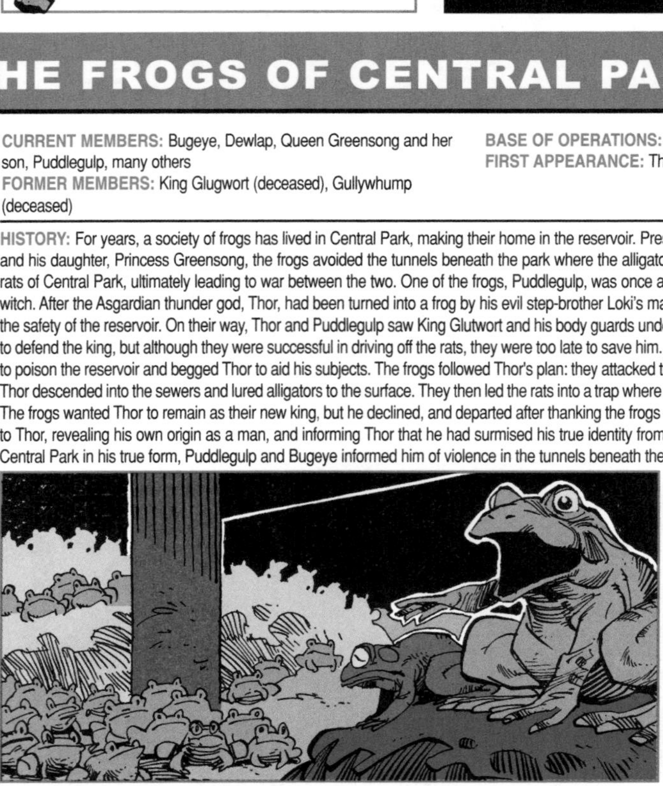

Art by Walter Simonson

# HELLCOW

**REAL NAME:** Bessie
**ALIASES:** Bovine Blood-Beast, Cowled Cow, Farm Killer, Recreant Ruminant
**IDENTITY:** Secret
**OCCUPATION:** Former milking cow
**CITIZENSHIP:** None
**PLACE OF BIRTH:** Kleine Scheidegg, Switzerland
**KNOWN RELATIVES:** None
**GROUP AFFILIATION:** None
**EDUCATION:** None
**FIRST APPEARANCE:** Giant-Size Man-Thing #5 (1975)

**HISTORY:** Three hundred years ago, Bessie was old Hans' favorite milking cow. One night a desperate Dracula — finding the local Swiss village locked tight — fed on Bessie. Unable to bear eating her, Hans buried her instead. Three nights later, Bessie rose as a vampire and began a vengeance-seeking pursuit of Dracula. Centuries later, in the farms around Cleveland, Ohio, the Hellcow fed on farmer Jubal Brown

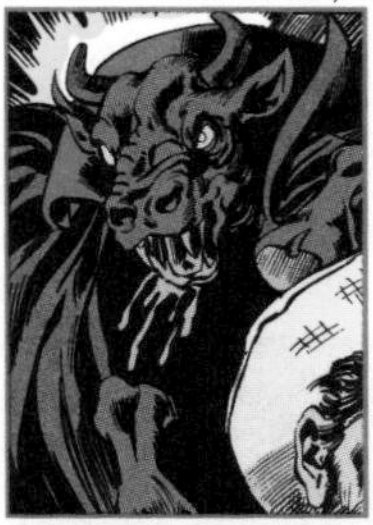

and four others. Howard the Duck determined that the killer could not be human but was likely a chicken, since he never trusted chickens. Howard sought to capture the killer, hoping to get a police job. Impersonating a man, he strolled Cleveland's streets at 2AM. Thinking he might be Dracula, Bessie swooped down and butted Howard through an auto parts shop's window, snapping a wooden post into a sharp stake. Howard grabbed a cross-shaped lug wrench to ward off Bessie. As he put it down to pick up a mallet, Bessie leapt at him, missed, and landed in a tire heap, her fangs imbedded in a whitewall. Using the stake and mallet, Howard destroyed her, but didn't get a police job for doing it. A fulfilled prophecy involving Blade presumably resurrected Bessie along with virtually every destroyed vampire but no sightings of her have been reported.

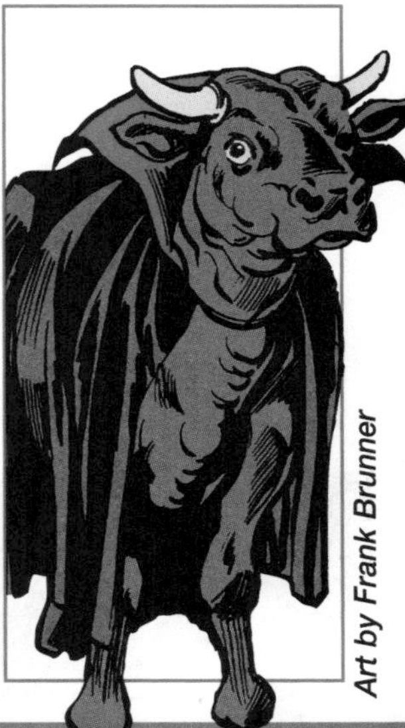

Art by Frank Brunner

**HEIGHT:** 4'6" at shoulder **WEIGHT:** 575 lbs. **EYES:** Red **HAIR:** Brown

**ABILITIES/ACCESSORIES:** Bessie's fangs could drain victims of blood and her Dracula cape could turn into leathery wings allowing her to fly. She could turn to mist and had a distinctive laugh: "hahahamooo."

**INTELLIGENCE:** 2 **STRENGTH:** 4 **SPEED:** 3 **DURABILITY:** 4
**ENERGY PROJECTION:** 1 **FIGHTING SKILLS:** 1

# HELLHORSE

**REAL NAME:** Elendil
**ALIASES:** None
**IDENTITY:** No dual identity
**OCCUPATION:** Steed of the Dreadknight (Bram Velsing)
**CITIZENSHIP:** Property of Bram Velsing
**PLACE OF BIRTH:** Unrevealed
**KNOWN RELATIVES:** None
**GROUP AFFILIATION:** None
**EDUCATION:** No formal education
**FIRST APPEARANCE:** Tales to Astonish #52 (1964)

**HISTORY:** Criminal scientist Nathan Garrett used his biology knowledge to engineer his horse Elendil to possess wings that could bear it aloft while

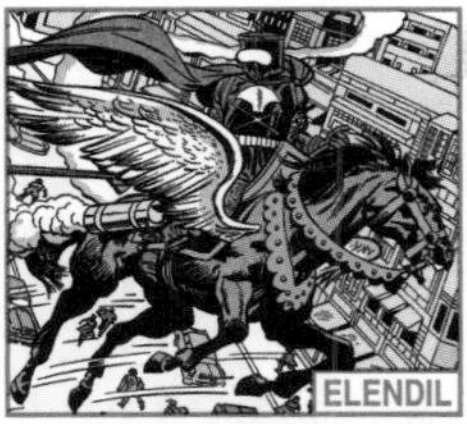
ELENDIL

Art by Jack Kirby

carrying a passenger. Garrett dubbed himself the Black Knight and became a costumed criminal, clashing repeatedly with his foe Giant-Man (Henry Pym) and the Wasp (Janet Van Dyne) astride Elendil. He also joined the ranks of Baron (Heinrich) Zemo's Masters of Evil. However, while in an aerial battle with Iron Man (Tony Stark), Garrett fell from Elendil and was gravely injured. Elendil fled and was eventually found in Switzerland by Victoria Frankenstein, a descendant of the famous Victor Frankenstein. Victoria attempted to restore the horse to normal with her ancestor's techniques, but unfortunately mutated the steed further. Dubbed the Hellhorse, it was stolen from Victoria by the Dreadknight who used it in battle with Iron Man and Frankenstein's Monster. Over the years, the Hellhorse also bore the Dreadknight into battle with the Black Knight (Dane Whitman), Captain Britain (Brian Braddock) and Spider-Man (Peter Parker). After the Dreadknight's last defeat, the Hellhorse was transferred to the property of Dane Whitman, who arranged for it to be held at New York's Central Park Zoo.

**HEIGHT:** 5'4" (at withers) **EYES:** Red
**WEIGHT:** 1000 lbs. **HAIR:** Black

**ABILITIES/ACCESSORIES:** The Hellhorse possesses wings that enable him to fly at speeds up to 125 miles per hour while carrying one or more passengers. The Hellhorse's hooves have been replaced with claw-like appendages and its body has been modified to withstand the pressures of high speed flight; the Hellhorse can also extract oxygen at high velocities. The Hellhorse has possessed a strong rapport with each of its masters (Nathan Garrett and Bram Velsing) enabling him to understand and obey complex commands.

**INTELLIGENCE:** 1 **STRENGTH:** 4 **SPEED:** 3 **DURABILITY:** 2
**ENERGY PROJECTION:** 1 **FIGHTING SKILLS:** 3

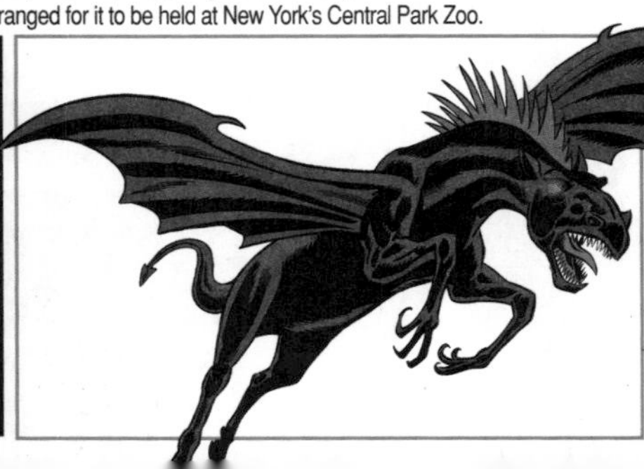

Art by George Tuska

# INA & BIRI

**REAL NAMES:** Ina and Biri
**ALIASES:** (Ina) the Spotted; (Biri) the Dark One
**IDENTITY:** No dual identities
**OCCUPATION:** Pets, adventurers
**CITIZENSHIP:** Property of Shanna O'Hara

**PLACE OF BIRTH:** Manhattan, New York
**KNOWN RELATIVES:** Julani (mother, deceased)
**GROUP AFFILIATION:** None
**EDUCATION:** No formal education
**FIRST APPEARANCE:** Shanna the She-Devil #1 (1971)

**HISTORY:** Ina and Biri were the cubs of Julani, a leopard who was brought to the Manhattan municipal zoo by Shanna O'Hara. Shanna raised Julani from a cub and Julani birthed Ina (a spotted leopard) and Biri (a panther) in captivity, but one day a sniper broke into the zoo and slaughtered most of the giant cats; although Julani survived, a panicked zookeeper shot and killed her. Shanna took custody of the cubs and moved them to the Dahomey Reserve in Africa; donning Julani's pelt as her garment, Shanna raised Ina and Biri in the wild and, when they were mature, she brought them with her as she took action against poachers. Ina and Biri aided Shanna against "Ivory" Dan Drake, slave trader el Montano, a colony of lost Minoans and the mutants Silver Samurai, Nekra and Mandrill. Along the way, Ina and Biri befriended Shanna's allies Patrick McShane, Jakuna Singh of SHIELD

**BIRI (LEFT), INA (RIGHT)**

*Jim Steranko*

and Daredevil (Matt Murdock). Unfortunately when Ina and Biri joined Shanna on a mission to India to confront the cultist Raga-Shah, he cast their souls into Ghamola, an elephant statue, animating it to life as his weapon. When Shanna destroyed the statue, she accidentally killed Ina and Biri as a result.

**HEIGHT:** 2'5" (Ina, at the shoulder); 2'7" (Biri, at the shoulder)
**WEIGHT:** (Ina) 40 lbs.; (Biri) 52 lbs.
**EYES:** Green (both)
**HAIR:** (Ina) Blond w/ black spots; (Biri) Black

**ABILITIES/ACCESSORIES:** Like most leopards, Ina and Biri could run at a peak of 37 miles per hour. Ina and Biri possessed keen eyesight, night vision along with sharp hunting and tracking instincts. They possessed a strong rapport with Shanna and were capable of following simple verbal commands.

**INTELLIGENCE:** 1 **STRENGTH:** 2 **SPEED:** 2 **DURABILITY:** 2
**ENERGY PROJECTION:** 1 **FIGHTING SKILLS:** 3

# KERBEROS

**REAL NAME:** Kerberos
**ALIASES:** "Kirby"
**IDENTITY:** No dual identity
**OCCUPATION:** Hunter, former pet
**CITIZENSHIP:** Property of Amadeus Cho
**PLACE OF BIRTH:** New Mexico desert

**KNOWN RELATIVES:** Unidentified mother (deceased), unidentified mate
**GROUP AFFILIATION:** None
**EDUCATION:** No formal education
**FIRST APPEARANCE:** Amazing Fantasy #15 (2006)

**HISTORY:** Kerberos was a young coyote pup when its mother was struck and killed by a car. He was found by the youthful genius Amadeus Cho who took the coyote under his protection. Aware that a coyote could be killed for suspicion of carrying rabies, Amadeus refused to allow strangers near the pup; Amadeus was himself a fugitive from the law and kept the coyote inside his jacket during their travels. Amadeus named the pup Kerberos ("Kirby" for short) after the Kerberos network authentication protocol, a secure identity software application (Kerberos was also derived from the Greek name for the hellhound Cerberus). Amadeus brought Kirby with him as he attempted to recruit allies sympathetic to the Hulk (Bruce Banner), eventually gathering the Olympian god Hercules, Angel (Warren Worthington) and Namora into the Renegades. For their actions, Hercules and Amadeus were taken into

*Art by Takeshi Miyazawa*

SHIELD custody. During the debriefing process, a Skrull that had replaced a SHIELD agent confiscated Kirby and replaced him with a Skrull imposter. The Skrull continued to travel with Amadeus and Hercules and was nearly killed when the Black Widow (Natasha Romanoff) struck Amadeus from behind, causing him to fall on top of the Kirby-Skrull. Amadeus nursed the seeming-pup to health, only for it to assume its true form as Hercules and his allies were attempting to combat the Skrull gods; the imposter was devoured by Demogorge. Amadeus eventually traced Kirby to the desert where he had been released back into the wild, only to find that the now grown coyote had taken a mate who was pregnant with his litter. Kirby refused to abandon his mate, forcing Amadeus to sadly leave his pet in the wild.

**HEIGHT:** 2' (at the shoulder)
**WEIGHT:** 20 lbs.

**EYES:** Black
**HAIR:** Brown

**ABILITIES/ACCESSORIES:** Kerberos possesses keen tracking senses and sharp teeth and claws. He was implanted with a tracer that allowed Amadeus track his movements.

**INTELLIGENCE:** 1 **STRENGTH:** 2 **SPEED:** 2 **DURABILITY:** 2
**ENERGY PROJECTION:** 1 **FIGHTING SKILLS:** 2

# KRAVEN THE HUNTER'S MENAGERIE

**CURRENT MEMBERS:** Nickel
**FORMER MEMBERS:** Rajah, Simba, Zmbuku, many others

**BASE OF OPERATIONS:** Mobile, including Nairobi, Manhattan and New Jersey
**FIRST APPEARANCE:** Amazing Spider-Man #15 (1964)

NICKEL

*Art by John McCrea*

**HISTORY:** The big game hunter and costumed criminal Kraven the Hunter (Sergei Kravinoff) kept a variety of animals in his custody during his lifetime. Many of these animals were captured by him personally in the wild. Kraven kept menageries both at his home in Africa and in the various bases he made in the USA. Among the animals Kraven held were varieties of bears, elephants, elk, gorillas, leopards, lions, rhinoceroses and snakes. Kraven would keep the animals both to test his prowess before a battle and to involve the creatures in his various battles with Spider-Man (Peter Parker) and other heroes including the Human Torch (Johnny Storm) and Tigra (Greer Nelson). While Kraven was affiliated with the Maggia, he used his Zmbuku snakes to harvest the ZMB chemical that the Maggia

traded as a narcotic ("zoomers"). Kraven's collection included the lion Simba and the leopard Rajah. Kraven also considered the powerful extraterrestrial Tsiln named Gog as something like a pet. Following Kraven's death, his son Alyosha assumed his identity and kept his own menagerie of animals. Although Alyosha used the animals in his initial clashes with Spider-Man and Calypso, he later adopted the wolf Nickel as a primary companion. At various times, both Kravens kept animal-like humans in their care as though they were actual animals, including Bushmaster (Quincy McIver), Frog-Man (Eugene Patilio), Gargoyle (Isaac Christians), Grizzly (Max Markham), Kangaroo (Brian Hibbs), Man-Bull, Mandrill, Mongoose, Rhino (Aleksei Sytsevich), Swarm, Tiger Shark (Todd Arliss), Tigra and the Vulture (Adrian Toomes). Other beings caught by Alyosha included Dragon Man and the Vatican's Black Knight's steed Aragorn, who was killed by Alyosha.

*Art by Steve Ditko*

# KRILL

**KNOWN MEMBERS:** None named
**BASE OF OPERATIONS:** Carlsbad County, New Mexico

**FIRST APPEARANCE:** Incredible Hulk #61 (2003)

**TRAITS:** The Krills' bodies were a synthesis of organic and silicon-based cybernetic parts. The Krills' eyes contained video cameras and microphones to transfer data back to Home Base. Their fangs were constructed from titanium and rendered hollow to store samples of the Hulk (Bruce Banner)'s blood; successful receipt of a blood sample would be instantly relayed to Home Base. The Krills' eyes were extremely susceptible to light and so they would shun both fire and moonlight. The Krills' cybernetics were also easily shorted out by exposure to water.

**LENGTH:** 2'        **WEIGHT:** 30 lbs.        **EYES:** Red        **SKIN:** Grey

**HISTORY:** The Krill were produced by Home Base, a conspiracy operation organized by longtime Hulk foe the Leader (Sam Sterns). Desiring blood samples from the Hulk, the Krill were manufactured to procure and deliver their portions to the Leader. The Krill were genetically engineered lizards modified by synthesized samples of the Hulk's DNA and enhanced with bionic parts. Swarms of the Krill were released to the home of Nadia Dornova in the New Mexico desert, a locale that the Hulk had visited earlier. However, former Home Base operative Betty Banner was present with Nadia and helped defend her from the Krill's attack. Home Base helped facilitate Banner's safe travel to Nadia's home so that the Krill would have an opportunity to obtain a blood sample. Although Banner became the Hulk to save Betty and Nadia, one of the Krill succeeded in taking a sample and escaping. While the

Hulk pursued the Krill back to Home Base's facility, Doc Samson and former Home Base agent Sandra Verdugo arrived and helped Nadia and Betty with the remaining Krill by shattering open a water tower, shorting out the Krill. The Krill carrying the Hulk's blood sample was destroyed and Samson, Betty and Verdugo subsequently invaded the facility and destroyed it, eliminating any remaining Krill.

**NOTE:** The Krill created by Home Base should not be confused with the Krill, an extraterrestrial race.

*Art by Mike Deodato Jr.*

# MAN-OO

**REAL NAME:** Man-oo
**ALIASES:** Man-oo the Mighty
**IDENTITY:** No dual identity
**OCCUPATION:** Wildlife protector
**CITIZENSHIP:** None
**PLACE OF BIRTH:** Nigeria
**KNOWN RELATIVES:** None
**GROUP AFFILIATION:** None
**EDUCATION:** No formal education
**FIRST APPEARANCE:** Jungle Action #1 (1954)

**HISTORY:** Man-oo was a powerful yet gentle gorilla who defended the weaker animals in the Nigerian jungles. When the antelope family of Tondo, Riba and Wabbi were threatened by the lion Numa, Man-oo defended them, ultimately slaying the lion with his bare hands; Tondo returned the favor by saving Man-oo from a poisonous snake. Later, Man-oo saved the antelope Adawna from a white hunter, taking a bullet in her stead. The animals of the jungle nursed Man-oo's wound and restored him to health. When the great snake Serpo tried to assault the weakened gorilla, the animals defended him until he finally regained enough strength to kill Serpo himself. Another gorilla named Kago tried to usurp Man-oo's authority by abducting a baby gorilla and leaving it for hyenas to kill. Although Man-oo outfought the hyenas and saved the baby, the parents mistook Man-oo for the kidnapper. Anticipating Man-oo tracking him down, Kago fashioned a noose hoping to catch Man-oo unawares, but was himself taken by surprise when Man-oo attacked him from behind. Startled, Kago fell into his own noose and was killed. Man-oo later bested another challenger, the ape Babu.

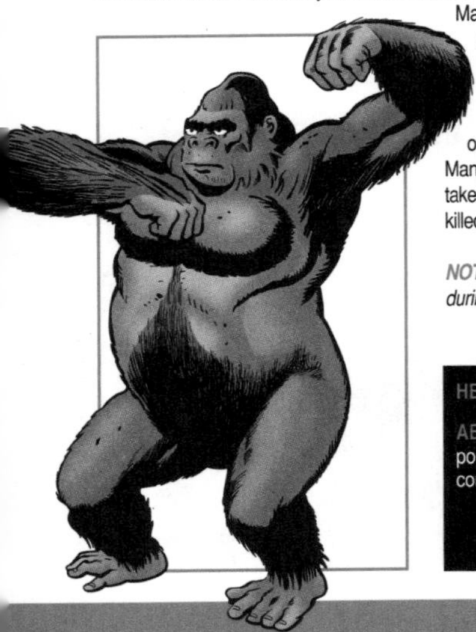

***NOTE:** Man-oo should not be confused with either of the two extraterrestrials called Manoo, both active during different eras at Farnsworth College.*

**HEIGHT:** 5'6" **WEIGHT:** 325 lbs. **EYES:** Brown **HAIR:** Brown

**ABILITIES/ACCESSORIES:** Like most gorillas, Man-oo was stronger than an average human, possessed superb climbing skills and could manipulate simple tools. Man-oo was an able combatant, wrestling even lions in battle.

**INTELLIGENCE:** 1 **STRENGTH:** 3 **SPEED:** 2 **DURABILITY:** 3
**ENERGY PROJECTION:** 1 **FIGHTING SKILLS:** 2

# MAX

**REAL NAME:** Max
**ALIASES:** None
**IDENTITY:** No dual identity
**OCCUPATION:** Watchdog; former pit fighter
**CITIZENSHIP:** Property of Frank Castle
**PLACE OF BIRTH:** Unrevealed
**KNOWN RELATIVES:** None
**GROUP AFFILIATION:** None
**EDUCATION:** Attack dog training
**FIRST APPEARANCE:** Punisher #54 (1991)

**HISTORY:** Max was the pet of a Connecticut cocaine dealer whose operations were brought down by the Punisher (Frank Castle). Finding that Max was half-starved, the Punisher adopted him and employed him as a watchdog at one of his safe houses in Queens, New York. Equipped with an automatic feeding machine a 5000 gallon sandbox, and unwavering in his loyalty to the Punisher, Max successfully guarded the weaponry warehouse until its location was discovered by George Wong, an employee of the Kingpin (Wilson Fisk) who had trailed Punisher's ally Microchip to the location. Max bit George, who shot the dog before running to a hospital. The Punisher soon arrived and treated Max's injuries. With the warehouse's location compromised, Max was relocated to a new Queens safe house, which was wired with explosives to deter intruders. After the Punisher visited the safe house with his ally Lynn Michaels, a gang called the Ghetto Rangers recognized him and tried to break in after they departed. After some were killed by the explosives, the remainder faced Max, who tore up several of them before being knocked unconscious. The gang leader sold Max to Ty Fetters, who trained attack dogs for underground fight clubs in New Jersey. Max became a successful pit fighter in Fetters' operations until the Punisher and his ally Mickey Fondizzi ultimately raided the fight club and retrieved Max, who happily rejoined his master.

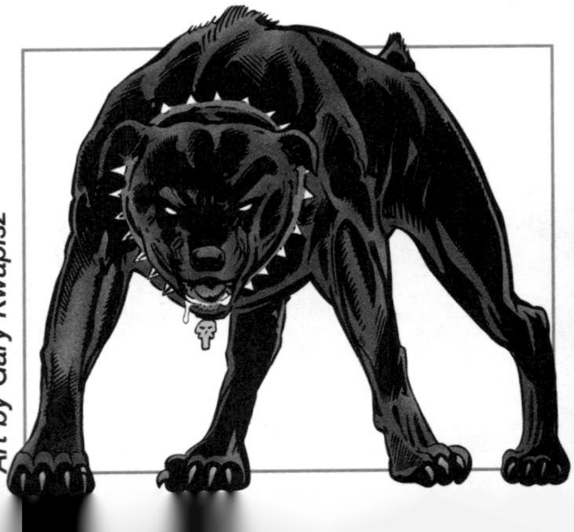

Art by Gary Kwapisz

**HEIGHT:** 2'4" (at the shoulder) **EYES:** Yellow
**WEIGHT:** 150 lbs. **HAIR:** Brown

**ABILITIES/ACCESSORIES:** Max is a particularly savage rottweiler who would use both claws and teeth in combat against dogs and humans; his jaws are strong enough to crush bones or throats. Max is trained not to bark at intruders, keeping his presence a secret until he is ready to attack. The only human who can prevent Max from attacking a target is the Punisher.

**INTELLIGENCE:** 1 **STRENGTH:** 2 **SPEED:** 2 **DURABILITY:** 2
**ENERGY PROJECTION:** 1 **FIGHTING SKILLS:** 3

# MONKEY JOE

REAL NAME: Monkey Joe
ALIASES: None
IDENTITY: No dual identity
OCCUPATION: Adventurer
CITIZENSHIP: Property of Doreen Green

PLACE OF BIRTH: Presumably somewhere in southern California
KNOWN RELATIVES: None
GROUP AFFILIATION: Great Lakes Avengers, partner of Squirrel Girl
EDUCATION: Trained with Squirrel Girl
FIRST APPEARANCE: Marvel Super-Heroes #8 (1992)

HISTORY: Monkey Joe was a California squirrel befriended by mutant teen Squirrel Girl (Doreen Green), who could communicate with squirrels. Joe helped her audition as a potential sidekick to Iron Man (Tony Stark); though Stark turned her down, she subsequently rescued Iron Man from mad Latverian tyrant Dr. Doom. Joe played a key role in that unlikely victory, helping disable Doom's airship and armor, even tearing away Doom's cloak and mask as the beaten dictator escaped. When Doreen moved to New York, Squirrel Girl and Monkey Joe fought crime in Central Park, where they rescued Great Lakes Avengers (GLA) members Doorman and Flatman from muggers. Offered GLA membership, Doreen and Joe accepted, aiding the team against Batroc's Brigade; but disgruntled ex-GLA member Leather Boy, angered by news of the team's new recruits, invaded GLA headquarters and brutally murdered Monkey Joe, who was on monitor duty. Monkey Joe's ghost briefly watched over the GLA thereafter, but has since moved on to whatever awaits heroic squirrels in the afterlife.

Art by Paul Pelletier

LENGTH: 2'3" (including tail)
WEIGHT: 2.2 lbs.

EYES: Black
FUR: Brown

ABILITIES/ACCESSORIES: Monkey Joe was a fox squirrel (Sciurus niger), also known as a monkey-faced squirrel. An extremely swift, agile climber and acrobat, he could make high jumps up to 6 feet or horizontal leaps up to 15 feet, landing safely from falls of 20 feet or more. His tail enhanced his sense of balance, also serving as a makeshift parachute, landing cushion or blanket as needed. Joe could run up to 15 miles per hour and was an unusually strong swimmer, even capable of underwater diving. He could chew through wood, wiring, and thin or soft metals. He had a unique, possibly empathic or quasi-telepathic rapport with Squirrel Girl (perhaps the source of his remarkably high intelligence); they communicated fluently with each other, and Joe apparently understood English. Smarter than the average squirrel, Joe could also operate computer equipment.

INTELLIGENCE: 2 STRENGTH: 1 SPEED: 3 DURABILITY: 2
ENERGY PROJECTION: 1 FIGHTING SKILLS: 2

# MUNIN & HUGIN

REAL NAMES: Munin and Hugin
ALIASES: (Munin) Memory, Muninn; (Hugin) Thought, Huginn
IDENTITY: No dual identities
OCCUPATION: Messengers
CITIZENSHIP: Property of the Asgardian throne

PLACE OF BIRTH: Asgard
KNOWN RELATIVES: Unrevealed
GROUP AFFILIATION: None
EDUCATION: No formal education
FIRST APPEARANCE: Thor #274 (1978)

HISTORY: Hugin & Munin are two ravens that have served the All-Father Odin, and later his successors, by acting as the ruler's eyes and ears. Each morning Odin sent the pair though the Nine Worlds to return at night and convey what they heard and saw. The pair served Odin faithfully for years, remaining out of the Asgardians' sight. Hugin & Munin told Odin of the coming of Ragnarok, which Loki brought about through the seeming death of Thor (Red Norvell) who seemingly perished in Thor (Odinson)'s place. When Odin sought to atone for his sins of avarice and pride, he had Hugin & Munin use the Rhinegold ring-halves of the Ring of Power to nail him to the Yggdrasil, the world ash tree. They returned to his service after he learned the Nine Songs and secrets to the runes. When Odin sent the ravens into the demon Surtur's realm, the Burning Galaxy, Surtur used Twilight, the sword of the gods, to destroy Hugin while Munin escaped to inform Odin of Surtur's impending attack. After Odin was seemingly slain by Surtur, Munin served Balder, who in turn used the water from the Well of Life to restore Hugin. When Thor restored the Asgardians to life, after previously breaking the Ragnarok cycle, Hugin & Munin helped Thor find Odin in Valhalla. It remains to be seen if they will serve Balder, who has regained the throne of Asgard.

LENGTH: (Both) 3'5"
WEIGHT: (Both) 20 lbs.

EYES: (Both) Black
FEATHERS: (Both) Black

ABILITIES/ACCESSORIES: Hugin & Munin possess enhanced strength, endurance, and agility. They can travel across any dimensional barriers and are immune to all holding spells. Hugin & Munin are highly intelligent, capable of speech and able to differentiate between individuals like all Midgard ravens. They possess a wingspan of 4'5" with black shiny feathers with an almost oily appearance and can perceive their surroundings while moving at high speeds and execute aerial maneuvers.

INTELLIGENCE: 3 STRENGTH: 4 SPEED: 3 DURABILITY: 3
ENERGY PROJECTION: 1 FIGHTING SKILLS: 2

Art by Marko Djurdjevic

# NIELS

**REAL NAME:** Niels
**ALIASES:** The Bouncing Cat, "P-Cat, the Penitent Puss" (allegedly), "Kitty Kitty," "Dumb Cat," "Little Pest," "Fur Ball," "Pesky Pussy," "Peculiar Projectile," "Stupid Cat," "Mangy Fleabag," "Flea-bitten Dirtbag," "Darn Cat," "Little Pain"
**IDENTITY:** The general public is unaware of Niels' existence
**OCCUPATION:** Domestic housecat; former research laboratory cat
**CITIZENSHIP:** Property of Robert Baldwin
**PLACE OF BIRTH:** Springdale, Connecticut
**KNOWN RELATIVES:** None
**GROUP AFFILIATION:** None
**EDUCATION:** No formal education
**FIRST APPEARANCE:** Speedball #1 (1988)

**HISTORY:** Once the pet of Hammond Lab research scientist Dr. Nicholas Benson, the always underfoot Niels led a simple life until an extradimensional energy experiment released a swarm of kinetic energy bubbles that accidentally enveloped him and high school student Robert Baldwin, essentially transforming both into kinetic bouncing balls. Wanting to study the effects of the energy, Dr. Benson assigned his assistant Claude and Baldwin — now secretly the costumed adventurer Speedball — with catching Niels for study, but both were consistently unable to apprehend the elusive, antisocial cat. Some time later, Niels was briefly caught and studied by the genius Mad Thinker, then secured by a number of Speedball's enemies hired by criminal scientist Clyde Bodtchik. When Clyde attempted to steal the cat's powers for himself, he was stopped when Niels coughed up a highly destructive kinetic hairball, which destroyed Clyde's machinery. Having dislodged the hairball, Niels' disposition changed for the better, and he was subsequently taken to Manhattan to live with Baldwin. Later, Baldwin, now the mentally unstable Penance, claimed Niels had become the armored and spike wearing "P-Cat, the Penitent Puss." Whether this is true remains unconfirmed.

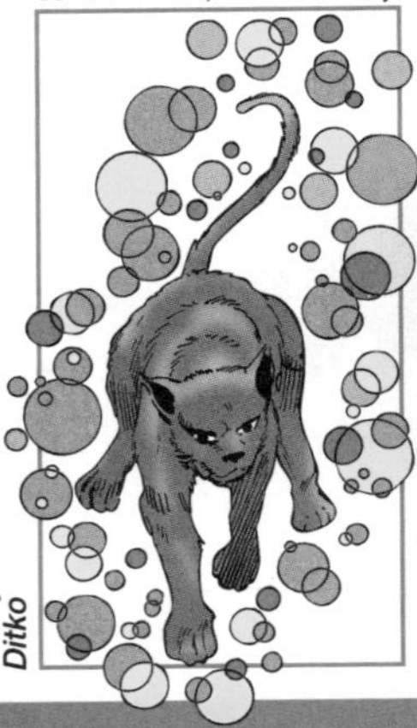

Art by Steve Ditko

**HEIGHT:** 1'2" (at the shoulder) **WEIGHT:** 10 lbs. **EYES:** Yellow **HAIR:** Orange

**ABILITIES/ACCESSORIES:** Niels projects an energy field around him that absorbs, amplifies and redirects kinetic energy. This field activates with any impact, causing him to rebound and bounce at high speeds, usually in the opposite direction. When the field is active, he is immune to physical harm, and is surrounded by multi-colored kinetic energy "bubbles." On at least one occasion, Niels coughed up a hairball that was imbued with enough kinetic energy to do massive damage upon impact. Niels has sharp teeth and claws, and senses of hearing and smell more acute than humans. He can see in the dark, yet has terrible depth perception and trouble seeing colors or immobile objects. He is an excellent hunter with quick reflexes, is very agile, flexible and always lands on his feet.

**INTELLIGENCE:** 2 **STRENGTH:** 1 **SPEED:** 3 **DURABILITY:** 6
**ENERGY PROJECTION:** 3 **FIGHTING SKILLS:** 2

# NIMO

**REAL NAME:** Nimo
**ALIASES:** None
**IDENTITY:** None
**OCCUPATION:** Parent, hunter
**CITIZENSHIP:** None
**PLACE OF BIRTH:** Santo Cristo Mountains, Colorado
**KNOWN RELATIVES:** Tama (mate), two unidentified sons
**GROUP AFFILIATION:** None
**EDUCATION:** No formal education
**FIRST APPEARANCE:** Kid Colt, Outlaw #7 (1949)

**HISTORY:** Nimo is a mountain lion (cougar) who lived in the Santo Cristo Mountains, where he was regarded as a "king," much as the lion is familiarly called the "king of the jungle." Nimo and his mate Tama had two spotted male cubs who Nimo taught hunting and survival. Nimo's family was threatened from a variety of sources, notably fellow giant cats. In addition to driving off rival cougars, Nimo once rescued Tama from a jaguar that had wandered north, finally killing it in battle. In another instance, a Bengal tiger with a deep hatred of humans escaped from a nearby circus, and Nimo slew it to save the local humans. Local ranchers such as Ned Parks and Jed Norris knew of Nimo but left him and his family alone. Nimo was once suspected of slaughtering local sheep, but the culprit proved to be a giant eagle, which Nimo slew when it threatened one of his cubs. Nimo's enmity with some rival predators, such as local wolves, led him to sometimes defend other animals threatened by them, on separate occasions saving a horse and a moose from wolf packs. When a forest fire drove Nimo's family from the hills and into the path of a hostile grizzly bear, Nimo bested the grizzly in combat and drove him from the territory.

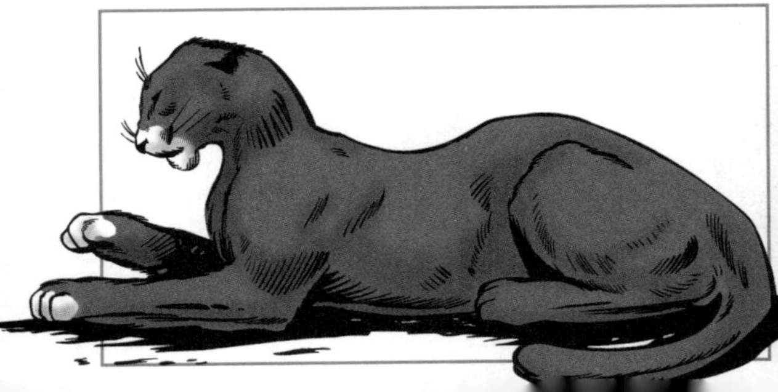

**HEIGHT:** 2'7" (at the shoulder)
**EYES:** Green
**WEIGHT:** 155 lbs.
**HAIR:** Brown

**ABILITIES/ACCESSORIES:** Like most cougars, Nimo could run at a peak of 45 miles per hour, possessed sharp fangs, a prehensile tail and a set of claws on each of his paws. Nimo was an excellent hunter and considered an experienced fighter amongst cougars.

**INTELLIGENCE:** 1 **STRENGTH:** 2 **SPEED:** 2
**DURABILITY:** 2
**ENERGY PROJECTION:** 1 **FIGHTING SKILLS:** 3

# OLD LACE

**REAL NAME:** Old Lace
**ALIASES:** None
**IDENTITY:** No dual identity
**OCCUPATION:** Pet, adventurer
**CITIZENSHIP:** Chase Stein's property; formerly Gertrude Yorkes' property
**PLACE OF BIRTH:** Earth (87th century)
**KNOWN RELATIVES:** None
**GROUP AFFILIATION:** Runaways
**EDUCATION:** None
**FIRST APPEARANCE:** Runaways #2 (2003)

**HISTORY:** Unknown to their daughter Gertrude, Dale and Stacey Yorkes were time travelers and part of the criminal Pride. As a present, they brought a genetically engineered Deinonychus-like dinosaur, designed with an empathetic connection to Gertrude, from an undefined 87th-century Earth to the modern era, and placed it within a secret lair in their LA home where it was to await Gertrude turning 18. However, Gertrude and the other Pride members' children learned of their parents' murderous activities and while investigating further they discovered the dinosaur. The teens fled, but it followed them and won their acceptance after it saved them from the Pride during a confrontation. When the children chose code names, Gertrude picked Arsenic for herself and named the dinosaur Old Lace. Eventually the Runaways destroyed the Pride, but were caught by the authorities; Old Lace was remanded to a Stark warehouse, but the Runaways escaped and freed it. Though fiercely loyal to Gertrude, Old Lace wandered away at one point, leading to a confrontation between the Runaways and the X-Men. Recovered by the X-Men's Emma Frost, Old Lace returned to the Runaways. During a battle with a new Pride incarnation, Gertrude was murdered. With her last breath, she passed on Old Lace to her teammate and boyfriend Chase Stein. Old Lace accompanied Stein when he left the team to try to resurrect Gertrude, but both returned after the plan failed. It remains an integral part of the Runaways.

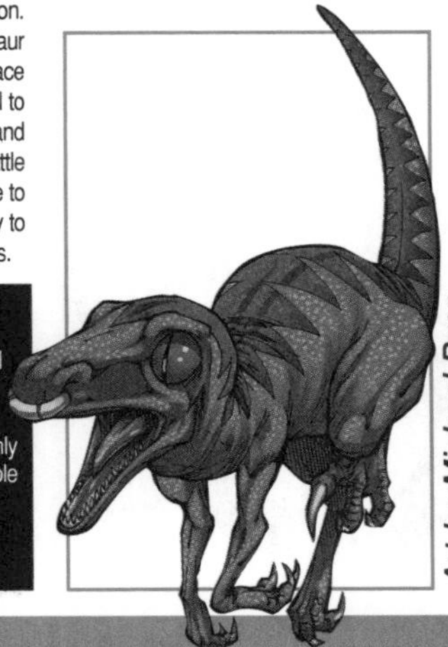

Art by Michael Ryan

**HEIGHT:** 6'11" (including tail) **WEIGHT:** 334 lbs. **EYES:** Red **HAIR:** None

**ABILITIES/ACCESSORIES:** Old Lace possesses razor-sharp teeth and claws, and a powerful tail that it uses for striking. Its senses are very keen and reflexes are more pronounced than a human's. Through its empathetic link, it and its owner feel each other's emotions and pain, and it even knows its owner's thoughts; however, if its owner dies with the link intact, Old Lace might die too. It will only follow the commands of others if its owner tells it to. Surprisingly intelligent, it has shown itself capable of disobeying orders it disagrees with.

**INTELLIGENCE:** 2 **STRENGTH:** 3 **SPEED:** 3 **DURABILITY:** 3
**ENERGY PROJECTION:** 1 **FIGHTING SKILLS:** 3

# PREYY

**REAL NAME:** Preyy
**ALIASES:** None
**IDENTITY:** No dual identity
**OCCUPATION:** Pet, predator
**CITIZENSHIP:** Property of Erik Killmonger
**PLACE OF BIRTH:** Unrevealed, presumably Wakanda
**KNOWN RELATIVES:** None
**GROUP AFFILIATION:** Former member of Madam Slay's leopard pride
**EDUCATION:** No formal education
**FIRST APPEARANCE:** Jungle Action #6 (1973)

**HISTORY:** The African leopard Preyy was Erik Killmonger's only true friend. When Erik went after Black Panther (T'Challa) for the first time, Preyy was ordered to kill T'Challa, but the Wakandan monarch nearly broke the cat's neck. Erik saved Preyy, but eventually died himself battling T'Challa. Preyy then joined the leopards serving Erik's ally Madam Slay, who caught T'Challa and his security chief W'Kabi. Madam Slay bound T'Challa to Preyy and another leopard, who dragged T'Challa across the harsh terrain until he jumped on their backs and rode on them back to their mistress. After Madam Slay's defeat, Preyy was once again alone. After Erik's resurrection, Preyy rejoined him. Finding T'Challa's former fianceé Monica Lynne in the jungle near N'Jadaka Village, Preyy protected her. Joined by Erik they went on a hunt, and Preyy had to be held back by Monica when Erik fought W'Kabi and other Wakandan soldiers. Not long after that, Erik became the new Black Panther and took Preyy to America. They sought to join the Avengers and Preyy befriended Triathlon (Delroy Garret). As part of a plan to get Erik killed, T'Challa antagonist Achebe hired Deadpool to bring him Preyy. He claimed Preyy was named Ukatana and stolen from him. Deadpool teleported Preyy and, accidentally, Triathlon to Achebe's Wakandan hideout, and Achebe killed Preyy after his plan failed. Erik held T'Challa personally responsible for Preyy's death. Erik later obtained a new leopard named Preyy II.

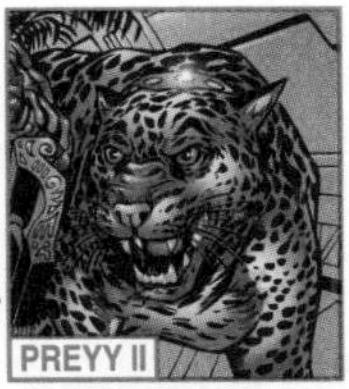
PREYY II

Art by Patrick Zircher

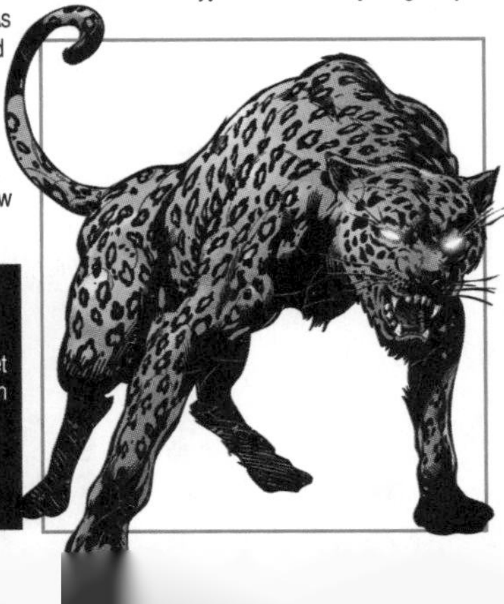

Art by Sal Velluto

**HEIGHT:** 3'5" (at the shoulder) **EYES:** Green
**WEIGHT:** 176 lbs. **HAIR:** Cream-yellow to orange-brown with black dots

**ABILITIES/ACCESSORIES:** Preyy can run up to 40 mph, leap in a single bound 50 feet horizontally or 10 feet vertically and carry up to 220 pounds with his mouth. Preyy is skilled in using his sharp claws in combat and instinctively knows how to kill a victim with a neck bite.

**INTELLIGENCE:** 1 **STRENGTH:** 2 **SPEED:** 3 **DURABILITY:** 2
**ENERGY PROJECTION:** 1 **FIGHTING SKILLS:** 3

# PRINCESS PYTHON'S PYTHONS

**FIRST APPEARANCE:** Amazing Spider-Man #22 (1965)

**HISTORY:** As performer and criminal in the Circus of Crime, Princess Python unfailingly retained the service and devotion of at least one twenty-five-foot Indian rock python (python molurus). These snakes possessed unique traits such as enhanced speed and flexibility; un-python-like fangs; ability to "hear" vibrations from much further away than ordinary snakes, and sufficient intelligence to carry out reasonably complex verbal instructions. In an early adventure, Princess Python set her python Precious against Spider-Man (Peter Parker), who tied the overconfident snake in knots. Months later, when Circus members stole the Golden Bull statue, Precious accompanied his mistress to overpower a security guard, although Thor (Odinson) intervened. The Circus subsequently infiltrated the Yellowjacket (Henry Pym)/Wasp (Janet van Dyne) wedding, and Precious sprang from a cake to entwine Wasp but was dislodged. When Princess Python attempted a non-Circus crime, Precious accompanied her and was exposed to experimental chemicals, growing strong enough to potentially crush even Iron Man (Tony Stark)'s armor, but Iron Man hurled him into an acid vat to perish. Precious' successor, female "Precious II," met a quick end battling Daredevil (Matt Murdock). Training a third "Precious,"

*Art by Sal Buscema*

Princess Python joined Viper (Madame Hydra)'s Serpent Squad, and her new pet survived two fights with Nomad (Captain America/Steve Rogers). Months later, Howard the Duck tangled with the Circus, and Precious almost killed him, only to abandon the duck to attend his injured mistress. Precious fared less well against the Hulk (Bruce Banner) and the Thing (Ben Grimm), and Princess Python left him behind to briefly serve in Sidewinder (Seth Voelker)'s Serpent Society. Months later, Precious accompanied his mistress to Superia's Femizon gathering but sat out the action when Captain America and Paladin intervened. Princess Python expanded her act to include several snakes, and Precious may have died, since another, Benny, became her favorite. When John Blaze sought recruits for Quentin Carnival, Princess Python won herself and her snakes a place; although Benny proved himself by retrieving Blaze's hellfire shotgun at a critical moment, Blaze soon dissolved the carnival. When Benny and mistress rejoined the Circus of Crime, Benny was briefly transformed into a six-winged flying snake by temporary ally Relf. Later, Circus manipulation of Devil Dinosaur attracted Spider-Man, and Benny attacked the hero but fared no better than his predecessor. When Princess Python and others branched off into a smaller unit, Benny achieved the greatest victory of any Circus python by rendering an admittedly befuddled Hulk unconscious. When Princess Python abandoned crime, however, she resurfaced with seemingly ordinary python Pythagoras, suggesting Benny had met disaster or perhaps remained in Circus or police custody. She married Stilt-Man (Wilbur Day), who was soon killed by the Punisher (Frank Castle); Pythagoras accompanied his mistress to Stilt-Man's wake, which Punisher disrupted with explosives. Soon afterward, Pythagoras died, and Princess Python's new husband Gibbon bought her a replacement.

# PUPPY

| | |
|---|---|
| **REAL NAME:** Unrevealed | **PLACE OF BIRTH:** Unrevealed |
| **ALIASES:** None | **KNOWN RELATIVES:** Unrevealed |
| **IDENTITY:** Secret | **GROUP AFFILIATION:** None |
| **OCCUPATION:** Former companion to Fantastic Four | **EDUCATION:** Unrevealed |
| **CITIZENSHIP:** Unrevealed | **FIRST APPEARANCE:** Fantastic Four #9 (1998) |

**HISTORY:** Having made his way into the basement levels of Four Freedoms Plaza under unrevealed circumstances, the canine-like creature later dubbed Puppy, hungry and lonely, began howling. New York City officials hired Alyosha Kraven to investigate the noise, but the Fantastic Four's Human Torch (Johnny Storm) and his allies Caledonia and Spider-Man (Peter Parker) intervened, and Caledonia, recognising the cries for what they were, became the first to befriend Puppy. The trio brought Puppy to the Fantastic Four's then-home, Pier Four, and Johnny presented Puppy as the perfect companion to lonely young Franklin Richards. The two bonded, and quickly became inseparable; Franklin even occasionally rode Puppy like a horse through their home. While Puppy's resemblance to the Inhumans' Lockjaw suggested some connection, Franklin's father Reed chose not to investigate Puppy's origins for fear of upsetting his son should the Inhumans lay claim to Puppy. When first Bounty and then the Bacchae came after Caledonia and the Four, Puppy demonstrated his ability to teleport himself and others across space-time, bringing himself and his companions after the Bacchae to Tartarus (after a brief misstep into Hela's realm). However, the chaos of the underworld left Puppy too frightened to teleport them back; fortunately Franklin's parents rescued them. When a "chaos wave" threatened Earth, the Fantastic Four sent Franklin to the extragalactic boarding school Haven, accompanied by Caledonia and Puppy. They were soon joined there by Franklin's sister Valeria, and all four returned home on occasion, once going on a mystical adventure with the legendary Sinbad. When Abraxas threatened Earth, Valeria brought herself and Franklin home, but Puppy and Caledonia did not accompany them.

| | |
|---|---|
| **HEIGHT:** 2'6" (at the shoulder) | **EYES:** Brown |
| **WEIGHT:** 260 lbs. | **HAIR:** Brown & White |

**ABILITIES/ACCESSORIES:** Puppy can teleport interdimensionally, carrying others with him, though he is not yet highly skilled at this. He can track others interdimensionally as well. He has a forked antenna on his forehead, similar to Black Bolt's and Lockjaw's, and wears a dog tag bearing the Fantastic Four's "4" logo

INTELLIGENCE: 1 STRENGTH: 3 SPEED: 2/7* DURABILITY: 3
ENERGY PROJECTION: 1 FIGHTING SKILLS: 1
*PUPPY IS A TELEPORTER

# SAINT

**REAL NAME:** Saint
**ALIASES:** None
**IDENTITY:** No dual identity
**OCCUPATION:** Vampire hunter, bodyguard, companion
**CITIZENSHIP:** Property of Quincy Harker
**PLACE OF BIRTH:** England
**KNOWN RELATIVES:** None
**GROUP AFFILIATION:** Quincy Harker's vampire hunters
**EDUCATION:** Specially trained attack dog/service animal
**FIRST APPEARANCE:** Tomb of Dracula #7 (1973)

**HISTORY:** Years after Dracula crippled him, aged vampire hunter Quincy Harker acquired German shepherd Saint as a pet, training him to attack vampires and other enemies as necessary. When Dracula returned to Harker's native England after years of absence, Harker's operatives, including his protégé Rachel van Helsing, Taj Nital, and others, fought the vampire lord under his orders. At home, Harker was at times attacked by Dracula, Dracula's daughter Lilith, and human enemy Jason Faust's employees, but Saint defended him each time. Occasionally Harker, with Saint, accompanied his operatives into action against Dracula, Dr. Sun, and others, but Saint, devoted to Harker, left his side only when ordered. Over a year after Dracula's return to England, Harker, aware a heart condition would kill him within a year, traveled to Transylvania's Castle Dracula, which Harker meant to destroy with Dracula in it; expecting neither Dracula nor himself to survive the confrontation, he left Saint behind. Harker killed Dracula and was himself killed when his bomb destroyed the castle, although Dracula revived soon afterward. Saint's ownership was presumably willed to Rachel van Helsing.

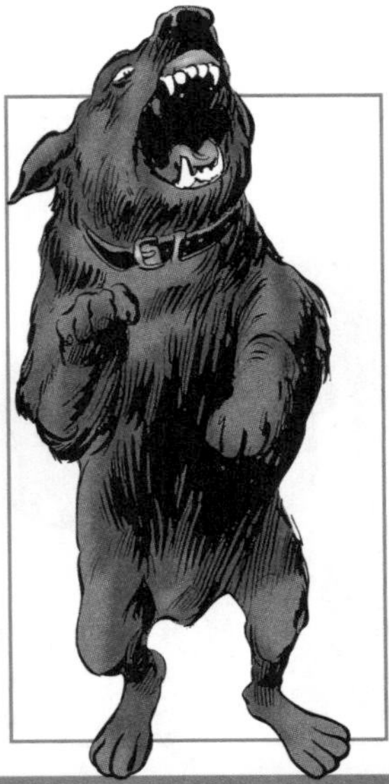

*Art by Gene Colan*

**HEIGHT:** 2'4" (at the shoulder)
**WEIGHT:** 105 lbs.
**EYES:** Blue
**FUR:** Light brown

**ABILITIES/ACCESSORIES:** Saint is a powerful attack dog as well as a trained assistance dog. Although most animals avoid vampires if possible, Saint is specially trained to attack them on command. He excels at detecting evil intent in people, whether human or vampire. He wears a collar studded with silver crosses, which are anathema to vampires and certain other supernatural beings; when Saint attacks a vampire, the victim often instinctively tries to dislodge Saint by grasping at his collar, which burns and weakens the vampire.

**INTELLIGENCE:** 2 **STRENGTH:** 3 **SPEED:** 2 **DURABILITY:** 2
**ENERGY PROJECTION:** 1 **FIGHTING SKILLS:** 4

# SASSAFRASS

**REAL NAME:** Sassafrass
**ALIASES:** "Sassy," "the dog filled with fear"
**IDENTITY:** No dual identity
**OCCUPATION:** Pet
**CITIZENSHIP:** Property of Henry McCoy
**PLACE OF BIRTH:** New York City, New York
**KNOWN RELATIVES:** None
**GROUP AFFILIATION:** None
**EDUCATION:** House trained
**FIRST APPEARANCE:** Defenders #122 (1983)

**HISTORY:** While out jogging one morning, the Beast (Hank McCoy) passed a pet shop and couldn't resist buying a small puppy he saw therein, naming her Sassafrass. She came to live with the Beast and his Defenders teammates at their New York brownstone home where she was often looked after by the Defenders' housekeeper Dolly Donahue. Sassafrass accompanied Beast to the wedding of former Defenders Daimon Hellstrom (Hellstorm/Son of Satan) and Hellcat (Patsy Walker) and helped oppose an attack by Hellcat's ex-husband Mad-Dog (Buzz Baxter) and the Mutant Force by biting Slither (Aaron Salomon). When Beast and the Defenders fought the Secret Empire, Sassafrass was cared for by his teammate Angel (Warren Worthington)'s girlfriend Candy Southern until their return. Sassafrass then accompanied the Defenders when they relocated to Angel's New Mexico home, complete with a safety bunker for her to retreat to in times of crisis. A very friendly dog, Sassafrass took a liking to all of the Defenders except for Moondragon, who once used a mental blast to shoo her away. Sassafrass even tried to befriend the villain Manslaughter after his failed attempt at killing the Defenders. Sassafrass also provided the inspiration for one of Candy's holographic defense programs. When Moondragon was corrupted by the Dragon of the Moon and turned against the Defenders, Candy and Dolly took Sassafrass and fled. When the military took up brief residence at Defenders mansion, Sassafrass came to like one soldier in particular that would regularly leave chocolate bars for her to eat, though chocolate is poisonous to dogs. One time, the soldier also left the Beast's holographic game system running, leaving Sassafrass to dodge its laser blasts until it was shut down by a returned Manslaughter. Following a climactic battle with the Dragon of the Moon, the Defenders disbanded and Sassafrass stayed at the mansion with Candy.

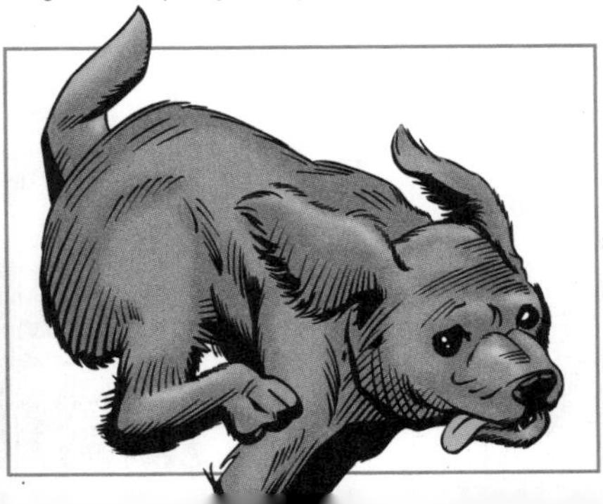

*Art by Don Perlin*

**HEIGHT:** 1'11" (at the shoulder)
**WEIGHT:** 45 lbs.
**EYES:** Dark brown
**HAIR:** Brown

**ABILITIES/ACCESSORIES:** Sassafrass possesses various canine traits including heightened senses as well as natural fangs and claws.

**INTELLIGENCE:** 1 **STRENGTH:** 2 **SPEED:** 2 **DURABILITY:** 2
**ENERGY PROJECTION:** 1 **FIGHTING SKILLS:** 1

# SLEIPNIR

**REAL NAMES:** Sleipnir
**ALIASES:** "Gliding one"
**IDENTITY:** No dual identity
**OCCUPATION:** Steed to the throne of Asgard
**CITIZENSHIP:** Property of the Asgardian throne
**PLACE OF BIRTH:** Asgard

**KNOWN RELATIVES:** Grane (aka Grani, son), Svadilfari (aka Svaðilfari, father), Loki (mother)
**GROUP AFFILIATION:** None
**EDUCATION:** No formal education
**FIRST APPEARANCE:** Thor #274 (1978)

**HISTORY:** Ages ago, the Asgardian trickster Loki convinced Odin to wager the goddess Freya in a bet that an itinerant stonemason, actually a Frost Giant in disguise, couldn't rebuild Asgard's walls in a set time period. To ensure Odin would win the bet, Loki, who noticed the mason's horse did most of the heavy hauling, took the form of a young mare, and lured the stallion away, ensuring the work was not complete on time. When Loki returned, he brought with him an eight-legged colt named Sleipnir and gave it to Odin. Later, Odin used Sleipnir to travel to Hel, the Asgardian realm of the dead, to learn of the coming of Ragnarok from the prophetess Volla. Upon discovering Balder's seeming death, Odin sent Hermod, the god of speed, into Hel with Sleipnir to learn how to restore Balder to life and prevent Ragnarok. Over the years, Odin used Sleipnir to travel to the realms of other pantheons and dimensions; however, Sleipnir's speed has been used by others in times of desperation, as when Nanna used Sleipnir to stop the Norn Queen Karnilla from forcing Balder into marriage.

*Art by Victor Olazaba*

**HEIGHT:** 8'5" (at whithers)
**WEIGHT:** 3500 lbs.
**EYES:** Black
**HAIR:** Black

**ABILITIES/ACCESSORIES:** Sleipnir possesses superhuman strength (able to carry 2 tons & pull 10 tons), endurance, and agility. Sleipnir is an eight-legged steed that can gallop at the speed of light (up to 186,000 miles per second) over land, sea, or through the air and can even outrun the god of speed Hermod. He is symbolic of time itself and can travel between the realms of spirit and matter. His intelligence is higher than normal horses.

**INTELLIGENCE:** 2 **STRENGTH:** 4 **SPEED:** 6 **DURABILITY:** 3
**ENERGY PROJECTION:** 1 **FIGHTING SKILLS:** 2

# STRIDER

**REAL NAME:** Strider
**ALIASES:** None
**IDENTITY:** No dual identity
**OCCUPATION:** Steed of the Black Knight
**CITIZENSHIP:** Property of Dane Whitman

**PLACE OF BIRTH:** Avalon
**KNOWN RELATIVES:** None
**GROUP AFFILIATION:** None
**EDUCATION:** No formal education
**FIRST APPEARANCE:** Heroes for Hire #2 (1997)

**HISTORY:** Strider is an enchanted horse from Avalon, the otherdimensional realm where King Arthur Pendragon's body reposes. When the Lady of the Lake presented the Black Knight (Dane Whitman) with vestments including the Sword of Light and Shield of Night, Strider was given to him as his new steed. The Black Knight soon rode Strider into adventures alongside the Heroes for Hire, his new team of comrades. Strider first bore the Knight into battle with Nitro and later carried him underwater to battle the Deviants of Lemuria. When the Heroes for Hire engaged in battle with the Master of the World (Eshu), the Black Knight and Strider clashed with a clone of Whitman called Knight Errant. Strider also bore Whitman to a confrontation with the dragon Malcolm Drake, who proved to be a new ally. Strider later carried the Black Knight into battle with the Knights of Wundagore and Acolytes as well as an excursion into the realms of Avalon and Otherworld. Recently, the Black Knight has joined the ranks of MI13 and accepted Excalibur (Faiza Hussain) as his steward. Strider occasionally bears both heroes into their adventures.

*Art by Pasqual Ferry*

**HEIGHT:** 5'5" (at withers)
**WEIGHT:** 1,100 lbs.
**EYES:** Black
**HAIR:** White

**ABILITIES/ACCESSORIES:** Strider possesses wings that enable him to fly while carrying one or more passengers. Strider can also travel underwater without apparent need for oxygen; the Black Knight's enchantments enable him to be likewise supported underwater. Strider can be mystically summoned to the Black Knight's side when he activates his enchantments by invoking Avalon. Strider possesses a strong rapport with its master, Dane Whitman, enabling him to understand and obey complex commands.

**INTELLIGENCE:** 1 **STRENGTH:** 4 **SPEED:** 3 **DURABILITY:** 2
**ENERGY PROJECTION:** 1 **FIGHTING SKILLS:** 3

# TIPPY-TOE

**REAL NAME:** Tippy-Toe
**ALIASES:** "Tip"
**IDENTITY:** No dual identity
**OCCUPATION:** Adventurer
**CITIZENSHIP:** Property of Doreen Green
**PLACE OF BIRTH:** Milwaukee, Wisconsin
**KNOWN RELATIVES:** None
**GROUP AFFILIATION:** Great Lakes Initiative, partner of Squirrel Girl
**EDUCATION:** Trained with Squirrel Girl
**FIRST APPEARANCE:** GLA #4 (2005)

**HISTORY:** When the mutant Squirrel Girl (Doreen Green) joined the Great Lakes Avengers (GLA) in Milwaukee, she recruited many local squirrels to aid the GLA against Maelstrom and his minions, Batroc's Brigade. The GLA won, but only one squirrel survived, a female dubbed "Tippy-Toe." She became Squirrel Girl's new partner and joined the GLA, later renamed the Great Lakes Initiative. The former agent of Oblivion called Deathurge, stripped of his cosmic duties and trapped in squirrel form after failing to collect the soul of Squirrel Girl's slain original partner Monkey Joe, has sought to win back his old job by killing Tippy-Toe and collecting her soul, but all his murder attempts have failed miserably. In addition to helping the GLI defeat AIM, Deadpool and the Skrulls, Squirrel Girl and Tippy-Toe have also vanquished major menaces such as Bi-Beast, MODOK and Thanos, proving little creatures can help fell the biggest foes.

**LENGTH:** 2' (including tail)
**WEIGHT:** 1.8 lbs.
**EYES:** Black
**FUR:** Gray

**ABILITIES/ACCESSORIES:** Tippy-Toe is an eastern gray squirrel (Sciurus carolinensis). An extremely swift, agile climber and a natural acrobat, she can make high jumps up to 6 feet or horizontal leaps up to 17 feet, and can land safely from falls of 20 feet or more. Her tail enhances her sense of balance, also serving as a makeshift parachute, landing cushion or blanket as needed. She can run up to 20 miles per hour, and can chew through wood, wiring or thin/soft metals. An aggressive and fearless fighter willing to use her claws and teeth on opponents, she sometimes makes kamikaze assaults via the "fuzzball special" maneuver, in which Squirrel Girl hurls Tippy at their foes. She has a unique, possibly empathic or quasi-telepathic rapport with Squirrel Girl (perhaps the source of Tippy's remarkably high intelligence); they communicate fluently with each other, and Tippy apparently understands spoken English, though she is said to be incapable of reading written English. Proficient in basic handicrafts, she can also use items such as matches, fuses, explosives, scissors, screwdrivers and blenders (for making acorn smoothies).

**INTELLIGENCE:** 2 **STRENGTH:** 1 **SPEED:** 3 **DURABILITY:** 2
**ENERGY PROJECTION:** 1 **FIGHTING SKILLS:** 3

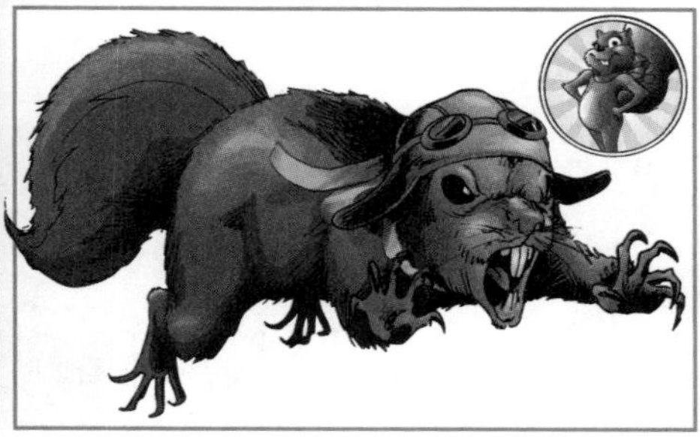

Art by Matt Haley

# VALKYRIOR STEEDS

**CURRENT MEMBERS:** Cloudrider, Dark Horse of Death, many others
**FORMER MEMBERS:** Aragorn, Brightwind/Darkwind
**BASE OF OPERATIONS:** The Aerie, Valhalla, realm of Asgard
**FIRST APPEARANCE:** Thor #132 (1966)

**HISTORY:** Throughout the history of Asgard, home of the Norse gods, the Valkyrior have been the choosers of the slain, selecting fallen gods to reside in the land of Valhalla. During the times when the Asgardians had worshippers on Earth, the Valkyrior would also carry worthy mortals to Valhalla. The Valkyrie performed their tasks astride winged horses native to Asgard. These horses, similar to Pegasus of Olympian myths, possessed a strong empathic bond to the Valkyrior who rode them. The Valkyrior's horses could bear their masters interdimensionally between Earth and Asgard. The steeds were held in stables at the Valkyrior's Aerie between missions. Among the named steeds of the Valkyrie was Cloudrider, who was sent by the Valkyrior to the mortal Eilif Dragonslayer so that he could accompany Thor into battle with the dragon Fafnir of Nastrond. When Eilif died in battle, Cloudrider bore him to Valhalla. Another steed is the Dark Horse of Death who carries fallen Asgardians to Valhalla while the Valkyrior escort him on foot. The horse Brightwind formed its bond to the human mutant Danielle Moonstar after she saved him from warriors sent by the death goddess Hela; Moonstar's bond to Brightwind caused her to become a Valkyrie. The horse Aragorn was the product of biological experimentation by the human Dane Whitman, but served Brunnhilda the Valkyrie on Earth and later joined her for a time in Asgard until she gave Aragorn to the Earth-based Valkyrie Samantha Parrington.

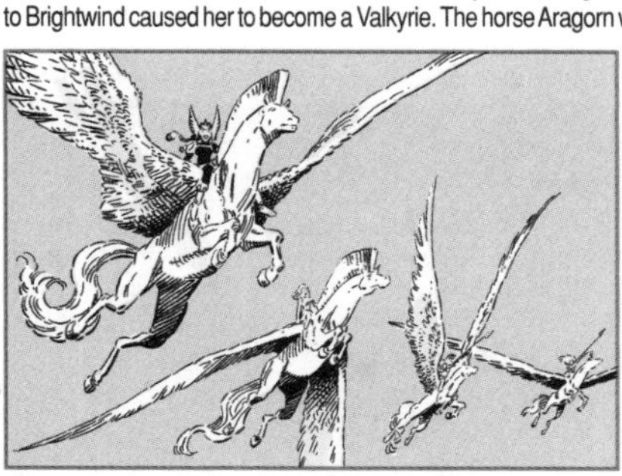

Art by Art Adams

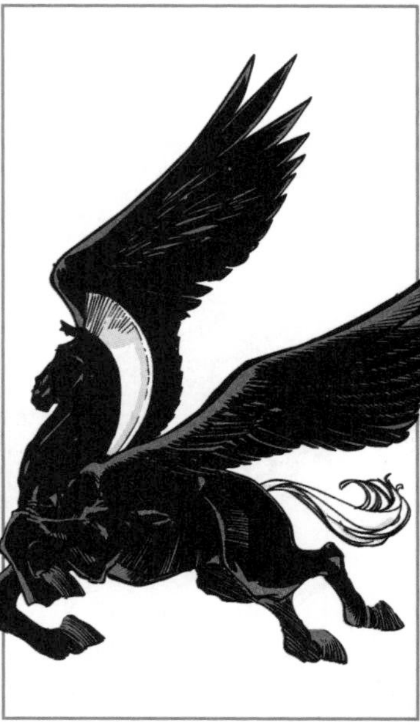

Art by Walt Simonson

# WATCHDOG

REAL NAME: Normie
ALIASES: "Woof-Woof"
IDENTITY: Secret
OCCUPATION: Pet, adventurer
CITIZENSHIP: Property of Robert and Lindy Reynolds

PLACE OF BIRTH: Unrevealed
KNOWN RELATIVES: None
GROUP AFFILIATION: None
EDUCATION: Unrevealed
FIRST APPEARANCE: The Sentry #1 (2000)

*Art by John Romita, Jr.*

*Art by Jae Lee*

HISTORY: Watchdog is believed to have been a normal dog named Normie until he obtained superhuman powers from the Sentry (Robert Reynolds). Donning a blue cape he became the Sentry's occasional companion in his adventures and eventually welcomed Lindy Lee as a shared master when she married the Sentry. Watchdog befriended some of the Sentry's heroic allies including the Fantastic Four and the Hulk (Bruce Banner) (who called him "Woof-Woof"). The Sentry was ultimately struck with amnesia-inducing illusions by Mastermind (Jason Wyngarde), which also affected every person who knew him, including Watchdog. With no memories of their costumed identities or powers, the Sentry and Watchdog became simply Bob Reynolds and Normie. Although Reynolds eventually regained his memories and powers, Normie evidently remained a normal dog. To replace Watchdog, Sentry had his computer CLOC construct a robotic Welsh corgi with all the powers of the original Watchdog. The robot joined the Sentry and Lindy when they took up residence in the Sentry's headquarters the Watchtower, which had merged with the Avengers Tower. Watchdog continued to accompany the Sentry on occasional missions.

HEIGHT: 12" (at the shoulder)
WEIGHT: 30 lbs.
EYES: Black
HAIR: Brown

ABILITIES/ACCESSORIES: Watchdog can fly at superhuman speeds up to 500 miles per hour. Watchdog also has superhuman strength, enabling him to lift up to one ton (in his mouth or upon his back). Watchdog's fangs are extraordinarily strong and sharp, able to puncture the flesh of the Sentry. Watchdog is capable of understanding and obeying simple commands from the Sentry.

INTELLIGENCE: 1 STRENGTH: 4 SPEED: 3 DURABILITY: 3
ENERGY PROJECTION: 1 FIGHTING SKILLS: 3

# ZAR

REAL NAME: Zar
ALIASES: Zar the Mighty
IDENTITY: No dual identity
OCCUPATION: Pet, adventurer
CITIZENSHIP: Property of David Rand
PLACE OF BIRTH: Belgian Congo (later Democratic Republic of the

Congo)
KNOWN RELATIVES: Sha (mate), Zoro (son), Sulani (daughter)
GROUP AFFILIATION: None
EDUCATION: No formal education
FIRST APPEARANCE: Ka-Zar: Lord of Fang and Claw (1936); (Marvel) Marvel Comics #1 (1939)

HISTORY: Zar was a lion who lived with his mate Sha in the Belgian Congo of the 1930s when he witnessed the arrival of the Rand family as their plane crashed in the jungle. Over time John and Constance Rand died, but their son David survived and befriended Zar by saving him from a pit of quicksand. Thereafter, Zar served as David's friend and protector, earning the name "Brother of the Lion" — or "Ka-Zar." Soon after Zar brought Ka-Zar to live with him in his cave, Sha gave birth to two cubs, Zor and Sulani. Bardak the ape kidnapped Zoro as part of his ongoing clash with Ka-Zar, but Ka-Zar saved Zoro's life; after this, Sha accepted Ka-Zar just as Zar had. Ka-Zar and Zar had many adventures together in the jungles, clashing with Paul de Kraft (the

*Art by Ben Thompson*

man who slew Ka-Zar's father), N'Jaga the leopard and unusual outsiders including escaped murderer London Jack. When Zar was captured by Rajah Sarput who transferred him to the hunter Bradley, Ka-Zar trailed his companion to New York, breaking Zar out of a zoo. The duo returned to Africa to find that Nazi forces were on the march and clashed with them. Ka-Zar and Zar finally bested Rajah Sarput, who was slain by the elephant Trajah. Ka-Zar and Zar's adventures continued at least as late as 1941.

HEIGHT: 4' (at the shoulder)
WEIGHT: 400 lbs.
EYES: Black
HAIR: Brown

ABILITIES/ACCESSORIES: Like most lions, Zar could run at a peak of 36 mph, possessed claws on each paw, a tail and sharp fangs. Zar was an excellent hunter and tracker. Zar and Ka-Zar possessed a rapport that enabled them to glean meaning from each other's every sound and motion as if they were literally speaking to each other.

INTELLIGENCE: 1 STRENGTH: 2 SPEED: 2 DURABILITY: 3
ENERGY PROJECTION: 1 FIGHTING SKILLS: 3

# APPENDIX: COWBOY HORSES OF THE OLD WEST

Many of the heroes of the "old west" era of the USA's 19th century rode horses in their adventures. These horses tended to be fiercely loyal to their masters, able to understand simple commands, fast runners and capable of performing unusual feats such as chewing through ropes. Notable among these horses was Banshee, who wore the same phosphorescent dye as his master the Phantom Rider and the Black Rider's steed Satan, who doubled as Ichabod in his master's secret identity of Matthew Masters.

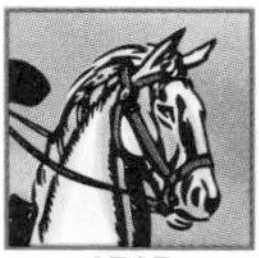

**ARAB**
Steed of Ringo Kid
Ringo Kid #2
(1954)

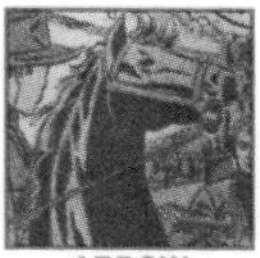

**ARROW**
Steed of
Arizona Kid
Arizona Kid #1
(1951)

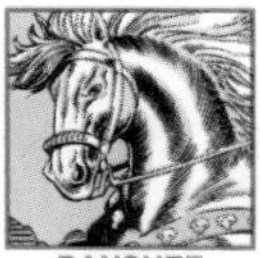

**BANSHEE**
Steed of Phantom
Rider
Ghost Rider #1
(1967)

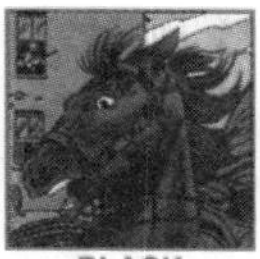

**BLACK**
Steed of Gunhawk
Western
Gunfighters #1
(1970)

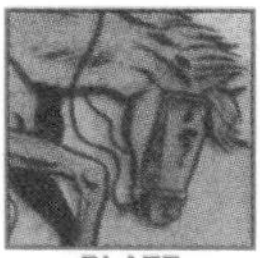

**BLAZE**
Steed of Red
Larabee
Gunhawk #12
(1950)

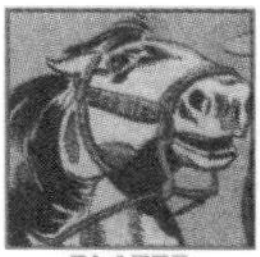

**BLAZER**
Steed of Outlaw
Kid
Outlaw Kid #10
(1972)

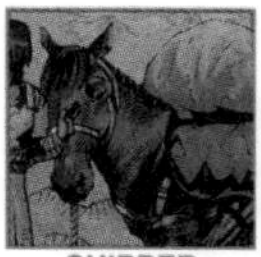

**CHIPPER**
Steed of Hurricane
Western Legends
#1 (2006)

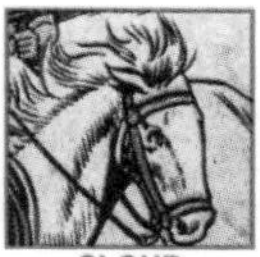

**CLOUD**
Steed of Lobo
Tex Morgan #1
(1948)

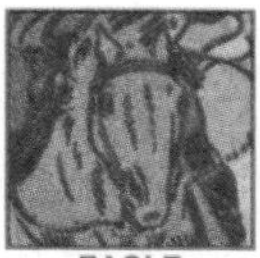

**EAGLE**
Steed of Matt Slade
Matt Slade,
Gunfighter #1
(1956)

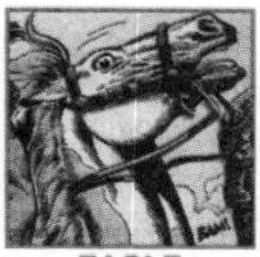

**EAGLE**
Steed of
Arrowhead
Arrowhead #1
(1954)

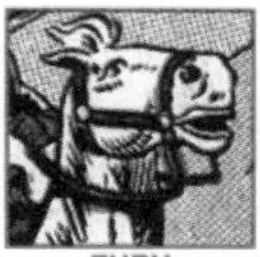

**FURY**
Steed of Prairie Kid
Wild Western #12
(1950)

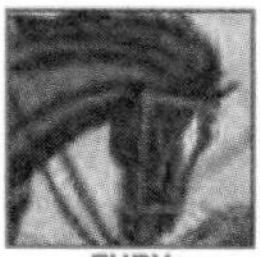

**FURY**
Steed of Tex Taylor
Wild West #1
(1948)

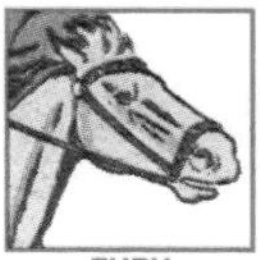

**FURY**
Steed of Red
Hawkins
Wild Western #13
(1950)

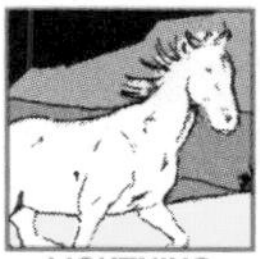

**LIGHTNING**
Steed of
Masked Rider
Marvel Comics #1
(1939)

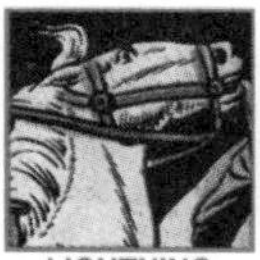

**LIGHTNING**
Steed of
Tex Morgan
Tex Morgan #1
(1948)

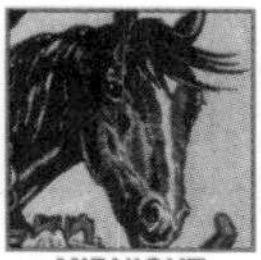

**MIDNIGHT**
Steed of
Blaze Carson
Blaze Carson #1
(1948)

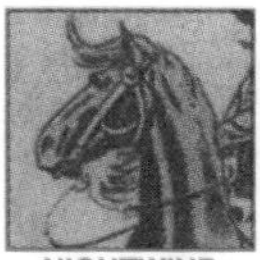

**NIGHTWIND**
Steed of
Apache Kid
Apache Kid #53
(1950)

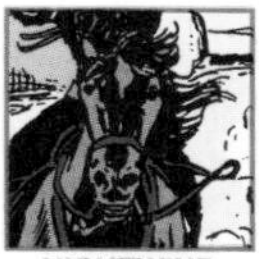

**NIGHTWIND**
Steed of
Rawhide Kid
Rawhide Kid #17
(1960)

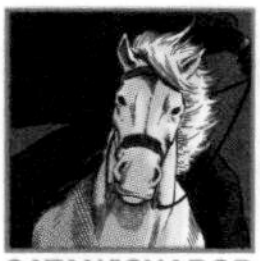

**SATAN/ICHABOD**
Steed of
Black Rider
All-Western
Winners #2 (1948)

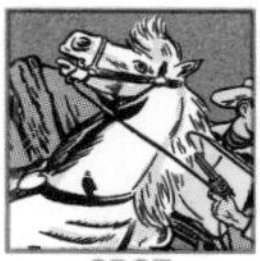

**SPOT**
Steed of Texas Kid
Daring Mystery
Comics #1 (1940)

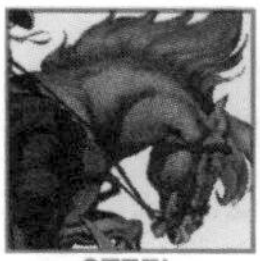

**STEEL**
Steed of Kid Colt
Kid Colt #1 (1948)

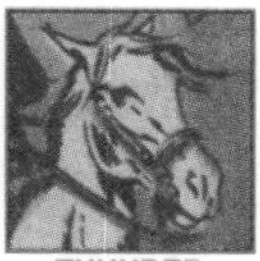

**THUNDER**
Steed of
Outlaw Kid
Outlaw Kid #1
(1954)

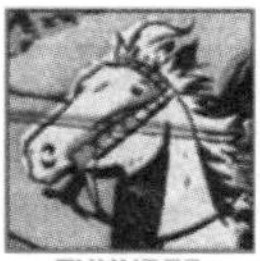

**THUNDER**
Steed of Texas Kid
Texas Kid #1
(1951)

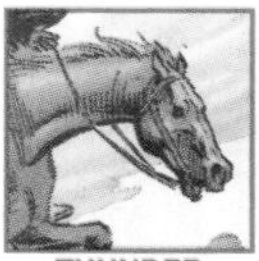

**THUNDER**
Steed of
Two-Gun Kid
Two-Gun Kid #60
(1962)

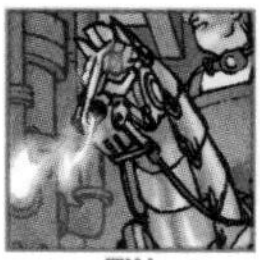

**TIN**
Steed of
Steam Rider
Amazing Fantasy
#20 (2006)

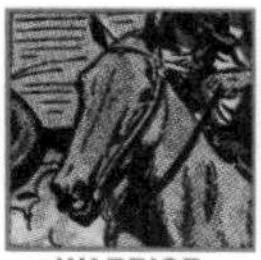

**WARRIOR**
Steed of Rex Hart
Rex Hart #6 (1949)

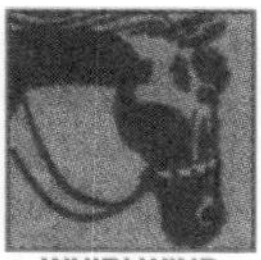

**WHIRLWIND**
Steed of Tex
Dawson
Western Kid #1
(1954)

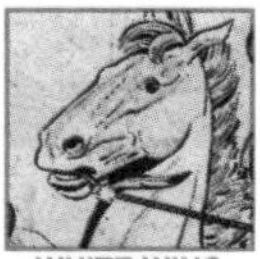

**WHITE WING**
Steed of
Red Warrior
Red Warrior #1
(1951)

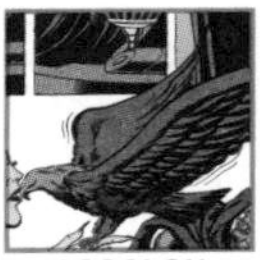

**ACCOLON**
Eagle, pet of
Morgan Le Fay
Iron Man #150
(1981)

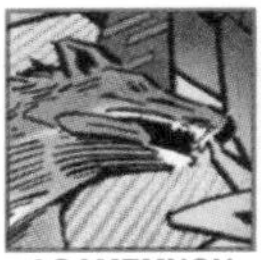

**AGAMEMNON**
Dog (deceased), pet
of Elektra Natchios
Elektra: Root of Evil
#3 (1995)

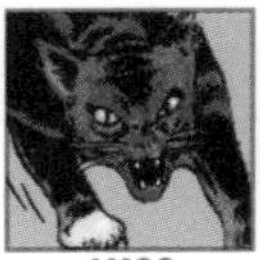

**AMOS**
Cat, pet of Max
Yadow
Thor #309 (1981

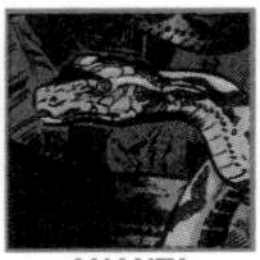

**ANANTA**
Snake, pet of
Shanna
Rampaging Hulk
#9 (1978)

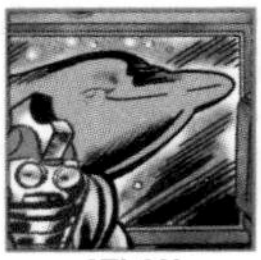

**ATLAN**
Dolphin (deceased),
member of
Conspiracy
Rampaging Hulk #8
(1978)

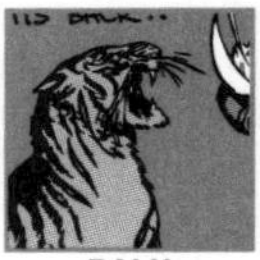

**BALU**
Tiger,
pet of Trojak
Daring Mystery
Comics #2 (1940)

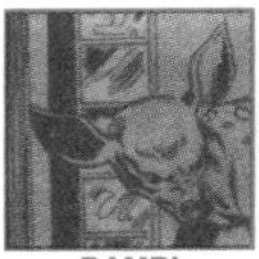

**BAMBI**
Deer,
possessed by
Chondu the Mystic
Defenders #31 (1976)

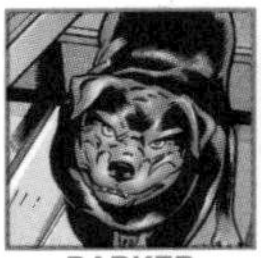

**BARKER**
Dog, pet of
Caryn Earle
Peter Parker: Spider-
Man #30 (2001)

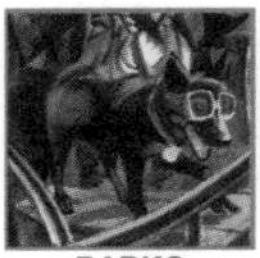

**BARKO**
Dog, member of
Confederates of the
Curious
Immortal Iron Fist
Annual #1 (2007)

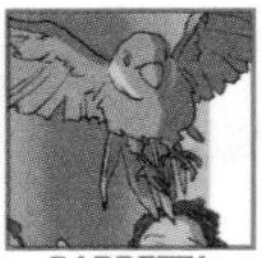

**BARRETTA**
Bird,
pet of
Tatiana Caban
NYX #4 (2004)

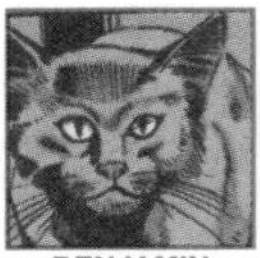

**BENJAMIN**
Cat
(Earth-148611),
pet of Kathy Ling
Psi-Force #4 (1987)

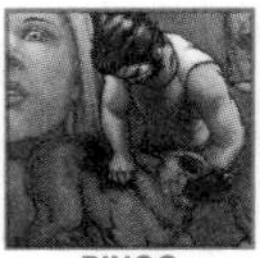

**BINGO**
Dog, pet of
James MacKenzie
X-Men Unlimited
#48 (2003)

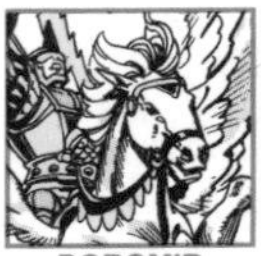

**BOROMIR**
Horse, steed of
Thundersword
Secret Wars II #1
(1985)

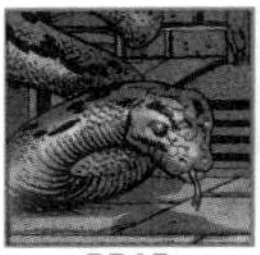

**BRAD**
Giant snake, servant
of Amanda Sefton
Nightcrawler #2
(2004)

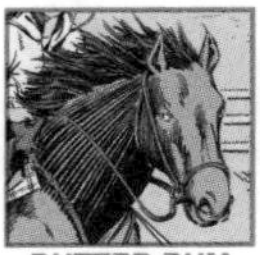

**BUTTER RUM**
Horse (deceased), pet
of Angelica Jones
Firestar #2 (1986)

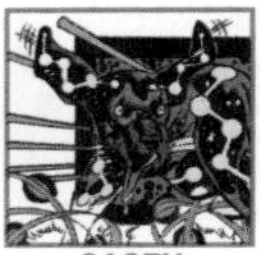

**CASEY**
Dog, pet of
Glenn Herdling
What If #31 (1991)

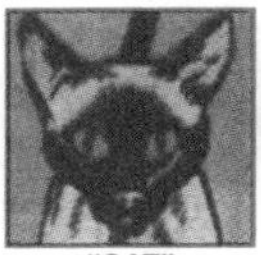

**"CAT"**
Cat, pet of Shang-Chi
Master of Kung Fu
#38 (1976)

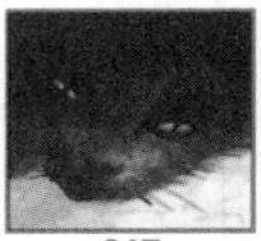

**CAT**
Cat, pet of Night
Raven
Night Raven: House
of Cards (1992)

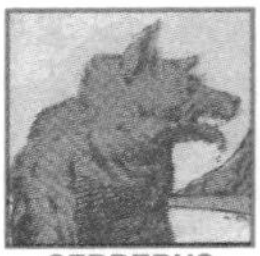

**CERBERUS**
Wolf/dog, pet of
O.Z. Chase
Dazzler #38 (1985)

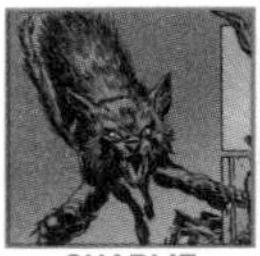

**CHARLIE**
Cat, pet of
Howard the Duck
Howard the Duck #1
(2002)

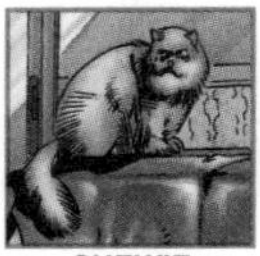

**CHEWIE**
Cat (Earth-58163),
pet of Carol Danvers
Ms. Marvel #4 (2006)

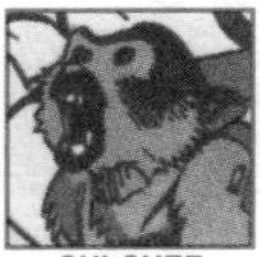

**CHI-CHEE**
Chimpanzee,
pet of Warlock
Warlock #1 (1998)

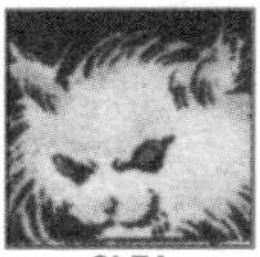

**CLEA**
Cat, pet of
Vincent Stevens
Dr. Strange #62
(1994)

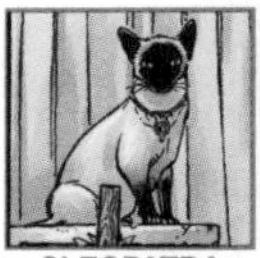

**CLEOPATRA**
Cat,
pet of the Roman
Wolverine #183
(2003)

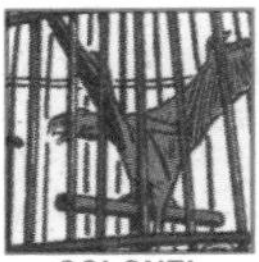

**COLONEL PTERODACTYLEE**
Miniature Pterodactyl,
pet of Nightcrawler
Special Edition X-Men
#1 (1983)

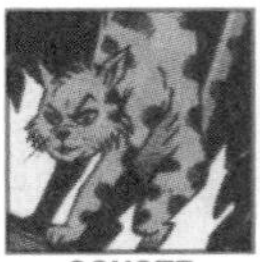

**COYOTE**
Cat, pet of
James Proudstar
X-Force #-1 (1997)

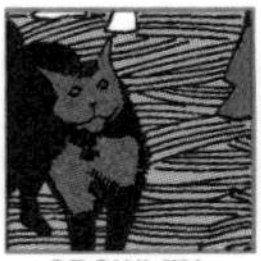

**CROWLEY**
Cat (Earth-712), familiar
of Arcanna Jones
Squadron Supreme #1
(1985)

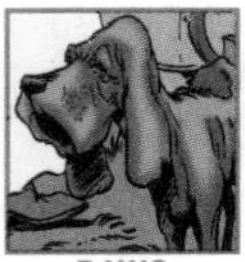

**DAWG**
Dog (deceased),
pet of Ezekial Tork
Man-Thing #9
(1974)

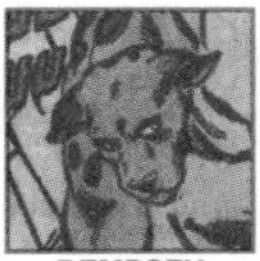

**DEMPSEY**
Dog (deceased), pet
of Herbert Wyndham
Thor #135 (1966)

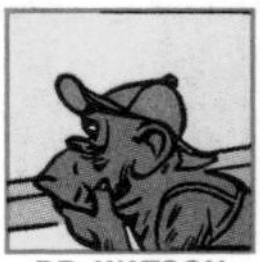

**DR. WATSON**
Chimpanzee, pet of
Terry Vance
Marvel Mystery
Comics #10 (1940)

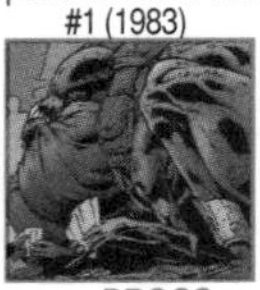

**DROGS**
Extraterrestrial mounts,
steeds of Lunatik
Cosmic Powers
Unlimited #3 (1995)

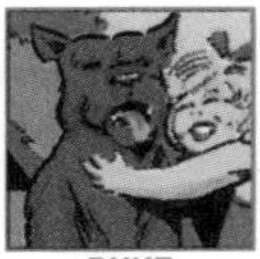

**DUKE**
Dog, pet of Barbara
Norriss
Defenders #21
(1975)

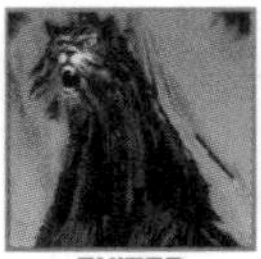

**EXITER**
Cat (deceased),
familiar of Satana
Haunt of Horror #2
(1974)

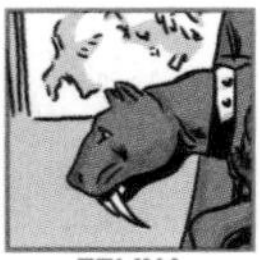

**FELINA**
Giant cat,
pet of Leanne
Ka-Zar the Savage
#1 (1981)

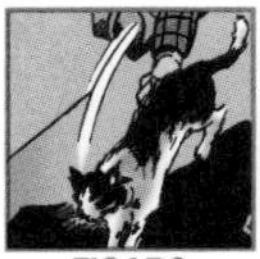

**FIGARO**
Cat,
pet of Sam Wilson
Captain America #137
(1971)

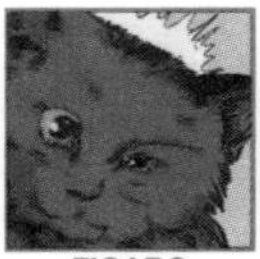

**FIGARO**
Cat
(Earth-148611), pet
of Angie Tensen
Justice #26 (1988)

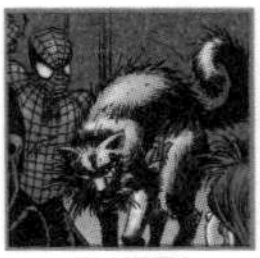

**FLUFFY**
Cat, pet of
Randy Robertson
Amazing Spider-Man #27 (2001)

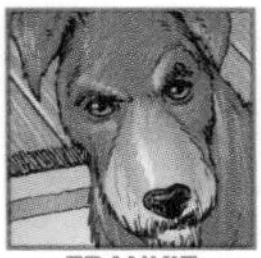

**FRANKIE**
Dog, pet of
"Joan the Mouse"
Punisher #19 (2003)

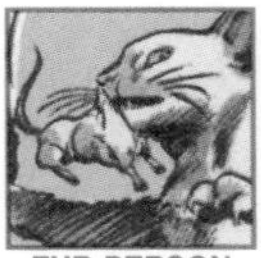

**FUR-PERSON**
Cat, pet of Samson Scythe
Captain America Annual #5 (1981)

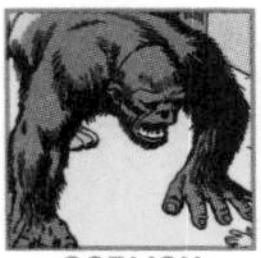

**GORLION**
Gorilla/lion, pet of the Ancient One
Amazing Adventures #1 (1961)

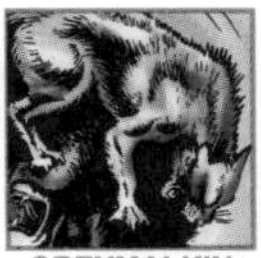

**GREYMALKIN**
Cat, pet of
Sarah Mumford
Hulk Comic #1 (1979)

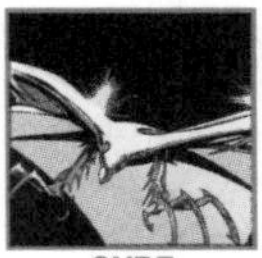

**GYRE**
Robot hawk (destroyed),
pet of Lure
Gun Runner #4 (1994)

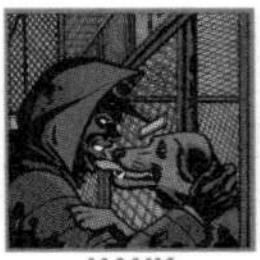

**HANK**
Dog,
pet of Shatter
Morlocks #2 (2002)

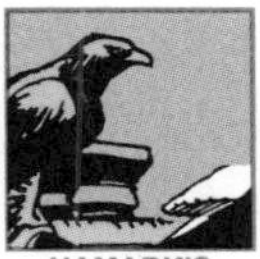

**HAMARKIS**
Eagle,
pet of Ashake
New Mutants #32 (1985)

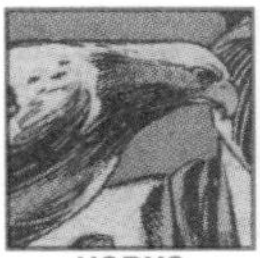

**HORUS**
Falcon (deceased),
pet of
Anubis the Jackal
Moon Knight #1 (1985)

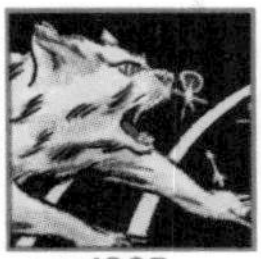

**IGOR**
Cat, pet of Gary & Susan Daley
Tower of Shadows #4 (1970)

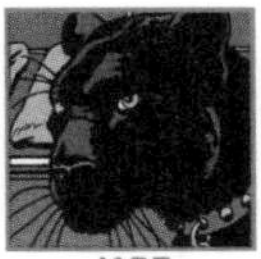

**JADE**
Leopard (deceased),
pet of Shanna
Marvel Comics Presents #68 (1991)

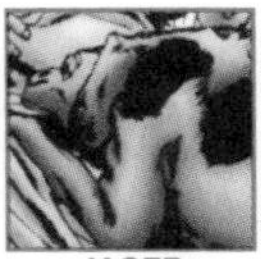

**JAGER**
Dog, pet of Karl Lykos
X-Men #60 (1969)

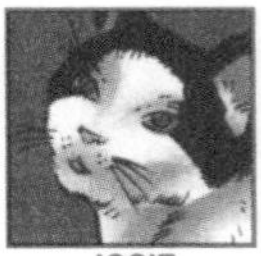

**JOSIE**
Cat, pet of
Pepper Potts
Iron Man: The Iron Age #1 (1998)

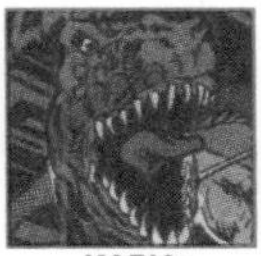

**KARIA**
Giant lizard, steed of Arkon
Avengers #358 (1993)

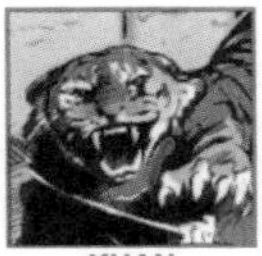

**KHAN**
Tiger (deceased),
pet of Yi Yang
Hulk Comic #17 (1979)

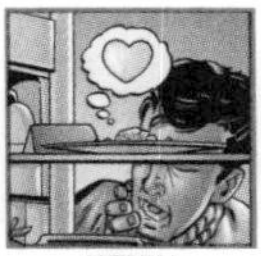

**KEVIN**
Moldy cheese, pet of
Peter Parker
Peter Parker: Spider-Man #21 (2000)

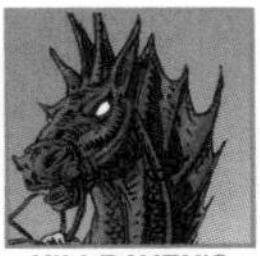

**KILLRAVEN'S SERPENT HORSE**
Earth-691
Amazing Adventures #26 (1974)

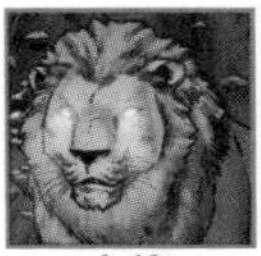

**L-10**
Robot lion (Earth-1119, destroyed),
Black Panther's pet
Exiles #1 (2009)

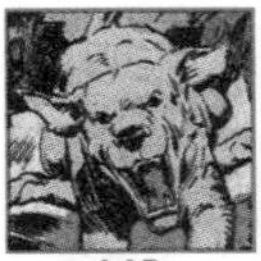

**LAD**
Dog, pet of
Bruce Banner
Incredible Hulk #219 (1978)

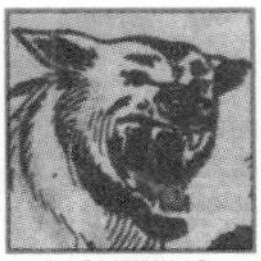

**LIGHTNING**
Dog, pet of
Tex Dawson
Western Kid #1 (1954)

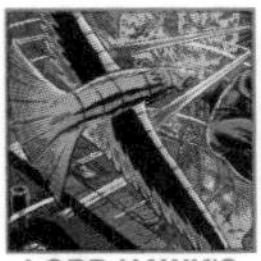

**LORD HAWK'S HAWK**
Robot hawk
Captain Britain #27 (1977)

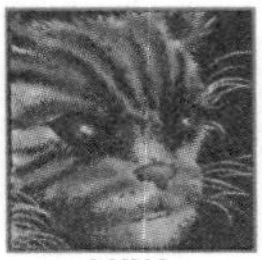

**LUNA**
Cat, pet of
Vincent Stevens
Dr. Strange Annual #4 (1994)

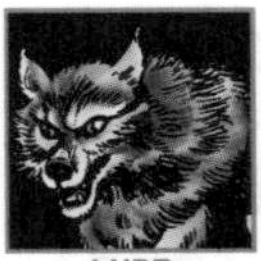

**LUPE**
Wolf, pet of
Vortigen
Hulk Comic #6 (1979)

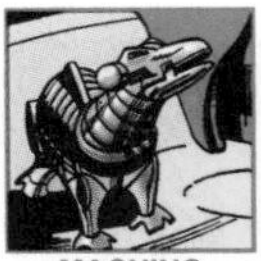

**MACHINO**
Robot dog, pet of Anelle
Captain Marvel #2 (1968)

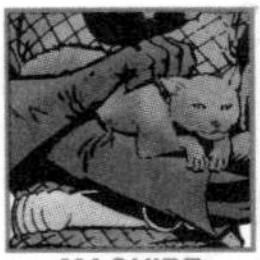

**MAGUIRE**
Robot cat, pet of Mad Jack
Spectacular Spider-Man #242 (1997)

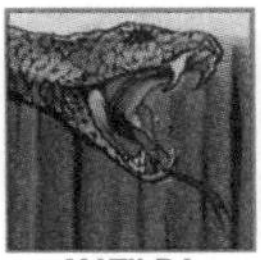

**MATILDA**
Snake (deceased),
pet of Venomm
Black Panther: Panther's Prey #2 (1991)

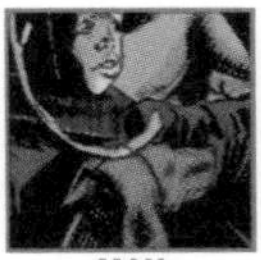

**MAX**
Dog, pet of Cindy Lou
Thor #444 (1992)

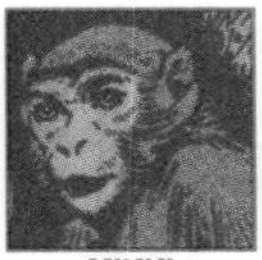

**MIKKI**
Chimpanzee,
pet of Lorna
Lorna the Jungle Girl #1 (1953)

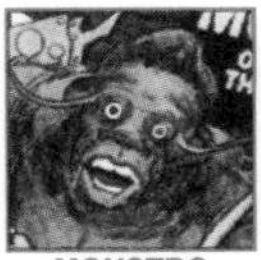

**MONSTRO**
Giant ape, former circus performer
Journey into Mystery #54 (1959)

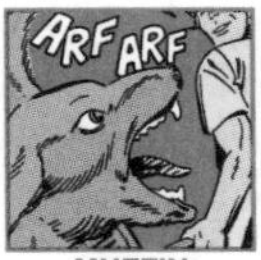
ARF ARF

**MUFFIN**
Dog, pet of
Ray Coffin
Micronauts #2 (1979)

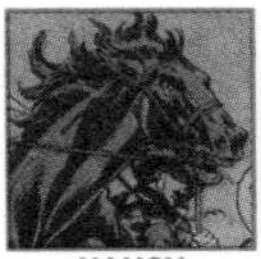

**NANCY**
Horse, steed of
Two-Gun Kid
Marvel Tales #100 (1979)

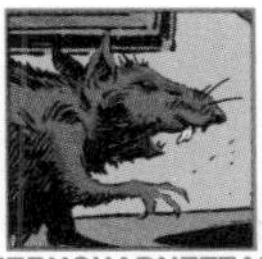

**NEBUCHADNEZZAR**
Rat, familiar of
Cyrus Black
Defenders #6 (1973)

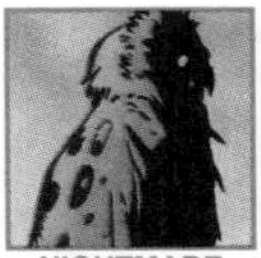

**NIGHTMARE OWL**
Demon owl,
pet of Nightmare
Nightmare #2 (1995)

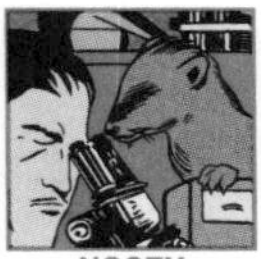

**NOSEY**
Ferret, pet of the Ferret
Marvel Mystery Comics #4 (1940)

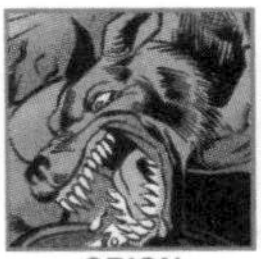

**ORION**
Dog, pet of
Truthsayer
Darkhold #16 (1994)

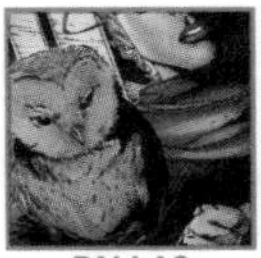

**PALLAS**
Owl,
pet of Athena
Incredible Hercules #115 (2008)

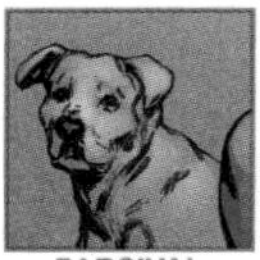

**PARSIVAL**
Dog, pet of
Howard the Duck
Howard the Duck #1
(2002)

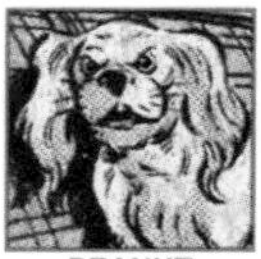

**PEANUT**
Dog (deceased),
pet of Vic Martinelli
Iron Man #146
(1981)

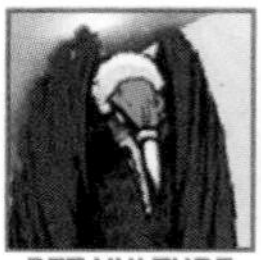

**PET VULTURE**
Vulture, pet of
Death's Head
Dr.Who Magazine
#140 (1988)

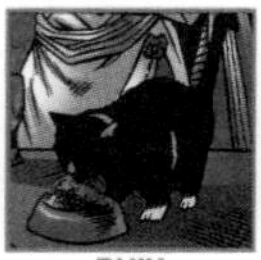

**PHIX**
Cat, familiar of
Ashake
New Mutants #32
(1985)

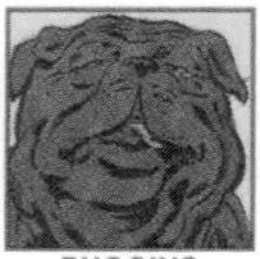

**PUGGINS**
Dog, pet of
Kathy Dare
Iron Man #234
(1988)

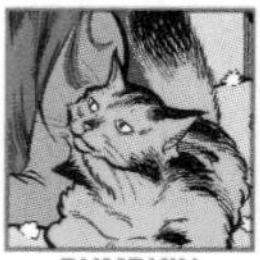

**PUMPKIN**
Cat,
pet of
Angelica Jones
Firestar #1 (1986)

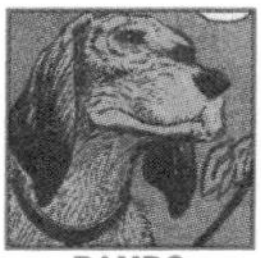

**RAMBO**
Dog, pet of
Rick Sheridan
Sleepwalker #1
(1991)

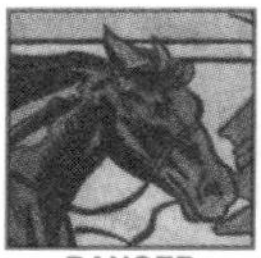

**RANGER**
Horse, steed of
Red Wolf
Marvel Super-
Heroes #2 (1990)

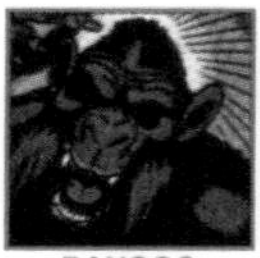

**RANGOO**
Chimpanzee, pet of
Tigerman
Daring Mystery
Comics #6 (1940)

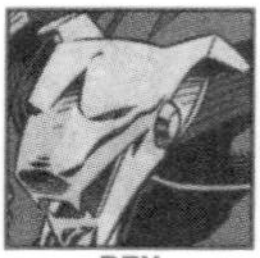

**REX**
Robot dog
(destroyed),
pet of Ultron
Blackwulf #3 (1994)

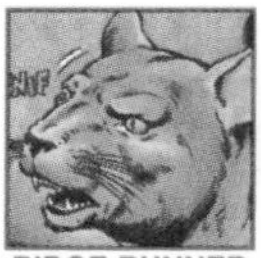

**RIDGE-RUNNER**
Cougar (deceased), pet
of Danielle Moonstar
Marvel Graphic Novel
#4 (1982)

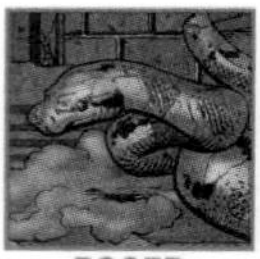

**ROGER**
Giant snake, servant
of Amanda Sefton
Nightcrawler #2
(2004)

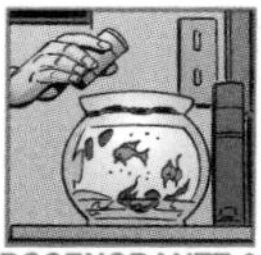

**ROSENCRANTZ & GUILDENSTERN**
Fish (deceased), pets
of She-Hulk
She-Hulk #9 (2005)

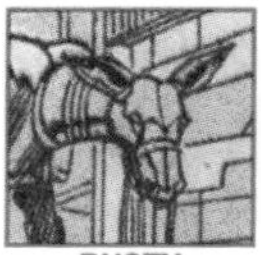

**RUSTY**
Robot horse, steed
of Shabby Allus
Captain Marvel #42
(1976)

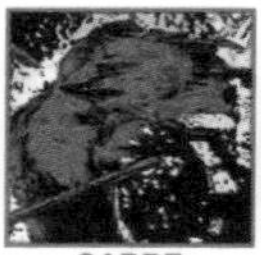

**SABRE**
Dog (deceased),
pet of Angela
Cleaver
Fury/Black Widow:
Death Duty (1995)

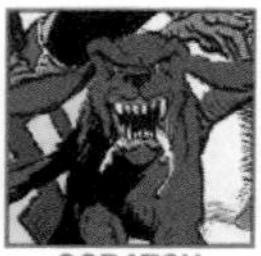

**SCRATCH**
Dog (Earth-5555),
pet of Scavenger
Dragon's Claws #1
(1988)

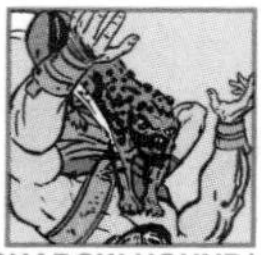

**SHADOW-HOUND/ LAELAPS**
Dog, pet of the
Huntsman
Ka-Zar #1 (1974)

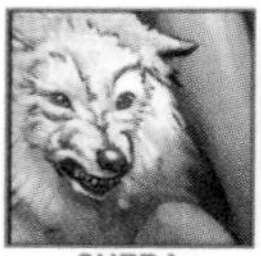

**SHEBA**
Wolf, pet of Shanna
X-Men Unlimited
#48 (2003)

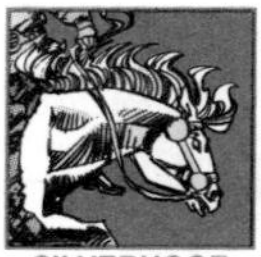

**SILVERHOOF**
Horse, steed of
Balder
Thor #344 (1984)

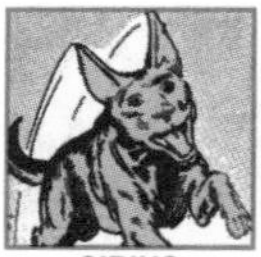

**SIRIUS**
Dog (deceased), pet
of Douglas family
Incredible Hulk #294
(1984)

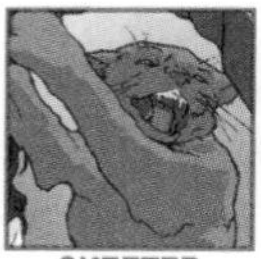

**SKEETER**
Cat, pet of
Tatiana Caban
NYX #4 (2004)

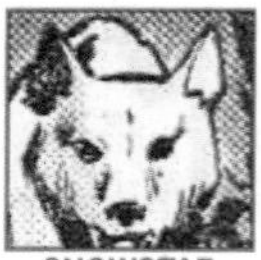

**SNOWSTAR**
Dog, pet of Glazier
Incredible Hulk
#262 (1981)

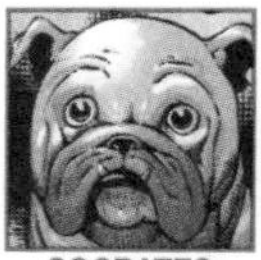

**SOCRATES**
Dog, pet of
Pepper Hogan
Iron Man #2 (1998)

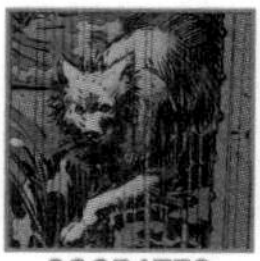

**SOCRATES**
Dog, pet of Zuras
Eternals #5 (2006)

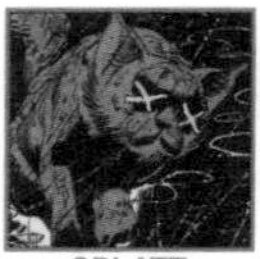

**SPLATT**
Cat, pet of Roadkill
Dr. Strange #38
(1992)

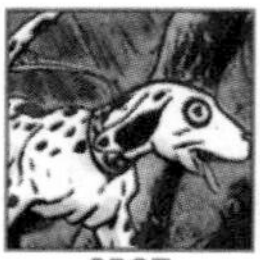

**SPOT**
Dog, pet of John
Warren
Journey into
Mystery #57 (1960)

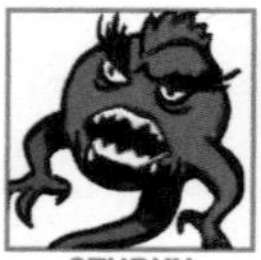

**STURKY**
Artificial being, pet
of Bereet
Incredible Hulk
#269 (1982)

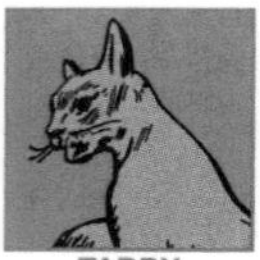

**TABBY**
Cat, pet of Henry
Pym
Tales to Astonish
#65 (1965)

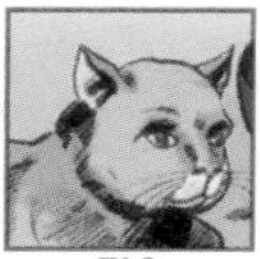

**TAO**
Cat, pet of Lin Sun
Deadly Hands of
Kung Fu #9 (1975)

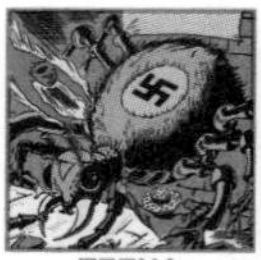

**TEENA**
Spider (deceased),
pet of Black Talon
Young Allies #2
(1941)

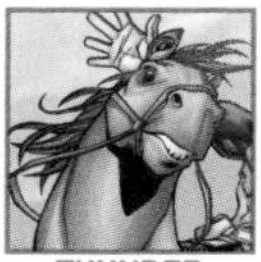

**THUNDER**
Horse, steed of
Major Mapleleaf
Alpha Flight #1
(2004)

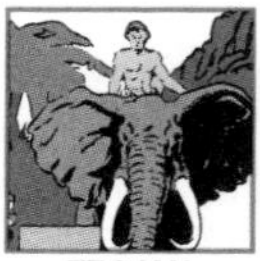

**TRAJAH**
Elephant, ally of
Ka-Zar
Marvel Comics #1
(1939)

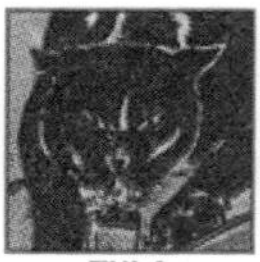

**TULA**
Panther (deceased),
pet of Dr. Agony
Captain America
Comics #37 (1944)

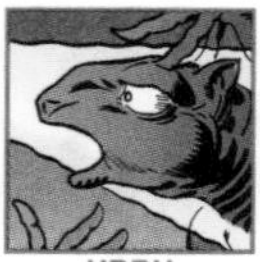

**UBBU**
Imp, pet of
Shazana
Strange Tales #133
(1965)

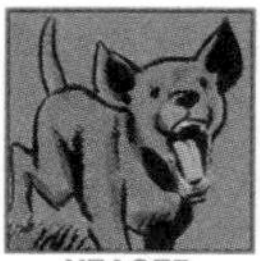

**YEAGER**
Dog, pet of Hal
Chandler
Incredible Hulk
#251 (1980)

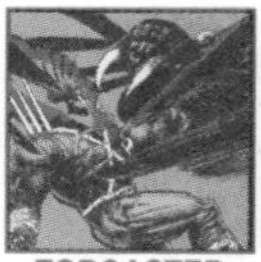

**ZOROASTER**
Spider (deceased),
pet of Diabolique
Darkhold #10 (1993)

# VARIANT COVER GALLERY

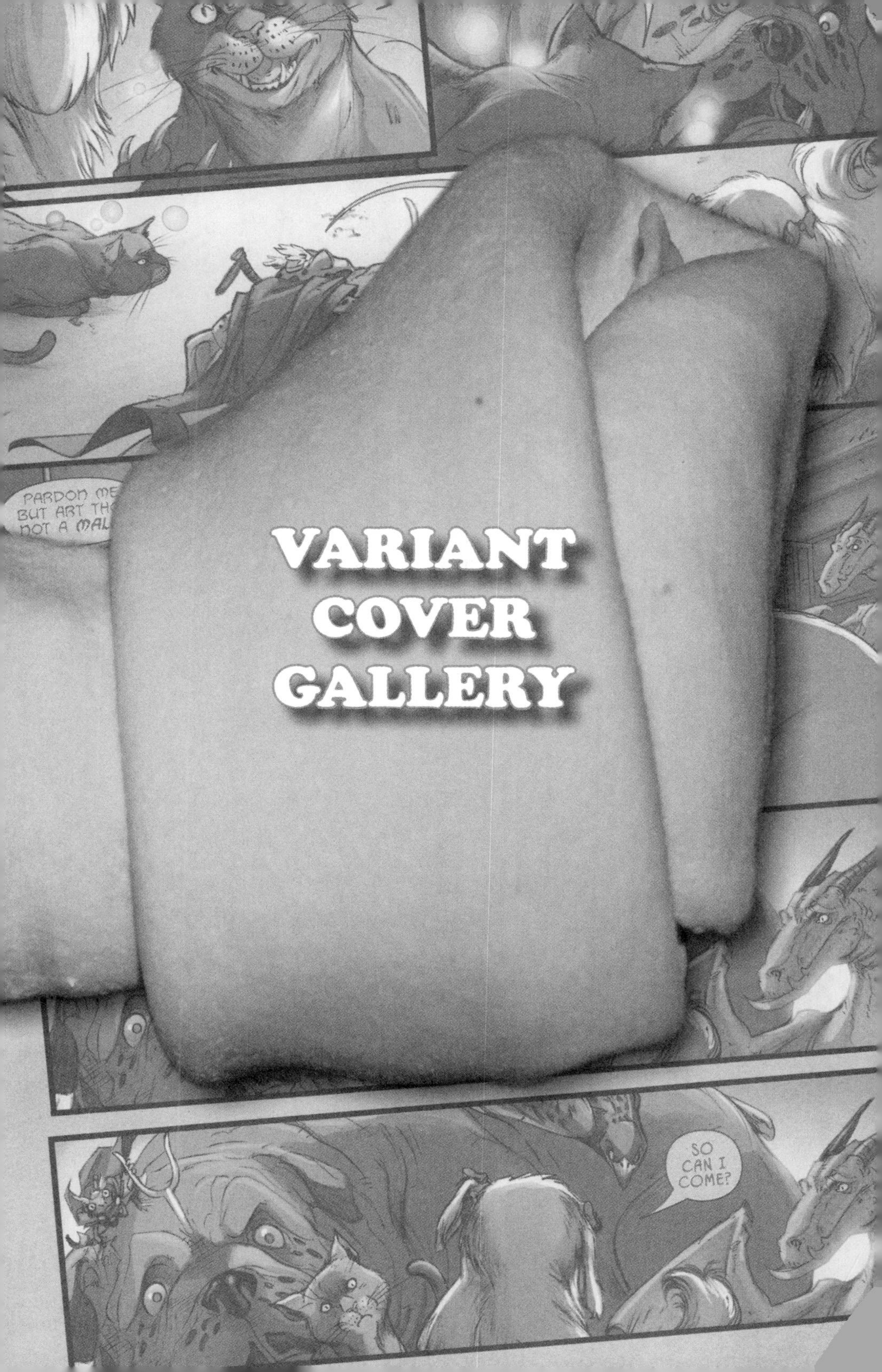
PARDON ME BUT ART THO NOT A MAL
SO CAN I COME?

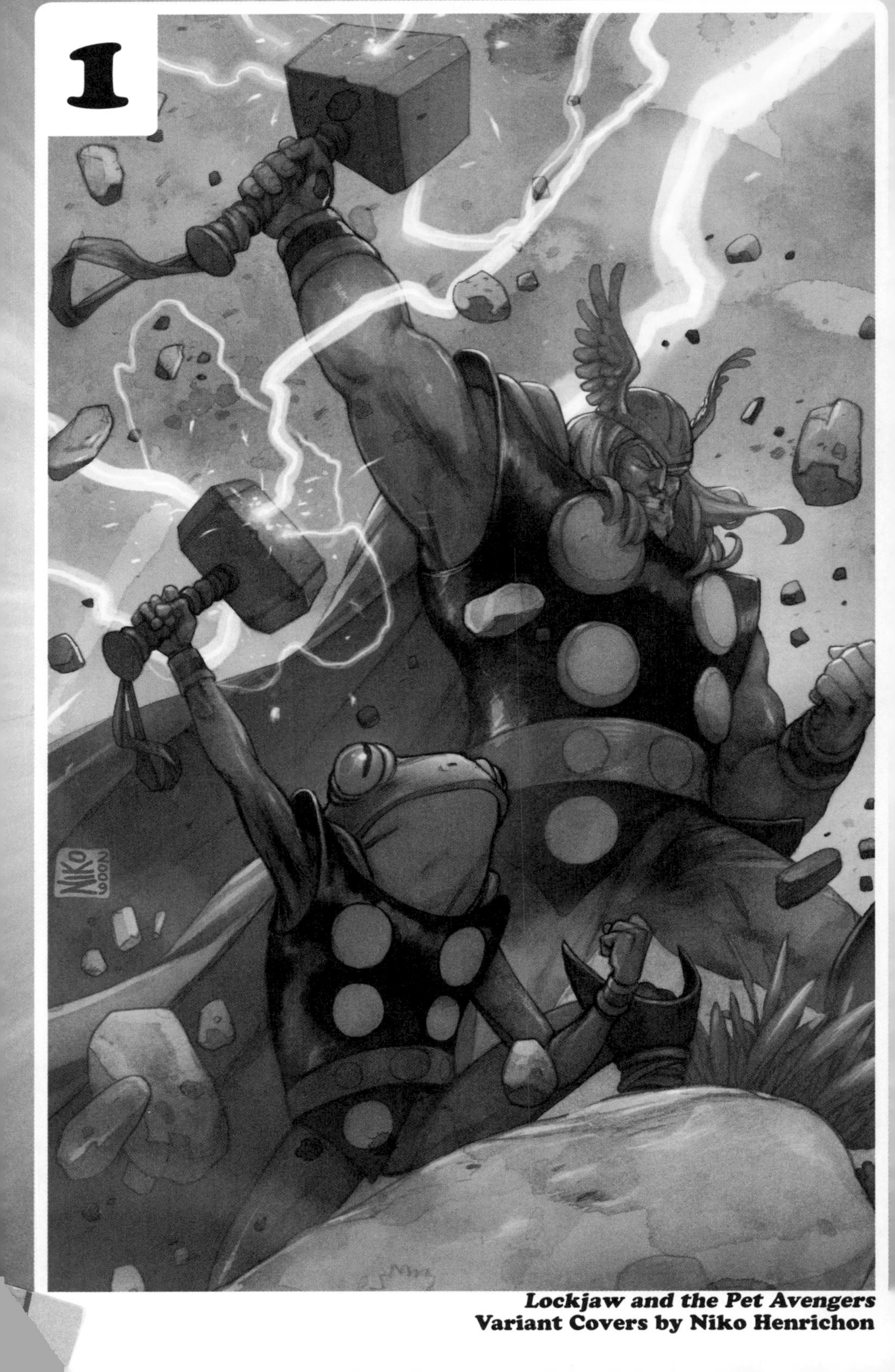
1

***Lockjaw and the Pet Avengers***
**Variant Covers by Niko Henrichon**

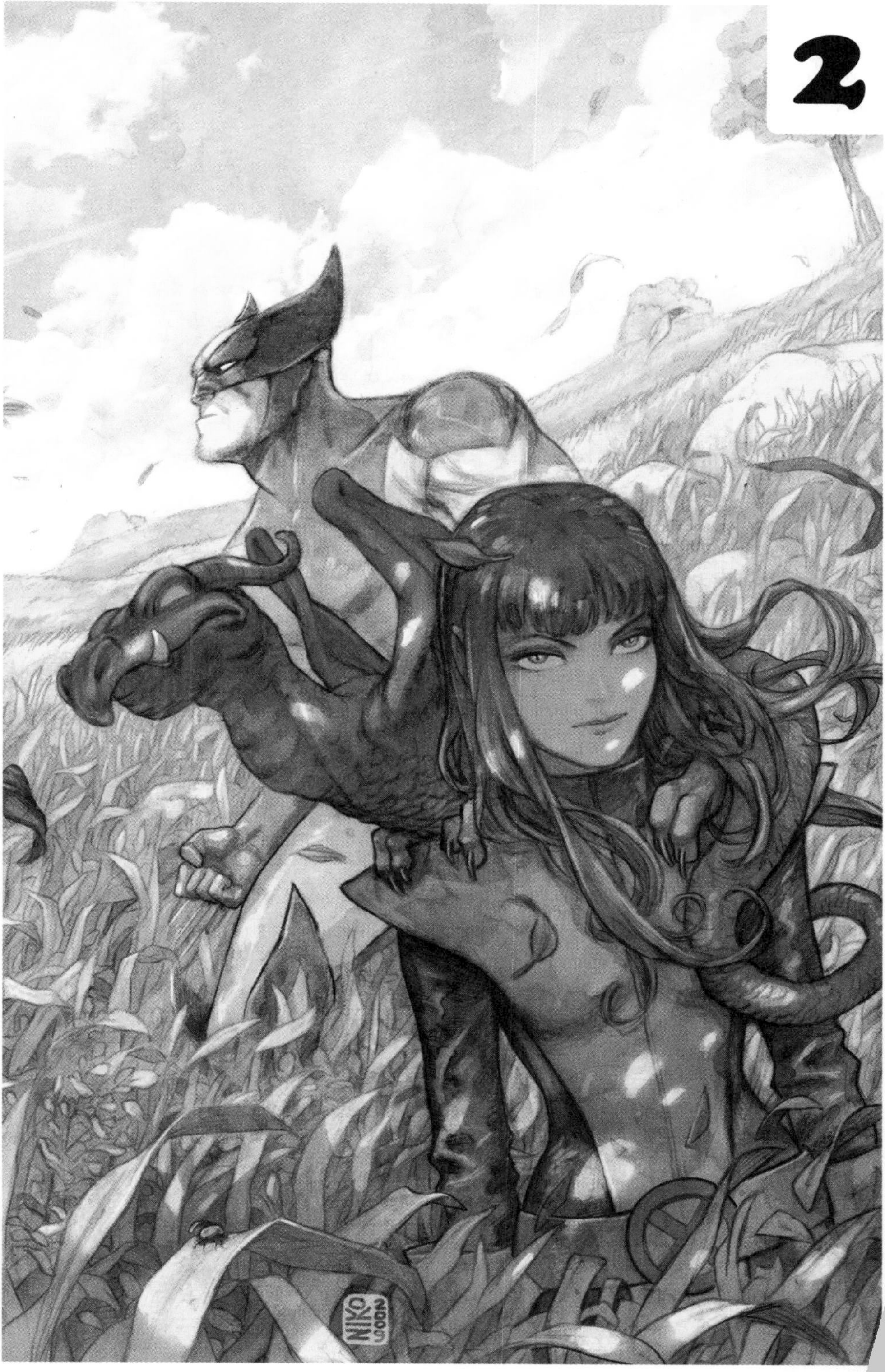
2
NIKO

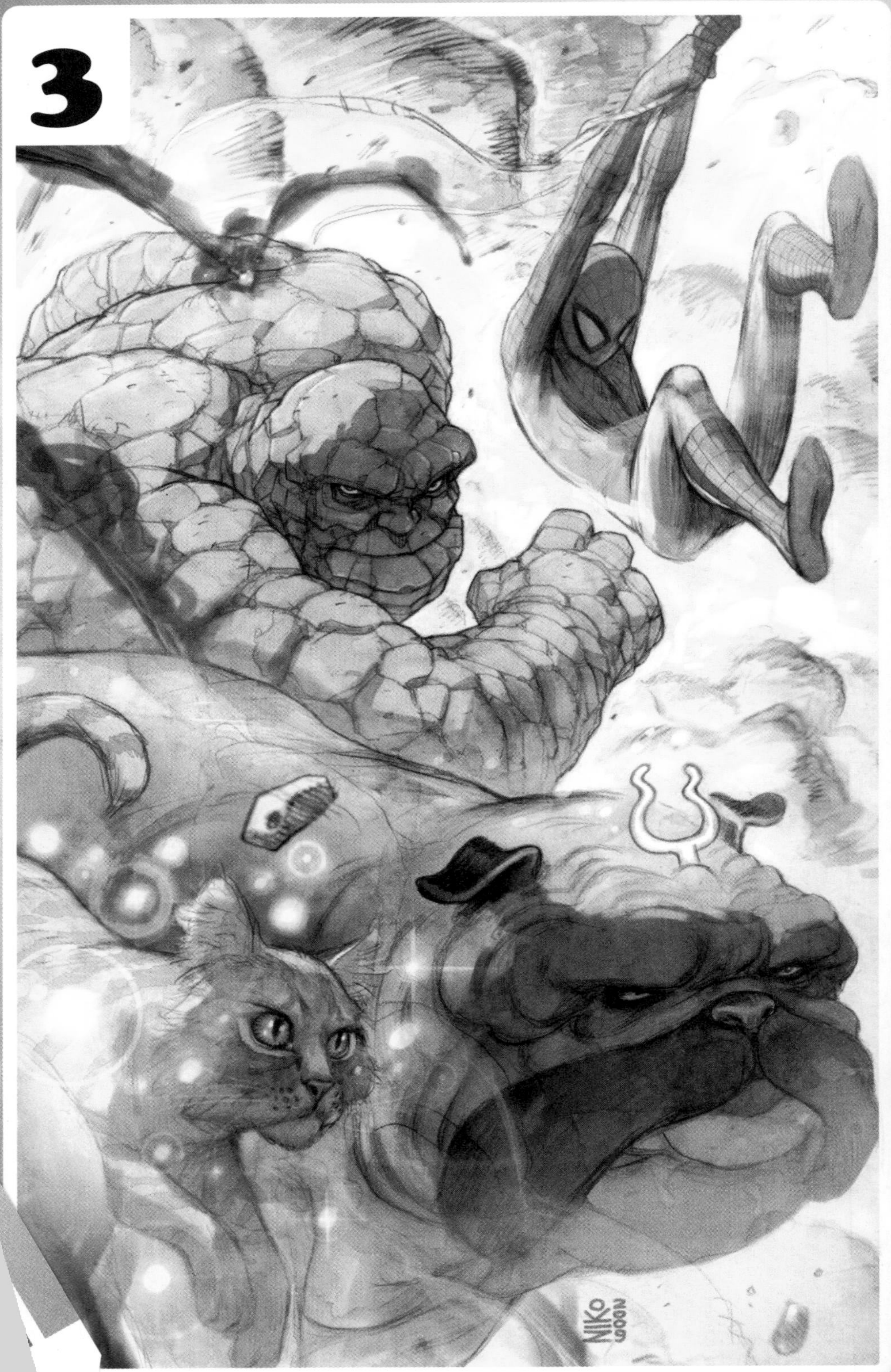
3

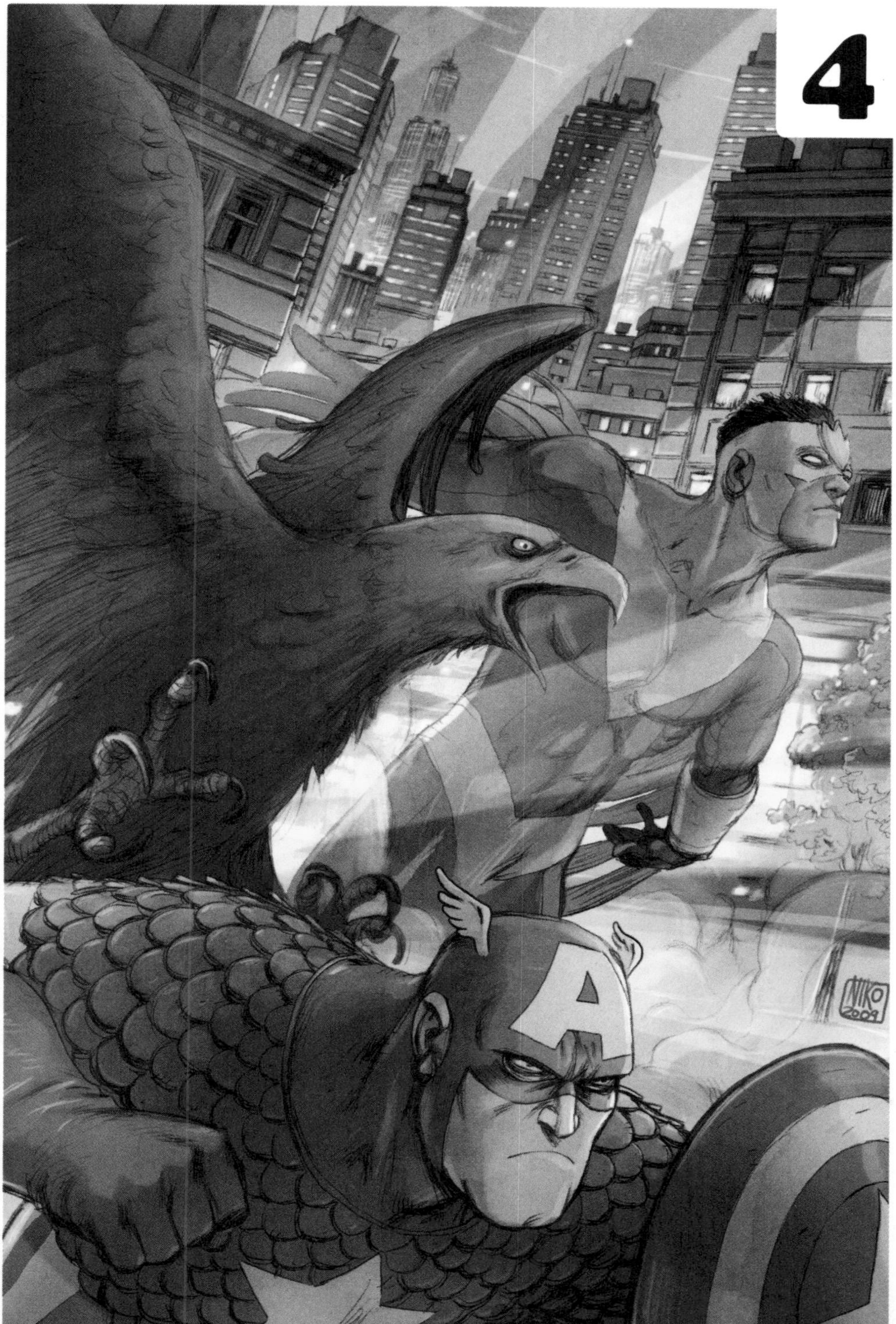
4
NIKO
2009

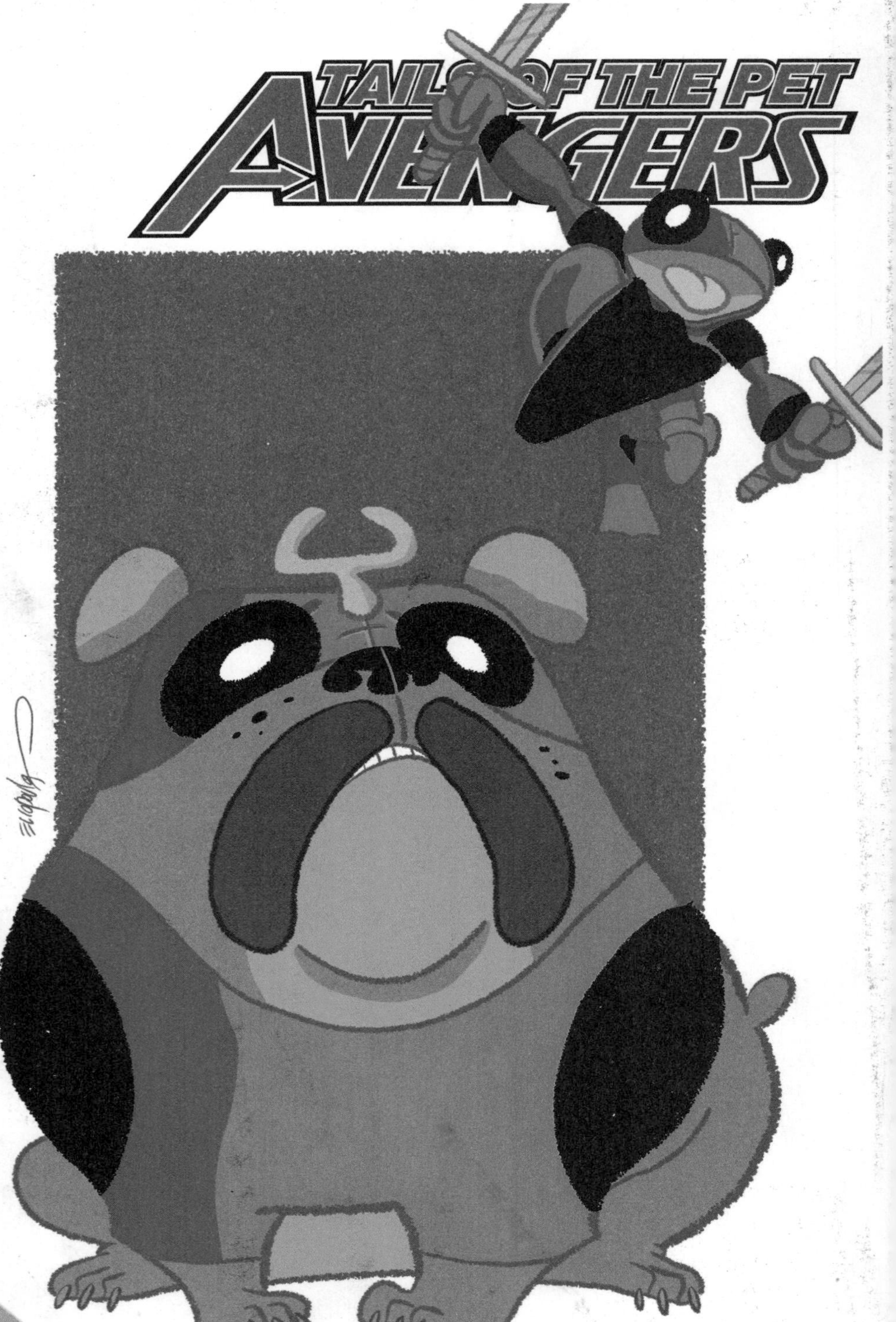
TAILS OF THE PET
AVENGERS

**Deadpool Variant**
**by Chris Eliopoulos**